VELER FOR

Qty _____ Date _____

Qty _____ Date _____

Cut By: _____

Scanned By: _____

Scanned B

PRAISE FOR DEBORAH COOKE'S DRAGONFIRE NOVELS

KISS OF FIRE

"Cooke, a.k.a. bestseller Claire Delacroix, dips into the paranormal realm with her sizzling new Dragonfire series...Efficient plotting moves the story at a brisk pace and paves the way for more exciting battles to come."

—Romantic Times

"Paranormal fans with a soft spot for shape-shifting dragons will definitely enjoy *Kiss of Fire*, a story brimming with sexy heroes, evil villains threatening mayhem, death and world domination, ancient prophesies, and an engaging love story...An intriguing mythology and various unanswered plot threads set the stage for plenty more adventure to come in future Dragonfire stories."

—BookLoons

"Deborah Cooke has definitely made me a fan. I am now lying in wait for the second book in this extremely exciting series."

—Romance Junkies

"Wow, what an innovative and dazzling world Ms. Cooke has built with this new Dragonfire series. Her smooth and precise writing quickly draws the reader in and has you believing it could almost be real...I can't wait for the next two books."

—Fresh Fiction

KISS OF FURY

"Those sexy dragons are back in the second chapter of

Cooke's exciting paranormal series...The intriguing characters continue to grow and offer terrific opportunities for story expansion. Balancing a hormone-driven romance with high-stakes action can be difficult, but Cooke manages with ease. Visiting this world is a pleasure."

—Romantic Times

"The second book in Deborah Cooke's phenomenal Dragonfire series expertly sets the stage for the next thrilling episode."

—Fresh Fiction

"Entertaining and imaginative...a must-read for paranormal fans."

—BookLoons

"Riveting...Deborah Cooke delivers a fiery tale of love and passion...She manages to leave us with just enough new questions to have us awaiting book three with bated breath!"

—Wild on Books

"Epic battles, suspense, ecological concerns, humor, and romance are highlights that readers can expect in this tale. Excellent writing, a smart story, and exceptional characters earn this novel the RRT Perfect 10 Rating. Don't miss the very highly recommended *Kiss of Fury*."

—Romance Reviews Today

"Deborah Cooke has only touched the surface about these wonderful men called the *Pyr* and their battle with the evil dragons...I am dying for more."

—Romance Junkies

Kiss of Fate

"Second chances are a key theme in this latest Dragonfire

adventure. Cooke keeps the pace intense and the emotions raging in this powerful new read. She's top-notch, as always!"

—Romantic Times

"An intense ride. Ms. Cooke has a great talent...If you love paranormal romance in any way, this is a series you should be following."

—Night Owl Reviews (reviewer top pick)

Winter Kiss

"A beautiful and emotionally gripping fourth novel, *Winter Kiss* is compelling and will keep readers riveted in their seats and breathing a happy sigh at the love shared between Delaney and Ginger...Sizzling-hot love scenes and explosive emotions make *Winter Kiss* a must read!"

—Romance Junkies

"A terrific novel!"

—Romance Reviews Today

"All the *Pyr* and their mates from the previous three books in this exciting series are included in this final confrontation with Magnus and his evil Dragon's Blood Elixir. It's another stellar addition to this dynamic paranormal saga with the promise of more to come."

—Fresh Fiction

Whisper Kiss

"This is a terrific Kiss urban romantic fantasy...The author has 'Cooked' another winner with the tattoo artist and the dragon shape-shifter."

—Alternate Worlds

"Cooke introduces her most unconventional and inspiring heroine to date with tattoo artist Rox...Cooke aces another one!"

—Romantic Times (four and a half stars)

"Deborah Cooke has again given readers a truly dynamic story in her Dragonfire chronicles."

—Fresh Fiction

"*Whisper Kiss* by Deborah Cooke is now my unofficial official favorite!...Bursting with emotions, passion and even a real fire or four, I count myself lucky not to have spontaneously combusted! Don't miss this sizzling addition to Deborah Cooke's Dragonfire series—it is marvelous!"

—Romance Junkies

DARKFIRE KISS

"Deborah Cooke's Dragonfire novels are impossible to put down. *Darkfire Kiss* is no exception. I dare any reader to skim any part of this terrific story!"

—Romance Reviews Today

"Quick action, engaging prose, and hot sex."

—Publishers Weekly

"Another book not to be missed!"

—Fresh Fiction

"An action-packed, fast-paced romantic read."

—TwoLips Reviews

FLASHFIRE

"Deborah Cooke is a dragonmaster of a storyteller...Lorenzo fills the pages with enigmatic glory only rivaled by his mate,

Cassie, and I did not stop turning pages until the firestorm was ended."

—The Reading Frenzy

"Cooke's long-running series continues to be a sexy and thrilling winner!"

—Romantic Times

"Thrilling and unpredictable...*Flashfire* is another great addition on one of my favorite paranormal romance series."

—Paranormal Haven

EMBER'S KISS

"The Dragonfire series continues to delight its fans with the dragon shifters finding their destined mates and the danger they face as they complete their trials. If you love dragons, this series is sure to please."

—Romance Reader's Connection

"*Ember's Kiss* is another well-written, fascinating and amazing storyline in Deborah Cooke's Dragonfire series. Deborah creates a world of beautiful dragons and timeless love. I have loved Deborah's dragons since the very beginning and I was immensely pleased that she brought together the *Pyr* in this amazing tale."

—The Reading Cafe

The Dragon Diaries

Flying Blind

"Zoë is a wonderful heroine—smart, strong and sympathetic. Bring on book two!"

—#1 New York Times Bestselling Author
Kelley Armstrong

"Whether you're young or just young at heart, you will equally enjoy this brand-new series by Ms. Cooke...It's entertaining, it's exciting and it's adventurous...a wonderful new series."

—The Reading Frenzy

"This. Book. Rocks."

—One a Day YA

"The first of a new dragon series sure to become a classic...Cooke has written a fantastic offshoot of her *Pyr* universe...After turning the final page, I sat for a moment with a sense of excitement I haven't felt since I finished my first of Anne McCaffrey's Pern books."

—Fresh Fiction

"This story crosses the boundaries. It will appeal to both teens and adults across the board. The story is engaging and fun. It's bringing to life a world of dragons and magic that appeals to all."

—Night Owl Reviews (5 stars, top pick)

"The writing is swift and fun, just like I'd imagine flying on the back of a dragon...If you're looking for a break from vampires and werewolves or you're a fan of Cooke's adult Dragonfire series, you won't be disappointed."

—All Things Urban Fantasy

WINGING IT

"[Cooke's] clever ability to convey what it means to be going on sixteen while being faced with dark, world-altering dilemmas has created a unique and compelling young-adult series bursting with magic, mayhem, and danger."

—Fresh Fiction

"Zoë is as kick-butt as ever...another fast-paced, well-thought-out novel in [Cooke's] Dragonfire universe. Teen readers will love that Zoë and her friends get to be the stars."

—Romantic Times

BLAZING THE TRAIL

"There are so many twists in this book, I loved it. I could not put it down, and read it in a day. If you have read Deborah's adult books, with the adult dragons, then you will love this series with the kids!"

—Books Complete Me

"I have been a huge fan of Deborah Cooke for many years. When a new release comes across my path, I truly do a happy dance. Cooke has lived up to her previous work with *Blazing the Trail*. I loved how Zoë deals with the everyday issues in front of her while trying to save the world with the *Pyr* and fellow shifters."

—Fresh Fiction

HERE *Be* DRAGONS

THE DRAGONFIRE NOVEL COMPANION

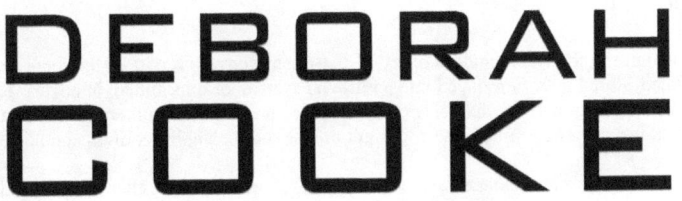

Here Be Dragons: The Dragonfire Novel Companion
By Deborah Cooke

BOOKS BY DEBORAH COOKE

Paranormal Romances:
The Dragonfire Series
KISS OF FIRE
KISS OF FURY
KISS OF FATE
Harmonia's Kiss
WINTER KISS
WHISPER KISS
DARKFIRE KISS
FLASHFIRE
EMBER'S KISS
Kiss of Danger
Kiss of Darkness
Kiss of Destiny
SERPENT'S KISS
FIRESTORM FOREVER
HERE BE DRAGONS:
The Dragonfire Novel Companion

The Dragons of Incendium
WYVERN'S MATE
Nero's Dream
WYVERN'S PRINCE
Arista's Legacy
WYVERN'S WARRIOR
Kraw's Secret
WYVERN'S OUTLAW
Celo's Quest
WYVERN'S ANGEL
Nimue's Gift

The DragonFate Novels
Maeve's Book of Beasts
DRAGON'S KISS

Paranormal Young Adult:
The Dragon Diaries
FLYING BLIND
WINGING IT
BLAZING THE TRAIL

Urban Fantasy Romance
The Prometheus Project
FALLEN
GUARDIAN

REBEL
ABYSS

Short Stories
Coven of Mercy
An Elegy for Melusine
A Berry Merry Christmas

Contemporary Romance:
The Coxwells
THIRD TIME LUCKY
DOUBLE TROUBLE
ONE MORE TIME
ALL OR NOTHING
Christmas with the Coxwells

Flatiron Five
SIMPLY IRRESISTIBLE
ADDICTED TO LOVE
IN THE MIDNIGHT HOUR
SOME GUYS HAVE ALL THE LUCK
Going to the Chapel
BAD CASE OF LOVING YOU

Secret Heart Ink
SNOWBOUND
SPRING FEVER
ONE HOT SUMMER NIGHT
UNDER THE MISTLETOE

For Claire Delacroix medieval romances,
please visit
http://delacroix.net

HERE BE DRAGONS

DEBORAH COOKE

Dear Reader;

When I first had the idea of writing about a society of dragon shape shifters hidden amongst us, I had no expectation that the world of *Dragonfire* would become both so intricate and so compelling. I certainly didn't imagine that there would be so many books in the series. As the world has evolved, I've been keeping notes for my own reference. This volume has grown out of those notes—augmented and expanded from my scribbles—in response to reader demand.

I'm thrilled that so many of you find my *Dragonfire* world and my *Pyr* heroes so interesting, and that enthusiasm is why I'm continuing to write more stories set in the world of the *Pyr*, with the *DragonFate* novels. This is a good point to do some documentation, though, as the original *Dragonfire* series has come to is completion, plus we've had a spin-off young adult series set in the future. *DragonFate* picks up the story of the *Pyr* several years after **Firestorm Forever** and features the younger dragon shifters of the Dragon Legion as they face a new challenge from Maeve, the Queen of the Dark Fae. Maeve is introduced in **Firestorm Forever** but there's only a glimpse of her plans by the end of that book.

This guide is organized in sections. First is a section on the books themselves. This includes a brief overview of the world of Dragonfire, a discussion about reading order, then summaries of the individual books in order with comments from me on each book. The detailed summaries were compiled by Carol Malcolm and edited by Mary Dieterich—I appreciate the assistance of both of them. Amber Carpenter also did an excellent proofread.

The second section is an alphabetical Glossary of Terms. This describes the detail of the *Dragonfire* world—if you haven't read all of the books, be warned that there are spoilers here. Many of the elements of the realm of the *Pyr* evolved over the course of the series—thanks to the influence of the darkfire—or changed outright over time, and those transitions are documented here for reference.

The third section is an alphabetical List of Characters, independent of their nature and whether they survived to the end of the series. Throughout these two sections, you'll find quotes from the books, chosen to illustrate a point or just because I like them.

Following the List of Characters, you'll find family trees for the *Pyr*. These are also available as free PDF downloads on the Dragonfire website, if you'd like to print them out in a larger format.

Next, you'll find interviews I did with the first six of the *Pyr* featured in the *Dragonfire* series. Each of those *Pyr* is interviewed on a specific facet of the *Pyr* world or nature. These were posted on my website in 2009 and were popular there, so I've included them here.

Finally, you'll find **Harmonia's Kiss**. This short story evolved from an out-take of **Whisper Kiss** and features Drake and the Dragon's Tooth Warriors, who choose in this story to call themselves the Dragon Legion. This story is available on its own in ebook, but has not been included in a print edition until now.
The *Dragonfire* novels have their own website, which features all the books set in this particular fictional world. You can find it at:

http://DragonfireNovels.com

There's also a Facebook page for the series and there are Pinterest boards showing some of my inspiration. You'll find links for both of those on the *Dragonfire* website. You can also sign up for my newsletter, **Dragons & Angels**, which features my paranormal romances.

I hope you find this volume helpful and interesting. I had a wonderful time compiling it and have used it extensively in its pre-published form myself.

Happy reading and all my best—
Deborah

Table of Contents

THE BOOKS

THE WORLD OF DRAGONFIRE

For millennia, the shape-shifting dragon warriors known as the Pyr *have lived peacefully as guardians of both the four elements and the earth's treasures. But now the final reckoning between the* Pyr, *who count humans among these treasures, and the* Slayers, *who would eradicate humans and the* Pyr *who protect them, is about to begin...*

There are ten novels, three novellas and a short story in the *Dragonfire* series of paranormal romances. The arc of the entire series takes place over an eight year period in our time, beginning March 3, 2007 and ending October 1, 2015. Each book is a romance, but the series should be read in order to follow the over-arching story of the Dragon's Tail Wars.

In order, the books are:

1. **Kiss of Fire** - Quinn, the Smith, and Sara

2. **Kiss of Fury** - Donovan, the Warrior, and Alex

3. **Kiss of Fate** - Erik, leader of the *Pyr*, and Eileen

4. **Winter Kiss** - Delaney and Ginger

5. **Harmonia's Kiss** - a short story about the Dragon's Tooth Warriors (who become the Dragon Legion)

6. **Whisper Kiss** - Niall and Rox

7. **Darkfire Kiss** - Rafferty and Melissa

8. **Flashfire** - Lorenzo and Cassie

9. **Ember's Kiss** - Brandon and Liz

10. **Kiss of Danger** - Alexander and Katina

11. **Kiss of Darkness** - Damien and Petra

12. **Kiss of Destiny** - Thad and Aura

13. **Serpent's Kiss** - Thorolf and Chandra

14. **Firestorm Forever** - Sloane, the Apothecary, and Samantha; Drake, leader of the Dragon Legion, and Veronica; Marco, the Sleeper, and Jacelyn.

There are four digital boxed sets available of the series. **The Dragon Legion Collection**, includes **Kiss of Danger, Kiss of Darkness** and **Kiss of Destiny**, is the only bundle available in both digital and print editions.

Dragonfire Quest includes **Kiss of Fire, Kiss of Fury** and **Kiss of Fate**. **Dragonfire Elixir** includes **Winter Kiss, Whisper Kiss** and **Darkfire Kiss**. **Dragonfire Reunion** includes **Flashfire, Ember's Kiss, Harmonia's Kiss, Kiss of Danger, Kiss of Darkness** and **Kiss of Destiny**. **Dragonfire Triumph** includes **Serpent's Kiss** and **Firestorm Forever**.

All of the individual books are available in ebook, trade paperback and hardcover collectors' editions. There are links on Deborah's website to buy signed copies of the entire series from Deborah in trade paperback or hardcover.

OVERVIEW OF THE SERIES

Before we look at the individual books and stories, let's examine the underlying assumptions and details of the world of *Dragonfire*.

The Dragon's Tail Wars are the final conflict between *Pyr* and *Slayers*, a foretold battle which only one kind of dragon shifter will survive. The Dragon's Tail is an astrological event—the moon takes nineteen years to complete a circuit in the sky visible from earth. Each half of the cycle is called a node and takes about nine and a half years. The first half is called the Dragon's Head, because the moon appears to be ascending. This node is said to favorably influence expansion and growth. The other node of the moon is called the Dragon's Tail, because the moon appears to be descending in the sky. This node is believed to favor balancing of debts and rebuilding foundations.

The first Dragon's Tail of the twenty-first century began in June 2006 and is believed to be a phase particularly geared to reorganization, the establishment of balance and karmic reckoning. It was forecast to be a phase of severe weather, and a period in which it was critical for us to rebalance our relationship with each other and with the earth. The first lunar eclipse after in this node of the mood was on March 3, 2007 and it sparked the first of the Dragonfire firestorms, Quinn's in **Kiss of Fire**. The moon's node turned again in October 2015, which made the last total lunar eclipse of this phase the blood moon on September 28, 2015. This eclipse sparked Sloane's firestorm in **Firestorm Forever.**

The *Pyr* are an ancient species of dragon shape shifters with a mission to defend the four elements and the treasures of the earth. They include humans amongst those treasures. Their name is derived from the Greek word for 'fire'. The *Pyr* have become divided over the centuries, partly because of the actions of humans. In the Middle Ages, dragons were hunted by humans, both because they were seen as wicked and because their bodies were believed to be the source of magical cures for human ailments. In this era, the *Pyr* divided ranks, some of them no longer seeing humans as treasures to be defended. These dragon shifters became known as *Slayers*—the *Pyr* say that they denied the divine spark of the Great Wyvern by rejecting their original mandate. The blood of *Slayers* is black and caustic, and they cannot have firestorms. They are still *Pyr* in terms of their abilities, though, so some distinguish between "*Pyr*" and "true *Pyr*". The dragon shifters have a saying that *Pyr* are born but *Slayers* are made.

In the world of Dragonfire, individual *Pyr* live long lives but aren't immortal. Each *Pyr* comes into his shifting powers at puberty and once he grows to maturity, he ages very slowly. Each *Pyr* will have one firestorm in his long life. This is an opportunity to conceive a son. The firestorm sparks between the *Pyr* and his destined mate—quite literally, sparks fly between them, so the *Pyr* can't mistake the identity of the woman fated to conceive and bear his son. The firestorm creates light and heat which are both stronger with closer proximity, but also kindles sexual desire. The firestorm cannot be denied, and grows in intensity the longer it remains unfulfilled. When the *Pyr* and his mate satisfy the firestorm, the sparks disappear and a child is conceived that first time. The *Pyr* in question will also begin to age after the fulfillment of his firestorm. There are those who believe that his body will match its aging process to that of his mate, at least if they remain together.

The *Pyr* have sons the vast majority of the time. There is only one female *Pyr* at any given time, known as the Wyvern, and she has additional powers. The Wyvern at the beginning of *Dragonfire* is Sophie. Traditionally, the Wyvern has been so elusive that the *Pyr* seldom see her and many Pyr have believed her to be almost divine. Sophie is determined to take a more active role in ensuring the survival of her kind because she knows the Dragon's Tail Wars are pending.

The spark of a firestorm can be felt by all *Pyr*—including *Slayers*, so it tends to create a gathering of dragon shifters. *Slayers* may come to interfere with the firestorm's satisfaction, out of spite or a desire to ensure there are fewer *Pyr* born. In contrast, the *Pyr* are drawn to support the *Pyr* in question, by assisting in his defense and that of his mate.

Since each of the *Dragonfire* novels is a paranormal romance, each one features a firestorm. (**Firestorm Forever** is the exception: since it's the series finale, it features three firestorms.) The *Pyr* also believe that firestorms of key importance to the survival of their kind (such as those during this Dragon's Tail node of the moon) are ignited by a total lunar eclipse.

The *Dragonfire Novels* fall into groups for me, with each group having a specific role in the recounting of the overall arc of the story of the Dragon's Tail Wars. The first three show the launch of the Dragon's Tail Wars, but also orient the reader in the world of the *Pyr*. These books introduce the continuing characters, the world of *Dragonfire*, and many of the concepts that are developed over the series. In **Kiss of Fire**, we meet the *Pyr* through the perspective of Quinn, a dragon shifter who is alienated from his kind yet should perform a key role for them as the Smith. In **Kiss of Fury**, we experience the firestorm with an established fighter in the *Pyr* who isn't interested in permanent relationships. In **Kiss of Fate**, we share the transformative power of the firestorm with the *Pyr* most invested in the community of dragon shifters yet the one whose own firestorm failed and whose son turned *Slayer*. This trilogy shows that the Dragon's Tail is about more than the war with the *Slayers*, but is a time of testing assumptions and challenging the *Pyr* to change.

The second trilogy within the Dragonfire saga is focused on the Dragon's Blood Elixir and the battle against its creator, the *Slayer*, Magnus Montmorency. This is accomplished in three steps by the *Pyr*. First, the source of the Elixir has to be found and destroyed, which is Delaney's chosen mission in **Winter Kiss**. It's a personal quest for him, since he was infected with the Elixir against his will, but one he can only successfully complete with the help of Ginger, his destined mate, and the firestorm. Secondly, those *Slayers* infected with the Elixir have to be hunted down and destroyed. This is Niall's quest in **Whisper Kiss**, one that becomes very personal: Niall discovers that his dead twin brother, Phelan, has not only become a shadow dragon but means to steal Niall's mate,

Rox. Finally, Magnus himself has to be killed, no small feat and one that falls to Rafferty, who has the longest and most bitter enmity against the *Slayer*. Stakes are raised in **Darkfire Kiss** when Rafferty's firestorm sparks and his destined mate, Melissa, proves to have a vendetta against Magnus as well.

The third grouping of stories involves bringing the outsiders of the *Pyr* into the community of the greater group. Lorenzo has long avoided the *Pyr* and is actually courted by Chen to turn *Slayer* in his book, **Flashfire**. A master illusionist, Lorenzo is good at disguising his true intention and feelings, at least until he meets Cassie, who sees right through him. Brandon is an exile from the *Pyr:* as a result of his parents' divorce, he knows little of his skills, and he's been taught his mother's distrust of them. That ignorance makes him an easy target for the *Slayer* Chen in **Ember's Kiss** as well as skeptical of the *Pyr* who try to help him—at least until his mate, Liz, becomes determined to save him from Chen.

The Dragon Legion novellas can be considered to be part of this grouping of "outsider" stories, but are also a group in their own right. This trilogy of stories takes the Dragon's Tooth Warriors back in time to their firestorms, which they've missed since they were enchanted for several millennia. These stories include time travel and some mythical journeys, too. In **Kiss of Danger**, Alexander is returned to the destined mate and son he left behind. In **Kiss of Darkness**, Damien travels to the underworld to retrieve his pregnant lost love. In **Kiss of Destiny**, Thad's firestorm sparks on Mount Olympus with a nymph who steals his heart forever. Drake, the leader of the troop, is the only one to return to contemporary times.

Ember's Kiss and the Dragon Legion novellas could also be considered a group in their own right, as each of them features a heroine who is an elemental witch. These four firestorms fulfill a prophecy which allows Thorolf to eliminate Viv Jason, an ancient foe of the *Pyr* in his book, **Serpent's Kiss**.

The short story **Harmonia's Kiss** was published between **Winter Kiss** and **Whisper Kiss**, but really could be considered part of two different groups: it could be a prologue to the Dragon Legion novellas, as it concerns the quest of the Dragon's Tooth Warriors to find meaning in their situation. (This is why it's included in the digital bundle **Dragonfire Reunion**.) It also could be considered a prologue to Drake's firestorm in **Firestorm Forever**, because Drake met Ronnie for the first time in **Harmonia's Kiss**, and actually she's responsible for him finding hope in his future.

There are four firestorms in the last two books of the Dragonfire series, all of which contribute their part to ridding the world of *Slayers* and ensuring the *Pyr*'s triumph. In **Serpent's Kiss**, Thorolf destroys three foes with the help of his goddess-mate, Chandra: Viv Jason, from the ancient curse, the *Slayer* Chen and the Jormungand, which accelerates the healing of the world. In **Firestorm Forever**, Drake's firestorm with Ronnie exposes Jorge and his plan; Marco and his mate, Jac, hunt both Jorge and the clones of the *Slayer* Boris Vassily that are hatching with each eclipse; and Sloane and his destined mate Sam work together to find a cure for the disease ravaging the world. Sloane and Sam's firestorm sparks at the very end of the book, closing the entire series with a firestorm, just as it began.

The portal opens to the realm of the Fae in **Firestorm Forever**, and Maeve, the Fae Queen, is introduced in that book. She's not vanquished, even though she's on a quest to eliminate all shifters and "half-breeds" from the world. The battle against Maeve is left to the Dragon Legion and is the storyline of the *DragonFate Novels*.

We'll also learn more about the origin of the *Pyr* in the *DragonFate Novels*.

READING ORDER

It is best to read the *Dragonfire Novels* in order as the entire series recounts the events of the Dragon's Tail Wars.

There is, however, a spin-off paranormal young adult series featuring the coming-of-age of Zoë Sorensson, the daughter of

Erik, leader of the *Pyr*, and his mate Eileen. As mentioned above, there is only one female *Pyr* at any given time and at the beginning of *Dragonfire*, the Wyvern is Sophie. Sophie dies in **Kiss of Fate**, during Erik and Eileen's firestorm. The resulting child is a girl, Zoë, whom Erik hopes will be the new Wyvern. The timing of Sophie's death is regrettable, since the *Pyr* come into their powers at puberty: Erik fears that the Dragon's Tail Wars will be over before Zoë claims her abilities. His concern with his daughter's abilities is an ongoing thread in the subsequent books. Zoë appears to have some abilities of a Wyvern—like casting dreams—but these occur less often after she begins to talk. *The Dragon Diaries* is a paranormal young adult trilogy that tells of Zoë's coming of age. When her powers begin to manifest, she has to figure out how to use them all by herself since there are no other Wyverns. She also realizes that the *Pyr* face a new challenge, one that the older *Pyr* don't take seriously. It's up to Zoë and the next generation to save the day. The trilogy has one story arc, so it is best to read these three books in order.

When should you read this series? Well, I wrote it at the same time I was writing **Darkfire Kiss** and it was published shortly afterward. The first option is to read it after **Darkfire Kiss**. The other is to read it in terms of chronological time since the *Dragonfire Novels* are set in real time. Zoë is conceived in 2008 and born November 16, 2008. The *Dragonfire Novels* finish with the epilogue in **Firestorm Forever** in October 2015. **Flying Blind**, book #1 of the *Dragon Diaries*, begins in April 2024. So the second option is to read Zoë's story after you've read all of the *Dragonfire Novels*.

But then, there's another spin-off series, which complicates things even more. *The DragonFate Novels* are set in the same world as *Dragonfire* and features a new challenge to the *Pyr*, one that is faced primarily by the Dragon Legion. Other *Pyr* we know and love will make cameo appearances, but the focus will be on new firestorms and new battles. **Maeve's Book of Beasts**, the prequel to the *DragonFate Novels*, is set in October 2019, putting it right between the *Dragonfire Novels* and the *Dragon Diaries* in terms of chronological time.

I also plan to write some historical romances set in this world, to explain—for example—the source of the Dragon's Egg, and more. Reading in chronological order is going to become complicated, so you might want to read the books in the order they were written.

In the following section, you'll find each book in the series in order, beginning with the cover copy, the prophecy, and a summary of the story. Each book's entry concludes with my comments on the book and an excerpt of my choice.

KISS OF FIRE

ONE KISS CAN CHANGE THE COURSE OF DESTINY...

When ace accountant Sara Keegan decides to settle down and run her quirky aunt's New Age bookstore, she's not looking for adventure. She doesn't believe in fate or the magic of tarot cards, but when she's saved from a vicious attack by a man who has the ability to turn into a fire-breathing dragon, she questions whether she's losing her mind—or about to lose her heart.

Self-reliant loner Quinn Tyrrell has long been distrustful of his fellow Pyr. *When he feels the firestorm that signals his destined mate, he's determined to protect and possess Sara, regardless of the cost. Then Sara's true destiny is revealed and Quinn realizes he must risk everything—even Sara's love—to fulfill their entwined fates.*

THE PROTAGONISTS

Kiss of Fire recounts the firestorm of Quinn Tyrrell, who is both the Smith of the *Pyr* and an outsider. He decided long ago to avoid his fellow dragon shifters, for various reasons, and intends to continue on that path. Quinn is a good ambassador for readers meeting the *Pyr* for the first time, because he doesn't know their history or relationships either. He also has some details wrong, thanks to the meddling of a *Slayer* who pretended to be his friend. His mate, Sara, who likes to solve riddles and believes everything is logical, asks a lot of questions, compelling him to delve deeper into the lore of his kind and learn where he has it wrong.

Dragons are said to have an affection for virgins (or maidens), damsels in distress and princesses. There aren't many virgins in *Dragonfire*—just one!—although there are plenty of damsels in distress, many of whom are being targeted by *Slayers*. Sara is the only princess: the name Sara means 'princess', and she also has that delicate prettiness we associate with the role. Her nature is in contrast to her appearance, though, as Sara is pragmatic and logical. She's stubborn enough to not let go of a riddle once she's found it, and is an innovative problem-solver. She challenges Quinn's assumptions and makes him re-think what he believes he knows, as well as stealing his heart away forever.

THE ELEMENTS

In **Kiss of Fire,** Sophie reveals that each *Pyr* has affinities to two elements and that his destined mate will have affinities to the remaining two.

The Smith commanded earth and fire, whether he knew it or not, bringing the persistent power of earth and the passion of fire to all he touched. The Seer held the reins of winter and air, again whether she knew it or not, bringing the intuitive understanding of water and the cold reason of air to every puzzle she encountered. The four elements would join with their union and create a greater fusion of their abilities.
—from **Kiss of Fire**

Quinn's affinities are for earth and fire, a fitting combination for the Smith who works with fire and metal. Sara's affinities are to air and water—she's analytical, as shown in her past in finance and her desire to be organized, and that's the side of herself that she knows best. Water governs her ability to have psychic dreams and visions, which is harder for her to accept.

THE SETTING

Quinn's firestorm is sparked by the total lunar eclipse of March 3, 2007. Although he feels the heat of his firestorm from his home in Traverse City, Michigan, he's in no hurry to go to his mate, since he expects the *Pyr* to meet him there. He meets Sara in Ann Arbor, Michigan when he exhibits his work at the Outdoor Art Exhibition in July.

THE PROPHECY

When the Dragon's Tail demands its price,

And the moon is devoured once, not twice,
Seer and Smith will again unite.
Water and air, with fire and earth
This sacred union will give birth
To the Pyr's sole chance to save the Earth.

THE STORY

Prologue: On March 3, 2007, six members of the *Pyr* high circle meet in southern Libya to use the Dragon's Egg to determine the location of the next firestorm, shown to be Ann Arbor, Michigan. Erik Sorensson tells the group they will all go, as a final battle is forthcoming. In the Kalahari desert, six others have gathered, having captured a seventh, the female Wyvern They torture her by threatening to cut off her wings to learn the name of the human woman (Sara Keegan) and the *Pyr* who will be her mate via the firestorm (Quinn Tyrrell, the Smith). In Traverse City, Michigan, Quinn changes into his dragon form for the first time in centuries and realizes his firestorm is coming.

Chapter 1: Four months later, July 2007: as Sara Keegan leaves the New Age bookstore she inherited from her aunt, she spots a gold coin on the threshold of the shop, then gets attacked by a man who knows her name. She is on the verge of being choked when the pressure suddenly disappears. When Sara looks up, she sees a silver and blue dragon, and her attacker runs away. Sara passes out briefly, and when she comes to, she no longer sees a dragon. There is a man there who helps her up and offers to walk her to a safe area. Despite her misgivings, Sara allows him to do so, at which point he disappears. After watching to ensure Sara makes it safely home, Quinn adds protections around her house.

Chapter 2: The next morning, Sara wakes to a woman's cry for help, but cannot find anyone in distress. At an art show the same morning, Quinn sees another *Pyr*, who approaches him and tells him it is his duty to breed. Sara arrives at the fair and spots Quinn in his booth. She thanks him for his assistance the night before and learns both his name and his trade: blacksmith. Very aware of her growing attraction to Quinn, Sara then spots a mermaid door knocker she insists upon buying for her shop. Quinn offers to install it for her.

Chapter 3: While working in the book shop updating the accounting records, Sara is interrupted by an unusual man who enters the shop and asks where he can find the books on mythology. The mermaid doorknocker lights up orange and becomes hot to the touch. The customer comes to the counter with three books, and Sara briefly sees green flames in his eyes. The man tells Sara he chose the books, all titles on dragons, for her and then says, "It is prophesied that the Seer and the Smith will be the first partners of the new age." Sara realizes he is the man she saw at Quinn's booth. He says the *Slayers* will kill her to keep the prophecy from coming true. He also introduces himself as Erik Sorensson, leader of the *Pyr*. After Erik abruptly leaves, Quinn arrives and transforms into a dragon in front of Sara—the same one she'd seen the night before. Quinn changes back and explains a bit about the mystical characteristics of being the Smith. Sara shares some information about her past and why she took over her aunt's shop, leaving her previous life as an accountant behind. Quinn demonstrates the firestorm by touching palms with Sara and reveals that they are destined mates. He then recites the prophecy of the Seer and the Smith, which says their child will save the Earth. Sara then asks to touch one of Quinn's talons.

Chapter 4: Sara's reaction to the idea of destined mates lets Quinn know she is not quite on board yet. Once he learns Erik has visited Sara, he becomes more concerned, due to a past history with the *Pyr* leader. Quinn tries to convince Sara to come with him right then so he can better protect her, but she balks and remains at the shop. Quinn does blow a trail of protective dragonsmoke around Sara's store, which also identifies him as her protector. Sara tries to adjust the thermostat on the air conditioning system, which has been acting up. While trying to fix the air conditioning, Sara finds a velvet bag containing her aunt's tarot cards. She wonders to herself if her aunt meant for her to make the discovery, and the air conditioning comes back on. Fearing a fire due to faulty wiring, Sara turns off the breaker to the system. As she works with the tarot cards, the same one keeps coming up: the Lovers. Then the air conditioning comes back on, without a power source. A book falls from a shelf to the floor—three times: *Awakening the Psychic Within*. In his booth, Quinn hears another *Pyr*, in his mind, using old-speak, which he believes only *Slayers* can do, though at first, he thinks it sounds like his old friend, Ambrose. Sara reads some of the book on psychics and pulls the High Priestess card from the tarot deck. She has a vision about a woman with the same voice that had woken her that morning, and also hears the words, "It is forbidden to injure the Wyvern!" Disturbed, Sara locks up the shop to leave, and sees the same gold coin at the doorstep as was there the night before. She decides to go see Quinn about it, but does not notice the man following her.

Chapter 5: Sara arrives at Quinn's booth, tells him about her vision, and asks about the Wyvern. Quinn explains that the Wyvern is the only female *Pyr*, until she dies and her ability gets passed on to another who carries the *Pyr* gene. The Wyvern has the gift of prophecy, knowing which male will experience the firestorm next, and who his mate is. Quinn also explains the role of the *Pyr*: to protect the Earth, including humankind. *Slayers*, however, see the humans as destroyers of the Earth and want to get rid of them. Sara and Quinn surmise the Wyvern must be a captive of the *Slayers*, which explains how they knew to look for the two of them. They arrange a meeting with Erik, even though Quinn doesn't trust him. As both men change into their dragon forms, another dragon group attacks.

Chapter 6: While watching the dragon battle from the bell tower, Sara sees a huge golden dragon sneaking up on her. He talks about Quinn as though he knows him, and she realizes it is the same man who attacked her the night before. When he breathes fire on Sara, Erik arrives and pushes her over the edge of the tower, but Quinn catches her and takes her far away from the action. Erik comes to them and arranges a meeting where they can talk. Sara wants to go along, and Quinn agrees. They go to Sara's place to shower first, during which they have a pre-sexual interlude.

Chapter 7: When Quinn and Sara arrive at Erik's hotel room, four other *Pyr* are also in attendance. Quinn learns Erik knew his father.

The other *Pyr* take Quinn to task for not remaining with them, but he states he had no wish to after the death of Ambrose, his mentor. Erik says Ambrose was a *Slayer*, but Quinn does not believe him. The other men are also unhappy over the death of Delaney, lost in the battle earlier that night, and at the fact his body was taken away by the *Slayers*, to dishonor it, they think. Sara tells them according to one of the books Erik suggested she read, what they really wanted to do was make sure he stayed dead. The others realize the *Slayers* took the bodies of their own dead in order to revive them. Despite his reluctance to believe that Ambrose was a *Slayer*, Quinn remembers being introduced to his former mentor with a gold coin like the one he'd found the night before when fighting the dragon who attacked Sara. Back at her home, Sara realizes she forgot to show Quinn the coin she had found that morning before he left. She holds it to see if she can summon a vision, but when nothing happens, she goes to bed.

Chapter 8: Sara has a dream/vision about a four-year-old boy witnessing the destruction of his village, and she feels the boy must be Quinn. When she wakes, Sara then hears the Wyvern again, and feels actual pain from cuts, though nothing shows on her body. She meets Quinn downstairs and tells him they need to help the Wyvern. Quinn dismisses the idea, mainly because they don't know where to start looking, and he refuses to place Sara in additional danger. Sara describes her dream/vision and asks if Quinn will send Erik to her to explain all he knows about the Wyvern. He does not want to summon Erik, despite Sara pointing out she thinks Erik has been watching out for Quinn, and that she believes it was Ambrose who threatened her in the tower the night before. In the street, Sara and Quinn indulge in a literal traffic-stopping kiss before he leaves her at her shop. Inside, since she now accepts Aunt Magda's existence as a ghost, Sara asks for help finding information on the Wyvern, and a book falls to the floor. Back at the art fair, Donovan, Erik's cohort, walks up and tosses Quinn a coin, challenging him to a blood duel in response to the death of Delaney in the battle the night before. At first, Quinn tries to talk Donovan out of fighting, but then agrees. Back at her shop, Sara discovers information in the book Magda pulled out for her about the Cathars and the destruction of the town of Béziers. She thinks this is what she witnessed in her vision, though that would make Quinn over eight hundred years old. Sara decides to head over to Quinn's booth on her own. Donovan and Quinn begin their duel, but in the midst of it, the *Slayer*, Lucien, shows up, and the two *Pyr* team up to face off against him. On her way to Quinn, Sara gets stopped by two men: Ambrose and a Russian man, who puts Sara in some kind of thrall and entices her into their car. Back at the dragon fight, Quinn and Donovan kill Lucien, but then Quinn realizes Sara is in danger, and he and Donovan leave together to find her.

Chapter 10: While Ambrose drives the car with Sara asleep in the backseat, Boris muses on how difficult it has proven to kill Sara, and devises a plan to permit Sara to escape and lead the *Pyr* into a trap when trying to save the Wyvern. Donovan and Quinn go get the others to plan the rescue of Sara. Sara has a dream/vision of Quinn as a young man beginning to come into his abilities, but not understanding what they are, and she sees him meet Ambrose for the first time. Quinn, Erik, Donovan, Niall, and Rafferty form two groups to go look for Sara, Niall's air affinity giving them a trail to follow. Sara wakes in strange surroundings, once again to the sound of the Wyvern's voice, but this time the woman herself is there. Sara cleans the Wyvern's (Sophie's) wounds, while she tries to figure out a way to escape.

Chapter 11: Rafferty, with his earth affinity, opens a hole in the ground near the cabin where Sara is being held. Inside, Sara and Sophie discuss the firestorm and what it means, and Sophie explains to Sara about coins and blood duels when she sees the one Sara has. Sophie points out the prophecy regarding the Seer and the Smith does not specifically state they will give birth to a child, implying the words may refer to something else. Sara feels the ground tremble, and then a large hole opens in the floor of the cabin, out of which Quinn appears. Quinn sends Sara through the tunnel and tries to get to Sophie, but three *Slayers* appear and use their dragonsmoke as a weapon against Quinn. Sophie tells him to go, as he is the one they really want. As Quinn runs down the tunnel with Sara on his back, they get almost all of the way out before smoke hits one of Quinn's legs, injuring him. After Niall and Rafferty pull Quinn out of the ground, Sara suggests they breathe their dragonfire on Quinn so he can heal. Sara suggests to Quinn they head home and take care of the firestorm.

Chapter 12: Back at the cabin, Sophie realizes the *Slayers* are using her as bait to trap the *Pyr*. She also reflects upon Sara and Quinn as the Seer and the Smith, understanding their respective gifts (Quinn with earth and fire, Sara with water and air) would join the four elements together with their union, creating more power. Sophie also sends Sara a dream. Quinn learns Ambrose did not teach him everything he needed to know about being *Pyr*, and Sara suggests their first meeting was also supposed to be a challenge from Ambrose. Sara tells Quinn, Niall, and Rafferty they should all be able to learn how to wield the power of all elements. This would increase their power immensely in the battle against the *Slayers*. Sara encourages Quinn to talk to Erik about the past, and they agree to meet the next morning. At Sara's, she and Quinn explore the firestorm by having sex for the first time (or three). The next morning, Quinn finds a silver hair in his temple, understanding this means he is aging after satisfying the firestorm.

Chapter 13: Quinn meets with Erik and learns the truth about his family's murders, that Ambrose was responsible, and that Erik and Quinn's father were close friends. Erik also gives Quinn a coin that had belonged to his father, with the comment that his father had said he could make it his own. Quinn realizes Erik has been telling him the truth and so invites him up to Sara's for coffee. Meanwhile, Sara has a dream of Elizabeth, who had been Quinn's wife in colonial America, seeing her be burned alive by Ambrose. Sara then asks the men when they all (including her) will rescue the Wyvern. When Sara suggests Quinn needs to work with the *Pyr*, Quinn objects. Sara says she knows he still suspects Erik of Elizabeth's death, but she knows it was Ambrose because she saw it.

Chapter 14: Sara assures Quinn that Elizabeth did not blame him for anything. Sara explains about her own parents' deaths in a fire following a car accident. They realize that Ambrose killed her parents, believing Sara to be in the car with them at the time, as she originally planned to be. While the *Pyr* train together for their assault on the cabin to rescue the Wyvern, Rafferty teaches Sara how to resist beguilement. She asks Rafferty if the firestorm is only about mating, and he responds that it depends. When the group (including Sara, who convinced Quinn she must go as she can cross dragonsmoke without being harmed) meets to leave, Sara notices there are no longer literal sparks when she and Quinn touch. She asks if the firestorm is over, but Quinn doesn't give a direct answer. When they arrive at the cabin, Erik warns them some of the *Slayers* may be concealing themselves. Sara goes inside to get Sophie, then hears Ambrose outside, setting the cabin on fire. Sara asks Sophie to change into a small shape to escape her chains, and the Wyvern changes into a salamander, which Sara puts in her pocket. Then she screams.

Chapter 15: As the dragon battle rages, Erik faces off against a smaller green dragon that is blocking him from going after Boris. It turns out to be Sigmund, Erik's only son, who has turned *Slayer*. He uses the name Sigmund Guthrie and is the author of the book on how to kill the *Pyr*, one of the titles Erik pulled out of a shelf in Sara's shop for her to read. Though taunted, Erik refuses to kill his son, flinging him away. Sigmund recovers and hits Erik twice from behind while Boris breathes dragonfire on him. As Ambrose flies up to meet the *Pyr*, Sara grabs onto his tail to escape the fire. Quinn distracts Ambrose by throwing his coin and issuing a challenge. Ambrose drops Sara, but Quinn cannot dive into the smoke after her, since it would kill him. Then a sleek white dragon saves Sara from falling, and they realize it is the Wyvern. Despite his injuries, Quinn determines to fight Ambrose alone, telling the other two to protect Sara as she already carries the next Smith. Donovan helps by breathing dragonfire across Quinn's back. As Sophie tries to heal Erik, Sara learns from the others about her pregnancy.

Chapter 16: Quinn uses Ambrose's main weakness—his pride— against him, taunting him to anger. As they battle, Quinn learns Ambrose had abducted Quinn's mother when she was a young woman, and Quinn's father had rescued her. Quinn tricks Ambrose into thinking he is weakening and dying, making use of dragonfire from the surrounding burning trees. He takes Ambrose by surprise and kills him. Sophie leaves after repairing Erik's spirit, necessary for his physical healing. Sara and Quinn discuss what it may mean now that the firestorm is over, and Quinn assures her he has no plans to leave unless she wants him to. Sara also wonders why the four elements together only harm the *Pyr* and not heal.

Chapter 17: Over the next few weeks after the battle, Sara and Quinn commute to see one another, she gets her pregnancy confirmed by a doctor, and Quinn experiments at his forge to see if he can come up with a way to use the four elements together to heal the *Pyr*. On the day of the next eclipse, when another firestorm will be revealed, Donovan is visiting Quinn's farm and collects a pair of custom metal talons made by Quinn which are like Lucien's. Together Sara and Quinn use the elements to heal the exposed area over Quinn's heart, now missing a scale due to his love for her. Quinn gives Sara an acorn to plant by their home, which prompts a vision of their shared future and sons.

DEBORAH'S COMMENTS

I like that the firestorm challenges the assumptions of both Quinn and Sara in this book, and they test each other's beliefs as well. Sara is sure that the world is a sensible place, but things happen in Quinn's presence that can't be logically explained. Although she doubts the suggestion that she could be the Seer, she becomes convinced of it through her experiences with Quinn and finds a hidden side of herself. Quinn, meanwhile, is sure he has no need of the *Pyr* in his life, even if his future is to be with Sara. It's Sara who convinces him that it's better to have more dragons at his back when there are *Slayers* around, just as it's Quinn who convinces Sara to believe in her dreams. They heal each other, proving to the other *Pyr* that Quinn's father was right about partnership with a mate. When Sara and Quinn join forces with each other and with the *Pyr*, Ambrose doesn't have a chance.

There are two passages in this book which stick in my mind. The first is Erik's explanation to Quinn of the *Pyr* view of firestorms, and how that's changed. Erik and Thierry had argued over

Thierry's determination to make a permanent bond with Margaux, as this was uncommon for the *Pyr* at that time, but is becoming convinced that Thierry was right. Here's what he tells Quinn about it:

"There is an old conviction among our kind that love is a whimsy of mortals, that to love a woman is to lose something of what makes one *Pyr*. To link oneself to a mortal woman is to create a binding tie with one place and time, to rip asunder our connection to infinity. According to such thinking, women serve their purpose in bearing our young and have no merit beyond that. We may protect them and we may honor them by force of that debt, but it is inadvisable for us to surrender any of our affection to them. I have known many who have lived to that code."

Quinn said nothing.

Erik pursed his lips and shoved his hands into the pockets of his jacket. "There is power in that choice and for a long time, I respected it as the truth."

Quinn was intrigued by the implication. "But?"

"But your father argued otherwise. Your father bound himself to your mother, in every possible way, and did so against much protest from the others."

"What do you mean?"

Erik held Quinn's gaze. "I mean that he loved her, and he was unafraid as to who knew as much."

Quinn looked at the sidewalk, remembering. There certainly had been affection between his parents and he knew his father must have been *Pyr*. He hadn't ever seen his father in dragon form, but he remembered the tricks his father used to play with flames. It had been as if the fire listened to him, but as a child, Quinn had believed his father could do anything.

Erik continued his story. "Your father insisted that he gained more by his surrender to love than he lost."

—from **Kiss of Fire**

This is an intriguing passage, because it implies that the *Pyr* are— or can be—immortal. In fact, in *Kiss of Fire* there is another similar suggestion. The *Pyr* suggest to Quinn that saving Sara might come at too high of a price if it means his own death. Rafferty notes that Sara's soul will be reborn, and that Quinn will have a later opportunity for a firestorm, while Donovan insists that Quinn not risk his life since the *Pyr* need him. Are the *Pyr* immortal? No. We see that when Quinn finds his first grey hair after consummating his firestorm with Sara. He's begun to age.

The more interesting question is whether the *Pyr* were ever immortal. That's something we'll explore in subsequent books.
The second quote is a passage that is my favorite in the book. Quinn creates a door knocker that is a mermaid as a talisman in the prologue. It has some magical powers, like heating and alerting him when Sara's in danger, and I love the passage that tells of Quinn crafting it. It's the night of the first eclipse after the moon of the node has turned to the Dragon's Tail. He knows his firestorm has sparked, although he knows nothing of Sara yet. In a way, she's a treasure to be won. It's snowing and Quinn's alone in his workshop, with the fire burning high in the forge, and is in his dragon form, scaled in sapphire and steel.

With his talons, Quinn removed the mermaid door knocker from the fire where she waited. She was red-hot, gleaming and glowing, on the verge of turning into liquid. He finished the end of her tail with sure strokes. He had known when the iron took this feminine shape beneath his hand that his turn had come; he had known that he could finish the work only in dragon form.

His firestorm was coming.

The others, good and bad, would follow the beacon of its heat.

This time, he would triumph.

This time, he would protect what was his to defend.

He exhaled mightily, spending sparks dancing throughout his workshop, infusing the hot iron with his desire. The mermaid glittered as if she were made of fire, caught in a magical wind of Quinn's making. She looked to be filled with sparks, but in truth, she was filled with the power of his will.

He was the Smith.

His talisman was struck.

Let them try to stop his firestorm.
—from **Kiss of Fire**

KISS OF FURY

ONE ACT OF PASSION CAN SAVE THE WORLD...

Scientist Alexandra Madison was on the verge of unveiling an invention that would change the world. Then her partner was murdered, their lab was burned, and their prototype was destroyed. While Alex is in the hospital recovering from burns suffered in the fire, recurring dragon-haunted nightmares threaten to land her in the psychiatric ward, but she knows she has to escape to her lab to rebuild the Green Machine.

Handsome, daring and impulsive, Donovan Shea is more than willing to do his part in the Pyr/Slayer war. Assigned to protect Alex, Donovan is shocked when her presence ignites his firestorm. He has no desire for a destined mate, but Alex's intelligence and determination inspire him to join the fight to save her invention. With the Slayers closing in, Donovan knows he would surrender his life for Alex...and lose his heart to possess her.

THE PROTAGONISTS

Donovan is what many readers would expect a dragon shifter to be. He's handsome and powerful, said to be the best fighter of his kind, loyal and true. He's also disinterested in making permanent connections, although he admires and enjoys women. He adores his Ducati motorcycle, is a bit reckless and daring. He's trouble, and he draws women like moths to the flame.

The challenge for Donovan is that of the firestorm, or at least with the permanent connection the *Pyr* are coming to believe it requires. He has no issue with consummating the firestorm, but because of his own family history, he's less enamored of the idea of conceiving a son. Fortunately for Alex and for us, Erik is on the side of the firestorm and tricks Donovan into encountering his destined mate. The firestorm has its own power to wield after that, and its heat compels Donovan to explore its allure and learn more about Alex.

In a way, Alex and Donovan are two of a kind. Alex is a scientist, driven to succeed, focused on her work and her end goal of creating a vehicle that is more environmentally friendly. When her partner is killed by *Slayers* before her eyes, she wants payback. Her ferocity and passion make her an equal match for Donovan, and fills this story with action. In another way, they're very different and have things to teach each other. For example, Alex relies upon her family in challenging times, while Donovan distrusts his father completely. Alex's romantic conviction that love is key to a relationship combines with the firestorm's heat to persuade Donovan to try to win her heart—and makes the satisfaction of their firestorm combustible.

THE ELEMENTS

Donovan's affinities are with with water and fire, and water is an unusual affinity for the *Pyr*. We'll see that this particular affinity might run in families, as Delaney shares it. Alex's affinities are with air and earth. Here's an excerpt from the book about their respective affinities:

Alex was thinking. "You're obviously fire," she said to Donovan. "All passion and fury."

"Thanks a lot," he teased. "I'll guess that you're air, with all those brilliant ideas."

"I'm feeling smarter all of a sudden," Niall joked.

"Earth," Rafferty said, pointing at Alex. "Possibly the most pragmatic and practical person I've ever met."

"And determined." Donovan nodded. "You'd give Rafferty a run for his money on determination." The *Pyr* laughed at that and Sloane nudged Rafferty.

"My grandmother taught me that giving up accomplishes nothing," Alex said with pride. "What about water? Is that always about tears?"

"Intuition," Sloane said. "Understanding and emotions."

Sara pointed a finger at Donovan. "That's you and your gut-level trust of people. You also fight well because you respond instinctively."

THE SETTING

Donovan's firestorm is sparked by the total lunar eclipse of August 28, 2007, which was visible in America. Donovan is in Minneapolis-St. Paul during the eclipse, where Erik has sent him to protect Alex. Alex is in the hospital with burns after the *Slayers* burned down the lab of Gilchrist Enterprises and tortured her partner, Mark, to death. Not unsurprisingly, Alex is having recurring nightmares of dragons.

THE PROPHECY

There are two prophecies in *Kiss of Fury*, one about the firestorm, and one about the powers of the foretold Warrior.

> *The Dragon's Tail demands recompense*
> *Owed the land for man's violence;*
> *Both human and Pyr must sacrifice,*
> *To earn the chance to make matters right.*
> *A portal has opened to the past*
> *Making possible what has been lost;*
> *Time to muster forces for the final battle,*
> *In which Pyr and Slayer learn their mettle.*

> *Elements four disguise weapons three,*
> *Revealed if love harnesses fury.*
> *The Wizard can work her alchemy*
> *Only with the Warrior's lost key.*
> *Transformation in the firestorm's light,*
> *Will forge a foretold force for right.*
> *Warrior, Wizard and Pyr army*
> *Shall lead the world to victory.*

THE STORY

Prologue: On August 28, 2007, Erik Sorensson returns home after meeting with others in the high circle of the *Pyr* where a ceremony revealed the next firestorm will take place in Minneapolis. He finds Sophie, the Wyvern, on his couch, having somehow gotten through his protections, saying she has a portent. Sophie alludes to Erik's gift of foresight, then recites the prophecy she came to deliver, which refers to a portal to the past. Sophie then retrieves the Dragon's Egg from where Erik keeps it, and chants to bring forth a picture of what is to come: *Slayers* are after a human in an office building. Sophie identifies the human as Alex Madison, a woman scientist leading a group working on environmental change—something that must occur before the *Pyr* can effectively aid humanity. Sophie says Alex is the Wizard, foretold in the story of the Wizard and the Warrior. Erik believes the *Pyr* referred to as the Warrior must be Donovan.

Chapter 1: In October 2007, Alex Madison wakes up from a hellish dream to find herself in a hospital. She realizes her dream was a memory, that she and her colleague, Mark, were attacked in their lab—it was destroyed, and she is sure Mark was killed. Feigning sleep, Alex overhears a nurse and doctor discussing her, learning she has been there two weeks, and the doctor wants her moved to the psych ward since she dreams every night and talks about dragons. Alex resolves to disappear before she can be moved. Donovan, sent by Erik to remove Alex from the hospital, poses as an orderly and arranges her escape. Alex is not sure about Donovan, or about the odd way he makes her feel when he's close by or touching her. After loading Alex into a hearse, Donovan confirms to Rafferty, the driver, that he and Alex are indeed experiencing a firestorm. Then Alex escapes from them, stealing a car, and goes to her office to retrieve a small package. When she returns to the car, Donovan is in the back seat.

Chapter 2: Donovan joins Alex in the front seat, and when their shoulders touch, Alex sees and feels a spark. She continues to feel heated and aroused around the man. As Donovan asks what she took from her office, suddenly something big lands on the top of the car. When she sees the tail, Alex knows it's a dragon. Donovan changes into his dragon form to pursue the *Slayer*, but ends up going back to get Alex before the *Slayer* returns, shocking her further by appearing in his dragon form. Alex faints, and Donovan wonders why the *Slayers* allowed her to live yet again. In a hotel room, Donovan, Rafferty, and Erik discuss Alex and the firestorm.

Alex wakes up in an adjoining room and sees her chance to escape so she takes Donovan's Ducati. Upset with Erik for tricking him into rescuing his destined mate without being told, Donovan does not hear Alex leave until the bike starts up.

Chapter 3: While on the run, Alex gets stopped by Donovan (whose name she still doesn't know) in dragon form. Rather than follow his demand to get off the bike, Alex takes off, the dragon following her. They encounter the same amber-colored dragon who had attacked the car earlier. During their fight, Donovan learns his adversary, Tyson, was the mentor of a *Slayer* killed in the recent battle with Ambrose. When Tyson leaves, another dragon appears, calling Donovan "son." Donovan realizes this is indeed his father, Keir, whom he has only seen once, in human form. Meanwhile, Quinn arrives at Erik's, leaving Sara in the *Pyr* leader's care as he goes to help Donovan. Quinn chases off Tyson, then makes sure Alex gets somewhere safe, mentioning Donovan by name and the firestorm. At this point, Alex begins thinking of Donovan as "her dragon." Alex watches as Donovan and Quinn destroy Keir, who seems to feel no pain and has no blood from his wounds.

Chapter 4: Donovan and Quinn convince Alex to come with them to stay safe, explain to her the difference between *Pyr* and *Slayers*, and Quinn tells her about Sara, his human wife. Alex rides with Donovan on his bike to Erik's, and in the parking garage, they have a very heated embrace, which Donovan breaks off since he intends to refuse the firestorm. At the hotel, Sloane treats Donovan's wounds, asking about his repaired armor. The process did not work for Niall or Rafferty, but only for Quinn and Donovan, the two who had or were experiencing firestorms. When Donovan tells the others he killed his father, Rafferty says that's impossible, as he saw the man die in a bar fight centuries earlier. Now the *Pyr* wonder what *Slayers* have learned to do.

Chapter 5: While Alex showers, Sara resolves to fill in the details for Alex about the firestorm. The *Pyr* discuss how it could be possible for Keir to have reappeared. Sloane has a manuscript he's attempting to decode which may have answers. Erik says Sophie told him this period of the three eclipses may open doors not possible before, and Donovan tells them about the new *Slayer*, Tyson. The *Pyr* come to the conclusion the reason Alex was not killed yet was so she could retrieve all of the information on her invention, the Green Machine, first. Alex has a dream reliving Mark's death at the lab, and when she wakes, she tries to leave but Donovan stops her. Sophie experiences Gaia trying to regain balance by sending disasters, but manages to soften them so they don't have a devastating impact. The Wyvern wonders about the *Slayers'* secret academy and also decides since the *Slayers* aren't playing by the rules, she will get a bit more involved in the lives of the *Pyr* than she is supposed to. Sophie sends dreams to Sara, Quinn, Rafferty, and Donovan, and the ability to decipher the beginning of the manuscript to Sloane. Donovan's dream suggests Delaney, killed in Kiss of Fire, was actually his brother.

Chapter 6: Sara and Alex go shopping for the latter to get some clothes, while Quinn and Donovan stand guard. Boris and Tyson, in human form, show up, taunting the *Pyr*, and Donovan throws his challenge coin at Tyson, who accepts it. The women notice the exchange, and Alex suggests they split up, seeing her chance to escape. After the *Slayers* leave, Donovan spots Alex leaving and follows her. She returns to her apartment to find it ransacked, though the Green Machine plans she came for are undisturbed. While leaving, a man (Sigmund Guthrie, Erik's son turned *Slayer*) speaks to Alex, but she gets away, at which time Donovan arrives.

Chapter 7: Alex agrees to work with Donovan rather than go off on her own with *Slayers* after her. She tells Donovan she first needs to stop at the bank to pick up plans and then at the drugstore for birth control. She's suggesting they give in to the firestorm so they can get past it and focus on work, but she wishes to avoid pregnancy. Donovan senses a *Slayer* nearby and breathes dragonsmoke to once again chase off Sigmund. When she comes out of the bank, Alex suggests they drive to a place one hundred miles away. When they stop at a diner for gas and food, they discuss the Green Machine, which is an engine that runs on water, and how Alex needs to get to the second prototype and get it up and running before an important meeting in a few days. Drawn to the firestorm, Boris, Tyson, and a third *Slayer* arrive. With Alex driving his bike, she and Donovan leave.

Chapter 8: Alex drives far out of their way to lose the vehicle following them, but they spot two dragons in the sky ahead. Donovan takes to the air and Alex continues down the road, but is stopped by a *Slayer*. Donovan fights with Tyson, then calls upon a smaller *Slayer* he refers to as Donovan's friend to continue the fight. Boris tells Alex the Green Machine is really what he is after, and when he moves to kill her, Alex shoots him. Donovan recognizes the small *Slayer* attacking him as Delaney, his friend he now knows was his brother. He knows the same sort of thing that was off with Keir also is with Delaney. Though he gets through to Delaney briefly, the smaller dragon yanks out Donovan's Dragon Tooth protection on his chest, and Donovan falls to the ground. After the *Slayers* all leave and Alex sits with Donovan, trying to figure out how to help him, a woman approaches them. The woman obviously knows who they are, recites the Warrior and the Wizard prophecy, and changes into her dragon shape to aid Donovan.

Chapter 9: Alex realizes this must be the Wyvern. She asks the white dragon if Donovan can be healed, and Sophie says it is up to her: "It is the Wizard whose alchemy can heal the Warrior." Sophie picks up Donovan and transports him to the location Alex visualizes, the country home of her brother Peter. Alex then drives there herself. Donovan dreams of Olivia (a woman from his past) and her betrayal, sacrificing him to obtain the Dragon's Tooth. When Alex arrives at Peter's, a smart house, she finds Donovan, still in what appears to be a deep sleep, on the couch. Alex sees a message on the glass front of the fireplace: "You know in your heart what to do." Still puzzled, Alex then hears Sophie's voice, and something resembling a movie appears on the television screen. The scene picks up the story where Donovan's memory left off, and Alex sees past Donovan descending the stairs to an underground chamber to fight.

Chapter 10: When Donovan changes to dragon form to fight his opponent, Alex notices he doesn't have the pearl embedded in his chest, the one she currently has in her pocket. Another dragon appears, and Alex recognizes Rafferty. As they battle, the two *Pyr* get the upper hand and Rafferty tells Donovan to look for Magnus' weak spot, the one he received by caring for someone. This statement leads Alex to understand why the dragons fear love, since it can leave a flaw in their armor. Alex watches Donovan plunge into the water to retrieve the Dragon's Tooth, and Alex overhears Magnus say to himself only he knows the secret of the pearl, and it will die with him. The picture ends then, and Alex wonders how she can help Donovan. She speculates on the power of the firestorm perhaps being useful, and it does indeed begin to work, especially when she kisses him. Meanwhile, Delaney feels the pull of the firestorm, and it brings what little is left of his true self to the fore, enabling him to make his way to Donovan's location. When Donovan wakes, he and Alex are in the process of giving in to the firestorm when he hears a scratching sound on the roof.

Chapter 11: Tyson comes to finish the blood duel, and he shorts out the security pad to get inside. The two dragons fight. On the roof, Boris and Sigmund listen to what is happening below, and when he realizes Alex is also there, Boris wonders why she chose to come to that location. He spots the boathouse and finds the Green Machine prototype. He decides to sabotage it by having the engine removed, and he also plans to meet with the investor to dissuade him from getting involved. Boris also says he wants the Dragon's Tooth. An offhand comment from Boris about wishing he had a dozen clones of himself leads Sigmund to say that gives him an idea. Inside the house, Alex shoots Tyson in his vulnerable spot, though the *Slayer* has sent dragonfire her way. Having seen Magnus use an opponent's fire by harnessing the energy, Alex tells Donovan to try it, and he does so successfully. They make sure Tyson is dead by using the four elements, Then Alex says she wants to see Donovan go through his change slowly.

Chapter 12: Donovan refuses, though he does not tell Alex the reason why—humans can go mad watching the transformation. Alex shows Donovan she has the Dragon's Tooth and will give it to him in exchange for showing her his change. They are interrupted by the arrival of Alex's brother, Peter, who was notified when the door alarm was destroyed. Donovan beguiles Peter to forget seeing the conservatory destroyed and a dead body in the pool, convincing the man to leave. Niall in dragon form follows Peter to keep an eye on him. The *Pyr* and Sara arrive, and Alex meets Erik for the first time. He explains they plan to guard Alex while she completes her work on the Green Machine, as part of their mission to save the earth. Donovan reasserts his position that there will not be a child from his firestorm, but that he will protect Alex until the next eclipse, when their firestorm will pass. Alex is disappointed, as she had been looking forward to thwarting the firestorm through protected sex.

Chapter 13: Donovan continues to worry about the firestorm and about how witnessing his change may harm Alex. Rafferty tells Donovan they ought to give into the firestorm so it can stop, and therefore not draw the *Slayers* to their location. Both men wonder if the sex itself stops the firestorm, or if conception does. Rafferty suggests perhaps Donovan was attracted to Olivia due to her physical resemblance to Alex, saying perhaps he had a sort of vision of his future mate. Donovan tells the group about encountering the no-longer-dead Delaney. Sloane says the manuscript he's been working on may have the answer to what the former *Pyr* has become. The divine spark of the Great Wyvern animates *Pyr* bodies. When *Slayers* choose to abandon the divine spark and work for their own ends, the Great Wyvern removes her favor from those choosing darkness by turning their blood black. The ones without any blood at all have no soul. Sloane explains the *Slayers* have learned how to plant a shadow in the body of dead *Pyr*, in place of their soul, which has been returned to the Great Wyvern. As Erik states someone needs to stop the *Slayers*, Sophie pops into the room and says, "None of you," telling them an older *Pyr* will be the one to do so, though she doesn't know who. Then she disappears as quickly as she appeared. Alex goes to the boathouse so she can get some rest, away from the houseful of dragons. She and Donovan talk, but he remains outside since she locks the door. He puts a strong dragonsmoke protection around the building. Soon Alex falls asleep, but then screams. Erik leaves for Minneapolis with Sloane, sensing a *Slayer* problem. Rafferty senses someone burrowing under the earth, and traps it, unable to tell whether the being is *Pyr* or not.

Chapter 14: Alex assures Donovan her cries were due to a nightmare, but Donovan wants to see her to confirm that's true. In exchange, Alex wants to see him shift. When Donovan says no, Alex says it must be because he loved Olivia and doesn't want to be reminded of her. Donovan insists he did not love Olivia: he lost his scale over care for someone else (Delaney, also explaining it can happen over other types of love besides the romantic variety). He then tells Alex how Olivia went mad when she saw him change. He showed her his change after learning of her betrayal, but had not realized what would happen. Alex convinces him seeing him change may help her get over her fear of dragons and make the nightmare stop. After Donovan changes to his dragon form, Alex examines his body, and when she touches his chest, another scale falls off. Meanwhile, Erik and Sloane join Niall at Peter's home in Minneapolis. They combine their smoke to make a super-strong protective field, and Peter's four-year-old son catches sight of Niall. In the boathouse, Alex asks what she did wrong to make a scale fall off, and Donovan tells her she didn't do anything. Alex shows Donovan the Green Machine's hiding place, and then they kiss. They return to the house and Alex's room. While she sleeps, Sara has a dream about a dragon, a warrior named Cadmus, and the Dragon's Tooth.

Chapter 15: Alex and Donovan give in to the firestorm, with protection. Afterward Alex notices the firestorm has not abated, and thinks it may be a bit stronger. She then wonders if she may indeed be able to have it all—love, children, and her work. After Donovan wakes up, Alex wants to know his favorite movies, saying that's how you can tell if you are compatible with someone or not. His list passes her test. Alex also opens up a bit about Mark and talks about seeing him die, how the *Slayers* killed him— tortured and then ate him alive. Alex decides she wants to be with Donovan for the duration, but will not beg—she will take what she can get.

Chapter 16: Downstairs Rafferty tells Donovan in old-speak where Erik and Sloane have gone. Sara is on a computer doing research. Alex and Donovan tell Sara and Rafferty about Sophie showing Alex, via the television, the incident with Donovan, Olivia, and Magnus. Alex says she thinks Sophie showed her that scene so she'd know about places with missing scales being weak spots. Donovan points out that's how Alex killed Tyson. Sara says the Dragon's Tooth is the key, and Alex recites the verse of the prophecy. Tyson's body has dissolved, a result of it having been exposed to all four elements. At the boathouse, Alex discovers the engine is missing from the Green Machine and immediately suspects the *Slayers*. Donovan then catches one area of scent Sigmund did not erase. The *Pyr* declare they will help rebuild the engine. Quinn and Rafferty tell Donovan the firestorm will transform him into the Warrior, which he finds difficult to believe, but begins to think giving in to the firestorm may be inevitable. Sara tells the group the story of Cadmus and the buried dragon's teeth, which sprouted warriors. She wants to bury Donovan's Dragon's Tooth pearl to see what happens. Somewhat reluctantly, Donovan agrees with Sara's plan. Rafferty now wants to see who or what he has trapped below the earth, so has Quinn dig in a particular spot, and the ground breaks open.

Chapter 17: The digger comes out of the ground, in dragon form, and tries to take the Dragon's Tooth away from Donovan, but Alex gets to it first. Donovan shifts, using dragonfire on the other dragon, who shifts to human Delaney. Alex and Donovan use the power of the firestorm to try to heal Delaney. Rafferty tells Donovan he is now becoming the Warrior, as he used fire to heal, which he points out is also a weapon against evil. Alex recites "Elements four disguise weapons three," and Rafferty says they will know the other two when they see them. Alex and the *Pyr* work on the Green Machine all of Tuesday, into the night. By singing to the metal, Quinn is able to make the needed changes. Meanwhile, Jared, Alex's young nephew, is lured outside by a dragon beckoning to him. Peter rushes outside to stop a man from carrying Jared away, with only a letter opener as a weapon. To Peter's shock, the man becomes a dragon, but Peter continues to stab at him. When Peter is injured, three other dragons appear and take care of the kidnapper dragon (Sigmund). Erik refuses to beguile a child, but convinces Peter he needs to take his family to the cottage (where everyone can be protected in one place). The *Pyr* break from repairing the Green Machine for the night. Alex and Donovan discuss trying again to see if they can trick the firestorm.

Chapter 18: Donovan and Alex return to the house to discover Peter, his wife, Diane, their two children, and the three *Pyr* who had been looking out for them all there. Diane is visibly upset over recent events, so Rafferty beguiles her. When Alex calls Mr. Sinclair, her Green Machine investor, he expresses doubt and some disinterest in the project, citing the lab incident and suspicion being cast on Alex since she left the hospital. He then tells her she can in the future speak to his new assistant, Boris Vassily. Erik resolves to go see Sinclair on his own, and ensure the man makes it to his scheduled meeting with Alex. Erik declares he will rid the earth of Boris if it's the last thing he does, at which point Sophie materializes briefly to state that is pretty much how it will go. The rest of them remain behind to help Donovan and Alex with the machine and repairing Donovan's scale. Peter's children, Jared and Kirsten, watch the process, unknown to the others. After the repair, Donovan vows to himself to win Alex's heart—after the Green Machine work is done.

Chapter 19: Erik tracks Boris to Chicago, and tosses his challenge coin to the *Slayer*. They take their battle to the docks. It seems to go Erik's way. Thinking he has destroyed Boris with the four elements, he leaves to go and help the others before he can see Boris crawl along the ground, revived with the legendary Dragon's Blood Elixir. Back in Minnesota, Alex successfully starts the engine of the Green Machine, but a stranger appears just outside the smoke, introducing himself as Jorge. He is joined by Magnus, who says he has unfinished business with Rafferty. He offers the *Pyr* the chance to, "join the winning team." When they refuse, they sense a disturbance in the elements. Sara says, "the dark academy is opened," and a number of soulless "shadow" dragons appear, all of them related to the existing *Pyr* present. Donovan tries to get Alex to promise she will stay inside the smoke barrier before the *Pyr* begin their battle. Magnus tries to control Delaney, who fights against the influence and makes a decision. Young Jared comes outside and is upset to see Sloane being hurt, referring to him as "my dragon." Alex crosses the smoke barrier to get Jared, getting boxed in by Jorge and Magnus. Inspired by fear for and love of Alex, Donovan reaches inside himself and acquires the power of earth and realizes he has become the Warrior. A new black and silver dragon appears in the sky—the dragon born of the planted Dragon's Tooth. Magnus says he could have made a whole army from the teeth he had.

Chapter 20: Nikolas, the black and silver dragon, sees the shadow dragons are on the side of evil, so he joins in the fight beside the *Pyr*. Delaney comes to Alex's aid. After joining the others in casting the shadows into an abyss formed in the earth, Nikolas meets the others, Donovan assuring him they will help him get caught up and acclimated to his new time and surroundings. Erik returns, meets Nikolas, and tells everyone Boris is dead. Delaney expresses concern he may never be free of the *Slayer* influence, but the others are ready to help, and Sloane says he has the treatise to guide them. The *Pyr* discuss Magnus and his knowledge of old lore, how the *Slayers* have been able to create new shadow dragons out of fallen *Pyr*, and Rafferty mentions the Dragon's Blood Elixir, which Erik dismisses as myth. Sophie arrives, and though she does not show it, is very intrigued by Nikolas, who falls to his knees when he sees her. Erik says there is now only one more firestorm to go in this cycle. Rafferty says the only pair left of the high three revealed to him in a dream is King and Consort. The others feel it must be Erik, as he is their leader, but he says he's already had a firestorm, when he fathered Sigmund. Sophie tells young Jared that he will need to forget everything, and she kisses his forehead, leaving a silver mark that fades. Alone, Donovan and Alex admit their true feelings for one another and give in to the firestorm with no cheating, looking forward to their future. Alex meets with Mr. Sinclair the next day, and he is now on board with everything Green Machine-related, ensuring the *Pyr* are furthering their quest to protect the earth and its treasures.

DEBORAH'S COMMENTS

There are several details in *Kiss of Fury* that I really like. One is the introduction of Jared as a young boy. He's Alex's nephew and fascinated with dragons. We meet him when the *Pyr* stand guard over Alex's family to keep them safe, and Jared sees Sloane out the window of the family home. Here's a bit with Jared after he's seen Sloane, when he wants to be with dragons—but he doesn't realize that the dragon he sees out the window is the *Slayer*, Sigmund:

Jared Madison kicked at his running shoes.

His mother refused to change his Halloween costume. He didn't want to be Spiderman anymore, even though his costume was all ready to go. He had wanted to be Spiderman more than anything else.

Until last night.

Until he had seen a real live dragon on the roof.

It had been a beautiful dragon, so shiny and powerful and magic, and Jared knew it was still up there. No one else had seen it and no one believed him. No one had seen it today when he had pointed to the roof, but he was sure the dragon hid behind the chimney.

He wanted to be just like it: big and beautiful and strong and magic. But his mother said it was too late to change his costume, that he had wanted to be Spiderman and he was going to be Spiderman this year, and next year he could be a dragon.

Jared wanted to be a dragon *now*.

He'd refused to eat spaghetti for dinner because he was quite sure that dragons didn't eat pasta. He would be a dragon and he would eat... roast chicken. With French fries. Jared was sure that was what dragons ate, and even his mother's insistence that Spiderman ate spaghetti hadn't been good enough.

He'd been sent to his room to think about eating his spaghetti.

So, he kicked his running shoes around his bedroom and sulked. He didn't want to color and he didn't want to play computer games and he really didn't want to talk to his stupidhead sister. He didn't want to eat spaghetti, even if he was kind of hungry.

He looked out the window. It was getting dark, exactly the right time to be seeing a dragon. He had seen one at this time the night before. He went to the window and pressed his nose against the glass to look into the backyard.

Sure enough, there was a dragon out there.

A different dragon, but a dragon all the same.

This one was green, swirly green, whereas the other one had been green and purple and gold. Jared thought the first dragon had looked more magic. This one waved and beckoned to him instead of looking surprised like the first one.

Maybe Jared couldn't be a dragon, but he could be with one. That might just be magic enough.

He held up a finger to the dragon, telling him not to leave. The dragon nodded and Jared grabbed his running shoes. He crept down the stairs, hearing his mother and sister in the kitchen, his father in his library on the phone. Jared silently opened the front door. He shut it behind him, pulled on his shoes, then ran around the back of the house to find the dragon.

He didn't have to look far.

The dragon was waiting for him.

—from **Kiss of Fury**

We'll meet Jared again in the *Dragon Diaries* trilogy, when he's grown up to be a rebel and a rocker, and steals Zoë's heart away. The fact that he's been entrusted with Donovan's beloved motorcycle by that time and gives Zoë her first bike ride doesn't diminish his bad boy appeal in the least. Here's a bit from *Flying Blind*, when Jared and Zoë meet:

Jared laughed. He had a great laugh, a hearty, deep one, which surprised me. In fact, it made him look like a different person. I liked how his eyes twinkled when he laughed, but he still looked wicked.

"No. But that doesn't mean I can't get roped into Donovan's plans."

So, Mr. Urban Pirate knew something about the *Pyr*.

Interesting.

"You could say no," Garrett suggested.

"Not a chance. Not to Donovan." Jared slapped his gloves again and eyed me. "Let's go. I haven't got all day."

"What are you supposed to do?" Liam asked.

"Give someone named Zoë a ride." Jared pointed at me. My heart leapt to my throat, right on cue. "That must be you."

My face burned. "Wild guess?"

He wasn't daunted by my tone. If anything, his grin got wider. He had a dimple on the left side, a deep one.

"Well, Zoë is a girl's name." He indicated Isabelle, his gesture almost dismissive. "And she's not *Pyr*. I know I'm giving the Wyvern a ride, so that leaves you."

I nearly choked. How could this human guy know about my destined role? It was against the Covenant...

"Forget it," Alex protested.

"Donovan's orders." Jared watched me. There was a dare in his eyes and I understood that it was up to me.

He didn't think I had the nerve.

That made me decide instantly that I was going to do it.

I stood up. He *was* taller than me, but I refused to be daunted. "First you have to tell me something. You can't know anything about Wyverns. It's against the rules."

He shrugged, unapologetic. "Well, I do. Screw rules." He winked at me as Alex glared at him. Then he proved that he knew some Wyvern lore. "Send me a dream, Zoë. Or maybe you already have."

The guys hooted and Nick gave a wolf whistle. But Jared just smiled at me, smiled in a way that made me get even warmer and more flustered.

"On the other hand, you might be right. Maybe I don't know nearly enough about this particular Wyvern." His voice dropped low. "Yet."

—from **Flying Blind**

I also like how Alex and Donovan use their firestorm to begin Delaney's healing from the forcible injection of the Dragon's Blood Elixir. The firestorm cauterizes wounds, burns away debris and makes the *Pyr* new. That's quite an endorsement for the power of love, which the *Pyr* are realizing the firestorm should mean.

"You were Delaney." Alex's voice was soft. "What are you now?"

Delaney, still on his knees, shook his head mutely as if

powerless to comprehend what had happened to him. Rafferty didn't think he would speak, but was surprised.

"Lost," Delaney whispered, sounding on the verge of tears. "Lost in darkness." He trembled again and couldn't stop shaking his head "It goes on forever. Except here." He raised his head and stretched out his hand as Donovan shielded Alex again.

"Let me touch him," she urged, and pushed Donovan's claw aside.

The spark of the firestorm leapt between them.

Delaney gasped in wonder. Rafferty saw the hunger in his expression, a yearning that far exceeded Rafferty's own. Delaney reached for the spark as if he couldn't do otherwise. In the same moment, Rafferty saw an answering light leap in Delaney's eyes.

"Your firestorm," Delaney said with awe, and his shoulders shook as he began to weep. He stared at Donovan, the tears tracing tracks on his cheeks as he remained on his knees. "Help me, Donovan. Light my way back."

The old Donovan would have destroyed such a creature, such an abomination of all the *Pyr* knew to be right. Rafferty braced himself to intervene, but he felt the change in the warrior he had tutored.

And he was glad. Rafferty knew the moment that Donovan allowed compassion in his heart, that he let sympathy temper his power to mete justice. He knew the moment that Donovan accepted the threat in order to try to heal his brother.

The transformation was occurring. The Wizard was working her alchemy. Rafferty dared to hope for their collective future.

KISS OF FATE

ONE FORETOLD LOVE DESERVES A SECOND CHANCE...

Haunted by dreams of a lover who takes the form of a mythical dragon, Eileen Grosvenor searches for the truth. She never expects to find a real dragon shape shifter, let alone one who awakens her passion and ignites memories of her own forgotten past.

Erik Sorensson is focused on leading the Pyr to triumph over the Slayers, even if it costs him his life. When an ancient relic that can turn the tide of the battle reveals itself, Erik knows he has to retrieve it from Eileen's possession. But when he tries to do so, he's shocked by an incredible firestorm that compels him to confront the truth about Eileen's identity. Her presence reminds him of mistakes he's determined not to repeat, and Erik is forced to make a choice: duty or love.

Only by unlocking the secrets of the past can Erik and Eileen fulfill the prophecy of the Pyr. Can they face their deepest fears and claim their destined love in time to defeat the Slayers?

THE PROTAGONISTS

By the third book in a linked series, it's time to mix things up a bit. Erik isn't just the oldest of the *Pyr* featured in the series so far, but is the one who has been most closely involved in the affairs of dragons. His father, Soren, was the leader of the first Council of Seven, and in fact, orchestrated its development. Erik has also already had a firestorm and a son, although that relationship ended badly: Louisa committed suicide and Sigmund turned *Slayer*, rejecting all that his father represented.

I wanted Erik to have a second chance. He also is the kind of *Pyr* who could do with some shaking up. Erik was very confident of his conclusions up to this point, so it was time to challenge his assumptions and open his eyes to alternatives. He already has the gift of foresight, but needed to broaden his perspective to use it better. When his firestorm sparks, his gift of foresight disappears.

Eileen is a scholar who works in comparative mythology. She's the one who believes that myths which resonate for people are the ones that 'have their toes in the truth'. In a way, it's easiest for her of all the mates thus far to accept that dragons are real, simply because dragons feature in so many human stories. It makes sense to Eileen that the *Pyr* are the truth behind these dragon tales. Eileen needed to be tested in other ways, then, and she is in this story. Not only must she accept that she's the reincarnation of Erik's mate, but that she chose to end her own life that time. She also needs to get out of her library and actively engage with the world in order to make her life complete. Trying to keep a stolen treasure while being pursued by *Slayers* is a good way for her to start.

THE ELEMENTS

Erik, with his gift of foresight, has an affinity with the element of air, as well as with fire. Eileen's affinities are to earth and water, exhibited in her practicality and her compassion. Erik finds another meaning to Eileen's affinity with earth, identifying her as the treasure of his hoard.

Sara stepped forward then, lifting the runestone from Eileen's hand. She closed her hand over it and lifted it to her ear, as if listening to it, then nodded. "The proper union requires all four elements to be present and accounted for. The *Pyr* generally have fire covered and an affinity for one other element. The mate brings the other two to the equation."

"Eileen brings water," Erik said with conviction.

Eileen couldn't deny that she had a strong link to that element, for better or for worse.

"Compassion and understanding," he added, and she was sure he smiled at her with affection. "Sensitivity and intuition."

Eileen thought about the Wyvern's comments beside the pond. It seemed as if Eileen had gotten her water back this weekend.

"Erik must be air, as well," Sara mused. "He's the thinker of the *Pyr*, the one most concerned with abstractions and ideas."

"And plans," Donovan interjected.

"Logic," Quinn added.

"Doesn't air govern the gift of foresight?" Sloane asked.

"Yes," Erik said. "And the ability to conjure visions."

Eileen stared at him and remembered how he brought the past to life in the ocean's dark mirror. "That leaves earth, then," she said. "What's its association?"

"Practicality, determination, resilience," Sara said.

"Gold," Alex said with a smile, touching the ends of Eileen's hair.

"Treasure," Erik said with approval. "Where no one has had the wits to seek it before."

"Dross into gold?" Eileen teased, and he laughed.

"No." His eyes shone as he regarded her, the intensity of his attention making her heart skip. "The extraordinary discerned where others have overlooked it."

They stared at each other, a new kind of heat kindling between them, and Eileen half wished the other *Pyr* would disappear.

—from **Kiss of Fate**

THE SETTING

Erik's firestorm is ignited by the total lunar eclipse of February 21, 2008 and sparks in London, England. Eileen is there on a research trip, on sabbatical from her teaching job in Boston. The story concludes in Chicago, where Erik's lair is located.

THE PROPHECY

Third match of three demands sacrifice,
A blood cost of enormous price.
Then King and Consort in union complete
Choose trust over ancient deceit;
Shed blood alone can give the power
To aid the Pyr *in their darkest hour*

THE STORY

Prologue: On February 21, 2008, in Chicago, the *Pyr*, along with

Sara and Alex, gather on the roof of Erik's lair during an eclipse to observe as the Dragon's Egg reveals the location of the next firestorm. This is the third and last eclipse before the great battle between *Pyr* and *Slayers*. A map appears on the Dragon's Egg specifying the location of the next firestorm. Sophie, the Wyvern, in human form, appears and announces London as the location. She also teaches Erik how to coax the Egg into giving additional information. Erik is shocked to see his long-dead wife's face appear on the surface of the Egg. He calls out, "Louisa?" The woman replies she was called that name once, but now she is Eileen Grosvenor. Erik can hardly believe the firestorm will be his, since he had one before. Rafferty feels that Erik should be chosen at the dawn of the important battle. Boris Vassily recovers in a hospital room after his recent fight with Erik. He swears vengeance against Erik who had also killed his father a long time in the past. Boris leaves, tracks down the doctor who worked on him, and sets the man and his home on fire. Eileen Grosvenor wakes up in her London hotel, having dreamed of swimming—something she never does due to her fear of the water. She has been dreaming about a man and wonders if it means she will finally meet a good man. When she looks in the mirror, Eileen notices a leaf in her hair, which is wet.

Chapter 1 (February 29th, 2008, in London, England): Erik has been staying at Rafferty's London home, waiting for his firestorm to manifest, but they have been avoiding each other. Rafferty returns home from work as an antiquities dealer and tells Erik that the Dragon's Teeth have been discovered during the construction of a new tube station, and the government plans to sell them, of course not realizing what they are. Rafferty says they can buy them and grow a whole army of *Pyr*. Erik is unhappy at having lost his gift of foresight, and then the firestorm hits Erik. Erik dismisses the old stories and myths, and Rafferty suggests, in his anger, that perhaps Erik has led the *Pyr* astray. Rafferty recites the prophecy about the third firestorm, which speaks of sacrifice and blood cost. Erik interprets the words to mean he will die. Erik searches for the woman sparking his firestorm, and finds her walking down a street late at night. She looks both similar to and different from Louisa, but her smile is the same. She sees him, and their gazes lock, but then Erik senses *Slayers* in the area, and abruptly leaves. Eileen is surprised to see the man from her dreams and is confused when he suddenly leaves. She continues to a meeting her friend, Teresa, who called regarding some artifacts (actually teeth) that her company has come into possession of. The late-night meeting is completely secret, and the items have been securely locked up.

Chapter 2: Teresa tells Eileen the teeth have been carbon-dated to fourthousand years old, but the DNA is of no known animal. Teresa explains she feels they must be really special, as an antiquities dealer, Rafferty Powell, is so interested in them. She hopes Eileen, who specializes in urban legends, myths, and lore, can make some connections to figure out what they may be. Teresa leaves the room to take a call, leaving Eileen to examine the huge three-inch teeth in their box. Then Eileen hears a shot so she turns off the desk lamp and then she sees two men, one of whom shoots Teresa. Eileen hides under the desk with the box. Magnus, waiting in a car outside, instructs Jorge and Mallory to get the hoard— especially the teeth. Jorge finds Eileen, but gets distracted by a noise in the other room, and Eileen runs. When she sees a large black dragon, Eileen wonders if she's imagining things, but she then sees the other intruder change into a dragon, as well. Somehow the black dragon's eyes seem familiar—reminding her of the man in her dreams. After she gets away from another dragon, Eileen sees the man from her dreams appear and tell her to come with him. Erik tries to hide his shift from Eileen, then uses his tail to knock a hole in the wall and they fly out through the hole.

Chapter 3: Aside from the fact she is flying through the air being carried by a dragon, Eileen is astounded to feel desire. When the dragon lands in Hyde Park, he covers Eileen's eyes and changes back into a man. Eileen asks him to give her the box with the teeth, and he does so. When the two of them bump hands, a spark appears. Eileen learns her dream man has also dreamed about her, and he tries to convince her to come with him so he can keep her safe. She wants to go to the police about Teresa, but he says they wouldn't believe her if she mentions dragons. Aggravated, Eileen stalks off, but stops when she sees the car that was outside of the building earlier. The man in the car (the reader knows it's Magnus) calls Erik by his name. Erik senses *Slayers* nearby and feels Boris' presence but is confused because he thinks he killed him. Erik convinces Eileen to give up the case with the teeth in the morning. Eileen asks what "firestorm" means and Erik demonstrates by kissing her. After Erik leaves her in a hotel lobby, Eileen catches a cab to her sister's house, where she's been staying.

Chapter 4: When she gets upstairs to her room, Eileen sees Magnus' car outside and realizes she is putting her sister at risk by staying there Erik has followed Eileen, and while he's setting up a dragonsmoke barrier around the house, Sophie arrives. She asks Erik which comes first in his priorities: himself, the *Pyr*, or Eileen. When Erik answers the *Pyr*, Sophie tells him that's the wrong answer, then disappears. Eileen wonders how her trip to England to further research the story "The Dragon Lover of Madeley" has ended up with her seeing and meeting real dragons. Her work collecting and analyzing urban myths has shown her not everything can be explained by logic. Eileen takes the teeth from the case, wraps them, and places them in an overnight bag. She writes her sister a note about making sure the contents go to Rafferty Powell. After making her preparations, Eileen dozes off, dreaming about a baby—a dream she has had before. In the morning, her sister, Lynne, talks to her and says she believes Eileen is avoiding intimacy in her relationships. She also says, "...you're writing down other people's stories instead of living your own." Eileen then leaves to catch a train. On her way to her platform, a man with a chest wound and flames in his eyes tries to take the case from her. Eileen manages to get away from him, and when she boards her train, Erik is behind her. He takes the case from her hands and chastises her with, "you promised."

Chapter 5: Sophie senses a dark taint and follows it to Chicago, to Erik's lair. When a *Slayer* rejects the divine spark within himself, his blood turns black, giving him a different scent than that of the *Pyr*. When Sophie arrives, she is surprised to sense Boris, who is supposed to be dead. Sophie shifts into a small salamander so she can watch Boris undetected. Boris penetrates Erik's smoke barrier unscathed and hovers between forms—both abilities limited to the

Wyvern. Sophie changes back to her human form and Boris catches her. After stating she is too involved in earthly affairs, Boris holds one of his talons against her carotid. He says he is there to destroy the Dragon's Egg. Nikolas appears and Boris forces him to choose between Sophie and the Egg, which he throws out the window.

Chapter 6: Back at the train station, Erik and Eileen manage to evade two *Slayers* following them. Shortly thereafter Erik gets overwhelmed by the feeling something terrible has happened. When Eileen asks what is wrong, he tells her he doesn't know. She can't quite come to terms with recent events, but she says that she also realized long ago that there were things in the world that defied easy explanation. Eileen tells Erik she wants full explanations, not halfway versions. She decides to trust Erik and tells him her destination, so he buys a ticket for the same place. Then Erik explains about dragonsmoke.

Chapter 7: Nikolas chooses to save Sophie, so he grabs Boris. When Boris lets go of Sophie, she changes to a salamander to escape. As he is beating up Boris, Nikolas hears the Dragon's Egg break outside and feels a physical shock so strong he lets go of Boris. The *Slayer* leaves through the window and tells Sophie in old-speak it isn't over yet. Sophie changes back to her human form, and Nikolas realizes he feels more than just reverence for the Wyvern. Near his home in New York City, Niall finds an unknown *Pyr* he has sensed in the area. He suddenly feels as though the wind has been knocked out of him, and when he finds the unknown *Pyr* in pain on the floor of a club he has just entered, it's obvious he had a similar reaction. Niall asks, in old-speak, if he knows what he is, and when the other *Pyr* answers in the affirmative, Niall brings the man with him. Niall tells the newcomer they must go to England. In Michigan, Sara wakes up from a nightmare, and Quinn says he felt it, too. They know Quinn needs to go to Erik, but Quinn won't go without her, though she is seven months pregnant. Rafferty's reaction is akin to heart attack, and he goes outside to lie on his patio and touch the earth. Sloane and Delaney are working in Sloane's greenhouse when they both feel the shock, and they determine to go to Erik's lair in Chicago.

Nikolas retrieves the pieces of the lifeless Egg, broken in half, with one part in three pieces. Nikolas explains he didn't have a choice, pledging himself to her defense. Sophie feels desire for him, though intimacy is forbidden to her. She accepts his offer of protection, but tells him he needs to keep his distance.

Chapter 8: Erik explains dragonsmoke to Eileen, describing the high-tone resonance of a closed circle. Eileen doesn't like that he refers to her as his mate, and he replies, "the firestorm is the mark of destiny." When she asks if he means "destined love," he says "destined sex." Erik tells Eileen he's not British, but Viking, and though not immortal, the *Pyr* age very slowly until their firestorm. When Eileen says they are headed to Ironbridge to research the story "The Dragon Lover of Madeley," Erik suddenly gets quiet. Eileen tells Erik she teaches at a university in Boston, and has just recently become very focused on that one story. Erik says he will tell her the story behind the story, in exchange for the case (which he believes still contains the teeth). Eileen agrees, and they seal their bargain with a kiss.

Chapter 9: Magnus, Jorge, Mallory and Balthasar follow the train in their car. Unhappy with his minions, Magnus threatens to kill Jorge, which leads to a discussion about shadow dragons and invincibility. Jorge surmises Magnus has the Dragon's Blood Elixir, which Magnus does not deny. Magnus tells Jorge to practice hovering between forms. Erik and Eileen both feel the power of the firestorm. Erik also thinks to himself he should not be surprised at Eileen's interest in her own story. He sends out a query to Rafferty via old-speak to find out what happened that caused the physical shock he felt, and eventually gets a response that the Dragon's Egg has broken. Rafferty says everyone is gathering at Erik's lair in Chicago. Erik says he will be there with the teeth, after satisfying the firestorm. Rafferty says he will not be there. Erik tells Eileen that he was married before, but his wife killed herself over what their son had become. Erik asks her to tell him what she knows of the Dragon Lover story.

Chapter 10: Eileen reads the story aloud, the tale of two sisters, called Shadow and Sunshine (not their real names). The two sisters are close, and Shadow, the eldest, refuses to marry, angering their father, and Sunshine will not marry before her sister does. One day Shadow (Louisa) admits she is pregnant, but before she leaves, she gives her sister a painting of a dragon. Eventually Sunshine (Adelaide) marries, and one day while outside gets visited by a dragon, who gives her a lock of hair and says, "my son." Adelaide understands who the dragon must be, and asks after her sister. Though the sisters never saw each other again, on her deathbed Adelaide told her eldest daughter the story, and gave her the painting and lock of hair. Erik tells Eileen the story contains truth, but not all of the truth. Then Erik realizes Magnus is following them so they get off the train and get a rental car to try to elude the *Slayers*. When Magnus catches up to them, Erik steers their car right at Magnus' car.

Chapter 11: Magnus has his driver swerve to miss Erik, but the maneuver results in Magnus' sedan flipping to its roof. Magnus speaks to Erik in old-speak, demanding the teeth or he will take Eileen. Erik fears for her safety, wondering if the others will keep her safe after his death. Erik feels he must get the teeth away from her to keep her safe, but resolves to tell her the rest of the tale first. He and Eileen continue until they arrive at a bridge, where Eileen feels afraid. To get her past her fear, Erik begins to tell her the rest of the Dragon Lover story. Knowing the importance of the firestorm, the *Pyr* told Shadow he would deny his nature if she would lie with him. When she became pregnant, he agreed to live in human society, but away from her family, until their son came into his abilities. Shadow agreed, and all went well until their son turned into a *Slayer*. The *Pyr* was unable to save his son, and when he shifted to his dragon form and broke his promise to his wife, her heart was broken. The other *Pyr*, except Rafferty, have gathered at Erik's Chicago lair to inspect the Dragon's Egg. They argue with Nikolas that Boris could not be alive, but Sophie appears and backs up Nikolas' story. However, the Wyvern does not look well, and the wound on her neck still bleeds. Sloane realizes this means the Dragon's Blood Elixir actually exists. Delaney believes they gave the Elixir to the dead to create shadow dragons, but if a living dragon survives it, they become more or less immortal. Sophie says Boris, Magnus and the shadow dragons must be destroyed.

Alex asks if the Egg can somehow be repaired. Sophie says it cannot. As it was a gift from Gaia, she agrees to ask for another Egg. Sophie wonders aloud if it would be better for her to be less involved. As she shimmers in advance of leaving, Nikolas rushes to her and they both disappear.

Chapter 12: Continuing to feel overpowering dread on the bridge, Eileen focuses on Erik's story. Erik says the *Pyr* of the story never told Shadow about going to visit her sister, fearing she would want to leave and return to her family. Believing herself betrayed by her husband and in despair over their son, Shadow took her own life by jumping off the bridge. As he speaks, Eileen realizes Erik is the *Pyr* in the story and she kisses him. As the firestorm overtakes them once again, Erik reluctantly breaks off the kiss so they do not draw *Slayers* to them. Once they arrive at the small hotel, Erik begins to set up a smoke barrier. While Eileen prepares for her bath, she wonders how old Erik is, and lays out condoms on the counter.

Chapter 13: Erik and Eileen give in to the firestorm, having sex in the bathtub. Meanwhile, Sigmund walks into town, following the firestorm. As he gets closer, he realizes it is his father's firestorm and swears vengeance on his father for his mother's death. He also believes Erik killed his grandfather, Louisa's father. Magnus arrives and makes a deal with Sigmund, saying he can have the mate, but Magnus wants Erik, using the Elixir as a bargaining chip. Magnus insists Boris does not hold the power. Sigmund agrees to the arrangement, satisfied that he will be able to kill his father's mate.

Chapter 14: Though he regrets doing so, Erik prepares to leave Eileen and take the case of teeth to Chicago. Opening the hotel room door, Erik is surprised by Magnus who grabs the case and flies away. Erik pursues him. Eileen dreams of water, and in her terrified struggles, she hears a voice telling her not to fight it, but to embrace its nature. Once she does so, Eileen stands up and finds stones weighing down her dress, realizing she was once Louisa. A blond woman with turquoise eyes tells her to trust in goodness and surrender to the water. Eileen submerges herself and swims. The blond woman disappears, but then Erik helps her out of the water before she wakes up. Awake, Eileen wonders if she does have a connection to Louisa. When she finds Erik is gone, she realizes she wants more time with him. Determined to focus on her research, Eileen heads out to the archive. Erik chases Magnus through the sky, and also encounters the *Slayer's* minions. With the uneven odds, Erik resolves to survive the encounter to be there for Eileen. Using Quinn's technique of absorbing dragonfire to enhance his own energy, Erik next uses his dragonsmoke to draw life force from Mallory. After fighting off the two minions, Erik learns from Magnus that the Dragon's Blood Elixir is real, right before the *Slayer* attacks.

Chapter 15: Eileen is working in the archives, when a young man asks if he can help with her research, claiming he's an expert on the town. When Eileen refuses his help, the man doesn't leave and begins to get a bit too pushy. Eileen has a bad feeling about him. He introduces himself as Sigmund Guthrie, and she asks him about Louisa Guthrie. Sigmund immediately says she died in March 1782. Eileen then finds an article about Louisa and learns the name of her son. Sigmund confirms that he is, indeed, Erik's son, and Eileen runs out. As Erik and Magnus battle, Erik notices Magnus has a scale missing. Magnus suddenly drops the chest of teeth and starts chanting. Erik realizes he is attempting to influence the weakened dragon soldiers trapped in the teeth, calling them to the *Slayer* side. Both Erik and Magnus get a big surprise when the case breaks and it is empty. Eileen drives away quickly, letting the firestorm guide her toward Erik. Close in pursuit, Sigmund breathes dragonfire at the car. Realizing he needs to get to Eileen, Erik impales Magnus on a fence in a cemetery and heads to the hotel. When he finds the room empty, Erik feels Sophie was correct—that in choosing the *Pyr* over Eileen, he made a mistake. Erik catches her scent and follows it to her current location but is not pleased to also smell Sigmund.

Chapter 16: Magnus strikes a deal with Jorge to help Magnus get free of the fence in return for Dragon's Blood Elixir. If the Elixir kills Jorge, he'll be rid of him; if it works, he'll have a faithful ally who will do just about anything for more of the potion (a side-effect detail he has kept to himself). Eileen drives on a side-road she knows she has never traveled before, yet it feels familiar. The road ends in a clearing, with only a building foundation. Eileen is confronted by Sigmund and another man, and as she drives toward them, they shift into dragon form and she hits a tree. The second man opens her door and beguiles her. Eileen can't look away. Boris is pleased that Eileen ended up at her old homestead. and decides he will share her story with her, also removing the spell. After introducing himself, Boris calls Eileen Shadow, explaining to both she and Sigmund she is Louisa reincarnated. That is why Erik was gifted with two firestorms. Eileen runs off as Erik races down from the sky to Boris. He is surprised to find Boris alive, even though he had scented him earlier. Erik knows he cannot let the *Slayer* win their unfinished blood duel, so he tricks Boris into thinking he has been injured while they fight. Sigmund, shocked to learn Eileen's identity, follows her, resolving he won't allow Boris to kill her. Eileen learns Sigmund turned *Slayer* when she rejected his dragon nature. She tells him of the dreams she has of a baby boy.

Chapter 17: Boris sets the trees around them on fire. Eileen sees Erik losing badly in his battle with Boris. After dropping Erik's limp body to the ground, Boris comes after Eileen, but Sigmund rushes to her defense. Surprised, Boris calls Sigmund a coward, saying he should have killed the *Pyr* leader to take over, just as Erik did—an accusation Eileen does not believe. Boris uses dragonfire and smoke on Sigmund, stealing his life force. Then Erik grabs Boris and carries him far above the earth and drops him, though the *Slayer* tries to bribe him with Dragon's Blood Elixir. On the ground, Eileen goes to the dying Sigmund, now in human form, his blood both black and red, and the two make their peace. Sigmund talks to Erik, asking for the four elements. Erik wants to know how to kill those who have taken the Elixir. Sigmund dies before he can tell Erik more than that there is just one way. Erik disposes of Sigmund's body in the way needed to keep him from becoming a shadow dragon. Eileen realizes she wants a future with Erik, and they fly off.

Chapter 18: As Boris falls, he tries another of the Wyvern's abilities he thinks he may have due to the Elixir. He concentrates on Sophie's location and is able to manifest right on Sophie's back, as she lies on the sand, asking Gaia for another Dragon's Egg. Boris puts his talons around her neck, and though she shifts between her three favored forms, she is unable to escape Boris' grasp. Nikolas, though ordered to maintain a distance, comes to her aid and takes on Boris. Boris drops Sophie, and Nikolas and Boris battle. Nikolas seems to get the upper hand, but as he is about to swallow Boris in his salamander form, both Boris and Sophie disappear. Devastated, Nikolas blames himself. Sophie, who has hidden, witnesses Nikolas' distress, and decides to embrace her desire for him. She manifests as a salamander in his shirt pocket, resolving to take care of a couple of things first. As he flies carrying Eileen, Erik learns that she put the teeth in a locker and sent her sister the key. She is then supposed to take them to Rafferty. Erik explains who Rafferty is, and that her sister, Lynne, may be in danger until she hands off the teeth to Rafferty. Erik and Eileen head back to London. Erik lets Magnus think he has the teeth, contacting him through old-speak. He also calls to Niall, who brings the new recruit with him. In his home in London, Rafferty feels somewhat responsible for Teresa's death He also wonders why he has been unable to contact Erik via old-speak.

Chapter 19: Erik and Eileen land on Lynne's roof, and he quickly changes to his human form. Niall arrives with a third dragon, not as graceful as the others. Erik recognizes the new dragon, saying he is of noble Viking lineage—Erik knew his father and grandfather. Erik accuses him of denying his legacy, which is why Erik didn't know he existed. The new, silvery dragon lands clumsily on the rooftop. He says his name is Thorolf, though he thinks it's weird and generally prefers to go by T. Eileen tells Thorolf she is Erik's destined mate, and when he sees the stone she has found in her pocket, he identifies the symbol on it as the Helm of Awe, a protective rune. Eileen thinks the stone was put in her coat pocket by Sigmund. Thorolf mentions someone named Rox, who he claims is his sister, but Eileen doubts it. Erik feels hopeful about the *Pyr's* chances now, and wonders if Thierry's theory that one who commits to his mate during a firestorm becomes stronger is true. Thorolf doesn't just want to stay at the house with Niall, and he asks how he can tell who the good guys are, between *Slayers* and *Pyr*. Erik asks Thorolf to fly with him and Eileen while he explains the difference, so the newcomer can make his choice. Erik tells Thorolf the creation story of the *Pyr*, explaining how they were created out of the void as guardians set to protect the four elements. Eileen is shocked to hear how men killed dragons in hopes of acquiring their powers, which led to the race dying off over time. Division between dragons began during this time, one side choosing to still defend humans while the other decided to kill humans. The Great Wyvern changed those who would become known as *Slayers* to have black blood, and took away their chance at a firestorm. Erik tells Thorolf to make his choice, but Thorolf asks how he knows Erik isn't a *Slayer* himself.

Chapter 20: Shocked, Erik cannot immediately find the words to respond to Thorolf, but Eileen points out Erik bleeds red, has an active firestorm, and that the *Pyr* have been teaching Thorolf about his own abilities. Thorolf admits that is all true and states he is on board. Erik sends Thorolf to join Niall to guard Lynne's house. As they continue their flight, Eileen tells Erik she would like to discuss the possibility of a shared future. Meanwhile, Boris drags himself to the sanctuary where the Elixir is kept. He needs more Elixir to repair his body—one sip is not sufficient. He realizes Magnus means to create an army of addicts who will do his bidding to get more Elixir. As he pulls himself up to the large vial of Elixir, powered by the blood and body of a dragon suspended in water, Magnus comes out of the Elixir and grabs Boris. As Erik flies over the Atlantic back to Chicago, Eileen awakens and wants to hear the story of the dragon who killed his father to take control of the *Pyr*. Erik begins by saying his father, Soren, was the first leader of the *Pyr*, and he put together a council of seven advisors. Rafferty also served on that first council. After some members died, Erik's uncle, Sigmund, wanted Erik on the council. Soren wanted a broad base comprised of *Pyr* from all over the world, but those could not be found. Erik states that he learned fear from alchemists, as they believed dragons possessed the secret of the philosopher's stone location, if not the gem itself. Then Erik tries out a new ability, projecting images upon the ocean surface. Eileen gets a glimpse of Louisa, but then the scene switches to a room with two dragons in a large glass bottle, whom Erik identifies as Soren and Mikhail, Boris' grandfather. The two dragons fight, and the victorious Soren wants his prize—to be set free. The alchemist says he wants the philosopher's stone. When Soren says he does not have the stone, the alchemist lowers him to the fire.

Chapter 21: In the vision/reenactment, Eileen sees a large black dragon arriving, who smashes the glass bottle. Eileen sees the stone she now has in her pocket stone roll from a table onto the floor. A boy comes into the room, and the large black dragon says, "Sigmund." Eileen learns the alchemist was Louisa's father, having captured both Soren and Boris, working magic upon them. After Louisa told Sigmund to leave, he went to his grandfather. During this event, the alchemist attacked Soren with a knife, digging in his head. Erik killed the man with dragonfire, and Soren asked his son to do what needed to be done (kill him). Louisa comes in and sees the fire that has now spread, but she did not witness what happened before. Back in London, Thorolf has been working with Niall on learning how to breathe smoke, use dragonfire, and even rudimentary beguiling. Niall points out a *Slayer* in human form on the sidewalk, explaining how to identify their scent. Suddenly another Slayer attacks from behind them, and Niall is knocked out. Thorolf battles the two *Slayers*, and ultimately runs the two off, but not before humans become aware of fighting dragons. Niall and Thorolf now have some beguiling to do. Eileen wakes in a strange room but realizes it must be Erik's place in Chicago. When she gets up, she sees a small blond woman with turquoise eyes and an injured foot. Eileen recognizes the woman from her dream about water, and her visitor introduces herself as the Wyvern. The Wyvern asks Eileen to share her innermost dream, but when she doesn't do so, the Wyvern says she knows Eileen dreams of a child. She counsels Eileen to commit herself wholly, and then disappears. Eileen hears Erik in the shower.

Chapter 22: Erik realizes Eileen has become very important to him. When he gets out of the shower, she is standing there, and asks him if he wanted her or the Dragon's Teeth. Erik answers he came to her because of the firestorm, left for the Teeth, and returned for her. When she asks about Louisa, Erik explains the ways the two of them are different. When Eileen asks him why he doesn't want a child, Erik tells her about the portent about blood and sacrifice, saying he feels it would be unfair to leave her alone with a *Pyr* child. Everyone gathers in the living room, including Alex and Sara. Donovan and Quinn tease Erik, throwing his own words back at him — how satisfying the firestorm and breeding is a duty. Eileen asks to hear the prophecy, which Erik recites. Eileen then states childbirth involves a lot of blood, and there are other kinds of sacrifice.

Chapter 23: Eileen believes the prophecy is actually a metaphor referring to the connection between the health of the land and that of the king. She points out Erik has not really been balanced since Louisa. She learns the other two couples (Sara and Quinn, Alex and Donovan) stayed together out of choice, and the two *Pyr* were made stronger. Eileen tells Erik she will have his child, and if he isn't around to help, she will call upon the others. Everyone then leaves to take care of various tasks. Delaney agrees to try hypnotism in order to discover information about the Elixir and/or the *Slayer* dark academy. Sara offers to help, by accepting his visions. With the others all gone, Eileen and Erik revel in their firestorm. Eileen feels even more satisfied when Erik calls her by her name, knowing for sure it is her he wants, not Louisa.

Chapter 24: Sophie returns to Nikolas, stepping into his arms rather than running away. In Chicago, Eileen wakes up while Erik still sleeps, and notices a scab on his forehead from fighting Magnus. Thinking of what Thorolf had told her, Eileen places the runestone on Erik's wound. His frown disappears. Eric dreams of his first Viking voyage with his father, who gave him the runestone. When he wakes up, finding the runestone in his lap, Erik feels full of purpose, and is aware his gift of prophecy is back. Crediting Eileen with the change in his attitude, Erik also accepts the Great Wyvern may not wish for him to always be shown everything. The other *Pyr* gather for the session with Delaney on the roof of Erik's building. The hypnotized Delaney is able to tell them the *Slayer* academy is in a tunnel under the earth, near water. Suddenly he has an overwhelming desire to take Sara's unborn child. Delaney now understands why Magnus let him go: he is to take the *Pyr* babies and deliver them to Magnus. Horrified, Delaney fights off both Donovan and Quinn and then leaves, banishing himself from their presence. Erik explains the runestone was the source of the alchemist's power against Soren. He then says she needs to call her sister and tell her to accept whatever offer Rafferty makes for the Teeth.

Chapter 25: Lynne Williams meets Rafferty at his shop with her two daughters and a small suitcase. He makes her a very generous offer for the Teeth, but Lynne is unsure since she hasn't talked to Eileen about any of the details. As if on cue, Lynne's phone rings with a call from Eileen, encouraging her to accept Rafferty's offer, after an additional twenty thousand dollars gets added. Rafferty is pleased to realize Erik's gift of foresight has returned, and it likely means he has consummated his firestorm and plans to stay with Eileen. Sophie wakes up next to Nikolas but panics when she is unable to hear and sense the earth and other elements. She is unable to shift to her salamander form, though she can still transform into a dragon. She interprets this as meaning she no longer serves as the Wyvern after becoming intimate with Nikolas. Sophie feels guilty about leaving the *Pyr* without a Wyvern to guide them, but feels there may not have been a choice due to a feeling of an impending deadline. Realizing Nikolas will never leave her side to go and fulfill his destiny as the one to take down the dark academy, Sophie flies off in dragon form to the *Slayer* location, knowing he will follow her. She believes they will be the sacrifice spoken of in the prophecy. On the rooftop of Erik's home, with Sara, Alex, Quinn, Donovan and Sloane, Eileen witnesses Erik's slower transformation from human to dragon form. She sees the place on his brow where a scale is missing, and they perform the ceremony to repair the weak spot, using the runestone.

Chapter 26: In his garden, Rafferty, with the help of Niall and Thorolf, plants the Teeth, then sings to them. A few hours later, the earth rumbles and the dragon warriors rise from the ground. The naked men change into dragons, and in pairs, fly off. Rafferty thinks they have been summoned by someone, likely Nikolas. Rafferty talks to the one who appears to be the leader and the three

Pyr are asked to accompany the warriors. Nikolas follows Sophie into a tunnel underneath the ocean, but she disappears behind a door he cannot open. When the other dragon warriors arrive, they help him break down the door, but must fend off attack from shadow dragons. Rafferty wonders if he will be the sacrifice. Meanwhile, in Chicago, Magnus tries to trade a vial of the Elixir for the teeth, but Erik throws the vial against the wall, shattering it. Three other *Slayers* move in for the attack and a red salamander goes after the liquid from the vial. Erik knows it's Boris and goes after him. Boris shifts to a dragon and grabs Eileen, forcing Erik to choose between saving her or capturing him. As Erik moves to catch Eileen, Magnus catches her first.

Chapter 27: Thorolf helps Rafferty, who is fighting the shadow of his grandfather. After they destroy that shadow dragon, the two *Pyr* go to help Niall. Then the door finally gives way, and all of the remaining shadows race to the inside. Rafferty and Niall follow the Dragon's Tooth warriors inside, where they find a ball of whirling white energy, which Rafferty realizes is Sophie, in dragon form, having her life force sucked out of her. Nikolas immediately goes to her, becoming entwined with her, their combined vitality creating an energy that the dark academy cannot withstand. Sophie and Nikolas are enveloped in bright light, and they disappear. Rafferty hopes the two will be reborn and reunited at some point in time. He begins to sing to the earth, and the ceiling begins to crack and fall onto the warriors. Many perish. The *Pyr* and the surviving dragon warriors gather, and the leader of the warriors gives Rafferty a black and white ring he says Rafferty should have., He says he and his warriors will follow Rafferty. Rafferty wants them to meet Erik. In Chicago, Magnus plans to kill Eileen, but he suddenly gets a sense of something being very wrong and the shadow dragons all leave. He decides it is better to leave than to face the *Pyr* on his own. Sara cries out that Sophie is gone. Boris then blows dragonfire through the window of Erik's apartment. Quinn and Donovan take their wives away while Sloane pulls the fire alarm. Erik kills and then burns Boris, and he and Eileen drop his ashes into Lake Michigan so all four elements are involved. As Eileen and Erik watch the fireworks display (from those ignited in Erik's pyrotechnic warehouse), she tells him she would like a month to figure everything out, and he agrees.

Chapter 28: Back home in Boston, Eileen knows within two weeks she is pregnant, and she spends her evenings writing the history of the *Pyr*. She wants to do this for her child and to serve as a manual for mates. Sara sends her the book written by Sigmund, *The Habits and Habitats of Dragons, a Compleat Guide for* Slayers. After a month, Erik comes to her. Eileen notices some silver in Erik's hair, and he explains how *Pyr* begin to age more quickly after their firestorms. He also says his friend Thierry, Quinn's father, told him he believed *Pyr* could choose to die after the loss of their mates. Later, as Erik sleeps next to Eileen, he hears Sigmund talking to him. Sigmund gives him a vision of where the Elixir is kept, telling him the source of it must be destroyed and showing him the cinnabar dragon that fuels the potion. When Erik asks how Sigmund was able to come to him, Sigmund answers, "the Wyvern." Erik states there is no longer a Wyvern, but Sigmund replies, "Isn't there?" Eileen awakens briefly and tells Erik they are having a daughter, though he thinks this impossible. Then he realizes their daughter will be the new Wyvern.

DEBORAH'S COMMENTS

There are so many things I like about this book. I love reincarnation stories, and I love when old wrongs are set to rights. I also like second chance romances. The reconciliation between Erik and his son Sigmund, who turned *Slayer*, is very powerful for me. Of course, it only happens because of Eileen.

"[Eileen] was even more pale as she watched [Sigmund] and her eyes seemed more vibrantly blue. "You turned *Slayer* because I rejected you," she murmured, guessing his truth.

"I lost a scale for you!" Sigmund cried. "I loved you, but you refused to love me once you knew that I was like my father."

"I'm sorry," she said, and he heard a new compassion in her words. She swallowed and her eyes filled with tears. "I have this dream. I have it all the time. I dream that I'm holding a baby boy. And in that dream, my heart is so full of love for my son that I'm afraid it will burst."

She stretched out her hand toward Sigmund, seeking reconciliation, and he was tempted to meet her halfway. He held his ground, though, his mouth dry.

"I thought it was a dream for something that might never happen, but it's of you. It's a memory of your birth. And in that dream, my greatest fear is that my beloved son will be taken away from me."

Eileen shook her head. "I can't have meant to send you away. I must have spoken in anger. I'm sorry. Sigmund, I am so sorry."

Sigmund felt that old wound ache again, but the pain was less sharp. Sunlight could have touched the ice that encased his heart, beginning the slow melt of spring. Her words lit a spark where there had been darkness for so long, and tempted him to forgive her. He stretched out a hand to Eileen, more than ready to meet her halfway. The sympathy she offered was all he wanted and more.
—from **Kiss of Fate**

If I had to pick a favorite of the *Pyr*, on many days, that would be Erik. I like how he tries to balance his personal responsibilities with his obligation to the *Pyr*—not always with success—as well as serving his notion of the greater good. I admire how Eileen challenges him, continuing to do so even after their firestorm. Here's a bit from the very end of their book, after Erik awakens from a dream of Sigmund. They converse in old-speak, which appears in italics.

Sigmund straightened, then looked steadily at Erik. He looked as he had when he was younger, not burned and broken, not bitter. He was less substantial, though, perhaps ghostlike. *"I didn't let you down this time."*

"No."

"You kept your promise to me. Did you know I would return to keep mine?"

"No." Erik smiled. *"I only hoped. It was time for one of us to trust."*

Sigmund inclined his head once at the truth of that *"Thank you."*

"Thank you."

And in the dream, Erik's son offered his father his hand. Erik wished it weren't a dream, as he would have liked to have felt that last handshake with his own son.

"How did you do this? How did you come to me?" Erik asked, wondering what other secrets Sigmund had unearthed.

"The Wyvern."

"But there is no Wyvern," Erik argued. Before he could explain that Sophie had died after Sigmund's death, his son smiled mysteriously.

"Isn't there?" Sigmund asked quietly. He smiled, waved, then turned away. Before his back had fully turned, he faded to nothing.

Erik blinked and stared at the ceiling, his throat tight that he had had one last precious exchange with Sigmund. His heart leapt that Sigmund had given him the piece of the puzzle he needed to eliminate Magnus, the *Slayers* he made immortal, and the shadow dragons. And he wept that he had not made peace with his son sooner.

Eileen stirred in the darkness and pressed a kiss to his shoulder. "What's wrong?" she asked sleepily. "You were gone."

"No, just dreaming."

She braced herself on her shoulder and looked down at him sleepily, then touched her fingertips to his cheek. "And what kind of dream makes the leader of the *Pyr* weep?"

"I dreamed of our son," Erik admitted, his words thick.

Eileen shook her head and yawned, nestling down beside him. "Don't be silly; we aren't having another son."

"But the *Pyr*..."

"Yes, I know, but your big myth is going to be proven wrong. We're having a daughter. I know it as well as I know my own name."

"How?" Erik whispered.

"I dreamed of her." Eileen opened one eye to give him a look. "Definitely a girl." Then she smiled at his shock and settled back to sleep again. "You'll see in seven or eight months," she threatened, her words already slowing.

Erik couldn't sleep then because his heart was pounding. The stories of the *Pyr* weren't being proven wrong at all. There could only be one female *Pyr,* a prophetess who returned to flesh time and again to aid the *Pyr* in their quest.

Another Wyvern was coming into the world.

She would be their daughter.

We see here that there's a bond between Sigmund and his half-sister Zoë, who hasn't been born yet. Sigmund also appears in Zoë's dreams in *The Dragon Diaries*, and is one of the only sources of information she has in trying to fulfill her destiny. Of course, being her big brother means that he also teases her and isn't very quick to reveal everything he knows.

WINTER KISS

ONE KISS CAN MELT HIS FROZEN HEART...

The mysterious Dragon's Blood Elixir gives immortality to Magnus, the Pyr's greatest enemy, and his minions. The Pyr must destroy this source of power, and outcast Delaney vows to complete the quest himself. Delaney was exiled because of his dangerous impulses, and success in eliminating the Elixir will either redeem him or end his suffering.

But his plans don't take into account his sudden firestorm—or fiery Ginger Sinclair. The firestorm revitalizes Delaney, restoring him to his old self. And when Ginger learns about Delaney's mission, she realizes she cannot resist a strong man with a noble agenda.

THE PROTAGONISTS

Delaney Shea is a *Pyr* who has been turned into a shadow dragon against his will. He was injured in the fight in Ann Arbor in **Kiss of Fire**, and his body taken by the *Slayers* to Magnus' hidden Academy, where he was compelled to consume the Dragon's Blood Elixir. The firestorm of his brother, Donovan, started his healing process in **Kiss of Fury**, but Delaney doesn't trust himself so has exiled himself from the *Pyr*. He intends to destroy the Elixir, no matter the cost, fully expecting that it will be a suicide mission. I had to give him a firestorm on the evening before his assault on Magnus' sanctuary, as well as a feisty mate who has no intention of being left alone. Ginger is fearless and determined, a tiny woman with a huge heart and a lot of resolve. As soon as I met her and knew the firestorm would be on her side, I recognized that Delaney didn't really have a chance.

THE ELEMENTS

The affinities take a bit of a switch in this book: because Delaney has been turned to a shadow dragon and lost his fire, his mate provides that element. Ginger is fire and earth, while Delaney is air and water.

He smiled. "Ginger is the fire in this partnership."

"Ideas are associated with air and the wind," Niall said. "Even though I have a strong bond with the wind, Delaney always has the best ideas."

"That's two," Sara said with approval. "What about water?"

"Swimming?" Ginger asked.

"It's often shown by empathy and understanding," Eileen said. "Compassion, an attempt to reconcile or create unions, soothe troubled waters." She shrugged and smiled. "Or other things."

Ginger was already shaking a finger at Delaney. "That's you. You went back to your mother, and you were worried about the planet in your nightmare. You're air and water."

"And you're earth," Delaney agreed. "You're completely in touch with the land and its cycles, with the rhythm of life."

"You said you missed that feeling," Ginger said, and he nodded agreement.

"Practical, problem solving," Alex mused. "I think we can agree that Ginger has an affinity for the earth."

"So we need a token, willingly given, that represents the earth and the fire that you bring to this union," Sara said. "That's what will heal Delaney's scale."

Ginger knew instantly what it had to be. She pulled off her mother's amber earrings and offered them along with the scale to Quinn. "Can you use these? They look like fire to me, and they come from the earth, and they were my father's first gift to my mother."

"Ginger!" Delaney protested. "You don't have to do this."

"Yes," she said with conviction. "Yes, I do."

Quinn took the earrings in his broad hand and turned them over as he examined them. "Set in silver," he said. "They resonate beautifully."

"What do you mean?"

He smiled at her. "They continue to be given in love. Gems know these things."

Ginger could believe that. "Can you use them?"

"I'll go one better," Quinn said. "I can work the sterling easily. I'll use just one for the scale."

"What will I do with one earring?"

"Quinn can make the other one into a ring," Delaney said, coming to Ginger's side. He took her hand in his. "Make a ring that I can give back to Ginger."

She looked at him in surprise and his crooked smile made her chest tighten. "Wear it on your right hand for now. By the time the baby comes, you'll know whether you want to move it to your left hand or not. Either way, it'll always be yours."

But Ginger didn't need that much time. She already knew that this man would always be in her heart.

—from **Winter Kiss**

THE SETTING

Because Delaney is being changed to a shadow dragon against his will, his eclipse is fired by a penumbral lunar eclipse, specifically the one on February 9, 2009. The book is set in Ohio, where Delaney has located Magnus' lair. The Dragon's Blood Elixir is hidden nearby in a sanctuary beneath the Serpent Mound, an ancient earthwork. Ginger's family farm is also in the vicinity. There's a blizzard during this book, perhaps echoing the chill that has quenched Delaney's fire.

THE PROPHECY

The Outcast patrols shadows deep,
Defending the Pyr *while they sleep.*
When darkness becomes his domain
He risks losing his path back again.
Vigilant in the endless night
Yet drawn by the firestorm's light,
But how can one so at ease in dark
Surrender fully to the firestorm's spark?
Will he dare to leave his task,
Choose himself first instead of last?

THE STORY

Prologue: (Chicago, February 9, 2009) In his apartment, Erik tries to calm three-month-old Zoë, feeling restless himself. Another full lunar eclipse is not expected until December 2010. Eileen wakes and informs Erik there are three penumbral (partial) eclipses, one of which takes place that very morning. She thinks that since they are shadows perhaps they will involve the shadow dragons. The two discuss Delaney, how he refused becoming a *Slayer,* but sold off his assets and has moved on, not answering old-speak. While trying to communicate with Zoë to see if she has any of the Wyvern abilities already, Erik tries to and conjure a vision using a bowl of water. He speaks to his daughter in old-speak. The baby stretches her hand down toward the water, and a scene appears— that of the holding place for the Dragon's Blood Elixir, and Delaney in a parked car outside the location. Erik realizes this means Delaney hopes to destroy the Elixir's source on his own. Lines of latitude and longitude appear, marking a place in Ohio. Knowing he can't take his family into danger, Erik delegates the trip to Sloane, Niall, and Thorolf. Driving along a country road in Ohio, Delaney suddenly begins to change forms without his control., The rental car ends up in a ditch, and as the change comes violently, he feels an uncontrollable need for the Elixir. Using pain to gain control over his senses, Delaney also experiences a familiar nightmare: the earth and humanity being destroyed, knowing it is due to the Elixir not being destroyed as it should be; men becoming selfish and greedy like *Slayers,* Gaia fighting back to protect herself, and a great shadow covering everything. Four hours and three minutes after the eclipse passes, Delaney shifts back to human and resolves to find and destroy the Elixir, even though he expects the action to kill him.

Chapter 1: Delaney plans to attack the Elixir sanctuary the next morning, taking away the *Slayers'* ability to make more shadow dragons. He has been preparing himself physically and mentally for a year to be ready for this task, which he considers to be a suicide mission. Back on the road after the violent shift, Delaney sees lights ahead and craves human company, so he stops at a roadhouse. While ordering his drinks, a woman touches his elbow and sparks result. Delaney realizes he has been blessed by the Great Wyvern with a firestorm and plans to honor it during what he feels to be his last night alive. The short, curvy redhead with bright blue eyes introduces herself as Ginger, and the two of them begin to dance. With both of them feeling a strong attraction, and after he passes her "good guy" test, Ginger asks Delaney to go home with her. She lives on a dairy farm and hopes to expand to organic foods in the future. Delaney uses his father's surname for the first time, and the two kiss.

Chapter 2: Delaney and Ginger have sex, indulging in their firestorm. While Ginger sleeps beside him afterward, Delaney wishes he could stick around to build a future with her, but feels he can best protect her and their child by destroying the Elixir. Contacting Erik via old-speak, Delaney asks him to watch out for Ginger. Erik agrees but also asks Delaney to wait for him, which the latter replies he cannot do. Delaney reluctantly leaves. When Ginger wakes to find Delaney gone, she decides to go after him since it seems he left not long before. Starting up her old pick-up, Ginger sets out to find Delaney.

Chapter 3: Delaney heads to the Serpent Mound, an earthwork state memorial, which he knows hides the entrance to the location of the Elixir. One theory about the Mound has it based upon the constellation Draco, which Delaney thinks must be why Magnus chose this location. Delaney notices a break in the dragonsmoke perimeter, as well as a house from which he scents the *Slayers* Jorge, Mallory, and Balthasar, and two others he cannot identify. He reaches a hole that is a tunnel opening, and Delaney sends a message to Magnus in old-speak, to come and get him. He slides down, and at the bottom, discovers an iron grate covering an opening, behind which he sees a glow of red light. He uses dragonfire to melt the bars. Ginger finds Delaney's rental car in the monument parking lot, and she decides to follow his footprints, after grabbing her rifle. Delaney's tracks lead to a hole, then disappear. She also spots another set of footprints next to the hole. She slides down the opening, only then does she recall that the second set of prints seemed to have appeared out of nowhere. Delaney finds the large vial containing the Elixir and tries to destroy it. When his energy flags, Delaney hears a voice tempting him to drink of the contents to enhance his strength. He overcomes the temptation and continues to beat at the vial. When he sees the source of the Elixir inside he is horrified. Magnus appears, and the two fight in dragon form. Delaney notices Magnus' missing scale.

Chapter 4: Ginger hears the sounds of fighting, and fearing Delaney may be in trouble, she readies her rifle and enters the room. Aside from the red glow emanating from within, Ginger is astounded by the sight of two dragons fighting: one emerald and copper, the other jade. Watching the two battle, Ginger is surprised and disturbed by two things: she feels desire, and when the emerald dragon speaks, his voice sounds like Delaney's. The jade dragon notices Ginger and moves in to attack. She shoots him, but the jade dragon grabs her and starts to breathe fire. Though shocked to see her there, Delaney knows he must protect Ginger, while at the same time puzzling over why the firestorm feels as strong as ever. Delaney attacks Magnus, and the *Slayer* attempts to control him, but Delaney is able to resist, possibly due to the strength given him via the firestorm. He tears into Magnus, though he stops himself before killing him, not wishing to become like those he fights against. Now holding Ginger, Delaney decides it is more important to get her out of danger than it is to destroy the Elixir right then. Changing to human form, Delaney carries the unconscious Ginger outside. When she wakes, she demands answers, having difficulty believing what she saw. Frightened when Delaney almost changes due to the *Slayers* closing in, Ginger runs from Delaney, and he tells her to move faster. As they reach the top of the hill, Ginger sees four additional dragons and hears a man speak to her.

Chapter 5: Delaney thinks it may be a good thing for Ginger to be afraid of him, especially if it makes it easier to leave her. The tall, blond man standing near Ginger watches the battle overhead. As he pushes her rifle muzzle away, Ginger notices a dragon tattoo on the back of his hand. Ginger knows it is impossible for men to turn into dragons, but can't explain where Delaney could have gone. The blond man says the emerald and copper dragon is Delaney — they are dragon shifters — and points out Delaney is protecting her. As the copper and emerald dragon, along with two others, comes toward Ginger, she recognizes Delaney's eyes. The man tells Ginger she may want to close her eyes since viewing the transformation is not typically good for humans. She doesn't and Ginger faints when Delaney shifts. Realizing he feels more for Ginger than just as the bearer of his child, Delaney feels guilty. Along with Niall, Sloane, and Thorolf, Delaney is confused as to why the firestorm has not been sated. Niall remarks that he sensed the firestorm very strongly, likely due to the bond he shares with Delaney. Niall chastises Delaney for trying to destroy the Elixir alone because no one could have been there to prevent the *Slayers* from turning him into a shadow dragon. Delaney shows the others his blood now runs completely red. Ginger comes to, and tells Delaney he has some explaining to do. He acknowledges the other three *Pyr* as his friends, and Ginger agrees they can all go to her farm to talk.

Chapter 6: Still processing the information she has been given regarding dragon shifters, Ginger drives her truck back to her farm, with Delaney as passenger. The others follow in the rental car. On the way, Ginger learns about the word *Pyr* (Greek for fire), finds out Delaney is four hundred and fifty years old, that dragon shifters are not immortal but age slowly, about the Elixir, and about *Slayers*. She learns Delaney was forced to drink the Elixir. Delaney then describes shadow dragons, and what the *Slayers* attempted with him. While listening to Delaney's story, Ginger is reminded of veterans she has seen suffering from PTSD. Satisfied her instincts about Delaney had been correct—he was one of the good guys—Ginger is somewhat taken aback to hear about mates and the firestorm. Still in the truck after they arrive, Delaney demonstrates with a kiss. Ginger and Delaney join the others to go inside for coffee, where they find Rafferty waiting for them. Somewhat soothed by Rafferty's manner (due to his affinity with earth), Ginger learns about old-speak, and Delaney agrees to forgo using it in front of her after Rafferty points out that the *Pyr* always stop using it in front of their mates.

Chapter 7: Ginger, a chef by trade, makes breakfast for the group, and then learns the purpose of the firestorm—to create a child. This revelation angers Ginger, given the fact Delaney left her the next morning. Sloane examines Delaney's wound and asks Delaney when his blood became solely red. Delaney tells him it was only the day before, and all agree the firestorm must be responsible. Over breakfast, the *Pyr* discuss the destruction of the Elixir, trying to convince Delaney he cannot do it alone. Ginger then understands he expected to die in the underground chamber. Just when she has decided to forgive Delaney a bit for leaving her after he thought he'd done his duty by impregnating her, Ginger learns he told the others they had sex. Angry, Ginger tells them all to leave.

Chapter 8: Delaney tries to explain himself, but Ginger stops him, saying she believes in love and romance and states that she is not interested in the firestorm/mate idea unless he wishes a long-term relationship. She also points out that if the firestorm is still going, either her pill is working or Delaney is impotent. She then leaves to go work in the barn, saying she expects them gone by the time she returns. Delaney tells the *Pyr* to leave so he can talk to Ginger alone. Niall tries to get him to promise not to go after the Elixir by himself, but Delaney won't do so. As they are leaving, Rafferty tells Delaney the Great Wyvern puts mates together who are two halves of a whole, and also says, "choosing to live can be harder than choosing to die." But Delaney thinks his experience with the *Slayers* and the Elixir is different. He goes out to the barn to talk to Ginger. In the barn, Ginger thinks about her move from farm to city and back again, and about the farm and cows. As she works, Ginger notices something seems off with a couple of the bulls. Thinking a stray wild creature had found its way in, Ginger is surprised to come across a stranger with a scary smile and laugh. When she sees the signs of him beginning to transform, Ginger runs out of the barn.

Chapter 9: As he thinks over his plans for betraying and overthrowing Magnus, Jorge shifts and catches Ginger. Pursued by Delaney, the two battle, Jorge using Ginger as a pawn by dropping her, though Delaney manages to catch her in time. Jorge gets her back, but Delaney severs his foot and retrieves Ginger, placing her safely on the ground once again. The fight goes against Delaney, and he is badly injured, enabling Jorge to once again get Ginger, and this time he flies away with her, to Magnus.
Meanwhile, at a local diner Thorolf, Niall, and Rafferty discuss

Delaney's situation. Rafferty thinks Magnus' attempted manipulation of Delaney is a ploy to get Delaney to try to destroy the Elixir alone, as he has been. Rafferty believes the treatise Sloane has been working on and just went to get from his home may have the answers as to why. Rafferty leaves to consult with Erik. Niall and Thorolf agree to stay behind and back up Delaney, but they will pretend to leave, in order to draw out Magnus. Meanwhile, Magnus sips at another glass of Elixir to aid in his healing and watches the captive Ginger pace. Jorge, who Magnus suspects is untrustworthy, is sporting a cast enclosing his Elixir-dipped stump and severed foot. Magnus decides to entertain himself by talking to Ginger. He ends up telling her the story of Cinnabar, the dragon fueling the Elixir. Named Sahir, then Sylvanus Secundus, a *Pyr* in Roman times who did not know who or what he was, he worked in a mine of cinnabar (mercury). The mineral did not poison the *Pyr* as it did humans, but his metabolism was affected by the cinnabar. When Magnus came upon him many years later, he got the idea for the Elixir. He imprisoned the *Pyr* in the vial, creating the Elixir with his life force, which is being slowly drained away. After telling her the story, Magnus locks Ginger in an outdoor courtyard, using her to lure Delaney but also to kill her. In his room, Magnus retrieves a bloodstone from an urn that previously housed Aurelia's ashes. He thinks back on her manipulation of him, her death, and how he sent Cinnabar to retrieve the bloodstone from her corpse. With a syringe, Magnus makes his way to the Elixir.

Chapter 10: Delaney dreams of the earth dying, the *Pyr* dead but preserved under ice, and of Ginger dying. He awakens to find Ginger and Jorge gone, but Niall has returned and is tending to his wounds. Thorolf arrives, displaying more skill with shapeshifting. Niall discovers a small bead of mercury in Delaney's shoulder wound, and when Delaney puts the bead on his finger, his skin has a strange reaction. The three speculate that perhaps the Elixir contains mercury, as Delaney says he saw the same beads on the outside of the vial. Niall and Thorolf follow Delaney as he tracks Ginger's scent, which he is not surprised to discover leads to the new house he spotted earlier. Thick dragonsmoke prevents his friends from getting too close, but Delaney ignores the pain when he spots Ginger in the courtyard below. Realizing that he needs to leave before the smoke pulls the life force from him and strengthens whoever set the barrier, Delaney flies away to come up with a plan. Trapped outside in the cold, Ginger regrets having told off and kicked out the *Pyr* from the farmhouse. While trying to scale the wall, Ginger also notices a large bowl containing red liquid. She is pretty sure it contains Elixir. Thinking back to Magnus' story about Cinnabar slowly dying, she guesses that she is being used as bait to lure Delaney so he can become the next Elixir fuel. Then Ginger senses Delaney overhead, due to the firestorm. When she sees him depart after coming closer to check on her, she knows he's leaving because of the dragonsmoke, since Thorolf told her about it.

Chapter 11: Delaney and Niall come up with a plan to blow off the front of Magnus' house using fertilizer and the rental car, creating an escape route for Ginger, so Delaney can get to her and move her to safety. Delaney shifts and feels the dragonsmoke even more acutely in dragon form, but manages to tear down the gate. In human form, Delaney drives up to the house, hitting the front. The noise gets the attention of Balthasar, who comes out to investigate. He shifts and comes after Delaney, who sets the gas tank on fire, which then causes the car to explode. Though Balthasar gets away, the front of the house explodes. Ginger decides to create a distraction so the *Pyr* can enact whatever their plan may be. She starts kicking at the bowl containing the Elixir and manages to create a crack. Jorge and Mallory come out to see what she is up to. Jorge tells Ginger that she no longer serves a purpose, since Delaney now knows where she is and will be coming for her, so they want to find out how toxic the Elixir is to humans. Jorge tells Mallory to grab her and he takes her over to the bowl, trying to force her to drink. Ginger remembers Mallory's injuries, and digs her fingers into his partially-healed wound. She escapes when the *Slayer* loosens his hold on her and throws her against a wall. Then an explosion occurs, and Ginger runs free. Outside, Niall attacks Balthasar, and Thorolf provides back-up for Delaney when he goes to get Ginger. Delaney wonders to himself if the *Pyr* will watch out for Ginger after he is gone, and realizes he is beginning to feel a lot for Ginger beyond just responsibility for her safety. Later

Ginger mentions Luke, her neighbor, and Delaney is jealous. Niall points out someone intent on heading into a suicidal situation shouldn't care that much about Ginger's neighbors or employees.

Chapter 12: Arriving back at the farm, Ginger wants Delaney to change to his human form while still holding her, which he does. Ginger makes an effort to distance herself physically from Delaney, but after he sends Niall and Thorolf off to start fixing the barn roof damaged by Jorge, Delaney tells Ginger he needs to talk to her, hoping to explain his actions. Ginger accepts the firestorm as a primal need, but asks Delaney to consider that if he was chosen to have a firestorm, it must be because he is special in some way. She compares the firestorm to love at first sight. Delaney says he has a taint, but she responds she would like to make that determination on her own. Ginger tries to tell Delaney about Magnus' plan for him, but he distracts her with a kiss. Delaney promises Ginger he will stick around that night, then goes off to help with the barn. Ginger gets a call from her friend, Tanya, who insists Ginger bring Delaney with her to Tanya's wedding the following weekend. After the call, Ginger reads a poem left by Rafferty, which she believes may be a prophecy about Delaney. Their roof repairs complete, the *Pyr* start cleaning the barn for Ginger.

Chapter 13: While cleaning the barn, Niall and Thorolf argue about the latter's lack of ambition and initiative, then Ginger arrives. A comedy of errors involving Thorolf, the rooster, and a bull ensues. While at first enjoying himself, Delaney then becomes quiet and withdrawn after realizing he cannot have the things he really wants, due to his task to destroy the Elixir. During dinner, Ginger tries to talk about Magnus, but Delaney says he knows all he needs to about the *Slayer*. Ginger relates the story of Cinnabar, which Delaney has to admit he did not know. Ginger shares her belief Magnus wants to put Delaney in the Elixir vial. Niall raises the point Rafferty made about Magnus using some of his commands to Delaney as a distraction to get him closer to the Elixir vial. Delaney scoffs at the idea and leaves the table to go outside. Niall follows shortly thereafter, as does Ginger. The two men tell Ginger about their eco-travel business, and Niall wants

Delaney to return. It worked well since Delaney came up with the ideas and Niall put them into action. Upset about one more thing he believes he cannot have, Delaney describes a bit about what the Elixir has done to him. The other two notice his skin has taken on a red hue, much like what happened to Cinnabar. Delaney begins to believe he is being transformed.

Chapter 14: A few hours later the redness has dissipated from Delaney quite a bit. As Ginger heads upstairs to go to bed, Delaney convinces Ginger he needs to stay in her room to protect her from the *Slayers*, since they have figured out a way to break through dragonsmoke. Ginger hears about the Wyvern for the first time. As they discuss the firestorm, Delaney says it cannot be denied, and he kisses her. Despite her desire, Ginger tells him how her parents died in a car accident when she was just a year old, and she insists she will not have a child alone. Delaney agrees to spend the night on a chair in her room, but when he has his nightmare again—seeing each of the *Pyr* destroyed by the elements they have affinities with, or in ways related to their calling, and his mother talking to him—he awakens chilled and moves toward the heat of the firestorm, climbing into bed with Ginger.

Chapter 15: At Erik's Chicago home, Rafferty thinks of Sophie and Nikolas, missing them both. He stops outside baby Zoë's room, she reaches toward him, so Rafferty picks her up. He is unsure if she is the new Wyvern, but he begins to wonder when Zoë puts his black and white ring from Sophie and Nikolas into her mouth, causing Rafferty to have a powerful vision. He sees a lunar eclipse, and the number 6585.322. Rafferty takes the sleeping Zoë with him to do some research on Erik's laptop. He learns eclipses occur in Saros cycles, which are 6585.322 days, or the equivalent of eighteen years. Digging deeper, Rafferty discovers it may be necessary for Magnus to create more Elixir by 2013, so he assumes that's why the *Slayer* is manipulating Delaney now. Erik joins Rafferty, having had the same dream, and they discuss the toxin in Delaney being mercury. After Eileen wakes, they decide to all go to Delaney. In Michigan, Sara wakes from a dream about Nikolas looking for Sophie, unable to find her. She tells Quinn they need to go to Delaney, because in her dream Nikolas gave her a scale, saying she would know what to do with it. Sara knows it is one of Delaney's scales, and insists they need to go to him so Quinn can fix Delaney's armor. Donovan wakes in Minneapolis, knowing his restlessness comes from resolving to avoid the call to his brother's firestorm. Donovan has a memory of when he first met Delaney. Quinn contacts him via old-speak, telling him Sara says they need to go. Alex is not thrilled at the prospect at first but agrees they need to help.

Chapter 16: Delaney wakes Ginger with a yell, from his nightmare. He says she was dead, and it was all his fault. When she soothes him, the firestorm kicks up and they begin kissing. Delaney stops short of intercourse, sure she would regret it in the morning. He gives her several orgasms, but then leaves the bed, and she finds a bead of mercury on the pillow. He goes downstairs and senses a *Pyr* presence just before Erik appears. Delaney is stunned Erik brought Eileen and the baby with him, given his previous encounter with the pregnant mates. Erik forbids the younger man to go to the sanctuary alone to prevent Magnus from being able to make Delaney the new source of the Elixir. Ginger joins them in the kitchen, and Delaney says he has a story to tell them. Rafferty goes to Serpent Mound Park, wondering if he can use any of Sophie's powers, possibly aided by his connection with her through his ring. He wishes to be where Magnus is, and in salamander form. He manifests in an underground chamber with Magnus. Rafferty challenges him using his coin, depicting St. George and the Dragon, and Magnus tosses his, as well. The two begin to fight. Back at the farmhouse, Delaney tells the story of his mother, who suffered from some form of mental illness. He knew nothing of his powers until he was fourteen and was angered by a man who cheated him. Not understanding what was happening, he shifted and killed the man. His mother guessed what he had done and wanted him to show her his other form. When he did, she cried out about demons. The healer he had hired to help his mother told him he should probably leave. He did, but he sent money for her care, and asked neighbors how she was doing. He went to see her when she was dying and told her about the *Pyr*.

Chapter 17: Ginger hears the gathered *Pyr,* with Eileen's help, tell the tale of the creation of the four elements (earth, air, fire, and water) and of the race of guardians created to protect them. Delaney says his mother told him she didn't know why he was made the way he was, but that she loved him, and believed he must have some purpose. She gave him her silver cross to wear and made him promise to use his powers in the service of good. Delaney tells the group he believes destroying the Elixir will allow him to keep his promise to his mother, as well as to protect the earth and the other *Pyr*. Ginger follows Delaney outside to the old barn, and she shows Delaney the poem Rafferty wrote, which seems to indicate he has a future. She said maybe the Elixir was unable to completely transform him because he was given a second chance. Ginger makes a deal with him: if he agrees to try to come back, not to be set on self-destruction in his task, then she will have his child. He agrees, and they give in to the firestorm.

Chapter 18: Later, when Delaney touches the sleeping Ginger, there is no longer a spark, so he knows the firestorm has been sated and Ginger must be pregnant. Delaney notices one of his thumbnails has turned red. Though he hopes to live and return to her, Delaney still believes he needs to destroy the Elixir. He leaves his cross in Ginger's hand, gets the remaining fertilizer, and flies off with it. Rafferty and Magnus continue to fight. Rafferty decides to conserve his energy by pretending to be badly hurt so Magnus will leave him alone. Niall comes into the barn looking for Delaney as Ginger wakes up. When they go into the house, Ginger meets Quinn, Sara, Donovan, Alex and their children. She likes that they have all gathered to help Delaney. Ginger shows the others the poem Rafferty wrote down and fills them in on some of the other news about Magnus. When they realize Delaney must have gone to destroy the Elixir, Erik assigns tasks. Alex and Donovan's son then points at the counter, saying "no" over and over, and they see a garnet red salamander.

Chapter 19: Delaney arrives at the sanctuary and begins putting bags of fertilizer around the Elixir vial, noticing the liquid now appears more pink than red. Magnus shows up and confirms Ginger's supposition about his plans for Delaney and the Elixir, explaining about the Saros cycle. Delaney changes to his dragon form and sees he is becoming more red. At the farmhouse, the red salamander breaks through a window and jumps out, changing to its dragon shape and flying away: Mallory. They don't know what he was doing there, but Quinn and Donovan go off in pursuit. The others analyze Rafferty's poem, and Alex realizes the Elixir may be destroyed with nitric acid. Erik sends Donovan, Quinn and Alex after the chemical, says he's going to look for Rafferty while Sloane, Niall, and Ginger go after Delaney, and assigns Thorolf the task of guarding Sara, Eileen, and the children. As Niall flies with Ginger closer to the sanctuary, he says he smells Jorge, Balthasar, and Mallory. The *Pyr* and *Slayers* begin to fight, and shadow dragons join in. Ginger gets passed off to Erik when Niall gets attacked by the shadow version of his twin brother. Back at the farmhouse, baby Zoë will not stop crying. Sara and Quinn's son, Garrett, goes up to the baby and she grabs his hand. Garrett's eyes get big, and he tries to open the door to go outside. Realizing Zoë told the toddler something, they follow him out the door. Garrett brings back a planter from the porch, which has a bead of mercury on it. They figure out Mallory had been there to poison the water with mercury to create replacements for Cinnabar. The battle between *Pyr* and *Slayers* rages on, with Niall using the air to create a funnel cloud. Two new *Slayers* join the fray.

Chapter 20: Delaney tries to use dragonfire to ignite the fertilizer, but exhales only cold air. Magnus laughs, saying his transformation has begun. The *Slayer* surrounds Delaney with dragonsmoke, draining Delaney's energy to bolster his own. Delaney notices he now has a scale missing in the middle of his chest, a sign of his care for Ginger. Unable to move, Delaney shifts to his human form. Magnus injects him with quicksilver and places a stone in his mouth. Rafferty arrives—too late, he fears—and takes on Magnus once again. Donovan uses his ability to turn the elements into weapons, and the *Slayers* retreat during an onslaught of ice. Ginger determines she is the only one who can get through the dragonsmoke to deliver the canisters of silver nitrate to the Elixir. She taunts Magnus, trying to draw his attention and his fire, and when her plan works, Cinnabar rises from the vial to protect her, drawing the dragonfire to himself. The vial cracks, the Elixir is lit by the fire, creating a crimson smoke, and the liquid changes to crystals on the ground. Rafferty continues to battle Magnus, energized by the black and white ring. The earth begins to crumble down around them. Ginger realizes Cinnabar is protecting her, and then he turns his attention to Delaney, drawing the mercury out of Delaney's body. When Delaney is healed, Ginger thanks Cinnabar, using his real name, Sahir. He shifts to his human form and then fades away. Delaney wakes up, asking about Magnus. Rafferty tells him the *Slayer* is now buried beneath the earth and the Elixir is gone. Delaney gives him the stone that Magnus had put in his mouth. Rafferty crushes the "piece of wickedness" in his hand. Ginger, Delaney and Rafferty escape the collapsing chamber.

Chapter 21: When they arrive at the farm, Ginger asks Delaney if he will be her plus-one at her friends' wedding, and he says yes. He tells her he plans to stay for as long as she wants him to. The other *Pyr* and their families all gather around Ginger and Delaney. Sloane shows them a scale he has in his hand, and Ginger knows it belongs to Delaney. While the others wait, Ginger figures out that the missing scale means Delaney loves her and that Quinn will be the one to replace it. She wants to know what to do to aid in the repair. Since Delaney's affinities are air and water, Ginger offers up her earrings as representations of earth and fire, filling out the four elements needed for the ceremony. Quinn uses one earring to make the repair and says he will make the other into a ring. After a successful ceremony, the others all leave, Ginger and Delaney alone together at last.

DEBORAH'S COMMENTS

One of my favorite parts of this book is the chemistry between Ginger and Delaney. Not only are they electric together—with or without the spark of the firestorm—but Ginger is fearless. She tells Delaney off, even knowing he's a dragon shifter, and I love that. Here's when she finds out what the firestorm means:

Ginger put the eggs down and placed one hand on her hip. "What aren't you telling me? Come on, cough it up."

"The firestorm also means that the mate conceives the *Pyr's* son," Delaney admitted.

Ginger made a dismissive wave of one hand. "No such chance. I take the pill." She would have turned to the stove, but Rafferty spoke.

"That doesn't matter," he said, and Delaney wished he hadn't.

"Excuse me?" Ginger turned on Rafferty again.

"The pill is known to have a small failure rate in preventing conception." Rafferty shrugged. "I guarantee you that the firestorm will ensure that is what happens between you and Delaney."

Delaney winced to have that detail aired. As much as he was glad to have the support of his fellow *Pyr,* they did have a tendency to be annoying.

Life would have been a lot easier if they had just shut up.

Ginger's eyes flashed as she turned to Delaney again. "You *knew* that?"

He felt the back of his neck heat. "Well, yeah. That's the point—"

Ginger interrupted him. "You *intended* to get me pregnant without talking to me about it first?" she demanded, her voice rising. "Don't you think that I might have had other plans for the next twenty years of my life? Don't you think you ought to have *asked?*" She threw out her hands. "Oh no, that's right—you *left* this morning without even talking to me!"

"Ginger, I..."

She shook a finger at him and he took a step back from her anger. "You planned a one-nighter to knock me up! You *planned* to leave me pregnant. Just who in the hell do you think you are?"

Delaney didn't have a good answer for her. He'd thought only of his duty to the *Pyr,* not of the implications for Ginger, and felt foolish as a result. "It's my responsibility—," he began, but she interrupted him again.

"Responsibility? What am I? Just a womb for the taking? I can't believe I thought you were a gentleman." She practically growled as she opened one carton of eggs. "I can't believe I thought you were a keeper."

"Ginger, I—"

She turned on him again. "You really think it's that easy for a woman to raise a child alone?" Ginger flung out a hand. "Never mind a child who's going to be a dragon shape shifter..."

"We *Pyr* don't come into our abilities until puberty," Rafferty interjected softly.

"Great!" Ginger said, facing the older *Pyr*. "That would give me twelve or thirteen years to figure out how to explain that to the school." She glared at Delaney, her hands on her hips, and he thought again that she was a little spitfire. "What was in your head? Or maybe your planning was being done a bit lower down."

Delaney shuffled his feet, feeling as he did whenever he'd been called on the carpet by Erik, leader of the *Pyr*. "I guess I wasn't thinking clearly..."

"Well, neither was I." Ginger growled in irritation, then whirled and headed for the stove. She dropped a second cast-iron skillet onto the burner so hard that he feared one or the other would crack.

She was furious and every *Pyr* in the kitchen knew it.

—from **Winter Kiss**

Another detail I enjoy about **Winter Kiss** is learning more about Thorolf—particularly that he's afraid of cows. That's not very helpful when Ginger and the *Pyr* muck out the barn, or when the protective rooster, Reginald, takes exception to the change in routine:

"The fresh hay is over there," Ginger called. "Put half a dozen bales on each side." Niall did as she instructed and Delaney started to shovel the floor of the stalls the cows had left.

Thorolf hung back and Niall muttered something about laziness.

"I'm not lazy!" Thorolf shouted, and the cows shied away from the sound.

"Calm," Ginger scolded. "Quiet and routine. That's what they like."

"Get a shovel already," Delaney said with impatience.

He looked up in time to see Thorolf's dismayed expression. "You mean, like, go in there, close to them?"

Ginger laughed. "They're mostly cows!"

"You go in the stall next to them, not with them," Niall said.

Thorolf held his ground. "Hey, I'm a city dude." He put a hand over his heart. "I do mongrels and stray cats, sparrows and pigeons. Raccoons and skunks, maybe. Bats. Rats. Pigeons and crows. Bulls are a whole other thing."

"You do steak," Delaney couldn't help noting.

Thorolf's eyes lit with enthusiasm. "Well, yeah! But it's not going to attack me from the plate."

"Just don't annoy them," Ginger advised. "Move slowly and talk to them in a calm voice. They like having the stalls mucked out, so they should be cooperative."

"Should be," Thorolf repeated with a shake of his head. "Did anyone else hear the uncertainty in that? How much do these things weigh, anyway? They're huge!"

"Move it," Delaney said. He'd already shoveled a quarter of one large paddock.

"Courage," Niall mused as he leaned into it. "Another admirable trait."

Thorolf swore.

Niall smiled.

Ginger seemed to be trying to hide a laugh as she came toward Delaney, challenge in her expression. Delaney could have watched her eyes dance for the rest of the day—never mind the sway of her hips—but he focused on his job. He remembered the satisfaction of heavy work, of using his body to make a difference.

Honest work.

Ginger joined him, showing that she was far from frail in the way she put her shoulder into it, too. "Chute at the back right corner," she instructed. "Luke can move it out from there whenever he gets through the snow."

Luke. There was the mention of that man again. Delaney felt a hot stab of jealousy, one more like dragonsmoke than the firestorm, and resented this man he didn't even know.

"Moo," Thorolf said to a small dark bull in a paddock by the door. The blond *Pyr* was holding a shovel, obviously uncertain of the wisdom of proceeding further.

"That's Darian," Ginger said. "He's quite gentle."

"Uh-uh," Thorolf had time to say before Darian bellowed.

Thorolf bolted toward the door of the barn, his eyes wide with terror. "He's going to kill me!"

"He knows about the steaks," Delaney said deadpan. "He wants to get even."

Niall laughed. Ginger giggled. Thorolf lifted the shovel high in self-defense as Darian bellowed again.

Reginald took exception to Thorolf's quick move and flew to the rail of the paddock, squawking and flapping furiously. Thorolf swore and grabbed the broom, holding both the broom and the shovel aloft.

"Don't hit him with the shovel," Niall advised. "I think Ginger's teasing about the coq au vin."

Thorolf looked momentarily confused, glancing between broom and shovel, rooster and bull. Reginald made his move, flying at the *Pyr* with his talons extended. Thorolf bellowed and retreated. Darian charged the rim of the paddock. Thorolf dropped both tools and bolted from the barn.

The snow spiraled through the open door. Reginald crowed with pride as he strutted along the rail. Darian exhaled, the incident already forgotten as he bent to nuzzle his fresh hay.

Niall cracked up. Ginger joined his laughter, the two of them doubling over. The sound of Ginger and Niall's laughter was so infectious that Delaney found his own smile forming. When he laughed himself, the sound was so unfamiliar that he didn't recognize it as coming from him.

Ginger caught his arm and leaned against him, her voice low with merriment. "You have a great laugh," she said, her eyes glowing and her curves pressed against his side. Delaney caught his breath at the sudden intensity of his desire for her. "You should laugh more often."

When he looked down into her sparkling eyes, Delaney could almost believe it possible that he could have the future he craved, that he could learn to laugh again and to sleep without fear.

Almost.

But not quite.

—from **Winter Kiss**

HARMONIA'S KISS

Enchanted for thousands of years, the shapeshifters known as the Dragon's Tooth Warriors have awakened to find the world a vastly different place. Their leader, concerned for their morale, dares to take them on a mission to confront the fullness of everything they've lost.

Little does Drake realize that this dangerous mission will give him a renewed purpose. And if they succeed these Pyr will have to question everything they thought they knew about the past—and confront a quest for the future.

THE PROTAGONISTS

The Dragon's Tooth Warriors, led by Drake, have been cast through time by the spell of Cadmus. Drake names Lidio, Aeson, Cletus, Milo, and Alexander in the company, but this short story is mostly about Drake and his first meeting with Veronica Maitland. Taking a commission to find her missing husband leads him to the Cadmus: the defeat of that viper and the completion of his quest gives Drake new hope and purpose for the future.

THE SETTING

The Dragon's Tooth Warriors, disguised as a soccer team, travel through Europe, Greece and into the Middle East. Their exact location is not disclosed in the story.

THE PROPHECY

When the Dragon's Tail demands its price,
And the moon is devoured once, not twice,
Seer and Smith will again unite.
Water and air, with fire and earth
This sacred union will give birth
To the Pyr's sole chance to save the Earth.

THE STORY

Chapter 1: (Summer Solstice, June 2010) Erik meets Drake, the leader of the Dragon's Tooth Warriors at the Callanish standing stones. Many of the warriors were lost in an earlier battle, bringing their number down from one hundred to less than twenty. All of them are dark and very similar in appearance, in both dragon and human form, and they carry no scent. Drake tells Erik he fears the warriors may not be to pledge their hearts to Erik's cause until they see proof with their own eyes that the world as they knew it no longer exists. Before he makes a decision, Erik asks to hear the history of the Dragon's Tooth Warriors. Drake tells Erik of the warriors being led by a man named Cadmus to hunt vipers, creatures who turned men into teeth in the vipers' mouths. Though he had great success against the vipers, Cadmus ensnared Drake and his men with a spell. Drake wants to search for proof of Cadmus' death so his men will believe there is hope for the future. Erik scrys with his challenge coin, and gives Drake and the men permission to go, though he won't say what he saw. As the Dragon's Tooth Warriors leave, Erik thinks to himself how it will be up to them to resist their old leader, still alive, and keep from turning *Slayer*.

Chapter 2: Sitting in a bar in a city in the Middle East, Drake feels despondent over what he and his men discovered—the end of the world as they knew it, the people gone, the way of life different. He thinks back upon his earlier life there, his wife, Cassandra, and their son, Theo. Drake feels the effects of a distant firestorm but does not plan to get involved. Drake is surprised by a young boy asking if he knows his father, another soldier. The boy says his father has been missing for two months. Then a harried, yet lovely, woman comes in looking for her son, Timmy. Drake asks the woman if she wishes to know the truth, whatever it may be, and she says she does. He realizes the despair he and his men have been feeling is the work of a viper, whose chant he can hear when he listens very closely. Drake introduces himself, learns her name is Veronica Maitland, or Ronnie, and promises that he and his men will find out what happened to her husband.

Chapter 3: Following the trail of the missing man, the call of the viper grows stronger, and Drake believes there is a connection between the two. Some of the warriors fall, unable to continue. As they progress, the voice becomes louder, and Drake realizes Cadmus is still alive. The warriors fight some enthralled humans and find the cell with Maitland's body: he is clutching a photo of his family. Drake tells his second, Alexander, to take the soldier's body to the embassy while he continues to hunt and then destroy his old adversary.

Chapter 4: Fighting the viper's voice, Drake forges ahead and finds Cadmus. His former mentor now resembles a worm more than a dragon and refers to Drake as his apprentice, which Drake denies. Cadmus points to a skeleton in the corner, which Drake understands is that of Cadmus' wife, Harmonia. The old viper rails against women, and Drake argues with him. Then he kills Cadmus. Though feeling some sadness over the act, Drake also feels a new purpose. He thinks about how Harmonia could have made Cadmus' life different if he had let her in. Drake believes Veronica's sprit and love for her husband helped that man resist the viper's call.

Chapter 5: Ronnie wonders what she was thinking to come to the Middle East to search for her husband, Mark, and why she trusted Drake. After a week without word from him, she is packing to go home when he arrives at her hotel. Drake hands Ronnie an envelope, and she knows it must be the photo Mark said he would always keep with him. She sends Timmy into the other room, and Drake says he wishes he had better news. Ronnie is devastated but knows learning the truth is better than always wondering. Drake is touched by the kiss on the cheek Ronnie gives him, and when she asks if she will see him again, he leaves without answering.

Chapter 6: In the hotel courtyard, Drake can hear Ronnie's crying. Drake and the other Dragon's Tooth Warriors take to the sky, on their way to see Erik and pledge their loyalty. Drake thinks upon how the firestorm can balance a *Pyr*. He plans to one day look for Ronnie, not knowing what her reaction will be.

DEBORAH'S COMMENTS

I love when characters have second chances and this is the beginning of Drake's second chance. He starts to heal because of his interaction with Veronica and her son—in a way, he starts to live again. I don't think anyone who reads this story will be surprised that Drake and Ronnie ultimately experience a firestorm.

Here are Drake's thoughts at the beginning of this adventure:

Dust, all dust.

Drake sat in a café in a modern Middle Eastern city and faced the truth. Everything he had known, everything he had loved, was lost to time. He had known it would not be easy for him and his men to revisit the lands they had known so well, so many centuries before. But the experience of coming home was far worse than expected.

Home. That was a cruel joke. The cities they remembered were ruins, if they survived at all. The homes they had built were lost to the hills. The verdant valleys they had known were barren. The people they had loved, the children and wives, brothers and parents and neighbors, were lost without a trace. The past was dust and ash, desolation that hung a weight on Drake's heart.

He had seen each of his men survey what had once been familiar without recognition. He had watched hope die, over and over again. Theirs was an irrational hope, they all knew it, but they each sought some crumb of what they had lost. They had marched off to war thousands of years before and never returned. While they had been trapped in enchantment, lives had ended, borders had shifted, the world had changed.

They were perennially homeless now. All the money in the world, all the traveling possible, couldn't take them back to where they longed to be.

Ever.

—from **Harmonia's Kiss**

And here's his perspective after delivering the bad news to Ronnie. I don't think the difference could be more striking.

Drake hoped that in return, one day when Veronica Maitland's grief had diminished, one day when she least expected it, she would meet a man who didn't exactly remind her of her lost husband but who kindled the same feelings within her as that man once had.

Drake hoped that maybe, just maybe, Ronnie would one day see her future instead of her past.

It would take time, but Drake intended to hope for her healing. He'd hope for her son to grow up strong and proud.

And one day, one day after her tears had dried, Drake would make a point of finding her again. Veronica Maitland might be glad to see him. She might not.

The choice would be hers.

In the interim he'd know, with every blow from his talons and every volley of dragonfire he exhaled, that he was continuing the fight that he and his kind would pay any price to win.

—from **Harmonia's Kiss**

WHISPER KISS

ONE MAN'S MISSION IGNITES ONE WOMAN'S FIRE...

Niall Talbot has volunteered to hunt down and destroy all the remaining shadow dragons—who were weakened by destruction of the Dragon's Blood Elixir—before they can wreak more havoc. Among them is his dead twin brother, making Niall's mission not only dangerous but personal.

Tattoo artist Rox believes the world is a canvas to be made more beautiful. An unconventional spirit who isn't afraid of anything, she doesn't even flinch when a shape-shifting dragon warrior suddenly appears on her doorstep. And as a woman who follows her heart in matters of passion, she makes the perfect mate for a firestorm with Niall...

THE PROTAGONISTS

Niall Talbot is the *Pyr* who has offered to eliminate the shadow dragons left after the destruction of the Academy. This is a personal battle for him, as his twin brother Phelan is a shadow dragon and has attacked Niall in the past. Roxanne Kincaid is a tattoo artist, another tiny and feisty woman who is even more fearless than Ginger—because Rox is fascinated by dragons. Having a firestorm with a sexy dragon shifter in real life is her every dream come true—even if she isn't Niall's dream, at least at first glance.

THE ELEMENTS

Niall has a very strong affinity with air. From the beginning of the series, he shows an ability to conjure storms and summon a wind. In his book, his abilities are enhanced when he learns to become the DreamWalker, which allows him to journey through the dreams of others. This is Wyvern-like power, so it's apt that the toddler Zoë helps him to learn it.

Niall's other affinity is to fire, while Rox's affinities are water and earth. Of course, given Rox's business, tattoos feature in this book. At the end of the book, Niall and Rox have large back pieces that nest together and represent their union.

Rox's dragon was now colored in hues of amethyst and blue, accented in white to mimic platinum. The dragon curved like a letter C, his tail rising high on her left shoulder and his head curving up from below. Those orange stylized flames flowed behind him, but they looked more brilliant now that he was colored.

The dragon represented earth and water.

Rox liked that they each had the two elements of their own affinity represented on their backs, along with a symbol of the other's role in their partnership. She was earth and water to Niall's air and fire, but she was his Phoenix and he was her Dragon. The yin and yang symbol on his back represented the balance of their union, while the pearl on hers indicated—to Rox's thinking— the richness of the life they were making together.

Maybe even the precious gem of their son.

—from **Whisper Kiss**

THE SETTING

Because Niall must battle his dead twin brother, who has become a shadow dragon, his eclipse is tied to a partial lunar eclipse. It's triggered by the partial eclipse of June 26, 2010. The book is set in Manhattan, where Rox is a partner in a tattoo shop called Imagination Ink, which is located reasonably close to the office for Niall's eco-tourism business.

THE PROPHECY

The Phoenix sheds her former skin,
Clothes herself to begin again.
Injuries and debts unearned,
Consigned with her hide to fire's burn.
The Dragon loses but one scale,
To keep nigh intact his coat of mail.

But not all things should survive,
And not all burdens help him to thrive.
Can he learn the Phoenix's song,
And leave his past where it belongs?
Learn the Dreamwalker's dance
And usher in the world's new chance?

THE STORY

Chapter 1: (New York City, June 26, 2010): Rox is pleased to have found a job for her under-employed roommate, T. She believes T has incredible potential (especially since she knows about his other nature), but he lacks initiative, so she views him as a project she can fix. When she arrives home to tell him about his new job, she finds him packing his bags to leave, saying he's going to live with a guy named Niall who runs an ecotourism business. He now wants to be called by his name, Thorolf. He also tells Rox that Niall is "like him," and he has a lot to learn from the other man. Rox is suspicious and determines to find out what is going on. Niall, frustrated with his mentee, Thorolf, senses something unusual in the night air. He has been busy, sometimes with Thorolf's help, getting rid of the shadow dragons—a responsibility he took upon himself. So far he has destroyed twenty but thinks he must destroy the rest before the next total eclipse in December to avoid war. He also felt a partial eclipse that same morning. Unusual wind scent and activity coupled with a power outage make Niall move more quickly toward his home. He sees a light upstairs in his building, obviously from someone who doesn't belong there. As he gets closer, Niall sees a woman trying to get into the apartment. When he gets closer, feels a huge jolt, recognizing a firestorm. He can't imagine a less suitable woman to be his destined mate than this tattooed brunette. Niall is sure the firestorm must be wrong, Niall asks who she is, and when Rox tells him her name, he recognizes it as Thorolf's friend. When the building suddenly cracks in half, Niall's protective reflex kicks in and he changes to his dragon form.

Chapter 2: Amazed Niall is also a dragon shifter, Rox then admires the amethyst and platinum dragon next to her, also feeling an unusual physical response. Niall feels the same, but he knows the reason why. After he shifts back to his human form, Rox takes Niall by surprise by knowing he's a dragon shifter. They briefly discuss Thorolf, sharing their mutual exasperation at his behavior, but Rox adamantly suggests everyone deserves a second chance— sometimes even more than two. As she thanks him for saving her during the earthquake, Rox kisses Niall, and he kisses her back. Thorolf arrives, responding to Niall's earlier call to him via old-speak. When Thorolf mentions a firestorm, Rox has no idea what he means. Niall grabs some papers and his laptop from his office, and tells Thorolf to try to sense what is going on with the building. Feeling the structure's imminent collapse, the two men shift, Niall grabs Rox, and they leap out the window.

Chapter 3: When they land, Niall demands an explanation of why Thorolf let Rox see his shift. Still unhappy over the prospect of a firestorm during such an inopportune time, Niall tells Rox, "I haven't got time for this right now." When Thorolf joins them, Rox learns what beguiling is, but Thorolf assures her he never tried to do it to her. He also explains to Niall how Rox saw his shift during a bar fight, and he changed before he could stop the change. Thorolf gets upset at Niall for giving him a hard time about not being reliable, but Rox says her encouraging approach does not seem to be as effective as Niall's tough love. Thorolf agrees to buckle down and try harder. Thorolf insists Niall needs to protect Rox, even though she says she doesn't need to be protected. She does feel the attraction between them and tries to kiss him again, but Niall walks away, still not explaining the firestorm. Rox says Niall must have his dragon shifter abilities for a reason. Then Rox sees a homeless kid on the street and offers him a place to stay if he will work at her tattoo shop. Niall asks why she puts herself in such danger, and she explains she had a similar story. Before she leaves, Rox kisses Niall again, and gives him her card, saying it's up to him to call. Unobserved by either *Pyr*, a jade and gold salamander is on the sidewalk in front of Niall's building, and an elderly Chinese man picks it up and puts it in a plastic bag.

Chapter 4: Niall thinks about Rox, but thinks they are too different to be compatible. He learns from Thorolf she does not drink or use any drugs at all, just like Niall. Thorolf shows Niall the dragon tattoo Rox gave him to remind him of what he was capable of. Niall checks his email and finds an updated list from Ginger about missing *Pyr* who may be enlisted to fight against the *Slayers*, and also the names of the deceased, with notations if they might be turned into shadow dragons. Niall wonders if Rox maintains the physical appearance she does for a specific purpose, to keep people away. Thorolf reminds him that his firestorm is a duty to the *Pyr*. Niall scents shadow dragons, so he and Thorolf leave the cafe in pursuit. At work, Rox thinks about Niall and ends up drawing a dragon tattoo design. She decides to leave work a bit early and go after him, but then she sees Niall, in sunglasses, at the front counter. Chen, a *Slayer*, goes into an underground chamber beneath an apothecary shop, where shadow dragons are kept, taking Magnus, in the plastic bag, with him.

Chapter 5: Niall and Thorolf kill two shadow dragons, both with tiger-shaped marks on their necks, which they had not seen before. They wonder where the shadow dragons are hiding out. Niall decides to go see Rox. As they get closer, Niall scents another shadow dragon, this time his twin, Phelan. He realizes his brother must be near Rox, so Niall and Thorolf hurry to the tattoo shop. Rox is happy to see Niall, but everything about him seems different, and the outline of his body appears indistinct. When he touches her hand, his skin is cold, and the sparks are missing. Rox says she can't leave, but he grabs her and shifts to dragon form, which doesn't look the same as before. When she looks in his eyes, she realizes her captor is definitely not Niall. When Niall arrives, Phelan tries to convince him he was saving Rox from Jorge and the *Slayers*, and that he is on Niall's side. Phelan says he had no choice but to become a *Slayer*. Niall wonders to himself if Phelan can be saved the way Delaney was, so decides not to kill him during their fight. Rox hears the rumbling of old-speak, but doesn't yet know what it is. Thorolf catches her when Niall drops her, and Phelan leaves when an opal and gold dragon appears.

Chapter 6: Phelan dreads returning to Chen's lair where he is being held captive with the other shadow dragons, even though the *Slayer* provides him with the powder that clears his mind, enabling him to be cognizant for short intervals. Chen is furious Phelan has failed. Chen claims to be the last of the dragon kings, then recites a rhyme about the Phoenix and Dragon mating in the year of the tiger. In Ohio, Ginger complains to Delaney that Erik is ignoring her request for information on Gaspar's bloodline, which she needs for her research on potential allies and possible shadow dragons. Sara wakens from a dream, which sounds like one of the prophecies of the *Pyr,* referencing a Phoenix and a Dream Walker. She thinks about many things before she goes back to sleep: her pregnancy, which she has told no one about yet; whether or not Erik and Eileen's daughter, Zoë, is really the new Wyvern; and why the prophecy came to her when another firestorm is not due for several months. Magnus, still in his salamander form, is dumped out of the plastic bag and sees a large red dragon with gold-tipped scales. He identifies him as Chen, one of the last *Slayers* he gave Elixir to. Chen has imprisoned the shadow dragons and controls them. Chen admits that he released Magnus in order to follow him. He traps Magnus in an airtight jar and mentions dragon rain.

Chapter 7: Niall questions his decision to let Phelan go, but knows he was unwilling to do something as final as killing him if there was a chance he could be saved. Rafferty, who arrived during the fight, gets introduced to Rox, who mentions Phelan's tiger mark on his neck. Rox says it may be like a gang tattoo, which isn't always by choice, but they may have to live by whatever code it represents. Rox guesses the old-speak sound she has been hearing is a form of communication, but also wants to hear about the firestorm. Niall states she has been identified as his destined mate, and they are supposed to conceive a son for the firestorm to abate. Rox is astounded to learn Rafferty is twelve hundred years old, Thorolf eight hundred, and Niall two hundred. Rafferty explains they age slowly until they have their firestorms. Despite her fiery attraction to Niall, Rox is put off by the mention of a child, and decides she needs to go home to distance herself from Niall. Meanwhile, Niall talks to Rafferty about Rox and Phelan. Rafferty points out Phelan was deceptive even before he became a *Slayer,* which Niall acknowledges is true. He still wants to find a way to save his brother. He feels this may be the lesson his firestorm has for him. Niall goes to Rox's place to see if she will allow him to stay and protect her. He and Rox talk through a crack in her door. He says it's his job to protect her and that he is ready to explain to her the point of his abilities.

Chapter 8: Niall tells Rox the story of the four elements, and how the *Pyr* were created to be the guardians of the earth and its treasures, including humans. After Niall touches her hand to prove he is not his brother, Rox lets him inside the apartment. He sees her walls are covered with very realistic paintings of dragons, and Rox explains her fascination with the creatures since she was a child. She was inspired by their inherent strength after the death of her father. Niall tells Rox about the shadow dragons, suggesting that perhaps the lesson he is being taught from the firestorm is to give second chances. Niall notices the tattoo of a small blue heart with a line through it next to one of her eyes, and Rox says it's a reminder to her every day of the price of trust. Unable to resist their attraction to one another, they pleasure each other without intercourse. They are interrupted by Thorolf and Rafferty coming inside to get out of the rain. Rox agrees to let them all stay, but she locks her bedroom door, sending a clear message to Niall. Niall decides he wants a relationship with Rox and determines to win her over while he works on dispatching the shadow dragons.

Chapter 9: When Rox wakes up she feels safe hearing Niall's breathing in the other room. She realizes that she doesn't fear having a child after the firestorm, but does fear being abandoned after the birth of that child. Rox decides to wear her "armor" of black make-up and studded leather to turn Niall off, if all he is interested in is appearances. However, when she discovers him, in dragon form, lying over the threshold to her bedroom door in protection, she momentarily forgets her decision and admires his dragon form. Rox wants him to change in front of her, but he refuses, worried he may damage her mentally by doing so. When she runs her hands over his dragon body, Niall moves away from her and shifts quickly, telling her she must not do that again or he will not be able to restrain himself. Niall believes Rox must be trying to scare him off. While Thorolf complains about the lack of what he considers to be a substantial breakfast, Rox and Niall learn their eating habits are very similar, as are their lifestyles in many ways. Rox finds that her armor doesn't seem to put Niall off. She meets Sloane, who arrives with Rafferty. She learns about dragonsmoke and some of the differences between *Pyr* and *Slayer*. Niall discusses his brother, Phelan, with Sloane, saying he wonders if he can be healed the way Delaney was. Niall points out Phelan doesn't act like a typical shadow dragon anymore, which Sloane finds odd. Rox goes to work with Niall along for protection. When they get to the tattoo shop, they find the boy from the night before lying in front of the door. The boy, Barry, asks if she is still offering him a job. Niall wonders about Rox's tattoos—how many, where they are, and what they mean.

Chapter 10: Working at his laptop, Erik feels completely frustrated by the spreadsheet Ginger sent to him, the one detailing the lineage of each known *Pyr*. One particular box highlighted in red he cannot read at all when looking straight at the page and can catch only a glimpse of when looking out of the side of his eye. When Erik asks Eileen to look at the section of the spreadsheet he can't read, she tells him right away: the name Gaspar. However, Erik cannot keep the name in his mind for long, though he knows he does know who Gaspar is, or was—a friend of his father. Eileen says it sounds as though he was beguiled. He initially scoffs at the idea, since *Pyr* are not supposed to do this to one another, but Erik eventually accepts that he was indeed beguiled in the past, likely by either Gaspar or by Gaspar's son. Erik decides they need to go to New York. At the shop, Niall learns about tattooing in general and Rox's work in particular. After watching her work on a client, doing a memorial tattoo, he realizes there is more to her process than meets the eye.

Chapter 11: Niall tells Rox he believes she takes on the burden of grief from her clients when she does memorial tattoos. The burden is lightened by leaving behind some of that energy. Niall says his air affinity likely helped him sense what happened, and then he explains how each *Pyr* has an affinity for one or two elements, and that Rafferty believes the firestorm brings together two people who combine all four elements. Niall asks who provides healing energy for Rox, and what caused her to put up the walls around herself.

Niall and Rox kiss, feeling the heat of the firestorm. Niall feels the need to shift, and then grabs her as the earth begins to rumble, signaling another earthquake. Niall's tail gets caught in a crack, and he is unable to pull free. Rafferty and Thorolf arrive and try to free Niall: Rafferty by singing to the earth and Thorolf by tearing at the debris. Rafferty's song seems to be making progress, and Rox tells him to sing more loudly, while she pulls Niall by one talon, urging him to fight. When they extricate Niall, he flies away after grabbing Rox. She asks why the earth tried to kill him, since he has an affinity with it. Rafferty says it was another song that seduced Gaia to do its bidding — an old voice that he did not recognize, but also heard yesterday. Back at Rox's apartment, the *Pyr* give her a bit of background on the shadow dragons and the Elixir, puzzling over why their behavior has changed and why the shadow dragons haven't all come at the *Pyr* at once Rafferty tells the group he knows the other singer is not Magnus, whom they all presume dead. He explains to Rox having an affinity means the element responds to the songs once mastered. When learning water affinities are unusual amongst the *Pyr,* Rox says according to Chinese folklore, Chinese dragons can control rain. Niall remarks he has wondered if the elements have consciousness once awakened, since they seem to make their own decisions once called, and Rafferty says he has been wondering the same. Sloane wants to heal Niall's tail and tells him he needs to sleep.

Chapter 12: Phelan feels himself wakening, knowing it is due to Chen's use of the magical dragon bone powder. Phelan resents his brother and is jealous of Niall's firestorm. Chen tells Phelan to retrieve Niall's mate quickly, before the powder wears off. Phelan also hopes for his brother's death, but Chen tells him Niall will wish for death first, and then recounts his own use of the elements against the *Pyr* recently, even claiming he controls the level of heat in the firestorm. In the car on the way to New York, Zoë awakens, becoming aware of her true self as the Wyvern. She thinks of the Dragon's Tail adjustment associated with the eclipses, and how the second set of three total eclipses and their firestorms will occur in December. Zoë then sends dreams to the *Pyr* and those close to them. Rox dreams of what she believes is a scene from the past, involving Niall's parents, Phelan, and Rafferty. She wonders what terrible thing happened to Niall's mother, and then senses someone else nearby. Sara wakens with another prophecy involving the Dragon and the Phoenix, the Dragon's Tail, and the elements. Quinn, also awake, tells her he has been dreaming about his brother, Michel, now a shadow dragon, and believes they need to go to New York to help Niall. Though she hasn't told him yet, Quinn is aware of Sara's pregnancy. The rest of the *Pyr* sense the need to go to Niall because of trouble with the shadow dragons — Alex and Donovan from their vacation in the South Pacific with their son, Nick, and her brother's family, and Delaney and Ginger from their farm. When Eileen mentions Gaspar to Erik and he struggles to remember, Zoë touches Erik's forehead, and the memories come back. He tells Eileen that he had been friends with Gaspar's son, Salvatore, who took his Venetian mother's surname. Eileen thinks it is a weird coincidence that she was researching Venice the day before. Erik recalls it was Salvatore's son, Lorenzo, who beguiled him, and Eileen resolves to get to the bottom of what happened. Rox discovers Phelan outside her bedroom window. He tries to convince her that he and Niall are the same. He tells her he knows of a *Slayer* who can make shadow dragons. He also tells Rox she should ask Niall about how Phelan died. Even though she knows it's happening, Rox is unable to counteract Phelan's beguiling of her. In his room, Niall dreams of a young Rox then awakens with the fear that she's in danger: he breaks down the door to her room.

Chapter 13: Niall sees Rox at the window, right before Phelan snatches her and flies away, laughing. Niall pursues, wondering at his brother's behavior, since shadow dragons do not typically express any emotion. Phelan drops Rox onto the debris left from Niall's building, and the two fight in dragon form. He tells Niall they will be twins again when Niall is turned into a shadow dragon. Chen appears and knocks Niall down with his tail. Pretending to be more hurt than he is, Niall realizes that Chen intends to brand him. He wonders if the brand has the power to control him. He escapes Chen, but Phelan then holds him in place. Before Chen can use the brand, Rafferty, Sloane, and Thorolf arrive to help Niall fight. Chen turns into a salamander and disappears, at which point Phelan also leaves. Rox describes her experience with Phelan, and Niall explains to her about beguiling, which he says he only uses to "fix" human memories so they don't recall seeing dragons. After a brief romantic interlude, Niall and Rox talk to the others. Niall tells the others about the brand, and about his brother not acting like a shadow dragon anymore. Rafferty realizes Chen is the singer who caused the earthquakes. Rox suggests perhaps Niall is being targeted for his affinity with air, which Chen must need for some particular purpose. Rox asks about Phelan's claim Niall killed him. While Niall says he failed to help Phelan when he was thinking of turning *Slayer,* Phelan threatened their mother and their father, Nigel, killed Phelan. Niall says he cannot destroy Phelan until he knows beyond a doubt that his brother can't be saved.

Chapter 14: Back to Rox's apartment, Niall sleeps on the floor near her bedroom window, for protection The next morning, Rox asks the already-awake-and-working Niall where Chen went after attacking him. Niall says he turned into a salamander and vanished into the building rubble. Rox declares she may know where Chen and the shadow dragons are hiding. Underneath the city are countless tunnels and passages from subways, trains, and other underground projects. Rox has been there, and says she will take them. She even has a key to one entrance, located in the basement of her building. Niall doesn't want to put her in danger, but Rox insists she must go. The group moves through the tunnels and see a man approaching, whom Niall identifies as a shadow dragon. Separated from the group, Sloane follows the scent of shadow dragon. While Niall battles his foe, Chen drags Rox away, but Thorolf is in pursuit. Thorolf and Chen fight.

Chapter 15: Rox watches as Chen pulls Thorolf beneath the murky water and disappears. Niall arrives after having destroyed the shadow dragon, and Rox tells him he must go after Thorolf. He and Rox dive into the water. He changes to his dragon form, and when Rox grabs hold of a scale it comes off. She puts the scale in her pocket to ask about later. They follow a white, pulsating light, and when the water recedes, Niall returns to his human form. Niall and Rox go through a small opening, and they come out into a bigger room with a railroad car turntable and water-filled tunnels, from which a talon appears, holding the iron brand which produces light. Talons of shadow dragons reach out of the tunnels, and chants of "Chen, Chen, Chen" surround them. Chen himself then rises from the water, with a lifeless Thorolf. He offers Niall a choice: he will take either Niall or Thorolf as a new recruit. Niall attacks and gets the brand away from Chen and gives it to Rox. Then she gets dragged away and through the water, but she hits her attacker with the brand. Niall severs Chen's tail, but Chen gets away. Niall sees Rox come up from under the water, while the chamber begins to collapse around them. As they make their way out, with a struggling Thorolf, shadow dragons fly out above them. Phelan attacks them from behind, going after Rox, and Niall fights with his brother. Phelan knocks him unconscious, then goes after Thorolf. Rox heads toward Sloane, but Phelan catches up to her and cuts her with a talon down the length of her back. Rox falls but Sloane decides to work on Niall first, as he is the most likely to heal, sucking poison out of his wound. When Niall comes to, he and Sloane work their way aboveground with the injured Rox and Thorolf.

Chapter 16: As Quinn flies into New York with Sara and Garrett in his arms, the shadow dragon Michel—Quinn's brother—attacks. The two fight and Quinn destroys the shadow dragon. Rafferty joins Sloane and Niall in moving Thorolf and Rox aboveground. They come into a familiar tunnel, and they see an attractive Asian woman who catches Thorolf's eye. On the street, the group notices an apothecary shop, but the woman seems to have disappeared. The unconscious Rox experiences a memory she has tried to forget—that of her stepfather sexually abusing her when she was fifteen. Sloane says her injury is worse than he thought. Her wound is silvery in color and very cold to the touch, At Sloane's urging, Niall uses the warmth of the firestorm to help heal her wound. As he chants, the other *Pyr* join him, working together to heal Rox. Sloane states that the dark fluid in the wound helped the shadow find a hidden darkness in Rox's mind and make it stronger, keeping her unresponsive to them. Sara shows Niall the prophecy about the Phoenix and the Dream Walker, and he realizes they represent Rox and himself. Zoë shows Niall how to dream-walk, to help Rox. Niall goes into Rox's memory, helping her to work her way out of it. Rox's breathing and color improve, though she still does not wake up. Niall praises Thorolf in front of the other *Pyr*, for his loyalty, bravery, and dedication to perfecting his innate skills, such as beguiling. Quinn relates his experience with the shadow dragon, and Rafferty gives him Chen's brand to look over. When Erik asks if he can reshape it, Quinn says it would be too dangerous, as the metal has a charm woven into it that could be released. Sara then shares her second prophecy, which says after gaining control of all four elements, the thoughts of everyone on earth could be controlled. They realize Chen wants Niall so he can complete the set of four. They decide to lure Chen out with both the brand and Niall.

Chapter 17: Rox wakes up and decides she is now ready to commit to Niall. Niall speaks to Rox about the dragon tattoo on her back, learning the original plan was for a phoenix to also appear. The two discuss how Niall came into Rox's dream. Rox tells Niall she is ready for more with him, says the world needs another *Pyr*, and they satisfy the firestorm. Afterward, Rox thinks about how the firestorm and/or Niall has helped her see the world with new possibility. Niall asks about Rox's sister, Suzie. She tells him about their stepfather, who sexually abused both girls. When their mother didn't believe them, Suzie left home at age sixteen, and Rox shortly thereafter at fifteen. Rox has never been able to locate Suzie, and has no idea of her fate. A shadow dragon appears and breaks the window with a rock. Niall and another *Pyr* go after the shadow dragon Phelan appears in human form and tricks Rox into passing through the protective smoke barrier. He then shifts shape, grabs Rox, and flies off.

Chapter 18: In Rox's living room, Erik has an awareness of the other *Pyr* around or in the building, as well as the firestorm being sated. He then senses danger and sees a dozen shadow dragons on their way to the apartment. He warns the others in old-speak, shifts, and goes after the intruders. Donovan, flying above Manhattan holding Alex and their son, Nick, sees Quinn below him, as well as the shadow dragons. He joins the fray, using the gloves with metal talons Quinn made for him. Delaney joins the fight, and they destroy three shadow dragons. Back at the apartment, Chen appears outside the window and then cuts through the dragonsmoke to enter the living room. He wants to retrieve his brand and intends to brand the children first to see if he can gain control of the *Pyr* without them being shadow dragons. When Chen fixes his gaze on Zoë, Eileen screams her name, hoping to attract Erik's attention. Hearing Eileen's cry, Erik leaves Niall, and heads off to protect his daughter. Once he arrives, Zoë communicates with Erik via old-speak, saying, "Venice." He understands she is referring to his encounter with Lorenzo. Erik manages to beguile Chen into destroying the brand himself, making him believe it could be used against him. Chen gets away by shifting shape a few times. Rafferty scents Magnus and teleports to the apothecary shop. Magnus tries to convince him to let him out of the jar so they can complete their challenge, but Rafferty hides when he hears someone coming. He is surprised to learn the attractive Asian woman they saw earlier is actually one of Chen's forms. Magnus and Chen fight, but both disappear as salamanders. Rafferty leaves to join the *Pyr*. Rox plays along with Phelan's advances, getting him to admit his deception in the past as well as the present. Niall hears everything, and realizing none of the divine spark remains within Phelan, Niall grabs his brother and destroys him. Meanwhile, the Dragon's Tooth Warriors arrive, aiding in the obliteration of the shadow dragons.

Chapter 19: Niall chooses a yin and yang symbol for his tattoo over the spot of the missing scale, thinking they will have to wait a few weeks for his wound to heal. In the meantime, he sets up his business in a new location near Rox's shop, Imagination Ink, and hires Barry as an assistant. Sloane also decides he'd like a tattoo. Niall surprises Rox with the news he thinks the phoenix tattoo should go on his back, connecting to Rox's dragon, a demonstration of their commitment. Rox produces his missing scale, which he had thought lost. Quinn performs the ceremony to replace it, with the other *Pyr* all present. Niall then surprises Rox by using his Dream Walker skill to find her sister, Suzie, and her mother. Niall brings Suzie and her husband to Rox and produces train tickets to go see her mother. That night, Niall notices Rox's broken heart tattoo has been filled in, and she says she had it done because she didn't think hers would ever be broken again. Niall agrees.

DEBORAH'S COMMENTS

One of the secondary characters I really like in this story is Chynna, the senior partner at Imagination Ink. Although Chynna doesn't appear often on the page, her influence is felt. By her actions, Chynna inspired Rox to pay it forward, and to create a family of choice when she was without a family of blood.

"The only home I have is the one I've made for myself. I made myself a new life, one without those people." [Rox] tipped her head back and held his gaze, knowing he would understand her anger. "Ink is stronger than blood."

Niall nodded. "I'm sorry, Rox. I'm sorry that no one believed you or defended you."

"I had Chynna. She found me. I think at first she just felt sorry for me, but once she saw me draw, she took me as her apprentice. She talks tough, but she's a good person."

"She takes care of her own."

Rox nodded. "She gave me a chance, the only one I needed."

"She became your family of choice," Niall said, proving that he understood completely. He looked down at Rox, his smile warming his eyes. "I'm thinking it's time you met my family of choice." He winced. "Seeing as they've probably already emptied your fridge. Isn't that just like family?"

Rox appreciated that he tried to make her smile.

"Just like," she agreed.

—from **Whisper Kiss**

I liked Chynna enough that I sent her to *Flatiron Five*: in that contemporary romance series, she opens a tattoo shop at the fitness club and is featured in a spin-off series called *Secret Heart Ink*. Chynna has a pet raven and a broken heart by the time she sells Imagination Ink and moves uptown to F5. Her second chance romance is told in **Under the Mistletoe**.

Another detail I enjoy in this book is Thorolf's character growth. Thorolf provides the perfect contrast to Niall, who is quite uptight at the beginning of this firestorm, and also gives Niall and Rox one point of agreement. The only thing Niall and Rox appear to have in common at the beginning of their firestorm is their disgust with Thorolf for his refusal to master his abilities.

"He takes care of his peeps," Thorolf said, his admiration clear. He brushed off one of the office chairs and sprawled in it happily. Thorolf could never just sit on furniture—he overwhelmed it, drooped on it, lounged on it. His casual manner made Rox a bit less concerned.

She perched on the other chair. The pieces didn't match, as if they'd been bought used. Rox approved of that. "What people are those?"

"I told you—Niall runs an eco-travel business. There are tour groups all over the world at any time."

Rox remembered that, and how she'd thought it a lie. No wonder she hadn't paid much attention.

Thorolf nodded approval, his gaze locked on Niall. "I think Brett is the tour leader for the group coming back from Machu Picchu tomorrow."

The ceiling creaked again and a chunk of wood fell into the middle of the apartment. Rox noticed that Niall caught the laptop against his chest with the same protectiveness he'd shown toward her earlier.

Niall frowned as he listened to Brett, zipping the bag and slinging it over his shoulder. "Yes, if people want me to check on their families, give me phone numbers and e-mail addresses. Thorolf can help us get through the list. Right. I'll get back to you when I find a place to work. Right."

What was wrong with working here?

"Work?" Thorolf frowned. "He can't work during a firestorm." He leaned forward and braced his elbows on his knees, his eyes brightening. "I've got to talk some sense into him."

Rox didn't understand what he was talking about, but to her surprise, Niall had heard Thorolf's soft words. He disconnected, then glared at Thorolf.

"That's not what you've got to do," Niall said angrily.

"What do you mean? We all have to support the firestorm."

"What you need to do first is use the talents you were born

with."

Thorolf looked confused. "I don't think shifting shape is going to solve anything right here and right now."

"That's not everything you can do!" Niall said, his voice rising in frustration. "If you were paying attention, you'd know it's not safe to stay here."

"Huh?" Thorolf straightened.

Niall continued to lecture, his eyes snapping. "You have keen senses, courtesy of your *Pyr* blood, but you never use them. *That's* how we almost got killed last night."

"What had happened last night?" Rox got to her feet, concerned.

Niall pointed at Thorolf. "If you're not going to pay attention, then we're both dead meat. We've got to watch each other's backs, which means we both need to use our abilities."

"But..."

"But nothing. Now or never."

"But Erik said..."

"I don't care. Listen to the building!" Niall shouted, as uninterested in Thorolf's excuses as Rox usually was. His voice dropped low enough to make her shiver, and his eyes glittered a vivid blue. "Smell the extent of the damage," he urged, his words low and compelling. "It's your responsibility to defend humans like Rox, not to sit around yapping when there's danger."

Rox looked between the two of them. "What's he talking about?"

Niall pointed at Thorolf, ignoring Rox. "This is how you get surprised by shadow dragons."

What were shadow dragons?

"So, what should I do?" Thorolf was defensive, as he always was when challenged to change his ways.

"Listen," Niall hissed. He looked dangerous, a predator hungry for lunch, and she was glad he was angry with Thorolf and not with her.

All the same, she found his intense manner really sexy. It was exactly how passionate she thought a dragon should be.

Instead of passive, like Thorolf

That explained the power of that kiss.

Thorolf narrowed his eyes and breathed deeply, focusing in an uncharacteristic way. Rox was surprised that Niall had gotten through to Thorolf.

Maybe he *was* the perfect mentor for him.

—from **Whisper Kiss**

DARKFIRE KISS

FOR ONE WOMAN, HE WILL RISK MORE THAN HIS LIFE...

Rafferty Powell has exchanged challenge coins with his arch-nemesis, Magnus Montmorency, and their next battle will be their last. But Rafferty never expects to meet a woman whose desire for Magnus' downfall matches his own—and whose presence sparks Rafferty's long-awaited firestorm.

Since facing her own mortality, investigative reporter Melissa Smith has resolved to live without fear. She's determined to make the seemingly untouchable Magnus pay for his role in ending her friend's life—no matter what the price to herself.

When Melissa's quest entwines with Rafferty's, she finds herself risking more than she ever thought possible. Because the heat between them unleashes the darkfire—an awesome force of Pyr legend, one that won't be sated until everything they know has been tested and remade.

THE PROTAGONISTS

Rafferty Powell is one of the older *Pyr*, with a strong affinity to the earth and a fan favorite. This might be is because he's a romantic, and the one to always argue the merit of making a permanent relationship with a destined mate. He's opal and gold in his dragon form and originally from Wales. In his book, we learn about his family's association with the Arthurian legends. Melissa Smith is a reporter determined to expose Magnus as an arms dealer, no matter what the cost: to her thinking, she doesn't have a lot left to lose. Her marriage dissolved when she was diagnosed with uterine cancer and her work has become everything to her. Who better than Rafferty to teach her to restore the balance in her life—and which *Pyr* other than Rafferty could look beyond his destined mate's inability to conceive to realize why she's the perfect partner for him. I love that Melissa and Rafferty create a family of choice.

THE ELEMENTS

Rafferty's affinities are with earth and fire.

"The Smith commanded earth and fire, whether he knew it or not, bringing the persistent power of earth and the passion of fire to all he touched. The Seer held the reins of winter and air, again whether she knew it or not, bringing the intuitive understanding of water and the cold reason of air to every puzzle she encountered. The four elements would join with their union and create a greater fusion of their abilities."
—from **Darkfire Kiss**

Melissa's affinities are with water and air, echoed in her empathy and her dexterity with ideas and ideals.

THE SETTING

Rafferty's firestorm is sparked by the total lunar eclipse of December 21, 2010. The story begins in Washington, D.C. where Magnus keeps a lair, and continues in London, England.

THE PROPHECY

Darkfire's flame burns bright as ice;
No hint of compromise will suffice.
Darkfire's heat will not fade
Until much that is has been unmade;
Until all that is hidden has been revealed,
Until all that was clear becomes concealed;
Until the Sleeper wakes to his fate,
Until the Cantor's legacy is claimed.
But out of ruin rises new growth;
The flames of mercury know this truth.

THE STORY

Prologue: The *Slayer* Chen hides deep in the Himalayas, with the dark purple crystal containing a spark. Legend says there were once three stones, but Chen knows only of the one he possesses. Chen remains in his chamber for weeks, nurturing the spark and singing to Gaia, urging her on to greater destruction. He plans to rule over the earth alone. Eventually, the darkfire is released and Chen is confident the *Pyr* will not be able to overcome it. In Chicago, Erik Sorensson feels a dark shock run through his body. The *Slayer* Jorge, recovering from his leg injury, has been deserted by Balthasar and betrayed by Chen, who trapped Jorge within his own lair. To gain more strength and break out, Jorge attacks the hibernating Mallory to make use of the Elixir running through the unsuspecting *Slayer's* veins.

Chapter 1: (Washington, D.C., December 20th, 2010) Former reporter Melissa Smith argues with herself over putting her ethics aside to uncover the truth about the death of her friend, Daphne. She needs to break into the home of Magnus Montmorency to prove he is an arms dealer and that he killed Daphne. Two days earlier Melissa received a note and a key in the mail from Daphne, which led to a bag belonging to Daphne, along with a journal that included the security code to Montmorency's home. The proof Melissa needs to take down the man would be in a journal kept on his desk. Still seeing Daphne's charred remains in her mind, Melissa resolves to go through with her plan. Rafferty, outside of Magnus' home, tries several times to manifest inside but is unable to. He wants to settle things between them once and for all. Rafferty sees a woman walk up to the house after a black sedan drives away, and he feels a very distinct attraction to the woman. He watches the visitor use the keypad to enter the house and manages to sneak in behind her before the door closes all the way. Melissa feels unsettled by both the pitch-black environs and the feeling someone is following her. She continues until she finds the office, where she turns on her flashlight, then hears a man behind her say, "bad choice." While studying the striking man, whom she dubs Mr. Conscience, she hears yet another say, "very bad choice." She points her flashlight in his direction sees Montmorency himself, holding a gun. Melissa sees the outline of the first man begin to shimmer blue. Thinking she must be imagining things, Melissa blinks, only to find the men gone and two dragons in front of her. She then picks up the gun Magnus dropped. Rafferty and

Magnus begin fighting, with Rafferty wondering about the lady thief. Though Rafferty has the upper hand, Magnus begins to breathe his dragonsmoke.

Chapter 2: Rafferty manages to evade Magnus' energy-draining dragonsmoke while Magnus taunts him about the woman they hear driving away. Rafferty resolves to save the woman before Magnus can get to her. While driving away from Montmorency's home, Melissa wonders if she really saw dragons. Suddenly a car from a side street slams into the passenger side of Melissa's car, and she realizes getting hit was no accident. Melissa tries to open the door to escape, and suddenly, her door is torn off, by Mr. Conscience. Her rescuer once again changes into a dragon and flies into the air, carrying her, followed by the driver of the other car, who also changes into a dragon. Melissa gets out her phone to document the experience. Rafferty fights with Balthasar and puzzles over his attraction to the woman in his arms. When he realizes she's taking pictures, his feelings turn to indignation. Melissa wonders why the two dragons have blood of different colors—her rescuer red, the other black. After Mr. Conscience gets the best of the other dragon, he puts her on the ground of the deserted National Mall. She sees him, in human form now, watching her from across the reflecting pool. Realizing she needs to leave before he can destroy her photos, and wishing they could have met under different circumstances, Melissa flees.

Chapter 3: Rafferty beguiles the guards at the Washington Monument, and follows the scent of the woman thief to retrieve her camera, still puzzling over his reaction to her. He finds her home, knocks at the door, and demands her camera. She agrees but only lets him in as far as the foyer. When Rafferty mentions Montmorency's book, Melissa asks if they are friends, which Rafferty vehemently denies. After destroying the camera's SD card, Rafferty tells her goodnight, but she asks if that is all, invitation clearly on display in her eyes. Rafferty decides to let his desire flow, and takes her up on her offer, on her couch. When he awakens and Melissa is still asleep, Rafferty takes the book she stole from Magnus' office, in order to protect her from Magnus. Rafferty flips through the journal and sees a notation mentioning

Jorge. Knowing he needs to leave, Rafferty nevertheless wants to touch her once more. When he does so, he sees a line of blue fire along her skin and coming from his fingertips. Surprised, Rafferty then remembers the old portent about darkfire, which no one has ever seen in the twelve hundred years he has been alive. Darkfire is supposed to be connected to a firestorm, but Rafferty does not feel the typical reaction. He leaves and contacts Magnus via old-speak and tells him he has his book.

Chapter 4: Melissa awakens languid and satisfied, sorry to see Mr. Conscience gone. She retrieves the hidden memory card with the dragon pictures on it, loading them onto her computer. She plans to post the pictures to draw attention to her blog, exposing Montmorency's deeds to a wider audience. She questions if she should post the pictures since that would reveal Mr. Conscience's secret. She decides to check Montmorency's book to be sure he reveals in writing the evidence she needs against him. When she cannot find the book, Melissa realizes Mr. Conscience must have taken it. In her anger, she posts the first set of dragon pictures. Erik's old-speak wakens Rafferty from a deep sleep, asking, "who is Melissa Smith?" Erik sends a link to pictures of he and Balthasar in their dragon forms. Rafferty chastises himself for not beguiling the woman. As he readies himself to return to Melissa's place, Thorolf arrives, sent by Erik to "help" Rafferty with his problem. Rafferty is annoyed at himself and is perturbed the undisciplined Thorolf is his "help." Feeling unsettled, Rafferty feels a tingling throughout his body, which typically means a firestorm is happening. He thinks it may be Thorolf, who quickly dismisses the possibility. Rafferty realizes it may indeed be him, with Melissa, and determines he needs to find out for sure. Melissa's old boss calls and asks whether her pictures are real, and if she can get more. He offers her a lot of money, but she would rather have a job again. She sends the man a photo of herself to prove she is doing fine. He tells her to get the photos, and he'll see what he can do about the job. Melissa then hears a knock at the door and knows who it is. When she doesn't answer after the second knock, her door is pushed in, and she sees Mr. Conscience, along with a friend. The former, very angry, holds her up off the ground and asks if she knows what she has done. His hands feel very hot against her skin, and she sees a blue flame. When she asks about them, Mr. Conscience replies, in a whisper, "darkfire," but refuses to explain what that means.

Chapter 5: Upset that an opportunist like Melissa seems to be his chosen mate, Rafferty demands she take down the pictures. When he insults her integrity as a journalist, Melissa slaps him. She explains she wants Magnus' date book for "justice." They both get sidetracked by the firestorm, almost satisfying it with Thorolf in the other room, but Rafferty stops himself. saying he will not allow himself to be seduced. They are surprised when Magnus shows up, wanting to make a deal for the book. He asks Melissa to come out to the porch so they can discuss it. Rafferty tells her not to look at Magnus, but she does so and is beguiled. Rafferty is trapped inside by the *Slayer's* dragonsmoke barrier. Magnus takes Melissa away in a helicopter. Rafferty sings to the earth and causes a small earthquake, making a crack through and beneath the house so he can get out past the dragonsmoke. He heads out in pursuit, to save Melisa and to act in defense of the Sleeper, awakened by the firestorm.

Chapter 6: Erik thinks Rafferty will understand that he sent Thorolf because he had confidence in Rafferty's ability to fix things. With Sloane guarding Eileen and Zoë, Erik leaves their Nevada hotel to track down Lorenzo, the *Pyr* who beguiled him long ago, to ask for his help against the *Slayers*. Erik meets with Lorenzo in a room of mirrors, making it difficult to tell the difference between image and actual person. Lorenzo says he will not aid in the fight against the *Slayers,* saying, "war does not create peace." Lorenzo questions Erik's leadership, bringing up Quinn, Drake (a Dragon's Tooth warrior), and Brandt, and Erik finds himself telling Lorenzo things he should not be, wondering if he is being beguiled again. Lorenzo brings up darkfire, the Cantor's last charm, and the Sleeper, though Erik does not know what the last two items are. As he drives away, Erik sees images of the dead, including himself, in the dust in his rearview mirror. Donovan tells Alex they are leaving for Wales since he had promised to help Rafferty if the Sleeper ever woke. When Alex comments it seems unfair for Rafferty to get the "rotten" kind of firestorm, Donavan responds Rafferty may be "the only one who can turn darkfire to good." Sloane senses the darkfire firestorm, and while watching little Zoë play, asks, in old-speak, if she can feel it, but she gives no indication of hearing or understanding him. Eileen tells Sloane that since Zoë started talking a few days earlier she no longer responds to Erik's old-speak. She hopes this will give Zoë a chance to be a child before taking on the responsibility of Wyvern. Sloane says the appearance of darkfire is supposed to signal a time of great trial for the *Pyr*. Erik arrives back at the hotel and tells them Lorenzo won't help, but he also got Erik to speak of things he should not. Erik sends Sloane, who resists, to go after Brandt, his cousin, as he fears for the latter's safety. While they are working in Niall's New York office, Barry sees a video of Thorolf shifting into dragon form after escaping the earthquake at Melissa's. Assuring Barry it is all just a trick, Niall goes off in pursuit of Thorolf, so he can hide him for a bit. Sara notices blue fire on the mermaid doorknocker at her shop and finds an entry in Sigmund's book on darkfire, which lists a number of undesirable effects, including loss of prophetic ability. Deciding to ask her dead Aunt Magda for help, Sara reads tarot cards and pulls up the one for Death. Quinn tells Sara they will not go to Rafferty's firestorm due to the risk. Viv Jason feels the darkfire while she works at a coffee shop in Manhattan, leading her to the one who had set it free. She knows she needs to go to Asia. Though waking, the Sleeper continues to doze.

Chapter 7: In the helicopter, Melissa regrets not having listened to Rafferty about not looking into Montmorency's eyes, and she resolves not to do so again. Magnus wants to know how she knew about the book and the security code. Rafferty, in his dragon form, approaches the helicopter, but before he grabs her, Magnus vanishes and all she sees in the cabin with her is a salamander. As they fly off, Melissa wonders why Rafferty protects her while seeming to disapprove of her. After they land, Rafferty remembers Melissa from her reporting days, but she doesn't tell him why she no longer has that job. Rafferty explains about dragonsmoke, and Melissa tells him about Daphne, and her goal of exposing Magnus. Erik then contacts Rafferty via old-speak and sends him the video link of Thorolf's shift. Rafferty shows her the video and also tells her she is his destined mate. Not sure what to think about the mate business, Melissa says her job chance is now blown, anyway, so they can work together to bring down Magnus. Drawn together by their firestorm, they begin to kiss. Then they hear Magnus' voice, yelling about Daphne, and a salamander appears between them, biting Rafferty on the chest, initiating a shift.

Chapter 8: Both Rafferty and Magnus shift—unfortunately before human witnesses. Before Rafferty can deal the final blow, after making reference to Maximilian's son, a gold dragon suddenly appears and takes Magnus away. The crowd of onlookers turns on Rafferty, calling him names, though Melissa tries to explain he is the good guy. Rafferty picks up Melissa and flies off. Disgusted by his behavior in front of so many people, Rafferty realizes he revealed the secret of Maximilian's son to Magnus and possibly put the Sleeper in great danger. He thinks about his grandfather, who wished to teach him the Cantor's songs. As they make their way across the ocean, Melissa learns her house was destroyed, and Rafferty explains the difference between *Pyr* and *Slayer*. When he mentions Jorge, Melissa realizes he was Magnus' bodyguard in the Middle East, who she had seen kill someone. Melissa tells Rafferty how she feels she owes it to Daphne to get justice. Since she can't do much while they are flying, Melissa takes the opportunity to get some sleep.

Chapter 9: The captured and badly-injured Magnus attempts to bargain with Jorge—his life for some of the Elixir. When Jorge relaxes his hold just a bit, Magnus shifts to his salamander form and escapes. Melissa wakes what she knows must be Rafferty's home since the surroundings reflect his personality and character. She follows the blue flame downstairs, thinking about her brother's home where she'd gone to heal, as well as the house she had shared with her former husband. She finds Rafferty in his library, and they discuss briefly how Magnus can manifest at will in different locations. Rafferty says the two times he was able to do it may not have been his doing. Melissa asks about the mate bond, and Rafferty explains, "the destined mate is the one who can conceive that *Pyr*'s son." It can also bring together two people for a more lasting partnership. Melissa wants to be with Rafferty again, but does not tell him a key element of her own history, fearing he would reject her. She tells him she wants to satisfy the firestorm and they do so. Afterward, the darkfire is still active, so Rafferty realizes something is wrong.

Chapter 10: In his Tibetan lair, Chen senses the darkfire, the firestorm, the Sleeper stirring, and a *Pyr* gaining a rare affinity — air. He devises a trap to ensnare that *Pyr*, since it is the one affinity over which he does not have mastery. Sara dreams of a young girl and wonders who it could be. Thorolf wakes from a hedonistic dream that ends with Chen in his seductive female form, resolving not to involve Niall or Rox in his plan to take care of the *Slayer* on his own. Melissa's plan to share her story with Rafferty is interrupted by a man present in Rafferty's kitchen. Upset, the visitor shows them a picture and headline from a newspaper, with Rafferty, in dragon form, flying away with Melissa. Melissa then asks to use the phone so she can call her brother to assure him she's safe. She is surprised to learn her brother recognizes Rafferty's name (on the caller ID) as a well-known antiquities dealer. Melissa remembers the dreams that died with her illness. Erik chastises Rafferty for his reckless behavior, but also for not sating the firestorm. Rafferty replies he tried, and Melissa says she has something she needs to tell them.

Chapter 11: Melissa confesses that she cannot have children as she had uterine cancer and all of her necessary organs were removed. Rafferty shows concern and compassion, while Erik is puzzled, asking how his destined mate could be someone unable to have his child. Rafferty suggests that more may be gained from an alliance between he and Melissa than a child. Melissa apologizes for having revealed the dragons, but thinks maybe they are supposed to work together with humans to save the planet. Since darkfire likes to disrupt the status quo, she asks to be told what they know about it. Rafferty recites the prophecy regarding darkfire, learned from his grandfather. Melissa goes through line by line, asking specific questions, most of which Rafferty does not know the answer to. At this point, Eileen and Zoë come in from outside, the little girl climbing onto Rafferty's lap. When she starts touching his black and white ring, he hopes she will send him a sign, but nothing happens. Melissa suggests they should try to draw out Magnus while he is weak, allowing Rafferty a better chance of destroying him. She says they can use Magnus' book as evidence to turn public opinion in their favor. Erik doesn't want to reveal dragons to humans, but both Rafferty and Eileen see the merit in Melissa's proposal.

Chapter 12: Erik lies down and reaches out to the other *Pyr*, finding Delaney in Ohio, not planning to come to Rafferty's firestorm; senses Donovan somewhere nearby in the west of England, but isn't sure what he is doing; sees Quinn at home, not planning to endanger his family by coming near the darkfire; Niall and Thorolf together for the latter's protection; and Sloane with Brandt, the two having fought but not seriously harming one another. Unable to sense either Lorenzo or Drake (or any of the Dragon's Tooth Warriors), Erik fears his leadership of the *Pyr*, now divided, may be at an end. Erik then hears his dead son, Sigmund, in his mind, telling him the Sleeper stirs, is under a spell, and they must find the third Cantor's crystal: one created the Sleeper, one held the darkfire. Rafferty begins to tell his tale and shows a crystal to the ladies, saying he was given it as Guardian of the Sleeper. The darkfire flame within has diminished as the Sleeper gets closer to waking up. The darkfire may be the price Rafferty has to pay for having refused his grandfather all those years ago, and he tells Melissa firestorms are also about healing— so it may change her feelings about the future. Rafferty tells the story of his grandfather, who came when Rafferty was a young boy to take him under his wing. His grandfather, as a younger man, had a firestorm with a woman living in a convent, and his uncle was Merlin of Arthurian legend. Rafferty's father, Owen, was killed shortly after conceiving him.

Chapter 13: Melissa asks about Magnus' ability to take on the salamander shape, and Rafferty tells her that some *Slayer*s who have drunk the Elixir have that ability. Melissa says she will not reveal anything else about the dragons without his permission. She wants to work together to prove Magnus' guilt. When Rafferty tells her about Chen taking six forms, and maybe not having imbibed any of the Elixir, Melissa asks how Rafferty's grandfather managed to get into a convent without being seen. Eileen adds that in some forms of the legend, Merlin takes on a stag shape. Rafferty says Melissa has brought him a gift in the possibilities she has revealed. Donovan waits to cross the small stretch of stormy water to Bardsey Island, to be there to defend the Sleeper. Rafferty asks Melissa why she no longer believes in the future, and learns her husband deserted her when she was diagnosed with cancer, since she would not be able to give him children. Rafferty is appalled by her husband's behavior. He knows what he needs to do to convince Melissa of his intentions, so he gives her Magnus' book to reveal on her blog, and she begins writing the article. Magnus materializes in his salamander form in Rafferty's cellar, feeding off the energy from the firestorm to heal. Since he is too weak to face both Rafferty and Jorge, he resolves to bide his time.

Chapter 14: A despondent Erik tells Eileen he has failed the *Pyr*—and in fact will die, killed by Brandt, after breaking a blood oath not to disturb him. Erik plans to meet Brandt somewhere away from where she and Zoë are, and even states he now doubts Zoë is the Wyvern. Eileen realizes the Sleeper may be connected to Arthurian legend, and Erik says he won't stand in the way of change for the better. Eileen refuses to give in to Erik's plan. Melissa and Rafferty work on Melissa's story, posted in parts, including pictures sent to her by her cameraman friend. At one point Doug, her former boss, calls, saying she is putting herself in danger. Melissa sends Doug the file containing the photos of all of Magnus' datebook. Eileen tells Melissa and Rafferty what is going on with Erik, who has already left. Rafferty tells the two women Brandt has been in solitude since his mate spurned him when she learned the truth of what he was. When Zoë wakens, Eileen brings her downstairs, and the little girl holds her arms out to Melissa. Reluctant at first, Melissa takes Zoë and is moved to tears. The child enjoys watching the blue flames of the firestorm. Brandt finds Erik in flight, Sloane closely following.

Chapter 15: Rafferty tells Melissa and Eileen the story of his history with Magnus, whom he met a thousand years ago in Venice. Rafferty and Magnus became friends, but soon Rafferty realized there was an unpleasant side to Magnus. He dealt in dragon hide and even killed his own brother over jealousy when the latter got his firestorm. Rafferty resolved to protect the brother's mate and child, taking them to his grandfather, Pwyll, the Cantor, for protection. Magnus sensed the birth of the child and fought with Rafferty. Magnus feigned injury and followed Rafferty to the mate and child. The woman had died, and there was a dead child there, too, but after Magnus left, Rafferty learned it was a human child, killed by his grandfather. The *Pyr* child was spirited away, enchanted by Rafferty's grandfather to become the Sleeper. Pwyll begged Rafferty to take on the guardianship of the Sleeper, but Rafferty refused, as he believed the power his grandfather wielded was too dangerous. Upon his grandfather's death, the crystal appeared in Rafferty's hoard. Eileen suggests perhaps the Cantor's power could be used for good. Magnus materializes as a salamander, biting Rafferty in the jugular. He then appears on Melissa's shoulder, saying she is going with him. Eileen grabs Zoë, and Melissa disappears with Magnus, ending up in a room under the earth. Rafferty decides he must concentrate on using the Cantor's power to help him save Melissa, to materialize wherever she may be.

Chapter 16: Magnus appears in salamander form, and Melissa steps on his tail, breaking it off. When he shifts to his human form, it's obvious Magnus is injured. He tells Melissa that he arranged to meet Rafferty in Venice, as he wished to harness the Cantor's power for himself. He hopes to use some of the Sleeper's spell to gain a form of immortality. Magnus sets the chamber on fire and disappears, though she can hear him chanting and feels the earth begin to rumble and crack. Melissa realizes she now has a lot to lose. Rafferty materializes beside her, but his energy is drained so he shifts to dragon form and knocks down the door. The darkfire from Melissa's touch heals the wound on Rafferty's neck, and one of his scales drops off. Back in his human form, he gives the precious item to Melissa to hold on to. As they come out of the tunnels in Highgate Cemetery, the earth is heaving, and Rafferty realizes the subway line is collapsing. Melissa suggests she reports on the earthquake while Rafferty goes to help those in need. The two acknowledge how much they mean to one another, and Rafferty drops Melissa off at the station entrance. She gives her report, and he goes looking for survivors. At one point he has to change into dragon form to remove debris from a woman's trapped leg. She and another man who also helped mention the dragon hero to Melissa while she is on the air. When they speak privately, Melissa tells Doug she cannot give him any more details on the dragons.

Chapter 17: Jorge follows Donovan's scent into a cottage and through a trapdoor into a tunnel. He finds Donovan guarding the Sleeper, and the two fight in dragon form. Following Magnus, Rafferty materializes inside the control room of the Thames Barrier. The *Slayer* intends to flood the city. When Magnus opens the gates, the men in the control room realize he's the bad dragon, not Rafferty. Magnus breathes dragonsmoke into the place of the missing scale on Rafferty's chest, and he relaxes his hold just enough that Magnus can escape. He also hears Jorge tell Magnus in old-speak he has found the Sleeper. Erik and Brandt fight above London, but Erik realizes the younger *Pyr* is working out his anger over losing his mate. Sloane urges them to work together to save the city from flooding. After Erik agrees to help Brandt with his son, the three dragons head below to close the barrier. Melissa interviews a man on-air, a worker at the Barrier who recounts the tale of a dragon fight and the three dragons who saved the city. In the cave underneath Donovan's cottage, Rafferty sees Magnus, in salamander form, making his way toward the Sleeper. Rafferty smashes his foe with a stone. The dying *Slayer* cycles through his forms, and Rafferty makes sure the body, now a dragon, is exposed to the four elements. Jorge begins eating Magnus' corpse, saying he is the last source of the Elixir. Donovan takes the Sleeper out of the chamber, and once aboveground, calls to the elements and seals the chamber with stone. Jorge is trapped, but Rafferty thinks of Melissa and wills himself away.

Chapter 18: Sophie's soul, striving to be reborn so she can eventually be reunited with Nikolas, who was reborn quickly as Donovan's son, Nick, is having difficulty, until she hears a child wishing to die. The Sleeper thinks of Pwyll and feels the darkfire loose. He knows this is wrong and wills himself to the site of the flame, ending up in a soft bed. Rafferty finds himself in front of a church near his home. He can feel the darkfire, so knows Melissa is close. He sees a little girl in the doorway of the church, who calls him by his name. He asks about the girl's parents, and she says she will show him where Isabelle's parents are. Thinking it strange she refers to her parents in that way, Rafferty goes with her to a house, where he sees the building has collapsed on top of the two. The girl explains they are dead, Isabelle wanted to go with them, so she and Isabelle traded. She reveals that she is Sophie and she wants to live with him. Rafferty explains there are procedures to follow, but says he will do his best. Melissa can feel Rafferty's approach, and when she notices the little girl, Rafferty introduces her, saying Isabelle has suggested they adopt her. Rafferty shares the news about Magnus. Chen senses a woman, wakened by the darkfire, getting through his barriers. She arrives in the form of a snake and then shifts into human form. She introduces herself as Viv Jason, thanking him for releasing the darkfire. She wishes to work together to destroy the *Pyr*, saying they owe her. Chen wonders if she can bring him the *Pyr* with the air affinity. Eileen is surprised to find a naked young man asleep in a bed in the house. Then the others arrive, And Erik sees the ghost of Pwyll. Eileen suggests that perhaps Erik's vision of being with the dead means he can now see them. Erik reports Pwyll confirms her idea. Relieved, Eileen then points out the visitor. Melissa recites the part of the prophecy about the Cantor's legacy being claimed. Eileen thinks someone has to learn his art before the Sleeper can fully wake. Erik tells them Pwyll says the craft was not his only legacy, and Melissa realizes it is the crystal. Melissa gives the crystal to Rafferty, saying the darkfire may awaken his memories of the Cantor. Rafferty begins to sing.

Chapter 19: Amazed that he could still be the heir to his beloved grandfather's ability, Rafferty is also pleased to understand Pwyll did not do ill with his gift, but only good. As he sings, Rafferty wishes for the darkfire to be extinguished and that the recent trials experienced by the *Pyr* be over. When he points the crystal at the Sleeper, a crack and a flash of light occur. A blue spark hits the Sleeper right in the heart, waking him. Once learning Rafferty's identity, the Sleeper tells him how much Pwyll loved him. The Sleeper claims the crystal as his and says that the darkfire was released by someone with wicked intent. Eileen guesses Chen. The Sleeper, who identifies himself as Marcus, says the responsibility to contain the darkfire has passed to him, as Rafferty has fulfilled his duty to protect him. Rafferty translates for Erik and the Sleeper, who only understands Welsh. When Erik uses a nickname for him, Marcus knows for sure Erik speaks for Pwyll. Rafferty asks Melissa to marry him, and she accepts. The darkfire no longer burns between them, since Marcus now has the stone. The ceremony to replace Rafferty's scale takes place on New Year's Eve at Sara and Quinn's home in Michigan, with all of the *Pyr* present. Sara recognizes Isabelle as the little girl from her dream and believes she is indeed Sophie. Rafferty asks Melissa to allow herself to cry for all she has been through. She does so, and her tears are used in the ceremony.

Epilogue: Melissa's friend, Daphne has a well-attended funeral, and soon thereafter Melissa and Rafferty are married. They formally adopt Isabelle, who has stopped talking about Sophie, though sometimes the little girl gets a faraway look in her eyes. Melissa then does a story from the Middle East, with Erik's blessing, revealing the *Pyr* and their history, with a plea for all to work together to save the planet. Erik's stipulation: they cannot reveal their human forms or names. Rafferty appears on-camera in his dragon form, then soars in the sky carrying a very happy Melissa.

DEBORAH'S COMMENTS

By the sixth book in an ongoing series, it's time to challenge the underlying assumptions of the series. What if a *Pyr* had a firestorm with a woman who couldn't conceive? What if the *Pyr* ceased to be hidden from human society? These two possibilities challenge the *Pyr's* view of the world and their place in it. They might be Erik's worst nightmare come true—although I have worse ones in store for him. I hoped from the beginning of *Dragonfire* that I'd get to the point that I could turn things around like this. I also knew that the *Pyr* who could succeed in the face of such challenges would be Rafferty, with his complete faith in the firestorm. Can he convince Melissa to surrender?

"So, about this mate thing," [Melissa] said.

Rafferty spun suddenly to face her, his move deft and elegant. Once again, he had moved more quickly than she had anticipated. What else could he do? "What about it?"

"It has something to do with the firestorm, with these flames, right?" She lifted her hand, and the blue-green fire danced predictably from her fingertips, angling toward Rafferty as if burning in a stiff breeze. Or yearning for a connection. Melissa's mouth went dry, and she felt a yearning of her own as Rafferty's gaze brightened.

"The firestorm and its flames are a sign that a *Pyr* has found his destined mate."

"I don't believe in destiny," Melissa said. "Do you?"

"Then believe in biology," he said, avoiding her question and her gaze. This conversation made him uncomfortable, which was interesting. "The destined mate is the one woman who can conceive that *Pyr's* son."

There was no chance of that happening, but Melissa saw no reason to tell all of her secrets just yet. "So the flames are a sign?"

"And the firestorm's heat mounts, until it is sated." Rafferty arched a brow. "It becomes increasingly difficult to deny."

Melissa leaned toward him, knowing that the white robe would gape at the neck. Rafferty's eyes shone and his fist clenched, but he didn't move closer. It seemed his entire body had become taut, which only fed Melissa's urge to touch him.

Everywhere.

"So, the firestorm is about making more dragons?"

Rafferty frowned and glanced away. He was turning that ring again but seemed unaware of what he was doing. "There are those who believe as much. There are others who think the firestorm is a chance for a deeper partnership, one that endures after the firestorm is sated."

Melissa could guess which perspective was Rafferty's. She respected his sense of tradition and longevity. She wished she'd met him sooner, when she had still believed in the future, in love lasting forever, and in the possibility of happily ever after.

Her short marriage had destroyed that particular illusion.

Rafferty flicked a potent look in her direction, and she glimpsed how important this notion was to him. "There are those who believe the most successful firestorms are those that become permanent partnerships. A union that is more than the sum of the parts."

—from **Darkfire Kiss**

It wouldn't have been fair for Rafferty to have to deal with complications created by other forces—darkfire, then, with its ability to turn things inside out and upside down, is his family legacy. This makes Rafferty both part of the root of the change and its resolution. Not only does he have to ally with his mate, but he has to embrace the rest of his own legacy to become whole.

"Wait a minute," Melissa said, noticing something in the verse. Maybe she had the solution. She indicated Erik. "You're seeing Pwyll, Rafferty's grandfather, right?"

Erik nodded.

"And Pwyll's the one who enchanted the Sleeper in the first place, right?"

Rafferty nodded. "He could enchant anyone or anything. The Cantor's song was potent."

"And you refused to learn it. And Pwyll refused to teach anyone else, because he was determined to teach only a *Pyr* with a pure heart about his skill, so it wouldn't be used for ill."

The *Pyr* looked at her in amazement.

Melissa nodded. "Magnus told me that he tried to learn Pwyll's gift. He said he befriended Rafferty in the first place to try to learn the Cantor's song." She saw that they hadn't guessed this.

"Could he have targeted you?" Erik asked.

Rafferty nodded thoughtfully. "I was not that suspicious in those days. And he always collected arcane knowledge."

"Until the Sleeper wakes to his fate; until the Cantor's legacy is claimed," Melissa said, repeating the verse.

"Someone has to learn Pwyll's skill to end the darkfire," Eileen guessed.

"I'll bet that you have to use what you know of Pwyll's abilities, in order to awaken the Sleeper," Melissa said to Rafferty.

Rafferty frowned. "But it is a complicated art, and I never learned much of it from him. It is not something with which one would err."

"I'll bet you remember more than you think you do," Melissa insisted, sensing that she was right. "Who watched Pwyll sing the most? Who saw him at work most often? Who heard the most of his stories?"

Rafferty looked shocked by the notion, but he rubbed his chin. "I always believed it to be wrong to use enchantment."

"What if you chose to use it for good? To end the darkfire?" Melissa demanded. He eyed her, and she saw that he was becoming convinced.

"Pwyll says his craft wasn't his sole legacy," Erik said.

"He left you the stone!" Melissa said with sudden realization.

"Sigmund said there were three stones; that the Cantor and his kind were the custodians of them," Erik said.

"And of the Sleeper," Sloane said. "My father was fascinated by the potential power of darkfire. He spent his whole life wanting to see it for himself." He sighed and shook his head. "You have no idea how many crystals he collected, or how many expeditions we took, in search of one with darkfire locked within it."

"Pwyll knows," Erik said softly.

Melissa didn't need any more assurance than that. She bolted down the stairs and retrieved the crystal. It was still lit with the darkfire's blue light, and the spark inside it became brighter when she picked it up. Melissa raced back up the stairs, even as she heard the rumble of thunder overhead. She skidded into the room and smiled at Rafferty.

"I'm sure I'm right," she said with her old confidence. She took the crystal and put it into Rafferty's hand. "You're Pwyll's grandson and the closest thing he has to an heir. You need to try."

—from **Darkfire Kiss**

Melissa has the ability to reconsider the facts and see them in a new light. In a way, this skill is like darkfire. She's the one who realizes that it could be better for the *Pyr* to be revealed to human society, and also the one with the connections to make it happen. I like that Rafferty is the first to see the merit of her idea, too.

My favorite scene in this book is when Rafferty meets Isabelle, but that's excerpted elsewhere in this volume. It only makes sense that the darkfire resolves the central issue of Rafferty and Melissa's firestorm, allowing them to create a family of choice.

FLASHFIRE

HE'S LOST ALL HOPE...UNTIL SHE CHANGES EVERYTHING.

Master illusionist Lorenzo wants nothing to do with the Pyr. *His dragon nature is just another secret to hide and another detail to juggle, like ensuring that each of his Las Vegas magic shows is a true spectacle. Until he feels the burn of his firestorm and his whole world shifts...*

Cassie Redmond is tired of photographing celebrities. She wants to pursue her dream of serious photography—despite the lucrative offer for a shot of a dragon shifter. Las Vegas is the last place she wants to be, but Lorenzo arouses more than her curiosity when he shifts shape at the finale of his show. Instead of forcing him to reveal his secrets, Cassie gets swept away by this illusionist's masterful touch.

Lorenzo wants to satisfy the firestorm and put it behind him. But Cassie is hard to forget—and he can't ignore the danger when Slayers *target the mate Lorenzo didn't believe he wanted...*

THE PROTAGONISTS

Lorenzo is the first of the "outcast" *Pyr* to be brought back into the fold. He's a *Pyr* who doesn't want to be a dragon shifter and a master illusionist. He also doesn't want a firestorm, but he gets one—with a pragmatic photographer on the hunt for pictures that either prove or disprove the existence of the *Pyr*. Cassie is fearless in pursuit of her goals—even if a certain dragon shifter wishes she would give it up.

THE ELEMENTS

Lorenzo's affinities are to fire and water, while Cassie's are to earth and air. Lorenzo's affinity to water helps with his beguiling skill, while Cassie's affinity to earth means she's skeptical of anything that is unproven—like the existence of dragon shifters.

THE SETTING

Lorenzo's firestorm is sparked by the total lunar eclipse of June 15, 2011. He's in the middle of a performance when the firestorm lights, and integrates its flame into his illusionist show. He's such a control freak that I enjoy how this—and actually the whole firestorm—messes with his game.

THE PROPHECY

Flashfire lights the solitude
Of the Pyr *with most to lose.*
Firestorm plus an ancient spell
Fuels lust that sees his sense dispelled
Flashfire's promise is a lure
To cheat the Pyr *of his true power.*
Will he see through the disguise
Forget the song, seize the prize?
The future hangs upon his choice
Between life and love, or sacrifice.

THE STORY

Prologue: (Hawaii, January 19, 2011) Chen sits in a beach bar, thinking over his mistakes with the darkfire and his new plan involving the aid of Viv Jason. He anticipates a power struggle will eventually occur between them. He waits for, Brandon, a young *Pyr*, to arrive, and they make their usual trade: Brandon provides Chen with one of his scales, Chen gives Brandon some of the Dragon Bone Powder. The young *Pyr* gets a high from the substance, not realizing it will have repercussions. As Brandon leaves, Jean-Pierre, a *Slayer*, arrives. Chen plans to use him as a pawn to round out the collection of *Pyr* he needs for their affinities (Lorenzo/water, Brandon/earth, Thorolf/air). Quinn and Donovan killed JP's brother, Lucien. Chen suggests getting Lorenzo to turn against the *Pyr* and become a *Slayer* would be an effective way for JP to get his revenge.

Chapter 1: (Las Vegas, June 15, 2011) Cassie Redmond has joined her recently-jilted best friend, Stacy, on a girls' trip to Vegas. Stacy's idea of a good time means catching every show she can, especially since she won $2,200 in the slots. They are on their way to the next show when Cassie receives a message from an editor offering to pay top-dollar for photos of one of the *Pyr* shifting from human to dragon. Surprised, Cassie wonders if the woman would be just as interested in proof of fraudulence, as Cassie finds the whole story unbelievable. Stacy reminds Cassie they are on vacation and tells her about the show they plan to attend: the illusionist named Lorenzo is reputed to perform amazing feats with fire. While discussing this topic, the man himself drives by in his sports car, and they agree he is gorgeous. When they arrive at the surprisingly classy theater, Cassie finds out from her editor friend that she could be paid a huge amount of money for proof of fraud, as well. Lorenzo is edgy and knows he needs to relax before his performance. He had asked his father earlier in the day about the disappearance of the darkfire crystal six months before (which he had been given for safekeeping by the Cantor, Rafferty's grandfather, many years ago, in exchange for the flashfire song the Cantor placed in his mind). He is also feeling the effects of the eclipse and someone's impending firestorm. Lorenzo just wants to concentrate on doing his last few shows before his escape, no longer being connected to the *Pyr*. Once on stage, Lorenzo begins his show, but then observes the light of a firestorm coming from his own fingertips. He sees a woman in the front row encircled by golden light. Cassie feels the effects, but has no idea why.

Chapter 2: Cassie, puzzled by the intense desire she feels for Lorenzo, figures she must be sitting in a rigged seat of some sort. Lorenzo goes through his various tricks and illusions, working up to a very dramatic one where he somehow escapes a tank of water. Cassie is chosen to ask a question, and she asks where she would find one of the dragon shifters revealed by Melissa Smith. Lorenzo raises the flames on stage to conceal his shift, and then everyone sees a gold dragon above them in the theater. He flies down and picks up Cassie, carrying her around the theater. Landing on the stage, Cassie soon just sees Lorenzo. She still feels that overwhelming desire she cannot explain or control. Lorenzo then seals their experience with a kiss.

Chapter 3: Lorenzo marvels over the woman, whom he has dubbed Ms. Practicality in his mind, and her reaction to him. While he never took Erik's oath against revealing himself in public, it does bother him a bit that he shifted shape for the first time in centuries. He blames the action on the firestorm. Lorenzo takes the woman to his dressing room, where he continues her seduction through both the firestorm and slight beguiling. He is surprised that her lingerie seems out of character for the persona she presents. Since she seems eager and willing, he feels satisfying the firestorm quickly will be to his advantage. The two have sex. Leaving his bed a few hours later, Lorenzo feels a bit guilty about having beguiled his partner, then realizes he had not continued to after catching sight of her underwear, feeling her response to him was from something else after that point. He regrets that he will likely never see her again. Before leaving, Lorenzo confirms that the firestorm is no longer burning. He thinks of Caterina, a long-ago love who betrayed him. Cassie wakes in Lorenzo's dressing room and learns that it is 6:00 p.m. and Lorenzo's assistants are getting ready for the next show. Cassie walks back to her hotel and finds Stacy in the bar with a handsome guy. Lorenzo goes to the site of his upcoming spectacle, making sure everything is ready for the event. He still worries about the missing crystal, and then senses Erik in the vicinity. Lorenzo drives off in his car, happy to be making a little more trouble for Erik. Stacy introduces her gentleman friend as Jean-Pierre (JP). Cassie takes a dislike to the man immediately. Stacy tells him Cassie is a photographer, and the two women talk about the dragon in Lorenzo's show. Stacy leaves with JP. Cassie resolves to figure out Lorenzo's dragon trick.

Chapter 4: Cassie learns from the waitress at the bar that the dragon trick is definitely new. The waitress tells her about Lorenzo's upcoming event—being buried alive in his car for a month. Cassie decides to go back to the theater and watch the night show. Erik confronts Lorenzo in his dressing room. Lorenzo refuses to join the *Pyr* in their battle against the *Slayers* and tells Erik the firestorm has been sated already since he used beguiling to hurry the process along. Shortly thereafter, Lorenzo realizes Cassie is close by and will have heard his every word. Angry, Lorenzo tries to concentrate on his show. Cassie approaches Erik, and asks about beguiling, which he gives a very brief explanation of. She asks what firestorm means, but he tells her she needs to talk with Lorenzo about that. As he leaves, he tells her he has done what he can, and now it's up to her. Puzzled by the comment, Cassie stays to watch the show, but no dragon appears. Cassie wonders if Erik was implying both he and Lorenzo are dragon shifters. She wants to find out the truth. Back at the hotel, JP stops her in the lobby and asks her to check on Stacy since she is sick. The *Slayer* goes to the bar, releasing Dragon Bone Powder in the air. He plans to lure Lorenzo with Cassie's presence.

Chapter 5: In the hotel room, Stacy wakes up and tells her about flames in JP's eyes, which sounds very familiar to Cassie. When she goes to the bar to find JP, she asks him about Lorenzo's magic trick of the flames in the eyes, and then states perhaps beguiling has something to do with the firestorm. When JP responds that the two are unrelated, he realizes he fell into Cassie's trap. She asks him for information, so he tells her a bit about the *Pyr*, not confirming whether dragon shifters are indeed for real. He also says he believes beguiling/hypnotism can only be done once on the same person. He wanted to get it out of the way with Stacy so whatever relationship they end up having will remain free from it. Cassie tells JP about the big offer being made for photographs of the dragons. When JP tells her about the firestorm and the resultant child, Cassie worries when it occurs to her she and Lorenzo did not use protection when they had sex. After his show, Lorenzo scents a *Slayer* outside and finds Balthasar waiting for him. As usual, Balthasar attempts to recruit Lorenzo, since he is trying to fill the leadership void left by Magnus' death. When Lorenzo refuses, Balthasar starts baiting him by talking about "her." He threatens he could get to her whenever he wants. Lorenzo doesn't let on this idea bothers him but resolves to go to the woman's hotel and check on her. Lorenzo enters the bar, and Cassie feels the same attraction she did earlier. He and JP don't get along, and she thinks they may be competing magicians/illusionists, which suits Lorenzo just fine. Lorenzo finally learns Cassie's name, and JP reveals she is a photographer looking for dragons. Lorenzo wants Cassie to leave with him but, fed up with both men and their arguing, Cassie leaves by herself. In old-speak, Lorenzo warns JP to stay away from Cassie.

Chapter 6: Lorenzo catches up to Cassie, and admits he had to see her again. She decides she wants to find out if the attraction between them is just as strong without the tricks. Lorenzo offers to get a room there at the hotel, and Cassie agrees, but states there will be condoms this time. Lorenzo promises no beguiling. Cassie and Lorenzo have sex in their huge suite, but Cassie wakes up and leaves at 4:30 a.m., deciding it will be easier to make a clean break. Lorenzo, aware of Cassie leaving, lies in the bed also thinking of Caterina, and how her betrayal is characteristic of human behavior. Even though he thinks it's likely for the best that Cassie leaves, he feels he would enjoy spending more time with her. When leaving the hotel, Lorenzo discovers an unknown *Pyr* in his car, who asks for the darkfire crystal, which Lorenzo tells him he no longer has. The stranger identifies himself as Marcus Maximus, now called Marco, also known as The Sleeper. Hoping the guy doesn't ask for the flashfire song, Lorenzo agrees to let him come to his lair to see if he can sense the crystal. As they are driving, Marco shocks him by saying, "diavolo," the very word Caterina said to him, and which he had just been thinking about.

Chapter 7: Thorolf has been laying low in Bangkok after his transformation was caught on camera and appeared on YouTube. Though he's also supposed to be looking for Chen, this evening he's in a bar where he spots a lovely redhead. A thief takes the woman's wallet, and Thorolf gives chase outside. Though he manages to get the wallet back, he gives the thief fifty dollars of his own money, remembering what it was like to be on the streets and desperate. He returns the wallet to the woman, who introduces herself as Viv Jason. When she asks Thorolf about a place to stay, he volunteers his own. Chandra stole the wallet to find out the name the red-headed woman was currently using. Chandra knows the woman as one of the Liliot, Lilith's Daughters, and knows her being in the same place as the dragon shifter cannot be a fluke. Since she feels she now owes a debt to the dragon shifter, Chandra returns to the bar to keep an eye on him.

Chapter 8: Lorenzo wonders if the unusual *Pyr* can read his thoughts, which Marco then confirms. Marco tells him he cannot deny his nature and that the *Pyr* will come and help when he calls them, even though Lorenzo doesn't want anything to do with them. After confirming the crystal is indeed gone from Lorenzo's home, he says, "I should have known it would choose its own destiny." When Lorenzo asks who took it, Marco tells him to talk to his father. He then shifts and flies away. Lorenzo goes to check on his father, Salvatore, who has spent most of the last few years sleeping. The older man also prefers his dragon shape, counter to Lorenzo's own practice. Since his father doesn't want to move with him, Lorenzo decides he will contact his lawyer to will Salvatore the house so he can remain there. As he leaves the room, Lorenzo never sees Salvatore open his eyes and smile. Cassie refuses to give Stacy details of her time with Lorenzo. She then learns about Lorenzo's upcoming spectacle, and that many are expecting him to die. Deciding she needs to investigate further, Cassie researches as much as she can about Lorenzo, learns where he lives, and goes there while Lorenzo is performing. When she arrives at Lorenzo's compound, Cassie notices a couple of the security cameras freeze, then she sees a man beckoning to her from a window. When she goes inside, the older gentleman introduces himself as Salvatore, Lorenzo's father.

Chapter 9: Salvatore leads Cassie into a huge, elaborate room with a large painting on the wall. The painting looks like the room in which she is standing, but it seems to be of a house of pleasure, with a woman at the side of the picture gesturing toward the others shown. Salvatore says the woman in the painting is Angelina, Lorenzo's mother and that Lorenzo was born in 1585. She wonders at the man's lucidity, but he insists he is not confused. He says that femininity is Lorenzo's weakness, and that is how she will win him. Salvatore disappears, and Lorenzo arrives. He is obviously pleased to see her, but then there is a blue shimmer around Lorenzo, and he changes into a dragon in front of her and jumps through the window. As Lorenzo and another dragon fight, Cassie considers taking pictures, but decides not to since Lorenzo seems to wish to keep it secret. She hunkers down behind the couch to watch. Lorenzo is surprised and pleased to find Cassie in his home.

He is even more amazed to sense that Cassie is already pregnant, meaning the *Pyr* stories of the firestorm are true. Before he can enjoy Cassie's presence, he smells Balthasar, and shifts to fight. After besting the *Slayer*, he restrains himself from killing him so as not to indulge that part of his dragon nature he despises. Lorenzo shifts back into his human form in front of Cassie. He is worried when he sees her camera, but he can tell it hasn't been used, and when she tells him why, he thinks that maybe not all humans are like Caterina. The two surrender to desire once more.

Chapter 10: Cassie questions Lorenzo about the *Pyr* and he answers, but when she mentions his father and Lorenzo's birth year, he is angry that his father has been deceiving him. He abruptly gets up to confront Salvatore when they hear an explosion outside—Balthasar has destroyed Cassie's Jeep. Lorenzo confronts his father and asks what he did with the darkfire crystal. Salvatore says he put it where it belonged. He says though the firestorm has been sated, "it has not been extinguished." Lorenzo admonishes his father for trying to bring he and Cassie together in a lasting relationship, and Salvatore admits he promised Angelina he would ensure Lorenzo's happiness. Lorenzo says Salvatore got Angelina killed, leaving her undefended. As Lorenzo leaves in anger, Salvatore asks if he will really use the flashfire song. While Lorenzo is gone, Cassie sees Angelina beckon her to come toward the painting and then Angelina pulls her into the painting. Lorenzo doesn't see Cassie in the room when he returns but then sees her in the painting, with his mother. Angelina leads Cassie to a man who acts as translator, and Cassie learns about the firestorm and that she is pregnant, which shocks her. Before Cassie leaves, Angelina gives her a piece of parchment with what appears to be a verse written on it, telling her to get Lorenzo to tell her what it says. Angelina hugs Cassie, but when the clock chimes, gives her a gentle push back out of the painting.

Chapter 11: Cassie finds Lorenzo waiting for her when she returns. He says he saw her in the picture. Cassie asks why Lorenzo never told her about the firestorm and conception, and he says he didn't mention it because he never believed it. When Cassie asks about his upcoming spectacle, she figures out he plans to use the event to stage his disappearance. She gets very upset, accusing him of leaving everyone and everything behind, and she doesn't appreciate his referring to humans as vermin. Lorenzo asks her to take part in the ruse with him, but she storms out, taking his Ferrari.

Chapter 12: Lorenzo follows Cassie, in dragon form. He wonders about the prophecy, and why both *Pyr* and *Slayers* are after him. He resolves to call upon Erik to ask for his help. Cassie decides to drive to the site of Lorenzo's big spectacle, and since the car is recognized, she gets in easily. She parks and uses Lorenzo's leather jacket to cover herself. Thinking she could have loved Lorenzo, she cries herself to sleep. Lorenzo spots Cassie and hears her cry. After shifting and breathing dragonsmoke, Lorenzo settles in to keep watch, and contacts Erik via old-speak. Back at the hotel, JP leaves Stacy after a night of sex, only to be cornered in the elevator by Chen, in the guise of an attractive woman. Chen is not pleased with JP's progress so he marks him with one of his talons. Salvatore visits the realm of the Wyvern, where he has been only once before. He seeks to turn a memory into a dream. Cassie dreams of Angelina and a baby she knows must be Lorenzo. Angelina and her maid run from some men who are after them. Angelina manages to hide the baby and the maid gets away, but Angelina is raped and killed by one of the men. Cassie sees Salvatore in his dragon shape descending. In his Las Vegas hotel room, Erik is startled when he sees the ghost of Sigmund, who has brought along Angelina. She asks Sigmund to give Erik a message, then Erik hears Lorenzo's old-speak. Angelina confirms he means it. Erik then has a vision of two shadows, Angelina and a silver dragon, and he knows a *Pyr* will be leaving them soon.

Chapter 13: Erik arrives quickly, and Lorenzo gives him the paper with the prophecy, which speaks of a spell and flashfire. Erik tells him Sophie wrote the prophecy years ago and wanted to be sure it would eventually make its way to Lorenzo, so she entrusted it to Angelina. Erik asks about flashfire and says he knows it brings about change for an individual *Pyr*, unlike darkfire which affects them all. When Lorenzo describes the scent of the *Pyr* who he believes took the crystal from his lair, Erik thinks it must be Drake.

They discuss the *Slayers*, and Lorenzo realizes he will do whatever is necessary to keep Cassie safe because he loves her. Erik leaves, assuring Lorenzo he will help him in any way he can. Cassie wakes to find Lorenzo getting into the car. She tells him she had a dream about what happened to his mother. He explains he blames his father because Salvatore was a gambler and was not careful where he exposed his dragon nature. Salvatore taught Lorenzo how to beguile at an early age, so he could make his own way in the world. Lorenzo took his father in when Salvatore came to him years later. Lorenzo tells Cassie he realizes not all humans are vermin. He offers her the chance to take pictures of him shifting, feeling the money she will earn will provide a safety net for her and their child. They go to a spot in the desert and Cassie gets hundreds of pictures, none of them showing Lorenzo's human face. While they are flying, Cassie touches a loose scale and it falls off. She puts it in her pocket for safekeeping. While she is taking the photographs, Cassie realizes she loves Lorenzo. He asks her what she truly wants to do, since she doesn't seem to be happy as paparazzi.

Chapter 14: Cassie tells Lorenzo that it comes down to making a choice between getting the picture and whatever money or fame it would bring, and doing the right thing. She tells him she had to make that choice and now she wants to take pictures that matter. Lorenzo encourages her, insisting she is, indeed, good enough. Cassie and Lorenzo give in to their passion for one another once again, there in the desert. Salvatore knows he has to enter the Wyvern's realm one last time, and he does—to see his beloved Angelina. He apologizes to her for the past, but also lets her know all will be well with Lorenzo. Angelina asks him to take her flying one last time, and even though he knows he will not be able to find his way back out, Salvatore acquiesces. In his bed in Vegas, the silver dragon becomes an old man, then takes his last breath. Lorenzo tries to convince Cassie to disappear with him, via the spectacle, but she explains she is terrified of the dark and being underground. Lorenzo decides he needs to eliminate threats to Cassie, so he taunts Balthasar in old-speak, to get the *Slayer* to come to him. Cassie is frustrated Lorenzo walked off, but then realizes it's his nature to pretend he doesn't care when he really does. When they get in the car to leave, they see Balthasar headed toward them, and he lands on top of the car.

Chapter 15: The *Slayer* picks up the car and flies with it, but Lorenzo shifts and gets the car away from him and moves it somewhere safe. While the two dragons fight, Lorenzo comes up with a plan on how to deal with Balthasar in a way that doesn't involve deadly force—he beguiles him so Lorenzo can have a body to take his place in the spectacle. Lorenzo and Cassie admit to loving each other, and when she asks, Lorenzo tells Cassie a bit about Caterina, how she had been sent to expose him. Lorenzo says he will put her under Erik's protection if she doesn't get buried in the car with him. Cassie goes to the hotel to get her stuff and to sell the pictures, while Lorenzo takes his car to have the windows replaced. Instead of going straight back to Cassie as he had planned, he goes home first, after a frantic call from the housekeeper who has been unable to get his father to answer the door to his room. When he arrives, Lorenzo finds Salvatore dead. Lorenzo calls Erik for help with the proper disposal of his father's body, exposure to the four elements. He wonders if the flashfire will demand more of him than what he is now willing to give up. He tells the housekeeper he is going to call a collector who will pick it up the painting. When Cassie returns to the hotel room, Stacy is upset because JP stood her up for breakfast, and she can't reach him. Cassie wonders if he may be a dragon shifter, too. After Cassie texts Lorenzo to say she will meet him at the theater a bit later, Stacy tells her a federal agent came looking for her, a T. Chen, who is investigating dragon shifters for serious crimes. Erik calls Lorenzo and tells him only Sloane and Brandt will be coming to town. Lorenzo is disappointed, but not surprised, since he has never helped any of the other *Pyr*. They still plan to meet at midnight for Salvatore's ceremony, and Lorenzo plans to go to Cassie's hotel.

Chapter 16: Cassie meets Mr. Chen in the bar, with Stacy in tow. After Cassie tells him she believes the dragon portion of Lorenzo's show to be an illusion, he suggests they go to a quieter room to finish the interview. When Mr. Chen pushes her inside and she sees JP, she knows all is not well. Chen tries very hard to beguile her, and though she tries to fight it, she can't completely. She overhears Chen and JP discussing getting more material for Dragon's Bone Powder—from Salvatore and Erik. Though she tries to stay awake, Cassie loses consciousness. On his way to the appointed meeting place in the desert, Erik has a sense of doom. He sees Cassie staggering on the side of the road, but when . he stops to put her in the car, she runs in the opposite direction. He catches her quickly, then spots Chen in dragon form. Erik realizes Cassie is not drunk, but beguiled. She mentions Dragon Bone Powder, and Erik understands what Chen wants—Salvatore—but Cassie also points to Erik. He then goes after Chen. Unable to reach Cassie, Lorenzo is distracted during his final show, so much so that he misses a crucial step in freeing himself during his tank illusion. He has to shift briefly to break the bonds, and when he does so, his two assistants see him. He realizes he will need to beguile them later. After he escapes and completes the trick, Lorenzo hears old-speak, but not from any dragon he recognizes. The speaker threatens to raise Lorenzo's son as his own. Lorenzo cannot sense any dragons in the vicinity, so understands it must be a *Slayer* who drank of the Dragon's Blood Elixir. Lorenzo quickly leaves the theater, hurrying to get to Cassie, and finds the *Pyr* Brandt outside by his car. On the way to get Cassie, Brandt suggests Chen has more planned than just taking his mate. Since Lorenzo has not chosen a side in the fight, he is a good candidate to turn *Slayer*. When he doesn't find Cassie at her hotel, Lorenzo decides to go get more information out of the beguiled Balthasar, and learns about Chen, the Dragon Bone Powder, and the brand. Brandt sees him talking to Balthasar and assumes the worst, which suits Lorenzo just fine as part of his illusion.

Chapter 17: Cassie wakes up in a cave, with Erik beside her. He re-ties her bonds so it appears she is still restrained, but they are loose enough for her to work her way free. After asking if she trusts him, he beguiles away her beguiling from Chen, but wants her to act as though she is still under the *Slayer's* spell. Once JP leaves, Erik asks about an area with the four elements, and Cassie says Lake Mead. He gives her the keys to the hearse with Salvatore's body in it and lets her know he wants her to drive there when she sees the darkfire. In her pocket, Cassie finds the scale

Lorenzo lost earlier, and Erik seems very pleased. Lorenzo arrives where Cassie and Erik are being held, then sees a small red salamander, knowing it is Chen. The *Slayer* shifts to his dragon form, and Lorenzo allows himself to be bested in a brief fight, telling Chen he wants to join him. Brandt arrives, and deciding to use him as part of his ruse, Lorenzo attacks the *Pyr*, who then ends up being held with Erik and Cassie. They both understand Lorenzo is pretending, though they don't say anything, allowing the illusion to continue. Chen wants to brand Lorenzo, but when Chen gets close to him, Lorenzo grabs the brand and blows fire on it. He beguiles Chen, learning the *Slayer* wishes to control him for some reason. Lorenzo continues to breathe on the brand, and a blue-green spark appears. Lorenzo then uses the brand on Chen. Cassie sees her chance and leaves the cave, heading to the car. She drives toward Lake Mead and manages to shake off both Chen and JP. When Lorenzo appears, she tells him he will make a good father, and Lorenzo beguiles JP to reset the permissions on his dragonsmoke back at the cave.

Chapter 18: Cassie observes Salvatore's funeral ceremony conducted by Lorenzo, Erik, and Brandt. Afterward, Lorenzo tells her she has to come with him in the car the next day, because he is concerned about her safety with Chen and JP still around. She agrees. The next day, Lorenzo can smell both *Slayer* and *Pyr* in the area. Cassie is hidden on the floorboards, covered with a blanket. Once the car is buried, the video feed is changed so it looks as though Lorenzo remains in place, but he actually has an escape hatch through which he and Cassie leave, dropping down a hole into a tunnel. Once they are there, Balthasar appears, and once again Lorenzo beguiles the *Slayer*. He convinces Balthasar to give him the location of and the key to Magnus' library. Lorenzo then uses the flashfire song on Balthasar, cutting his ties to all dragons. When Balthasar collapses, Lorenzo takes him to the car. When Lorenzo returns to the tunnel, Chen has Cassie in his grasp, saying he will trade her for his brand. Lorenzo pretends not to care about Cassie. Then he shifts, throws the brand down the tunnel, and pulls Cassie away from Chen. The *Slayer* makes goes after the brand, but the brand disintegrates from darkfire. Marco is there, aiming his crystal at Chen, who shifts into salamander shape and leaves.

Marco tells Lorenzo he didn't claim the flashfire song from him because he knew Lorenzo would need it. Marco also says he hasn't gotten the other crystal back because it isn't ready to return to him yet. When Marco leaves, Lorenzo asks Cassie if she wants to go to the Caymans with him. He plans to give Magnus' library to Erik. They discuss a Vegas wedding and a Caymans honeymoon.

Epilogue: One month later, all of the *Pyr* and their partners gather at Lorenzo and Cassie's restored Venetian villa for a party to watch the raising of the car from the desert. Stacy is also there, having been let in on the secret of the *Pyr*. As expected, Balthasar's body passes for Lorenzo, making his disappearing act a success. Erik and Cassie then surprise Lorenzo: she has his missing scale and the others have all come to witness the repair of Lorenzo's armor. The ceremony gives Lorenzo hope for the future.

DEBORAH'S COMMENTS

What if a dragon shifter didn't want to be a dragon shifter? That was the question that Lorenzo asked when he sauntered into my office. What if he thought shifting shape was revolting and uncivilized, never mind becoming a fire-breathing dragon? I was intrigued. The one thing Lorenzo has refined to an art is his *Pyr* gift for beguiling: it's not only a useful skill for a master illusionist, but he even dares to beguile Erik, to ensure his own privacy. I like those who bend the rules—or refuse to even acknowledge them—so Lorenzo had me at hello.

One of the things I enjoy about Lorenzo's firestorm is how it proves that he can't ignore his own essence. I suspect we all have moments when we'd like to be someone else or at least be different, but Lorenzo's firestorm compels him to not only accept his own nature but to embrace it.

Lorenzo nodded at his staff and strode to his place at center stage, where he would await the rising of the curtains. He fought his awareness of the slow burn of the eclipse, teasing at the edge of his thoughts. He felt the firestorm light for some poor *Pyr* and ignored it, just as he had a hundred times before.

Even though it was close.

It was *not* his problem.

Lorenzo was in the act of donning his top hat when the music swelled. One pair of curtains swept back and the other curtain rose skyward.

Right on cue.

Perfect.

The audience stared at him in expectant awe. Lorenzo had a moment to think that everything would be just fine.

Then he raised his hand in a welcoming gesture, and the light of his own firestorm sparked from his fingertips.

Lorenzo was astounded.

His firestorm launched an arc of fire that illuminated the space between him and a woman in the front row. She was lit suddenly with radiant golden light.

The audience gasped.

Lorenzo wanted to swear.

— from **Flashfire**

Lorenzo wants us—and the *Pyr*—to believe that he's independent and likes it that way, even while he's secretly caring for his elderly and weakened father. Once we hear Salvatore's story of his great love for Angelina, we have to believe that the inspiration of the love will overcome Lorenzo's hurtful memories. It's not just the firestorm that undermines Lorenzo's assumptions: it's Cassie herself and the emotional response she awakens in a man who doesn't want to feel anything anymore. What's not to love about that?

Lorenzo marched through the broken glass and snatched up the camera. He might have destroyed it, but he saw that it was turned off. A flick of his thumb revealed that the memory card was empty.

He looked at Cassie, uncertain what to think.

She was a professional photographer. He knew that pictures of the *Pyr* were worth a fortune, thanks to Melissa Smith's television specials. He had spent his entire life convinced that humans were self-motivated and untrustworthy. He was so convinced of it that the empty memory card shook his world.

Was it possible that there were humans who were different? Was Cassie different from Caterina?

Or was this an illusion?

"I didn't take any pictures," she admitted quietly.

"Why not? Isn't that your job?" His tone was sharp, but Lorenzo couldn't help it. He felt vital and alive, but also within a hair of losing control.

Again.

Cassie exhaled. "I'm on vacation." She smiled.

"Don't shit me." Lorenzo spoke with force, having no patience for games. He could have guessed that he was shimmering around his perimeter, hovering on the cusp of change. His eyes were probably glittering, half dragon, his body coiled to fight again.

He knew he was right when Cassie's smile disappeared. She looked him over, then swallowed. She took a shaking breath and glanced around the room before meeting his gaze again.

But she answered him. She wasn't a coward. He liked that.

His dragon loved it. He'd never been much for fainting virgins or damsels in distress—and princesses were generally too much trouble.

"It would be great publicity for you to reveal what you are, but you haven't done it," she said. "In fact, you've hidden that truth really carefully. I have to think you have a good reason for that, that you know more about the risks than I do." She shrugged. "You're not stupid, and neither am I."

Lorenzo was astounded by her observations and how much they revealed her understanding of him. "You trust me?"

Cassie's smile was quick and genuine. "I guess I do." If he was shocked by the prospect of a human trusting him, her confirmation amazed him even more. "So what don't I know about all of this dragon stuff? Will you fill me in?"

It was a fair question. A fair exchange.

Even if answering her defied every choice Lorenzo had made in over three hundred years.

Was she tricking him?

Did he dare to trust her?

What about their son?

Lorenzo put down the camera with care, shaken by his emotions. He wasn't used to being overwhelmed, not by detail or by passion or by his own base instincts, but he was certainly shaken in this moment. He wasn't thinking clearly, his body still demanding pleasure with such vehemence that his pulse was pounding.

She trusted him.

He wanted to reciprocate in kind.

—from **Flashfire**

EMBER'S KISS

ONLY ONE WOMAN CAN PERSUADE HIM TO EMBRACE HIS POWERS...

Brandon Merrick is determined to banish his shifter nature forever. The charismatic tattooed surfer is on the cusp of the ultimate challenge—to prove himself on the whitecaps of Hawaii and secure his future as a pro surfer. But his dragon isn't prepared to be tamed so easily...

One look at marine biologist Liz Barrett ignites the spark of a firestorm: Liz is his destined mate and his chance for happiness. Brandon sees their first night together as just the beginning, but then his dragon seizes the upper hand. Awakening in the company of a raging dragon challenges Liz's ability to believe her own eyes. Can Brandon accept his inner beast in time to make it work with Liz?

Neither one realizes Brandon is caught in an ancient Slayer's scheme to enslave him. When the deadly plot ignites, the very island will be at risk...and Brandon and his mate could be the ultimate sacrifice.

THE PROTAGONISTS

Brandon and Liz are both outcasts from their family's paranormal tradition, but Liz chose to abandon the family magick when she saw her mother die. Brandon doesn't know much about being Pyr and doesn't want to: thanks to his mother's dislike of his father's nature, he thinks of his dragon as the beast within. He's always trying to banish it, as if he can be cured of being Pyr, instead of embracing it. His lack of knowledge about his own nature and his distrust of the *Pyr* combine to make him easy prey for the *Slayer* Chen. The firestorm brings Brandon exactly what he needs in Liz, whose history allows her to recognize Chen's spells for what they are, and to speculate on how to break them. She has to embrace her own powers in order to help Brandon, which means they pretty much save each other.

THE ELEMENTS

Brandon's affinities are to earth and water, while Liz's affinities are to fire and air. Liz is also a Firedaughter, from a family of elemental witches. I like this conversation which compares Brandon, Sloane and Liz's expectations of how affinities manifest:

Sloane cleared his throat. "We *Pyr* each have an affinity to two elements. Usually, fire is one. The affinity often manifests in more intellectual or emotional ways, though. My own affinity to water, for example, appears as empathy. That helps with my ability to heal, because I can diagnose more effectively."

"So, you can't create rain, then?" Liz asked. "Or be a waterfall?"

Sloane seemed startled by the idea. "I don't know. I've never tried."

"I can summon waves," Brandon said, and both Liz and Sloane looked at him in surprise. "Sure. There are days, you know, when the surf is low and there are no good breaks to be found. If I really want to surf, I sit on the beach and I think about the ocean. I feel its rhythm. I watch the waves and I visualize how they could break better. I think of them becoming higher and more regular, and they do. It takes time, but it works."

"Have you ever made it rain?" Liz asked him with excitement. His affinity with water was more similar to what the Waterdaughters in her family could do.

"Never tried," he admitted with a smile. "You can't surf in the rain." His eyes twinkled and his fingers slid into her hair in a slow caress. "But I do have a thing for a marine biologist," he murmured, his voice so low that Liz felt all tingly. "Does that count?"

—from **Ember's Kiss**

THE SETTING

Brandon's firestorm lights during the total lunar eclipse of December 10, 2011.

As a side note, 2012 was the year of the dragon in Chinese

astrology, so this firestorm was perceived by the *Slayer* Chen to be his last opportunity to complete the spell that would give him domination.

THE PROPHECY

Dragon lost and dragon found;
Dragon denied and dragon bound,
Down to embers, his fire chills,
In thrall to one whose intent is ill.
Firedaughter's spark can ignite the flame,
Give him strength to fight again.
Or will both be lost on ocean's tide,
Surrendered as a failed test's price?

THE STORY

Chapter 1: (Oahu, Hawaii, December 9, 2011) *Slayer* Chen sits in the bar waiting to meet his targeted *Pyr*. He blames his failures on the darkfire. The components of his plan need to be completed by January 23, 2012 (when the year of the dragon will begin) so he can gain power over all of the dragon shifters. Tonight's eclipse will signal a *Pyr's* firestorm, and since he feels the effects so strongly, he is sure the recipient will be his target, Brandon. The *Slayer* already possesses three of Brandon's scales, given in exchange for Dragon's Bone Powder, which the young *Pyr* does not understand the purpose of. After Chen gets the fourth scale, he will control Brandon's dragon thanks to old dragon magic. The firestorm will hasten what Chen wants to do. Brandon will not listen to the other *Pyr*, as they are allies of his estranged father. When Brandon arrives, Chen gifts him the last vial of Dragon's Bone Powder, not even asking a scale in return, since he plans to get it after the firestorm begins. Liz Barrett, a marine biologist, arrives in Hawaii to attend a conference. As her friend, Maureen, drives her toward a tunnel, Liz gets a bad feeling that she cannot explain. When they drive through, she hears a whisper saying, "Firedaughter," a term she has not heard in many years. Liz knows the voice must be in her head, which greatly worries her. When she starts seeing auras again, Liz becomes even more concerned. She wonders if her powers, gone for fourteen years, are now returning. Brandon and his two friends, also surfers, end up at a restaurant where he sees an attractive dark-haired woman. One of his buddies challenges Brandon to see which of them she responds to. Liz notices the handsome auburn-haired surfer, but has no interest in his friend.

Chapter 2: Brandon admires the lovely brunette and her group of friends, for seeming like serious people who can still enjoy themselves. He thinks about his own goal—ridding himself of his dragon nature he so despises. When the woman and her group move outside to watch the eclipse, he follows them. Then he notices orange sparks building around his hand. One spark flies from his finger straight to the brunette, who is glowing. Brandon tells himself it wasn't Chen's powder bringing him good luck, but the possibilities presented by the firestorm. He walks over to her, they touch hands, watching the sparks, then kiss. Liz hears the rest of her group, and breaks off the kiss. Brandon and Liz introduce themselves to each other. The mood is broken when Brandon's friend, Matt, flings the contents of the vial into the air. The powder has an immediate effect on the *Pyr*, as a blue shimmer appears around his body and one eye turns red, with a vertical pupil. Liz recognizes the feel of magic—and not the good kind—then leaves with her group. Meanwhile, in Chicago, Erik knows it is Brandon's firestorm and that it burns somewhat hotter this time. He realizes there is something different about the mate. Via old-speak, he contacts Sloane to go, and texts Brandt, Brandon's father, to stay away. Erik decides to take Quinn along. After receiving Erik's message, Brandt plans to go see Kay, his former wife and Brandon's mother. As he rides in the back of his friend's jeep, Brandon has to wrestle down the dragon while experiencing aggressive and violent feelings. He discovers that thinking of Liz makes him calmer, so he wonders if the firestorm is the way he can control his dragon. At her hotel, Liz cannot sleep. She thinks of her powers that she had lost contact with when isolating herself from the earth and wonders if they have returned. As she looks at the sky, she sees a dragon. Her mother had told her other beings share the world with them, often hiding from mortal eyes. The daughters of Hecate witness their presence, though they say nothing of it unless they are asked for help. Liz hears footsteps outside and sees Brandon. She goes out to meet him, and he tells her about the firestorm, though he doesn't mention being a dragon. They kiss.

Chapter 3: Brandon and Liz satisfy the firestorm in her bed, and later in the night, Liz notices the sparks are gone when they touch, though the attraction remains. Brandon wakes to find his dragon restless within him, but doesn't know why, since he thought that sating the firestorm would give him greater control. He can sense something is wrong, and then an earthquake hits. Brandon shifts, feeling the need to protect Liz. When Liz wakes and sees a dragon, she fears it has done something to Brandon, so she kicks it where a scale is missing and she is released. Liz tries to hide, but the dragon tears down the door and flies off with her, even thinking to bring some of her clothes and her purse. When the dragon sets her down, Liz tries to run off again, and the dragon picks her up and flies again. On the ground below, they spot a woman and child in danger, and the dragon picks them up, as well, flying them to safety. Liz wonders if Brandon and the dragon are one and the same. He puts her down on the island and leaves. Brandon is upset his dragon seems to have taken ascendency—he is unable to change back to his human form—and that his chances with Liz may be ruined. He also worries about his upcoming surfing competition, which will take place any day, depending upon the waves. Brandon resolves to stay away from Liz until he can contain the aggressive and bloodthirsty beast within him.

Chapter 4: Much to his dismay, Brandon remains unable to shift back to his human shape. He goes to an out-of-the-way beach so the waves can calm him, and he is able to shift back. He gets a ride back to his part of the island and learns that Honolulu was hit hard by the earthquake. Brandon resolves to control his dragon by consulting Chen, who he thinks has helped him in the past. Liz does some research, looking for the article she had seen before on dragon shifters and learns they are called the *Pyr*. Liz feels Brandon is trustworthy, based upon his deep blue aura. She decides that when she next sees him, she will just ask him for the truth. Jorge sees Chen as the tool to help him get revenge on the *Pyr*, so he has come to Hawaii. Jorge gets through Chen's dragonsmoke barrier in his lair (which he can do because of the Dragon's Blood Elixir), and finds an area of sand inside, with three dragon scales. It looks like a spell of some sort so Jorge takes one of the scales to use as leverage. He then allows just a small amount of his scent to alert Chen to his presence. He wonders if breaking the scale will hurt the *Pyr* it came from. A very tired Sara has just gotten her youngest son, Ewan, to sleep. He'd been restless all night, as had Quinn, but she attributes her partner's sleeplessness to a firestorm somewhere. Suddenly she hears a loud crack, and she and Quinn see the mirror above their dresser is covered in flames, spelling out words. Sara realizes it is a portent, so writes it all down. The verse speaks of a Firedaughter (which Quinn explains is a witch who can take the form of fire) and a dragon in thrall to someone with evil intent. Shortly thereafter Erik arrives, tells Sara and Quinn whose firestorm it is, and asks them to go with him. After having Erik scry to make sure things are safe, Quinn and Sara agree to go. Determined to find Brandon, Liz goes back to the restaurant from the night before. After learning where the surfers typically stay, she heads out.

Chapter 5: When Brandon arrives back in Hale'iwa, instead of Chen, he finds his friend, Kira, who owns a surf shop. She has adapted a wetsuit for him, and hopes he will wear it in the surf competition. When he says he can't pay her for it, she tells him her shop logo on the wetsuit will be advertising for her. Brandon tries it on, and it fits perfectly. He then heads to the beach. As Liz drives through the tunnel on her way to find Brandon, a bright blue-green light flashes in her car, and a symbol is branded onto her arm. Chen takes pride in the earthquake he caused and looks forward to claiming Brandon's power and affinities, in addition to using him as a slave. If the *Pyr* dies, he will provide a new source of Dragon Bone Powder. He is pleased to see Brandon's mate stop to ask if he would like a ride. When she touches his arm, he recognizes she is also a Firedaughter and wonders if she is aware of it. Liz picks up the old Chinese man, but is disturbed by his lack of an aura, and then even more so when he begins talking about a dragon whose mother is Pele, the volcano goddess. Liz wants to help the old man but also feels an aversion to him. After she drops him off, he tells her on which beach she can find the dragon. Liz finds Brandon in the water there, trying to catch a wave, against the advice of all of his friends. He seems to be holding his own, but when he sees Liz, he loses his concentration and balance, falling under the huge wave. When Brandon does not come up, but the black dragon does, Liz feels sure he is a *Pyr*.

Chapter 6: Matt is also getting ready to take on a big wave. The dragon swoops down to get him, but Matt falters when he sees it and falls. The dragon manages to get him out of the water, and the others come to get him. Liz decides to follow the dragon. Brandon, still in dragon form, feels guilty about what happened to Matt. He believes his dragon nature is evil, just as his mother had told him. Brandon feels no hope for the future, but then sees Liz's car coming toward his location at the national park, and he plans to tell her everything. The closer she gets, the more control he has over his dragon, and he shifts back to human. Liz tells him she guessed what he is, and Brandon is ecstatic. They discuss how he has been experiencing a loss of control. When he says physical exertion helps, they begin kissing. Suddenly, Brandon feels himself change, then has a huge pain strike his chest. Both he and Liz see there is a wound in one of the missing scale spots. Liz's presence and touch seem to calm his beast, and she asks him to change back to human form. They see he does indeed still have a wound when he is in human form, and Liz asks about the scales. When she hears Brandon traded them, and what for, Liz walks away. Brandon thinks she must be angry, but he soon learns she is scared.

Chapter 7: Liz realizes someone has cast a binding spell on Brandon, even preventing his hair and nails from growing in his human form. She learns it is the powder in the vial that has been the source, but Brandon finds it hard to believe of the man he thought was helping him. Brandon tells Liz she has sparks coming from her hands and hair when she gets upset. He's curious about why, but she refuses to talk about it. As they ride back to where he lives, Brandon notices the brand on her arm, knows it wasn't there before, and resolves to look it up. When they arrive back in town, Liz notices a dark-haired man watching her, who smiles strangely at her. She knows the mark signifies a test will be coming soon, and she thinks it would be best to stay away from Brandon until after her test. Brandon and Liz tell his friends he was caught in a riptide and washed up down the shore, but they keep asking about the dragon. When they say they are going off to look for the creature, a man walks up and tells them there isn't a dragon. Liz turns away when she sees the flames in his eyes. He somehow convinces the others to give up their pursuit and to forget that they saw a dragon at all. The man, obviously a *Pyr*, says he beguiled Brandon's friends, explaining it is a kind of hypnosis. He introduces himself to Brandon and Liz as Sloane Forbes, saying he was sent by their leader to help Brandon. Brandon isn't interested, telling Sloane he can only help if he can take the dragon out of him, which Sloane tells him is impossible. Liz wants to hear more, but Brandon spots Chen, and tries to take Liz to see him. Halfway there, she excuses herself and looks for Sloane.

Chapter 8: Liz follows Sloane to the parking lot. When she tells Sloane the man who gave Brandon the powder is an old guy, Sloane knows exactly who it is, and explains to Liz about *Slayer*s. He wants some of the powder so he can test it. He also suggests Liz can heal Brandon, since he can shift when she's present, and wants to know what her powers are. She says she gave them away years ago, but he says they seem to be back. He makes reference to the firestorm and their son, which shocks Liz, as Brandon had omitted that particular detail. Angry, she goes into the bar to confront Brandon, and sees his friend is the same old man to whom she gave a ride. When Brandon follows her outside, Liz confronts him about the pregnancy. He says he was planning to tell her but got sidetracked by everything going on. She says she doesn't ever want to have children because of what she will pass on to them. Liz tells him her suspicions about Chen, but Brandon is unwilling to believe. After Liz leaves, saying she's not sure she'll be back, Brandon resolves to get the vial to her for testing, rather than Sloane. While Brandon is gone, Chen is angry that someone broke into his lair, took one of Brandon's scales, and then destroyed it. He knows it must be Jorge, out for vengeance. When Brandon returns, he tells Chen his dragon is gaining more control. Chen reminds him that can be changed by removing a scale or two more. Brandon says Liz doesn't think it's a good idea for him to remove them, confirming Chen's suspicions that her influence is a hindrance to his plan. Chen begins to shimmer a pre-shift light, which Brandon notices, but as Chen gets up to leave, acting very feeble, Brandon says he will walk him home. He also asks for more of the bone powder, which Chen says he has in his room. Chen plans to attack and enslave Brandon that very night. In New York, Niall shows Rox a picture of Brandon's tattoos, and she explains they are tribal symbols. One of them is for protection and the other was drawn by a shaman. They decide they will all go to Hawaii.

Chapter 9: Brandon has a bad feeling and asks Chen what is in the powder. Another voice answers, "dragon bones," and Brandon sees a big blond guy appear. Chen shocks Brandon by turning into a red dragon, and the other guy turns into a yellow one, flying off talking about, "fresh mate." Brandon shifts shape, planning to protect Liz, but Chen traps him behind dragonsmoke. Brandon tries to contact the *Pyr* via old-speak, but has no idea if anyone hears him. Liz approaches the tunnel with trepidation. She hears and smells burning, and the goddess Pele appears in the passenger seat. She tells Liz she is the one who can break the spell that wakens the earth, and that Liz cannot change what she is—her powers are not gone, just slumbering. Pele also says only Liz can break the spell binding Brandon. When Pele disappears, the road ahead cracks and lava pours out. Liz heads toward the water and sees a blond man ahead of her who calls her "the mate." The man shifts and comes after her, but Liz calls upon her power and manages to singe him a bit. She then jumps in the water and swims across to Coconut Island, the *Slayer* still in pursuit. Liz then sees the yellow dragon battling with a red dragon. The blood coming from both of them is black, so she knows both are *Slayers*. After the yellow one disappears, the red one comes after her. Sloane responds to Brandon but cannot cross the dragonsmoke to get him out. Brandon begs Sloane to help him defend Liz. Sloane tells him he needs to accept and embrace his dragon nature and make a choice. Brandon agrees, and Sloane promises to do his best. After Sloane leaves, Brandon messes up Chen's spiral design in the sand.

Chapter 10: Liz sees a blue-green light, the same kind she saw before the mark was left on her arm, and then a dark-haired man (the same one she had seen watching her in Hale'iwa) appears. He aims a crystal at the red dragon, and a bolt of blue-green light hits the dragon, which falls toward the water but then disappears. Marco introduces himself and asks Liz about her powers. He explains that the darkfire answers to him, and it "introduces unpredictability, challenges expectations, and turns possibilities into reality." Marco convinces Liz she can help Brandon, and gives her the crystal, saying it wants to be with her, and he will retrieve it after her son is born. Marco then flies away. Brandon decides to retrieve his two remaining scales from Chen's sand area. Then Jorge appears and destroys one of the scales, causing Brandon a lot of pain. They fight over the second one, with Jorge stealing some of Brandon's power via a dragonsmoke conduit. Brandon pretends to be on the verge of death, shifting back and forth between forms, then latches onto Jorge when he starts to manifest elsewhere and ends up going along with him. In her soggy purse, Liz finds the pendant that once belonged to her mother. She cries when she thinks of her mother's death in a trial of fire and spirit, but hears her voice telling her she's strong, especially as the third daughter of a third daughter. Liz realizes she had muffled her powers before coming to Hawaii, but knows she has to call upon them now. She makes a sanctuary area at Maureen's. Brandon and Jorge manifest on a cliff and continue their fight. Brandon tears off Jorge's other wing, and figures out how to make his own dragonfire conduit to sap the *Slayer*'s strength and power. He drops Jorge into the water and leaves to go find Liz. At a party, Liz spots a Chinese woman who has no aura and is watching Liz closely. She goes outside, assuming the woman will follow her, which she does. Brandon races to Liz's location, and sees her turn to fire in a fight with Chen. She seems to have the upper hand, making use of a crystal he doesn't recognize and shadows that surround her, but then a bolt of lightning penetrates her protective shield and she cries out in pain. Both she and Chen disappear. Brandon fears the *Slayer* plans to drown her.

Chapter 11: The lightning strikes Liz's pendant, demolishing it, and leaves a burn mark on her chest. Chen begins diving to the bottom of the sea with Liz in his clutches, but she manages to poke him in the eye with the crystal, causing him to release her. He swims off, and she begins swimming to the surface. Brandon searches for Liz's scent, finding her in the water, and in human form does mouth-to-mouth. He then shifts and flies her to safety. Sloane joins him and suggests they hole up to recover and plan while Chen and Jorge are weakened. Some of the *Pyr* are on the way to help. Liz wakes up, naked, in a huge hotel bed, with Brandon lying beside her. Brandon then gives Sloane the vial, and the Apothecary confirms the residue is from Dragon's Bone Powder. He also wants to hear about Liz's powers. She tells him Firedaughters, Airdaughters, Earthdaughters, Waterdaughters, and just witches exist in her family line, and they are watched as youngsters to see which affinity they display. When Liz was eighteen, her mother faced her test, but lacked the ability with fire. When Liz tried to give her some of her power, her mother disappeared, and after that Liz left home and determined never to use her powers. Since her powers returned when she came to Hawaii, Brandon suggests perhaps the firestorm sparked their return. Sloane leaves, and Brandon and Liz have a brief sexual interlude. Liz asks to see Brandon's dragon, to check his wounded areas. He finally feels positive about being *Pyr* and honors her request.

Chapter 12: Liz heals two of Brandon's wounds by using her power, cauterizing and purifying while he is in dragon form. The area of the third missing scale is just a smooth spot. The angry Chen decides to go after Thorolf next, since killing him will give him more power to cast spells and more effectively control Brandon. He notices all of Brandon's scales he had collected are now gone. When Brandon and Liz wake, Brandon notices Liz now has a tattoo in the spot where the burn mark left by the pendant was. The mark on her arm is darker. Liz and Brandon meet Erik, Quinn, and Niall, along with their partners and families. They discuss the binding spell, which Liz explains creates a connection that goes in both directions. Liz suggests they use the spell to draw Chen out while he's weak. Brandon and Liz learn that dragons are only supposed to lose scales when they fall in love. Liz thinks Brandon must have had some sort of heartbreak to have been able to remove his scales himself, and together the *Pyr* and Liz convince him he ought to call his mother and let her know he's okay.

Chapter 13: Kay Merrick is missing her son (and worrying about him since the earthquake) when she gets a phone call from an unknown number. It is Brandon calling to apologize to her, as she does to him. He tells her he has met someone. Kay resolves right then to go see her son and meet his destined partner. While Brandon is on the phone, Sara shows Liz the prophecy, asking if she understands what it means. Then Rox asks her about the mark on her arm, and she explains to both women about her family. Liz tells the group she knows she can get Chen to them, but isn't clear on what to do when he gets there. To keep Brandon free from Chen, she will try a protective circle such as is used against demons. All of the group go to a secluded beach where Liz makes the circle. She places the *Pyr,* in their dragon forms, in particular spots: Erik in the north, Niall to the east, Sloane to the west, and Quinn to the south. The women hold hands, and their children are there, as well. When she raises Brandon's hand holding the vial toward the sky, a streak of lightning strikes the vial. It is then filled with white light within which Liz sees her mother's image. But the *Pyr* have no auras. In bed with Viv in Bangkok, Thorolf wakes and is attacked by Chen. Viv seems to sleep through everything, and during the struggle with Chen, Thorolf thinks he sees the thief from earlier. A green snake lies in Viv's place, and it bites Chen, after saying, "we had a deal." Then suddenly both Chen and the snake are gone, Viv telling him he has had a bad dream. Chen knows he has been pulled away by Liz's spell. He's also upset at Viv, who seems to want Thorolf for herself. He plans to first destroy Liz and Brandon, then take on Viv and Thorolf. On the beach, Brandon's dragon takes over once again, and he realizes Chen is controlling him. Both Chen and Jorge appear as salamanders, which Brandon tries to pick up. Jorge gets away, but Chen shifts shape into different forms. Darkfire also appears. Young Garrett chases after the gold salamander who escapes Brandon's grasp. Garrett catches the salamander, but then it transforms into Jorge's dragon form and flies off with the boy. Liz aims the crystal at the *Slayer*, he drops Garrett, and Liz picks him up. As she turns to take him back into the circle, she sees a pillar of fire—her test is upon her.

Chapter 14: Brandon uses a dragonsmoke conduit to weaken Chen by sending a tendril through a wound in Chen's eye. Chen moves through his different forms and finally to salamander, which Brandon crushes. He feels the body go limp and tosses it into the flames gathered around Liz during her test. An earthquake hits, making Brandon wonder if Chen is really dead, and he grabs Liz to keep her from falling into a crevasse. Brandon is struck by a searing pain, realizing the last scale must have been broken. Liz disappears. Zoë runs across the sand and picks up a scale that dropped off of Brandon when he went after Chen. She puts it in her pocket and goes back to the others, the *Pyr* fathers then taking flight with their families. Jorge, in human form, has Liz. He wants to trade her for Chen's body, as he can still get some Elixir from it. Brandon plays along, all the while concentrating on using his water affinity to create a huge wave. As Jorge gets closer, Brandon attacks, Liz calls fire, and Pele also shows up. The goddess takes Jorge—in dragon form—back down into the flaming ground. A tsunami threatens the shore, but between them, Liz and Brandon manage to contain it to one small beach. The mark on Liz's arm disappears, and the last two points of the pentacle show up, signifying the completion of her test. She then heals the spot on Brandon from which the third destroyed scale came. Brandt walks along the Australian beach where he and Kay had often met. To his surprise, he sees Kay arrive, and they apologize to one another for their behavior in the past. Kay tells Brandt she has a flight to Hawaii to watch Brandon compete in the surfing competition and asks him to come along. Brandt asks her if she'd like to fly with a dragon. She accepts. Back at the hotel, Liz is surprised by little Zoë bringing her one of Brandon's scales. The others explain about the repair process, how the scales get replaced with something else holding them in place. When Brandon shifts to his dragon form, everyone sees scales are beginning to grow back in the spots Liz healed. Quinn says this means the loves he lost are returning to him. His mother and father are the obvious candidates, and Liz suggests the third may have been himself, because he hated his dragon. The ceremony to affix Brandon's scale begins, with Liz offering her grandmother's earrings for Quinn to use. When leaving the celebratory meal later on, Liz and Brandon see the spirit of Liz's mother. She tells Liz not to feel guilty, that her death was not Liz's fault. She says she has always been with her, and will continue to be.

Epilogue: The *Pyr,* Liz, and her friend Maureen all gather to watch Brandon compete. Liz has been offered the opportunity to do some research at the Institute so she can stay in Hawaii. As he rides the wave, Brandon feels in tune with the ocean and everything else in his life. He succeeds in riding the Pipeline, wins the competition, and gets offered a spot on the international team. Reaching that goal gets somewhat eclipsed by the arrival of his parents, who have mended their own rift and now want to do so with Brandon.

DEBORAH'S COMMENTS

With Brandon, I wanted to write a *Pyr* hero who not only was outside the company of the *Pyr* but one who was young and vital, and who didn't understand his own nature. I needed a heroine who wasn't surprised to find dragon shifters in the world, or shocked by a firestorm. I also needed one to understand Chen's sorcery.

Elemental witches were the solution. What's not to love about adding heroines with powers of their own to the world of *Dragonfire*? I loved this idea as soon as I had it, and Liz fulfilled all my expectations. Here's the passage where she first realizes Chen's influence over Brandon:

A binding spell.

Liz felt sick. Someone had cast a binding spell over Brandon. He couldn't control his dragon because somebody else was in charge of that side of his nature. And the spellcaster had succeeded because he or she had a physical part of Brandon to anchor the spell. Nail clippings, blood, hair, or scales; a physical souvenir from the victim was critical to a successful binding spell.

The sorcerer had chosen scales because the real target was the dragon.

She had sensed dark magic, evil magic. She hadn't expected to be engulfed in the world of her childhood again, or to need all those lessons she'd been taught. She didn't want to revisit the past or reopen those old memories.

But she wanted to help Brandon.

Liz was pretty sure that Brandon was bleeding because that scale had been destroyed. It all made a kind of sense that had once been so familiar to her as to be second nature.

The mark on her arm made Liz reluctant to embrace the realm of magic again. It reminded her that there could be a price to pay — and soon. Even so, there had to be a way to break the spell that had snared Brandon. If they could get the scales, maybe, or if she could find the scientific basis for whatever was happening to him.

The other *Pyr* might be able to help him. They might recognize this situation and be able to deal with it themselves.

Liz turned to find Brandon watching her in obvious confusion, waiting for her to explain. How could he not know more about his own nature? How could his father have not taught him more?

"So, you traded three scales, thinking they'd grow back. Have they grown back at all?" she asked, already knowing the answer. A binding spell sapped the power of the victim, and a lack of routine regenerative growth on the body was the first sign of the spell's power.

Brandon shook his head.

"When did you last get a haircut?" she asked, her mouth dry.

"What?"

"When?"

"I don't know. It's been a while, actually."

"When did you trim your nails last?"

His grin flashed. "What is this — a personal-hygiene test?"

"When?" Liz barked.

"Whoa! You're all flashy again."

"What do you mean?"

His gaze roved over her and he looked awestruck. "There are sparks coming from the ends of your hair. It looks like you're filled with fire! Or maybe becoming a flame."

Liz averted her gaze, shocked that her true nature was so visible to him. "I'm just angry because it's important," she said, not wanting to talk about her challenges just yet.

Brandon wasn't the only one who wasn't fully in control of his powers, which wasn't the most reassuring realization possible.

Brandon looked at his fingernails. "Come to think of it, I haven't had to bother with them. I thought they were growing more slowly because it was winter."

There *was* a binding spell on Brandon. Who had cast it? What was the spellcaster's plan?

— from **Ember's Kiss**

Liz's spell to trap Chen is one of my favorite scenes in *Dragonfire*. Here's a bit of it:

To his surprise, Liz was outside of the circle she'd cast. There was a pillar of flame in front of her, and Brandon remembered her story.

This was her test! The mark on her arm was glowing red, lit by an inner fire. Garrett stood behind Liz, watching the flames with awe.

Liz visibly took a breath, then stepped forward, fearless and confident. Brandon could feel the rapid pounding of her heart, though, and knew she was afraid of failure. What could he do to help? Liz raised her arms before the column of crackling flames and recounted a spell. Brandon didn't understand her words or recognize the language, but he smiled as he felt the change in the air around him.

Air. She was proving her mastery over air first.

At Liz's command, the wind tore over the beach in silent fury, bending the trees to the ground and making the sand fly. It swirled around Liz and the column of fire, making sparks dance high into the air and Brandon's ears pop.

Liz spoke again and the wind calmed at her dictate, reverting to a gentle breeze.

Brandon was amazed by what she could do.

Air. She'd nailed air.

She swallowed, then gestured to the pillar of flame. She called another invocation. The flames grew higher and brighter, the column of fire turning to a pillar of white heat. Brandon shifted back to human form and stepped forward, wanting to be closer to her. He felt her heart skip because his did the same. She didn't look away from her task, her concentration intense. Brandon flung the crushed carcass of Chen into the flames, certain the old *Slayer* deserved no less than incineration, and went to her side.

He and Liz would both put their challenges behind themselves today, then step into their future together.

He smiled as Liz coaxed the fire to burn higher and hotter yet. It seemed to touch the sky or even become one with the sun. When the pillar of crackling flames was blinding in its heat and intensity, Liz spread her hands and spoke again. She steadily damped the flames until they were embers, glowing red in the sand.

She cast Brandon a proud smile, and he grinned at her.

Garrett clapped in approval.

Liz took a deep breath, and Brandon felt her confidence falter. He realized that she had addressed the elements that were easier for her first. He reached out and took her hand, not certain whether his touch would hamper or help her. She squeezed his fingers once, as if in gratitude, then walked around the pile of embers.

Was she choosing a cardinal point of the compass? Or just summoning her strength? Brandon wasn't certain, but he trusted Liz to know what she was doing.

The mark on her arm, after all, was half-gone. He could see that two of the points of the pentacle that had been emblazoned on her chest were flickering with golden light, too.

Those must be the elements she had proven herself able to command.

Brandon glanced back at the *Pyr*, who still stood frozen in the remnants of Liz's protective circle with their mates. He didn't like that they were snared like that, but didn't want to interfere with Liz's concentration by asking questions. Maybe only some people could witness the test of a Firedaughter.

He was glad to be one of them.

—from **Ember's Kiss**

KISS OF DANGER

THEY WILL SACRIFICE ANYTHING TO REGAIN THE LOVES THEY'VE LOST...

Alexander knew he had to fulfill his duty to his kind, the dragon shape shifters called the Pyr, even at the price of abandoning his new wife and young son. After he and his fellows were enchanted for centuries, then finally set free in a future long after their own time, Alexander feared he would never return to his love. Against all odds, the darkfire crystal makes his dream come true, flinging him across the centuries to the world he left behind. Is this his chance to regain the life he lost? Has Katina waited for him? Or has the darkfire crystal sent him back in time for some mysterious purpose of its own?

THE PROTAGONISTS

The Dragon Legion Novellas introduce time travel into the *Dragonfire Novels*. This seemed to me to be the ideal solution to the Dragon's Tooth Warriors recovering their destined mates, and the darkfire crystal made it possible. Alexander, Drake's second, had already experienced his firestorm and had a son, just like Drake, both of whom had been left in the past when the Dragon's Tooth Warriors were enchanted by Cadmus. For Alexander, there can be no other woman but Katina—but Katina, a pragmatic woman left alone with a young son, has married again by the time Alexander returns to her. The attraction between them is still combustive, but there are complications to be conquered for this second chance romance to have a happy ending.

THE ELEMENTS

Alexander's affinities are to fire and earth, a classic combination for a *Pyr* warrior. Katina is the second of the elemental witches to appear in the series: she's a WaterDaughter, a detail which Alexander did not know before his return. In fact, she had been brought to Delphi as an offering by her parents when she met

Alexander, because they feared they wouldn't be able to find her a husband, given her powers. Here's a passage about the reception of the water at the temple of Delphi, when Alexander and Katina arrive:

They continued in thoughtful silence to the Kastalian spring and Katina wondered if she were the only one feeling a tentative hope for the future. "We wash ourselves here," she told the boys. "To purify our bodies before we enter the temple."

"Isn't Kastalia a naiad?" Alexander asked quietly and Katina nodded. "Maybe she's the forebear of your kind."

Katina didn't know. It was difficult to learn much about her powers, since revealing her nature usually meant being ostracized by others and she'd been rejected at the shrine.

But when she reached for the water of the spring, it surged toward her like a tide. The water splashed high, sprinkling her, as if greeting her home.

"Did you do that?" Lysander asked, but Katina could only shake her head.

"The water recognized you," Alexander murmured and Katina thought he was probably right, even though nothing like that had ever happened to her before.

She reached into the water as if to embrace it and was startled to see a dozen women's faces in the water. They smiled at her, their hair streaming back over their shoulders and their voices as light as a rippling stream. "Welcome, sister," they said, and Katina realized that her companions hadn't heard them.

Welcome, sister.

When she raised handfuls of water to her face, the water caressed her skin like a thousand kisses.

Could her home be at Delphi?

—from **Kiss of Danger**

THE SETTING

The Dragon Legion novellas are sparked by the partial lunar eclipse of June 4, 2012. It's a partial eclipse because the Dragon's Tooth Warriors aren't entirely in our time. There's only one eclipse influencing these three stories because the Dragon Tooth

Warriors travel through time to their destined mates and even into other dimensions. In our time, the events in these stories take place in the blink of an eye.

THE PROPHECY

There are two prophecies in this story. The first is the one given to Katina's parents by the Pythia at Delphi, which indicated that she couldn't be offered to the shrine. The women who serve at the shrine remained virgins, but the prophecy spoke of the child Katina would bear:

> *Your future lies in fire and earth;*
> *the world's in the son you birth.*

When Katina and Alexander visit Delphi at the end of their story with their son Lysander and Theo, the Pythia offers this prophecy:

> *Evil must face its just defeat,*
> *By* Pyr *trained to soldiers elite.*
> *Apollo makes this task your price,*
> *A life of service will suffice.*
> *You, naiad-spawn, lost and found,*
> *Have gifts beyond any count.*
> *Here you will learn skills still unknown;*
> *Here you will bear sons more of your own;*
> *Here you and* Pyr *will live as one;*
> *Here you will lay future's cornerstone.*

Katina had believed her place was at Delphi in service, since she has borne that foretold son, but this prophecy reveals (to her satisfaction) that she should remain with Alexander.

THE STORY

Prologue: (Las Vegas, December 10, 2010) Salvatore dreams of the realm of the Wyvern, where all possible realities exist at the same time. He realizes he must pass on the darkfire crystal from the hoard he shares with his son, Lorenzo, to another. He sends out a summons via dreams, and when he wakes, retrieves the crystal from the hoard. While Lorenzo is waiting for Erik to visit him, a group of seventeen *Pyr* he cannot identify appears. The leader introduces himself as Drake and says they are the Dragon's Tooth Warriors. They have come for what was promised to them. Drake says they were summoned, but Lorenzo has no idea what he is talking about. Lorenzo asks them to wait while he deals with Erik, but when he returns to where he left them, the Dragon's Tooth Warriors are all gone. He checks on his father, thinking he might have had something to do with this, but he finds Salvatore sleeping, as always.

Chapter 1: Alexander, Drake, and the other Dragon's Tooth Warriors, prepare themselves for being pulled through time yet again by the darkfire crystal. The puzzling phenomenon has occurred four times, the first right after they acquired the crystal. Drake insists they are the guardians of the crystal so getting rid of it is not an option. Those standing close by all end up traveling together, but they are losing men at each location. There are now only twelve of their company left. After deciding to call themselves the Dragon Legion, the darkfire flashes brilliantly and they are all sent to another place and time. When they get their bearings, Alexander realizes they are in his old village. His only thought is to see his wife, Katina. As he goes to find her, following her scent, the crystal activates again, and he runs further away, to make sure he is not taken along with the rest of the Dragon Legion. Katina, working on a clay pot, thinks of the oracle's words from many years ago, which led to her life with Alexander. She still thinks of him all of the time, and still wears his ring, but is surprised when he shows up at her door. The two are still very attracted to one another and end up having sex in Katina's bed.

Chapter 2: Katina then tells Alexander he needs to leave because she has remarried. He is shocked to learn he has been gone eight years, and Katina though he was dead. His son, Lysander, was just that day taken into service in the Spartan army. She and Lysander would have starved if Cetos hadn't married her, despite the rumors about her. Katina resists telling Alexander her own secret and leaves to meet her husband in the courtyard. As Cetos approaches his home, he is pleased that he has sold Katina's son to a merchant. He plans to get Katina pregnant to provide him with his own son. Alexander, hiding in the bedroom, catches a bothersome scent, though he doesn't understand how he could since *Slayer*s do not yet exist in this time, Alexander resolves to be sure of Katina's safety or to free her. When Cetos finds out Lysander is already gone, thereby killing his deal with the merchant, he gets violent, grabbing Katina by the hair and throwing her down. As he is about to hit her, an ebony dragon appears. Cetos releases Katina, who runs away. After breathing fire on Cetos, the dragon grabs Katina and takes to the sky. Katina is wary but understands the dragon means her no harm. Alexander does not regret his actions, but fears he may be required to pay for them with more years of service. He feels he must have been sent back to that time to reunite with his mate. The merchant arrives to collect Lysander and finds Cetos lying on the ground badly burned. When the man learns the boy is gone, he becomes angry, and then seemingly disappears. A yellow dragon then appears, and with flames in its eyes, asks Cetos where the boy may be. After he tells him it could be Sparta or Delphi, the dragon breathes fire on him, attacks the other people there, and flies off with another boy.

Chapter 3: Flying with the dragon, Katina wonders if Alexander got away. The dragon surprises her by speaking to her, and she realizes he and Alexander are one and the same. She asks to see him change, and though he warns it may make her go mad, Katina insists. She now feels she can share her own secret with Alexander, when the time is right. Katina wants to go away with Alexander, but he says he must consult the Pythia at Delphi to learn the appropriate course of action. Katina learns Lysander is also *Pyr*. As they fly off, Katina notices Alexander is missing a scale on his chest. Meanwhile, Alexander smells *Slayer*. He explains a bit to Katina about *Pyr* and *Slayer*s, then they spot a yellow dragon, which Alexander knows is Jorge. A soldier is battling the dragon— defending a boy. Alexander and Katina realize the two in danger are Lysander and Pelias, Alexander's friend who came to retrieve Lysander. Alexander distracts Jorge while Katina gets Lysander away. Pelias manages to stab Jorge. Alexander and Jorge fight, with Alexander getting the better of the *Slayer* until he forms a dragonsmoke tendril to draw power. He targets another young boy—Drake's son, Theo. Jorge says he killed the boy's mother, and he plans to go after all of the sons of the Dragon's Tooth Warriors. Lysander tells his mother Pelias told him about who and what he is, and about the other boy. Lysander sees Jorge with a scale, and then Alexander is on the ground bleeding, alternating between forms. Lysander rushes toward him.

Chapter 4: While Alexander seems to have the upper hand in his fight with Jorge, the *Slayer* shows him a dark scale, which he crushes, sending Alexander into paroxysms of pain. He realizes the scale is his, lost at Katina's when he returned to her. To protect Lysander, Alexander forms a dragonsmoke tendril of his own to turn Jorge's back toward him. As Jorge sucks out his power and his life, Alexander suggests to Jorge he should return to his own time to face Chen while he is strong. Jorge agrees and disappears. Pelias makes a conduit to Alexander, gifting his own life force to save him. Before he dies, Pelias instructs Lysander to gather all of the pieces of the broken scale and keep them safe until they are needed. Alexander awakens, finding out Pelias' fate, and he is shaken. He didn't know the man was *Pyr*, as he'd always denied it. Alexander explains to Katina about needing to expose Pelias to the four elements. When they lack any water, she says she can help with that. Katina then demonstrates her Waterdaughter ability she has kept secret, awing both her husband and her son. On the way to Delphi, Alexander tells Lysander the story of how Apollo avenged the death of his mother by the dragon Pytho, by killing it and leaving the body in a crevasse. The fumes cause visions in those of purity, hence the Pythia oracle. Apollo had to spend eight years in service to mankind for his transgression against Pytho in his home. Katina understands Alexander fears this may be his fate, even though he did not kill Cetos. Alexander tells Lysander he will learn about his abilities and how to control them in Delphi.

Chapter 5: Alexander, Katina, and the boys rent a room on their way to Delphi. Alexander asks Katina if Theo can stay with them. She agrees, and says she will take care of him even if Alexander has to leave. He also tells her about what happened to him, the enchantment and how it changed all of them. They make love again. When they arrive in Delphi, Katina remembers the prophecy told to her many years ago and suggests perhaps Alexander represents the fire she needs. He says in the future the *Pyr* and their mates each have two affinities apiece, thus making a whole. The Pythia makes her pronouncement, saying Alexander will remain there training young *Pyr*, as will Katina, so she can nurture her own abilities. As the Pythia moves to heal Theo, time is frozen and Jorge appears as a salamander, attempting to bite the boy. Alexander's dragonfire has no effect on the *Slayer*, but darkfire flashes out of his talon toward Jorge, and Jorge vanishes. A firestorm is then rekindled between Alexander and Katina. The Pythia mends Alexander's scale, acting as a Smith, using fire and Katina's ring to hold the scale in place. The assembled young *Pyr* hail their new leader.

DEBORAH'S COMMENTS

I am a sucker for a second-chance romance, which is what Katina and Alexander have in this story. These two are a good pair: Alexander is a warrior who keeps his word (my favorite kind) while Katina is a woman unafraid to find solutions to her own predicament. I like that she doesn't need to be saved—and I love that she first shows Alexander her abilities as a Waterdaughter so that he can perform the *Pyr* death ritual for his mentor, Pelias. That's teamwork.

Alexander was incredulous.

He watched as Katina lifted her hands over her head and closed her eyes. She was as graceful and elegant as ever, but to his amazement, her figure began to ripple. He thought his eyes deceived him, but the rippling grew more emphatic. She was murmuring some chant that sounded like the dancing of a brook over stones and with every passing moment, her figure looked more fluid.

More silvery.

More ethereal.

Her hair seemed to flow around her body like a dark river, one that ran far past her hips. As he watched, her form became disguised by a column of water, a pillar that bubbled at its top and stretched toward the sky. Or had she become the water? Alexander couldn't tell, but he saw the water pooling on the ground where Katina's feet had been. It ran over the dry soil. He heard the distant rumble of thunder and watched dark clouds conjure themselves from the clear sky. They rolled closer with remarkable speed, converging from every direction in a way that wasn't natural at all. The storm clouds collided overhead, tumbling into each other where the pillar of water reached into the sky.

There was a crack of lightning and the first drops of rain fell.

—from **Kiss of Danger**

KISS OF DARKNESS

THEY WILL SACRIFICE ANYTHING TO REGAIN THE LOVES THEY'VE LOST...

Damien, the Heartbreaker of the dragon warriors called the Pyr, can't forget Petra, the only woman who could both captivate him and destroy him. He's haunted by their firestorm, the prophecy that compelled him to leave her—and her subsequent death. When the darkfire crystal takes the Dragon Legion to the underworld, Damien seizes the chance to save his son. To his surprise he finds Petra just as enticing as ever...and still pregnant. When his kiss makes their baby stir to life again, they both hope for a different future. Can they learn from the past and trust each other? Even if they solve the riddle of the prophecy, will they be able to escape the underworld, save their son and claim the promise of the firestorm?.

THE PROTAGONISTS

Dragon Legion Warrior Damien has no desire to ever commit to one woman, but Petra is an elemental witch who makes him re-think what he believes he knows, as well as stealing his heart away forever. This is a second chance romance with a secret baby.

THE ELEMENTS

Damien's abilities are to fire and air, while Petra's are to earth and water. Petra is an Earthdaughter, and like Alexander before him, Damien didn't know about his destined mate's powers before the darkfire crystal reunited them. Petra's affinities are to earth. In fact, as an Earthdaughter, she has a very strong connection to that element.

THE SETTING

Damien follows Petra to the underworld of Greek myth. He doesn't do it willingly, but once he's there, we see his true nature.

DEBORAH COOKE

And yes, I love that he's afraid of snakes.

This is the first *Dragonfire* story to take place in an alternate realm.

THE PROPHECY

A lost child mourned for many years;
A mother who will shed no tears;
A dragon warrior turned to stone;
A woman abandoned, all alone.
Firestorm's promise will fade to naught,
Until stone and fire pay death's cost
After a Pyr sacrifice is made,
Destiny's promise can be claimed.

THE STORY

Chapter 1: The Dragon Legion Warriors find themselves in another unknown place and time thanks to the darkfire crystal. Damien thinks they are likely in southern Europe, and from the style of people's clothing, he thinks they may be in Italy in the 1970s. Only eight of the men remain. The conversation turns to the crystal, and Thad suggests the crystal is taking the Legion members to either their past or future mates. Not long after, a firestorm ignites between Orion and a woman across the square. The others encourage Orion to get far enough away from the crystal as it brightens again. The other seven men are transported to a place Damien recognizes—Hades. He knows his mate Petra must be there, with their son, whom he plans to take back with him. He steps into Charon's boat, and the others disappear. Damien needs to figure out how to get past the hellhound, Cerberus, and get out of Hades alive. Petra finds being dead, and in Hades, boring. She is perpetually full-term pregnant, and she is angry at Damien for leaving her. Suddenly she sees some flashes of blue-green sparks and decides to follow them. To her amazement, she sees Damien standing in Charon's boat. He comes face-to-face with Cerberus, and tries to change to his dragon form. Damien doesn't understand why he can't shift, but he tries to fight

182

Cerberus in human form. After the hellhound wounds him, Damien hears Petra begin to sing, which puts Cerberus to sleep. Petra tells Damien she knew she couldn't speak to him until he shed blood. Damien asks for his son, but then he sees she's still pregnant. Damien picks Petra up and carries her over to the boat.

Chapter 2: Petra thinks he is only interested in their son, not her, so she kicks him in his wound. She gets away and runs. A blue-green light crackles and forms an orb of light ahead of her, into which she can't stop herself from running. Damien follows her, and they are thrust into the past, reliving the night they met, the night of their firestorm. Damien and Orion are in a tavern where a beautiful woman is singing, and it becomes apparent Damien is having his firestorm with her. She sings to him and then they go outside. Damien tells her about the firestorm, and his being *Pyr*. She has heard the stories and is thrilled to learn they are true. She wishes to see him change and to go flying. Back in Hades, Damien notices Petra is now lifelike in her coloring. Damien says he wishes to save her and their son, but she says it's too late. Damien admits he's afraid of her. As an Earthdaughter, she can change people to stone. She did so in the past, but she says she only put the village in that state to protect him, as they were about to capture him. She left them that way only a day and a night before releasing them. Petra asks Damien if he's still a dragon, and when he responds that he can't shift, she says everyone has to sacrifice something when they come to Hades. Damien wonders if Petra has also lost her powers, thinking that might be for the best. He asks why she took the ferry to Hades early, but Petra says she didn't— his son was too stubborn to be born.

Chapter 3: Though Petra feels alive again, Damien appears to be losing color and fading away. She needs to get him out of Hades very soon. Damien explains the darkfire, and she feels it means they are being given a second chance—especially since she can feel the baby move again, though she does not tell Damien. Petra tells Damien she wants a true partnership with him if he wants them to be together. He realizes what she proposes is what the future *Pyr* have with their partners. He asks her to show him her powers, and Petra does so, making the ground vibrate, and creatures of darkness appear. Petra becomes afraid when the baby stops moving, but he kicks and she knows all is well. When Damien tries to reach Petra, a crevasse opens and he falls into it. He wakes up in a forest of trees with people trapped inside, and memories take over. Damien relives the memory of returning home to Petra and finding the villagers turned to stone. He learned some of what she could do, and told her of the prophecy he had been given (which mentioned a dragon warrior turned to stone). Damien now realizes the prophecy was not about Petra turning him to stone, but about the viper doing so. He sees a woman ahead of him, she looks like a monster and attacks him. After an intense fight, Damien prevails, leaving the lifeless body of the creature on the ground. Petra arrives and is alarmed.

Chapter 4: The monster was one of the Erinyes, half-divine creatures who torture the dead undeserving of rest, leading Petra to believe they must be in Tartarus. Damien tells Petra about his mother having enslaved his father with a potion. He also explains that he and the others were enchanted for so long. Petra tells Damien she took the ferry to seek out the Mothers for help when the baby stopped moving. She also confesses she invoked the Erinyes in her anger. Damien asks Petra to be his partner, to leave with him, and they realize they must petition Hades. The darkfire seems to have left them, so they know they are on their own. They must cross the River Leche to get to Hades on the other side of Tartarus. As they make their way through the snake-infested waters, Damien talks about the belief of the contemporary *Pyr* that they should make a permanent bond with the women who bear their children, since it makes them a stronger unit. In front of him, Petra stumbles and falls into the water. Petra relives the memory of her drowning and invoking the Erinyes in her despair. Damien kisses her several times in hopes of reigniting the darkfire to revive her, and it works. When she awakens, they both say they love each other. They see the other two Erinyes coming toward them from the sky. At that moment, Petra's water breaks, signaling the beginning of labor. Though Petra tells the Erinyes she invoked them in error, they still want vengeance on Damien for having killed their sister. Hades himself appears, and the group has now moved to the stone tree forest. Hades demands more in recompense than Damien's apology for the dead Erinyes. He revives Tisiphone and sends her to the world of the living, where she may exact her vengeance upon her murderer and his kind. Petra and Damien realize they must escape and warn the other *Pyr*. While she labors, Petra uses her powers to crack open the ground and the realm above them. Damien, now able to shift into his dragon form, picks up Petra and they fly through the opening. She notices he is missing a scale on his chest and that his scales have changed to gold with green tips. Petra asks to be taken to the Mothers, an area of standing stones on a peak.

Chapter 5: At first confused, Damien finally realizes that the stones contain women. Petra tells him they are the Earthdaughters who, "never met a man who was more than a man." The Mothers guide both Petra and Damien through the birth of their son. The baby has blond hair, as does Damien now, due to his visit to the Underworld. Petra suggests they name him Orion, after Damien's good friend. A snake approaches, drops something in the grass, and then leaves. Petra finds a scale. Damien explains the scale falling off means that he has fallen in love. He says they need to go to Delphi to have his armor repaired, but then senses the approach of Alexander and other *Pyr*. Petra meets Alexander and Katina, as well as Lysander and Theo. After the ceremony to replace Damien's scale, a flash of darkfire touches baby Orion, leaving a small mark on his arm like the one his father has. When Damien says Orion is "one of us," Petra knows he is also one of her kind and looks forward to the future.

DEBORAH'S COMMENTS

Damien appears at first to be similar to Donovan, in that he seems to be a warrior who thinks love is for other people. The truth is more complex, though, because Damien's heart has already been surrendered to Petra. He's lost his true love and knows there will never be another woman to hold his heart—he just doesn't admit that detail to anyone else. Petra is hard on Damien, unafraid to speak her mind or make her accusations, but he needs someone who isn't easily charmed by him. I love that the Earthdaughters have customs of their own, including giving birth in the circle of the Mothers, as Petra does:

Damien shifted back to his human form in time to watch Petra endure another contraction. It was hard to watch her in such pain, yet he felt lucky to be in her presence. He was amazed that his son might be saved, after all, and terrified that the infant might not survive. It seemed that Petra always prompted a mix of emotions in him, all powerful, all impressive. He watched as Petra clenched her teeth at the pain and he hoped their son would arrive quickly. She was panting when this one was completed, her fingers dug into the moss and sweat on her brow.

Damien tried to distract her with a comment.

"You knew that spring would spout," he said as he knelt beside her.

"It's the gift of the Mothers," Petra said, gesturing again to the circle of stones around them.

Damien barely spared the stones a glance. If she wanted to call stones by a particular name, that was fine by him. He was more concerned that he knew nothing about the arrival of children and they were on an isolated mountaintop.

Surely he couldn't make another mistake that would cost him Petra?

"This is where you intended to come?" he asked as she caught her breath.

"I thought it superstition that Earthdaughters should give birth in the presence of the Mothers. I thought the rules didn't apply, not if I'd found a man who was more than a man."

"But when the baby stilled..."

Petra nodded. "I feared that I'd broken the rules. I tried to come here then."

Damien took her hand, because he didn't know what else to do. He tried to hide his concern and speak calmly. "But Petra, we're on the top of a mountain and I know nothing about the birth of children. Should I find someone to help?"

"The Mothers are here," Petra said through her teeth. He could tell from her expression that another contraction was coming.

"But..."

Petra cast him a smile. "Look, Damien. *Look* at the forebears of my kind."

And Damien looked. To his astonishment, he saw faces in the standing stones that surrounded them. Women. Old women. Wise women. Kindly women. As the next contraction ripped through her, Petra gripped his hand hard. Damien saw that the Mothers had moved closer, as if they bent over one of their own. He could see concern in those frozen faces, a concern that hadn't been there a moment before.

He looked at Petra in amazement.

She laughed a little at him. "You think you have all the marvels?" she teased and he was embarrassed that he had thought as much. "They come out of their stones for a birth," she said, bracing herself for another contraction. "They ensure that all is well. I can see them and those of my kind can see them." She spared him a look, then asked a quick question. "Can you see them?"

Damien smiled. "It's like the stones are melting," he whispered. "They're breaking free of the rock."

"The Mothers are eternal," Petra winced.

"But what are they? Why are they like this?" He had to wonder if this would be Petra's fate, and as much as she held the Mothers in esteem, he hoped not.

"They are Earthdaughters who never met a man who was more than a man."

Damien's gaze locked with hers. "And what of those who do?"

Petra smiled tightly. "Who would sacrifice a partnership like ours to become a standing stone?" Damien had only a heartbeat to smile at that, then Petra screamed as the next contraction ripped through her body.

Damien saw the stones move even closer, one bending over on either side of Petra. When he narrowed his eyes, he could see the forms of elderly women, their hair grey and their faces lined, their eyes filled with the wisdom of the ages. When he strained his ears, he could hear them murmuring, like pebbles falling into a crevasse.

He knew they were advising Petra, because she nodded and smiled at them, following their instructions. He sat back and simply witnessed the birth of his son, within the circle of the Mothers, so wise and kind and giving.

—from **Kiss of Darkness**

KISS OF DESTINY

THEY WILL SACRIFICE ANYTHING TO REGAIN THE LOVES THEY'VE LOST...

When the darkfire crystal takes the dragon shape shifters Thad and Drake to an unknown location, only fulfilling his firestorm matters to Thad. Little does he know that in following its light to his destined mate, he's stepping into the realm of the gods, a place so forbidden to mortals that any who enter it must die. Aura has always been skeptical of long-term promises—but Thad is irresistible. No sooner does Aura surrender than the gods demand their due of her dragon shifter. Can she save Thad and make the dream of the firestorm come true?

THE PROTAGONISTS

Like Damien, Thad is taken to another realm by the darkfire crystal. He is the last of the Dragon Legion warriors to leave Drake, but neither of them perceive that he has a choice when the firestorm sparks. The firestorm leads Thad to Mount Olympus and a nymph who steals his heart away.

THE ELEMENTS

Aura is an Airdaughter, and her association with the element of air is closely linked to her ability as a nymph. She can appear and disappear at will, become a breeze, and evade a dragon shifter if she so chooses. Thad's affinities are to fire and earth, making him a practical dragon shifter who is prepared to solve riddles—like how to convince his destined mate to trust him.

THE SETTING

Thad and Aura's firestorm is set in the realm of the Greek gods, Mount Olympus and the Garden of the Hesperides. These are mythic locations, but their descriptions in **Kiss of Destiny** are evocative of the lands around the Mediterranean. Hera's garden, for example, could be in modern Morocco.

THE PROPHECY

Across the centuries and the years,
You will wait and shed your tears,
Until the darkfire is freed again,
Your vengeance can cause the Pyr no pain.
I close the portal, for once and all,
To see those I love out of your thrall.
When darkfire will burn once again,
Your sister's death can be avenged.
When daughters of all elements are mates
Then will the dragons face their fates.

THE STORY

Prologue: Drake and Thad sit on the edge of a fountain in a park, likely in a twenty-first-century American city. They are the only two Legion members remaining. Thad insists the darkfire has a purpose for where it takes them, but Drake is still not convinced. While he would like to see his son again, he wonders if he and Cassandra would be happy together now. Once again the crystal lights up, moving Drake and Thad somewhere new. Very pleased, Thad begins to experience his firestorm and says goodbye to his leader and friend. Drake is moved yet again and realizes from the scent he is on Erik's roof. The darkfire appears completely extinguished, leading Drake to believe the crystal's mission is now over, and Drake's place is with Erik.

Chapter 1: Thrilled to be having his firestorm, Thad shifts to his dragon form as he follows the sparks toward his partner. He never knew his own father, in part because the attitudes at that time did not typically view the firestorm as meaning anything other than procreation. Thad hopes to build something more with his own event. Aura wonders about the sparks surrounding her, especially as they seem to be associated with lust. Then she sees, in her mind, a handsome man smiling at her. As a nymph she should be able to disperse the sparks, but they won't cooperate. Her vision of the man becomes increasingly erotic, and then she sees him change into a dragon. When the dragon arrives and changes into his human form, he and Aura are drawn to one another, and they kiss. He explains they are experiencing a firestorm, and says when they create their son, the sparks will fade. Aura wants nothing to do with having a child, and after telling Thad so, she disappears. He resolves to follow her and convince her they belong together. Aura joins her fellow nymphs in a glade on Mount Olympus, hoping to find out if anyone else has ever been part of a firestorm. The gathered women discuss —a tale they heard of a man who came to the Underworld to take his lover back, and she was an Earthdaughter. Aura finds herself impressed by the dedication of the man who risked so much for the woman. Thad finds Aura, and he tells her what he is and the *Pyr*'s purpose. He says he wants to remain with her and the child as partners. She demonstrates some of her powers, asking him if it matters. He says no and asks her to be with him. She tells him to catch her, then takes a whirlwind to the clouds. Thad follows.

Chapter 2: Aura races through the sky as a breeze, deciding she will take him to the Garden of the Hesperides to eat a golden apple, compelling him to tell her the truth. When Thad gets closer, he tells her he most admires the *Pyr* who stay with their mates. Aura remains somewhat skeptical due to her own mother's experience. She asks Thad to accompany her somewhere, and he agrees. Thad knows what the garden is and is aware of different stories about the apples. Suddenly, a large green dragon with nine heads attacks. Aura tries to get him to stop, saying Thad is her friend, but the dragon, whom Thad realizes must be Ladon, the guardian of the apples, says only nymphs are allowed in the garden, by order of Hera. Ladon attacks and Thad fights back, But Aura tells him not to kill Ladon, as Hera would then curse him. As they battle, Ladon is surprised to learn Thad is *Pyr*, since he is only a dragon, not a shifter. Ladon is curious about the firestorm, telling Aura the *Pyr*'s most valued treasure is their mate. He then taunts Thad a bit about Cadmus, and shortly thereafter Thad tells Aura what happened with the viper, and about being a Dragon's Tooth Warrior. Thad agrees to eat of an apple and insists he means everything he has said to her. Convinced, Aura agrees to satisfy the firestorm. Jorge is tired of the darkfire moving him around, but is pleased to find himself in the garden where a firestorm is taking place, meaning a human will also be nearby. Then he catches the scent of Viv Jason

Chapter 3: While Thad believes the firestorm will lead to conception, the apple showed Aura there was not a child in her future. She feels free to be with him, and they satisfy the firestorm in the garden. Meanwhile, in Chicago, June 1, 2012, Erik is restless, keeping an eye on Drake, who has not woken or moved in three days. Through his connection to each of the *Pyr*, he can tell they are all on edge. He sees a bright light, a fireball of sorts, in his mind, and doesn't understand what it means. Back in the ancient world, a sick pilgrim stops on his way to the garden to petition Hera to heal him. He notices a woman who seems thirsty, and he offers her his water. They talk, and she stays with him when he coughs up blood, saying she will tell him a story. When Thad wakes, he sees a spark when he kisses Aura's forehead, and realizes the firestorm has not yet been sated. She tells him she knew she wasn't going to have his son, explaining she sees the future. She asks him what he wants more: her or the child. At first, he says he wants both, but after thinking about Rafferty and his union, Thad decides he should love his partner even though she cannot get pregnant. He wants to learn why Aura does not want children. She says she will tell him a story if they go to a particular tree outside the garden. When they take flight, a scale falls off of Thad's chest and lands in Aura's hand. Aura tells the story of a nymph tricked and raped by Zeus, whom Hera takes pity on. She offers to raise the daughter the nymph would bear and then turns the nymph into a tree to keep her safe from men. Thad finishes the story himself in old-speak, understanding Aura is the daughter, and she has brought the *Pyr* to meet her mother.

Chapter 4: Aura and Thad arrive at the tree, where they also see the sick pilgrim and the cloaked woman, who Aura knows is really Hera. Suddenly another woman appears and attacks Thad with a knife. She turns into a winged hag, accusing the *Pyr* of killing Tisiphone. Jorge, in his salamander form, is very interested in the disease the dying pilgrim suffers from. Since he can't identify what the sickness is, it will be especially deadly in the twenty-first century. He plans to hitch a ride to the future with Viv, along with a part of the sick man to spread the disease. Thad and the creature battle, and she mentions Damien. Then he smells *Slayer* and sees a yellow salamander headed for the sick pilgrim. Thad leaves the fight to make his way to Jorge. Aura watches the salamander become a large yellow dragon who fights Thad. Aura offers herself to the hag she believes is Tisiphone. Before the creature can kill her, Hera intervenes and forbids the action,. There is a flash of blue-green light, and Jorge tears off the dying pilgrim's arm. Hera utters a command, changing the hag back into the red-headed woman. Hera closes the portal until the darkfire is freed again and when daughters of all of the elements are *Pyr* mates. When the Erinys gets banished, Jorge hitches a ride via the darkfire, and ends up in Seattle in his dragon form. Jorge flies through the air, dripping blood from the infected arm over the city, being filmed by many humans,. He then leaves to get Chen to help with his plan. Tisiphone finds herself in an unfamiliar place and time and takes on the form of the red-haired woman once again. A woman with dark hair and red lips, wearing a silver bracelet in the shape of a snake, introduces herself as Viv Jason. She offers to help Tisiphone, who goes along with her, thinking the woman may be useful. Hera heals the pilgrim makes him a caretaker in her garden. Aura asks Hera if she can also heal Thad, but the goddess says only his own people can help him. She tells Aura she cannot complete the firestorm with him since she is immortal, so Aura asks to be made mortal. She wants to be an Airdaughter so she will still have powers to work together with Thad. Hera changes her, and Aura realizes the firestorm is gone and knows she must be pregnant. She then uses old-speak to try to contact the *Pyr* to help Thad.

Chapter 5: Erik and Eileen watch the various recordings of Jorge in Seattle, noticing the flash of darkfire preceding his appearance. Neither can figure out what he is doing, or why. The next evening, Alexander and Damien, as well as Katina and Petra, arrive at Aura and Thad's location. The *Pyr* give Thad some of their life force to heal him. Aura mentions his missing scale, and the other women tell her only she can replace it. Thad learns Aura became mortal for him. When Alexander wonders how they can help the *Pyr* of the future, Thad says they are doing so already by providing an army. Damien suggests they can mark the flesh of their sons so they can be identified down the line. Now awake, Drake sits with Erik and tells him what he knows and remembers. Eileen and Zoë arrive, and Zoë gives Drake a picture of two men sitting by the fountain where he and Thad had last been. Erik heads to his front door, just before a knock sounds. A few dozen unfamiliar *Pyr* are there, the one in front introducing them as descendants of the Dragon Legion. The leader is descended from Drake's son Theo, and also named Theo. He shows Erik a paper with Hera's prophecy written on it. Erik says, "So, it is time." Meanwhile, the ceremony to replace Thad's scale takes place, and Aura has a vision that she and Thad will have twins.

DEBORAH'S COMMENTS

One of my sources of inspiration for *Dragonfire* were the many stories about dragons in various cultures around the world. I enjoyed digging into Greek myth for the adventures of the Dragon Legion, including the story of Cadmus (in **Harmonia's Kiss**), Pythia (in **Kiss of Danger**), and Ladon in this story.

He was over the trees, preparing to land, when another dragon erupted from the shadows of the orchard below.

The dragon was of deepest green, and he had nine heads, each of which was breathing fire at Thad. His eyes could have been burning coals and his talons were as sharp as knives. There was something of a snake in his agility and form, and Thad knew instinctively that he was ancient.

The other dragon had surprise on his side. He had latched a talon on to Thad's tail before the *Pyr* could respond.

Ladon, Thad realized. This must be Ladon, the guardian of the golden apples, and another myth come to life.

—from **Kiss of Destiny**

Aura is also the fourth and last of our elemental witches, accounting for the final element. In mystical thought, the union of four elements invokes a fifth element—often spirit—which is an idea prevalent in Dragonfire with the union between Pyr and mate bringing all four affinities together. In this story, the fourth elemental witch to mate with a *Pyr* after a firestorm brings another change to the world of my dragon shifters: many more warriors of their kind.

Drake was on his feet in a moment, knowing something was wrong but unable to name it. Before he could speak, Erik's eyes flew open and he stared at the door. He crossed the room with long strides, and Drake guessed that he had felt a breach of his dragonsmoke barrier.

There was a knock at the door. Erik inhaled deeply, frowned, then cast open the door.

The corridor was filled with unfamiliar men, young and vigorous men who held themselves with determination. There had to be three or four dozen of them.

They were *Pyr*. Drake stood behind Erik and breathed deeply, not believing his own senses. How could there be so many *Pyr* of whom he knew nothing?

"We are the descendants of the Dragon Legion," said the *Pyr* in front. He tugged up his shirt sleeve, showing a tattoo on his upper arm that was the same as the tattoo Drake and his men had gotten as a sign of solidarity. Drake considered the young man with wonder, liking the intelligence that shone in his dark eyes. "I am named Theo, for my forebear, the son of Stephanos who became Drake," he said, his words startling Drake. "We come to pledge ourselves to the leader of the *Pyr*, Erik Sorensson, as we pledged to our fathers, who pledged the same to their fathers and their fathers before them."

"So this is what I sensed," Erik said, almost under his breath.

Theo offered a piece of paper. "We surrender to you this prophecy, made millenia ago but for these times. We have kept it in trust, preserved it and awaited the moment it should be revealed." He handed an envelope to Erik.

Erik opened the envelope and removed a sheet of paper. Drake could see that it had eight lines of script, though he couldn't quite read the words. Erik read it in old-speak.

"Across the centuries and the years,

You will wait and shed your tears,
Until the darkfire is freed again;
Your vengeance can cause Pyr *no pain.*
I close the portal, for once and all,
To see those I love out of your thrall.
When darkfire will burn once again,
Your sister's death can be avenged.
When daughters of all elements are mates
Then will the dragons face their fate."

"So, it is time," Erik said aloud. He offered his hand to Theo. "Welcome, Theo. Welcome to you and all your company. Please, cross my dragonsmoke and share your tidings with us." He turned and indicated Drake with a slight smile. "This is Drake, who was Stephanos. He has been weary, but I think you may bring him joy."

Against Drake's every expectation, a son of his line stood before him. Theo smiled and there was a gleam of tears in his eyes. He stepped forward and gave a crisp salute. "I have always dreamed of meeting you. It is an honor beyond all, sir."

"Not sir," Drake said hoarsely. He took Theo's hand and shook it, liking the firmness of this young man's grip. "I would have you call me Drake." And then he embraced Theo, glad beyond belief that the darkfire had brought him this gift.

—from **Kiss of Destiny**

SERPENT'S KISS

ONE SPARK CAN BANISH EVERY SHADOW IN HIS HEART...

The dragon shape shifter Thorolf is known for an impressive lineage, raw power in battle, and the impulsive indulgence of his appetites. The last has made him an outcast from his fellow Pyr, *and even his hunt for their dangerous opponent, the* Slayer Chen, *hasn't helped. Seduced by Chen's ally Viv Jason, Thorolf finds himself drawn into a trap, as bait to lure his fellow* Pyr *to extinction. The only one to come to his aid is a woman he already knows to be a thief—does he dare to trust her with not just his own life but the survival of his kind?*

Chandra has planned for centuries for a battle against evil that she knows will determine the world's future. She's never wasted time on the pleasures of the physical realm, much less experienced passion—until the firestorm sparks between herself and Thorolf, demanding more from her than she ever expected to give. Will the firestorm provide new power, or be a dangerous distraction that gives Chen the chance to triumph over the Pyr *forever?*

THE PROTAGONISTS

Thorolf is old and powerful, and his firestorm challenges all of his assumptions. The woman he trusts—Viv Jason—proves to be bent on the destruction of the *Pyr* as well as in league with Chen, the *Slayer*. Thorolf's mate Chandra is a goddess who can change shape herself and challenges him to give more of himself.

THE ELEMENTS

Thorolf's affinities are to fire and air. He's been targeted by Chen for his affinity to air and is known for his fighting abilities and his passion. Chandra's affinities prove to be to earth and water, perhaps indicating both her blunt manner and the fluidity of her appearance.

THE SETTING

Thorolf's firestorm is sparked by the first of the four blood moons that mark the end of the moon's node in the Dragon's Tail. This total lunar eclipse occurred on April 15, 2014, and Thorolf was in Bangkok. In a strange twist of fiction and reality, there was civil unrest in Bangkok during this eclipse.

THE PROPHECY

A union of five will tip the scale
When the moon aligns in Dragon's Tail;
This Pyr *alliance can defeat the scheme*
And cheat the Slayer *of his dream.*
Fulfilling a pledge long been made
Will put darkness in its grave.
Know Pyr *and* Slayer *can share on curse:*
A vulnerability wrought of their birth.
Keep the pledge and defeat the foe,
So the Dragon's Tail brings triumph not woe.

THE STORY

Prologue: (Chicago, June 15, 2012) Erik senses something bad is going to happen and fortifies his dragonsmoke barrier in his home. Drake has left with the new *Pyr* recruits to train them. Sickness is spreading in Seattle in the area where Jorge in his dragon form spread the diseased blood. Erik goes to check on JP, the *Slayer* who remains imprisoned in an apartment downstairs. Erik realizes something is wrong, and then sees Chen, in one of his human forms, disappearing with JP. When Erik checks all of the *Pyr* to make sure they are okay, he can't find/sense Thorolf. He feels guilty he hasn't kept up with Thorolf. Erik finds a large spiral burned into the apartment floor, the same design as the brand on JP's neck. He steps into the area and immediately realizes his mistake, as he is unable to move. Chen taunts Erik via old-speak, saying he could take him then if he wanted. All he needs is the element of air. Thorolf wakes in his room in Bangkok, very sore, to find a huge snake in bed next to him. The snake bites him, its venom acting as a paralytic. Thorolf hears Chen's laughter and worries Chen could use the brand to enslave him. Niall walks in the dream of an unknown *Pyr,* one who witnesses the death of a woman named Astrid and blames the *Pyr* for her death. Niall will experience the same basic dream, with variations, for twenty-two months.

Chapter 1: (Bangkok, April 15, 2014) Thorolf walks through the streets of the city, and can't figure out why the area just doesn't look like it did the night before. His skin burns all over, and he finds spirals have been traced all over him, including over his existing tattoo from Rox. An eclipse begins, and Thorolf can feel the effects of a firestorm, but he thought the next one was a couple of years away. Thorolf worries about Viv's safety if both *Pyr* and *Slayer*s come to the area, and has thoughts of Astrid and her death. Racing up to his apartment, which also looks odd, Thorolf finds a man who won't tell him where Viv is. He starts choking the strange guy, but suddenly, he feels the heat of the firestorm very close. Then he sees the thief from an earlier encounter climb through the window. Apparently, the thief wasn't a boy, after all. When the woman gets closer and touches his forehead, Thorolf realizes it is his own firestorm he's feeling, with the thief. She tells him the man he is holding does not know anything so Thorolf lets him go. Thorolf kisses the woman, who changes images countless times, the variety pleasing him. Then someone hits him in the back of the head. Chandra is annoyed at Thorolf for having delayed the completion of her quest by disappearing for almost two years, as had Viv Jason. Unused to the level of physical lust she is experiencing around the *Pyr*, Chandra is grateful the man knocked him out. She decides to take Thorolf to her sanctuary to find out what he knows of Viv and her plans. To keep the apartment resident from calling the police, Chandra concocts a story to explain Thorolf's anger and the appearance of sparks between them. Then she throws his phone out of the window, and Thorolf and Chandra leave.

Chapter 2: As they try to get away, Chandra varies between her vow of chastity and the desire to give in to her lust. A police officer and several people, including the guy from the apartment, find them, and they have to run. Thorolf tells Chandra to go ahead, he'll find her. After throwing aside but not hurting the officer, Thorolf takes off after Chandra. Thorolf gets worried when he can't see Chandra, and begins to think the only way to keep her safe is to eliminate all of the *Pyr*. He then smells both *Pyr* and *Slayer*, and sees another dragon. Thorolf shifts, roars, and goes after the dragon, even tossing his challenge coin. The other dragon calls him by name, but Thorolf attacks. He only stops when Chandra gets near him, the effect of the firestorm seeming to calm him down. Thorolf then realizes the other dragon is Rafferty. Thorolf says he smelled *Slayer*, and Rafferty says he did, as well. When Thorolf wipes blood from his face and discovers his blood is dark—not black, but a darker red than it should be, he realizes the *Slayer* scent came from him. He learns he's been missing for twenty-two months, and tells the other two the last things he remembers. Rafferty asks Thorolf about the two small holes on his arm and the crude spiral tattoo that covers Thorolf's body. Chandra's touch soothes the pain. She now isn't so sure Viv was responsible for Thorolf's disappearance. It seems to Chandra someone is using the firestorm against them and wonders if her brother is involved.

Chapter 3: The three try to figure out what happened to Thorolf, and Rafferty is surprised that Chandra knows so much about the *Pyr*. Thorolf says he wanted to protect Viv from the *Pyr* when he came back, and they realize he had been turned against his own kind. Rafferty feels sure this must be the work of Chen, a name Chandra has not heard before. Thorolf suggests he must be having his firestorm at just the right time, to save him from being turned. Chandra says she will not consummate the firestorm but offers her sanctuary as a place to hide. Rafferty volunteers to take them there via his ability to spontaneously materialize, and all she has to do is think of the place. Once they arrive, Thorolf is startled to notice there aren't any people around. Chandra says she thinks the location may be part of Myth, and she introduces him to her silver falcon, Snow. To Chandra, her sanctuary feels different, and the firestorm's light is now like the moon rather than like the sun. She wonders if the firestorm has changed her in some way and resolves to continue with her mission.

Chapter 4: Chandra asks Thorolf once again where Viv is, and he says he'll answer if she answers a question for him. But when he asks her what she is, she won't say. She claims her knowledge of the *Pyr* comes through research in her library. Chandra says she needs to complete her quest—to save the *Pyr*. They arrive at the library, a small stone building with a large smiling face above the opening, and Thorolf realizes Chandra's appearance has changed. She is now Caucasian, with longer hair and blue Celtic tattoos. He asks which is the real her, and she asks which is he, really, the dragon or the man. Despite being creeped out by the entryway, Thorolf follows Chandra in and sees the room is filled with skulls. He asks if the ghosts she sees are from the skulls, and she says maybe. She asks him to pick one, and he chooses the one the falcon sits upon. He immediately finds himself alone, in a place raining blood. Rafferty travels as a salamander to Erik's home, since he finds rematerializing less unpleasant that way. He changes form and moves to the couch next to Melissa. He knows Erik will be angry since he defied his orders by going to Thorolf. Sloane and Melissa put salve on his wounds. Erik enters and shows him a new YouTube video of Thorolf in dragon form, including Rafferty, as well. Rafferty fills the group in on what he believes happened to Thorolf. Erik and Sloane believe Chen released Thorolf as a trap. Erik reminds everyone there will be four full eclipses in the next two years and that will mark the end of either *Slayers* or *Pyr*. Sloane says he needs to figure out how to stop the plague. Melissa suggests they do another television special giving the public more information on the *Pyr*. Once again, Erik and Rafferty disagree about how to handle Thorolf, but Rafferty says he'll go to help Thorolf no matter the result. At that point, Erik relinquishes his role as leader to Rafferty and retires to his hoard. Rafferty tells Melissa to get things started for the show.

Chapter 5: Thorolf feels blood all around him, and then realizes he is reliving his own birth. He sees his father, Thorvald, come in, showing tenderness toward his mother, which he never saw his father express. He hears Thorvald tell the midwife what he will name his son, and that he will wield the sword called the Avenger of the Aesir. Then a woman appears in the room—Chandra. Thorvald and the midwife recognize her as a Vanir, a goddess who walks among humans. She says she has come to choose a hero, and she chooses his son. She gives the baby a blessing upon his head, and states he will be, "the salvation of the *Pyr* and of the world." Thorolf is angered by all he learns, as he feels his firestorm is a lie, designed to manipulate him to take on this role he never wanted. Thorolf returns to the present, accusing Chandra of not wanting to sate the firestorm because he has not yet done what she wanted. She says that isn't true, but that he does have a destiny to save the *Pyr*. Thorolf takes off into the jungle. In his lair, Chen sleeps, dreaming Thorolf's dreams, and sees who and what Chandra really is. For the first time, Chandra questions how her methods affect those she has chosen to fulfill her goals. She doesn't like the idea of a world without Thorolf in it and wonders if there is a way to help him without losing herself. Thorolf runs through the jungle, and the landscape around him begins to change. He shifts shape and flies over the familiar terrain of his old village, going to Astrid. He doesn't get there in time to save her. He remembers going home, and Thorvald telling him she was a distraction. Thorolf realizes his father was behind the attack on the village that resulted in Astrid's death. He stops at the cliff where he'd thrown the sword Aesir into the chasm. He is sorry to be *Pyr* and feels his firestorm is another betrayal.

Chapter 6: Niall wakes up from the same dream he has had for the past twenty-two months, telling Rox it is Thorolf's. He says he must tell Erik, and they book a flight to go to Thorolf. At the bookstore, Sara receives another prophecy, this time mentioning a union of five, and that *Pyr* and *Slayer* can share a curse. Sara hasn't told Quinn about her pregnancy yet, but he knows. He says they won't go to the firestorm but he'll send Erik the prophecy via email. Chandra follows the light of the firestorm to Thorolf's location, thinking about her involvement in the death of Astrid. She went along with Thorvald's plan to make sure a group of raiding dragons went past the woman's village. She needs to convince Thorolf of his role in saving the *Pyr*, but also desires him and wants to make amends. She takes off her clothes and goes to Thorolf. When Chandra approaches, Thorolf is aroused and interested, but he is also suspicious. He asks her what kinds of powers she has and learns her Vanir name is Freya. In addition to shape-shifting, she can gather the dead, summon visions, and cast spells. When Chandra admits she will return to Asgard at the completion of her quest, Thorolf becomes angry, accusing her of putting duty and responsibility before the firestorm and love.

Chapter 7: Before Thorolf can walk off, Chandra admits she was willing to give up something in exchange for receiving something from him. She says she made a vow to her brother, to protect and save the *Pyr*, and that Thorolf plays a role in that goal. He argues he doesn't want the task. Chandra then tells him about her vow of chastity, surprising him, especially when he hears how long it has been—over two thousand years. Chandra and Thorolf share a sizzling kiss, but she is alerted by Snow that something has happened so she says she must go. Thorolf intends to go with her, to fight together as a team, and when she can't dissuade him, she knocks him out. Viv Jason is touring another house. She has made looking at new properties a regular activity. Though she is glad Chen is doing her work for her—destroying the *Pyr*—she feels guilt over him using Thorolf to do so. She liked Thorolf, as he was always good to her. She also wonders what will become of her after she completes her mission: will she be returned to Hades and her sisters? Chen manifests, first as a salamander then as a woman, demanding she trap Thorolf again for him. Suddenly Viv finds herself in a place of snow, with a blond warrior woman pointing an arrow at her. When the woman addresses her as Tisiphone, Viv knows she must have followed her from the Underworld and be an immortal, herself. Viv tries to bargain with the woman, saying she knows how to break the spell upon Thorolf. Just as the woman is about to shoot an arrow into Viv's neck, Thorolf arrives. Tracking her via the firestorm, Thorolf sees Chandra in the form of Freya of the Valkyries and that she is about to shoot Viv with an arrow. He knocks Chandra aside, telling Viv to run, which she does. Chandra tells him it is her quest to kill Viv because she is, in fact, his enemy. She tells him about Viv's snake form, and that she bit him. At first, Thorolf doesn't believe her, then he remembers the big snake in his bed.

Chapter 8: Chandra then tells him the "Jera" rune keeps turning up on each of her arrows, meaning "change toward completion."

When Thorolf moves to touch Chandra, he runs into a glass wall, then is caught up in a snowstorm, which abruptly stops. In his Venetian palazzo, Lorenzo hears a voice in old-speak saying, "meet me." He wonders if it is coming from *Pyr* or *Slayer*. Suddenly he sees the blue-green flash of darkfire, and Marco materializes in a chair opposite him. As Lorenzo thinks of Cassie, the voice speaks to him about her, and Marco mouths "Jorge" to Lorenzo. Without speaking, Marco lets Lorenzo know the current firestorm is Thorolf's. Jorge tells Lorenzo he has a proposition for him, and he agrees to go since Marco can guard Cassie and baby Antonio. Before Lorenzo leaves, Marco gives him the prophecy, and they figure out the five who can beat Chen if they band together are Lorenzo, Erik, Thorolf, Brandon, and Marco—those who had been targeted by Chen at some point. Lorenzo meets Jorge and learns the Slayer wants him to beguile Chen. In return, he will tell him how to release Thorolf from Chen's spell. Lorenzo's and Thorolf's grandfathers had been good friends, so Lorenzo feels an obligation to help him, trusting he can somehow turn the tables on Jorge after getting what he needs. Marco hears the darkfire speaking to him, telling him he must retrieve the last crystal. Thorolf finds himself in a city street, probably Bangkok. His t-shirt is gone and the blue tattoo burns. Thorolf smells *Slayer* and is immediately filled with rage, not noticing the scale that falls to the ground. He sees an opal and gold salamander, grabs the lizard, which tells him his mate is his salvation. Thorolf gets bound by dragonsmoke and then rematerializes with the *Pyr* in a hotel room, with two other *Pyr* in attendance. Erik thinks about the *Pyr* who have gone to Thorolf. He tells Eileen he let down a friend and needs to apologize. He goes to his hoard, taking out the box that contains the Avenger of the Aesir.

Chapter 9: As Erik looks at the sword and its protective sigils, he thinks over how he had known for centuries where Thorolf was. Because he did not think him worthy to wield the blade, he left him to his own devices and then rejected him to try to get him to come to his senses. Erik tells Eileen about the sword and its background, and she says it needs to be delivered to Thorolf. Erik doesn't want to take the chance of anything happening to it, but she says they have nothing left to lose. She shows him the fax from

Lorenzo with the prophecy and the names. Erik feels energized and positive. Erik contacts other *Pyr* via old-speak and has a Skype session going with Donovan, Delaney, and Quinn. Erik tells them what is going on and that he has passed leadership of the *Pyr* on to Rafferty. Quinn and Donovan agree to come to Erik's to guard his family, bringing their own along, as well. Delaney and Ginger plan to go to help Thorolf. Marco briefly appears to tell the group Chen has a brother, which may be his weakness. Chandra can still feel the effects of the firestorm from far away, making it difficult to think clearly. She has Viv trapped in a mirror spell, but as she watches, the mirror starts to reassemble itself. Her brother appears, in his Apollo form. He tells her he had something to do with the firestorm, so she could experience physical pleasure before the portal closes and deities have to remain in Myth forever. Once she realizes she cares about humans and what happens to their world, she resolves to do what she can to help them. Her brother warns her that if she is on the other side when the portal closes, she will be stuck there. Niall looks over Thorolf, wondering if his friend can be saved. Rox joins them and says Thorolf's scales look tattooed. They wonder if Thorolf's firestorm is only a trap and who exactly Thorolf's mate is. Suddenly Thorolf shifts to his human form and sounds like himself. While the group wonders what brought on the change, Chandra appears, saying it is the firestorm healing him.

Chapter 10: Thorolf thinks perhaps Chandra marking him at birth is like a firestorm in reverse. Niall and Rox conclude the spirals in Thorolf's tattoo are Chen's brand, but rather than ink, they have been made in *Slayer* blood. Chandra asks if the firestorm can be used to heal Thorolf best if allowed to burn longer, or if consummated. Sloane, the Apothecary, says he first has to know what was done to him. Thorolf tells Chandra to show the others what she can do, so she creates a vision of the Underworld, where they witness Hades revive Tisiphone and give her the chance for vengeance. Then the scene changes to Hera banishing Tisiphone until the darkfire is once again set free. They see Tisiphone change into a snake They also see Jorge tear the arm from the sick man, the source of the disease in Seattle. Chandra tells Thorolf that Viv was both the snake and the hag, Tisiphone. She also says she took an oath to protect the *Pyr*. Suddenly, Chen, in his female form, appears in the room, grabs Chandra, and disappears. Rafferty tells Thorolf to focus on the firestorm to follow them.

Chapter 11: Chandra and Chen manifest on top of a mountain. They fight,, but when Chen throws Chandra over the side, Thorolf in dragon form arrives in time to grab her. He asks her to hold Rafferty, in salamander form, who is worn out from all of the manifesting. Chandra holds Rafferty close to her while she rides on Thorolf's back during his battle with Chen, the firestorm seeming to help them both. Everywhere she touches Thorolf, his scales return to their former luster, so she runs her hands along his body to aid the process. As Chen drains Thorolf with dragonsmoke, Rafferty sends Chandra and Thorolf to her sanctuary. She resolves to heal Thorolf. The light of the darkfire wakens Liz and Brandon in their home, and they go into their sons' room to find Marco there. He says, "brothers," and the other two adults are not sure of the significance of his statement. Marco has come for the darkfire crystal and also tells them about the alliance of five needed against Chen. Rafferty arrives back in the Bangkok hotel room and tells the others what has happened with Chen, Thorolf, and Chandra. He says they need to get the sword Chandra mentioned, which Sloane suggests is likely the one Erik is trying to get to them. Since getting the sword through airport security poses a problem, the group comes up with a plan for several of the *Pyr* to take turns flying it.

Chapter 12: Thorolf wakes up in Myth to find Chandra on top of him, seemingly interested in fulfilling the firestorm. She also surprises him by saying he has a strong moral code. While they pleasure each other with oral sex, Thorolf feels the heat of the firestorm healing him, and Chandra changes through many different forms. One of them is Ulrike, the friend of Astrid, his first love. This situation kills the mood for Thorolf, and he decides to investigate by touching one of the skulls on Chandra's belt, asking to see Ulrike. Chandra now feels great regret over her past actions, and realizes Thorolf will see what she did as treachery. As Ulrike, she had pretended to be the lone survivor of a dragon attack in a nearby village and had befriended Astrid. She had told Astrid there was a rumor about one man being able to shift into a dragon form, and that perhaps it was Thorolf. When Astrid asks Thorolf, he shifts and lets her see him. Ulrike tells people in the town Astrid had sex with a dragon, and the village decides to sacrifice her as a way to appease the dragons. Astrid was stoned, and the villagers all died in the dragon attack. When the vision clears, Chandra tries to apologize to Thorolf, saying she didn't understand at the time. Thorolf suggests she somehow conjured the firestorm, but she insists that it is real. She says they make good partners, and that she doesn't want there to be a world without him. Thorolf says he needs time away from her so he can think.

Chapter 13: Niall tries to dreamwalk through Thorolf, but can't find him. He hears Marco's voice telling him Thorolf is in Myth, so Niall can't follow him. After seeing a flash of darkfire, Niall does have a vision of the past—the *Slayer* JP is drained of blood, and it is converted into what Niall believes is the ink used to tattoo Thorolf. Tisiphone manages to pull the pieces of the mirror back together. Now she needs a mortal to look into it, freeing her. She is determined not to be stuck in Myth when the portal closes. Thorolf shows up, and in her Viv form, she begins to cry. Thorolf, disturbed to see Viv crying, talks to her. When Viv puts her hand on the glass, Thorolf does, also, causing it to ripple. Then he sees Viv cry tears of blood, as he saw Tisiphone do in the vision Chandra showed him. He realizes she may indeed have been a distraction for him, meaning Chandra had been telling the truth. When she emerges from the mirror, she has changed to her Erinyes shape, and then to a huge snake, which bites him in the throat. Chandra arrives and uses her knife on the snake, cutting off its head. After witnessing Tisiphone go through her different shapes, all of them decapitated, Chandra knows her foe is dead. Thorolf is not moving so she works to suck out the poison. She pulls her last arrow from her quiver and puts it in his mouth, since the rune upon it signifies regeneration. Then Chen arrives to collect Thorolf. While Snow tries to grab at Chandra to take her through the portal before it closes, she chooses to stay with Thorolf. She grabs onto Chen to hitch a ride to wherever he is taking the *Pyr*. In Chen's cave, he puts Chandra in a cage. She uses her magic (aided by a darkfire crystal she sees in the cave) on both the bit of arrow she used on Thorolf and the one she used against Chen. Thorolf dreams of Chandra, and he asks her why he was chosen to save the *Pyr*. She says before he was born, she saw a vision of his father's firestorm and knew he would be the one. When she tells him she has left the world of the gods behind to stay with him, Thorolf realizes he must embrace the firestorm and his destiny.

Chapter 14: Chandra and Thorolf discuss the signs of Ragnarok being upon the world, that Jormungand is in the sea, summoned for the end-of-the-world battle. Thorolf is supposed to kill the giant serpent, and he needs his sword to do so. Marco arrives in Chen's lair, behind a large oval stone with darkfire inside of it. When he touches it, he knows it wants to be broken, so he cracks it, then gets transported to an outdoor market. Delaney and Brandon make their way to Thorolf, taking turns carrying the sword as they fly. Sloane arrives, with Rafferty in salamander form. The two *Pyr* hope they will get transported to where they need to be. Thorolf awakens in Chen's cave, seeing the dead JP. Thorolf's memories return of how he had been infused with the Elixir and his thoughts manipulated. Chen appears to be asleep, and then Thorolf sees Chandra in her cage. He realizes he has one of her arrowheads in his mouth, which he can swallow in his dragon form, and does so. Chen then appears in his female form. Thorolf sees a yellow salamander, then Lorenzo appears. Lorenzo attempts to beguile Chen, but when Chen gets the upper hand, Lorenzo lets him think he's beaten him, and then forms a plan involving the darkfire. Chen moves toward Thorolf with a syringe, to inject him in the place where he'd lost a scale. Chandra activates the arrowhead she stabbed Chen with, causing pain. Thorolf fights back, destroying the syringe. The egg-shaped rock breaks open, darkfire beneath it, and a smaller dragon appears. The dragon stabs Chen with a piece of the darkfire crystal. The dragon, Chen's brother, disappears with the aid of darkfire. Jorge arrives, feasting on the blood and guts of Chen, still alive, and collapses the cavern ceiling on the others. Chen's brother, Lee, finds a dragon scale on the ground, then meets Marco in the marketplace, and they leave to go join the others. In the cavern, Rafferty, in salamander form, delivers the sword to Thorolf, then escapes with Thorolf, Chandra and Lorenzo. Thorolf and Chandra end up in the sea, the other two not with them. Thorolf knows he needs to fight Jormungand. Regretting that he never learned to swim, Thorolf battles the serpent, losing the sword inside its body. Jormungand dies, but not before spraying Thorolf with venom, which makes its way to his skin, in the spot of the missing scale.

Chapter 15: Chandra tries to revive Thorolf, but the venom burns her hands. Then black liquid comes out of his pores, the venom counteracting the *Slayer* blood. Chandra uses the firestorm to try to bring him back. She begins kissing and caressing him to encourage the flames to burn hotter. Her attempts work, and Thorolf comes around. Chandra says she is mortal now, but she can change form just one more time. Thorolf tells her to choose, and she picks the huntress form, since that was who she was when they first met. They both admit their love for one another and then sate the firestorm. Chandra wakens in the hotel room. While the mortal world escaped Ragnarok, the link between mortal and divine is now severed. Snow brings her a skull. Worried the bird may have missed its chance to go through the portal, she is relieved when she sees it join her brother, Apollo, in the sky. She remembers telling him to send her a man worthy of forgoing her vow of chastity, and she realizes he has done just that. Thorolf uses the skull to communicate with his father, who apologizes to him for Astrid, and the two make their peace. The *Pyr* gather at Angkor during the new moon for Thorolf's scale repair ceremony. Rafferty turns leadership back over to Erik. Rafferty, Niall, Sloane, Delaney, Brandt, and Brandon are all in attendance, many of the partners and children present, as well. Erik then uses the reflecting pool at the temple to conjure a connection with the other *Pyr* who are not there in person: Quinn, Donovan, Marco, Drake, Lee, and the other Dragon Legion warriors. The ceremony is completed successfully.

DEBORAH'S COMMENTS

I like Thorolf. I did from the moment he first stepped onto the page, even though I knew it would be a challenge to make a hero out of him. In the end, Chandra had to do a lot of the work herself.

This story is a favorite of mine in the *Dragonfire* cycle: not only does the most unwilling dragon shifter have to come to terms with his own past and change, but his mate is one of the most elusive and powerful of all the heroines in the series. Chandra is also pretty merciless when it comes to compelling Thorolf to confront the truth. At the same time, Thorolf challenges Chandra's assumptions, undermining her belief that her vow of chastity is a good thing, much less a permanent thing. I love that Chandra is a shape-shifter herself and how she dazzles Thorolf. (Several of those scenes are excerpted elsewhere in this volume.) I love the imagery of Myth and the intersection of Thorolf's firestorm with Norse stories.

But my favorite detail is Chandra's last choice. There is a medieval story in which knights are trapped by a fearful hag. She offers each knight the choice of having her beautiful by day (and a hag by night) or beautiful by night (and a hag by day). The implication is that any knight's answer reflects whether he cares more for his own pleasure (with a beautiful woman at night) or public appearances (with a beautiful woman at his side by day). The spell cast over the woman is broken when one knight tells her to make the choice herself and he will be content either way: the moral of the story is that what a woman wants most is to make her own choices. I like that when Chandra surrenders her immortality for love, Thorolf asks her to choose which form she will take.

"Will we even make a son?" he asked.
She smiled. "Isn't that the point of the firestorm?"
"But you're a goddess..."
Chandra shook her head. "Not any more. I'm mortal now."
Her choice still blew Thorolf away. It was epic. "You shouldn't have done that. You shouldn't have given up your powers."
Chandra smiled. "The alternative wasn't acceptable."
He stared at her, amazed and honored. "No one ever gave up anything that big for me before."
"Maybe they made the mistake of underestimating you," she said with a smile.
"You didn't have to save me."
"Maybe you saved me." Chandra rolled so that she was facing

him, and punctuated her words with taps of her fingertip on his chest. Each touch launched a spark, and each spark made his desire heat even more. "You said that you were tired of people saying they loved you because they wanted something from you, that love shouldn't be an exchange. You said you wanted someone to love you for your own self, and that the firestorm was supposed to bring that person to you."

"I did. So?"

She met his gaze. "I understood exactly what you meant. No one ever loves a goddess for her own self. It's all about what that goddess can do for you. It had never occurred to me that things could be different."

"I do love you for your own self," Thorolf admitted.

Chandra flushed a little again, his innocent seductress. "I know."

He ran one hand over her hip, savoring the insistent burn of the firestorm and trying to think straight. "Does that mean you can't shift shape anymore?"

She pursed her lips, considering. "Maybe one last time." She smiled at him. "Do you have a preference?"

Thorolf claimed her lips in a thorough kiss, one that left them both breathing quickly. "I love you," he said, his mouth the merest increment from hers. "And that doesn't change, no matter what you look like. Whatever you choose is good with me."

Her smile was blinding in its brilliance, and her hands locked around his neck to pull him closer. This kiss was hungry and passionate, a kiss that fed the core heat of the firestorm and took it to a fever pitch. When Thorolf opened his eyes, Chandra was the ebony-haired huntress, her blue eyes filled with sparkles. "Your fave?" he asked against her throat.

"It was how we met," she answered, her breath teasing his ear. She parted her thighs and wrapped her legs around his waist. Thorolf sank into the sweet heat of her, dizzy at the feel of her softness closing around him. The firestorm burned like an inferno in his veins, and his body matched its rhythms to hers in that amazing way. He stared into her eyes as they moved together, then she kissed him, drawing him deeper into her embrace, making their union complete. The pleasure consumed him, even as the firestorm burned hotter and hotter, driving him on to heights he'd never reached before. Chandra was right with him, her wonder and pleasure encouraging him to make it last.

He'd been right before: she just might kill him.

But Thorolf couldn't think of a better way to go.

—from **Serpent's Kiss**

FIRESTORM FOREVER

THIS FLAME WILL BURN FOR ALL TIME...

Three key firestorms mark the culmination of the Dragon's Tail Wars, pitting the dragon shifters known as the Pyr *against the evil* Slayers. The Slayers *have struck a blow against mankind, bringing a pestilence from the ancient world, which is spreading like wildfire. Sloane Forbes, the Apothecary of the* Pyr, *knows it is his duty to find the cure, but the solution is elusive, his beautiful neighbor is distracting, and time is running out.*

In moving to a remote farm in the California hills, Samantha Wilcox has left her demanding career behind by choice and on principle. It's too painful to remember her own failures as both mother and physician, so she's determined to start fresh. She's going to live differently, following her instincts and savoring life's pleasures—like the hot sex with no commitment offered by her mysterious neighbor. Sloane Forbes is no more an herb farmer than she is a tarot card reader, but Samantha is determined to keep their illusions intact—at least until she discovers that Sloane's one of the Pyr, *the dragon shifters responsible for the epidemic that stole her son's life. As* Slayers *and* Pyr *gather for the final battle, can Samantha and Sloane work together to save the world and build themselves—and their respective kinds—a future?*

THE PROTAGONISTS

Firestorm Forever is a big finish. It takes place over a year and a half and features three firestorms. The first is that of Drake, the leader of the Dragon Legion, whose firestorm with Veronica Maitland leads him back to the woman he's admired since **Harmonia's Kiss**. The second is that of Marco, the Sleeper and custodian of the darkfire, whose firestorm with Jacelyn, the dragon hunter, is tinged with unpredictability. The third firestorm sparks at the end of the book between Sloane Forbes, the Apothecary of the *Pyr* and Samantha, the woman he's helped to heal over the course of the story so they can build a future together.

THE ELEMENTS

With three firestorms come three pairings of affinities. First, Drake's affinities are to earth and fire, while Veronica's are to water and air. Drake is a pragmatic warrior while Veronica's dreams help the *Pyr* to save her, and her empathy means that Drake finds it easy to confide in her. Marco's affinities are to fire and air, while Jac's are to earth and water. Marco is the Sleeper who learned from Pwyll in his dreams, while Jac is both nurturing and a problem-solver. Finally, Sloane's affinities are to fire and water, while Sam's are to earth and air. Sloane's affinity to water helps him to heal, while Sam's affinities inform her practicality and her intellectual ability: she's good at solving puzzles.

What's interesting here is that the *Pyr* each have an affinity to fire and one other element, which means all four elements are covered by the three *Pyr* heroes. I thought we needed that kind of conjunction to heal the world.

THE SETTING

This book, in which three firestorms collectively heal the world, takes place over a year. During this period, there are three full lunar eclipses that are blood moons, and each one sparks a firestorm. The first, on October 8, 2014, ignites the firestorm of Drake and Veronica. The second, on April 4, 2015, signals the firestorm of Marco and Jac. The third, on September 28, 2015 and the last eclipse before the moon's node changes to the Dragon's Head in October 2015, sparks the firestorm of Sloane and Samantha.

Given the timeline of the story, it's no surprise that the characters travel as much as they do. The story begins in California, at the home of Sloane, the Apothecary. Ronnie and Drake's firestorm sparks in Virginia. Jac and Marco's firestorm sparks in Seattle, where the virulent disease brought from the ancient world by Jorge has launched a modern plague. The story also moves to Australia and culminates at Machu Picchu in Peru.

THE PROPHECY

Three blood moons mark the debt come due
Will the Pyr *triumph or be hunted anew?*
Three eclipses will awaken the spark
In thirteen monsters breeding in dark.
Three times the firestorm will spark
Before darkfire fades into the dark.
Firestorm, mate or blood sacrifice
None or all can be the darkfire's price.
When the Dragon's Tail has turned its bore
And darkfire dies forevermore
Will the Pyr *be left to rule with might*
Or disappear into past's twilight?

THE STORY

Prologue: (April 2014, Chen's lair in the mountains of Tibet) Jorge, still gorging himself on Chen's dragon corpse, manages to escape the chamber that Lorenzo and Thorolf have collapsed by clutching Chen's corpse as he thinks about manifesting somewhere safe. He then finds himself in a library and hears voices outside, speaking Russian. Then he sees a small egg-like stone, green with red veins. Jorge knows he is in the lost library of Ivan the Terrible, and in the presence of the Dracontias.

Chapter 1: (Wednesday, Oct. 8, 2014, California) As Apothecary of the *Pyr*, coupled with the duty to safeguard humans, Sloane has been working tirelessly to find a cure for the virus Jorge started in Seattle. Sloane knows there is a firestorm taking place that night, and he worries that with all the new *Pyr*, he may never get his chance before the next three firestorms signal the end of the Dragon Tail Wars. He wishes he could choose his own mate, since he feels his next-door neighbor, Samantha Wilcox, would be perfect. Taking a break, Sloane goes to his pool and swims vigorously with the intent of wearing himself out. He feels the firestorm begin, though it is not his, and then sees Samantha at the gate. Sloane has held back from starting a relationship with her, as he doesn't want to be unfair to her when he does get his firestorm.

However, when she takes off her bathing suit to join him in the pool and then kisses him, Sloane's restraint evaporates. In Virginia, despite always feeling he would return, Veronica is surprised to see Drake again. She had thought and dreamed of him a lot over the past four grueling years, as she worked to make a life for herself and Timmy, who is now eleven. Already feeling odd due to the eclipse earlier in the day, Ronnie also feels a physical response to Drake—one she has not felt for anyone since Mark's death. Since Timmy is spending the night with a friend, Ronnie invites Drake to dinner to thank him for his help. Drake says she gave him new purpose—understanding the importance of fighting for good people. Drake says he has returned to give her a choice. Then a spark moves from his fingertip to her shoulder, and she feels intense physical desire. Telling Drake she'd like to cook for him, she then kisses him. Meanwhile in Seattle, after watching the video of the dragon spreading the virus, Jacelyn vows revenge upon the *Pyr*. She has been researching them, trying to figure out their weaknesses, and has even contacted Maeve, the woman who posted the video, to see if she knows more. Jac dismisses Melissa Smith's information as pro-*Pyr* propaganda. Feeling slightly out of sorts, perhaps due to the blood moon, Jac decides to go to the gym. Her attractive neighbor is at her door with a package he says was delivered to him in error. He introduces himself as Marco. He suggests she open the package, and inside is a book: *Habits and Habitats of Dragons: A Compleat Guide for Slayers* by Sigmund Guthrie. Jac becomes engrossed in the book, which talks about how to hunt and kill the *Pyr*. Meanwhile in Chicago, Erik wakens from the same dream he has been having, with Sigmund telling him, "The blood moon will ripen the eggs." Confused by his dead son's meaning, Erik looks up some information about blood moons. He finds a Blood Moon Prophecy, written in the Book of Joel, about the event being a precursor to the end times. Erik tells Eileen the firestorm is Drake's, and she is pleased. Right after he tells her about the dream, Zoë comes in the room and repeats the very same words. Suddenly, a large ruby red dragon appears, one that looks a lot like Boris, a *Slayer* Erik killed.

Chapter 2: Ronnie feels overheated and frazzled in her kitchen with Drake. They both admit neither has been with another since their spouses died. Ronnie thinks about what Drake did for her in the past, and their kiss is so amazing she forgets to ask about the odd light between them. Drake has checked on Ronnie periodically over the past four years, and feels certain they are perfectly matched. He thinks her lack of questions and her readiness to be with him means she knows about the *Pyr* and the firestorm. Ronnie notices Drake's Dragon Legion tattoo and mistakes it for a military one, but he doesn't mind if she sees similarities between him and her late husband, as Drake thinks him an honorable man. Meanwhile, in Chicago, Erik shifts and takes to the air to take on Boris, who claims he has been reborn as himself. Just when Erik seems to have gotten the best of the *Slayer,* tearing off both of his wings, a second Boris appears. Erik is injured but ice pellets fall out of the sky, signaling Donovan's arrival. While Donovan takes on Boris, Erik makes his way to shore, aided by Delaney, who offers Erik some of his energy via a dragonsmoke conduit so he can heal. A few minutes later, Donovan reports the *Slayer*s disappeared, proving to them the effects of the Elixir do diminish. Meanwhile in Seattle, Marco gave Jacelyn the book he had taken from Erik's hoard so she could help track down Jorge. He knows she listened to Maeve's anti-*Pyr* diatribes, and she was also at the scene of the initial infection. Marco saw her on the video, with a young child, Nathaniel, who got the infected blood in his mouth and was the first to die. As he dozes, Marco thinks about the darkfire and as the firestorm begins, receives a prophecy. Liz, out on a research trip, feels something odd in the water, though Brandon does not. She describes it as a spark that burned hot, then cold, then was gone. She said it was like a quickening. Brandon says he will check with the others.

Chapter 3: Drake and Ronnie have sex in her kitchen, then move to her bathroom tub. Ronnie notices the light that enveloped them earlier now seems to be gone and wonders if she imagined it. Eileen, Alex, and Ginger all nervously await the return of Erik, Donovan, and Delaney. They discuss Boris, and how he has been dead almost seven years. When the *Pyr* arrive, Eileen is not pleased to see Erik's injuries. The group tries to decipher Sigmund's message to Erik, suggesting they should check Sigmund's book. Erik goes to his hoard for the volume, but he finds the book and the burned-out darkfire crystal are gone. He says Marco's scent is there, and the group hopes they don't have a traitor in their midst. After having sex twice, Sloane and Samantha wake up next to the pool. Sloane tries to get to know her better but senses she covers up an emotional wound of some sort. He learns Samantha is divorced and has determined never to marry again so she is not interested in anything permanent or complicated. When Samantha sees Sloane's dragon tattoo, she gets very upset, saying dragons are killers. She leaves in a huff, saying she has no more interest in being with him if he thinks dragons are okay. Sloane determines to find out more about his mysterious neighbor, right before he gets a call to go to Erik.

Chapter 4: Fuming, Sam goes home and researches Sloane's tattoo, confirming it is a caduceus, a symbol of Hermes, messenger of the gods. She scoffs at the idea of dragons being connected to gods. Taking a mug from the cabinet makes Sam think of Nathaniel, and she wonders what Sloane would say if he knew she thought herself a terrible mother, given the fate of her son. She realizes she owes Sloane an apology, but before she can go next door, she sees him drive off. She decides to investigate him further. After their second bout of lovemaking, Ronnie's mood quickly changes, and she says they didn't use protection. She is shocked when Drake states there will be a child. Blindsided, she asks what he means, and Drake realizes she has no idea about the firestorm, or what he is. As he tries to explain, she asks to see him shift, and about that time, a ruby and brass-colored dragon crashes through the window. From behind her, a grey and black dragon pulls Ronnie out of the way and fights the intruder. Ronnie realizes the grey dragon is Drake. He dispatches one dragon but two more appear, and he tells Ronnie to run. When she sees her car is on fire, Ronnie runs on foot, seeing red dragons in the sky. Drake is impatient to find Ronnie but must stay to answer police questions. He is relieved when Arach and Kristofer, two of the Dragon Legion warriors, appear to help him.

Chapter 5: Sam learns that Sloane bought his property twenty years ago, but the age he appears now does not make that likely. She notices the lights go on in his house, though his truck is not there. Just when she decides she will go over to apologize, the lights all go out. Sam resolves to check things out in the morning. Timmy can't believe his mom is missing. He insists to the police officer and his friend Dashiell's parents that Drake can find his mom. The officer asks Timmy about Drake. Upset with the adults, Timmy opens the front door to leave and finds Drake standing there. Timmy feels responsible for his mom's disappearance, but Drake tells him he was not. He tells Timmy he will search for Ronnie himself. While Timmy stays with Dashiell's family, there will be three men from his company keeping watch over him at all times, and Drake will check in every week. Ronnie wakes up on a cot in a strange room, with no idea where she is. Then she witnesses a dragon descend outside her window, carrying an injured dragon. Three identical men appear in the courtyard, shift into dragons, and three of the dragons attack and eat the dying one. Boris IV, the third clone of Boris Vassily, remembers his earlier life clearly, as well as his rebirth of being hatched from an egg and being transported by Jorge. For wanting to kill the *Pyr's* mate instead of capturing her, Jorge punishes him by denying him permission to eat any of the fallen clone. Boris IV decides he will figure out where the next batch of eggs will hatch in six months so he can consume one of them to gain strength. Then he can get his revenge on both Jorge and Erik. Drake is unable to track Ronnie at all. Erik says he will ask Niall to try to locate her through dreams, but he may need to talk to Timmy first to make his attempt more effective. Ronnie gets a visit from one of her captors, learning they plan to take care of her because they want the child she carries. She realizes that if she is there for nine months, it will give Drake time to find her, and she knows he will watch out for Timmy. Sam goes to Sloane's house in the morning but finds no sign of him.

Chapter 6: Cassie is annoyed and worried by the news report by Maeve O'Neill with video footage of Erik, in dragon form, battling a *Slayer*. She and Lorenzo plan to return to the U.S. Lorenzo says he has a plan: to make a returning-from-the-dead appearance, give Maeve an exclusive interview, and beguile her into thinking the *Pyr* are not the terrors she has been making them out to be. Ronnie is taken to have dinner with a man who introduces himself as Jorge. Explaining the difference in philosophy between *Pyr* and

Slayer, he also makes it clear he plans to keep her alive until she gives birth, asking if she'd like to play board games to pass the time. Sara gives birth to a fifth son, which she names Michel, after Quinn's brother who had been turned into a shadow dragon. She and Quinn discuss going to stay with Sloane in California so their family can be together with the rest of the *Pyr.* Niall tries to relax enough to dreamwalk and locate Ronnie. At first he is unable to do so, but when visiting Timmy's dream, he catches a dream thread in the hope it is the boy's mother's. Ronnie sees a man in her dream who shifts into dragon form. After confirming he isn't a *Slayer* by cutting himself and showing her his blood, he tells her Drake is there with him and allows her to see both Drake and Rox in the apartment. He shifts back to human, introduces himself as Niall, and asks Ronnie to think of what she has seen and experienced so they can figure out where she is.

Chapter 7: While Drake looks over Niall's notes from his dreamwalking conversation with Ronnie, trying to figure out where she is being held, Rox discovers a YouTube video that shows the same scene Ronnie described to Niall: four dragons ganging up on and eventually eating the fifth dragon—all of whom look like Boris. They can see a moss-covered building in the background. Rox calls a friend of hers, an urban explorer, to locate the building. It is Seaview Hospital in Staten Island, and he tells her which building. Rox tells the others there are tunnels underneath that part of the hospital. Despite being pretty sure they are walking into Jorge's trap, Drake insists upon going to get Ronnie, taking along a few of the Dragon Legion warriors to help. Jorge has Ronnie brought to him that evening, and asks her about how and when she met Drake. He says Drake abandoned Cassandra and their son, and then suggests he may have killed Ronnie's husband in order to get her for himself. Though she doesn't believe him, Ronnie realizes she doesn't know much about Drake at all. Angry, Ronnie asks to go back to her cell. Drake's Dragon Legion warriors start a fire in the tunnel as a distraction, and he goes up to get Ronnie, in dragon form. As they fly off, Drake explains what really happened regarding both Mark's death and his disappearance from Cassandra and Theo. He says he attempted this rescue, even knowing it was a trap, so he could ensure she knows the truth about him. Jorge shows up, and the two dragons fight, Drake managing to tear off the end of Jorge's tail.

Chapter 8: Sloane returns home worn out from healing Erik. With a vague sense of something being off at the house, Sloane is surprised to pick up the scent of Sam's perfume outside. Once inside, Sloane finds his lab destroyed and the vial of blood with the virus missing. Realizing Jorge is the culprit, Sloane also worries about Sam and rushes to her house. Sloane goes next door and tells Sam his house was broken into. She assures him she's fine. She apologizes for how she behaved, and they make up, agreeing not to pry into one another's lives too much. Sam does ask about the caduceus, though, and he says he has it because he's the Apothecary. He then mentions *Lives of the Necromancers* by William Godwin. Sloane gets a text summoning him to New York, and he regrets having to leave. Drake and Jorge continue to fight, then Jorge suddenly veers toward a group of humans on the ground, raising a vial over them. Drake makes the choice to save the humans rather than escape with Ronnie. When he makes the decision, he feels a scale fall from his chest. Theo, one of the Dragon Legion warriors, and a descendant of Drake's, sees Jorge turn on Drake, creating a dragonsmoke conduit to sap his energy. Drake drops Ronnie, but Theo makes the decision to save Drake, who could be killed, rather than Ronnie, who would only be injured. Unfortunately, Ronnie disappears, and the *Pyr* realize she has been taken again. In a cave with Jorge and the other *Slayer*s, Ronnie sees Jorge eat a fallen dragon. He explains why, telling her about the Elixir. He also confirms she is pregnant, saying he can smell the change in her. He tells her Drake is dead because he chose to save the humans. When Ronnie asks about Leftie, the *Slayer* who was missing an arm from the attack on her apartment, Jorge gets angry and disappears. The Dragon Legion warriors carry out the ceremony for their dead comrade, to ensure he does not rise again as a shadow dragon. While Drake watches, he fears for Ronnie and vows to change to be worthy of his second firestorm.

Chapter 9: Sloane arrives at Niall's apartment in New York to heal the badly-injured Drake. Sloane says Jorge stole the vial of blood, and Drake tells them what the *Slayer* did with it. Sloane realizes the Boris look-alikes must be clones. They decide to try to capture one to learn more. While watching the video of his mom and the dragons, Timmy hears her call the one holding her "Drake." He is sure he knows Drake's secret, but keeps the information to himself. Now Ronnie is only given horrible-tasting gruel to eat, and she thinks Jorge must put something in her food that keeps her from dreaming. She keeps Drake's scale hidden from Jorge, and wonders if her *Pyr* is truly dead. She is also now sure she is pregnant. Drake goes to see Timmy, who lets on to Drake that he knows his secret but hasn't told anyone. Drake tells Timmy and his friend, Dashiell, that he will stick around to be involved in Timmy's life, which pleases Timmy very much. Melissa's producer, Doug, shares a video with her of a woman telling Maeve O'Neill about her tour group in Easter Island witnessing the hatching of dragons. As usual, Maeve attempts to spin the story to the negative, and Melissa resolves to track the witnesses to get more information and to provide counter-coverage. Rafferty plans to take their daughter, Isabelle, to stay with the other children at Eric's place. He voices concern over the hatched dragons disappearing into thin air, suggesting they can manifest elsewhere.

Chapter 10: After having read Sigmund Guthrie's book three times, Jac starts a list of what she has learned: dragon shifters lose a scale when they fall in love; they have to be in possession of their hidden clothes in order to change back to their human forms; and they mate once in their lives, with a human woman. After watching videos and reading witness accounts, she begins to wonder if Melissa Smith is correct, that there are good dragons and bad dragons. Jac knows for sure which category the gold one who spread the virus in Seattle belongs in. Seeing the most recent video of the dragons hatching on Easter Island makes her want to go there, but she wants to ask Marco a question since she thinks he knows more about dragons than he is letting on. Marco finds Jac very enticing but realizes he needs to go to Easter Island to find out about the hatchlings. He packs a bag so he can leave quickly. When Jac comes into his apartment, she asks Marco if he sent her the book, and he confirms he did. She sees the prophecy written on his wall. When she sees the darkfire crystal and asks if she can touch it, the stone turns green in her hand. Marco puts his hand over hers, and the crystal seems pleased. As the two acknowledge their mutual attraction, Jac asks what the crystal is for, and Marco says it can kill a dragon shape shifter. She automatically thinks he is a dragon hunter, and when she learns where he is headed, asks to go with him. Jac leaves a message for her sister Sam, telling her she's going to a retreat. She takes along her dragon notebook but leaves behind the book. When she meets Marco at their cab, he whispers the prophecy in her ear, which talks about three blood moons, three eclipses, and thirteen monsters. Sam has a booth to do tarot readings at the local farmer's market. She feels good that she was able to look at some photos of Nathaniel and feel happiness as well as the sadness. She thinks about her sister, Jac, and wishes she were less impulsive, also knowing Jac blames herself for Nathaniel's death. She decides she doesn't want Sloane to know about her background yet. Then he shows up at her table, asking how much for a reading.

Chapter 11: When it becomes clear that Sam isn't very good at doing readings, Sloane ends up taking over and doing a reading for her. While this goes on, they also agree they would both like to have a relationship with no commitment and only an occasional question. Sloane asks why she decided to become a tarot card reader, and she says it was because it was so different from what she had been doing. The two decide they are in the mood for afternoon sex, so head to Sam's house. Jac wakes up in the hotel room bed she shares with Marco, both of them crashing immediately after their long flight. When Marco wakes, Jac asks him about his family, and they end up having sex. Neither of them see the darkfire crystal going wild while they do so. While Sam is in the shower, Sloane looks around her house, perusing the shelves of her library. He finds a framed picture of a young boy, labeled "Nathaniel" on the back. Sloane figures out he is the same boy who was the first to die of the mystery virus spread by Jorge. Sloane returns the picture to its place, and when Sam returns, he tells her he has read some of the same books. She scoffs at the idea, not imagining how he could possibly read and understand books on microbiology and germ warfare. Sloane takes offense at her attitude and leaves the room. Sam apologizes, and learns Sloane had wanted to attend medical school but was not able to. He wants them to at least be able to talk to each other. When she says she has trouble opening up, he suggests that may have something to do with her divorce. Sam thinks that if she talked to anyone about Nathaniel, it may well be Sloane.

Chapter 12: Sam and Sloane enjoy a nice meal and great conversation, with Sloane wondering if he is in too deep already. He does have the feeling he is supposed to heal Sam by allowing her to talk about her pain. As they drive over to the nest site on Easter Island, Marco thinks about how he trusted the darkfire when it led him to Jac. Melissa is at the site doing a report, and Jac makes disparaging comments about her. Marco begins to feel uneasy about the situation. The darkfire in his pocket has heated unbearably, so Marco pulls Jac aside so her can show her. A dragon (Rafferty) descends from the sky, Jac grabs the crystal from Marco, yells, "this is for Nathaniel," and shoots the dragon with it. Rafferty begins to shimmer, and Marco realizes Rafferty's identity is about to be revealed on video. Marco shifts, takes the crystal from Jac, catches Rafferty as he falls, and uses the darkfire to take his friend to Sloane. In Chicago, Erik, Eileen, Zoë, and Isabelle watch Melissa's newscast from Easter Island, but they don't see who shoots Rafferty with the crystal, only that it's there,. Then they see Marco take Rafferty away, thinking he's abducting him. Some of Thorolf's young self-defense students in Bangkok watch the video of Rafferty, and Thorolf decides he needs to go to the U.S. to find out what's going on. Still at Sam's, Sloane gets a message with the video of Rafferty being injured, and he shows it to Sam. She recognizes Jac, but doesn't tell Sloane. He returns to his house and finds a very distraught Marco there with Rafferty, saying the darkfire betrayed him. Sloane asks him if he can recite some of the Cantor's songs to draw the darkfire out of Rafferty's body, but Marco leaves, saying he has to finish what he started. Sloane tries to use his own songs and sees the darkfire crackle beneath Rafferty's skin. Jorge feels the darkfire, and thinks about how he animated the thirteen Boris clones made by Sigmund. He decides to leave one of the new clones in charge guarding Ronnie while he goes to a bar in Australia to watch the news. He sees the recent video and knows the darkfire crystal is active again. He plans to get it.

Chapter 13: Jac is ecstatic over her success in taking down a dragon, but can't figure out where Marco disappeared to. Since he had the keys to the rental truck, she starts walking back to the hotel. Shortly thereafter, Marco pulls up in the truck to pick her up. He's unhappy that she took the crystal, and his manner toward her seems very different. He says he trusted where he shouldn't have. He asks for the poem she had copied down into her notebook. She gives it to him, but after he drops her off, she writes it down again, from memory, resolving to figure out the poem's meaning, and to take down more dragons on her own. Sloane continues to work on Rafferty. Erik contacts him and refers to Marco as a traitor. Sloane tells him it was Marco who delivered Rafferty, and he seemed very upset. Erik, Eileen, and Sloane discuss which *Pyr* are headed to Sloane's to help, and Eileen hopes Sloane can work on Erik's wounds, too. Sam notices Sloane getting a lot of company at his house. She then gets a phone call from Jac. The two sisters argue a bit, but Sam makes clear she cares about Jac and offers to pay for her to fly back so they can talk about everything. Melissa, Thorolf, and Chandra all arrive at Sloane's, and he tells them Marco refused to use the Cantor's songs to try to heal Rafferty because he no longer trusts the darkfire. Sloane says he is trying to remember the songs that were used to waken Marco. Erik, Eileen, Zoë, Isabelle, and Brandt were also there at the time. Melissa says Erik saw Pwyll then, too, and suggests maybe he can contact the ghost again. Chandra says she feels some sort of ripple in Myth, but can't see clearly. The group joins hands (the *Pyr* in dragon form) to chant over Rafferty. In the small restaurant where she is eating dinner, Jac notices Maeve O'Neill there with her crew. Then a tall blond guy comes to Jac's table and congratulates her for shooting down the dragon. He says, "welcome to the League of *Slayers*," saying he hunts the *Pyr*, too. Though the guy seems friendly enough, something about him seems off to Jac. Jorge tells Jac Rafferty killed Marco's uncle so he had wanted to be the one to get revenge on the dragon she shot. She says she then understands why he was upset with her. Jorge learns about Marco's poem and the Guthrie book. He asks for her address, saying he can teach her more about killing dragons.

Chapter 14: Marco agonizes over what happened to Rafferty, not knowing how Jac was able to fire the crystal. He wonders if the darkfire was reacting to the desire of a *Pyr* or *Slayer* in her vicinity at the time and speculates whether Jac may be in danger. He also blames himself for not having explained the differences between the types of dragons. Marco sees Jac walking with Jorge, but picks up on her discomfort around the *Slayer*. He resolves to find out what Jorge is up to, without using the darkfire. At Sloane's, Erik is frustrated he cannot communicate with Pwyll to get the Cantor's Song. Eileen asks Chandra for specific details from her recurring dreams and connects them to myths, giving them a possible location for another nest of eggs. Thorolf will go to Easter Island to look for clues and will then take Chandra to Australia. Brandon and Brandt will assist from there. Sam picks up Jac at the airport, and they agree to start over, getting past their father's very high expectations for Sam and low ones for Jac. Jac also suggests she can help her sister make her house look as though someone lives in it. While they are resting, Rafferty stirs and says, "She's here. I smell her." Sloane has no idea who the injured *Pyr* is referring to, but is relieved when he realizes Sam's visitor is another woman, not a man. Marco arrives back at his apartment in Seattle to find it trashed and sees Jorge in salamander form on top of Sigmund's book. When Marco shifts and tries to reach for both, he gets trapped inside the spiral Jorge has drawn. The *Slayer* then proceeds to suck his energy through a dragonsmoke conduit. Sam offers a ride to a man walking on the side of the road, who says he needs to find the Apothecary. At Sloane's shop, a man working behind the counter recognizes her passenger, calling him Lee. Sloane then comes out and greets Sam.

Chapter 15: February, 2015: Jorge devises a terrible plan—he infects Ronnie with the Seattle virus, planning to release her, in the hope she will spread the virus to the other *Pyr* mates and their children. He breaks all of her fingers and damages her throat so she won't be able to tell anyone what has happened to her. Ronnie wakes up in a park next to a hospital, flags down a passing car, and the woman driving it gets paramedics to come help Ronnie. Drake senses both a *Slayer* presence and that of Ronnie, then makes his way to the hospital. Ronnie is relieved to see Drake, but refuses to let him send for Timmy. Drake is able to smell the virus and warns the doctor and nurse, who tell him he and everyone who came into contact with her will have to go into isolation. Drake tells Ronnie he wants to build a life with her, and that he will go along with the isolation in order to protect their secret. Sam's former boss calls her about coming back to work, telling her he needs her to work on Ronnie's case. She calls Sloane. After they make love, Sam tells Sloane about her son. She says her relationship with her ex-husband fell apart because their only true connection was Nathaniel. She thanks Sloane for helping her to heal, showing him the necklace Nathaniel had gotten for her but she has never worn. Sloane puts it on her neck. Sam tells him she will be leaving to go back to work and offers to sell him her house. Sloane accepts her decision since he will eventually have a firestorm and doesn't want to string her along. He feels he may have helped her to heal a bit.

Chapter 16: Drake gets released from isolation, since he does not have the virus present in his blood. He figures Jorge's plan was to infect the *Pyr* mates. Drake devises a plan to get a sample of Ronnie's blood from the hospital for Sloane to study. First, he beguiles a doctor into destroying all his blood samples so they don't discover his secret. Then Drake beguiles an orderly and takes one of Ronnie's samples. Sloane is glad he bought Sam's house, as Sara and Quinn are currently staying there. Drake and Theo then arrive, the former presenting him with the vial of blood. They wonder why Drake did not get infected since they had assumed it was the Elixir that prevented the disease taking hold of Jorge. When Theo suggests perhaps there is something special about Drake's blood, Sloane realizes he must have natural antibodies against it since he came from the time period of the infection. Drake's blood will be used to synthesize a vaccine. Ronnie is very pleased when the virus hunter, Dr. Wilcox, shows up in her room, giving Ronnie a tablet and stylus to use to communicate. Dr. Wilcox provides Ronnie with a laptop so she can help with research, since she had previous research experience, and to Skype and email with Timmy. Sam thinks perhaps her time working as a tarot reader put her a bit more in touch with other people. She realizes how much she misses Sloane. Sam resolves to leave no stone unturned in her quest to find a cure for the virus. Thorolf arrives at Sloane's just as Chandra goes into labor. Sara and Chandra have a vision together, of Snow as a white owl, dropping a rock into Chandra's hand, showing Australia, and Boris as a salamander. Eileen reports Rox just had twins again. Outside of Sloane's, Lee and Zoë plant a spiral garden of calendula and sunflowers, the seeds of which look like dragon claws and dragon eyes.

Chapter 17: (April 3, 2015) Ronnie has managed to keep herself occupied for two months in isolation, thinking about Timmy, her baby, and Drake. She learns the worst from Dr. Wilcox: her temperature has been steadily increasing in the last twenty-four hours. Ronnie will be transferred to Atlanta the next day. Crackling darkfire wakens Marco in his apartment, and he realizes the darkfire does things for the greater good rather than for individuals. He decides to use it to manifest wherever Jac is. A feverish Ronnie dreams, and Niall visits her, telling her the *Pyr* believe they have a cure and asking if she will consent to being taken by them rather than being moved to Atlanta. She agrees. Sam is both frustrated and saddened by her inability to help Ronnie. Sam decides to call Jac. When she gets voicemail, she leaves a long message for her sister, talking about Nathaniel and how he'd once told her he felt as though he had two moms, the second being Jac. Sam decides on the spur of the moment to accompany Ronnie to Atlanta. As she is being loaded onto the helicopter, four dragons descend from the sky, one of them picking up Ronnie. Very pleased to see one another, Ronnie and Drake share news about each other and Timmy. Ronnie mentions she had Drake's missing scale but Jorge took it. Drake doesn't want to worry her, so says he doubts it matters. They discuss how Drake continues to call her Veronica, and she decides that's fine, as her grandmother did, too. Sam is furious the dragons snatched Ronnie, and determines to go to Atlanta herself to search for a cure. Drake calls Timmy and explains his mom is being treated by the Apothecary with an antidote and is already getting better. When Timmy says he wishes he were a dragon shifter, Drake tells him he shouldn't wish that— that he has his own strengths and gifts. Then Timmy gets to speak to Ronnie. Since Jorge made all of Jac's travel arrangements for the lunar eclipse, she didn't know where she was going until the day she left—Australia. She has been training to face dragon shifters, but her thoughts turn to Marco. Though she has not seen him at all, she had sometimes sensed him. She feels particularly warm and aroused that evening and is surprised when Marco knocks on her hotel room door.

Chapter 18: After talking briefly, Jac lets Marco into her room. The two feel an intense attraction, and eventually have sex. Afterwards, when Marco runs his hand down the side of her face, he sees sparks. Jac sees them, also, and knows exactly what is happening, due to having read Sigmund's book. She accuses Marco of being "one of them," and he confirms it by shifting in front of her. Jac runs out of the room, to find Jorge waiting in a vehicle. After driving away, Jorge leaves the vehicle while it's moving, shifting to his dragon form, which Jac recognizes as the cause of the Seattle virus. Marco approaches. Brandon, Thorolf, Chandra, and Liz are all at Uluru, waiting for the eclipse and their task—to capture a hatchling for Sloane. Due to Sara and Chandra's vision, they also expect to see the armless Boris clone. They feel the firestorm ignite nearby. Sloane feels darkfire crackling and sees it flaming beneath Rafferty's scales. Erik gives Rafferty energy through a dragonsmoke conduit, and Sloane decides to try to remove the darkfire from Rafferty and trap it in the stone. Sloane senses the firestorm is Marco's and is relieved, as it means the Sleeper has not turned *Slayer*. Pwyll's ghost appears and begins the Cantor's chant, which Sloane, Erik, Lee, and Quinn all join in on. When the eclipse is over, the darkfire is trapped and Rafferty awakens.

Chapter 19: Jac grabs the wheel and speeds off. The two dragons begin fighting, and when she sees Jorge's black blood, she begins to believe the differences between *Slayers* and *Pyr*. Recalling that in the past people tried to kill dragons with saltpeter, Jac looks for and finds three flares in the glove box. She also notices four dragons fighting over Uluru. As the vehicle is about to crash, Marco gets there in time to get her out and flies off with her. Jorge attacks, but Jac fires one of the flares in his mouth, obliterating his lower jaw. Another *Slayer* taunts Marco and then attacks, and Jac throws a flare down inside of his mouth, as well. Jorge then uses dragonsmoke on Marco. Marco convinces Jorge he is in bad shape and he asks for the Elixir. Brandon tells Liz and Chandra he heard Marco ask for the Elixir, suggesting he plans to turn *Slayer* after his firestorm. They all try to figure out where Jac and Marco are staying. Jac wakes up in what appears to be a library, with an unconscious Marco next to her. She finds Sigmund's book there, as well as a dragon scale. Suddenly a dragon drops onto the floor, followed by a yellow salamander, who proceeds to eat the guts of the other dragon after it dies. Jac sees that Marco is conscious and has some sort of plan. After he shifts to his human form, Jorge tells Jac he had hoped there would be notes on how to create the clones in Sigmund's book, but there were not. The building begins to rumble and the floor vibrates.

Chapter 20: Jorge explains they are under a subway system, in Ivan the Terrible's lost library. He says the *Pyr* don't know the place exists. Jorge shows Jac a precious green stone called the Dracontias. The legend says a knight killed a dragon during the Middle Ages, removing the stone from its brow. It is supposed to have the ability to heal and to turn poison to water. Jorge says he'd like Jac's help to get something. Jorge then smashes Marco's scale he had torn off, causing Marco great pain, and the two begin to fight. Jac grabs Sigmund's book and the Dracontias. Sloane makes plans to refrigerate the captured *Slayer* clone once he's delivered, since he needs a live subject to test. Drake visits Ronnie and explains that he stayed away while she was in isolation to keep his nature a secret. Drake wants to prove to the Great Wyvern he is a worthy partner, so he tells her about his life with Cassandra, how he was imprisoned in the dragon's tooth, and that he wants their life together to be different from what he had before. Marco is losing his fight against Jorge, and he tries to manifest elsewhere with Jac but isn't able to. Jac then tells him to swallow the Dracontias, and then he uses a dragonsmoke conduit on the *Slayer*. Marco wishes them elsewhere.

Chapter 21: Marco and Jac end up in a motel room in Virginia, in the same city where Sam lives. They decide they are in Sam's town because the darkfire wants her to use the stone on the Seattle virus. Jac and Marco discus what will happen to the *Pyr* children if the *Slayers* win the war, Marco admitting he doesn't really know. Jac is resistant to the firestorm and having a child, since she doesn't want to be left alone. She wants to be more than just useful. Brandon, Chandra, and Liz find the room at the resort where Marco and Jac were, and they find Jac's notes about dragons and the prophecy, which makes Brandon doubt Marco even more. They scan and email the prophecy to Erik and wait for Thorolf to join them. Liz says they need to find the last batch of eggs sooner. Over a romantic dinner Drake tells Ronnie about Nikolas and Sophie, and their sacrifice. He says he will give up hunting vipers. She tells him after they win the war, that will be fine by her. Marco makes it clear to Jac it is her decision whether or not they will sate the firestorm. She says she never wanted a child to be just an accessory, as she often felt Nathaniel was to Sam and her ex-husband. She felt both her father and Sam left the care of her dying mother to her because she didn't have anything else to do. She felt they did not value what she did. Marco realizes he never had a family other than the current *Pyr*.

Chapter 22: Marco tells Jac about his father being killed by a *Slayer* and his mother being spirited away to a sanctuary by Pwyll, Rafferty's grandfather, until she gave birth to him. She died soon after, and Pwyll enchanted him to sleep to keep him safe—for fourteen or fifteen hundred years. Marco and Jac plan to check on Rafferty. He tells her he feels he never really was completely awake until she injured Rafferty and snapped him out of his lethargy. Jac checks her phone messages, and is touched by her sister's message. Jac asks Marco if he would stick around after she has a child. He says he would. She says he needs to prove he has good intentions and to survive the last eclipse of the moon's node. Jorge wakes to find his lair destroyed and his Elixir meal gone. Taunting old-speak tells him to come above to one of the subway stations. Jorge goes, grabbing the dragon scale he still has from his table. The formerly one-armed Boris clone is growing another arm, and the two fight. Jorge gets a couple of bites out of the dead clone, enabling him to manifest elsewhere. As Sam is packing up to leave for Atlanta, Jac visits her and tells her a bit about Marco.

She then tries to give Sam the Dracontias, saying it can cure anything, giving her a bit of the history. Sam refuses to believe any of it, but when Jac leaves, Sam realizes she still has the green stone. She briefly considers trying it, then dismisses the idea. Ronnie asks about the difference between the Dragon's Tooth Warriors and the Dragon Legion, and he explains how the Legion are the descendants of the original Warriors. He asks why she never removes her grandmother's pearl necklace, and she tells him her grandmother was the only family member to stand by her when she chose to marry Mark. Suddenly Drake senses an intruder. Maeve hears a knock at her door, and when she doesn't see anyone, conjures a sphere in her hand that shows her who is there. She recognizes the guy from Easter Island who identified himself as a dragon hunter. Maeve knows better, though, and assumes he is the last *Slayer*. She decides she would enjoy a bit of dragon before the *Pyr* and *Slayers* destroy each other so she lets him in. The man shows her a dragon scale, which he bites to destroy. The *Pyr* it belongs to screams in anguish, and Jorge notices Maeve hears it, too. In order to distract him from discerning her true nature, she kisses him.

Chapter 23: Marco goes to retrieve the darkfire crystal, so he can give it to Jac to defend herself. At Sloane's, he finds Rafferty holding it in a talon. When Marco touches the crystal, the darkfire flashes, and Rafferty, now in salamander form, looks at Marco. He puts Rafferty in his shirt pocket, hearing him say, "the firestorm," in old-speak. Melissa witnesses what happens. Sloane hears Melissa scream and goes into the main room to hear Erik yell that Marco took Rafferty. Erik seems to believe the worst of the Sleeper, still insisting he may be turning *Slayer*. Sloane is shown pictures of Jac's notebook, sent by Brandon. He stills wants to give Marco the benefit of the doubt. The group focuses on the sacrifice section of the prophecy. Sloane insists on bringing in a human doctor to help with the virus cure, even though Erik disagrees. The others decide to leave so they will not be at risk of public exposure. Then they all hear Drake cry out in pain. Jac decides it may be a good idea to use the firestorm to attract *Slayers* so Marco can then dispose of them, thereby ensuring the survival of the *Pyr*. Shortly after reaching this conclusion, Marco reappears with the darkfire crystal and a salamander he identifies as Rafferty. He hands both to her, and the firestorm begins to heal Rafferty. Marco and Jac cup their hands around him, the fire burns hotter, and soon he is fine. He thanks them, then disappears. Jac tells Marco of her idea, then he senses a *Slayer*. Niall gets a call from Sloane, who asks him to dream-walk into Sam's dreams, giving her an idea of Ronnie's connection to the dragon shifters. Niall agrees, and Donovan says he needs to go find Marco.

Chapter 24: Sam wakes up from a dream that causes her to put a few things together: Sloane's tattoo, the slogan on the work trailer in his driveway, Veronica Maitland, and Sloane being called the Apothecary. She realizes he treats dragon shifters and decides she's going to California to confront him and to find Ronnie. Marco finds the Boris clone in his living room. He says it was his idea for Sigmund to create clones, when their ranks were depleted during the time of Quinn's firestorm. Boris feels Marco would make a good co-ruler of the *Slayer*s, since he is the nephew of Magnus, that now-dead *Slayer* who created the Elixir. Boris tries to lure Marco by promising his son will live. Marco comes up with his own plan, telling Boris he has captured and imprisoned Rafferty as a possible source of the Elixir, but they decide Jorge would be a better choice, given how much Elixir he has consumed. Boris says he and the other hatchlings have one burning goal: to kill Erik. Marco lets Boris think they have a deal so he can work on his own plan. Jorge enjoys his time with the insatiable Maeve O'Neill, but is puzzled by her lack of scent and why he feels foggy around her. Maeve takes him into a trophy room of sorts, where she shows him items connected to the last mermaid, the last unicorn, the last elf, and so on. She states she "eliminates the unnatural creatures from this world." She wants Jorge's help to get rid of the *Pyr*, offering him immortality in exchange. Saying she is an immortal queen, she opens a portal to another dimension where she is addressed as Queen Mab. Jorge agrees to her terms—to destroy the *Pyr* and to love her as his queen in return for immortality—since it will be easier than making more Elixir. She gives him a key to the portal, and Jorge does not notice when he loses a scale, which one of Mab's minions picks up. Healing Drake has fallen to Lee, since it his dead brother Chen's methods (taught to Jorge) affecting the Dragon Legion leader. Lee takes Drake to the garden he and Zoë planted. He thinks about Chandra's vision of the two brothers, one with snakes coming out of his mouth and the other pearls. Lee takes his father's advice to heart, regarding intent rather than actual wording, and begins a chant. The other *Pyr* present join in, and not only is Drake healed, but Rafferty reappears. Lee feels as though he has a new family. Erik persists in his distrust of Marco, though Rafferty assures him the Sleeper is not turning *Slayer*. The *Pyr* disperse into various locations, with Erik going to see Lorenzo to find out what his plan is. Sam arrives at Sloane's, angry, demanding to see Veronica. When she does, she is astounded to see Ronnie looking so much better. Sloane tells her what he has done, about Drake, and the antidote made from his blood. Sam brings up the Dracontias, but Sloane says is it is a myth. Sam asks why he aids the dragon shifters, and he responds, "why do you think I do?"

Chapter 25: Sam guesses Sloane is a dragon shifter, and he explains the difference between the types of dragons. She asks which he is. They argue a bit, but Sam ends up agreeing to help him with Ronnie, specifying they will maintain a professional relationship only. Sloane gives her his notebooks, smarting that she would believe the worst of him even after all they had shared. Erik learns Lorenzo plans to beguile Maeve O'Neill during an interview, to change her attitude toward the *Pyr*, but he thinks it is a bad idea. Chandra has a vision of Machu Picchu as the next hatching site. After a few days, Sam has a conversation with Drake, in which he tells her about the firestorm. He says Sloane would not want to lead her on and hurt her when his destined mate is yet to be revealed. Drake suggests she watch the recent video from Australia, which shows a dragon shifter having a firestorm. She gains a new understanding from the video and resolves to do what she can to help. Sam tells Sloane what she has learned, and they discuss firestorms and Nathaniel. Sam admits she has missed him, and they share heated kisses.

Chapter 26: As Sam and Sloane work together, they marvel at Drake's white blood cells. Sam asks Sloane if the *Pyr* ever get sick. He says they typically only worry about battle injuries, but also explains what happens physiologically when one of them turns *Slayer*. None of the *Pyr* have caught the virus, though Theo and Kristofer were exposed when they helped bring Ronnie back. Sloane decides to inject himself with infected blood to compare his body's reaction to Ronnie's. Jac and Marco come very close to giving in to the firestorm but are interrupted when Boris shows up, saying they need to go. Marco tells Jac to bring the darkfire, and she decides then if he survives the fight, she will sate the firestorm. Erik and Eileen are driving across the desert after leaving Lorenzo's. Erik says he has a bad feeling about everything, especially because he caught a whiff of Jorge's scent on Maeve's business card. He left because Lorenzo told him to. Suddenly Erik feels a firestorm close by, tells Eileen to drive, and gets out of the car. A woman lands on the hood of the car. She says she's a mate, and when Eileen lets her in, the woman introduces herself as Jacelyn. She is holding a darkfire crystal. Eileen sees Eric fighting Boris, and Jacelyn explains about the clones. While Erik fights Boris, he sees Marco hanging back and thinks he may be correct about Marco turning *Slayer*. When the battle seems to be going against Erik, Marco intervenes. Jac uses the crystal on Boris, killing him. Zoë pours water on the *Slayer*'s ashes, and Marco and Jac use the firestorm to heal Erik. Erik says he should have talked to Marco before assuming the worst of him, but Marco says he had to trick Erik in order to convince Boris. Zoë touches the darkfire, which completely closes Erik's wound. A scale falls from Marco's chest into Jac's hand, and she says, "I love you, too."

Chapter 27: Jac and Marco sate the firestorm back at her apartment. Maeve goes to the construction site of Lorenzo's new Las Vegas theater and realizes right away Lorenzo is a dragon shifter. She plans to get all the information she can from him. When he tries to beguile her, she is able to fight the urge to succumb. Lorenzo wakes up at his theater, with no idea what happened. When turns on his phone, there are a bunch of messages from Cassie, as well as one from Maeve saying she had to cancel the interview. Cassie calls again, and Lorenzo says he's fine but doesn't know what happened. He catches a scent of an unusual perfume, sees images of stiletto heels, and has memories of divulging secrets. He thinks he must have been dreaming. For two

weeks Sam has studied Sloane's blood, and he has not contracted
the virus. His blood developed different antibodies than Drake's
did. She tries the Dracontias on Ronnie's blood, and it works. Sam
decides she needs to go to Atlanta to run trials. While this cure will
make her career, she says that doesn't feel quite as satisfying as it
once would have. Though they regret not being able to form a
permanent attachment, Sam and Sloane spend the afternoon
together making love. Then Sam decides to try the Dracontias on
the *Slayer* in the freezer. She opens the door before Sloane gets
downstairs, and the Boris clone wakes up, coming after her. Sloane
arrives in time to injure the clone enough to put him back in the
cold, and Sam sees his dragon form for the first time. Sam gives
him the Dracontias before she leaves. Ronnie saw one of Sloane's
scales fall off when he heard Sam's scream. She plans to give it to
Sam for safekeeping. Timmy is very excited that Drake is going to
take him to see his mom. Drake takes him to the house he has
purchased down the street from Dashiell and tells Timmy he is
going to have a brother soon.

Chapter 28: In July, the *Pyr* gather at Sloane's for Drake's armor
repair ceremony. At Ronnie's insistence, so as to raise awareness
of the nobility of the *Pyr*, the ceremony is being filmed, though the
identities of all the participants are concealed. Melissa interviews
Ronnie, who is wearing a mask, over topics ranging from losing a
scale to affinities and the elements. In her Atlanta hotel room, Sam
thinks about the success of the antidote in the trials, including the
nurse who was infected when helping Ronnie. She takes out the
scale Ronnie gave her. She then sees Melissa's broadcast,
recognizes Sloane's place, and tries to figure out who the various
dragons are. Afterwards, Sam sees a dragon overhead, and when
Sloane arrives at her door, she's ready. Sloane explains that he
hasn't been able to test the *Slayer* blood, since it burns through
everything. Sam suggests putting the Dracontias, or a piece of it, in
Boris' mouth, then drawing his blood to test it. She mentions her
sister Jac and Marco, surprising Sloane, and he tells her Jac and
Marco have had a firestorm. Sam is surprised but glad her sister is
happy. Sloane thinks it unlikely two *Pyr* would have firestorms
with two sisters, which saddens him. Erik thinks about the coming
end to the Dragon's Tail War and wonders what will happen if the

Pyr do not prevail. He is still ready to pay the price if it becomes necessary to sacrifice himself. Sloane arrives, telling him of the Dracontias and the possibility of using it to combat the effects of the Elixir, and Erik offers his help.

Chapter 29: (September 28, 2015) Sloane has taken a hiking vacation in Peru, giving him a chance to prepare for the upcoming final stand. The Dracontias has been shown to counteract the effects of the Elixir. Sloane has made a solution from the stone, distributing it to the *Pyr* to be administered via syringes. On the morning of the eclipse, Sloane meets Chandra, Thorolf, Liz, and Brandon at Machu Picchu. They split up to check out the most likely sites where the eggs will hatch. Marco, Quinn, Donovan, and Lorenzo are with Erik at Quinn's home in Michigan, along with their families. They know the clones will target Erik. The eclipse begins, but there are no signs of a firestorm. Darkfire suddenly explodes within the crystal, then a ruby and gold salamander appears. Marco shoots the crystal at the *Slayer,* who shifts into his dragon form and begins fighting Erik. Marco attacks a second clone, Lorenzo injects it with the antidote, and Donovan and Quinn fight and destroy it. During the fight, their stash of syringes gets broken, so Marco leaves to get more. The first clone to hatch gets away from Sloane and his group. They know the eclipse will only last an hour and thirteen minutes, and Sloane and Rafferty worry about the lack of a firestorm. Sloane, in his human form, goes through a crevasse into the chamber below where the clone appeared. They find several funerary bundles called *falsa.* This is where the eggs are hidden. Two more hatch, and Sloane catches and injects one, which Thorolf pursues, but another gets away. The earth rumbles deeply, and Rafferty says he can't sing to stop it. Gaia will have her revenge. Liz and Sloane manage to catch and inject another clone, which Arach goes after. Sloane turns to find Jorge with Chandra and her baby in the *Slayer*'s grip. When the *falsa,* begins to move, signaling another hatching, Jorge pushes Chandra away, shifts into dragon form, grabs the *falsa,* and leaves, ripping the roof off the chamber. Sloane goes in pursuit with a syringe. In the forest behind his home, Drake waits with Niall, Delaney, and Lee, as well as Theo, Kristofer, and Kade from the Dragon Legion. Lee has built a spiral of dragonsmoke to attract evil. Two *Slayers* appear, and the *Pyr* manage to get the antidote into both and destroy them. Sloane catches up to Jorge, and they battle, the syringe being juggled and dropped several times during the fight. Sloane determines to kill the *Slayer*, even without the antidote to help him.

Chapter 30: Marco manifests in Machu Picchu, grabs some of Sloane's antidote, and injects the *Slayer* Rafferty is fighting before he leaves to assist Erik in Michigan. Sloane and Jorge continue to battle, Sloane feinting to once again get his syringe. He notices Jorge does have a missing scale so Sloane injects him there. He sees a small cylinder fall from beneath the scales, Jorge saying, "She did it. I knew she was worthy." Sloane has no idea who the *Slayer* is referring to, but he kills Jorge, exposing his remains to all four elements. Marco arrives at Quinn's, helping Erik finish off the clone he has been fighting. While healing Brandt and Arach, Sloane sees fire on the tip of one of his talons, realizing he is having a firestorm. Marco helps him by manifesting with Sloane near where his mate is. He leaves him at Quinn's, where Sloane speaks briefly with the others, then continues his quest. Sloane finds himself outside of a hospital in Ann Arbor, Michigan, where he sees Sam—the other half of his firestorm. Sloane explains what is going on, and after a brief discussion (in which Sloane agrees Jac and Marco should live in Sam's former house), they go to where Sam is staying to enjoy the heat.

Epilogue: (October 1st, 2015) The *Pyr* have all gathered at Erik's in Chicago for the armor ceremonies of Marco and Sloane. Sam surprises Sloane by gifting the necklace Nathaniel got for her. The group also takes part in a ceremony to free the darkfire, so it may spread over the world and have its light no longer visible. When Marco breaks the crystal in half, the darkfire works its way around the circle of the gathered *Pyr*, touching each of them, before blinking out. Erik says it is time, and they fly off in pairs. In Chicago to cover the *Pyr* story, Maeve looks for a good candidate for her plan to hunt dragons. She spots a dark-haired young *Pyr*, who introduces himself as Kade. She gives him a stylus made of ice, which he can use it to make a door anytime he'd like to see her. The *Pyr* gather for their last public appearance, putting on a spectacle for the crowd below. After this, they will disappear from human view again, having taken an oath during the earlier ceremony not to expose themselves without good cause. At one point, darkfire crackles and a spark lands on Theo, seemingly signifying a firestorm.

DEBORAH'S COMMENTS

This is a big book. I'll pick a favorite detail from each of the component stories.

Drake and Veronica have their chance, finally, although their firestorm (and romance) is beset by challenges before their happy ending. I love when the firestorm sparks and they find each other again:

> The firestorm was a gift unexpected.
> That it should spark for Drake again was good fortune beyond any he had ever known.
> That it should burn between himself and this woman, this woman who had haunted him for four years, was a marvel he refused to question.
> He could have found Veronica even without the spark of the firestorm, for the scent of her was seared into his very being. It had been her blend of resilience and vulnerability that had snared him four years before, her fragility matched with a conviction that she could change her own circumstance. She wore her heart on her sleeve, and her thoughts were clearly read in her eyes, but she had a resolve that would surprise most people.
> Veronica fascinated Drake. Contrast seemed to characterize her, not just in her nature but in her choices. He had to think it would have been simpler for her to have married again than to have raised her son alone. He hoped she was a person guided by principle and that they had that trait in common. He liked that, though her life was modern, the necklace she wore was of pearls old enough that they'd been perfectly matched. Her home showed the same contrast, being simply decorated but elegant, with a few well-chosen pieces. It felt like a sanctuary.
> He'd known four years before that he could love this woman,

that he likely would idolize her, given half the chance, but when they had met, she had just lost her husband. He'd known she had to grieve her loss.

He'd checked on her at intervals, without her knowing of his presence, because he felt protective of her. He liked to think that someone had taken an interest in his lost wife Cassandra after he had failed to return from battle. Drake had noticed that on occasion, Veronica seemed to sense his presence, but he was sure she had never seen him.

He'd never dared to hope that she might remember him with more than kindness.

Never mind that she would melt into his arms so readily, a desire in her eyes that fueled his own. He was amazed that she had no questions, that she made no demands, that she needed no explanation of the firestorm and its sparks.

She must be one of those humans who now knew about the *Pyr* and must understand the import of the firestorm. Relief surged through him that there were no questions to answer and no explanations to make. It was all so simple between them that he could believe in destiny again.

That he had come to her appeared to be enough for Veronica.

That she wanted him was certainly sufficient for Drake.

—from **Firestorm Forever**

I like that Jac shakes up Marco so badly. He's always been so serene and composed, that I think it's good for him to be rattled, as he is in this scene when Jac surprises him:

At her urging, Marco removed his hand from his pocket, and they blinked in unison, shielding their eyes against the brilliant fire in the stone. The darkfire burned so brightly that it was almost white and impossible to look at.

"Wow," Jac whispered. "Something *is* going to happen."

"Stay close and stay down," Marco advised, then he heard the rumble of old-speak.

"Thunder!" Jac said, scanning the sky. "No, it's old-speak. They *are* coming!" Her eyes lit and Marco was afraid.

"Stay here," he commanded, but Jac seized the crystal from his hand and leapt over the rocky barrier.

To his dismay, she ran directly toward Melissa Smith and her crew, her gaze fixed on the dragon regally descending from the sky.

It was Rafferty, come to his mate.

"This is for Nathaniel!" Jac roared.

No. She couldn't.

She *wouldn't*.

But she did.

Marco watched in shock and horror as Jac shot Rafferty with the darkfire crystal. She hit Rafferty in the lower gut and the darkfire exploded into blinding light on impact. Then it crackled all around the wounded *Pyr*, like an electrical shock finding a hundred answering sparks. Rafferty lost the rhythm of flight and fell toward the earth, his massive opal and gold dragon form emitting a shimmering blue light.

Marco knew what would happen next. Rafferty would shift shape involuntarily, and the camera crew would broadcast it. Rafferty's human identity could be revealed, and the Covenant would be broken.

He had to intervene!

Marco shifted shape and leapt into the sky, snatching the crystal from Jac's outstretched hand as he flew past her. He plucked Rafferty out of the air, shielding his body from the view of the cameras just as the unconscious *Pyr* shifted to his human form. The crowd on the island shouted and cried out, but Marco was deaf to their cries.

It was Marco's worst nightmare come true. Rafferty was out cold and injured badly. And it was Marco's fault, because he'd been careless.

Because the darkfire had led him astray.

Marco soared into the sky, thinking furiously of what he should do. He heard the crowd roaring behind him, and he heard Melissa's cry of anguish.

He was shaken to his very marrow that the darkfire could have betrayed him like this and unable to even think straight.

Rafferty was injured, perhaps fatally so. His guardian, mentor and friend might die, because of his mistake.

It was up to Marco to make this mistake come right.

—from **Firestorm Forever**

And finally, there are Sloane and Samantha. There's an electric attraction between them right from the start, but issues to be resolved, too. I love that Sloane helps Sam to heal without any expectation of being with her for good, and that his efforts mean they can have a firestorm. Their firestorm is excerpted elsewhere in this volume, so here's their first scene together:

Sloane was beginning to feel as if he were being punished for his failure to solve the riddle of the plague.

In addition to that, the presence of his new neighbor made him resent the fact that he couldn't choose his own mate. He turned underwater and roared through another pair of laps. Samantha was exactly the kind of woman he'd have chosen for himself. She was blond and delicately built, but clever and sensitive. He suspected that she was stronger than even she knew. She was feminine but pragmatic, too, which had to be the most enticing combination.

He'd met her when she'd moved in and talked to her again when she'd come to buy herbs from his greenhouse. She was a tarot card reader who said she sometimes cast spells with herbs for her clients. She had a secret, though—Sloane could smell it on her—and a vulnerability that got him right where he lived. Something had hurt her badly and she'd made a big change in order to deal with that injury. Sloane wanted to help more than he knew was sensible.

The thing was that until he had his firestorm, he couldn't promise anything more than a short fling to any woman. He sensed that Sam needed more than that and plowed through another half dozen laps disliking that he didn't have more to offer.

The moon moved, the first shadow of the eclipse touching its radiant glow.

Sloane swam harder.

He closed his eyes as a firestorm sparked, his heart sinking with the realization that it wasn't his. He reached the end of the pool with a growl, pulled himself out of the water, then caught a whiff of jasmine and musk.

Sam's perfume.

She was standing at the gate, watching him in silence.

Sloane froze, braced on the side of the pool, and stared, transfixed. It was as if he had conjured her out of nothing, willing her to appear. He halfway thought she was a vision, but he could sense her uncertainty. He saw her swallow and wanted to reassure her.

No, he wanted to protect her forever from whatever she feared. And he wanted to spend the night making love to her first.

Sam evidently took his silence as an invitation, because she opened the gate and stepped into the paved yard. She slipped out of her flip-flops and eased the linen shirt from her shoulders. She was wearing a bikini so small that Sloane's mouth went dry. She flicked a glance at him, then smiled as she unfastened the clasp in the middle of the top. She bared her breasts to the moonlight, then slipped out of the bikini bottom. Sloane could have been turned to stone.

She walked toward him, and he told himself he had to be dreaming. The moonlight made her skin look silver and her eyes luminous. She sat down on the lip of the pool beside him and put her feet into the water. She smiled, licked her lips, then touched his shoulder.

"I was so hot," she whispered, her gaze clinging to his. He didn't dare survey her again, because he didn't want to spook her, but he could see the patina of perspiration on her upper lip. He wanted to kiss it off. "It made me think of you," she admitted, and her words astonished him.

She wasn't lying.

So, he wasn't going to.

"I was just thinking of you," Sloane admitted, and she smiled with pleasure.

"But you're too much of a gentleman to have done anything about it," she charged, then shook her head.

Sloane might have defended himself, but she was right. He wouldn't have gone knocking at her door on a moonlit night, no matter how much he wanted to do so.

"Is that why you were swimming laps so hard?"

Sloane dipped his head and grinned that she'd guessed at least part of the reason for his frustration. "Caught," he murmured, daring to look into her eyes once more.

She was pleased by that and her eyes started to sparkle. She looked good enough to eat, but whatever happened had to be her choice. Sloane was keenly aware of her vulnerability, an indication of an emotional wound, and instinctively wanted to help her to heal. He sensed she was trying to make a change, to move past something, and it was in his nature to facilitate that.

Which meant he had to wait.

He wasn't sure how long they stared into each other's eyes before Sam reached out and touched his mouth with her fingertip. "I'm hoping you're not too much of a gentleman to do something about this," she whispered, then bent closer and replaced her fingertip with her mouth.

Her lips were soft and sweet, her kiss gentle, her scent beguiling him as little else could have done. Her mix of boldness and vulnerability kicked all of Sloane's desires into overdrive. Before he could think twice—much less be cautious and responsible—she was in his arms and he was slanting his mouth over hers, deepening his kiss.

That distant firestorm burned hotter, sending fire through Sloane's veins.

It wasn't his firestorm.

It might have been a thousand miles away.

But the funny thing was, Sloane no longer cared.

—from **Firestorm Forever**

GLOSSARY

Every fictional world has its own terminology and that is particularly true of fantasy realms. Here is a glossary of terms that frequently are used in the Dragonfire novels. Although every attempt is made to include an explanation in context, sometimes a longer explanation is desired. Be warned that if you haven't read the entire series, you may find spoilers here!

ACADEMY, THE—The Academy was established by Magnus to raise dead *Pyr* and *Slayers*, force-feed them the Dragon's Blood Elixir and turn them into shadow dragons responsive only to his commands. In this way, he meant to build an invincible army to defeat the *Pyr*.

Although the Academy was hidden from the outset, certain of the *Pyr* had an awareness of its presence, though they might only have sensed that there was a new shadow in the world. In **Kiss of Fury**, Erik had been haunted by dreams of a place where "crimes are committed in the shadows", and Sophie sensed "the black void of the *Slayers'* secret academy." Sophie's awareness of the Academy had an allure and she feared it was a trap, that by drawing her attention, the *Slayers* would snare her and use her power for their own ends. Similarly, she warned Erik to stay away from the shadow of the Academy in his own dreams. Sophie associated a smell with the Academy "a scent of cinders and ash, of death and dark shadows." She believed the smell to be wicked.

"It will be an older *Pyr*. Older than any of you. Someone who was born before the notion of *Pyr* and *Slayer* was so well articulated, someone whose heart holds both shadow and light."
—Sophie in **Kiss of Fury**

Later in **Kiss of Fury**, Sophie revealed that a *Pyr* will destroy the Academy and free those *Pyr* trapped there, but it won't be one of the *Pyr* present. She was referring to Nikolas of Thebes, who was still enchanted at this point.

There was a low rumble, the sound of shackles falling and heavy doors being thrown back on their hinges to collide with walls. Donovan heard locks tumbling, although he couldn't see anything. The shadows seemed to be getting darker beyond the driveway, as if the light were being extinguished.

"The earth moans," Rafferty murmured, clearly as puzzled as Donovan.

"The fire flickers," Quinn added.

"The wind dies," Niall said, scanning the sky.

Sara raised her hands to her mouth. "The dark academy is opened," she whispered, her voice filled with dread.
—**Kiss of Fury**

At the end of **Kiss of Fury**, Magnus revealed his shadow dragons to the *Pyr*. As the figures became clear, the *Pyr* saw familiar, beloved and dead *Pyr* in the ranks of Magnus' shadow dragons including Rafferty's grandfather, Niall's twin brother Phelan, and three of Quinn's brothers.

AEGISHJALMUR—A protective Norse sigil also called the Helm of Awe. It's composed of eight Elhaz runes arranged in a circle. Thorolf has a tattoo of the Helm of Awe on his bicep, and the runestone given to Erik by his father, Soren, is  inscribed with the Helm of Awe. Soren gave the runestone to Erik on his first voyage with the Drakkir. Erik subsequently gave it to his son, Sigmund, but Sigmund let his human grandfather use it as a talisman to trap Soren. Soren's runestone is recovered in **Kiss of Fate** and used to repair Erik's armor. Thorolf recognizes the sigil and tells Eileen that the Vikings made small Aegishjalmur talismans of lead and wore them on their foreheads into battle. Erik's missing scale is on his brow: the runestone is only fully visible in his dragon form, and appears as a silvery freckle in his human form.

AFFINITIES—As custodians of the four elements (air, water, fire, earth), the *Pyr* have a strong relationship with them. Each *Pyr* has affinities to two elements. When any given *Pyr* experiences his firestorm, his destined mate will invariably possess affinities to the other remaining two elements. Their strengths and weaknesses are complementary, as a result, which makes a permanent union such a powerful alliance. When the mate gives a gift for her dragon's scale repair that gift often echoes her two affinities.

An affinity allows a *Pyr* to commune, communicate, influence or even control that specific element. This often is done through chants or Songs. In **Kiss of Fury**, for example, Rafferty—whose has an affinity with the element of earth—confesses that he asked the earth for confirmation that Keir had remained buried a month after that dragon's death. Water is considered to be an unusual affinity for a *Pyr*, but it appears to run in the Shea family and both Donovan and Delaney share it.

There are differences between *Pyr* and their abilities with respect to their affinities, so the same affinity can manifest differently between different *Pyr*. Quinn, the Smith, for example has an affinity to earth just as Rafferty does. Quinn's skill is linked to metal, either refined metals at use in our world, or those raw ores still buried in the earth. Rafferty's skill, in contrast, is more tuned to earth, rock and even bone. In **Kiss of Fury**, he even repairs the saltillo tiles in Peter and Diane's conservatory, using his affinity to influence the clay in the ceramics.

The Wyvern has affinities to all four elements. In **Kiss of Fury**, Sophie attuned herself to the planet, Gaia, and worked to save humans by diverting storms and natural disruptions from areas of dense population. This is an endless and exhausting task, and invariably, she had to stop to rest.

Chen's spell for domination requires him to master the four elements to gain control of the fifth, spirit. Since he hasn't mastered the element of air and time is of the essence, he tries to capture a *Pyr* with that affinity. His plan is to seize the mastery from that *Pyr* during his firestorm. He targets first Niall, then Lorenzo, Brandon, and finally Thorolf.

AFFINITIES OF THE *PYR*:
Brandon—earth and water
Brandt—air and fire
Alexander—earth and fire
Damien—air and fire

Delaney—water and air
Donovan—water and fire
Erik—air and fire
Gaspar—air and fire
Lee—air and fire
Lorenzo—air and fire
Lothair—earth and fire
Marco—air and fire
Maximilian—earth and fire
Myrddin—air and fire
Niall—air and fire
Nikolas—earth and fire
Owen—earth and fire
Pwyll—air and fire
Quinn—fire and earth
Rafferty—earth and fire
Sahir (Cinnabar)—earth and fire
Salvatore—air and fire
Sigmund—air and fire
Sloane—water and fire
Soren—air and fire
Thaddeus—earth and fire
Thierry of Béziers—earth and fire
Thorkel—air and fire
Thorolf—air and fire
Thorvald—earth and fire

ALTERNATE FORMS—All *Pyr* and *Slayers* can shape shift between two forms, dragon or man. There are exceptions to this rule of thumb, however. The Wyvern has the ability to assume additional forms, most commonly that of a salamander. The salamander form usually takes its coloring from the dragon form of that individual. Any injuries also are consistent between forms.

With the consumption of the Dragon's Blood Elixir, some *Slayers* were able to develop additional abilities generally reserved by the Wyvern, including the assumption of the salamander form. Magnus could take this form, and simply knowing it could be done prompted the *Pyr* Rafferty to conquer this skill as well. The salamander form, because of its size, is particularly useful for spontaneous manifestation elsewhere, another ability traditionally exclusive to the Wyvern but appropriated by *Slayers*.

The *Slayer* Chen is remarkable in his ability to assume multiple human forms, including a young woman, a young man and an old man. Chen can also become a snake, as well as a salamander.

AIRDAUGHTER — An Elemental Witch with an affinity for air. An Airdaughter can control the element of air but also can become it. Aura is the first Airdaughter introduced in the series: her story and the link between Elemental Witches and nymphs is told in the Dragon Legion Novella, **Kiss of Destiny**. Aura also has the ability to peek into the future, and she can see both of Thad's forms simultaneously when they meet. She refers to herself as a shapeshifter, because she can be either a woman or air, and sees that she and Thad have common ground.

APOTHECARY — The healer of the *Pyr*. Like the Smith, the Apothecary is a hereditary role, involving a long apprenticeship and training in the medicinal uses of herbs etc. for the specific treatment of *Pyr*. The Apothecary in the *Dragonfire* novels is Sloane Forbes, the son of Tynan Forbes, the previous Apothecary.

The Apothecary is the only one who can treat injuries and diseases specific to the physiology of the *Pyr*. The black blood of *Slayers*, for example, is corrosive and burns whatever it contacts. Sloane has a salve to treat this. In **Kiss of Fury**, when Peter is burned by Sigmund's blood, Sloane is quick to remove the blood and treat the burn before the paramedics arrive on the scene. Sloane is intrigued by the changing color of Delaney's blood, after that *Pyr* was compelled to take the Elixir: Delaney's blood is mingled, black and red. Each time Delaney acts for good, the red becomes more dominant. When Sloane tends Delaney's injury after the spark of Delaney's firestorm in **Winter Kiss**, he's pleased that Delaney's blood is all red and interprets that as a sign that the firestorm has helped Delaney triumph over the Elixir. At the end of **Winter Kiss**, Sloane gathers the cinnabar crystals to use for healing. After Niall becomes the Dreamwalker in **Whisper Kiss**, Sloane teams up with Niall for a better understanding of Rox's injury in order to heal her. The pair, who are friends and have been business partners, consult together after that. Sloane's greatest feat of healing in *Dragonfire* is solving the riddle of the virus inflicted on humanity by Jorge and creating an antidote that Sam has replicated and distributed in **Firestorm Forever**. He also creates an antidote to the Elixir, which allows the Slayers who have consumed the Elixir to be killed.

AQUA FORTIS—an ancient name for nitric acid, literally 'strong water'.

> *Elusive as water,*
> *Strong as earth,*
> *I work change inexorably;*
> *Fire takes blood to stone;*
> *The cycle can only end*
> *with my sacrifice.*

Sloane reads this riddle from his treatise in **Winter Kiss**, figuring out with Alex that it refers to the "sacrifice" of nitric acid in a chemical reaction. The *Pyr* use nitric acid to precipitate the mercury sulfide out of the Dragon's Blood Elixir and destroy it.

AVENGER OF THE AESIR, THE—a sword that is Thorolf's legacy, forged by his grandfather, Thorkel. Thorolf and his father were estranged when that *Pyr* died, so he entrusted the sword to his friend, Erik, for safekeeping.

The Avenger of the Aesir was a long and heavy sword, so massive that only a man of Thorolf's large stature could wield it. The blade was forged true and etched with runes to bless and protect whoever carried it. The hilt was bronze, simply designed, for it stole no attention from the pommel. That disk had been impressed with the most powerful rune known to Erik and his kind, the Helm of Awe.

The Helm of Awe was an insigil, a composite of individual runes resulting in an amulet. The Helm of Awe was a circle, with eight lines inside it, two intersecting crosses. In that, it looked like the points of a compass. Each arm terminated in a fork, and each had three crossbars halfway down its length. Erik found his fingertip tracing the incised line of the insigil, as if to draw protection and strength from it himself.

There was a dent in the pommel and several deep scratches in the hilt. They were all the evidence that remained of Thorolf's rejection of this duty. They'd been buffed out by a master swordsmith but had been impossible to completely remove. Erik supposed the blade had to carry the mark of Thorolf's refusal to be his father's son. He hadn't been surprised that after Thorolf and Thorvald parted, Thorvald had hunted the world for the missing blade.

He certainly wasn't surprised that Thorvald had found it.

—from **Serpent's Kiss**

BEGUILING—Both *Pyr* and *Slayer* have the ability to beguile humans, although it is a skill which must be learned and cultivated. The dragon shifter in question drops his voice to low murmur, speaks slowly, and conjures flames in his eyes. This is usually done while in human form and humans see a flame deep in the iris of the dragon shifter in question. This is so irrational and unlikely that the human looks more closely, then is snared by the dragon shifters' spell. The human feels compelled to repeat whatever the dragon shifter says, thus deepening the spell by power of suggestion. There is more than one suggestion in the series that it is better to do less beguiling than more: in **Kiss of Fury**, the *Pyr* avoid beguiling both Peter and Diane, until Diane loses her temper.

Beguiling is similar to hypnosis, and like hypnosis, yields better results if the suggestion is something the victim already wants to believe. *Pyr* have used it for eons to convince those humans who have seen them in dragon form not to believe their eyes. Erik tries to beguile Sara in **Kiss of Fire**, to convince her to learn more about dragons and later in the same book, Boris beguiles Sara in order to kidnap her. There is an indication that humans can learn to block beguiling with some success as Quinn asks Rafferty to teach Sara to defend herself against it.

Beguiling also requires skill and concentration to be done successfully. In **Kiss of Fury**, Donovan is so shaken by the spark of his firestorm that he fails in his attempt to beguile a human interfering with his rescue of Alex. (He decks the man instead.)

Beguiling is less effective on children, perhaps because they have fewer expectations in terms of what they should see and in fact, there's a suggestion that it's dangerous to even try to beguile a child. It's not clear whether it's the child or the *Pyr* who is in peril. In **Kiss of Fury**, Erik forbids Niall and Sloane to beguile Jared, even though the three *Pyr* beguile Peter and the arriving firemen. It is Sophie who tells Jared that he must forget, but she doesn't beguile him—or if she does, her beguiling is of a different kind.

"Close your eyes," she whispered. "And forget." On his forehead she planted a kiss, one that shimmered silver on his skin.

When it faded, Jared was asleep on Sloane's shoulder.

—**Kiss of Fury**

The *Pyr* frequently compare the persuasive abilities of humans—particularly of their mates—to beguiling. This may be either admiration or rationalization. In **Kiss of Fury**,

The *Pyr* believe that a dragon shifter can't beguile another dragon shifter or not—at least until Erik realizes he's been beguiled in **Whisper Kiss**, which is why he can't remember any detail of Gaspar's bloodline. Erik believes this must have been done by Salvatore, Gaspar's son, but actually, it's Salvatore's son, Lorenzo, who is responsible. Lorenzo, that master illusionist who wants no part of the *Pyr*, is the most adept of the *Pyr* at beguiling. (Donovan says that Rafferty is the best of the *Pyr* at beguiling, but this is likely because Lorenzo has been out of contact with his fellow *Pyr* and Donovan is unaware of that *Pyr*'s expertise.) Erik realizes the truth when Zoë touches the runestone in his forehead and dismisses the beguiling. In **Flashfire**, Lorenzo beguiles Balthasar, sending him to his death. In **Serpent's Kiss**, Lorenzo beguiles Chen with mixed results but enough success to defeat him.

Slayers sometimes use beguiling to stop a firestorm or draw out the *Pyr*: Sara is beguiled and abducted by Boris in **Kiss of Fire**; Phelan beguiles Rox in **Whisper Kiss**; Jorge tries to beguile both

Ronnie and Jac in **Firestorm Forever**.

BLOOD—The blood of the *Pyr* is red, like human blood, while the blood of *Slayers* is both black and corrosive. *Slayer* blood burns through all it touches. The color of the blood of a wounded dragon can reveal his true allegiance more clearly even than his actions. In **Kiss of Fury**, Alex knew she could trust Delaney (who had been partly turned to a shadow dragon and whose true intent was unclear) when she saw that his blood had turned red.

BLOODSTONE—a token used by Magnus as part of the spell to create the Dragon's Blood Elixir. The sorceress Aurelia tempted Magnus with the stone, and he both fell in love with her and married her, giving her wealth and position in exchange for it. When she died, he sent his slave Sahir to retrieve it from her, ensuring that the slave was condemned to work in the Roman cinnabar mines for defiling a corpse. The bloodstone is described as being the size of an egg and inscribed with symbols of the four elements. Magnus puts it in Delaney's mouth near the end of **Winter Kiss**, when Delaney is paralyzed and about to become the new source of the Elixir. When Delaney is saved, Rafferty crushes the stone in his hands, ensuring that the Elixir can never be created again.

CANTOR—A traditional role of the *Pyr*, which is usually hereditary because it requires a long apprenticeship. The Cantor is a kind of wizard, who can cast spells with the assistance of the elements. Rafferty's grandfather, Pwyll, was the last Cantor of the *Pyr*, and he enchanted Marco to sleep until the darkfire was sparked. Although Rafferty knows some of the songs of the Cantor, he doesn't believe he has the expertise to be the new Cantor. Over the course of Dragonfire, his confidence grows as he remembers and dreams his grandfather's songs. Rafferty sings, for example, to the Dragon's Tooth that is Nikolas in **Kiss of Fury**, then later to the other ninety-nine Dragon's Teeth.

In Hampstead Heath, Rafferty Powell planted a strange crop in his garden. He had planted many mysterious seeds in his time, but these were the oddest of all.

He planted ninety-nine enormous teeth.

Niall and Thorolf had appeared after the departure of Lynne Williams, and Rafferty put them to work. The soil in his neglected garden wasn't easily worked, but the younger *Pyr* were strong and determined.

Rafferty focused on his low song, the same chant he had repeated when the tooth that had become Nikolas was planted. He sang to the teeth; he murmured to them of the challenges ahead of the *Pyr*, he beseeched them to fulfill their destinies. He sang until he was hoarse and then he sang some more.

—**Kiss of Fate**

After **Darkfire Kiss** and the reclaiming of the darkfire crystal by Marco, Rafferty is called the new Cantor of the *Pyr*, even though he is still learning his grandfather's skills. Marco calls himself the heir of the Cantor, because he has taken command of the darkfire.

CELEBRATION—It is traditional for the *Pyr* to celebrate any victory or triumph with earthly pleasures. In past times, there was considerable eating, drinking and making love after a dragon fight, perhaps an expression of an unconscious desire to prove that one had survived.

There was nothing, in Nikolas' experience, better than a battle ended well, and the company of comrades in arms. He was ready to celebrate in the traditional manner, more ready than usual, given that he'd spent several millennia enchanted.

He glanced toward the two women who stepped out of the shelter, unable to decide whether the tall dark-haired one or the delicate blonde was more attractive. Donovan and Quinn bristled as one, though, and Nikolas knew he would have to look elsewhere for that particular pleasure.

It was reassuring how few things had changed.

—**Kiss of Fury**

CHALLENGE COIN—Dragons have a tendency to both fight and to vigilantly defend their honor. If a *Pyr* or *Slayer* tosses his challenge coin at an opponent, he is challenging the other dragon shifter to a fight to the death. If that opponent picks up the coin, the challenge has been accepted. The fight may be interrupted or delayed, but they will fight to death, as a matter of honor. Challenge coins are carefully chosen by each dragon shifter to be characteristic of his nature or background, and to be distinctive. Each dragon always has his challenge coin in his possession, and carries it between forms.

The first challenge coin exchanged in the Dragonfire series was tossed by Ambrose to distract Sara. It was a florin from medieval Florence, although Quinn changed the coin, remaking it into his own with his power over metal. When the coin carried his marks, Quinn placed it on the chimney of Sara's home as a protective talisman, making Sara's residence an extension of his lair. There is some suggestion that Quinn invited the coin to change shape but didn't guide its final form.

When he opened his hand, the coin had changed. A mermaid adorned one face of it and a hammer, the other. Quinn smiled at the appropriate combination. Sometimes the metal knew better than he did.
— **Kiss of Fire**

Erik gave Quinn his own father's challenge coin in **Kiss of Fire**, saying that Thierry gave it to him to pass on to his son. It's a gold Roman coin, and Quinn remembered his father rolling it between his knuckles and making it disappear, to entertain the children. He also recalls that his father never allowed anyone else to touch the coin. This implies that the coin carries a signature energy, much as tarot cards become embued with the energy of their owner and reader, and that each *Pyr* will keep his challenge coin close — until he uses it to provoke a blood duel. Quinn tests Erik's story by singing to the coin: the fact that he can change its shape to make it is own proves to Quinn that Erik is telling the truth.

"Thierry told me to tell you that the Smith can make any coin his own. I don't know what that means, but maybe you do."
— Erik in **Kiss of Fire**

Winning a challenge also meant that the victor gathered the spoils, i.e. he laid claim to the hoard of the defeated dragon. With growing animosity between *Pyr* and *Slayer* came doubt that this tradition would be maintained. In **Kiss of Fury**, Donovan threw his challenge coin at Tyson, creating an interruption before Quinn shifted shape to defend Sara in a crowded shopping mall. When Donovan triumphs, the *Pyr* question whether he will gain Tyson's hoard or whether Boris will defy tradition and appropriate it himself. The outcome is never clarified.

Erik challenges Boris with his challenge coin in **Kiss of Fury**, and believes he has won at the end of that book, unaware that Boris has drunk the Elixir and will recover from his injuries. Rafferty throws his challenge coin at Magnus in **Winter Kiss**, launching a battle to the death between the two old dragons. When Thorolf is under Chen's spell and turning *Slayer* in **Serpent's Kiss**, he tosses his challenge coin at Rafferty, not recognizing his friend and mentor. Rafferty gives it back to him, acting as if it was just dropped by accident. Jorge beguiles one of the clones of Boris in **Firestorm Forever** and compels him to toss his challenge coin at a second clone. The two battle to the death for Jorge's entertainment as Jac watches.

KNOWN CHALLENGE COINS OF *PYR* AND *SLAYERS*

Ambrose—a gold *florin*, struck 1252
Balthasar—a Byzantine gold *histamenon* Constantine X, struck 1057
Brandon Merrick—an Australian dodecahedron 50-cent piece struck in 1969
Brandt Merrick—silver George III halfpenny struck in 1805
Boris Vassily—a 5-kopecs copper coin Catherine the Great, struck 1789
Delaney Shea—a silver portcullis trade dollar of Elizabeth I, struck 1601
Donovan Shea—American sterling silver dollar
Erik Sorensson—Olaf Tryggvason penny
Jean-Pierre (JP)—a silver *denier* of Pepin I of Aquitaine, struck 817
Jorge—a Russian silver *denga* with a dragon, struck 1360

Lorenzo di Fiori—a Venetian gold *zecchino* of Paolo Renier struck in 1779
Marcus Maximus—1£ Cardiff coin with dragon, struck 2011
Magnus Montmorency—a silver-plated brass Roman *follis*, struck 295 by Diocletian
Mallory—a silver *franc* with Henry III on one side and 4 fleur-de-lis on the other, struck 1583
Niall Talbot—peacock *rupee*, struck in UK (but incised Burma) in 1852
Quinn—his own mermaid coin, which he can create out of any other coin
Rafferty Powell—an "angel", a gold English coin struck in 1465 with St. George and the dragon on one side, and a sun with emanating rays on the other
Salvatore di Fiori—a Venetian silver *ducato*, ca. 1200
Sigmund Guthrie—a silver Offa King of Mercia penny, ca. 757
Sloane Forbes—a Spanish gold *dobla de la banda* of John II struck in 1410
Soren—runestone of Helm of Awe
Thierry of Béziers—Roman gold *solidus* Emperor Honorius, struck 393
Thorolf—a silver Aethelstan penny, struck 933

CINNABAR—an ancient name for mercury sulfide and a key ingredient in the Dragon's Blood Elixir.

"Sisapo is called Almadén now, in Spain." He eyed her but she shook her head. "It remains one of the largest deposits of cinnabar in the world, and is still a working mine."
"What's cinnabar?"
Breathtaking stupidity. Magnus stifled a sigh. "Mercury sulfide. A red stone, which can be used to make the pigment vermilion. The Chinese used it to stain lacquer-ware. The Byzantines used it for coloring ink." Magnus took the final sip of Elixir from his glass, a long swig that he savored as the mate watched him with disgust. "It was also used medicinally, to promote immortality. Oh, and its colloquial name was Dragon's Blood." He smiled.
—from **Winter Kiss**

At the end of **Winter Kiss**, when the red crystals are falling in the sanctuary that once held the Dragon's Blood Elixir, Ginger collects some of the crystals for Sloane.

CLONING—A chance comment made by Boris Vassily in **Kiss of Fury,** and the subsequent promise of reward, tempts Sigmund to research the possibility of cloning *Slayers*.

"If only I could clone myself a dozen times, we would be rid of the *Pyr* and their pesky humans."
There was a pause, one that caught Boris' attention. He turned to find Sigmund looking thoughtful...
—**Kiss of Fury**

Sigmund set an experiment in motion before he died, and hid thirteen dragon's eggs around the earth to incubate the clones of Boris. These eggs had to be exposed to the light of a blood moon in order to ripen and hatch, which they did in **Firestorm Forever**, under three different eclipses.

CLOTHING—When a *Pyr* or *Slayer* shifts shape, he folds his clothing away quickly and tucks it beneath his scales. It is considered to be particularly important that no one ever witness exactly where the garments are hidden. No shifter can return to his human form without his clothing, so speed with this feat is key to survival.

In **Kiss of Fury**, Erik burned the clothing of the *Slayer* Boris while they were both in dragon form: Boris, however, had folded away his underwear, so survived this tactic. In **Winter Kiss**, Niall insists that Thorolf practice hiding his clothes more quickly, but in **Whisper Kiss**, Rox sees them even so.

This vulnerability of the *Pyr* is twisted in the *Dragon Diaries*, when the Mages managed to hold the older *Pyr* captive and in their human forms by seizing the coat of scales of each dragon shifter.

Do humans know we exist? Sure. Humans always have—thus the dragon stories they tell. But knowing dragons exist, believing that there are actually dragon shape shifters, and being convinced that your neighbor is one of them are entirely different things.

That's probably a good thing...

The fact is that most humans don't believe they could personally know a dragon shape shifter...So, in a way, we might as well be a myth.

Which is funny, if you think about it.

—Zoë Sorensson in **Flying Blind**

COVENANT, THE—The Covenant is a pledge that all *Pyr* must swear to uphold in order to keep the identity of individual *Pyr* secret and all of the *Pyr* safe. The notion behind it is that humans can know an individual Pyr in either human or dragon form, but not in both forms, and certainly, no human should witness the transformation if it can possibly be avoided. The Covenant was put into place by Erik Sorensson, at the end of the Dragon's Tail Wars. All adult *Pyr* had to pledge to it immediately and Zoë confided in **Flying Blind** that the next generation had to swear to it after Nick Shea was caught showing off for some girls. Zoë has provided the only known text of the Covenant outside of the *Pyr*:

"I, (insert name), do solemnly pledge not to willfully reveal the truth of my shape-shifting abilities to humans. I understand that individuals may know me in dragon form or in human form, but I swear that I shall not permit humans to know me in both forms, to to allow them to witness my shifting between forms without appropriate assessment of risk. I understand also that there will be humans who come to know me in both forms over the course of my life—I pledge not to reveal myself without due consideration, to beguile those who inadvertently witness my abilities, and to supply the names of those humans whom I have entrusted with my truth to the leader of the Pyr, Erik Sorensson."

DARKFIRE—An ancient magic that breeds chaos and unpredictability in the world of the *Pyr*. Darkfire was trapped in three quartz crystals in the past by the Cantor, Pwyll, who was Rafferty's grandfather. Darkfire burns with a blue-green light and crackles within the crystals as if there is lightning trapped within them. Sigmund tells Erik in a dream that there were once three crystals:

"Once there were three, a legacy passed from Cantor to Cantor. One created the Sleeper. One held the darkfire. Who has the third?"
—from **Darkfire Kiss**

The *Slayer* Chen has one crystal and breaks it deliberately, setting the darkfire free in the hopes of defeating the *Pyr* at the beginning of **Darkfire Kiss**. The second darkfire crystal is revealed to be in Rafferty's hoard, entrusted to him by his grandfather on that *Pyr*'s death. The spark in that second crystal is said to mirror the state of the Sleeper, the nephew of Magnus and a *Pyr* enchanted by Pwyll to ensure his safety. When Rafferty first sees the darkfire, he's skeptical that it is darkfire—he recalls that darkfire has been trapped in the crystals for most of his life.

She was human. She was one of the treasures of the earth he was charged to defend.

Not only that, but his firestorm was the fabled darkfire. He had another responsibility, one that Magnus didn't suspect existed but would be determined to derail if that *Slayer* learned the truth. The Sleeper would awaken, according to Rafferty's grandfather's ancient charm, because the darkfire burned and Rafferty was bound to defend the Sleeper until the darkfire was extinguished.

That he had never believed this day would come was irrelevant.
—from **Darkfire Kiss**

When Rafferty and Melissa consummate their firestorm in his study, all the crystals in his mineral collection light with darkfire. The prophecy governing Rafferty's firestorm says that the darkfire will only be extinguished when there's been sufficient change. Melissa suggests that one of the things that have to be changed is the *Pyr*'s tradition of hiding themselves from humans, and Erik argues against this plan. The revealing of the *Pyr* happens anyway. Erik fears that one of the things sacrificed to the darkfire is Zoë's dawning gifts as Wyvern. When Rafferty sings the song of the Cantor as well as he remembers it, holding the crystal entrusted to him, it sparks and awakens the Sleeper. The Sleeper claims the crystal as his own, as well as the quest of containing the darkfire, and confesses that his name is Marcus Maximus. (The *Pyr* subsequently call him Marco.) The darkfire also influences Viv Jason, who leaves her job when she feels its spark and travels to Chen's lair in Tibet. At the end of **Darkfire Kiss**, the darkfire is contained in the crystal that Marco takes from Rafferty:

The Sleeper continued, again indicating the crystal. "You have contained that measure of darkfire in this stone, adding it to the darkfire already there."

The stone did burn with a brighter flame.

"It is the legacy of the Cantor to contain the darkfire," he continued. "To command it and to ensure that it is controlled. It is a responsibility, passed through your line."

Rafferty frowned. "I do not know how to do this...."

"You do not have to," the Sleeper said with resolve. "You have defended me and fulfilled the prophecy." He stood with purpose. "The quest now is mine. Pwyll trained me for this."

"The son he never had," Rafferty said softly, regret in his heart.

"No." The Sleeper held his gaze steadily, with no censure. "He said his line had paid dearly for the burden of darkfire. He loved you. He respected you. He wanted you to have the gifts of darkfire — and this is one of them."

"I thought you slept through the ages."

The Sleeper smiled. "And in sleep, there are dreams. The Cantor sang in my dreams, teaching me what I needed to know."

Then he plucked the stone from Rafferty's hand, claiming it for his own. The flame in the crystal responded immediately, burning brilliantly and then settling to a blue-green glow.

The Sleeper smiled. "It is done, just as foretold."

—from **Darkfire Kiss**

Marco also says that darkfire gives him the gift of convening with the dead. He tells the *Pyr* that Pwyll's ghost is confirming that Erik should lead them.

In **Flashfire**, the third darkfire crystal is revealed to have been in

Lorenzo's hoard but is missing. Lorenzo made a deal with the Cantor to defend the crystal in exchange for Pwyll teaching him the flashfire song. It's been missing from Lorenzo's hoard for at least six months. It turns out that his father Salvatore dreamed of the crystal and its destiny, and surrendered it to Drake, the leader of the Dragon's Tooth Warriors, in **Kiss of Danger**. That crystal compels those *Pyr* to travel through time in search of their destined mates and firestorms, as told in the **Dragon Legion Novellas**.

In **Kiss of Danger**, the darkfire sparks in the sanctuary of Apollo at Delphi, sending Jorge back to the future (in his salamander form). It also reignites the firestorm between Alexander and Katina, indicating their second chance, and gives both Theo and Lysander the tattoo of the Dragon Legion.

In **Kiss of Darkness**, the darkfire empowers Petra's song so that she's able to enchant Cerberus and keep him from killing Damien. It also prompts visions of the past for both Petra and Damien, reminding them both of the power of their firestorm. A snake returns Damien's lost scale to him after Petra delivers their son, even though he lost it in the underworld. The darkfire also gives Damien's newly born son the mark of the Dragon Legion.

In **Kiss of Destiny**, the darkfire crystal takes Thad to a misty mountaintop where he feels the spark of his firestorm. It then delivers Drake, alone, to the roof of Erik's loft in Chicago where Drake sees that the darkfire in the stone has been extinguished. He knows the adventure of the Dragon Legion is complete as a result and goes to Erik's lair to sleep. The darkfire crystal remains in Erik's hoard.

In **Ember's Kiss**, Marco uses the darkfire crystal in his possession as a weapon in his battle against the *Slayer* Chen. He entrusts it to Liz because she can use it as a weapon, too.

Liz peered into the stone. There was a blue-green light flickering in its core, like a glint of lightning held captive. She nodded, wondering what it was.

"Darkfire," Marco said, turning the stone in his hand as he

watched the darkfire burn. "Trapped in this crystal. Obedient to me."

"Why?"

"Because I am the heir of the Cantor. Darkfire is my realm and responsibility."

"What does it do?"

"It introduces unpredictability, challenges expectations, turns possibilities into reality." Marco considered her. He didn't blink, and his perusal was so steady that she had the feeling he could read her thoughts. "Like you, your presence here, your powers, and your being part of the firestorm. There is a better reason for the *Slayers* to target you. You are more than human, aren't you?"

—from **Ember's Kiss**

In **Serpent's Kiss**, Marco retrieves the crystal from Liz and breaks it in Chen's lair, freeing Lee from his brother's captivity. In **Firestorm Forever**, Marco steals the third and last darkfire crystal from Erik's hoard and uses it as a weapon against the clones of Boris Vassily. It also heals Rafferty to some extent and Marco takes it from Sloane's lair—with Rafferty—to give Jac a means of defending herself. By the end of the book (and the end of the Dragon's Tail Wars) the darkfire appears to be extinguished from the crystal. At the final display by the *Pyr* for Melissa's documentaries, Marco breaks the third crystal and releases the darkfire. It touches the repaired scales of each of the *Pyr*, indicating that their firestorms will burn forever, then touches Theo, hinting that his firestorm will be soon.

DEATH RITUAL—It is traditional to expose the body of a deceased *Pyr* to all four elements within half a solar day of his demise.

"Once exposed to the four elements, the body of a fallen *Pyr* or *Slayer* returns to those elements."

"You mean he dissolves."

Rafferty nodded. "Pretty much."

—**Kiss of Fury**

The death ritual was considered to be a sign of respect but had lapsed from active practice until the Dragon's Blood Elixir was formulated again. With the Dragon's Blood Elixir, *Slayers* were able to raise the dead of the *Pyr*, and turn them into shadow dragons against their will, if their bodies had not been ritually exposed to the four elements after death within twelve hours.

Delaney frowned. "Let's backtrack a bit. The Elixir, you see, can raise the dead."

"Be serious."

"I am. The bodies of those *Pyr* who die but are not exposed to all four elements within half a solar day—twelve hours—can be raised if the Elixir is administered to them. They have no souls, because their spark has returned to the Great Wyvern, so their bodies are simply machines. They have no morals and can be commanded to do anything."

"Ghouls," Ginger said, negotiating a turn with care. She'd seen lots of late-night movies during her sleepless nights since Gran had died. "Zombies."

"Shadow dragons we call them. They have memories of their lives but no emotion, no morals, no soul. They're hard to destroy."
—**Winter Kiss**

In **Kiss of Fury**, Quinn and Donovan realize that there's something odd about the *Slayer* Keir because he neither feels pain nor bleeds when injured. They dismember him, and incinerate him. Quinn realizes that of the four elements, only water is missing, and Donovan spits on the ashes of his deceased father to ensure that he remains dead. Keir has become a shadow dragon and dismembering and incinerating becomes the protocol for ensuring that shadow dragons stay dead.

In **Kiss of Fate**, Sigmund, who was the one to develop the means of creating shadow dragons with the Elixir, begs his father Erik to expose him to all four elements. It's a mark of their reconciliation that Erik does as asked.

"Look away," [Erik] murmured. "You won't want to watch what must be done." Then he brushed his lips across her forehead, sending a frisson of heat to her toes.

Eileen turned away. She was aware that Erik changed shape.

She felt his strength and his power close behind her but she respected his judgment.

She didn't look. Instead she counted elements. There was air everywhere, so that took care of one. Sigmund was lying on the earth, which provided the second element. She supposed that the falling snow, which was melting against her own skin, would provide the third element water.

Which left only fire.

Erik would cremate his son, at Sigmund's own request. It wouldn't be an easy thing to do. Eileen shuddered.

She wrapped her arms around herself and walked to the perimeter of the clearing, her sorrow rising with such force that it nearly choked her. She looked up into the swirling dance of the falling snow. She heard dragonfire. She smelled flesh burning. She tightened her grip on her own elbows and prayed that Sigmund would find peace.

And when Erik caught her shoulders in his hands long moments later, Eileen reveled in his strength. She felt herself tremble and let him gather her into his embrace. She leaned against his chest and welcomed the heat of the firestorm as it sparked through her veins.

The firestorm reminded her that she was alive.

That she could make different choices.

That she could learn from the past.

—**Kiss of Fate**

We witness the full ritual in **Flashfire**, when Salvatore dies and Magnus intervenes, hoping to steal the corpse for a new source for a batch of Elixir.

DIVINE SPARK—the *Pyr* believe that the divine spark of the Great Wyvern is what gives them life. In essence, She is the blaze that feeds the fire within them all. When a *Pyr* dies, that divine spark is released and returns to the Great Wyvern.

"And there's a spark of Her divinity within each of us. The firestorm, according to this document, is a mark of Her favor. It burns because She's more emphatically present. She's indicating Her choice."

—Sloane Forbes in **Kiss of Fury**

This notion affects the *Pyr* understanding of the firestorm, and also the change that occurs within *Pyr* who choose to become *Slayer*, which is said to be turning away from the light. The Dragon's Blood Elixir, and the shadow dragons it creates, is another abomination of the Great Wyvern's gift.

"The spark of the Great Wyvern was yet within him," Rafferty said when the light faded to a glow. "It is said that no conjurer can extinguish the light in a heart that is good, that no *Pyr* can be turned *Slayer* against his will."
—**Kiss of Fury**

Delaney's healing is begun by his brother Donovan's firestorm, because the heat of the firestorm feeds the last of the divine spark within Delaney.

DRACONTIAS, THE—A green stone, rumored to have healing powers. In **Firestorm Forever**, Jorge reveals to Jac that he has it: it was in the library of Ivan the Terrible, which he uses as his lair.

He leaned closer. "Even the *Pyr* don't know this place is here, much less that the greatest prize of all has been safely kept within it."
Jac glanced to the display of treasures and her gaze was drawn to that green stone. "The stone," she said. "Was it here?"
"An aristocrat's prize," Jorge said, picking it up with obvious admiration. "A Dracontias. Perhaps *the* Dracontias."
Jac had read about the Dracontias but neither she nor the sources had believed it was real. "I thought that stone was a myth."
Jorge gestured to himself. "You stand in the company of a myth come to life."
That was true enough. Jac's gaze lingered on his jaw, which looked exactly as it had before. "There was supposed to have been a Dracontias cut from the brow of a fallen dragon in the Middle Ages."
"Chevalier de Gonzo, Grand Master of the Order of St. John of Jerusalem, slew a dragon on the island of Rhodes, successfully

extracting the Dracontias from its brow before it died."

Jac recalled all of the story now. It was in Sigmund's book. "But the dragon had lost his ability to taint the power of the stone at the point of his death, presumably because the knight had enchanted him."

"Beguiled, I would guess."

"I didn't think humans could beguile dragons," Jac said. "I thought it only worked the other way around."

"Perhaps the knight learned a new trick." Jac sensed that Jorge knew more of this than he was telling and wondered why he'd told her anything at all.

Was he just bragging about his treasure?

Meanwhile Jorge turned the stone in his hand. "The gem became a family heirloom."

"And was used to both cure illness and to detect illness."

"Put the Dracontias in water and it will cause the water to boil. When the water cools and the stone is removed, the antidote to any illness is in the cup." Jorge put the stone back down on the table with elaborate care. "Although I'm somewhat skeptical that there truly is a universal cure. The second version of the tale, that putting the Dracontias into a cup of poison will turn that poison to water, is more compelling to me."

—from **Firestorm Forever**

DRAGONFIRE—A stream of fire breathed by a *Pyr* or *Slayer*, often aimed at another dragon in battle. Dragonfire burns particularly hot. It will singe dragon scales and can leave a victim disfigured, if not dead. The Smith can endure dragonfire, because of his affinity to the element of fire, and can even draw power from dragonfire: in **Kiss of Fire**, Quinn's dragonsmoke injury is healed by the energy in the dragonfire of his fellow *Pyr*. In **Kiss of Fire**, Quinn begins to teach the other *Pyr* how to welcome the heat of dragonfire and turn it to good use, building their strength with it. Although they don't have the Smith's inherent ability to deal with dragonfire, it's clear that they can learn some skill for their own defense.

In **Kiss of Fury**, Alex (the scientist) sees a vision from Donovan's past of a battle with Magnus, and realizes that the *Slayer* has the ability not only to control flames but to claim the fire's energy to fuel himself. She reminds Donovan that energy is never destroyed. With this information, Donovan begins to learn to draw energy from fire and dragonfire, something that Quinn managed intuitively.

Erik also has some additional skill with dragonfire: in **Kiss of Fury**, when Boris hovers between forms to intimidate Erik, Erik breathes dragonfire at the *Slayer* while still in human form. This shocks Boris as well as commencing their dragonfight.

DRAGON BONE POWDER—in **Whisper Kiss**, Chen first uses Dragon Bone Powder to animate the shadow dragons when he sends them on missions. Otherwise, the shadow dragons are like zombies, with no initiative and the ability to follow only a single command. Niall's twin brother, Phelan, both loves and hates the powder: he loves having his faculties returned and the sensation of feeling more alive, but that also makes him aware of what he's lost. The effect of the powder is fleeting and he hates when it fades away. Chen never explains where or how he discovered this powder, although he says it's made of pulverized dragon bones. In this excerpt, the shadow dragon Phelan describes the influence of the Dragon Bone Powder upon him:

Phelan was surrounded by fog.

It was the darkness of impenetrable shadows, the fog that had initially been pierced only by Magnus's commands. He had been able to accept Magnus's dictates and act upon them, but no more than that. Initiative had been sacrificed long ago, along with the fire of life.

Until recently.

Phelan heard the old man murmuring to himself. He spoke a language Phelan didn't know and didn't understand—he assumed it was an Asian language, given the old man's appearance. It was rhythmic, though, like a chant, and its familiarity sliced through the fog that enveloped Phelan.

Eliminating it.

Dispersing it.

Creating anticipation. The brush of those cool fingertips

against his throat, then the imprint of the strange coin upon the mark that Chen had placed upon him, had Phelan following the old man.

Blindly and wherever he led.

They halted somewhere—Phelan didn't care where—and Phelan felt the old man force his mouth open. He tasted that strange metallic flavor on his tongue.

And his mind sparked.

Like an engine being restarted, his thoughts began to dart like quicksilver. He recalled more than this spell, more than Magnus, more than the fog that enveloped him as a shadow dragon. Phelan remembered everything, in fact, that he had ever known. He remembered everything he had lost, everything his twin had stolen from him, every injustice and imbalance.

And with the memories came the lust for vengeance, the power of initiative, the conviction that he could achieve whatever he desired.

Phelan wanted what Niall possessed. It had always been thus between them, and even choosing the darkness to gain more than his twin had only intensified Phelan's jealousy.

Now Niall had a firestorm and Phelan did not.

Now Phelan had been given the magical powder and remembered.

—from **Whisper Kiss**

The Dragon Bone Powder also has an effect on all *Pyr* and *Slayers*, increasing both the power of a firestorm as well as their awareness of it and response to it. Erik considers it to be Chen's way of distracting the *Pyr* during a firestorm.

"Dragon Bone Powder," Erik said without hesitation. "The *Slayer* Chen used it during Niall's firestorm, to heat the flames of the firestorm and distract Niall from pending attack."

"But my firestorm was sated."

Erik shrugged. "It fires the lust in all of us to some extent, feeding that primal desire to mate. So close after your firestorm's spark, it could fuel yours more."

—from **Flashfire**

In **Darkfire Kiss,** Rafferty tells Melissa about working for Magnus in Venice about a thousand years before, when Magnus sold oil and wine. Magnus also did a brisk trade in medicinal substances derived from dead dragons, although Rafferty first assumes this is deceptive labeling. Rafferty was first alerted to the real source of these items when he recognized the scent of *Pyr* in a vial said to contain ground dragon hide. Magnus also created dragon bone powder from the remains of his brother, Maximilian, who had recently come to tell Magnus about his firestorm. It appears that Magnus simply used the trade as a means to dispose of the bodies of his murdered enemies. It is also possible that Chen's Dragon Bone Powder included some ancient magic, so Magnus' dragon bone powder is not capped to distinguish between the two versions.

In **Flashfire**, we learn that Chen is trading Dragon Bone Powder for Brandon's dragon scales. Brandon uses the powder as a stimulant to enhance his performance and to seduce women—he has yet to realize that the substance is addictive and that Chen's possession of his scales will be used to cast a spell over him. Just the bit of it lingering in the air is enough to push JP to the cusp of change. JP later uses the powder to enhance the effect of Lorenzo's firestorm, at Chen's command:

JP tipped out a pinch of the dark powder within, then capped the vial tightly. He blew the dark dust off his palm into the air.

It twinkled, dissolving into nothing before his eyes.

But the invisible cloud it created was palpable.

JP felt a flush of heat.

Followed by a tightening in his own groin and a hunger that only a great deal of sex would satisfy. This was every bit as potent as Chen had warned.

The waitress wiped the table in front of him and for a heartbeat, he thought of jumping her bones.

"Drink?" she asked with a smile.

JP took a steadying breath. He tucked the vial back into his pocket, smiled at her, and ordered two glasses of the wine Cassie had been drinking earlier.

Chen had been convinced that the Dragon Bone Powder heated

a firestorm to a fever pitch, even after the firestorm was satisfied. He'd said that the powder sharpened the desire of all *Pyr*, making them insatiable.

JP, even having changed to the *Slayer* team, was feeling more insatiable himself than he could ever recall. He felt all tingly and could hear his blood thumping. He was aware of the scent of women's perfumes mingling in the hotel bar. He noticed the curves of cheeks and buttocks and breasts and wanted to claim them all. He wanted to go upstairs and check on Stacy himself.

No, he wanted to do more than check on her.

He decided that his reaction was a good sign, and that Chen's plan would work.

—from **Flashfire**

Chen also plans to add to his inventory of Dragon Bone Powder with the corpse of Salvatore in **Flashfire**, but is thwarted by Lorenzo and the *Pyr*.

In **Ember's Kiss**, Chen's spell over Brandon requires only one more scale from the younger *Pyr*. The *Slayer's* plan is to create more Dragon Bone Powder from Brandon so he gives the last of the powder to Brandon. Brandon's friend, Matt, tosses the powder into the air on the night that Brandon's firestorm sparks, and Brandon can't keep himself from shifting shape. Chen also runs out of Dragon Bone Powder, so tries to capture a dead *Pyr* to make more.

DRAGON LEGION, THE—The Dragon's Tooth Warriors who survived the challenge recounted in *Harmonia's Kiss* and were sent through time by the darkfire crystal distinguished themselves by the name the Dragon Legion and a dragon tattoo. They include Drake, Alexander, Damien, Thad, Orion, Peter, Ty, Ashe and Ignatio. There were sixteen warriors following Drake when he claimed the darkfire crystal from Lorenzo's hoard, as told in **Kiss of Danger**.

In the *Dragon Legion Novellas* (**Kiss of Danger, Kiss of Darkness** and **Kiss of Destiny**), it's revealed that the *Pyr* were considered elite warriors by the Spartans in ancient Greece—the

Spartans sent their sons for training at the age of eight, and when a boy showed signs of being *Pyr*, he was then sent to the sanctuary at Delphi to serve and learn about his shifter powers. The warriors who follow Drake all had this training. They realize that the darkfire crystal is taking them through space and time to leave each *Pyr* warrior at his firestorm.

At the end of **Kiss of Destiny,** the descendants of the Dragon Legion arrive at Erik's lair in Chicago to pledge their service to him. I love this scene, and how the time travel caused by the darkfire crystal has changed history in the blink of an eye:

> There was a knock at the door. Erik inhaled deeply, frowned, then cast open the door.
>
> The corridor was filled with unfamiliar men, young and vigorous men who held themselves with determination. There had to be three or four dozen of them.
>
> They were *Pyr*. Drake stood behind Erik and breathed deeply, not believing his own senses. How could there be so many *Pyr* of whom he knew nothing?
>
> "We are the descendants of the Dragon Legion," said the *Pyr* in front. He tugged up his shirt sleeve, showing a tattoo on his upper arm that was the same as the tattoo Drake and his men had gotten as a sign of solidarity. Drake considered the young man with wonder, liking the intelligence that shone in his dark eyes. "I am named Theo, for my forebear, the son of Stephanos who became Drake," he said, his words startling Drake. "We come to pledge ourselves to the leader of the *Pyr*, Erik Sorensson, as we pledged to our fathers, who pledged the same to their fathers and their fathers before them."
>
> "So this is what I sensed," Erik said, almost under his breath.

—from **Kiss of Destiny**

DRAGON'S BLOOD ELIXIR—An addictive concoction that promoted longevity in dragon shape shifters, expedited healing and increased vitality. It also gave the powers of the Wyvern to *Slayers* who consumed it over a period of time, particularly that of being able to take a third form (a salamander) and to spontaneously manifest elsewhere.

There is initially skepticism amongst the *Pyr* as to the existence of the Elixir and its reputed powers. At the end of **Kiss of Fury**, Rafferty noted that Magnus was said to have possessed its secret. Clearly, he was surprised to see Magnus alive again in that last fight, and wondering how the old *Slayer* had survived. Erik insisted, though, that the Elixir did not exist. One of the interesting things about the *Pyr* is the fact that the modern *Pyr* believe that many of the tales told of them are myth or fabrication, when, in fact, they are truth. This skepticism proves to have quite serious repercussions during the Dragon's Tail Wars.

The *Pyr* become aware of the truth in a number of ways: Erik begins to have dreams of the Academy as a place of great evil. Sophie has similar dreams, but doesn't share them with the *Pyr*. Donovan observes that his father Keir shed no blood and apparently felt no pain in their dragonfight. When Rafferty confides that Keir had died over three hundred and fifty years before, the *Pyr* want to discover how he could have been raised from the dead. Sloane discovers an ancient manuscript in his own collection which had been indecipherable, and managed to break the code with the help of a dream from Sophie.

"This treatise lists the way to steal a soul. Obviously, it can only be done when the *Pyr* in question is unable to defend himself."

"Exposed to only three elements, but not quite dead," Sara said.

"But what happens to the soul?" Rafferty asked.

"The spark is released and it returns to the Great Wyvern, just as it does when we die," Sloane said. "But there's a complex process of implanting a shadow in its stead, of embedding darkness where the light should be, and thus turning the *Pyr* into a *Slayer*." He swallowed and looked around the room. "Into a slave who does not bleed."
—**Kiss of Fury**

Sloane further reveals that, according to the manuscript, the process of conversion is risky and fraught with complications. Any residue of the personality of the *Pyr* in question could fight the change. It was evidently common for the victim to become violent or even be driven insane, so the manuscript suggested imprisonment until the transformation is completed.

It is Sophie who solves the riddle in **Kiss of Fate**, after she sees Boris cut Erik's dragonsmoke.

> The *Pyr* stared in horror. The Wyvern's blood had been shed.
> Sophie swallowed and averted her gaze, her fingertips playing with the end of the scarf. "I was attacked," she admitted.
> "She was assaulted by Boris Vassily, right here!" Nikolas interjected, his outrage more than clear. "He came to break the Dragon's Egg and lured her into Erik's lair..."
> Donovan swore and shoved a hand through his hair. The other *Pyr* were clearly just as upset. "But Erik killed Boris last summer."
> Sophie met his gaze steadily. "How do you know?"
> "Erik said so."
> "Then Erik was wrong."
> "But Erik said he exposed Boris to all four elements," Quinn insisted. "He said that he ensured that Boris was dead."
> Sophie shook her head. "He did not know what Boris had done." She turned to Sloane. "There is one thing Boris could have done that explains all of this, only one substance he could have consumed before his battle with Erik."
> "But Erik said he exposed Boris to all four elements," Quinn insisted. "He said that he ensured that Boris was dead."
> Sophie shook her head. "He did not know what Boris had done." She turned to Sloane. "There is one thing Boris could have done that explains all of this, only one substance he could have consumed before his battle with Erik."
> Sloane took a step back, his horror clear.
> "There is only one substance that could have pulled him back from the brink of death," Sophie insisted, following Sloane. "And you, Apothecary, you know its name."
> "The Dragon's Blood Elixir," Sloane whispered as the color drained from his face.
> Sophie nodded.
> "Then it's real," Sloane continued. "And it does convey immortality."

"Of a kind," Sophie agreed.

Donovan's heart sank to his toes. He glanced at his fellow *Pyr* and saw his own dismay echoed in their expressions. He had always believed the Elixir was a myth, or at least a legend lost in the past

But it was real.

The *Slayers* had it.

And they were drinking it.

Donovan felt a trickle of dread. Alex's hand slid into his and her fingers were cold.

Sloane swore and began to pace. "That ancient treatise talks about the powers of the Dragon's Blood Elixir and how it can be used to give immortality to anyone who survives the test of drinking it. I thought it was a metaphor...."

—Kiss of Fate

The *Slayer* Magnus (a collector of ancient lore) found the formula and shared first sips to build a company of loyal followers. These *Slayers* heal rapidly, but they always need to drink more of the Elixir, which puts them in thrall to Magnus. When Magnus saw its powers, he established a secret Academy to put it to work. He revived dead dragon shifters there with the substance, creating an army of shadow dragons from those dead *Pyr* whose bodies had not had the traditional Death Ritual. This is what happened to Delaney. Because Delaney had not turned *Slayer* or died, the Elixir wasn't completely successful in converting him to a shadow dragon. Those *Pyr* successfully converted to shadow dragons become like zombies, in that they can only follow commands. They can only be killed by dismemberment and incineration.

Magnus admits that he has consumed the Elixir to Erik in their final battle in **Kiss of Fate**, calling it a trick that trumps all others. It's Boris who reveals that the power of the Elixir fades over time, and that those who have drunk it always need more. Erik realizes that when those *Slayers* are injured very badly and far from the Elixir, they might not survive. He leaves Magnus impaled on a spike, which compels Magnus to negotiate with Jorge, and flings a battered Boris toward the earth from high altitude.

The sanctuary of the Elixir is revealed to be in Ohio, in **Winter Kiss**, under the Serpent Mound and near a lair built by Magnus. The house has a central courtyard with a fountain of Elixir. Magnus tells a captive Ginger how the Elixir was made from the body of Cinnabar, who had been exposed to mercury in Roman mines. The spell to create the Elixir is linked to the Saros cycle of eclipses and Ginger learns that Magnus intends to replace Cinnabar as a source with Delaney. Jorge and Balthasar threaten to force Ginger to drink the Elixir, just to see what happens, but she manages to trick them instead. The *Pyr* learn that the Elixir can only be made by a dragon shifter whose blood runs red, which makes Delaney's firestorm and recovery ideal for Magnus' plan.

Under the influence of the Elixir, Delaney has nightmares, as well as losing control of his dragon. It's revealed in **Winter Kiss** that as part of the preparation to take the place of Cinnabar, Delaney was injected with quicksilver by Magnus (under Sigmund's instruction). Delaney begins to chill from the inside, and also to precipitate beads of mercury over the course of the book, a sign that Magnus' scheme is working. It is Ginger who realizes the significance of this, because she's seen the mercury precipitating out of the fountain of Elixir in the courtyard of Magnus' lair. The *Pyr* work together to destroy the source and the supply of the Elixir by the end of **Winter Kiss**.

The lack of a source creates a problem for those *Slayers* who are addicted to the Elixir. It turns out that Jorge had stashed a personal supply of Elixir while in the service of Magnus and has used it to aid in his recovery. Jorge's leg was torn off in **Winter Kiss**, and he retreated to a clinic in Moscow to have it repaired, with Mallory and Balthasar acting as his bodyguards. After Jorge retreated to a sanctuary on the Caspian Sea, Chen deceived him and stole the last of the Elixir, drinking it before Jorge, then sealing Jorge into his own lair with dragonsmoke. Mallory hibernates, consuming his strength, never guessing that in desperation for more Elixir, Jorge will consume him for the Elixir's residue in his body. At this point, the only remaining Elixir is in the bodies of those surviving *Slayers* who consumed it, which gives Jorge a plan.

DRAGON'S EGG—A polished sphere of black stone, resembling obsidian, which shows the location of a newly-sparked firestorm under the light of a fully eclipsed moon. The Dragon's Egg is in the custody of Erik, leader of the *Pyr*, at the beginning of Dragonfire. Erik uses the Dragon's Egg to specify the location of a firestorm. There is a ritual to invoke the display on the obsidian stone. The Dragon's Egg was kept in a black velvet sack in Erik's lair, and the *Pyr* say a blessing whenever it is removed under the light of a lunar eclipse. In **Kiss of Fire**, Erik spins the egg three times in the sand of the desert, requesting an augury before releasing it. Golden lines appear on the surface of the Dragon's Egg, tracing the shorelines of continents and turning it into a globe. Ley lines triangulated the location of the firestorm. At this point, Erik believes only the light of an eclipse can power the Dragon's Egg.

At the beginning of **Kiss of Fury,** however, Sophie shows Erik that the Dragon's Egg can be used as a scrying glass with the use of a chant that is unfamiliar to him. In fact, his experience of events portrayed in the Dragon's Egg is so vivid that Erik feels as if he were actually there. (He witnesses the assault upon Alex Madison's lab by *Slayers*.) Although Erik attributes this sensation to the importance of the vision, it is the first hint that the Dragon's Egg can be used as a portal as well as a scrying glass. In **Kiss of Fate**, Sophie summons a vision to the Dragon's Egg beneath the light of the eclipse, which reveals the identity of Erik's mate to him and the other *Pyr*.

The Dragon's Egg is broken in **Kiss of Fate**, when Boris demands that Nikolas choose between Sophie and the Dragon's Egg. He chooses the Wyvern and the stone is shattered. All of the *Pyr* experience the breaking of the Dragon's Egg, regardless of their location: Niall is jolted in New York, but Thorolf collapses, thereby helping Niall to identify him as *Pyr*; Rafferty in London believes he's having a heart attack; in Michigan, Sara has a bad dream and Quinn is awakened by a sense of unease; in California, Sloane and Delaney first think it's an earthquake, then recognize that something is wrong and decide to seek out Erik.

The *Pyr* try to formulate a plan to repair the stone in **Kiss of Fate**, but Sophie tells them it can't be done. She also reveals that the stone was a gift from Gaia to the guardians of the elements.

From that point onward, Erik learns to scry by using other surfaces, and to develop his ability to feel the locations of all *Pyr*.

DRAGON LOVER OF MADELEY, THE—A story that Eileen is in England to research in **Kiss of Fate**. The story comes from the area around Ironbridge and is about two sisters, Sunshine, who has a merry nature and raven hair, and Shadow, who is quieter and is fair-haired. Shadow is the oldest and disinclined to marry. Sunshine insists that she won't marry until her sister does. Shadow goes into the countryside alone, supposedly to paint, but eventually reveals that she is pregnant by her dragon lover. Her father banishes Shadow in a fit of fury, but she returns to say farewell to Sunshine and gives her a painting of a black dragon. Sunshine believes this is a metaphor for her sister's secret lover. Sunshine marries the new minister and the next spring, a black dragon visits her in her garden at the manse. He brings her a lock of golden hair, from an infant, and Shadow's best wishes. Sunshine realizes that her sister has borne a child and that her lover really is a dragon. She keeps the painting and hair hidden until she is on her own deathbed, then surrenders both, along with the story, to the daughter she was carrying when the dragon came to visit. The sisters never saw each other again and Sunshine died after sharing the story. Erik recognizes this as the story of his first mate, Louisa, who he remembers being called Shadow, and her sister Adelaide. The lock of hair was from Sigmund, although the fate of the painting isn't mentioned.

DRAGONSMOKE—A stream of vapor breathed by dragon shifters— whether *Pyr* or *Slayer*—that is invisible to human perception and is used as a boundary marker. Perceptive humans may feel a chill when they breach through a dragonsmoke barrier, but they cannot see it.

Everywhere the dragonsmoke contacted Erik, it burned. It was a brand touched to his flesh, a burning weapon that eased beneath

his scales, seeking weakness it could exploit.
—**Kiss of Fury**

Dragonsmoke is not only visible to dragon shifters as a thick mist, but it has a resonant ring when formed into a complete circle. This protective barrier or boundary mark is created with embedded permissions: dragonsmoke will burn any dragon shifter who crosses it without the explicit permission of the dragon shifter who breathed the barrier. In **Kiss of Fire**, Quinn's leg is touched by the dragonfire of *Slayers* when Sara is rescued: his leg not only burns but atrophies, laming him, as a result of the contact. Because he is the Smith, he is subsequently healed by the dragonfire of the other *Pyr*.

Sara uses the nature of dragonsmoke against the *Slayers* in **Kiss of Fire**: although they have imprisoned the Wyvern and barricaded her within a circle of dragonsmoke, Sara volunteers to walk through the dragonsmoke to save the Wyvern. This is possible because she is human, although as the Seer, she feels a chill as she passed through the dragonsmoke barrier.

In order to breathe dragonsmoke, a *Pyr* or *Slayer* enters a meditative state, and directs the stream of dragonsmoke, weaving it into a barrier that is preferable high and deep. Some *Pyr* have preferences in how many circuits of dragonsmoke they like to breathe, or how they like to interweave it, but a stream exhaled in a single breath—with no breaks—is always strongest. Some *Pyr* can breathe dragonsmoke even while fighting and thus not in a particularly meditative state.

It is typical for a *Pyr* to breathe dragonsmoke around his lair, and his hoard, as well as around the vicinity of his mate, particularly during a firestorm. A dragonsmoke boundary will disintegrate over time, and some dragon shifters can tell the age of a smoke ring by its condition. Most *Pyr* and *Slayers* can tell whose dragonsmoke they sense, presumably because the dragonsmoke contains some of the scent of whichever shifter created it.

He had one misshapen scale, one lost scale that had grown

back, thick and unnatural. Erik didn't doubt that the smoke would writhe beneath it. He flew away from the smoke and it followed him with leisurely persistence. It caught him again, winding around his ankle to hold him captive, rising like a cobra before him, stealing his strength with its furtive touch.

Erik looked beyond the smoke to Boris and was shocked. The *Slayer* became larger and brighter, his eyes shining with triumph as his smoke tormented Erik.

The smoke wasn't just stealing Erik's strength: it was giving that vitality to Boris. It was a conduit between the two of them, cheating Erik to fuel Boris. Boris would see Erik sucked dry, a shell of his former self.

— Kiss of Fury

Dragonsmoke can also be used as a conduit between fighting dragons, first shown in **Kiss of Fury** when it is used by the *Slayer* Boris to steal life force from Erik during their fight. Note that the lost scale Erik mentions here is not one lost over a love: it does grow back, leaving a gap in Boris's armor but not a hole.

Erik's means of evading Boris's dragonsmoke in this fight is also worthy of note: he dives into Lake Michigan, and the smoke can't follow him beneath the water. It pools on the surface, spreading across the lake. Clearly Boris's intent is to seal Erik under the water, compelling him to choose between savage burns and death by drowning.

In **Kiss of Fate**, Erik uses dragonsmoke as a weapon against Mallory, having learned from Boris's example how to use dragonsmoke as a conduit.

When he and Mallory parted again, Erik exhaled dragonsmoke with power. He breathed it in one endless stream as he hovered, the dragonsmoke maintaining a conduit between himself and Mallory. The *Slayer* yelped and twitched as the smoke wound beneath his scales. It slipped into the wound on Mallory's chest, finding a way beneath the scabs to sting raw flesh. Mallory fought on despite the pain, but Erik kept breathing dragonsmoke.

The dragonsmoke stole vitality; that was its treacherous power.

A *Slayer* or *Pyr* ensnared in smoke would be eroded to nothing but skin, his life force cheated away by the smoke. But by keeping the link and breathing one continuous stream of dragonsmoke, Boris had used the smoke as a conduit to steal Erik's strength for himself.

Erik had to be able to do the same thing. Just as it had with Boris, the dragonsmoke cheated Mallory of his power, feeding it directly to Erik. To his delight, Erik felt himself grow stronger even as Mallory was weakened. The *Slayer* fought valiantly, his eyes widening in terror as he felt his strength slipping away, but his was a losing battle.

"You will leave me an empty shell!" Mallory cried.

—**Kiss of Fate**

Magnus uses dragonsmoke to defend his lair in **Winter Kiss**, and also to protect the Dragon's Blood Elixir. Delaney is able to endure the assault of the dragonsmoke on his body, even though it burns: this is because he's endured much worse torment with the Elixir.

In **Darkfire Kiss**, Chen uses dragonsmoke to trap Jorge within his own lair, after stealing the last of the Elixir from the *Slayer*. Jorge has to wear it down in increments, enduring severe burns, then recover before he can fritter away at it again.

Then Chen had sealed Jorge inside his own refuge. His song was intricate and ancient; primal and powerful. Chen had departed, the Elixir in his gut, and Jorge had been trapped inside a dragonsmoke barrier, the like of which he'd never seen. It didn't simply resonate—it tinkled like thousands of little bells. And he could see it, as thick and impenetrable as the densest fog.

A wall of ice.

But this dragonsmoke burned like a corrosive acid, ten times worse than regular dragonsmoke. Jorge had thrown himself at the dragonsmoke barrier, worn it down, forced himself to take the abuse of gradually destroying it. Each time, he had to retreat to let the burns recover. Each time, the Elixir still in his body was less potent, more dilute, and the healing took longer.

It was an infuriating process.

—from **Darkfire Kiss**

DRAGON'S TAIL—A nine year cycle during which the moon appears to be descending in the night sky, at least from the perspective of earth. This is a real astrological event in our world. The Dragon's Tail began on June 12, 2006. The full cycle of the moon's node will be completed on January 12, 2025, but the Dragon's Tail (the first half of the cycle) ends on November 13, 2015. The other half of the cycle of the moon's node is the Dragon's Head, in which the moon appears to be ascending.

In astrological terms, the Dragon's Tail is a period of karmic correction, in which debts are paid and new balances struck. Although this 17-year cycle occurs over and over again, the *Pyr* had a prophecy that in one Dragon's Tail cycle, they would fight the final battle against the *Slayers* for ascendancy over the earth, during a cycle that began with three potent firestorms.

DRAGON'S TAIL WARS—The original Dragonfire series is set during a period of trial for the *Pyr*, in which they will battle the *Slayers* for custody of the earth and survival of mankind. This test was foretold to commence during the Dragon's Tail, an astrological period believed to be a phase of karmic retribution and rebalance. The most recent Dragon's Tail began in June 2006 and ends in November 2015—the premise of the original Dragonfire series was that either the *Pyr* or the *Slayers* would have been exterminated by the end of the cycle of the moon's node.

The *Pyr*'s prophecy declared that there would be three important firestorms after the moon's node changed, sparked on three successive lunar eclipses, and that all had to be successful for the *Pyr* to have a chance against the *Slayers*. **Kiss of Fire** begins with the *Pyr* gathering to watch the Dragon's Egg during the first lunar eclipse after the Dragon's Tail began, which was on March 3, 2007. Quinn and Sara's firestorm sparked as a result. The illumination of the Dragon's Egg during that eclipse was witnessed by six *Pyr*: Erik, Donovan, Niall, Rafferty, Sloane, and Delaney, who is unnamed in the passage. Those first prophesied three firestorms are recounted in **Kiss of Fire, Kiss of Fury** and **Kiss of**

Fate.

DRAGON'S TOOTH—one of the many Dragon's Teeth, but the one possessed by Donovan, who believed it to be a large and irregular pearl. It *is* a pearl, but instead of being constructed around a grain of sand, this pearl was built around one of the Dragon's Teeth.

> "But wait—a tooth isn't a pearl," Alex argued.
> "An oyster will build a pearl out of anything," Sara told her. "I just looked it up. A round pearl is a grain of sand that has many coatings on it. People have put things into oysters over the centuries to get that finish on them."
> "You'd have to keep track of the oyster," Rafferty noted.
> "They don't move very fast," Quinn joked.
> —**Kiss of Fury**

Donovan's human lover, Olivia, tricked him by asking him to retrieve it for her from a grotto hidden deep in the ground. Once Donovan stepped into the darkness, she locked him into the grotto, confessing that she had traded him to the pearl's keeper in exchange for the gem. Afterward, Donovan kept it as a token of his survival and triumph. After **Kiss of Fire**, he had Quinn repair the missing scale in his armor with the Dragon's Tooth. In **Kiss of Fury**, the pearl is coveted by *Slayers* and ripped loose from Donovan's scale. After Sara dreams of the story of Cadmus, the *Pyr* plant the tooth in the soil. Like the teeth sowed by Cadmus, this tooth grows into a warrior: Nikolas of Thebes, who is *Pyr* and has been enchanted for millennia.

At the end of **Kiss of Fury**, Magnus reveals that there were once a hundred such teeth and that he possessed them all at one point. The *Pyr* are skeptical, because Magnus is known to tell lies to impress others, until Nikolas asks after the fate of his fellow warriors. This begins the search for the Dragon's Teeth Warriors.

> He was the one.
> The thought echoed in Sophie's mind with utter conviction. One glimpse of the new *Pyr*, with his rugged masculinity and dark good looks, was enough to tell her of his origin.

And his destiny. He alone was old enough to enter the dark academy and survive.

There was something else about him, too, something that made her afraid to look directly at him, something that made her flutter her feathers a little bit more as she landed.

There was something about him that made Sophie feel shy.

She was afraid she knew exactly what it was.

—**Kiss of Fury**.

Nikolas' disenchantment also creates another change for the *Pyr*, or more particularly, for the Wyvern, Sophie. He's smitten with her on sight, and his admiration is returned. Their love is forbidden by the traditions of the *Pyr*, though, and consummating their relationship leads them on a path of sacrifice.

DRAGON'S TOOTH WARRIORS—These warriors were enchanted for millennia and freed, just like Nikolas, when the enchanted teeth are planted in the soil by Rafferty.

Originally, these warriors formed a military unit of *Pyr* in Ancient Greece, charged with hunting down and exterminating those dragon shifters who had turned against men. They come from a time before the evolution of *Slayers*, and call their opponents 'vipers'. In fighting one viper named Cadmus, they were enchanted and cursed to take the form of additional teeth for that dragon's maw.

They are led by a taciturn general named Drake, and unlike the modern *Pyr*, they are all dark in color in dragon form and almost indistinguishable from each other in either form. Nikolas is said to have no scent by the other *Pyr* and to appear to be more reptilian.

The first Dragon's Tooth is planted and becomes the *Pyr* Nikolas in **Kiss of Fury**.

The Dragon's Teeth were once part of Magnus's hoard and secured in his underground lair beneath Greenwich—this is where Olivia led Donovan, sending him to retrieve a pearl for her. The lair was destroyed in the subsequent battle between Donovan,

HERE BE DRAGONS: THE DRAGONFIRE COMPANION

Rafferty and Magnus. The teeth were lost until the Jubilee subway line in London was extended in 1999 and the hoard unearthed. At the beginning of **Kiss of Fate**, Eileen is summoned as a consultant to identify them. Teresa MacRae tells Eileen that the hoard was found in a natural cave, to the south of Greenwich and closer to Blackleith. Because the museums aren't interested in them, they're going to be auctioned by the Fonthill-Fergusson Foundation.

The teeth were huge. They each had three peaks, like the back teeth of a dog, but each was a good three inches across. The box was filled with trays, each tray divided into ten compartments, each compartment lined with blue velvet. There were ten trays, only one lacking an index number and tooth.

Ninety-nine teeth.

Whatever the beast had been, it had had a big mouth.

She picked one up and turned it in her gloved hands. Her first thought was that it couldn't be real, but she could see the hollow on the bottom where it had been attached to the gum. There was even a dark speck, a mark that could have been dried blood.

This Rafferty Powell might just want them because they were odd. But then, Teresa knew him better and she was suspicious of his motives. Eileen put the first tooth back and picked up another. It was similar but not exactly the same. It hadn't been cast from a mold. She suspected that it really was what it looked to be.

A tooth.

Ninety-nine teeth, to be precise. But from what?

Eileen got no further in her thinking before she heard the shot.

—Kiss of Fate

Eileen's inspection is interrupted by an attack by the *Slayers* Jorge and Balthasar, under the command of Magnus. The battle for custody of the teeth occurs in that book, with Rafferty ultimately planting them in his garden in Hampstead Heath. The warriors spring to life and aid the *Pyr* in the destruction of the Academy.

The result of the Dragon's Tooth Warriors' decision to finish what they had begun is told in the short story, **Harmonia's Kiss**. Their adventures with the darkfire crystal are told in the Dragon Legion Novellas, during which they rename themselves the Dragon

Legion. The Dragon's Tooth Warriors come to New York in **Whisper Kiss** to join the battle against the shadow dragons.

DRAKKIR—Those *Pyr* who sailed with the Vikings as mascots and guardians. Erik remembers sailing with his father and the Vikings in **Kiss of Fate**, and is stern in reminding Thorolf of his lineage.

"You are the spawn of warriors," Erik snapped. "We were the *drakkir*. We were invincible and fearsome. We were the mascots of the Viking raiders and they carved their ships in our likeness in homage to our power. We feared not man or beast, not elements foul or even death."
–Kiss of Fate

DREAMWALKER—A traditional role of the *Pyr*, although this role may not pass through a family line. The talent appears in a *Pyr* with a strong affinity to air and grants the power to enter the dreams of others, even to influence their outcome. This talent is also held by the Wyvern, though she may not exercise it, and can be granted as a gift of the Wyvern to a specific *Pyr*. In **Whisper Kiss**, Niall becomes the Dreamwalker. His mate Rox is wounded by the shadow dragon, Phelan, and Sloane believes the wound to be poisoned. Sloane thinks the darkness of the shadow dragons has found a resonance within her. The *Pyr* work together to drive out the toxin and heal Rox—it is in seeking the cause within the memories of his unconscious mate (with Zoe's encouragement) that Niall claims his role as Dreamwalker.

In **Flashfire**, Lorenzo's father is hibernating and in a dream state when he is permitted to enter the realm of dreams and reunite with his lost mate. While he is not the Dreamwalker of the *Pyr*, it's clear that Salvatore has some ability to journey in dreams, as well. Salvatore has an affinity with air, which manifests in his skill with beguiling, but—as with Niall—also influences his ability to navigate dreams.

ELEMENTAL WITCHES—Women with power not only over an individual element but also the ability to become that element. The first elemental witch introduced in the chronology of the

Dragonfire novels was Liz Barrett, a Firedaughter, in **Ember's Kiss**. The history of the relationship between these women and the *Pyr* is more ancient than that, though, and is explored in the Dragon Legion Novellas, each of which features an Elemental Witch as the heroine. Elemental witches are mortal.

EARTHDAUGHTER—An Elemental Witch with an affinity for earth. An Earthdaughter can control the element of earth as well as become it. Petra is the first Earthdaughter encountered in the Dragonfire series: her story is told in the Dragon Legion Novella, **Kiss of Darkness**. Petra goes to a circle of standing stones which she calls the Mothers to deliver her child, explaining that the Mothers are her forebears. They've turned to stone because they didn't find a partner to love them in their mortal life, but are able to abandon their stones to help one of their kind give birth.

EXPRESSIONS—like most communities or species, the *Pyr* have their own expressions and figures of speech, which often reference their dragon nature. Below are a number of them, with their human equivalents.

Shard of my talon— Like father, like son.

"Deny it if you will, but you are my son—blood of my blood and shard of my talon."
—Keir Shea to Donovan in **Kiss of Fury**

The spark never falls far from the blaze—What's bred in the bone will out in the flesh.

The richest gem in my hoard—Reference by romantically-inclined *Pyr* to his mate.

Meet fire with fire, or fight fire with fire— Reference to fighting in dragon form, usually against *Slayers*.

Like moths to a flame— Reference to *Pyr* and *Slayers* being drawn to a firestorm

Sparks fly— reference to the visual display of a firestorm

Wyvern spawn!— An insult and taunt, typically from *Slayer* to *Pyr*

FIGHTING—Dragons fight, in defense of their lairs, their mates, and their principles. They can fight to the death as the result of a blood duel triggered by the tossing of a Challenge Coin. *Pyr* can fight each other, *Slayers* can fight each other or *Pyr* can battle *Slayers*. When they fight, however, there are traditions to be maintained.

It is characteristic for a fight to begin with the opponents locking claws, and such a common beginning to a fight that the *Pyr* call it the traditional fighting pose. Insults may be ritually exchanged, typically in old-speak, before, during or after the locking of claws. These taunts are intended to undermine the confidence of one's opponent and may be personal slurs, intimidation or information intended to frighten the other dragon. After that, there are no rules.

Dragon fights can be savage and spectacular. They often take place at least partially in the air, and involve biting, slashing and tearing. Wings are a favored target, as the destruction of one makes that dragon vulnerable in the air. The section of hide where a scale is missing is also an excellent target for it's a point of weakness. A talon or a tooth may be driven into this spot, dragonfire may be aimed at it, and dragonsmoke may be locked on to it. Those *Pyr* and *Slayers* with additional powers may invoke them during the conflict: Rafferty might sing to the earth and summon an earthquake, for example, while Donovan might summon the elements and use them as weapons.

Whenever a dragon fight takes place in an area densely populated by humans, it is typical to beguile as many of those humans who have witnessed the carnage as possible.

FIREDAUGHTER—An Elemental Witch with an affinity for fire. A Firedaughter can control the element of fire as well as become it. Liz Barrett is a Firedaughter and the first Elemental Witch introduced in Dragonfire: her story is told in **Ember's Kiss**.

FIRESTORM—Each *Pyr* is destined to experience one firestorm in his lifetime. A firestorm occurs when that *Pyr* meets the human woman who can bear his son. Sparks literally fly between the couple, causing an overwhelming sense of attraction and desire. The heat of the firestorm builds until the couple's relationship is consummated (known as "satisfying the firestorm").

One of the most potent sensations for a *Pyr* is that of his body matching its rhythms to that of his mate, which occurs when the firestorm is burning hot (and has been denied.) His breathing changes to the same rate to hers, as does his heartbeat. Because he is so attuned to her and her body's reactions, this synchronization can make him dizzy. This effect can survive the firestorm, as it does for Quinn and Sara.

> Quinn inhaled as she put her hand over his heart. He could feel her pulse through her palm and listened as his own heart matched its pace to hers. There was no firestorm, but maybe there didn't need to be.
> They seemed to be good at building a heat of their own.
> —**Kiss of Fire**

The first coupling in a firestorm always results in the conception of a son. It is possible that the firestorm can only spark when the mate is in the fertile phase of her cycle, but equally possible that the firestorm over-rides any biological concern, making conception possible in that moment, regardless of the phase of her cycle. In **Kiss of Fury**, Alex and Donovan use contraception because neither of them want a child (yet neither of them can resist the allure of the firestorm), and the firestorm continues to burn until they abandon this choice—they believe the change occurs because Alex conceives, but I am skeptical. The firestorm has the power to compel a woman to conceive, no matter where she is in her cycle when it sparks. I personally doubt that such a force would be stopped by a condom, and suggest to you that it's a greater purpose that keeps Donovan's firestorm alight. The firestorm is still burning when Alex and Donovan encounter Delaney again, and its heat helps him to heal.

Pyr only have sons, who come into their shifting powers at puberty. (For the exception to this rule, please see Wyvern.) Once the firestorm is satisfied and one son has been conceived, those couples who remain together can conceive again. There is no other woman and will never be another woman with the ability to bear that *Pyr*'s sons. (For an exception, please refer to Erik Sorensson's book **Kiss of Fate**.)

He'd been angry before, but it was beyond unthinkable that is destined mate should flee from him and his protection.

Women did not run away from Donovan Shea.

Ever.

—Donovan Shea in **Kiss of Fury**

The firestorm is believed to flare the way it does because it marks the presence and approval of the Great Wyvern: in her presence, the spark within each *Pyr* is kindled to greater strength and power. All *Pyr* and *Slayers* can feel the spark of a firestorm, and are instinctively drawn to its blaze. Firestorms of particular significance to the *Pyr* tend to occur during full eclipses of the moon.

"There is an old conviction among our kind that love is a whimsy of mortals, that to love a woman is to lose something of what makes one *Pyr*. To link oneself to a mortal woman is to create a binding tie with one place and time, to rip asunder our connection to infinity. According to such thinking, women serve their purpose in bearing our young and have no merit beyond that. We may protect them and we may honor them by force of that debt, but it is inadvisable for us to surrender any of our affection to them. I have known many who have lived to that code."

—Erik Sorensson in **Kiss of Fire**

"The firestorm forges new strength and resilience," Quinn said. "Just as the forge tempers iron into steel, the fire makes the blade more than it could have been otherwise."

"The firestorm transforms us into more than we could be otherwise," Rafferty agreed.

—**Kiss of Fury**

There are two competing views amongst the *Pyr* about the permanence of the relationship marked by the firestorm. Historically, the firestorm was believed to be a purely biological impulse, but the modern *Pyr* increasingly believe that a partnership of long duration with the "mate" is ideal. In **Kiss of Fire**, Erik confesses that Quinn's parents' relationship was the first he had witnessed that showed such love and commitment.

"You have to realize that the firestorm is very intimate, that many *Pyr* will never discuss it."
—Rafferty Powell in **Kiss of Fire**

There is a suggestion that firestorms have not been overly discussed amongst the *Pyr*, at least not before the Dragon's Tail Wars. This may be because dragons prefer to hide their emotions, rather than discuss them.

"Put that in a jar and save the world," she murmured. "Look at it. It's spontaneous combustion, clean burning. If we could figure it out, we could put that energy to work."
—Alex Madison, playing with the firestorm's spark in **Kiss of Fury**

In some instances, the firestorm can be a healing power: in **Kiss of Fury**, the injured Delaney is drawn to the heat of his brother Donovan's firestorm in search of salvation. It could even be said that in **Kiss of Fire**, the spark of the firestorm draws Quinn back to re-unite with his own kind. Delaney's own firestorm with Ginger, in **Winter Kiss**, is what saves him from becoming the next source of the Dragon's Blood Elixir.

The firestorm is a very potent experience, particularly for those *Pyr* who make a permanent commitment with their mates. Experiencing the firestorm of another *Pyr* at the height of its heat can be both nostalgic and invigorating for a *Pyr* who has savored his own. In **Kiss of Fury**, Donovan thanks Quinn for helping him defeat Keir and defend Alex, by inviting Alex to touch his hand in Quinn's company and conjure the spark.

In **Winter Kiss**, Donovan offers the first 'firestorm gift', bringing a new sports car to Delaney. The *Pyr* joke about this new obligation, but it's between brothers and meant to replace the car that Delaney sold when he decided to embark on a suicide mission to destroy the Elixir.

FLASHFIRE SONG, THE—A chant taught to Lorenzo by Pwyll, as payment for Lorenzo defending the third darkfire crystal in his hoard. The flashfire song severs the connection between any *Pyr* and the rest of his kind, and Lorenzo plans to use it to disappear. He's uncertain whether it will claim his *Pyr* powers, as well, but doesn't care. Instead, he uses it on Balthasar, so that *Slayer* disappears.

There appears to be an issue here, as Pwyll died hundreds of years before Lorenzo was born. It is possible that Pwyll taught the song to Lorenzo's grandfather, Gaspar, and that both song and crystal were passed down as a legacy. This might explain Salvatore's decision to surrender the crystal to Drake, in order to keep his son from denying his own kind. It is also possible that Pwyll's ghost, which was active in the dreams and consciousness of other *Pyr*, made the deal with Lorenzo. This would explain Lorenzo's fear that the flashfire song will disappear from his memory after the crystal vanishes from his hoard.

GARDEN OF THE HESPERIDES—The garden of the goddess Hera, where Aura leads Thad in **Kiss of Danger**. Aura intends to ask Thad to take a bite out of one of the golden apples that grow there, because then he'll be compelled to tell her the truth about the firestorm and his intentions. It's a long flight, but Aura helps Thad by becoming a favorable wind. The fruit of the trees is defended by Ladon, a nine-headed dragon, and Thad fights him, then he and Aura satisfy their firestorm in the garden. The illness that Jorge brings to the present day is from the pilgrim on the road to the Garden of the Hesperides—he's made the journey hoping that Hera will intervene and save him.

GENEALOGIES—After the shadow dragons are destroyed in **Whisper Kiss**, Alex and Ginger embark on a project to create genealogies of the *Pyr*, in order to identify as many dead *Pyr* and *Slayers* as possible. The plan is to determine which of them might have become shadow dragons and hunt them down. Erik helps with this, answering questions from his memories: this is how the *Pyr* discover that Lorenzo has beguiled Erik, ensuring that Erik forgets about Gaspar and his progeny.

GREAT WYVERN—The deity acknowledged by the *Pyr*. The *Pyr* swear by the Great Wyvern and attribute radical changes in fortune to her. Their lore insists that the Great Wyvern lit the divine spark within each of them. The Death Ritual ensures that the divine spark is fully extinguished when it should be. By this same logic, the blood of *Slayers* turns black because they willingly douse the divine spark in themselves, by turning their backs upon their sacred mission to defend the earth and its treasures. Just as the firestorm is a mark of the Great Wyvern's favor, the sterility of *Slayers* is a sign of her disfavor.

GREEN MACHINE—The invention of Alex Madison and her deceased partner Mark Sullivan, the Green Machine is a car with an engine that runs on salt water. The destruction of the labs at Gilchrist Enterprises and the demolition of the prototype right before its unveiling before investors left Alex in the burn ward of the hospital.

HABITS AND HABITATS OF DRAGONS: A COMPLEAT GUIDE FOR *SLAYERS*, THE—A book, written by Sigmund Guthrie, perceived by humans to be fiction but actually a thorough account of *Pyr* lore, published in the late 19th century. The leatherbound volume first appears in Sara's bookstore in **Kiss of Fire**, where it is discovered by Erik, although Sara doesn't remember it being in the inventory. In **Kiss of Fate**, Sara sends it to Eileen, who begins compiling a reference to the *Pyr*. Sigmund's book proves to be a tremendous resource for Jac in **Firestorm Forever**, although it is less useful to Jorge who steals the volume to find out more about Sigmund's cloning project. There's nothing in the book about that experiment.

HERE BE DRAGONS—The name of Quinn Tyrrell's business. He's an artisan blacksmith who travels to exhibit and sell his work at art shows. He also hoards wrought iron to use in the creation of special pieces.

HIBERNATION—The *Pyr* have the ability to slow their metabolism to a very low rate. This technique is used when the dragon shifter in question wants to pass a lot of time, without actively living it. It is not uncommon for a *Pyr* to hibernate after the death of his mate, for example, because he doesn't want to experience all the days and nights of solitude before his own death. An individual *Pyr* might also use this technique to avoid detection, to lull opponents into complacency or to savor a moment. In **Kiss of Fire**, Sara consistently has the sense that time slows when she's in Quinn's presence, and that he'll wait forever. Marcus, the Sleeper, does this but not by choice—he has been enchanted by the Cantor, Rafferty's grandfather, to sleep until the darkfire awakens, which it does in **Darkfire Kiss**. In **Flashfire**, Lorenzo's father, Salvatore has been hibernating for a long time and Lorenzo has been protecting him. Salvatore also dreams and considers himself to be visiting the realm of the Wyvern when he does so.

HIDDEN WORLD—The *Pyr* live amongst humans and once did so openly as dragon shifters. They believe this is the reason that virtually all human societies tell stories of dragons: they were real and they were visible. In the Middle Ages, however, when dragon hunting became popular and the *Pyr*'s numbers were vastly diminished by humans, the *Pyr* chose to disguise themselves. They still live in human society but they hide their capabilities as dragon shifters from view.

"The cohesive element of human history is that the humans who recorded it seldom knew what was truly at stake."
—Erik Sorensson in **Kiss of Fire**

In the Dragon's Tail Wars, when fighting between *Pyr* and *Slayer* becomes more heated, this policy is undermined by Thorolf, when he is filmed shifting shape during Rafferty's firestorm in **Darkfire Kiss** The video goes viral after being uploaded to YouTube, which destroys the last of Erik's tolerance for Thorolf's failure to take his nature and his quest seriously. Subsequently Melissa, Rafferty's mate and a television reporter, proposes that the *Pyr* reveal themselves as a protective race, and Erik reluctantly agrees, stipulating that the *Pyr* can only be filmed in their dragon forms to protect their human identities. In **Flashfire**, Cassie earns a hefty fee for photographing Lorenzo as he shifts shape—the session is a sign of trust between Cassie and Lorenzo, but infuriates Erik.

By the end of the Dragon's Tail Wars, Erik's determination to defend his kind is been shown to have merit, and the *Pyr* develop a new Covenant, which each must swear to follow when he comes into his powers at puberty. Key to this new creed is a review process, which must be followed before any human is permitted to learn the true nature of any *Pyr*. This proves to be a problem for Zoë when she comes into her powers (**Flying Blind**), because she can't initially control her shifting to dragon form.

HIGH COUNCIL OF SEVEN—A governing council of *Pyr* established by Erik's father, Soren, in the Middle Ages (in 1220), in an attempt to fight the plan of Mikael Vassily to turn dragon shifters against mankind. That initiative failed, the *Pyr*'s numbers were vastly reduced, and Mikael became the first *Slayer*. The original High Council included Soren (father of Erik), Gaspar (grandfather of Lorenzo), Lothair, Sigmund (the elder, brother of Soren), Thorkel (grandfather of Thorolf), Rafferty and Erik. Erik notes that his father didn't want his son on the council because he believed Erik to be too young, but ran out of options. At the launch of the Dragon's Tail Wars, Erik was attempting to locate and gather the remaining *Pyr* to re-establish that council.

HOARD—A collection of treasures kept by every *Pyr*. Although the *Pyr* in question perceives the items in the hoard to be precious, they may or may not be of monetary value: it is as likely for a *Pyr* to keep sentimental trinkets in his hoard—or stock certificates—as gold and precious gems. Some *Pyr* believe that their mate is the most valuable gem in their hoard.

IMMORTALITY—The *Pyr* are not immortal, even though Boris taunts Sara in **Kiss of Fire** that they are. The truth is that they tend to have extremely long lives. They come of age, much like human children, and develop their shape shifting abilities at puberty. Once grown to adulthood, they age very slowly until their firestorms. Once the firestorm is consummated, the *Pyr*'s aging may match that of his mate, if the pair remain together. It is unclear whether this is a deliberate choice on the part of the *Pyr*, the manifestation of an unconscious desire, or a physiological development as a result of his having experienced the firestorm and conceived an heir. In **Kiss of Fire**, Quinn finds his first grey hair after he and Sara consummate their firestorm, even though he's more than eight hundred years old at this point.

"Maybe the trouble is that I'm a sucker for a British man," [Eileen] said lightly, her eyes sparkling. "It's the accent."

"What a relief." Erik sat back, waiting for his moment.

"What do you mean?"

"I'm not British, so there's no issue between us."

"Of course, you are!"

Erik shook his head. "Viking."

She shook a needle at him playfully. "We have a deal."

"We do," Erik agreed easily.

"There've been no Vikings for a thousand years. You can't be Viking, Erik, so don't put me on. Those people are all dead."

Erik spoke with quiet heat. "But we're not *people,* Eileen."

She stopped knitting.

She stared at him as her lips parted.

She looked at the wooden chest [containing the Dragon's Teeth], then back at him. There was a question in her eyes, one that she obviously thought was too crazy to say aloud.

"Yes," Erik said, knowing exactly what that question was.

Eileen swallowed and looked down for a moment. It was a shorter interval than Erik expected, and he admired her resilience.

She nudged the box with her foot. "Anyone you know?"

—**Kiss of Fate**

Most *Pyr* survive their human mates, but few live long after their mates are gone. There certainly are those who believe that the souls of a *Pyr* and his mate are linked forevermore, and others who suggest that when a mate dies, the *Pyr* can choose to expire as well.

IMAGINATION INK—the tattoo shop owned by Chynna, introduced in **Whisper Kiss**, located in New York City. Roxanne Kincaid and Neo are partners with Chynna. After the end of the Dragonfire cycle, Chynna appears in my *Flatiron Five* contemporary romance series after selling Imagination Ink to Rox (who has bought out Neo's share).

INCREMENTAL SHIFTING—The ability to partially shift shape, or to do so incrementally. This is a challenging skill for a *Pyr* to master, and an exhibition of extreme self control. The chosen shift is usually the thumb: the dragon shifter in question allows only his thumb to shift into a dragon talon. Quinn does this to help Sara come to terms with his nature in **Kiss of Fire**, apparently unaware that it's an unusual ability among his kind. Sigmund believed to be impossible until Boris Vassily proved that he could do it.

When Boris tried to intimidate Erik before their final battle in **Kiss of Fire** by hovering between forms, for example, Erik spontaneously breathes dragonfire at the *Slayer*, while still in human form. It is unclear whether this skill is a different example of hovering between forms, or whether Erik's dragon and human sides had begun to interact and merge in new ways. In **Kiss of Fury**, Boris let his thumb change to a dragon talon but otherwise remained in human form.

In **Kiss of Fate**, Sophie is shocked to see Boris not only partially shift but use his talon to breach the dragonsmoke on Erik's lair:

Then Boris lifted a talon. He was in human form, but had a dragon talon on his right index finger. Sophie didn't believe her eyes. Boris was hovering between forms.

And he held the shift at only his right talon.

Neither *Pyr* nor *Slayer* hovered between forms: once the shift began, it was impossible to stop, although a few *Pyr* learned to shift more slowly or to hesitate during the change.

Boris was frozen between the two forms.

To Sophie's further surprise, Boris used that talon to slice an opening in the dragonsmoke. Sophie gaped. Erik's dragonsmoke was breached, but it still rang true.

Sophie was shocked to her marrow. Neither *Pyr* nor *Slayer* could cross dragonsmoke without the express permission of the dragon who had breathed it—and live to tell about the deed. It was impossible for Boris to be doing what he was doing.

But he did it all the same.

Only the Wyvern could breach dragonsmoke unscathed.

Only the Wyvern could hover between forms, if she so chose.

Sophie's eyes widened as she thought of the other feats she could do.

How was Boris stealing her tricks?

Had he adopted them all?

Meanwhile, Boris severed the dragonsmoke to the ground. He let his nail shift back to human form.

Then he stepped through the breach in human form. Sophie gasped and sputtered. The dragonsmoke did not injure him. There was no mistaking the evidence of her eyes. Boris picked the lock on the door and entered Erik's lair, unscathed.

It was up to Sophie to stop him.

—**Kiss of Fate**

Changing shape slowly, however, is viewed to be something any *Pyr* can do, if he or she has sufficient self-control. In **Kiss of Fury**, Sophie changed shape slowly for Alex, to show her the transformation in greater detail, because she knew that as a scientist, Alex would need detail to believe her eyes. Donovan admitted in that same book to changing shape slowly when he deliberately drove Olivia insane. Donovan also confessed to Alex that after a certain point, he couldn't control the shift any longer. When he changed slowly for Alex, at her demand, once the shift reached his shoulder, he lost command of it, and the remaining shift was quick.

There is apparently an impetus to shift beneath the light of the eclipse. In **Kiss of Fate**, Rafferty is impressed that Sophie doesn't share the *Pyr*'s compulsion to shift shape. There's a suggestion that this involuntary shift can be mastered with practice. In contrast, in **Winter Kiss**, Delaney, because he has consumed the Dragon's Blood Elixir, is completely unable to control his shift during the eclipse. This lack of control is part of what he finds intolerable about his situation, and fuels his determination to destroy the Elixir at any price.

KING AND CONSORT—The third foretold firestorm and match, and the one that is said to demand a blood sacrifice. Erik and Eileen's partnership fulfills this prophecy, and Erik fears that he will be the blood sacrifice. Instead, the loss of Sophie, the Wyvern, by her choice to surrender herself for the good of the *Pyr* proves to be the sacrifice.

KUPUA—Chen's name for the *Pyr* when he's trying to convince Liz that Brandon is responsible for the earthquakes in Hawai`i in **Ember's Kiss**. He says that the dragon is the son of the fire goddess Pele and inclined to destruction. In Hawai`ian mythology, the Kupua are both supernatural beings and shape-shifters, having one human form and a second that can be an animal, a plant or a mineral. They are often destructive but can also be kindly. (Chen omitted that detail.)

LAIR—Although each *Pyr* may have multiple homes, his one principle residence is considered to be his lair. The lair is usually where the *Pyr*'s hoard is secured, and is invariably defended by dragonsmoke barriers.

LEY LINES—Also called dragon lines, these are lines of energy on the surface of the earth, perhaps revealed by magnetic sensitivity, that show paths between points of power. It is thought that they echo magnetic fields and that ancient roadways follow them. In **Kiss of Fire**, the *Pyr* follow ley lines to find Sara when she is captured by *Slayers*.

LOSS OF SCALE/REPAIR OF MISSING SCALE—A *Pyr* will lose a scale when he loves, particularly when he loves and loses (or fears to lose). His emotional vulnerability is mirrored in his physical armor, which must be repaired by the Smith of the *Pyr*. This is not necessarily a mirror of romantic love: Magnus the *Slayer* lost a scale out of love for himself, while Sigmund lost one over his love for his mother. The place where the scale is missing—where the dragon's hide isn't armored—is a favored place for attack because of its vulnerability. In **Kiss of Fire**, Quinn sinks his tooth into the unprotected spot on Boris's chest.

When a *Pyr* loses a scale due to his love for his mate, his emotional vulnerability is echoed in his physical dragon shape. Although the Smith can repair the scaled armor of the *Pyr*, the mate is the only one who can ensure that the repair of a scale lost for love is permanently repaired. No scale will grow back in the unprotected spot, as it would in time elsewhere, so the skin will be exposed forever. In order for the repair of such a scale to "take", the Smith must have a gift from the mate, and it must be voluntarily given. Often the gift is symbolic, and more frequently, it aligns with the affinities to the elements of the specific *Pyr* and his mate. Sometimes the scale is retrieved or captured when it falls, and later affixed to the *Pyr*'s coat of mail, but other times it is lost completely and must be replaced. The repaired scale may be discernible when the *Pyr* is in human form.

In **Kiss of Fire**, Quinn has lost a scale due to his love for his first wife, Elizabeth. That scale grew back when he fell in love with Sara, but he lost another one, right over his heart. This gap in his armor was repaired with a wrought iron scale that he forged himself, which Sara realized represented earth and fire. She cried at the prospect of him being vulnerable, and her tears added the element of water. She guessed what was happening and kissed the scale after it was in place, breathing on it to provide the element of air. The scale changed color as it adhered, and appears like a sterling silver badge on his chest in dragon form. In human form, Quinn has a freckle on his chest in the same spot, which looks silvery in some light.

There's more than one suggestion that repairing the scale on the hide of the *Pyr* can also repair emotional wounds. He can be made whole again, both emotionally and physically, by the gift of his mate during his firestorm, if not by the firestorm itself.
Because Quinn had been isolated from his fellow *Pyr* and because he was too young when his father died to have learned many of the mysteries of the Smith, he didn't realize all of the variables associated with repairing scales. After seeing his own armor

mended, he believed he could repair the scales of any of the *Pyr*. By the time of **Kiss of Fury**, he has fixed Donovan's armor with the Dragon's Tooth, which Donovan perceives to be the treasure of his hoard. In **Kiss of Fury**, however, Quinn reveals that he was incapable of mending Sloane and Niall's scales, because the repair wouldn't adhere. Quinn was frustrated by his inability to help his fellows and the unavailability of anyone to mentor him on the secrets of the Smith—until Sophie opened a conduit between Quinn and his dead father, allowing the former Smith to instruct the new in dreams.

"Alex!" Quinn commanded, and she understood. She put the palm of her hand on the jet, replacing Quinn's claw, and pushed the scale hard against Donovan's flesh.

The pain was searing. Firestorm and dragonfire burned together to repair his armor. The new scale could have been a brand. It burned deep, sending a stab of pain through Donovan.

Donovan tipped back his head and bellowed as the heat cut straight to his marrow. The fire incinerated his old pains and injuries, even those that had left scars upon his heart. It cauterized the wound of Olivia's deception. It knit his flesh and burned away the detritus and left the image of Alex seared upon his very soul.
—**Kiss of Fury**

The loss of a scale is a portent in **Winter Kiss**: Sara dreams of Nikolas giving her a copper and emerald scale, which she recognizes as belonging to Delaney. She and Quinn interpret this as a sign that they have to go to Delaney's firestorm, so Quinn can repair that Pyr's armor. At the time of her vision, however, Delaney has not yet lost the scale. The dream is a portent that he will—and he does, just as he enters the sanctuary of the Dragon's Blood Elixir for his final confrontation with Magnus.

In **Whisper Kiss**, Niall loses his scale in the battle with Chen beneath the city of New York—it comes loose when Rox is riding him through flooded subway tunnels and she keeps it.

In **Kiss of Danger**, the Pythia at Delphi repairs Alexander's scale using the gold and carnelian ring that Alexander gave Katina at their wedding. In Kiss of Darkness, Damien's lost scale is repaired with a stone from the Mothers, the large stones that Petra says are the Earthdaughters who came before.

TOKENS USED IN SCALE REPAIRS IN DRAGONFIRE:

When a *Pyr* loses a scale due to his love for his mate, that scale can only be successfully repaired with a gift offered willingly by her and the presence of the four elements. Near the end of each Dragonfire Novel, the *Pyr* in question has his armor repaired by Quinn with that token from his mate. Quinn's scale repair is unusual as the scale is truly lost. He creates a replica out of wrought iron.

Quinn—wrought iron replacement scale plus Sara's love
Donovan—his scale plus a carved jet pin of a swan with a garnet eye given to Alex by her grandmother
Erik—a runestone that belonged to his father, lost and found by Sigmund and retrieved by Eileen
Delaney—his scale plus one of Ginger's amber and sterling earrings from her mom. Quinn makes a ring of the other one, which Ginger wears as a wedding ring.
Niall—a protective tattoo from Rox on the exposed skin, plus his scale
Rafferty—Melissa's tears (because she has nothing but herself to give, and Rafferty taught her that was enough).
Lorenzo—a pearl in a gold pendant, bought in Venice by Cassie because it reminded her of Angelina's earrings
Brandon—jet and sterling earrings owned by Liz's grandmother
Alexander—scale repaired by the Pythia plus gold and carnelian ring he gave to Katina when they married
Damien—his scale plus a pebble from the Mothers collected by Petra
Thad—his scale plus the golden apple of the Hesperides that Aura took from the garden (missing three bites)
Thorolf—three teardrops of amber, shed by Chandra before she surrenders her immortality
Drake—a string of pearls from Veronica's grandmother
Marco—a sterling silver rose that belonged to Jac's mother

Sloane—the gold necklace with charm of the Space Needle, bought for Sam by her son Nathaniel. Quinn arranges the chain in a spiral with the charm in the middle.

LUNAR ECLIPSE—The most important firestorms of the *Pyr* are indicated by lunar eclipses. The Dragon's Tail began on June 12, 2006, and the eclipses documented in the Dragonfire series are real dates, as well as events in our world. As the Dragon's Tail Wars progressed, the indicated firestorms lit more closely to the time of the eclipse, becoming simultaneous with the totality of the lunar eclipse. The times below are stated in Universal Time, which is Greenwich Mean Time, and the Saros cycle is included, although that was only important to the *Pyr*, Cinnabar.

March 3, 2007—a total lunar eclipse, from 22:43 UT to 23:58 UT, Saros 123
This sparked Quinn and Sara's firestorm the following July in **Kiss of Fire**.

August 28, 2007—a total lunar eclipse, from 09:52 UT to 11:22 UT, Saros 128
This sparked Donovan and Alex's firestorm the following October in **Kiss of Fury**.

February 21, 2008—a total lunar eclipse, from 03:00 UT to 03:51 UT, Saros 133
This sparked Erik and Eileen's firestorm in **Kiss of Fate**.

These next three partial eclipses sparked the firestorm of Ginger and Delaney, who was almost a shadow dragon when the light of the firestorm drew him back to the *Pyr*.

February 9, 2009—a penumbral lunar eclipse, from 12:36 UT to 16:39 UT, Saros 143

July 7, 2009—a penumbral lunar eclipse, from 08:32 UT to 10:44 UT, Saros 110

August 6, 2009—a penumbral lunar eclipse, from 23:01 UT

August 6 to 02:17 UT August 7, Saros 148

June 26, 2010—a partial lunar eclipse, from 10:16 UT to 13:00 UT, Saros 120
This partial eclipse sparked Niall and Rox's firestorm. Because Niall's twin brother had become a shadow dragon, his firestorm was shadowed.

December 21, 2010—a total lunar eclipse, from 07:40 UT to 08:53 UT, Saros 125
This sparked Rafferty and Melissa's firestorm.

June 15, 2011—a total lunar eclipse, from 19:22 UT to 21:03 UT, Saros 130
This sparked Cassie and Lorenzo's firestorm.

December 10, 2011—a total lunar eclipse, from 14:05 UT to 14:57 UT, Saros 135
This sparked Liz and Brandon's firestorm.

April 15, 2014—a total lunar eclipse, from 07:06 UT to 08:24 UT, Saros 122
This blood moon sparked Thorolf and Chandra's firestorm.

These last three blood moons, which end the Dragon's Tail cycle of the moon's node, spark the firestorms in **Firestorm Forever**, including that of Sam and Sloane.

October 8, 2014—a total lunar eclipse, from 10:24 UT to 11:24 UT, Saros 127

April 4, 2015—a total lunar eclipse, from 11:54 UT to 12:06 UT, Saros 132

September 28, 2015—a total lunar eclipse, from 02:10 UT to 03:23 UT, Saros 137

MAGIC—The *Pyr* do not believe in magic. They believe that there are many illusions, which can be explained by closer study or greater perception. This is probably due to the fact that much of what they take for granted about themselves and their powers appears to be magic to human observers, whose senses are not so keen.

"There is no such thing as magic." Quinn's tone was dismissive.

"But there are mysteries we have yet to understand," Rafferty replied.

— **Kiss of Fury**

The exception to this is the *Slayer* Chen, who does use magic and spells. The assumption is that this knowledge is either lost to the *Pyr*, or that the use of magic is specific to the *Lung Wang* of Asia and the *Pyr* never knew of it before the Dragon's Tail Wars. In **Whisper Kiss**, Chen confesses to casting a spell to consolidate his power—by demonstrating his command of all four elements, his spell will grant him power over the fifth element, spirit. He believes this will give him mastery of the world. The element Chen does not command is air and he tries to capture or enslave *Pyr* with that affinity, beginning with Niall, Thorolf, Brandon and Thorolf again.

MATE—The traditional term for the woman who prompts the spark of a *Pyr*'s firestorm. Most mates take exception to the use of this word, although it does perfectly describe their role as results from the firestorm.

NYMPH—An immortal being with the ability to change shape. In **Kiss of Danger**, Aura and her nymph friends are aware of both Katina's power as an Waterdaughter and Petra's abilities as an Earthdaughter. They note that neither are immortal, that Katina is not bound to a single water source as the naiad are, and are envious that both have made a lasting bond with a *Pyr*. Aura mentions the presence of several Anthousai, who are flower nymphs, noting that they are pretty, easygoing, and not overly clever. This one exudes a scent of hyacinths. She also observes that nymphs are of two types: those who choose to remain chaste and those who are insatiable (like flower nymphs).

OLD-SPEAK—The traditional way in which dragon shifters communicate. Old-speak is gutteral and tends to be terse. It is expressed at a level too low for human ears to understand: humans typically hear the sound of old-speak but attribute it to passing trucks, trains or thunder. Old-speak can be uttered at different volumes: it can be conversational, it can be broadcast and heard at a great distance, or it can be whispered in the mind of another dragon shifter. A very wily dragon shifter can meld his old-speak with the thoughts of his victim so that the two are indistinguishable. This skill is used by *Slayers* like Ambrose and Magnus to bend *Pyr* to their will.

Old-speak appeared in italics in the Dragonfire novels, to distinguish it from speech that humans could here. It was not styled that way, however, in the original edition of **Kiss of Fire**.

ORIGIN—The *Pyr* tell a story of their origin, which they have memorized.

"In the beginning, there was the fire, and the fire burned hot because it was cradled by the earth. The fire burned bright because it was nurtured by the air. The fire burned lower only when it was quenched by the water And these were the four elements of divine design, of which all would be built and with which all would be destroyed. And the elements were placed at the cornerstones of the material world and it was good.

But the elements were alone and undefended, incapable of communicating with each other, snared within the matter that was theirs to control. And so, out of the endless void was created a race of guardians whose appointed task was to protect and defend the integrity of the four sacred elements. They were given powers, the better to fulfill their responsibilities; they were given strength and cunning and longevity to safeguard the treasures surrendered to their stewardship. To them alone would the elements respond. These guardians were—and are—the Pyr."

In *DragonFate*, it becomes clear that this is only part of the truth.

PROPHECIES — The *Pyr* are particularly fond of prophecies and portents. The Wyvern can be a source of prophecies for them, as can their leader, Erik Sorensson. Prophecies were also received by Sara Keegan, the Seer who is the partner of Quinn Tyrrell, the Smith.

> [Sara] was the Seer of the *Pyr*, but these verses always came from outside of her. They could have been missives from another world, the world of the *Pyr*, which Sara didn't completely understand.
> — **Whisper Kiss**

Each *Dragonfire* novel contains a prophecy about the firestorm in question. Dragons are reputed to have an affection for riddles — since these prophecies tend to be enigmatic, even though they offer insight, I think of them as riddles from the Great Wyvern.

Kiss of Fire: Quinn knew this verse, and called it an old prophecy when he confided it in Sara.

> *When the Dragon's Tail demands its price,*
> *And the moon is devoured once, not twice,*
> *Seer and Smith will again unite.*
> *Water and air, with fire and earth*
> *This sacred union will give birth*
> *To the* Pyr's *sole chance to save the Earth.*

Kiss of Fury: Sophie recites this prophecy to Erik when she tells him that the *Pyr* must successfully conclude the first three firestorms of the Dragon's Tail to have a chance against the *Slayers* in the war that will leave only one kind of dragon shifter surviving.

> *The Dragon's Tail demands recompense*
> *Owed the land for man's violence;*
> *Both human and* Pyr *must sacrifice,*
> *To earn the chance to make matters right.*
> *A portal has opened to the past*
> *Making possible what has been lost;*
> *Time to muster forces for the final battle,*
> *In which* Pyr *and* Slayer *learn their mettle.*

There is also a second prophecy in **Kiss of Fury,** an old one which both Erik and Sophie know and which Rafferty learns in a dream. The dream is dispatched by Sophie, but it is Rafferty's grandfather Pwyll who shares the prophecy in the dream:

> *Elements four disguise weapons three,*
> *Revealed if love harnesses fury.*
> *The Wizard can work her alchemy*
> *Only with the Warrior's lost key.*
> *Transformation in the firestorm's light,*
> *Will forge a foretold force for right.*
> *Warrior, Wizard and* Pyr *army*
> *Shall lead the world to victory.*

Kiss of Fate*:* Rafferty recites this prophecy to Erik and the other *Pyr*. There's an implication that it's been known for a long while and he's reminding them of it—although Erik claims to have never heard it before.

> *Third match of three demands sacrifice,*
> *A blood cost of enormous price.*
> *Then King and Consort in union complete*
> *Choose trust over ancient deceit;*
> *Shed blood alone can give the power*
> *To aid the* Pyr *in their darkest hour.*

Winter Kiss: This prophecy is delivered to Ginger by Rafferty, who has written it down.

> *The Outcast patrols shadows deep,*
> *Defending the* Pyr *while they sleep.*
> *When darkness becomes his domain*
> *He risks losing his path back again.*
> *Vigilant in the endless night*
> *Yet drawn by the firestorm's light,*
> *But how can one so at ease in dark*
> *Surrender fully to the firestorm's spark?*
> *Will he dare to leave his task,*
> *Choose himself first instead of last?*

Whisper Kiss: There are two prophecies in this book. The first is recited by Chen to Phelan and explains both his spell and his intentions:

> *When the Dragon's Tail turns in the sky,*
> *When the year of tiger rises high,*
> *The Phoenix and the Dragon mate.*
> *Desire does their child create.*
> *But at this junction the old charm,*
> *Can be performed to make great harm.*
> *Elements four in union do conjure.*
> *The chance to invoke the fifth's measure.*
> *Master the four, command the thoughts*
> *of all Gaia's populace.*

The other prophecy is the first one to come to Sara in a dream. She believes this is because Sophie the Wyvern has died, so can't deliver prophecies any more. There's some suggestion that Sophie is still delivering the prophecies from beyond the grave, but now using Sara as a vehicle.

> *The Phoenix sheds her former skin,*
> *Clothes herself to begin again.*
> *Injuries and debts unearned,*
> *Consigned with her hide to fire's burn.*
> *The Dragon loses but one scale,*
> *To keep nigh intact his coat of mail.*
> *But not all things should survive,*
> *And not all burdens help him to thrive.*
> *Can he learn the Phoenix's song,*
> *And leave his past where it belongs?*
> *Learn the Dreamwalker's dance*
> *And usher in the world's new chance?*

Darkfire Kiss: Rafferty recites this prophecy, once again saying that he remembers it.

> *Darkfire's flame burns bright as ice;*
> *No hint of compromise will suffice.*
> *Darkfire's heat will not fade*
> *Until much that is has been unmade;*
> *Until all that is hidden has been revealed,*
> *Until all that was clear becomes concealed;*
> *Until the Sleeper wakes to his fate,*

Until the Cantor's legacy is claimed.
But out of ruin rises new growth;
The flames of mercury know this truth.

Flashfire: Darkfire mixes things up in Lorenzo's firestorm, allowing his mate, Cassie to step into a painting and meet Lorenzo's mother, Angelina. Angelina entrusts Cassie with a prophecy that was given to her at Lorenzo's birth. It's in Venetian, so Cassie can't read it, but Lorenzo can.

Flashfire lights the solitude
Of the Pyr *with most to lose.*
Firestorm plus an ancient spell
Fuels lust that sees his sense dispelled
Flashfire's promise is a lure
To cheat the Pyr *of his true power.*
Will he see through the disguise
Forget the song, seize the prize?
The future hangs upon his choice
Between life and love, or sacrifice.

Ember's Kiss*:* The prophecy is revealed to Sara, the Seer of the *Pyr*, written in letters of fire on a mirror that illuminate then fade, as if they never were.

Dragon lost and dragon found;
Dragon denied and dragon bound,
Down to embers, his fire chills,
In thrall to one whose intent is ill.
Firedaughter's spark can ignite the flame,
Give him strength to fight again.
Or will both be lost on ocean's tide,
Surrendered as a failed test's price?

Kiss of Danger*:* The Pythia gives a prophecy when Katina and Alexander return to Delphi.

Evil must face its just defeat,
By Pyr *trained to soldiers elite.*
Apollo makes this task your price,
A life of service will suffice.
You, naiad-spawn, lost and found,

Have gifts beyond any count.
Here you will learn skills still unknown;
Here you will bear sons more of your own;
Here you and Pyr *will live as one;*
Here you will lay future's cornerstone.

Kiss of Darkness*:* Damien journeyed to the Oracle for a prophecy about his firestorm with Petra, and received this one. His interpretation that he would be the sacrifice required was what compelled him to join Drake's forces, leaving Petra pregnant.

A lost child mourned for many years;
A mother who will shed no tears;
A dragon warrior turned to stone;
A woman abandoned, all alone.
Firestorm's promise will fade to naught,
Until stone and fire pay death's cost
After a Pyr *sacrifice is made,*
Destiny's promise can be claimed.

Kiss of Destiny*:* This curse was placed upon Tisiphone by Hera when Tisiphone threatened the firestorm of Aura and Thad in an attempt to avenge her sister's death at Damien's hand. Tisiphone survived as Viv Jason.

Across the centuries and the years,
You will wait and shed your tears,
Until the darkfire is freed again,
Your vengeance can cause the Pyr *no pain.*
I close the portal, for once and all,
To see those I love out of your thrall.
When darkfire will burn once again,
Your sister's death can be avenged.
When daughters of all elements are mates
Then will the dragons face their fates.

Serpent's Kiss*:* Marco presents this prophecy to Lorenzo, suggesting that they be two of the union of five:

A union of five will tip the scale
When the moon aligns in Dragon's Tail;
This Pyr *alliance can defeat the scheme*

And cheat the Slayer *of his dream.*
Fulfilling a pledge long been made
Will put darkness in its grave.
Know Pyr *and* Slayer *can share on curse:*
A vulnerability wrought of their birth.
Keep the pledge and defeat the foe,
So the Dragon's Tail brings triumph not woe.

Firestorm Forever: In this book, the prophecy seems to be elusive to the *Pyr* and their mates, but this is only because it appears to Marco who doesn't share it with them. He writes it on the wall of his apartment and Jac copies it down into her notebook about the *Pyr* when she sees it there.

Three blood moons mark the debt come due
Will the Pyr *triumph or be hunted anew?*
Three eclipses will awaken the spark
In thirteen monsters breeding in dark.
Three times the firestorm will spark
Before darkfire fades into the dark.
Firestorm, mate or blood sacrifice
None or all can be the darkfire's price.
When the Dragon's Tail has turned its bore
And darkfire dies forevermore
Will the Pyr *be left to rule with might*
Or disappear into past's twilight?

PSYCHIC POWERS — Although some *Pyr* have the power to see the unseen (like the Wyvern and Erik Sorensson), most rely upon their very keen observational powers to anticipate actions and events.

In **Kiss of Fury**, Rafferty suggests that Donovan knew what his mate would look like, long before he met Alex. Donovan dismisses this idea, even when Rafferty notes that Donovan had always been drawn to women with similar physical characteristics — tall, athletically built, with brown hair and brown eyes. Rafferty's suggestion is never confirmed and it is possible that there's another explanation — that the Great Wyvern chooses a mate for a *Pyr* who will complement him perfectly.

PYR (OR "TRUE *PYR*")—The *Pyr* are an ancient race of dragon shape shifters. Their role is to defend the four elements and the treasures of the earth, and they include humans among those treasures. They are not immortal, but live a very long time. Their senses are more keen than humans—they see more clearly, for example, and hear a wider range of sounds.

PYROTECHNICS—Erik Sorensson earns his living as a pyrotechnics specialist, creating massive fireworks displays synchronized with music. It's likely that his gift of foresight helps in making minute adjustments to the length of fuses and setting of timers. Part of the reason he lives in an industrial loft is that his lair is also his place of business: he has stored his fireworks in a room in the loft. Sophie remarks upon the distinctive scent of them, mistaking it for brimstone, in **Kiss of Fury**. Eileen, of course, can't discern that scent. Erik's entire inventory is ignited at the end of **Kiss of Fury**, when the Pyr are attacked at his loft and a fire is started. They ensure that the other people in the building are safe, then retreat to watch the display.

QUICKSILVER—an ancient name for mercury in its liquid form. The *Pyr* discover in **Winter Kiss** that Magnus has injected quicksilver into Delaney's veins to prepare that *Pyr* to become the next source of the Dragon's Blood Elixir.

Sloane reads a riddle from the treatise he's decoded to the *Pyr* in **Winter Kiss**, which supplies a clue for saving Delaney and destroying the Elixir.

> *I am the mirror that both heals and kills*
> *false silver and burning red;*
> *the stone that flows*
> *the blood that breathes;*
> *the source of an immortality*
> *without breath or pulse.*

"The Elixir," Ginger guessed, remembering the way Cinnabar floated in the liquid.

"No," Alex said firmly. "It's mercury."

Everyone looked at her in surprise.

Alex ticked off the clues on her fingers. "Mercury is silver, but not sterling. It was called quicksilver for a long time and is a reflective surface like a mirror. It was known to kill germs and consuming it was believed in the Renaissance to confer immortality."

"Paracelsus?" Erik asked, as if remembering.

"He said he cured syphilis with it. I remember that." Alex smiled. "Maybe that made him feel immortal."

"Why *burning red,* then?" Sara asked.

"Mercury poisoning is characterized by flushed skin and a burning sensation," Alex said. "And mercury is the only element that is liquid at room temperature."

"Delaney was turning red," Erik said.

"And Cinnabar *is* red," Ginger agreed.

"The stone that flows," Sloane mused.

"Doesn't mercury come from cinnabar?" Ginger asked, remembering Magnus's story.

"Yes!" Alex said. "That's one source, and it supposedly bleeds from the stone. That's how the ancients found the deposits."

"Blood that breathes?" Niall asked.

"Another old name for mercury and quicksilver is dragon's blood," Sloane said.

"And I remember that it's said to breathe when it's heated," Alex said, her excitement clear. "That's how they discovered the element of oxygen. You heat mercury and it takes in oxygen, then heat it more and it expels it all."
—**Winter Kiss**

REINCARNATION—The *Pyr* have a conviction that reincarnation is real, but they don't believe it happens to them. The *Pyr* are convinced that humans reincarnate, specifically that mates can do so. In **Kiss of Fire**, Donovan makes a joke that if Quinn loses Sara during their firestorm, he can just wait for her to reincarnate again. The suggestion that the Wyvern could reincarnate is not readily accepted by all of the *Pyr*, although Rafferty has no doubt of it once he meets Isabelle.

SALAMANDER—A third form which the Wyvern can also assume. Traditionally, she was the only one with this power, but the concoction of the Dragon's Blood Elixir made it possible for some *Slayers* to also take the form—most notably, Magnus, Jorge and Chen. Rafferty Powell is the only *Pyr* other than the Wyvern who can also become a salamander.

SAROS CYCLE—a sequence of linked eclipses.

Rafferty kept reading, his excitement rising as he found details. A Saros cycle was a period of time in which the positions of the planets were replicated in three ways. A synodic month is the time from one full or new moon to the next, and a full or new moon is a necessary element for a lunar eclipse. A draconic year is the time it takes the sun to travel through the moon's north node to the south and back to the initial starting point. An anomalistic month is the time it takes for the moon to move from perigee to perigee, from the point where it is closest to the earth to the point where it is farthest away and back again.

And all three of these cycles repeat roughly every eighteen years, or every 6585.322 days.

Even more important, when they repeat, another eclipse will occur that is very similar to the one eighteen years before. Thus, eclipses are grouped together and numbered to indicate their Saros family. Each Saros family had an eclipse roughly every eighteen years.

Because nineteen draconic years is eleven hours longer than 223 synodic months, the alignment isn't perfect—thus, Saros families have a beginning and an end. The entire life cycle of a Saros family of eclipses lasts centuries, including seventy or eighty eclipses. They begin as penumbral eclipses, become total eclipses, then diminish until they stop completely.
—**Winter Kiss**

The Dragon's Blood Elixir was created when Magnus injected Cinnabar with his final dose of quicksilver on the first eclipse in Saros cycle 110, which occurred in 747 AD. There are seventy-two eclipses in that cycle, which ends with the eclipse in July 2027. The potency of the Elixir faded as the Saros cycle waned, requiring a new "donor" to become the new source of the Elixir. Magnus planned to have Delaney captive by May 2013 to take advantage of

Saros cycle 150 beginning with the eclipse in that month. That Saros cycle would last through the year 3275.

SCENT—*Pyr* and *Slayers* can detect each other's presence by smell. Each leaves a distinctive scent, which lingers and can be identified, thanks to the keen senses of dragon shifters. In **Kiss of Fire**, however, Erik confesses that he couldn't find Quinn when the Smith's family was attacked because Quinn was so young—at four years of age, he had yet to come into his shape shifting powers and his *Pyr* scent was faint. Erik did catch a whiff of it, but couldn't find the hidden boy. This implies that each *Pyr*'s distinctive scent develops at puberty, in concert with his other abilities.

Pyr with sensitive noses say that *Slayers* have an odor so foul that even if they don't recognize the dragon shifter specifically, they know his orientation by his scent. Needless to say, a *Pyr* can track his mate very closely by her scent.

Erik's son Sigmund knows how to remove his scent from a location, thanks to his diligent research into old dragon lore. The *Pyr* analyze Sigmund's scent left on the second prototype of the Green Machine in **Kiss of Fury**, noting its inconsistency. In some places, the scent seems years old, but in others smells fresh.

Quinn folded his arms across his chest. "It makes me think of thieves wiping their fingerprints off the getaway car, as though Sigmund missed a spot."
—**Kiss of Fury**

Some *Slayers* who drank the Elixir developed the ability to disguise their scent by choice. In **Kiss of Fury**, Rafferty reminded Donovan that Boris could disguise his presence, by implication, his scent.

SEER—Sara Keegan, the foretold partner of the Smith, Quinn Tyrrell. Their union during the Dragon's Tail Wars was anticipated to provide the *Pyr*'s chance to save the Earth. Sara has the first vision of her life right after she meets Quinn, implying that it is their being together that awakens her latent powers.

SERPENT MOUND—an earthwork in Ohio, constructed in the shape of a snake with an egg in its mouth. The earth is mounded five feet high and the head of the serpent is aligned to the summer solstice. The reason for its construction is unknown but Serpent Mound is believed to be about nine hundred years old. In **Winter Kiss**, the sanctuary holding the source of the Dragon's Blood Elixir is in a cave beneath the Serpent Mound.

The sanctuary of the Dragon's Blood Elixir is reached by following a stream that flows underground from the river near the Serpent Mound. There are three caverns below, each one secured with an iron gate. In the third cavern is a massive rock crystal vial filled with the Elixir—and the dragon, Cinnabar, who is its source. The Elixir steams and simmers, emitting humidity into the cavern. Stairs wind around the vial to the summit, stairs which are carved out of the rock crystal. Delaney tries to shatter the vial by force in **Winter Kiss**, but Magnus tells him that force won't crack it.

SHADOW DRAGONS—*Pyr* raised from the dead with the Dragon's Blood Elixir. These *Pyr* were not exposed to all four elements within half a solar day of their death so can be revived by the Elixir and turned into zombies. Shadow dragons do not bleed and they fight on, without regard for any sustained injuries. They must be dismembered and burned to ashes to be destroyed, then exposed to all four elements to ensure that they can't be roused again. The first shadow dragon encountered by the *Pyr* in the Dragonfire series is Donovan's father Keir in **Kiss of Fury**.

Raising a beloved *Pyr* from the dead and turning him into a shadow dragon was a favorite trick of Magnus, and one intended to undermine the defenses of the *Pyr*. For example, Sloane's father appeared in **Kiss of Fury** and attacked Sloane. Sloane couldn't strike the killing blow, even knowing the truth of his father's state, so Donovan attacked and dismembered him. When he was dead, both *Pyr* incinerated his remains with their dragonfire.

When the Academy is destroyed in **Kiss of Fate**, the shadow dragons escape into the world. After the source of the Elixir is destroyed in **Winter Kiss**, Niall offers to lead the task of hunting down and eliminating the remaining shadow dragons, partly because his twin brother, Phelan, has been turned into one. In **Whisper Kiss**, Niall realizes the shadow dragons are localized in New York City and wonders why. He subsequently discovers that Chen has taken charge of the shadow dragons, bending them to his will with the use of his enchanted brand, and trapping them in a hidden refuge. When the *Pyr* locate the lair of the shadow dragons beneath the city and battle Chen, the remaining shadow dragons once again escape into the world. Rox is wounded by Phelan in the escape from the hidden lair. Sloane believes the darkness of the shadow dragons has found a resonance within her because of something in her personal history and the *Pyr* fear that she will die. In seeking that incident and helping her to heal, Niall becomes the Dreamwalker. At the end of **Whisper Kiss**, Donovan, Quinn, Rafferty, Delaney, Erik, Niall and the Dragon's Tooth Warriors eliminate the shadow dragons.

There is a continuity error about the shadow dragons in the original edition of **Kiss of Fate**: near the end of that book, in that version, Erik recognizes Niall's brother, Phelan, and Rafferty's grandfather, Pwyll, among the shadow dragons that attack the *Pyr* with Magnus and Jorge in Chicago. Those two shadow dragons are still at the Academy, though, battling with Rafferty, Thorolf, Niall and the Dragon's Tooth Warriors at the same time.

SHAPE SHIFTING—*Pyr* and *Slayers* change shape at will and by choice. A *Pyr's* decision to shift form is presaged by a shimmer of pale blue that illuminates his body. Sophie, the Wyvern, in contrast, is said to emit a pearlescent shimmer when she shifts shape in **Kiss of Fire**. The shift is generally voluntary, with three exceptions:

1/ When a dragon shifter is wounded, he will revert to his human form, whether he is able to choose to do so or not. This may be the result of the *Pyr* living so many centuries in human society. In addition, when a dragon shifter is wounded so severely that death is likely, he will unwillingly and convulsively rotate between forms. Often the speed of the shifting increases in this situation, until the dragon shifter dies.

2/ When touched by the light of a full lunar eclipse, all *Pyr* and *Slayers* feel a compulsion to shift to their dragon form. If they are ill, injured, inattentive or have not trained sufficiently well at controlling their shift, they may shift shape involuntarily at these times. Delaney, at the beginning of **Winter Kiss**, has no control over his body's urge to shift under the eclipse, which he interprets as a sign that the Elixir is destroying him.

3/ During the his firestorm, a *Pyr* may not be able to fully control his shift to his dragon form, particularly if he has not trained sufficiently well to have complete mastery over his body when under duress. If he perceives that his mate is at risk, the urge to shift shape in her defense may be impossible to contain, possibly because he has no desire to do so. In **Kiss of Fire**, when Sara was visited by Erik and the Smith's talisman sent a warning, Quinn couldn't keep himself from shifting to his dragon form, even though he could see that Sara was safe.

Sophie summoned the change and felt the shift shimmer within herself. As always, she reveled in the power that made her what she was. She felt the vibration of change and let her body do what it did best.

She shifted shape, in broad daylight, in the middle of a Minnesota country road. She did it slowly, as slowly as she could possibly do it, the better to let the Wizard see the truth of transformation. The slow transition was a sight that could drive a human to madness—as Donovan well knew—but Sophie had faith in her instincts. She knew Donovan would never do this to Alex, just as she knew it had to be done.

The Wizard must be as stalwart as the Warrior, yet have the ability to consider known matters in a new way. The Wizard must be able to make sense of what seemed to be madness. Or magic. The Wizard must be able to witness this transformation and survive to make use of what she had seen.

—**Kiss of Fury**

There is a persistent idea amongst the *Pyr* that it is dangerous for a human to watch the actual transition between forms, and that seeing a *Pyr* change shape to a dragon can make a human insane. This was proven to not be a universal response during the Dragon's Tail Wars. Alex is shown the shift by the Wyvern in **Kiss of Fury** and urges Donovan to let her see his transformation. Ginger sees Delaney's shift in **Winter Kiss**: she then challenges him to let her watch the transformation, thereby proving to him that she can witness it. Rox also witnesses Niall's shift with no ill effects in **Whisper Kiss**—this astonishes Niall because his mother saw his father shift on their wedding night and they became estranged. He subsequently realizes that Rox wasn't surprised because she must have seen Thorolf shift before, and they argue about Thorolf's carelessness.

All *Pyr* and *Slayers* have two forms—dragon and man—but some are able to assume additional forms. *Slayers* who have drunk the Elixir are able to shift to a salamander form, as is Rafferty. Only the *Slayer* Chen is able to take multiple human forms in additio to dragon, salamander and snake. It is said that Rafferty's uncle, Myrddin, was able to take many forms. Shifting to dragon form is a defensive pose for the *Pyr*, meaning that they will only shift involuntarily in defense of all that is precious to them, a fact that gives great reassurance to their mates with regards to lovemaking.

SINCLAIR FARMS—the dairy farm owned by Ginger Sinclair, where much of **Winter Kiss** takes place. Ginger calls her herd of a hundred dairy cows "the girls". They're mostly Guernseys, but she's added Kerrys and Milking Shorthorns. The farm has been going organic under Ginger's stewardship and also sells bull semen. The milk from the Guernseys is sold at a premium to Ginger's friend, artisan cheesemaker Tanya. The milking barn is ruled by an aggressive rooster named Reginald, who challenges anyone who enters: Ginger leaves a broom inside the door to defend herself.

SIZE—*Pyr* and *Slayers* are larger than humans in their dragon form, though it's not always clear how much larger. This may be an issue of proportions, since dragon tails take up considerable space but have no counterpart in human physiology. Alex noted that Donovan was twice as tall as her in his dragon form, in **Kiss of Fury**, but that his tail "coiled a long way across the asphalt." They tend to choose large spaces for lairs, so that there is sufficient room to shift shape anywhere in the abode. It's no accident that Erik lives in a loft, a residence in a converted industrial building.

SLAYERS—The *Pyr* have a saying: "*Pyr* are born and *Slayers* are made," Because becoming a *Slayer* is a choice. *Pyr* who have abandoned the mission to defend humans among the earth's treasures are known as *Slayers*. Their blood is black, which is said to be a sign that they have turned away from the light of the Great Wyvern, and is also considered a mark that they are selfish instead of interested in serving the greater good. *Slayers* also forfeit the opportunity to have a firestorm by changing their perspective, as well as the ability to reproduce (if they've not already had a firestorm). Like all *Pyr*, they retain the power to sense the spark of a firestorm, and are drawn to its flame. Over time, they have become inclined to interfere in the fulfillment of the firestorm. Motivations vary on this—individual *Slayers* may seek vengeance against an individual *Pyr* during his firestorm, while other *Slayers* may be jealous or driven to eliminate both *Pyr* and humans from the world.

"What else does the document say?"

"That to become *Slayer* is to choose the darkness over the light, to choose the cold rather than the heat. It is to step away from the fire of divinity, so to speak, and to deny the eternal spark within each of us. To become *Slayer* is to deny the will of the Great Wyvern, to extinguish Her spark and become self-motivated, instead of concerned with the fate of the collective."

—**Kiss of Fury**

Originally, as the *Pyr* tell it, there were no *Slayers*, only *Pyr*. During the Middle Ages, when humans actively hunted dragons (believing that parts of dragon bodies and dragon's blood had medicinal uses), some *Pyr* turned against humans, no longer able to believe that those who hunted and killed their kin were treasures worthy of protection. That change of perspective, and the *Pyr* who so changed, are the origins of *Slayers*. Erik talks about *Slayers* turning humans to their own purposes in **Kiss of Fire**, indicating that the attack upon Béziers in 1204 was a cover for the assassination of Quinn's father, the Smith of his time. The evolution of *Slayers* is explained in **Kiss of Fate**.

SLEEPER, THE—Marcus Maximus, later known as Marco, was called the Sleeper for many centuries. He was enchanted by Pwyll to hide him from Magnus Montmorency, with a spell that would cause him to awaken when the darkfire burned. That happens in **Darkfire Kiss**.

SMITH, THE—The armorer of the *Pyr* and the only one who can repair their "armor" of scales. The current Smith of the *Pyr* is Quinn Tyrrell and his story is told in **Kiss of Fire**.

The Smith is a hereditary position, generally passed from father to oldest son, and relies heavily upon blacksmithing skills. The Smith has a particular affinity with fire, and often can coax a blaze or extinguish it with his thoughts. He can also take an assault of dragonfire and use its energy to build his own strength without his scales being damaged. In the absence of his forge, Quinn has used the dragonfire of his fellows to make scale repairs.

SMITH AND SEER—one of the three foretold and potent unions between *Pyr* and mortal women at the beginning of the Dragon's Tail Wars. The Smith is the *Pyr* armorer who can repair the scales of his fellow dragon shifters, while his mate, the Seer, was anticipated to be able to see the future. Quinn is the Smith who had a firestorm with Sara, the Seer of the *Pyr*, in **Kiss of Fire**.

SONG—A *Pyr* with an affinity to a specific element (fire, water, earth or air) may be able communicate, influence or control that element, with a song. The *Pyr's* dexterity depends upon his skill (which improves with practice) and the strength of his affinity. These invocations may or may not have words, may or may not be in a modern language, may or may not be literally understood by the *Pyr* in question or his fellows. As with so much, tradition rules this sphere for the *Pyr*: if taught to sing a certain way, that dragon will continue to sing "as it has been done", without regard to his own understanding of the words or the mechanism.

He began to hum a low chant, a melody dispatched to the earth and attuned to her rhythms. [Gaia] responded slowly, as troubled as she was, but gradually she warmed to Rafferty's call. He was, in many ways, an old friend and an ally. Once she recognized him, she responded to his melody.
— **Kiss of Fury**

In **Kiss of Fire**, Quinn talks about singing the songs of metals in his work as the Smith. He whispers to a metal lock to convince the tumblers to move and unlock without use of a key. There is some intimation that these songs are secret, particularly those linked to hereditary roles like that of the Smith, and confided to a *Pyr* as part of his apprenticeship. In **Kiss of Fury**, Quinn sings to the metal to reshape the engine parts for the customization of Alex's Green Machine. All of the metal in the building vibrates in response to his song, including the rebar in the concrete foundation. The work is exhausting, but when Rafferty offers to help with the additional parts, Quinn insists that the song of metal is his to sing.

Songs and chants can also be used to reinforce the effect of other influences upon the *Pyr*. In **Kiss of Fury**, Magnus chants a spell that strengthens the hold of the Dragon's Blood Elixir over Delaney: his song tugs Delaney back to the darkness, so that he turns upon Donovan again. Also in **Kiss of Fury**, Rafferty sings as the Dragon's Teeth is sown into the earth, encouraging it to grow as it should. When the tooth acts as a seed and grows into Nikolas of Thebes, Rafferty sings the same song, which orients Nikolas. With the help of Rafferty's song, Nikolas recalled his own commitment to justice, and recognized who was friend and who was foe in the battle he joined. Rafferty's song later created an abyss, and defeated *Slayers* and shadow dragons were cast into the chasm before Rafferty's song closed it, sealing them beneath the earth.

In **Kiss of Fate**, as Magnus and Erik battle for custody of the trunk containing the Dragon's Teeth, Magnus sings to them in an attempt to bring them to the *Slayer* side before they even break free of the enchantment. This strategy fails because the teeth aren't in the trunk anymore. Eileen has hidden them. Instead, the warriors trapped in the teeth hear Rafferty's song as he plants them in the soil behind his house in Hampstead Heath with the help of Niall and Thorolf.

In **Whisper Kiss**, both Chen and Rafferty sing to the earth when the *Pyr* invade the hidden lair of the shadow dragon, and their songs compete for ascendancy. In **Darkfire Kiss**, there is a lot of singing to the earth, as both Rafferty and Magnus have affinities to that element. Ultimately, Jorge is trapped in the cavern at Bardsey Island with a song to the earth. The flashfire song, referenced in **Flashfire**, originated with Pwyll but is known only by Lorenzo. It's a bit different from the other chants and songs as the use of it breaks the connection between a *Pyr* or *Slayer* and the rest of his kind.

SPONTANEOUS MANIFESTATION ELSEWHERE—The Wyvern traditionally was the sole *Pyr* with the ability to move by will through space and time, which was part of the reason she was both revered and considered at least partly divine. The fact that she was seldom seen meant that many of the Wyvern's abilities were unknown by other *Pyr* until Sophie became more involved in the Dragon's Tail Wars. We (and Erik) first learn of her ability to spontaneously manifest elsewhere in *Kiss of Fury*, when she appears in Erik's lair, inside his protective dragonsmoke barrier.

The ingestion of the Dragon's Blood Elixir allowed some *Slayers* to develop additional skills, including this one. Magnus, Chen and Jorge were all able to spontaneously manifest elsewhere. Rafferty was also able to so this beginning in **Winter Kiss**, although he doesn't master the skill until his firestorm in **Darkfire Kiss**. It's not clear whether his ability to do this at all is because of his descent from the Cantor or the influence of the darkfire. Marco also shows an ability to spontaneously manifest elsewhere in **Firestorm Forever**, but this is because of his close association with darkfire. It is a grueling exercise, from all reports, to fling oneself into the void, and Rafferty experiences nausea, dizziness, exhaustion and dehydration as a result.

TABOO—Like all societies, the *Pyr* have behavioral taboos, or actions that are considered so unacceptable that they're not even expressed aloud.

• The *Pyr* don't participate in intimate relations with other *Pyr*.
The *Pyr* have powerful friendships with other Pyr, they guard each other's backs in battle and they are loyal to other *Pyr*, but they aren't sexually intimate with each other.

• The Wyvern is untouchable.
Until Sophie, the Wyvern was seldom glimpsed by the *Pyr*. Hers was a mystical role and one that made her enigmatic and her rare appearances awesome. Most *Pyr* hold the Wyvern in reverence, so Sophie's choice to engage actively with the material world is shocking to them. This combined with the taboo against intimate relations within their own kind means that the attraction between Nikolas and Sophie is so far out of bounds as to be unthinkable. Even though Nikolas and Sophie love each other, once their relationship is consummated, they know that they'll be exiled from the *Pyr*. They're caught between a taboo so profound that it's not negotiable and their consuming love for each other. They could part or lie to their fellows about their decision, but they choose instead to sacrifice themselves for the sake of their kind. This gives them a kind of immortality.

• The dead must be honored.
The *Pyr* honor the bodies of their fallen fellows by exposing the corpse to the four elements so that the *Pyr* in question can return to dust. They do not consume each other's bodies for any reason. When Jorge decides to eat *Slayers* who have had the Elixir—in order to harvest any residue of the Elixir from their bodies—the *Pyr* who witness this are disgusted that he would so defile a corpse.

TALISMAN—The Smith may forge a talisman for his mate when he senses his impeding firestorm or feels its spark. This talisman is protective and carries a link to the Smith—when his mate is in peril, the talisman will heat, summoning the Smith to her defense like a beacon. Talismans have been used to ensure the mate's personal safety either during the courtship or later, during her pregnancy after the consummation of the firestorm, if the *Pyr* is not with her. The mate may or may not understand its import: the talisman can be presented as a gift or token without explanation. The talisman that Quinn gives to Sara in **Kiss of Fire,** for example, is a door knocker in the shape of a mermaid which he installs on the door of her book shop. When she is in peril, it appears to Sara to be on fire.

TATTOO—The *Pyr* often have tattoos, some *Pyr* collecting them with greater enthusiasm than others. They may or may not consider them to be protective—certainly they tend to choose tattoos that feature dragons. The first tattoo documented in Dragonfire is the one that Donovan has on his right bicep: "a dragon, coiled and breathing fire, a dragon in the thick of battle." He considers it to be a mark of his identity, and admits to Alex in **Kiss of Fury** that he had gotten it in Atlantic City, after losing a bet with Rafferty.

Of course, once Niall has his firestorm with Rox in **Whisper Kiss,** there are more tattoos done because she's a talented tattoo artist. Rox did a dragon on Thorolf's left hand when he had passed out drunk, to remind him of what he was. She gives Niall a back piece of a phoenix, to represent herself, as well as a yin and yang symbol on the spot where he's lost a scale. Rox herself has a little cracked heart tattoo at the outer corner of her eye as a reminder of being hurt in the past—she shades it in solid, making the heart whole, after she and Niall have their firestorm. She also has 'carpe diem' tattooed beneath her collar bone and a dragon back piece done by Chynna, which she eventually has colored in the same amethyst and platinum as Niall in his dragon form.

Across Rox's back was a dragon in flight, or at least the detailed outline of one. The dragon was drawn in the Chinese style, coiled and powerful. His tail was at Rox's neck, his body winding from her nape down to the left and back up the right side. Wingless and sinuous, he was horned and had five talons on each claw. Flames were drawn all around his body, the brilliant orange accenting the fact that the dragon scales were only outlined in black. The dragon held a pearl in its front claw, and he snarled up and over Rox's right shoulder.

Niall's first thought was that this dragon was guarding Rox's back.

—from **Whisper Kiss**

In **Whisper Kiss**, Sloane asks Rox to give him a tattoo of a caduceus, but with two dragons instead of two snakes. The Dragon's Tooth Warriors agree to each get the same tattoo as a sign of unity in **Kiss of Destiny**. Brandon in **Ember's Kiss** has tribal tattoos of more abstract designs, chosen for him by South Pacific tattoo artists and shamen. He has a spiral on his arm, which Rox identifies as a protective tattoo.

In **Kiss of Danger**, the Dragon's Tooth Warriors have gotten a tattoo of a dragon rampant to show their bond to each other and their mission. The Pythia uses darkfire to mark the two boys (Alexander's son, Lysander, and Drake's son, Theo) as members of the Dragon Legion. The Pyr who come to Drake and Erik at the end of **Kiss of Destiny** all bear the same tattoo as a mark of their allegiance.

Chen uses Elixir as the ink for spirals tattooed on the captive Thorolf's scales in **Serpent's Kiss**, starting a slow process of turning that *Pyr* into a *Slayer* against his will. The presence of the Elixir dulls his scales, but the firestorm counters the Elixir's effect. In **Firestorm Forever**, Sam takes offense at Sloane's tattoo, both because it's a caduceus and because it has dragons instead of snakes. He asks Niall to send her a vision of his tattoo in a dream, provoking her to return to California and help him solve the riddle of the virus spread by Jorge.

TAUNT—It is traditional for dragons to taunt each other before a battle, exchanging insults in a ritual intended to undermine the confidence of one's opponent. They typically do this after having locked talons in the traditional fighting pose.

The *Slayer* Chen taunts in a different way: in **Whisper Kiss**, he manipulates his scent to disorient and confuse the *Pyr* who hunt him and the shadow dragons in the tunnels beneath the city of New York.

Niall smelled *Slayer* with sudden intensity and the scent stopped him in his tracks.

Chen's scent disappeared abruptly, as surely as if it had never been. Niall knew he hadn't imagined it. It was as if the scent were being revealed and hidden again, as if the *Slayer* were messing with Niall's mind.

Teasing him.

Trying to trap him.

They were close.

Niall listened and he looked; he felt the stone and the concrete, seeking the clue that would tell him what he needed to know. He was keenly aware of Rox's presence beside him, of her vulnerability in this situation.

Chen wasn't a lightweight. Only those *Slayers* who had consumed the Dragon's Blood Elixir could disguise their scent, though he'd never encountered one who could toy with it like this.

It came again, flicking across the end of Niall's nose like a cat's tail. Then it vanished.

Chen knew they were here.

There was no dragonsmoke in the vicinity, perhaps because Chen also could cross that barrier without trouble. Perhaps he couldn't be bothered with a defense that might be ineffective.

An unbroken ring of dragonsmoke, after all, resonated with a kind of clarity, a ring that could be heard by all of their kind. Niall supposed that dragonsmoke might be as much of a beacon in the darkness as the firestorm could be.

That the scent came and went made it difficult for Niall to assess the distance to his foe. Being underground meant that he couldn't ask the wind for assistance.

He had a very bad feeling about both the staircase that descended even lower and the tunnel ahead. He feared he was stepping into a trap either way. At the same time, he had a conviction that if he turned away, an opportunity would be lost.

That Chen was trying to distract them told Niall that the *Slayer* had been surprised.

—from **Whisper Kiss**

TIGER BRAND—In **Whisper Kiss**, Chen uses a tiger brand to enslave shadow dragons, placing its mark on their necks. It's a tiger because this book is set in the year of the tiger. Niall and Thorolf first notice the brand when they destroy the shadow dragons Anson and Barth, and later Niall sees it on his twin, Phelan. He first sees the brand itself when Chen tries to mark him.

"Not yet," the *Slayer* murmured. "First I must make him mine. Bring the brand."

Niall's heart leapt. What brand? He thought of the tiger mark on the throats of the shadow dragons he'd killed, and the identical mark on Phelan's throat. He saw the flash of dragonfire through his lids and felt the heat of Chen's flames. Niall dared to look.

Chen heated a tool, just as Quinn the Smith did at his forge. He held the iron form between his talons, breathing dragonfire at it. The metal heated, turning red, then orange, then yellow, until its color was lost in the flames.

Niall thought he knew what it was. He recalled Rox's assertion that gang tattoos could be applied against someone's will, but that person then had to live by the code of the gang.

Was Chen's brand magical? Did it give him control over those he claimed? Was this how he was able to make shadow dragons without the Elixir? Was Chen the force behind the shadow dragons?

The brand neared the left side of Niall's throat, held in Chen's talons and hot enough to burn. It radiated white heat and a ripple slipped over Niall's flesh.

Niall felt his scales singe. He waited; he waited until the hot brand was treacherously close to his hide; then he thrashed his tail, breathed fire, and erupted from Chen's surprised grasp. He scorched the *Slayer* before rearing out of his reach.

"No!" cried the *Slayer,* but Niall struck him across the face with his tail. Dark blood ran from Chen's brow into the debris, and the iron brand fell from his claw.

It was shaped in the silhouette of a tiger.
—from **Whisper Kiss**

When Niall, Thorolf and Rox find the hidden lair of the shadow dragons, Chen tries to brand Thorolf. Niall manages to seize the brand and Rox uses it as a weapon in the ensuing battle. Quinn recognizes it as old metal that has been reforged and believes there is sorcery in it—he hums to it and interrogates the metal. The brand is then used by the *Pyr* as bait to draw Chen into a trap. Chen declares that he will enslave the children of the *Pyr*, beginning with the new Wyvern, but that plan doesn't come to fruition—Erik beguiles Chen, convincing him that it is tainted and must be destroyed. Chen himself sings to the brand and shatters it into seven pieces. The power of the beguiling is broken then and Chen escapes.

In **Flashfire**, Chen has reforged the brand, though he wonders if it has been tainted by the darkfire. (He sees glimmers of blue-green light touch it sometimes.) It is now a spiral instead of a tiger. He uses it to snare JP when JP fails to follow his orders to trap Lorenzo.

Erik nodded. "Chen had a brand, which he used to enslave the shadow dragons—those dragons raised from the dead by Magnus to be his slaves—and force them to his will instead. The brand was broken and the shadow dragons destroyed, but he is not one to accept defeat. I believe he has a plan to put himself in charge of all of us, with the use of that brand. It is ancient magic. He has targeted Thorolf in the past, although I'm not sure why. It is possible that he has similarly targeted you. I would not be surprised if he possessed some ancient magic unknown to us. He is far older than any of us."
—from **Flashfire**

The brand is shattered again and Marco claims the pieces to ensure that Chen can't reforge it.

TREASURE—The dragon shifters created as the *Pyr* are charged with defending the treasure that is the Earth. The *Pyr*—or "true *Pyr*"—believe that the treasures of the Earth include humans, probably because of their firestorms. *Slayers*, as a result of the hunting of dragons which occurred in the Middle Ages, don't agree. *Slayers* believe that the treasure of the Earth itself can only be defended by the extermination of humans, and of the *Pyr* who defend them.

"We cannot save humans on our own. They must make reparation themselves for the injury they have done to Gaia—they must initiate change within their own society. Then and only then can we fight for their survival."
—Sophie in **Kiss of Fury**

WARRIOR, THE—a foretold role of the *Pyr*, claimed by Donovan in **Kiss of Fury**. As the Warrior, Donovan can summon the elements as weapons. From Alex, Donovan learned to use anger and fear to build his own fighting strength, rather than letting either weaken him. He used his fear that Alex would be lost to renew his attack on Tyson and killed that *Slayer*, thus saving Alex. In the final confrontation of that book, Donovan used his fury with *Slayers* and their unjust tactics to fuel his own fighting strength. When he did so, he felt a new connection with Gaia, and was able to summon the elements as the three foretold weapons of the Warrior: the first is the heaving of the earth itself, the second weapon is hail falling like arrows of ice from the sky and the third weapon is rocks taking flight as projectiles then falling on his opponents.

WARRIOR AND WIZARD—the second of two foretold matches to result from firestorms in the Dragon's Tail Wars. In making a partnership with Alex, the Wizard, and learning from her, Donovan becomes the Warrior, using his new skills to defend her.

VIRGINS, PRINCESSES AND DAMSELS IN DISTRESS—The traditional favored taste of dragons in women, which bears some similarity to the truth. The only one of the *Pyr* to express a preference for virgins was Ambrose, the *Slayer*, who captured Quinn's mother because of her chastity. Sara's first name means 'princess' and all of the Dragonfire heroines find themselves to be damsels in distress, thanks to the firestorm. Most of them are capable of defending themselves, at least against assailants other than dragon shape shifting villains.

WATERDAUGHTER—An Elemental Witch with an affinity for water. A Waterdaughter can not only control the element of water but become it. Katina is the first Waterdaughter introduced in the Dragonfire series: her story is told in the Dragon Legion Novella, **Kiss of Danger**. In **Kiss of Darkness**, Katina explains to Petra that some people call Waterdaughters "naiads" and that she has strong intuition in addition to her affinity with water.

WIZARD—Alex Madison, the mate of Donovan Shea, was identified as the Wizard of *Pyr* prophecies, by Sophie the Wyvern, before Alex and Donovan's firestorm sparked in **Kiss of Fury**. Sophie even confided Alex's name in eliciting Erik's protection, which both shocked him and made him realize how much Alex was at risk from *Slayers*. Erik concluded that Donovan must be the *Pyr* who could become the Warrior, since he was the strongest fighter of them all. He also knew that Donovan wasn't very interested in commitment, so Erik charged Donovan with defending the Wizard, essentially dispatching Donovan to his own firestorm. Erik didn't want any risk of the firestorm not being fulfilled and guessed that once the sparks flew, Donovan wouldn't be able to resist Alex. This choice subsequently created friction between Erik and Donovan, because Donovan felt that he had been tricked.

WYVERN—The only female *Pyr* is called the Wyvern. The Wyvern at the beginning of *Dragonfire* is Sophie. At any given moment in time, there is one female *Pyr*, who has additional powers to the other *Pyr*. These include the power of prophecy, the ability to take the form of a salamander in addition to human and dragon forms, the ability to dispatch dreams, and the power to spontaneously manifest elsewhere. Perhaps because of her prophetic abilities, the Wyvern's sense of smell is even more refined than that of the *Pyr*: in **Kiss of Fury**, Sophie can smell Alex's character traits and emotional state.

"I am the Wyvern," [Sophie] said without interest. "I know many tricks, both magical and mundane."
—from **Kiss of Fury**

The Wyvern has affinities to all four elements, the implication being that she (unlike the other *Pyr*) needs no partner to be complete. In **Kiss of Fury**, Sophie attunes herself with Gaia, the earth, in order to divert storms from areas of dense human population. Sophie feels like a failure during this exercise, convinced that she hasn't intervened soon enough in the affairs of *Pyr* and human, and that the planet is in anguish as a result. She's afraid that matters had progressed too far for the world and humans to be saved. Rather than despair, and rather than remain aloof from the affairs of the *Pyr* as was the traditional expectation of her role, Sophie chooses to intervene and cast dreams to those of the *Pyr* who could make a difference.

Sophie could read the thoughts of others on occasion: she gets directions to Alex's intended refuge by commanding Alex to think of the place in **Kiss of Fury**. While Alex travels to her brother's 'cottage' on Donovan's bike, Sophie carries the injured Donovan there.

The Wyvern has some ability to heal the *Pyr*, as Sophie heals the fallen Erik at the end of **Kiss of Fire** with a song. The *Pyr* believe that she has brought Erik back from the dead or from the cusp of death: they comment that by sheltering his body from the rain, she's keeping the fourth element from touching him and thus giving him the chance to be revived. Sophie teaches that song to Sloane, the Apothecary of the *Pyr*, while she sings it and he subsequently realizes she has healed Erik's wounded spirit.

Sophie heard the chorus of the *Pyr* throughout her days and nights. It was a constant hum in her thoughts. It was both her gift and her curse as the Wyvern. She was the first to hear a sour note or a voice cut short.
—**Kiss of Fury**

The Wyvern is aware of the individual *Pyr* at the beginning of the Dragonfire novels, and the implication is that she is the only one with this ability. Sophie's thoughts on the subject indicate that each Wyvern has had this ability, but that every Wyvern before herself has remained aloof from the affairs of the *Pyr* and the world. Sophie, in contrast, believes that it is her responsibility to engage and to act, in order to help the *Pyr* win the war against the

Slayers. She senses that she will pay a high price for her intervention, but can't live with the idea of standing aside. I believe that this active choice on Sophie's part also allows her to fall in love.

After Sophie's death, Erik begins to cultivate an awareness of his fellows, and can sense not only that each is alive but his location.

The Wyvern's motives are not always clear to the *Pyr*, and there is evidence that Erik (if not others) find her elusive references frustrating. She certainly doesn't confess all that she knows. For example, Sophie was tortured by *Slayers* in **Kiss of Fire** to reveal the name of the mate in the next firestorm before that firestorm sparked. Later in the book, Sophie confesses to Sara that she knew this would happen, thanks to her foresight, but she allowed it happen to ensure that Quinn and Sara's firestorm was successful.

This kind of self-sacrifice characterizes Sophie, though whether that was a trait of all Wyverns or of Sophie in particular is not clear. In **Kiss of Fury**, Sophie meets and falls in love with the *Pyr*, Nikolas of Thebes. Their love was both undeniable and a violation of the *Pyr* honor code. After they consummate their relationship, Sophie realizes that her powers are compromised: she can't become a salamander anymore or cast dreams. She knows that another Wyvern will be born if she dies, and she has already foreseen that Nikolas is the one who can destroy the Academy. Sophie dies in **Kiss of Fate** with Nikolas: knowing they could never be together, she led him to the Academy and they sacrificed their lives for the sake of their fellow *Pyr*. The black and white ring worn by Rafferty is all that remains of them.

That wasn't the end of Sophie or of the Wyvern, though. Rafferty and Melissa adopted a little girl named Isabelle, who Rafferty believes is the reincarnation of Sophie as a human. Donovan and Alex named their first son Nicholas, in honor of Nikolas of Thebes. Erik and Eileen's daughter Zoë was conceived in **Kiss of Fate**, after Sophie died, and was expected to become the new Wyvern. In *The Dragon Diaries*, Zoë connects with the former Wyverns in a dream, forging a connection and source of wisdom that defies time. In that series, Nicholas and Isabelle have an undeniable attraction. She's human and he's *Pyr*, but he's younger than her (and a minor) in that series so they face another taboo.

The Dragon Diaries trilogy tells the story of Zoë's coming of age as the new Wyvern.

YEAR OF THE DRAGON—Within the period of the Dragon's Tail Wars, there was one year of the dragon, in 2012. The *Slayer* Chen had high expectations of success within this particular year.

THE CHARACTERS

A long-running series like *Dragonfire* results in a large cast of characters. Here's a comprehensive list of the characters, including *Pyr*, *Slayers,* mates, children and secondary characters. Note that if you haven't read all of the books, there will be spoilers here.

AESON—one of the Dragon's Tooth Warriors. He is first named in **Kiss of Danger** and has disappeared from the company by the beginning of **Kiss of Darkness**.

AHERN TALBOT—son of Niall and Rox, twin of Ruark, younger brother of Kyle and Nolan. Ahern and Ruark were born in March 2015.

ALASTAIR—one of the *Pyr* of the Dragon Legion who appear at Erik's lair at the end of **Kiss of Destiny**. He is first named in **Firestorm Forever** when he helps with the rescue of Veronica. Alastair is hematite and silver in his dragon form and appears in the *DragonFate* series.

ALEXANDER—A *Pyr*, one of the Dragon's Tooth Warriors, and Drake's second-in-command. Alexander has ebony wavy hair and dark eyes, and is smoky amethyst and silver in his dragon form: the purple of his scales so dark that they are almost black. His affinities are to fire and earth, and he is said to have the keenest sense of smell of his fellows. He is originally from Sparta and met his mate, Katina, while serving in the sanctuary at Delphi. Their son is Lysander. Alexander first appears in **Harmonia's Kiss** and his second chance romance with Katina is told in the Dragon Legion Novella, **Kiss of Danger.**

In **Kiss of Danger**, the darkfire crystal takes the Dragon's Tooth Warriors through time and space: when Alexander realizes that it has brought him home, he leaves the Dragon Legion to find Katina, fully aware that the other warriors will journey on without him. He wants to be with Katina again. He defends Katina when her new husband, Cetos, assaults her and leaves Cetos burned by dragonfire. Together, they seek out their son, Lysander, who has been taken by Alexander's old mentor, Pelias, to begin his training, and fight the *Slayer* Jorge. Alexander and Pelias save Drake's son,

Theo, who has been captured by Jorge, and send the *Slayer* back to the future. Both Pelias and Alexander are wounded, but Pelias sacrifices himself to heal Alexander with his dragonsmoke. After his death and Alexander's realization that his mentor was *Pyr*, as well, Alexander wants to expose him to all four elements to keep Pelias from being raised as a shadow dragon. He learns then about Katina's powers as a Waterdaughter and she helps him with the ritual. They return to Delphi to seek a prophecy from the Pythia about their future, and choose to raise Drake's son, Theo, along with Lysander.

In **Kiss of Darkness**, Alexander leads a group of *Pyr* to Damien and Petra when she delivers her son at the sanctuary of the Mothers. Together, they heal Damien's missing scale. In **Kiss of Destiny**, Alexander and Damien heal the injured Thad by sharing their own power through a dragonsmoke conduit. They also repair Thad's scale with Aura's help. Alexander remains in the past— along with Damien and Thad—to start a new lineage of dragon warriors. Their descendants come to Erik's lair to pledge to follow Drake at the end of **Kiss of Destiny**.

ALEXANDRA (ALEX) MADISON—Partner and mate of Donovan, a scientist who developed the Green Machine engine, and the prophesied Wizard of the *Pyr*. Alex is also the mother of Nick and Darcy. Alex has short brown hair and brown eyes, is tall and has an athletic build. She doesn't give up easily. Alex has a fondness for espionage movies and used what she learned from them to try to stay a step ahead of the *Slayers* tracking her.

Alex's lab, Gilchrist Enterprises, is targeted by *Slayers* and burned, right before the Green Machine was unveiled for investors. The only prototype of the revolutionary engine is destroyed and Alex's partner, Mark Sullivan, is killed. Alex is traumatized by the sight of dragons and treated in the burn ward of the hospital. When she realizes her nightmares of dragons would send her to the psych ward, she escapes the hospital, and is saved from *Slayers* by Donovan as the firestorm sparks. Alex and Donovan's firestorm is recounted in **Kiss of Fury**.

In **Kiss of Fate**, Alex sees the Dragon's Egg at work for the first time. She later accompanies Donovan to Erik's lair to see the broken Dragon's Egg and tries to help the *Pyr* create a plan against the Dragon's Blood Elixir. She's the one who suggests that the sanctuary of the Elixir might be an old mine shaft when Delaney shares his memories of it. She and the son she's carrying are also targeted by Delaney (under Magnus' command) at the end of **Kiss of Fate**. In **Winter Kiss**, Alex is the one to solve the riddles that help the *Pyr* destroy the Elixir, and plans the chemical reaction that will eliminate its source.

In **Whisper Kiss**, Alex and Donovan take responsibility for hunting the remains of dead *Pyr* and *Slayers*, guided by Ginger's genealogical research. They search for graves (or final resting places) with Donovan's keen *Pyr* senses helping them locate the sites. Alex then tests the soil for three trace elements that exist where the Elixir has been administered. One of these elements is mercury. They are at a resort on a south Pacific island located close to an epic battle between *Pyr* and *Slayers*—purportedly on vacation with Alex's brother and family—when Donovan realizes they have to go to New York for Niall's firestorm. In **Darkfire Kiss**, Alex accompanies Donovan to Wales, when Rafferty asks the Warrior to defend the Sleeper.

In **Flashfire**, Alex and Donovan come to Venice for the repairing of Lorenzo's scale with Nick—even though Alex is very pregnant with their second son, they actively explore the city. In **Serpent's Kiss**, Alex and Donovan's images (along with Nick and Darcy) appear where Delaney's reflection should be at Thorolf's scale repair in Angkor. In **Firestorm Forever**, Alex and Donovan come to Erik's lair in Chicago after one of Boris' clones attacks and begin to unravel the puzzle of the clones. They later take refuge at Ginger and Delaney's farm in Ohio with their sons.

AMBROSE—A *Slayer* who courted Margaux, the mate of Thierry and mother of Quinn Tyrrell. Born around 900 AD, Ambrose made his way as a gambler: his keen *Pyr* senses allowed him to prey upon humans, because he could see the nuances of their reactions and bet accordingly. In dragon form, Ambrose was golden, with the lights of tiger's eye in his scales. In human form, he had brown hair, brown eyes with golden lights, and dressed with distinction. IIis challenge coin was a gold florin.

Ambrose vowed to eliminate the line of the Smith after he failed to win Margaux's affections and was responsible for the deaths of Thierry, Margaux and their four oldest sons. Quinn, the youngest, survived, but he blamed Erik for the death of his family. When Ambrose later befriended Quinn in order to betray him, Quinn trusted Ambrose. When Erik killed Ambrose, Quinn blamed Erik for the loss and refused to accept Erik as a leader as a result.

It was revealed in **Kiss of Fire** that Ambrose murdered Quinn's first wife, Elizabeth, by burning her alive. He also killed Sara's parents in the March before Quinn and Sara's firestorm by causing their car accident near Machu Picchu. Sara had been scheduled to take the vacation with them, but even though she decided at the last minute not to go, his action ensured that she was emotionally vulnerable and alone. **Kiss of Fire** begins with Ambrose's attempt to kill Sara, and thus eliminate the chance of the Smith having a successful firestorm. Ambrose is killed by Quinn in the finale of **Kiss of Fire**. His corpse is exposed to all four elements that day.

ANDREW MERRICK—second son of Brandon and Liz, born January 7, 2014.

ANGELINA—a Venetian courtesan, mate of the *Pyr* Salvatore, and mother of Lorenzo. She was killed when her neighbors burned down her house after seeing Salvatore, her partner, in his dragon form. Angelina chose to confront the mob to keep Lorenzo's hiding place secret and was killed in defense of her son. Salvatore arrived too late to help her, and the incident scarred him deeply.

In **Flashfire**, the darkfire—which makes the impossible possible—allowed Angelina to invite Cassie into a painting of her home in Venice, which hangs in Lorenzo's home. Although there is a language barrier between the two mates, Angelina entrusts Cassie with a message for Lorenzo, and gives Cassie's match with Lorenzo her blessing. Through this incident, Cassie witnesses the attack on Angelina's home, her bravery and her death, which shows Cassie why Lorenzo so distrusts humans.

ANNA—one of Lorenzo's stage assistants in **Flashfire**. She and Ursula bind Lorenzo for his escape trick, and see him shift shape when it goes wrong. He chooses not to beguile them. Ursula and Anna unveil Lorenzo's car after his final stunt, while Lorenzo watches from Venice.

ANSON—a shadow dragon killed by Niall and Thorolf in **Whisper Kiss**. He confesses that he is the son of Guthrie in exchange for a faster death. Niall sees the brand on Anson's neck before he dies and wonders what it is.

ANTONIO—oldest son of Lorenzo and Cassie, born March 27, 2012.

APOLLO—Greek god and one of the guises of Chandra's brother. In **Kiss of Danger**, Katina recalls meeting Alexander at Delphi, in the temple of Apollo. Alexander tells his son, Lysander, the story of Apollo's quest to avenge his mother and his subsequent service of eight years to atone for killing Pytho in his own sanctuary. The Pyr give eight years service in Alexander's time out of homage to Apollo. In **Serpent's Kiss**, Apollo acknowledges to Chandra that he sparked her firestorm with Thorolf, wanting to tempt her to break her vow of chastity. He believes that the *Pyr*, although his favorite creatures, are doomed and warns Chandra that the portal between the worlds is closing forever. At the end of the book, she sees him departing in his golden chariot, remembering his vow to be the last to leave the mortal realm.

ARACH—one of the *Pyr* warriors who arrive at Erik's lair at the end of **Kiss of Destiny**. He is aquamarine and silver in his dragon form, and volunteers for the mission to help Drake save Veronica from Jorge in **Firestorm Forever**. He also is one of the *Pyr* who Timmy can call. Arach is injured in the final battle, but survives with Sloane's help, and appears in the *DragonFate* series.

ARCHIBALD FORRESTER—In **Kiss of Fury**, Alex stole a taupe

Buick left at the entrance to the ER with the keys in the ignition in order to escape from *Slayers*. She discovered that the car belonged to Archibald Forrester from the tag on the keys. Subsequently the car was demolished in the dragonfight between Donovan and the *Slayers* and burned beyond repair. At the end of the book, Archibald has a scene of his own, in which he is released from the hospital and all is made right—although his new Buick is navy. This is particularly good timing for Archibald as he has finally convinced Berenice to go to the dance at the Legion with him, and he's sure she'll be impressed by his new car.

ARETHUSA—a naiad (a nymph of fresh waters) and friend of Aura's, who appears in **Kiss of Destiny**. She is hovering on the cusp of change due to her excitement in learning about Katina, a Waterdaughter. She was seduced by Alpheus, a river god, despite her desire to remain chaste. In **Kiss of Destiny**, she shares Damien and Petra's story with the other nymphs.

ASHE—one of the Dragon's Tooth Warriors. Ashe is stocky and practical and the son of a blacksmith. He is first named in **Kiss of Danger** and is one of the eight survivors who form the Dragon Legion in Kiss of Darkness. By **Kiss of Destiny**, the darkfire crystal has taken him to his mate, although the location isn't specified.

ASTRID—the woman Thorolf loved, who was stoned and burned by her neighbors after their village was destroyed by a dragon attack. They blamed her for drawing the dragons to them. She wasn't Thorolf's mate, but his father directed the dragons to the village, believing she was an unnecessary distraction for Thorolf. Niall dreams repeatedly of her death in **Serpent's Kiss**, though he doesn't know the name of the *Pyr* she confesses to loving.

AURA—An Airdaughter and mate of Thaddeus. Aura is a nymph and an Airdaughter. She has long dark wavy hair that falls to her hips and dark eyes, as well as the ability to become a breeze. Aura and Thad's story is told in the Dragon Legion Novella, **Kiss of Destiny**. Aura's mother was a nymph who was raped by Zeus and left pregnant, then came to Hera for help. Hera turned her into a tree with silver leaves so she could be free of men's desires, and gave her daughter, Aura, the ability to see the future so she could avoid her mother's situation. Aura knows that because she's immortal and Thad isn't, they won't have a son. Her hope is to be desired for herself, and when Thad chooses to remain with her—even though the firestorm will burn in perpetuity—she asks Hera for the gift of mortality, leaving her life and fellow nymphs to be with Thad. She retains her gift of foresight and after Thad's scale is repaired, she sees that they will have twin sons.

AURELIA—the wife of Magnus Montmorency in ancient Rome and a sorceress. Magnus lost a scale over his love for this seductress, but she didn't return his affection. Aurelia had found a bloodstone sacred to the *Pyr* and tempted Magnus with it. He married her in exchange for it, giving her wealth and position for the stone. He killed her when she wouldn't surrender the bloodstone to him, and betrayed Sahir, sending his slave to retrieve the stone which was with Aurelia's corpse and ensuring that Sahir was caught in the act of defiling a corpse.

The bloodstone is described as being the size of an egg and inscribed with symbols of the four elements. Magnus puts it in Delaney's mouth near the end of **Winter Kiss**, when Delaney is paralyzed and about to become the new source of the Elixir. The stone is evidently part of the spell—but when Delaney is saved, Rafferty crushes the stone in his hands, ensuring that the Elixir can never be created again. As a storyteller, I regret Rafferty's choice: I would have liked to have played a little more with that bloodstone.

BALTHASAR—A *Slayer* who is agate with gold in dragon form. In human form, he has dark hair and green eyes. He was born in Constantinople in 1250. Balthasar first appears in **Kiss of Fate**, where he is Magnus' driver and bodyguard. He has an ability to drive any vehicle with ease, and is characteristically taciturn.

In **Winter Kiss**, Balthasar is one of the three *Slayers* defending Magnus in his home in Ohio: the others are Jorge and Mallory. When Mallory is fatally injured in a battle with the *Pyr*, Balthasar defends his corpse and takes him back to Magnus' lair so he can be given the Elixir. Balthasar ends up being the one to ignite Donovan's car bomb with his dragonfire and his tail is burned badly as a result. He's caught up with a shadow dragon in a funnel cloud summoned by Niall at the end of that book.

In **Whisper Kiss**, Balthasar, Jorge and Mallory have disappeared, according to the *Pyr*. In **Darkfire Kiss**, we learn that they retreated to Moscow. Balthasar acted as Jorge's bodyguard in Moscow — along with Mallory — when Jorge had reconstructive surgery on his leg, injured in **Winter Kiss**. Jorge lets Balthasar kill the surgeon as compensation, then he abandons Jorge. Jorge thinks Balthasar has been summoned by Magnus and pursues him without success — Balthasar is once again Magnus' driver, and he's photographed by Melissa in his battle with Rafferty. He is badly injured and retreats, then pilots the helicopter for Magnus when Melissa is captured. The helicopter is sent crashing to the earth, on fire, by Rafferty with Balthasar injured within it.

In **Flashfire**, we learn that Balthasar has been trying to convince Lorenzo to join the *Slayers*, without success. Balthasar is beguiled by Lorenzo and takes Lorenzo's place in the car that is buried for Lorenzo's final disappearing act. His corpse is mistaken for that of Lorenzo.

BALTHASAR (2) — One of the *Pyr* of the Dragon Legion who appear at Erik's lair at the end of **Kiss of Destiny**. Balthasar aids in the rescue of Veronica in **Firestorm Forever**. He is citrine and gold in his dragon form and also appears in the *DragonFate* series.

BARRY — A young man found on the streets of New York by Rox in **Whisper Kiss**. She offers him a place to stay in exchange for him helping out at Imagination Ink, the tattoo shop of which she is part-owner. Barry shows up to accept her offer after he is attacked and has a black eye to show for it. Ultimately, he proves to have a gift with computers and by the end of **Whisper Kiss** is working for Niall at his eco-tourism company. When Barry is first introduce, Niall thinks he's twelve or thirteen, but he's actually seventeen.

In **Darkfire Kiss**, Barry recognizes Thorolf in the video of the earthquake in D.C. on YouTube and shares it with Niall. Niall convinces him that it's some kind of trick and/or CGI, reminding him that Thorolf will do anything for a beer. He leaves Barry in charge and calls to Thorolf in old-speak, meeting him and taking him home to safety.

BARTH — a shadow dragon killed by Niall and Thorolf in **Whisper Kiss**. He also has the brand on his neck which proves to be from Chen.

BARTHOLOMEW — second son of Lorenzo and Cassie, born May 5, 2014.

BILL — a cameraman Melissa worked with in the Middle East who gave her advice about keeping her cool in hot zones. He told new arrivals to "get a grip" when they became frightened. She admired his nonchalant attitude. He'd also advised her to focus on the story instead of worrying about her own survival, and to concentrate on what she could control instead of worrying about whatever she couldn't. Bill advised that there'd be time for nightmares later. Melissa found his advice helpful in her recovery from cancer. When she's creating the blog posts about Magnus, she emails him where he's working in Asia to get some images of Daphne. He complies and welcomes her back. When Rafferty is torn between his desire to protect Melissa and his need to pursue Magnus, Melissa tells him of Bill's conviction that no one dies on the air — because there are so many witnesses, in front of the camera is the safest place to be.

BORIS VASSILY — An ancient and particularly wily *Slayer*, spectacular in dragon form with ruby red and brass scales and trailing red plumes. (These colors are open to individual interpretation — Quinn, for example, described Boris' scales as garnets edged with gold in **Kiss of Fire**.) His wings are leather, the color of bronze, and his accent is Russian. In human form, Boris is a large man with fair hair and icy blue eyes. His challenge coin is copper, a 5 kopeks coin minted under Catherine the Great in 1789. He is the son of Mikail Vassily, the first leader of the *Slayers*, and believes himself to be leader by right of inheritance.

In **Kiss of Fire**, Boris exhibits his additional skills: he summons a violent thunderstorm, showing his mastery over the weather, and repositions the dragonsmoke he breathed (along with the other *Slayers*) with a gesture. He can hover between forms for long periods (although Quinn can do it willfully for short ones) and can disguise his own scent from other dragon shifters. The *Pyr* believe these skills are the result of training and practice, but actually they are evidence that Boris has drunk the Dragon's Blood Elixir.

Boris professes himself to be bored with battles, though he still fights with force when necessary. He finds humans to be weak and of interest only when useful—he has had many mistresses—and confesses to having killed many people. He is inclined to let other *Slayers* do the heavy work for him, even having Ambrose drive his gold SUV when they kidnap Sara.

Boris and Erik exchange challenge coins in **Kiss of Fury**, and battle near the end of the book. Erik believes Boris to be dead and exposed to all four elements when he leaves the fight to assist in the battle between Donovan and the shadow dragons. Boris, however, has drunk the Dragon's Blood Elixir and is already beginning to heal by the time Erik leaves him for dead. He subsequently has plastic surgery to repair the worst of his burn wounds, and kills his surgeon at the beginning of **Kiss of Fate** to ensure that the story is lost, before resuming the blood duel with Erik.

Boris is further motivated to kill Erik as retribution—it was Erik's father, Soren, who killed Boris' father, Mikail. In **Kiss of Fate**, Boris kills the plastic surgeon who has done his reconstructive surgery and hunts Erik. Boris is killed at the end of **Kiss of Fate** and Magnus assumes leadership of the *Slayers*.

This isn't the end of Boris, though. In **Kiss of Fury**, Boris made a chance comment to Sigmund that he should be cloned. In **Firestorm Forever,** it's revealed that Sigmund acted upon Boris' idea before his own death, creating and inoculating thirteen dragon's eggs with those clones of Boris. The eggs needed to be exposed to the light of a blood moon to ripen, which occurred in **Firestorm Forever**, hatching *Slayers* that looked identical to Boris and who shared Boris' need to destroy Erik.

BRANDON MERRICK—A *Pyr* and professional surfer, the rebellious son of Brandt Merrick and Kay Weatherby. He is in his early twenties, has dark auburn hair and blue eyes. He also has tattoos. Rox notes that they're tribal tattoos, and that the spiral tattoo on Brandon's arm is a protection tattoo. (South Pacific tattoo artists can also be shamen, who choose the right tattoo for the bearer.) Brandon's other tattoos aren't specified, although there's at least one more on his chest. In dragon form, he is black with orange-tipped scales—Rox notes in **Serpent's Kiss** that his scales make her think of lava simmering beneath a dark crust. Brandon's affinities are to earth and water.

Brandon's parents divorced before he was born and he lived with his mother until puberty. When his *Pyr* nature began to reveal itself, Kay sent him to live with his father. She wants nothing to do with dragons but misses her son and they talk regularly on the phone. Brandon's firestorm is with marine biologist Liz Barrett and recounted in **Ember's Kiss**. Because of his affinity with earth, Brandon was targeted by the *Slayer* Chen and intended as a sacrifice to fulfill the charm and build that *Slayer*'s power. Before they have even met, Liz notes that Brandon's aura is indigo, and concludes that he's loyal and dependable. The firestorm and Liz's powers as a Firedaughter help Brandon to break free of Chen's spell.

In **Serpent's Kiss**, Marco sees opportunity in an alliance of five suggested in the prophecy for Thorolf's firestorm as a means to defeat Chen. He invites Lorenzo to join him. Lorenzo adds Brandon and Thorolf because they've been targeted by the *Slayer* just as he has. Marco is part of the group because he commands the darkfire and Erik is the fifth because he's leader of the *Pyr*.

In **Firestorm Forever**, Brandon and his mate Liz are doing research near the Great Barrier Reef when she feels the quickening of the clones of Boris Vassily beneath the light of the eclipse. He leads a hunt with his father, Brandt, Liz, and Thorolf to Uluru in Australia, seeking the stones, and stakes out the area during a second eclipse with Liz, Thorolf and Chandra while his parents defend his sons. Liz locates the ripening eggs and hatching clones, thanks to her powers as a Firedaughter, but Brandon is injured in the battle against the clones. Marco comes to his rescue, and Brandon hears the injured Marco ask Jorge for the Elixir. This convinces the *Pyr* that Marco has chosen to turn *Slayer*, but Liz is skeptical. Together, they seek Marco and find his hotel room, as well as Jac's book for hunting *Pyr*, but Liz still believes that Marco is on the *Pyr* side. They both participate in the final battle at Machu Picchu, with Liz using her powers to find the remaining eggs. Brandon also is part of the final flight of the *Pyr* for Melissa Smith's broadcast and his firestorm is one of those that will burn forever.

BRANDT MERRICK — An embittered *Pyr*, estranged from his fellow dragon shifters and divorced from his mate, Kay; father of Brandon. Brandt is a distant cousin of Sloane Forbes. Brandt has auburn hair in human form and yellow and orange scales in his dragon form. He works as a firefighter and has a temper. He also has an alcohol problem when we first meet him because he wants to forget the failure of his firestorm.

Brandt was born in England in 1630. Wrongfully convicted of a crime in the late 19th century, he was transported to Australia. He is an outcast from the *Pyr* by choice, because his nature has cost him his love: because Erik revealed the truth of Brandt's nature to Kay, he has extracted a blood oath from Erik and Sloane that the *Pyr* will leave him alone forever.

Brandt first appears in **Darkfire Kiss** when Sloane comes to warn him about Lorenzo's ability to beguile other *Pyr* at Erik's command. This breaks the blood oath, but Erik has anticipated that Brandt won't injure his cousin. Instead, Brandt seeks out Erik, taking issue with the source of the command. They fight, but then are reconciled to defend humans from the attack by the *Slayers*. Brandt also asks Erik to help with Brandon's education — since he has little contact with his son, Brandon knows almost nothing about his nature, which makes him vulnerable. Erik agrees and Brandt joins the *Pyr* to defeat the *Slayers*. Brandt later helps close the Thames Barrier with Sloane during the battle with the *Slayers*. He's at Rafferty's home in Hampstead Heath when the Sleeper awakens, but declines Sara's invitation to join the *Pyr* on New Year's Eve in Michigan for the repair of Rafferty's scale.

Brandt meets Lorenzo in **Flashfire** and they take an immediate dislike to each other—Lorenzo sees Brandt as a *Pyr* who "botched his firestorm" and Brandt suspects that Lorenzo is turning *Slayer*. He's concerned that Lorenzo will betray the *Pyr*. Lorenzo uses Brandt's distrust as a feint, deceiving Brandt and injuring him slightly to trick Chen into believing that he is ready to turn *Slayer*. After the firestorm, Erik plays peacemaker between the two but Cassie notices that Brandt is drinking Lorenzo's brandy.

Erik perceives Brandt to be "passionate, volatile, and unpredictable" so he instructs Brandt to stay away from the firestorm of his estranged son, Brandon, in **Ember's Kiss**. Although Brandt is offended by this command, he does as instructed, because he does want the best for Brandon and knows he can't give his son good advice about making a firestorm last forever. Instead, he goes to the beach where he used to meet Kay, remembering their firestorm and the optimism he felt during it. He also recalls how Kay came to walk on this beach when dealing with fear or bad news, and reviews milestones in their shared life. He isn't really expecting to see her there (she's moved away from the area) but when she appears, he apologizes to her and admits that he loves her. He confesses that he doesn't know why he drinks as there isn't enough alcohol in the world to make him forget what he's lost. After confessions and apologies, they agree to start again. When Kay tells Brandt that they're going to be grandparents, he offers to fly her to Hawai'i—that she accepts is evidence that she's coming to accept the truth of his nature. Once there, Brandt reconciles with Brandon.

In **Serpent's Kiss**, when the *Pyr* gather to support Thorolf's firestorm, Brandt and Kay welcome their daughter-in-law and two grandsons (Christopher and Andrew) at Brandt's lair, leaving

Brandon free to go to Thailand. Erik and Ginger also stay, and Delaney continues on with Brandon. Brandt and Kay come to the repair of Thorolf's scale at Angkor, travelling with Brandon and Liz—Kay carries their youngest grandson, Andrew.

In **Firestorm Forever**, Brandt joins the hunt with Brandon, Liz and Thorolf in Uluru for rocks that might contain clones of Boris, without success. He then retreats to defend Brandon and Liz's sons at his home with Kay during the eclipse. He travels to Machu Picchu by train with Arach for the final battle, and is one of the six *Pyr* awaiting the hatching of the clones. (The others are Arach, Brandon, Sloane, Rafferty and Thorolf.) He's wounded in the fight so badly that he rotates between forms, even as Liz and Chandra tend to his injuries. Sloane heals him and the darkfire touches his repaired scale, indicating that his firestorm will burn forever.

It's never stated where or when Brandt lost his scale—presumably during his firestorm with Kay or when he realized he loved her—and the repair by Quinn is never shown. Brandt arrives in Hawai'i after Brandon's scale is repaired in **Ember's Kiss** and his scale isn't mentioned when Thorolf's scale is repaired in **Serpent's Kiss**. He also doesn't seem to have a point of vulnerability by then, so Quinn must have fixed it in Hawai'i after the end of **Ember's Kiss** with a token from Kay, who was also present. The repair would have been a good symbol of their second chance and fresh start.

BRETT—a tour leader who works for Niall's eco-tourist company. When the first earthquake strikes in New York at the beginning of **Whisper Kiss**, Brett checks in with Niall. Thorolf tells Rox that Brett is returning that night with a group from Machu Picchu.

CADMUS—A warrior and character in Greek mythology, Cadmus killed a dragon with the help of the goddess Athena. Athena advised him to take the dragon's teeth as a trophy, which he did, then instructed him to sow the teeth in the ground, like seeds. Cadmus followed her directions and the teeth sprouted, growing into an army of fighting men, stronger than any warriors Cadmus had ever seen. When they turned on him, he threw stones at them.

They blamed each other for that and began to fight amongst themselves, killing each other until there were only five left. These remaining warriors made a pact of peace and became the founding fathers of the Spartans, which means *sown men*. The story explains the foundation of Thebes and its warrior rulers.

"Myth," Donovan said.

"Fantasy dressed as truth," Alex agreed, and they exchanged a look of understanding.

"No," Sara said. "It's the story of the *Pyr*, disguised for human consumption. Maybe it's even the story of the *Pyr*'s origins."

—from **Kiss of Fury**

In **Kiss of Fury**, Sara dreams of the story of Cadmus and tells it to the *Pyr*, who subsequently plant the Dragon's Tooth pearl. The story of the hunting of Cadmus and the origin of the Dragon's Tooth Warriors. is told in the short story **Harmonia's Kiss**.

CASSANDRA—Drake's first mate and mother of his son, Theo. In **Kiss of Danger**, Jorge implies that he ate her: when Theo tells Alexander that his mother is dead at Jorge's urging, Jorge says he has developed a taste for mate. In **Kiss of Darkness**, Drake remembers Cassandra as being outspoken and self-reliant, and wonders if they would be happy together if reunited: he's sure that he's changed because of the influence of the modern *Pyr*. Having loved and lost a partner is something that Drake has in common with Veronica and that draws them closer.

CASSIE REDMOND—A former paparazzi photographer and partner of Lorenzo. Cassie is fair and has reddish-blond hair. She meets Lorenzo when she's on a girls' weekend in Las Vegas with her friend, Stacy. Cassie and Lorenzo's story is told in **Flashfire**.

In **Serpent's Kiss**, Lorenzo and Cassie are living in Venice, but he's aware that she misses living in the States. She's pregnant with their second son. When Jorge invites Lorenzo to meet him, he leaves Marco to stand guard over her. Cassie and Lorenzo's images appear where Sloane's reflection should be at Thorolf's scale repair in Angkor.

In **Firestorm Forever**, Cassie sees a video on television of Erik battling with one of Boris' clones. When Lorenzo decides to give Maeve O'Neill an exclusive interview to create an opportunity to beguile her, Cassie contacts Maeve and sets it up (because she's known as the photographer who took the pictures of a *Pyr* shifting shape.)

CATERINA—Lorenzo's former lover, who had trapped and revealed him after he confided in her. She'd called him *diavolo*.

CERBERUS—the three-headed dog that defends the gates of Hades. In **Kiss of Danger**, Damien tries to shift shape to fight the guardian of the portals and learns that his powers are curtailed in the underworld. He fights the hellhound in his human form and is losing when Petra sings to beguile the beast, which saves Damien. The darkfire adds to the power of her song and the hellhound goes to sleep. This gives her the opportunity to tell Damien what she really thinks of him.

CETOS—the second husband of Katina, the mate of Alexander. He first appears in **Kiss of Danger**. Cetos arranges to sell Alexander's son Lysander into slavery, not realizing that the buyer is Jorge, the *Slayer*, but not caring about the boy's fate anyway. His plan is thwarted by the fact that Katina has let Pelias take Lysander to train as a warrior in Sparta. He strikes Katina for this disobedience and Alexander shifts shape to defend her, burning Cetos with dragonfire. Jorge subsequently arrives to collect his *Pyr* slave and executes Cetos for breaking their bargain.

CHANDRA—A hunter and executioner of evil creatures whose own nature is initially a mystery, as is her agenda. Chandra has the ability to change her appearance and is ultimately revealed to be a goddess. She is unconstrained by time or space, and moves between our realm and Myth at will. She has a pet falcon named Snow, which resides in Myth and is her protector and familiar. She is an accomplished archer, and her arrowheads become marked with a rune when she chooses an arrow from her quiver. Chandra first appears in **Flashfire** when her pursuit of Viv Jason (i.e. Tisiphone) leads her to Thorolf, who is Viv's lover. An expert in both the martial arts and mythological creatures, she immediately recognizes Thorolf for what he is, as well as the danger he's in, and (unknown to Thorolf) takes him under her protective custody. Thorolf thinks Chandra's a homeless kid and pickpocket until their firestorm sparks in **Serpent's Kiss**.

> Chandra glanced toward him, then straightened. She might as well lay it all out for them. "I am Chandra, Freya, Selene, Artemis and Diana, the virgin goddess, the huntress, the daughter of the moon and the sister of the sun. I am the one who vowed to defend the *Pyr* against Tisiphone's vengeance."
> "Not just any goddess," Thorolf said with such approval that she found herself blushing. "A major kick-ass deity. I like it."
> —from **Serpent's Kiss**

In **Serpent's Kiss**, Chandra is hunting Viv Jason, mistakenly believing her to be one of the Liliot, on a quest to save the *Pyr*. That brings her to Thorolf and her brother, Apollo, sparks a firestorm between them to torment Chandra over her vow of chastity. When Thorolf kisses her, Chandra experiences sensual pleasure for the first time. Thorolf sees that she shifts shape during that kiss, as if she's a thousand different women. To keep the new occupant of Thorolf's apartment from calling the police after Thorolf's attack, she pretends to be a caregiver at a psychiatric hospital. The two manage to escape, but she doesn't keep Thorolf from shifting shape (to defend her) in a busy market, tossing his challenge coin at Rafferty or injuring Rafferty. She shows him that his blood is darkening, like that of a *Slayer*.

Chandra and Thorolf argue about the firestorm, because Chandra has no intention of satisfying it, abandoning her vow of chastity or having a son. She insists that she works alone. She lets Rafferty take them to her sanctuary, using his ability to spontaneously manifest elsewhere, rather than revealing her own powers. She tells Thorolf that her sanctuary might be Myth, and notices the changes—instead of it always being midday, it's always twilight now. She interprets this as a sign that an era is ending. She takes Thorolf to her library, with its collection of ghosts and their memories, and gives him a vision of their shared past—the day he was born, when she appeared to his parents, was identified as one of the Vanir by his father, and claimed him as her champion.

Chandra led Thorolf to a small stone building that was less derelict than the rest. It was built like a fat column, but with a rounded top. It was maybe twenty feet wide and twice as tall, and the stone exterior was heavily carved. There was one of those big serene smiling faces carved over the low opening. This time, Thorolf was reminded of a midway ride, the kind that you entered through some demon's mouth.

Maybe that was why he had such a bad feeling about going inside.

There were some gaps in the stone and some pieces missing, as well as those vines growing all over it, but this structure was clearly in better shape than the others.

Was that because she'd maintained it?

He looked at Chandra, only to find her watching him with a challenge in her smile. He'd come to expect her to push him, but the change in her appearance startled him. He blinked, but she stayed in this new form.

And watched for his reaction.

Her hair had grown longer and hung in ebony waves to her hips. She was Caucasian now, her features pretty and her breasts more full. She was still tall and athletic, but now her eyes were clear blue and thickly lashed. Her lips were lush and rosy, offering an invitation he was inclined to accept. She had a blue tattoo that wound around her arms, a network of Celtic knots that looked like chain mail.

Not snakes, thank the Great Wyvern.

His body responded with enthusiasm to the change. She could have been a new mate, a new conquest to be made, a whole new firestorm. The silver flame that danced between them burned with the same vigor and brilliance, turning her features to silver.

"Surely dragons aren't afraid of temples," she said as he took a step toward her, and he realized that her voice was lower, too.

Sultry.

Almost familiar. Thorolf frowned, trying to grasp an elusive memory. Did he know her already?

"Which is the real you?" He had to ask. "This form or the

other?"

The question seemed to amuse her. "Which is the real you? The dragon or the man?"

—from **Serpent's Kiss**

Chen dreams of the vision Chandra gives Thorolf, which provides the *Slayer* with more insight into Thorolf's ability to fight the Elixir. Chandra also shares Thorolf's anguish over the death of Astrid and begins to understand the power of love. As a goddess, she believes that everything is a transaction. She bares herself to him and answers his questions, hoping to use the firestorm to learn more about Viv Jason. Her plan is still to return to Asgard once her quest is complete, but Thorolf undermines her resolve with his touch.

"Freya," she managed to admit before he worked his magic on her other breast. Who could have believed that such pleasure could come from one small erogenous zone? Who could have believed she'd spill the truth so readily? Thorolf closed the warmth of his hand over her other breast, working that nipple with his finger and tongue at the same time. Chandra wasn't sure her knees could continue to support her.

But she didn't want him to stop.

And it wasn't just because she hadn't won his cooperation yet.

"Depending who you ask, of course." Her words fell quickly, as they seldom did. "Gerd, Godiva, Selena, Demeter, Diana, Isis; all facets of the same divine truth."

"Which do you prefer?"

"Chandra," she admitted. "For the moon."

Thorolf nodded, smiled and glanced over her. "And this guise?"

"Freya." She felt her cheeks heat. "I like Scandinavia."

His eyes gleamed. "Since when?"

"About nine hundred and fifty years ago," she admitted, referring to the date she'd chosen him as her champion.

He was pleased, but ducked his head to hide it. She gasped when he kissed her nipple again. "The huntress," he murmured against her skin. "Fertility, death, magic, beauty and war." He flicked her a glance and his eyes were a vivid blue. "You should

know that seriously works for me."
—from **Serpent's Kiss**

Thorolf intervenes when Chandra is about to execute Viv Jason, and Viv runs, but Chandra traps her in a mirror spell, which is shattered as a result of Chandra's argument with Thorolf. She tries to convince him that Viv is his enemy without success. She realizes that Viv is reassembling the mirror in a bid to escape, and her brother appears to confirm her suspicions that an era is ending. She resolves to finish her assignment in time and goes after Thorolf again, determined to finish up. She shows Thorolf, Niall and Sloane the incident in the Underworld between Damien and Tisiphone, then Jorge's assault on the pilgrim outside the Garden of the Hesperides, but that vision fades before it's done. Chandra realizes that her powers are fading, which frightens her. Chen abducts her, identifying her and the firestorm as the issue with his spell over Thorolf, and she tells the *Pyr* to bring the sword.

Because Rafferty is with him, Thorolf is able to follow Chandra and Chen and manifest in their presence. After the battle, they start to satisfy the firestorm, but when Chandra has her orgasm, she shifts shape—revealing that one of her guises was as Astrid's friend Ulrike, the one who betrayed her and who Thorolf blames for Astrid's death. Because he feels manipulated by Chandra, Thorolf helps Viv escape the mirror spell, realizing only too late what he's done. Chen comes for Thorolf just as the portal between realms is closing. Chandra ignores the warnings from Snow, choosing to remain in the mortal realm to save Thorolf. They defeat Chen together with Lorenzo's help, then confront the challenge of Jormungand as the era ends. When Thorolf kills the world serpent, he's doused in its venom, which wounds him when it spreads over the skin where he's lost a scale. Chandra uses the firestorm to revive Thorolf, having chosen to become mortal to be with him and bear his sons. Thorolf's missing scale is repaired in a ceremony at Angkor with three of her tears, which turn to amber when they fall.

In **Firestorm Forever**, Chandra and Thorolf are teaching self-defense classes in Bangkok, although Thorolf has taken over the work as her pregnancy progresses. She's developed an appetite for kim chee during her pregnancy and when she goes to stay with Sloane in California, her taste for pickles surprises Sloane. Chandra hears bits of stories about twin boys that don't make sense to her, but she knows they're clues from Myth about what's happening in the Dragon's Tail Wars. She also dreams about Australia and the world being on fire. While she's in labor with their son Raynor, she has a vision of Snow which Sara sees as well—the bird delivers a red rock to her, which cracks open to reveal Boris Vassily, which helps the *Pyr* understand about the clones. She goes to Uluru with Thorolf, Brandon and Liz to watch for hatchings during the eclipse. They discover that Liz has the prophecy about the firestorm. She later dreams that the dragon eggs are in a ruin in the jungle and Thorolf remembers that the first *Slayer* attack on a mate at the beginning of the Dragon's Tail Wars was Ambrose killing Sara's parents near Machu Picchu. She shares Incan lore with the *Pyr* before the final battle and a bird directs them toward the Temple of the Condor. (Even though the bird is a condor, Chandra sees it as a manifestation of Snow.) Chandra and Thorolf's firestorm is one of those designated to burn forever by the darkfire.

CHARON—the ferryman on the River Acheron who takes the dead to Hades. In **Kiss of Danger**, Damien is glad to realize he has two coins in his pocket when he realizes he needs a ride. He feels the darkfire crystal light, taking his fellow Dragon Legion Warriors away, as soon as Charon pushes away from the shore.

CHEN—A formidable *Slayer* who claims to be the last of the Dragon Kings (*Lung Wang*) Chen believes himself destined to be king of all dragons and to claim stewardship of the earth. Chen possesses the secrets of ancient dragon magic, lost to all dragon shifters but him. He is known to have the ability to take six forms: an attractive young Asian woman, an agile young Asian man, an elderly Asian man, a salamander, a snake, and a dragon. Chen also has the ability to disguise his scent, like other *Slayers* who have drunk the Elixir. In dragon form, he is lacquer red and gold, with gold horns and golden talons. He is manipulative and often underestimated by others.

Chen makes his first appearance in the *Dragonfire* series in the prologue of **Winter Kiss**, when he arrives in the courtyard at Magnus' Ohio residence to sip of the Elixir on the eclipse. As his power grows, Chen plans his ascendancy as king of all dragons.

By the beginning of **Whisper Kiss**, Chen knows that he needs to sacrifice a *Pyr* with an affinity to air to give him control of all four elements: that will complete his spell, giving him control over the fifth element of spirit, as well. Chen demonstrates his command of earth by launching earthquakes that target Niall during that *Pyr's* firestorm. His command of water is shown by the torrential rain he summons—which he calls dragon rain—and his mastery of fire is evident when he fights the *Pyr*. He also uses his command of the earth in an attempt to capture Niall. Niall is saved by Rafferty, Thorolf and Sloane, when Rafferty sings to the earth. Rafferty also hears Chen's song but can't immediately identify the singer.

Chen ticked off the elements on his fingers. "Gaia surrendered my enemy to my grasp in an earthquake, at my dictate, proof that I command the element of earth. A deluge continues to fall, at my instruction, as proof of my command of water. When the *Pyr* who commands the wind is a shadow dragon in my thrall, I shall control the element of air."

"And fire?"

"The firestorm, of course. I command its heat, as well. Didn't you know?" Chen smiled. "Look." He pulled some dark powder from his pocket and exhaled upon it.

As Phelan watched with astonishment, flames erupted from Chen's mouth and lit the powder. It glowed brilliant orange and shot sparks. Chen murmured a charm beneath his breath, then blew the burning powder across the room. The particles flared as they danced through the air, several exploding, others shooting sparks.

"We can guess what they will be doing when you arrive," Chen said, then smiled again.

"And then?"

"And the fifth element, that of spirit, will be within reach and its conquest will be mine." Chen folded his hands together. "Finally!"

—from **Whisper Kiss**

Chen also captures Magnus, when that *Slayer* escapes from the earth and imprisons him. (Chen's lair is hidden beneath an apothecary shop in Chinatown in New York.) Without Magnus' influence over them, Chen has taken command of the remaining shadow dragons, keeping them in fetters in the underground caverns of New York City. He binds them to his will with the use of a brand, which leaves a tiger mark on the neck of his victims. (It is the year of the tiger.) He releases the branded shadow dragons on specific missions, using Dragon Bone Powder to reanimate them so that their intellectual powers are greater. Because he is targeting Niall for his affinity with air, Chen gives the Dragon Bone Powder to Niall's twin and shadow dragon, Phelan, several times. The firestorm gives Niall the power to fight back and, once injured, Chen tries to claim Thorolf instead but is unsuccessful.

One of the moments I enjoy in **Whisper Kiss** is after the *Pyr* escape from the hidden lair of the shadow dragons. Both Thorolf and Rox are wounded and Rafferty is leading the way. Chen passes them in his female guise as they emerge from the labyrinth beneath the city, but the *Pyr* are as yet unaware that the wily *Slayer* can take this form. Remember that Chen, having drunk the Elixir, can disguise his scent:

An Asian woman in tight jeans and stiletto heels came out of one of the offices behind them. Niall didn't see which one; he only heard her quiet murmur when she wanted to pass them. He moved immediately to one side, knowing they were blocking the passage.

"I beg your pardon," Rafferty said quietly as he and Sloane moved to one side, as well.

She smiled as she drew alongside them, her gaze flicking over Thorolf with obvious appreciation. Her floral perfume was strong enough to make Niall's nose itch and her blouse was a vivid red. Her jeans could have been painted on, and Niall was surprised she could walk easily in heels so high. Thorolf stared after her as she made her way to the street.

The woman paused just before the door to the street and cast Thorolf a smile over her shoulder. There was a bruise on her cheek, albeit one she had tried to hide with makeup.

When Thorolf didn't respond to the invitation, she shrugged

and stepped into the street. She strode to the left without hesitating, the door swinging shut after her.

Thorolf then took a few steps in pursuit.

"Not dead yet," Sloane muttered, and rolled his eyes.

Rafferty chuckled and shook his head when Thorolf's neck turned red.

Niall caught the door before it closed. He was surprised to find them on Doyers Street near his ruined building.

There was a Chinese apothecary shop to one side of the door he held and a dim sum restaurant on the other. That explained the smells. The signage overhead acclaimed the services of the acupuncture specialist and several other professionals located in the corridor.

"Holy crap," Thorolf said, looking around with amazement.

"I've walked past here a thousand times, with no idea," Niall agreed.

"No." Thorolf shook his head. "She's gone."

And it was true. Despite the number of people on either side of the street to the left of the doorway, there was no sign of the striking woman in the tight jeans.

"As surely as if she'd never been," Rafferty mused.

"Maybe she went into a shop," Niall suggested, but he had a feeling that wasn't the case.

—from **Whisper Kiss**

Thorolf is haunted by dreams of this seductive version of Chen in **Darkfire Kiss**.

At the beginning of **Darkfire Kiss**, Chen has retreated to his lair beneath the mountains of Tibet to heal from his injuries sustained in the last battle with the *Pyr* in **Whisper Kiss**. He also has one of the three darkfire crystals, which hold the darkfire captive: he uses his authority over the element of earth to sing to the crystal, break it, and loose the darkfire on the world. He believes that the chaotic influence of the darkfire will destroy the *Pyr*. It isn't specified where or how Chen got this darkfire crystal—when the Sleeper awakens, he says that it is known that one of the three crystals is lost, which implies that it was taken from Pwyll, even before the Sleeper was enchanted.

Chen remains in his lair in Tibet, listening to the earth, and is aware of lightning striking Thorolf three times, indicating that *Pyr's* affinity with air. At this point, he forges two of the seven pieces of his broken brand together again, and plans to enslave Thorolf. Chen appears in Thorolf's dreams as an attractive young Asian woman: Thorolf recognizes this as a taunt and resolves to destroy Chen alone, in order to protect his fellow *Pyr*. The loosed darkfire actually undermines Chen's plan, against his expectation. It awakens the creature known as Viv Jason, who manages to enter Chen's lair despite the barriers and traps set against intruders. He proposes an alliance with her, in order to trap Thorolf.

In **Flashfire**, it is revealed that Chen plans to make his play for ascendancy in 2012, the year of the dragon, and must command all four elements to do so. His own affinities are for fire and earth, but he plans to solidify his mastery of the elements by enslaving three specific *Pyr*: Lorenzo for his affinity with water, Brandon for his affinity with earth and Thorolf for his affinity with air. Chen's alliance with Viv Jason should bring Thorolf beneath his command. Chen has himself been giving Dragon Bone Powder to Brandon as a performance enhancer, trading the powder for Brandon's dragon scales for a binding spell. He's content to let Brandon's addiction have time to build. Meanwhile, he dispatches JP to trap Lorenzo, using Dragon Bone Powder.

JP is distracted by the power of the Dragon Bone Powder and ends up seducing Cassie's friend and roommate, Stacy, instead of pursuing Lorenzo. Chen intervenes, confronting JP in the Las Vegas hotel elevator in his young female form. He brands JP for his disobedience, then takes hunts Lorenzo himself. Chen disguises himself as a federal agent (Mr. T. Chen) investigating the *Pyr* for "making things disappear" who is purportedly interviewing everyone who attended Lorenzo's show. He stammers and is easily under-estimated in his guise of a feeble bureaucrat — until Cassie is alone with him. He shifts shape, beguiles and captures her, revealing that he and JP intend to make more Dragon Bone Powder from Salvatore's corpse. In the battle that ensues, Chen is wounded, the brand is broken again and Marco claims the pieces.

At the beginning of **Ember's Kiss**, Chen has three of Brandon's dragon scales. He surrenders the last of the Dragon Bone Powder for the fourth scale, which he needs for his binding spell over Brandon. His plan is that Brandon will ultimately be the source for more Dragon Bone Powder. Brandon believes that Chen is the only one who understands his *Pyr* nature and trusts in the lies Chen has told him. Chen encourages an earthquake using his affinity with the earth, hoping to put Brandon's dragon in ascendance. He then chants to the volcano Ko`olau, intent on urging it to erupt. He also tries to influence Liz, thinking that an enslaved Firedaughter can only help his plan to dominate.

On the hunt for more Elixir, the *Slayer* Jorge has decided to target Chen. He pursues Chen, locates his lair in Hawai'i, manifests inside the dragonsmoke barrier, and sees the spiral of sand that is the binding spell against Brandon. He recognizes by the arrangement that it's incomplete with three scales and assumes Chen is collecting the fourth. Jorge steals one of the scales and leaves a tendril of his scent inside the lair, just to taunt Chen. Jorge later breaks the scale, infuriating Chen that he needs to get another one. Jorge confronts Chen when he's trying to trap Brandon, and Brandon sees Chen's truth. In the ensuing battle, Brandon is trapped inside Chen's lair. He finds the spiral spell and disrupts it, then is challenged by Jorge and escapes. Chen, meanwhile, has targeted Liz and she uses her Firedaughter powers to defend herself. She also uses the darkfire crystal entrusted to her by Marco to injure Chen. He summons lightning to strike her down and intends to drown her, but she survives.

Defeated, Chen attacks Thorolf in Bangkok, expecting an easy victory, but Viv Jason takes exception to him changing the rules of their deal. While they battle, Liz creates a spell to summon him back to Hawai'i and Chen is pulled back there against his will, due to her possession of his last vial of Dragon Bone Powder. In the ensuring fight, Brandon injures Chen and throws his broken body into the flames, believing the *Slayer* will be incinerated. Jorge wants to claim Chen, but Brandon deceives him, and both *Slayers* are swept away by the tidal wave summoned by the younger *Pyr*.

In **Serpent's Kiss,** Chen steals JP from the prison where Erik has locked him away, in Chicago. Chen leaves a burned mark in the shape of spiral on the floor, which Erik realizes is a spell that is drawing him closer. Chen taunts Erik that he could claim the leader of the *Pyr* (and complete his spell, given Erik's affinity with air) but says he'd rather let Erik watch. Thorolf has gone to Asia to hunt Chen, so Erik knows that *Pyr* is the *Slayer's* prey. Chen traps Thorolf and tattoos his scales with spirals embued with a spell—the ink is the blood of JP, a *Slayer* who has drunk the Elixir, and will gradually be absorbed by Thorolf and compel him to turn *Slayer*. He then releases Thorolf, knowing the *Pyr* will welcome him but that Thorolf will perceive them as enemies and kill them. Meanwhile, Jorge tries to make an alliance with Lorenzo against Chen, trading the ability to beguile the old *Slayer* with Thorolf's survival.

Chen isn't planning on Thorolf having a firestorm, much less one with a goddess. Chen abducts Chandra, believing that the weak point in Thorolf's union is his mate, and the pair battle. Chandra jabs an arrow between Chen's scales, burying the arrow head beneath his skin. After he takes her and Thorolf captive and retreats to his lair, she calls to the rune etched on the arrowhead to weaken him. Thorolf and Chandra compare Chen to Nidhug, the dragon of Norse myth who chews the roots of the world tree, Yggdrasil. Because Thorolf has lost a scale out of his love for Chandra, there's a gap in his armor that Chen is compelled to repair before completing his enslavement of the *Pyr*. (The other scales all had spiral tattoos on them.) Lorenzo tries to beguile Chen, Chandra injures him more with the arrowhead, Thorolf battles against him—and Lee, his captive younger brother, kills him with half of the darkfire crystal, driving it into Chen's gut and then his eye. Jorge begins to devour the *Slayer* for the sake of the Elixir in his veins as Chen's lair collapses.

CHRISTOPHER MERRICK—oldest son of Brandon and Liz, born September 16, 2012.

CINNABAR—A *Pyr*, originally named Sahir, used by Magnus Montmorency to create the Dragon's Blood Elixir. Sahir (which means 'wakeful') was born around 350 A.D. He was captured by the Romans in the eastern empire, made a slave, taken to Rome, then escaped his owner. He was living on the streets of Rome, supporting himself with petty thievery, when Magnus spotted him and knew that he was *Pyr*. Magnus took him in and gave him a Roman name, Sylvanus Secundus. It is unclear at what point Magnus decided to use Sahir to generate the Dragon's Blood Elixir, but he did send Sylvanus to retrieve the bloodstone from the body of Magnus' wife, Aurelia. Sylvanus was caught and condemned to work in the cinnabar mine in Sisapo (now Almadén, Spain). This was considered a death sentence, since the workers always died of mercury poisoning in a short period of time after being sent there.

Sylvanus, however, did not. His *Pyr* nature made it possible for him to metabolize the mercury. The mercury, in fact, made him immortal. His hair and skin turned red, and his scales in dragon form changed from citrine to scarlet, the tinge spreading from the root. Survival meant that he rose through the ranks to become custodian of the mines. He changed names at intervals to avoid suspicion, eventually calling himself Cinnabar, the name of the mercury sulfide mined there. The Moors questioned him closely when they took possession of the mines in the early 8th century. Magnus was spooked by this, so trapped Sahir and imprisoned him in the vial, thereby creating the Dragon's Blood Elixir.

The creation of the Elixir had to be linked to a Saros cycle of eclipses: this meant that the usefulness of the captive dragon was of limited duration. Sylvanus—who became known as Cinnabar once confined in the vial of the Elixir—had been confined at the beginning of Saros cycle 110, which will come to its conclusion in 2027. This meant that Magnus had to find a *Pyr* to replace Cinnabar in the solution well before that date, to ensure that the Dragon's Blood Elixir continued to be generated. Magnus targeted Delaney for this role and intended to make the replacement in 2009, to ensure that there was never a lack of this key substance. Cinnabar intervenes on Ginger's behalf at the end of **Winter Kiss**, using the last of his strength to defend the firestorm and a pregnant mate from Magnus' dragonfire. He holds Delaney above the flood of Elixir when the vial is broken, then drapes himself over the unconscious Delaney and hums, summoning the mercury to precipitate out of Delaney's body. He fades from this last effort, and knows he has given his last to ensure that there will be no more Elixir. Ginger has a glimpse of Sahir as a young man just before he disappears forever.

CHYNNA—founder of Imagination Ink, the tattoo shop where Rox works in **Whisper Kiss**. Chynna established the shop, then later made Rox and Neo partners in the business. Chynna found Rox on the street and gave her shelter and a job. Once she saw how well Rox could draw, she made Rox her apprentice. She is described as being outrageous and outspoken, fiercely talented and an unabashed romantic. Chynna also likes to "pay it forward" by passing good deeds along. In return for her kindness, Rox designed and tattooed Chynna's full sleeves. One is completed at the beginning of **Whisper Kiss** and one still being designed (Niall helps Rox to solve the puzzle of integrating Chynna's existing tattoos into the new design.)

Rox had done Chynna's left sleeve first because it had been the easier one. That sleeve wound from the back of Chynna's neck to her wrist, a dozen large full-color roses tumbling down her skin.

The roses were detailed and realistic, to the point of having dewdrops on their petals and even a few small insects lurking on the stems and leaves. Rox had had more than one customer come in for "a rose like Chynna's."

Roses were the perfect image for Chynna—pretty, lush, romantic, but thick with unexpected thorns. The dozens of insects and butterflies secreted between the flowers made Rox think of all the lives Chynna had helped along.

– from **Winter Kiss**

Chynna also tattooed the dragon on Rox's back, using Rox's own drawing. She is said to believe that tattoos can be protective talismans. Rox also has a tattoo labeled *Sisters of the Heart* which has a portrait of Chynna and one of her sister, Suzie. The portraits were done by Neo, the other partner at Imagination Ink.

Chynna also appears in Deborah Cooke's contemporary romance

series, *Flatiron Five*: she sells Imagination Ink to her partners and opens a boutique tattoo shop at Flatiron Five in book #3 of that series. Her decision to give away a tattoo every full moon that will bring love into the life of the bearer launches the spin-off series *Secret Heart Ink*, also set in the F5 world.

CONNOR SHEA—third son of Delaney and Ginger, born September 2014.

CYSGWR—Welsh for 'the Sleeper', and the name given by Rafferty's grandfather Pwyll to Marcus Maximus, the Sleeper of the *Pyr*. See more under Marco.

DAMIEN—A *Pyr* and Dragon's Tooth Warrior, known by his comrades as the "heartbreaker" because of his string of short relationships with women. In the Dragon Legion Novella, **Kiss of Darkness,** he has the chance to save Petra, the woman who stole his heart. Damien has dark hair, but it turns blond after his time in Hades. He is dark emerald in dragon form and his scales are tipped with gold. His affinities are to fire and air. He's a fearless warrior, but dislikes snakes.

When Damien reaches Hades, he can't shift shape to fight Cerberus and is attacked by the hellhound. Petra sings to lull the guardian of the portal to sleep, but not until Damien has been wounded—she explains to a disgruntled Damien that she wouldn't have been able to talk to him unless he shed blood first. They argue about his decision to leave her while she was pregnant and her abilities as an Earthdaughter—Petra turned an entire village to stone, which Damien found horrifying, but admits that she did it to save him from their plans to hunt and kill him. Damien understands belatedly that the prophecy about dragons turning to stone was actually referring to the curse placed upon the Dragon's Tooth Warriors, which he survived. When he braves a river of snakes to save Petra, he realizes that he loves her. He offers to remain in the Underworld in her place when she goes into labor, so that she and his son can live, but Hades refuses. This so angers Petra that she uses her powers to crack the vault of stone over the underworld. The light means that Damien's powers return, and he shifts shape to carry his mate and son to safety. He loses the tip of his tail when the vault snaps shut. She delivers their son in the living world before they realize that Damien's journey to the underworld has made his dark hair blond. His scales also change from deep emerald tipped with gold to gold dipped in green. Their son is also born with blond hair.

In **Kiss of Destiny**, Alexander and Damien come to the injured Thad and heal him by sharing their own power through a dragonsmoke conduit. They also repair Thad's scale with Aura's help. Damien remains in the past—along with Alexander and Thad—to start a new lineage of dragon warriors. Their descendants come to Erik's lair to pledge to follow Drake at the end of **Kiss of Destiny**.

DAPHNE—a lover of Magnus Montmorency whom he killed. It's the disappearance of Daphne that brings Melissa Smith to Magnus' home at the beginning of **Darkfire Kiss**. There was a scene featuring this murder that was removed from the original edition of **Winter Kiss** and restored to the 2018 version. In the first draft, Daphne's name was Mona and Magnus had met her in Azerbaijan.

DASHIELL PATTERSON—the best friend of Timmy, Veronica Maitland's son. Timmy is staying overnight at Dashiell's when Veronica is abducted by Jorge, and remains there until she's found. Joy Patterson, Dashiell's mom, quickly decides that Drake is a keeper. Recognizing the bond between the two boys, Drake buys a house near the Pattersons for their blended family and Dashiell becomes one of the few humans entrusted with the truth about the *Pyr*.

DARCY SHEA—second son of Donovan and Alex, born August 4, 2011.

DARCY (2)—One of the Dragon Legion, named for the first time in *DragonFate*.

DARIAN—the Kerry stud at Ginger's farm in Ohio. He's small, black and mellow, but the sight of him strikes terror into the heart of Thorolf.

DELANEY SHEA—A *Pyr* and younger brother of Donovan Shea, born in 1564 in Ireland. Delaney is married to Ginger Sinclair, and father of Liam and Sean. Delaney is emerald and gold in dragon form when he first appears in **Kiss of Fire**. He is tall, auburn-haired and green-eyed in human form. Delaney was banished by his mother when he was fourteen and unable to control his dragon: he killed a man who cheated him, because his mother was ill and they needed the money he was owed. His mother saw the blood and guessed what he had done. Although Delaney subsequently found Donovan and the other *Pyr*, it is possible that his doubts about the merit of his shifting abilities made him an easier target for Magnus. He and Donovan originally recognized each other as two of a kind, the *Pyr* having a distinctive scent, and only realized much later that they were actually siblings. While Donovan remained estranged from Mhairi, Delaney returned to their mother and reconciled with her on her deathbed. He wears a silver cross on a chain which his mother gave to him then in exchange for a promise to use his powers for good.

Delaney's affinities are unusual for a *Pyr*: they are to water and air. He tells Ginger in **Winter Kiss** that he once worked on a horse farm in Ireland that bred Belgians and Clydesdales. Niall credits Delaney with being the "idea guy" in the eco-travel company that they founded together.

Delaney was Erik's second in **Kiss of Fire**, although he wasn't named in that book. He was the *Pyr* who was struck down by the *Slayers* and his body was removed by them. At the time, the *Pyr* believed he was dead—but he was the victim of an experiment, and was force-fed the Dragon's Blood Elixir. Because Delaney had not actually died, the forced conversion to *Slayer* didn't fully take and his heart remained *Pyr* while his body turned *Slayer*.

"In the darkness of the night, a lost dragon felt the heat of his brother's firestorm. The flame that kindled between Alex and Donovan sent a pang of yearning through him. The light shone within him, sang to the last shard of his own spark, lit the corners

of forgotten memory."
—from **Kiss of Fury**

The spark of his brother Donovan's firestorm pushes back the shadow of the Elixir, giving Delaney new hope. Magnus' chant, though, tugs Delaney back to the realm of the shadow dragons. Snared between the two and in torment, Delaney chooses to sacrifice himself to ensure the survival of Alex, Donovan's mate. This act of self-sacrifice pushes the Elixir's shadow from his heart.

Still, Delaney is left in torment, because he doesn't feel he can trust his dragon, or control it during a lunar eclipse. In **Kiss of Fate**, Sloane tries to heal Delaney and drive out the remaining influence of the Elixir. Instead, a subliminal command from Magnus is triggered, and Delaney attacks the pregnant mates, Sara and Alex, against his own will. This convinces him that he will end up betraying his fellow *Pyr*: he exiles himself by choice and plans to destroy the Elixir. Although he's previously used his mother's surname, Connaught, after realizing the effects of the Elixir, Delaney begins to use his father's surname, Shea. Keir Shea turned *Slayer* by choice, so using that surname reminds Delaney of what Magnus has done to him.

At the beginning of **Winter Kiss**, Delaney is committed to destroy the Elixir, regardless of the cost to himself. He can't control his dragon anymore and knows he can't continue as he has been. He's sold his car, his share in the eco-travel business he started with Niall (to Niall) and his house in Seattle. He's located Magnus' hidden lair and the sanctuary of the Elixir in Ohio. Delaney's own firestorm with Ginger sparks the night before his planned attack, and he sees this as an opportunity to create a legacy. They consummate the firestorm and he leaves Ginger, fully expecting to die. Ginger, however, isn't so inclined to let him go. Delaney asks Erik in old-speak to defend Ginger and their son but declines to wait for Erik.

Delaney still didn't continue, so Ginger tried to prod him. "But I still don't understand how you were fed the Elixir."

Delaney straightened, as if the memory made him restless. "I was injured badly in a battle and the *Slayers* took my body so that it couldn't be exposed to the elements."

"You were killed?"

"Yes. They imprisoned me and fed me the Elixir, but my soul hadn't departed my body."

"What does that mean?"

"It means that I was an experiment. Usually shadow dragons are made of corpses that the soul has vacated. Usually *Slayers* who have already turned against the *Pyr* drink the Elixir by choice."

"But you were *Pyr* and still had your soul."

"Exactly." Delaney smiled, but there was no humor in his expression. "Which meant the battle that raged within me for dominance over my body nearly drove me insane."

He glanced down, frowning, and Ginger gave him time to collect his thoughts. His expression was drawn, and she was reminded again of vets who came home from war, not physically injured but not quite the same psychologically as they had been, either.

It was strange that she had initially assumed he was a serviceman. He had the same discipline and drive as men she'd known who joined the military, but was in the service of a different force.

It was still one fighting for good, though.

Delaney continued softly after a minute. "They released me and I thought I had triumphed over the Elixir's wickedness, but Magnus had submerged commands in my subconscious while I was in captivity. Each time the *Pyr* fought the *Slayers,* Magnus triggered those buried impulses and made me act against my own will."

"That's evil."

"It is." He looked up at her, his expression haunted. "I even tried to attack the mates of my brother and his friend, tried to steal their unborn babies." He swallowed, the shadows in his eyes more clear than ever. "I didn't want to do it, but I couldn't ignore Magnus' command."

Ginger could see how the memory pained him.

She also noticed that none of the *Pyr* she had met had been introduced as Delaney's brother.

Ginger frowned at the road. Delaney's confession made her

believe that the Elixir hadn't managed to turn him *Slayer*. It bothered him that he had been compelled to act that way.

He was with the good guys.

Her instincts had been right.

Ha.

—from **Winter Kiss**

In **Winter Kiss**, during a battle in the sanctuary of the Dragon's Blood Elixir, Magnus tries to command Delaney but fails: Delaney attributes the weakening of Magnus' influence to the firestorm and Ginger. Rafferty, however, fears that the commands Delaney can refuse are just feints, and that the real subliminal command is for Delaney to destroy the Elixir. The *Pyr* discover this to be correct, as Cinnabar needs to be replaced as the source and Magnus has chosen Delaney to take his place.

The successful completion of his firestorm—and the power of Ginger's love—banishes the Elixir from his body and restores him to health. Delaney leaves his mother's cross with the sleeping Ginger after they consummate the firestorm, as a signal to her that he means to keep his promise to his mother and to her. Ginger follows him with the *Pyr*. Ginger and Delaney destroy the source of the Elixir and its sanctuary, along with the help of the *Pyr,* by the end of **Winter Kiss**. At the end of the book, Donovan gives Delaney a red Viper sports car, which he calls a firestorm gift but is a replacement for the vehicle Delaney sold.

In **Whisper Kiss**, Delaney and Ginger are working on the genealogies of the *Pyr* with Erik's help, trying to create a spreadsheet of all dead *Pyr*, including where they died. Donovan and Alex are using the information to visit the graves, or final resting places, in an effort to identify the remaining shadow dragons. Delaney's recovery in **Winter Kiss** also inspires Niall's hope that his twin, Phelan, can also be healed. Delaney and Ginger go to Niall's firestorm and help him to heal Rox. He fights shadow dragons with Donovan and Quinn in the big finish.

In **Darkfire Kiss**, Delaney and Ginger attend the repair of Rafferty's scale on New Year's Eve at Quinn and Sara's home in

Michigan. They didn't come to the firestorm because Delaney didn't believe Rafferty would need any help, and because Liam was very young. In **Flashfire**, Delaney and Ginger come to Venice for the repair of Lorenzo's scale.

In **Serpent's Kiss**, Delaney participates in a conference call with Erik and Donovan about Thorolf's firestorm, and agrees to not only come to the firestorm but to carry the sword from Los Angeles to Hawai'i. Subsequently, he ends up flying all the way to Australia with Brandon, taking turns with the burden of the sword Thorolf needs. Delaney and Ginger attend the repair of Thorolf's scale at Angkor.

In **Firestorm Forever**, Donovan had a bad feeling and suggested that he and Delaney go to Chicago for the eclipse. They fight the first two clones of Boris with Erik there—when Erik is wounded, Delaney tells him to take some of his own power with dragonsmoke. Afterward, Donovan, Alex, Niall, Rox and their boys go to Delaney and Ginger's farm in Ohio to ensure that they're all defended. At the end of the book, Delaney goes to Drake's home with Niall and Lee to defend Drake's family along with some of the Dragon Legion. Delaney injects Sloane's antidote into the clones, then subsequently ensures that the fallen are all exposed to all four elements. He attends the scale repair at the end of the book, and also participates in Melissa's special on the *Pyr*, in his dragon form.

Delaney is described as emerald and gold in his dragon form in **Kiss of Fire**, but subsequently, after he's been given the Elixir, he's described as emerald and copper. While it's possible that the change caused by the Elixir inside him was manifested in his scales, none of the *Pyr* comment on the change in his appearance because it's actually a continuity error.

DEREK SULLIVAN—Samantha Wilcox's first husband and father of Nathaniel. Sam and Derek are divorced. Derek is a researcher who was Sam's boss on a research trip to Africa. They had a one-nighter and she became pregnant. They married for the sake of their son: after Nathaniel's arrival, Derek kept travelling but Sam transferred to work in the research labs for Isaac. Derek is mentioned in **Firestorm Forever**, but doesn't make an appearance. Jac refuses to even say his name. Note that Derek has no family connection to Mark Sullivan.

DONOVAN SHEA—A *Pyr*, lapis lazuli and gold in dragon form, a former duelist and the Warrior of the *Pyr*. In human form, Donovan has russet hair with a gold stud in his left ear, green eyes and a dragon tattoo on his left bicep. Donovan is the son of Keir Shea and Mhairi Connaught, and was born in Dublin in 1552. He ran away from home when he was twelve, because his shifter powers had begun to manifest and his mother believed him to be possessed by the devil. He later encountered Delaney in Dublin and they recognized that they were both *Pyr*. They decided they must be cousins, and Donovan took Delaney under his tutelage. They later learn that they are brothers.

Donovan's challenge coin is a sterling silver American dollar. He challenged Quinn in **Kiss of Fire** and the *Slayer* Tyson in **Kiss of Fury**. After they defeated the *Slayer* Lucien together in **Kiss of Fire**, Quinn was inspired by Lucien's sharp talons to create a pair of gloves for Donovan, with retractable knives on the fingertips. He rides a Ducati motorcycle, loves risk, and has no interest in having a firestorm, much less making a commitment to a single woman.

Because of this, Erik set him up for his firestorm. After learning from Sophie that Alex would be the Wizard, Erik realized that Donovan was the most likely of the *Pyr* to be the Warrior. Wanting to ensure that the old prophecy of the Warrior and the Wizard came true, and wanting the second firestorm of the Dragon's Tail to succeed, Erik assigned Donovan to protect Alex. He hoped that once the firestorm sparked, Donovan wouldn't be able to resist its allure.

"The woman could tempt a saint, and he was no saint."
—Donovan on Alex in **Kiss of Fury**.

Donovan spent time at the Elizabethan court, where he earned his living as a duelist and took Olivia (among others) as his lover. In **Kiss of Fury**, we learned more of Donovan's past adventures, and his history as a lover and fighter. Donovan spoke Spanish when he pretended to be a hospital orderly in order to abduct Alex.

"Donovan heard the distinctive rumble of a familiar motorcycle engine.

Fading.

"Sounds like she knows how to get your attention." Rafferty settled back in his chair with a satisfied smile. "Only your destined mate would have the nerve to steal your bike."

— from **Kiss of Fury**

Donovan's firestorm with Alex was transformative—what he learned from Alex not only allowed him to become the foretold Warrior of the *Pyr* but it helped his brother, Delaney, to begin healing from the effects of the Elixir. It also changed the perspective of many of the *Pyr*, convincing them that Rafferty's view of the importance of creating a permanent relationship with a mate was more than romantic whimsy. Donovan is acknowledged by his fellows to be the best fighter in the *Pyr* and he has looked to Rafferty as a mentor for years.

Donovan lost a scale before the beginning of *Dragonfire*. Rafferty assumed that this is a sign of Donovan's love for Olivia, partly because Donovan had Quinn use the Dragon's Tooth pearl for its repair, a gem which he obtained from Olivia. In fact, Donovan lost his first scale because of his love for his brother, Delaney. He lost a second scale, right beside the first, when he fell in love with Alex. His scale is repaired at the end of **Kiss of Fury** with Alex's help, when she gives him the jet and garnet swan pin that belonged to her grandmother. The pin symbolizes Alex's affinities for air and earth, which align with Donovan's affinities for water and fire. Donovan and Alex have two sons, Nick and Darcy. Nick was named after Nikolas of Thebes.

In **Kiss of Fate**, Donovan goes to Erik's lair when the Dragon's Egg is broken. In the battle against Magnus and the shadow dragons at the end of the book, Delaney is prompted by Magnus to attack Alex, who is pregnant, and Donovan defends his mate against his brother.

In **Winter Kiss**, Donovan originally stays away from Delaney's firestorm, wanting to protect Alex, but Zoë sends him a dream that reminds him of his bond with his brother. He decides then to go to the firestorm, reconcile with his brother and help Delaney with his firestorm. Donovan helps in the destruction of the sanctuary of the Elixir and gives Delaney a "firestorm gift" of a new sports car.

In **Whisper Kiss**, Donovan and Alex are assigned the task of tracking down dead *Pyr* to refine a list of potential shadow dragons. Alex has discovered that there are trace elements in the soil wherever a dead *Pyr* has been raised by the Elixir, and Donovan retrieves the soil samples for her. They abandon the task to go to New York for Niall's firestorm, to help him both defend Ginger and defeat the shadow dragons.

In **Darkfire Kiss**, Donovan keeps his old promise by going to Bardsey Island to defend the Sleeper while Rafferty defends his mate during his firestorm. The property that includes the refuge of the Sleeper is owned by Donovan — in this passage, he thinks about the technical details of keeping it in his custody without revealing his own longevity.

"I came to Bardsey Island as a young man, although it's been a long time." It had been longer even than this man anticipated, but Donovan didn't say that. "My distant cousin owned a house on the island."

"And who would that be?"

"Donovan Shea."

"Oh, he's been gone a long while." The man's manner warmed at the mention of the name. "Seems I heard he had passed away."

"Yes." Donovan shook his head, as if to marvel. In fact, he had started the rumor, as he did every sixty or seventy years, concurrent with another round of legalities to pass his own property to himself. It had gotten more difficult in the last century, and he wondered absently how rich the *Pyr* were making lawyers everywhere. "I guess it amused him that we had the same name, for he left the house to me. Quite a surprise, after all this time."

"That would be the old white house, then."

"It would." Donovan wasn't surprised the man knew it. "I'm eager to see it again, and to show my own son the island. I'm sure it's as magical as I recall."

—from **Darkfire Kiss**

Jorge locates the Sleeper by following Donovan, and they fight in the Sleeper's lair. When Magnus and Rafferty both follow and Magnus is defeated, it's Donovan who reminds Rafferty that Magnus' corpse must be exposed to all four elements to ensure that he can't be made into a shadow dragon.

In **Flashfire**, Erik forbids Quinn and Donovan to come to Lorenzo's firestorm, because JP is there and he believes the *Slayer* will be seeking vengeance for his brother Lucien's death—and may take it upon the mates and children of the Smith and the Warrior. Erik sends Eileen and Zoë to Donovan for protection in Sloane's care. Donovan and Alex attend the repair of Lorenzo's scale in Venice.

In **Serpent's Kiss**, Donovan and Quinn go to Chicago to defend Erik's lair, after conferring with Erik and Delaney on a conference call. Alex and Donovan's images (along with Nick and Darcy) appear where Delaney's reflection should be at Thorolf's scale repair in Angkor.

In **Firestorm Forever**, Donovan has a feeling that he and Delaney should be at Erik's lair in Chicago for the eclipse, and they battle two clones of Boris there along with Erik. He and Alex take refuge at Delaney's farm, along with Delaney, Ginger, Niall and Rox, and all the *Pyr* sons. He resolves to find Marco, then goes to Quinn's lair with Marco, Quinn and Lorenzo for the final battle of the Dragon's Tail Wars. Donovan and Quinn breathe a dragonsmoke barrier around the house to protect the mates and children. After the fight—in which he uses his skills as the Warrior—Donovan helps to ensure all of the fallen are exposed to the four elements. Donovan and Alex attend the scale repair in Chicago at the end of the book and he participates in Melissa Smith's special on the *Pyr*.

There was a continuity error in the original editions of the *Dragonfire* books: Donovan's scales changed to lapis lazuli and silver in **Winter Kiss, Whisper Kiss,** and **Darkfire Kiss,** then the original lapis lazuli and gold returned in **Flashfire.** The silver reappeared in **Serpent's Kiss** but the gold was back again in **Firestorm Forever.** In the new 2018 editions, his scales are lapis lazuli and gold throughout the entire series.

DOUG CAMERON—Melissa's former producer, who contacts her in **Darkfire Kiss** about the dragon pictures on her blog. Instead of taking payment for the use of the images, Melissa asks for her old reporting job back. They haven't talked during the three years since she was diagnosed with cancer. He prefers foreign correspondents with no ties and Melissa knows that she qualifies now that she's divorced. They subsequently work together on Melissa's special broadcast about the *Pyr*.

DRAGON'S TOOTH WARRIORS, THE/ DRAGON LEGION, THE—The Dragon's Tooth Warriors sprang from the earth, from the dragon teeth sown as seeds in the soil, much like the legend of the Spartans. The first dragon's tooth appears as a treasure in Donovan's hoard in **Kiss of Fire**, when Quinn tries to repair Donovan's missing scale with it. (The repair doesn't hold.) In **Kiss of Fury**, we learn how Donovan came to possess the massive pearl, which was claimed from Magnus' hoard, and is actually a tooth that has been pearlized. The pearl is planted and the ancient *Pyr* Nikolas is freed from the spell laid upon Cadmus. Magnus reveals that there are ninety-nine more of the teeth but that he lost them in the destruction of his lair outside London.

In **Kiss of Fate**, the remaining teeth are found during excavations for a new subway line and that story follows Erik's battle against Boris for possession of the prize. Rafferty plants the teeth as seeds in his garden, and a company of warriors sprout from the teeth. They take flight under Drake's leadership and aid in the destruction of Magnus' hidden Academy. Many of them die in this effort, although Drake and a dozen of his men survive, then pledge themselves to Erik's service.

Harmonia's Kiss tells of their return to their original homeland in search of meaning in their disrupted lives. It is in this story that some of the warriors' names are first mentioned, including that of Drake, and the story of their enchantment is told. They find it disheartening to confirm that the lives they'd known are lost forever in time. Drake names Lidio, Aeson, Cletus, Milo, and Alexander. Several succumb to the viper's song, and the survivors subsequently choose to call themselves the Dragon Legion.

In **Whisper Kiss**, the Dragon's Tooth Warriors arrive for the final battle against the shadow dragons, shifting the odds in favor of the *Pyr*. In **Darkfire Kiss**, when Erik confronts Lorenzo in his hall of mirrors, he realizes that he can no longer detect the presence of the Dragon's Tooth Warriors and that they are missing.

In **Flashfire**, Salvatore reveals that he dreamed of Drake wielding the darkfire crystal hidden in Lorenzo's hoard. That was why he gave the crystal to Drake without Lorenzo's knowledge. The *Pyr* are as yet unaware why the Dragon's Tooth Warriors have disappeared.

The Dragon Legion Novellas—**Kiss of Danger, Kiss of Darkness** and **Kiss of Destiny**—recount the adventures of the Dragon's Tooth Warriors after they claim the darkfire crystal, which takes them through space and time. At the beginning of **Kiss of Danger**, Drake and his men collect the darkfire crystal from Lorenzo's hoard. In terms of chronology, this happens just before Erik arrives at Lorenzo's lair in **Flashfire**. Lorenzo is aware of their arrival but can't identify their scent:

"This scent was faint, difficult to perceive. It was so strange that he couldn't quite place it. He chose to mull it over, keenly aware of Erik's increasing proximity.

Definitely *Pyr*, but ancient. More like the old perfumes that had been sold in Venice centuries before. Frankincense. Myrrh. Ambergris. Scents that could not be precisely described by anyone but which, once smelled, were never forgotten. This scent awakened something in Lorenzo that he would have preferred to have left slumbering.

Lorenzo returned to the atrium and pulled back the blind with a single smooth gesture. He hid his surprise that there was not just one *Pyr* there.

There were seventeen."

—from **Kiss of Danger**

Not all seventeen warriors are named. By the beginning of **Kiss of Danger**, there are twelve remaining warriors: Drake, Peter, Orion, Ashe, Aeson, Ignatius, Tyrone, Alexander, Damien, Thaddeus, and two unnamed warriors. Obviously, there were five more, lost by this time in the abrupt journeys caused by the darkfire crystal. By the beginning of **Kiss of Darkness**, there are only eight warriors still together. They figure out that the darkfire crystal is taking them each to their firestorms. Orion feels the spark and follows it before the crystal takes them all to the underworld, when Damien's beloved is trapped. Note also that at the end of **Kiss of Darkness**, when Alexander rejoins Damien, Alexander has already built a company of *Pyr*: there are six *Pyr* with him who Damien doesn't yet know. By **Kiss of Destiny**, only Drake and Thad are left of the original company when Thad follows the spark of his firestorm. The darkfire crystal then, its energy spent, returns Drake to Erik's lair in Chicago. Drake is both discouraged and defeated to have lost his company of warriors, until their descendants come to Erik and pledge to serve the leader of the *Pyr*. The darkfire crystal has changed history and added multiple lines of *Pyr* warriors. They now call themselves the Dragon Legion and each have a tattoo to commemorate that.

In **Serpent's Kiss**, the Dragon's Tooth Warriors help with relief efforts against the plague in Seattle and also defend Cassie and the children when Lorenzo fights against Chen. Thorolf is given a vision by Chandra in which he witnesses Damien's actions in the underworld from **Kiss of Darkness**, and also the battle on the road to Hera's garden in **Kiss of Destiny**. This helps him realize the identity of Viv Jason and the source of the plague. At Thorolf's scale repair, the Dragon Legion warriors and Lorenzo appear as reflections in the lake, attending in spirit if not in body.

In **Firestorm Forever**, Drake has his firestorm and Veronica calls his tattoo, the mark of the Dragon Legion, a dragon rampant. The Dragon Legion support and defend Drake during his second firestorm, and he explains his history to his mate:

She ran her hand over Drake's bare chest and smiled at him, then traced the dragon on his arm with a fingertip. "And how is the Dragon Legion different from the Dragon's Tooth Warriors?" she asked.

Drake kissed her thoroughly before he answered and tucked the blankets over both of them. Ronnie nestled against him with satisfaction, liking the rumble of his voice beneath her ear. "There is a force known to the *Pyr* as darkfire. It burns blue-green and challenges expectation wherever it appears. I never knew of it in my time, but during the Dragon's Tail Wars, three crystals were revealed, each holding a spark of darkfire snared within it. Two have been broken, loosing the darkfire into the world, but the one granted to me remains intact. Its spark, however, died."

"Why?"

"Because its power was expended. The Dragon's Tooth Warriors were beckoned by the gem and I claimed it, as it commanded me to do. Once I held it in my possession, each time the darkfire brightened in the stone, my company was cast through time and space. At each place, at least one of our members would be left behind."

"How horrible!"

"It was a wearisome journey and an ordeal, and when it was done, I alone was returned to this time with the stone, and its heart had gone dark. I thought I had lost my entire company and I was certain that my solitude was a mark of failure of the worst kind."

Ronnie stretched up and kissed his cheek.

"We had suspected on the journey that some of the men were being taken to the time and place of their firestorms. It subsequently turned out that all of the men in my company were taken to their mates. Because we had been enchanted for so long, I suppose we had missed our opportunities, and the darkfire made it come right."

"Oh! That's a wonderful story."

"More than that," Drake said with satisfaction. "They had their firestorms."

Ronnie felt her mouth fall open. "They had *sons*."

"And their sons had sons. Because of our travel through time, history was changed. Suddenly there were generations and generations of *Pyr* that had not existed before our departure. They all have this tattoo. I was urged to get one in honor of my role in their creation."

"The quest you thought a failure was a tremendous success."

"We have a better chance in the Dragon's Tail Wars because of our mission and the darkfire crystal. The men I asked to guard Timothy are of the Dragon Legion. Their leader is named Theo."

"Just like your son."

"He is descended from my son, so he is both comrade and blood kin."

—from **Firestorm Forever**

The Dragon Legion assist in the final battle of the Dragon's Tail Wars, and both Drake and Theo take part in the *Pyrs'* final public performance.

DRAKE (AKA STEPHANOS)—A *Pyr* and the commander of the Dragon's Tooth Warriors and leader of the Dragon Legion. He has dark hair and eyes and an olive complexion in human form, and a military discipline. In dragon form, he is originally described as grey and black with red talons. In **Firestorm Forever**, Drake is described as "the thorned dragon with scales that gleam like black pearls". His affinities are to fire and earth.

Drake has been separated from his mate, Cassandra, and his son Theo by the curse laid upon his company in ancient Greece. Although the curse is broken in **Kiss of Fate**, the Dragon's Tooth Warriors are centuries away from their loved ones and past lives. Drake first appears at the end of **Kiss of Fate** and helps in the battle to destroy the Academy, although he's not named in that book.

Drake finds new meaning in his life in **Harmonia's Kiss** and has a second firestorm in **Firestorm Forever**. His mate is Veronica Maitland, a widow with a young son he met in the short story and helped to learn the fate of her missing husband. Drake's faith in the importance of the *Pyr*'s mission to defend humans as the treasures of the earth was revived by this exchange, and he found it impossible to forget Veronica.

In **Serpent's Kiss**, Drake attends the repair of Thorolf's scale in Angkor, taking a place opposite Niall on the perimeter of the reflecting pool. The images of the Dragon Legion appear in the still water, replacing the reflections that should be there.

Drake and Veronica's firestorm is sparked by the first of three blood moons in **Firestorm Forever**. They satisfy the firestorm before Veronica is abducted by Jorge and forcibly infected with the Seattle virus. Jorge's plan to infect all of the *Pyr* mates in this way fails because of Drake. Subsequently, Drake's blood is used to create an antidote for the Seattle virus and Veronica agrees to be the first test subject. The antidote pushes the virus into remission but doesn't eliminate it from Veronica's system until Sloane and Samantha work together to refine the antidote. Drake's scale repair is televised by Melissa Smith and her team, broadcast from the forest behind Sloane's home in California.

DYLAN—one of Brandon's surfing buddies in **Ember's Kiss**. He's described as blond and easy-going, without a lot of ambition. Liz sees his aura as golden, like honey. He has a fondness for spring rolls and Brandon notes that Dylan can eat more of them than anyone he knows. Dylan drove to the restaurant in his Jeep with Brandon and Matt where Brandon's firestorm sparks with Liz, and Brandon fights the power of Chen's Dragon Bone Powder in the back of Dylan's car, pretending to be asleep as they drive home to Hale`iwa afterward.

EILEEN GROSVENOR—A university professor whose area of expertise is comparative mythology, partner of Erik Sorensson, mother of Zoë. Eileen is the reincarnation of Erik's first mate, Louisa Guthrie. Eileen is tall and slim with a lot of curly copper hair. She's 37 when she meets Erik in **Kiss of Fate**, divorced, and convinced that she has terrible luck with men. The truth is that her experience as Louisa is affecting her choices: she's waiting for Erik to reappear and unconsciously choosing men who will only disappoint her in the meantime. She has a sister, Lynne William, who lives in London, is married to Roger and has two daughters. Eileen dresses with artistic verve: when Erik first sees her, she is wearing a purple sheepskin coat and a lot of silver jewelry. She likes to knit while she thinks. She also tells Erik that he should wear color, instead of always black, and suggests that he wear red. When he comes to her as agreed at the end of **Kiss of Fate** to hear her decision about their future, he wears a red T-shirt—and she has knit him a red scarf. I love that the cover art shows Erik in a red T-shirt.

"The most enduring myths have their toes in the truth."
—Eileen Grosvenor in **Kiss of Fate**

At the end of **Kiss of Fate**, Eileen begins to compile a history of the *Pyr* as a legacy for the child she knows she's carrying. Sara sends her (on loan) the only copy of Sigmund's book, *The Habits and Habitats of Dragons: A Compleat Guide for* Slayers. Eileen tells Erik at the end of **Kiss of Fate** that she knows they're going to have a daughter, not a son, fueling his hope that the baby will be the new Wyvern.

In **Winter Kiss**, it's Eileen who wonders if the penumbral eclipse will be the herald of Delaney's firestorm, since he's consumed some of the Elixir that creates shadow dragons. The fact that Eileen comes with Erik to Delaney's firestorm, and they bring Zoë, makes Delaney realize how much the leader of the *Pyr* and his mate trust him. It's Eileen who ensures that Ginger and Delaney have some privacy for the consummation of their firestorm, keeping the *Pyr* from following or listening by telling them to breathe dragonsmoke instead.

In **Whisper Kiss**, Eileen helps Erik to realize that he's been beguiled. She drives Erik's Maserati for the first time when they take Zoë to Niall's firestorm in New York, and Zoë casts dreams to the *Pyr* on the way. She and the other mates (and children) are defended by Thorolf when the *Pyr* lure Chen into a trap with his brand.

In **Darkfire Kiss**, when Eileen and Zoë remain with Sloane while

Erik confronts Lorenzo about being beguiled, she complains about the burden of expectation on her daughter. She goes to London with Erik and Zoë for Rafferty's firestorm and is the one who encourages the *Pyr* to consider Melissa's suggestion that they embrace the fact that their existence has been revealed to humans. She argues with Erik about his conviction that he has to die for the *Pyr* to survive

In **Flashfire**, Sloane takes Eileen and Zoë to Donovan's lair when Erik goes to the firestorm. Eileen, Erik and Zoë all go to Venice for Lorenzo's scale repair.

In **Ember's Kiss**, Eileen and Zoë go to Hawaii with Erik for Brandon's firestorm, and Erik's choice convinces Quinn to bring Sara and their sons. They all take a commercial flight from Chicago, to save the *Pyrs'* strength. Eileen contributes to Liz's explanation of spells and helps to convince Brandon to call his mom, Kay. She stands at the north point of Liz's circle along with Erik when the spell is cast to draw Chen. Eileen is the first to add her voice to Liz's spell and helps Liz to understand how a dragon scale is healed.

In **Serpent's Kiss**, when Erik surrenders the leadership of the *Pyr*, Eileen is supportive of him and his choice. He retrieves the sword from his hoard and Eileen recognizes it:

"You never showed me that one before," Eileen murmured from behind him. Erik barely glanced over his shoulder. She shouldn't have entered his hoard without express invitation, but he supposed none of those old rules mattered much any more.

He lifted the sword from the case, struck again by its incredible weight. He had to support the blade on his palm to hold it horizontally when he turned to face Eileen. At his gesture, she stepped into the hoard, glancing about herself before bending over the blade. She lifted a finger as if to touch it, but her hand hovered over it. "These are runes carved into the blade." She glanced up. "Can you read them?"

"Blessings and protection spells," he said with a shrug, his gaze falling upon the Helm of Awe.

Eileen followed his glance. "But this one in the pommel is important."

"The *Aegishjalmur* is the old name for it," Erik said. "The Helm of Awe."

Eileen looked at him, hard. "That's in a story."

Erik watched her with a smile, loving to see her mind at work. Eileen's specialty was comparative mythology and she knew thousands of stories. He waited while she sought the right one.

It didn't take long. She shook a finger at him. "Sigurd," she said with satisfaction. "The dragon slayer."

"He killed the dragon Fafnir to claim the Helm of Awe," Erik said. He nodded. "Fafnir, the first dragon shifter."

"A man turned to dragon to defend the golden treasure that was more important to him than anything else in the world," Eileen said. She touched the pommel. "And Sigurd fought for this sigil because it gives power in battle, making the bearer invincible."

"Giving the bearer the power to conquer with both physical and psychic force," Erik agreed, eyeing the sword.

"And you have this, why?" Eileen asked. "Because you *Pyr* took it back?"

—from **Serpent's Kiss**

When Erik goes to Thorolf's firestorm, Eileen stays in Chicago with Zoë, defended by Donovan, Quinn and Delaney. Eileen's image appears where Erik's reflection should be when he attends Thorolf's scale repair in Angkor.

In **Firestorm Forever**, Eileen is snuggling Zoë (who is six) when the clone of Boris Vassily attacks Erik's lair, shattering the glass door to the balcony. She cleans up with Alex and Ginger who arrive immediately, thanks to Donovan's sense of foreboding. She persuades Erik to call Sloane to tend his injuries after the dragonfight. She watches Maeve O'Neill's broadcast of the eggs hatching with Isabelle and Zoë, never guessing that the girls will see Rafferty struck down by Marco and the darkfire crystal. She and Erik then drive to California to Sloane's lair with the girls, in the hope that Erik can buttress the song of the Apothecary to heal Rafferty. Eileen recognizes the story of Alinga from Chandra's dream, which leads the *Pyr* to Uluru. She offers to cook for

Thorolf when the *Pyr* hear that he's approaching California, and ends up taking turns with Lee in keeping everyone fed. She and Erik go to visit Lorenzo, where Erik argues with Lorenzo about his plan to beguile Maeve, then leave, only to have Marco manifest near them, carrying Jac and fighting one of the clones. Erik shifts shape to join the battle and Jac demands to be let into the car. She has the antidote, and when she shoots down the clone with the darkfire crystal, Eileen and Erik are convinced that Marco hasn't change to the *Slayer* side after all. She holds Ronnie's new son when Drake's scale is repaired by Quinn.

ELENA VAN VLIET—Ginger Sinclair's mother. She died in a car accident with her husband Sean when Ginger was about a year old. Her family owns a farm near Sinclair Farms where they raise dairy goats.

ELIZABETH—Quinn's beloved wife in colonial America. She was targeted and killed by Ambrose, who locked her in their house and set it aflame, taking advantage of the fact that Quinn was far from home. Although Elizabeth and Quinn did not have a firestorm— and thus no children—she defied her family to marry him out of love. Quinn lost a scale over his love for his first wife. Sara dreams of Elizabeth's death in **Kiss of Fire**.

Elizabeth does not scream and she does not beg for mercy. She has loved with all her heart and soul, and she has been loved in return. And that, for her, is eulogy enough.
—Sara's vision from **Kiss of Fire**

ERIK SORENSSON—A *Pyr*, onyx and silver in dragon form (sometimes described as black and pewter), the leader of the *Pyr*, a pyrotechnics expert who creates large fireworks displays synchronized to music, and the partner of Eileen Grosvenor. In human form, Erik is tall, has dark hair with a bit of silver at his temples, and has a British accent which becomes more pronounced when he is agitated. He is tall and lean, and can be impatient. His affinities are to air and fire, and he was born around 700 AD in Norway. His challenge coin is an Olav Tryggvason silver penny. His lair is in Chicago, and takes the entire top floor of a renovated warehouse. Erik and Eileen's story is told in **Kiss of Fate**.

Erik has had two firestorms, one with Louisa, which resulted in the birth of his son Sigmund Guthrie, and a second one with Eileen, who is the reincarnation of Louisa. He and Eileen have a daughter Zoë, whose coming-of-age story as the next Wyvern is recounted in the *Dragon Diaries* trilogy. Erik has a great affection for his car, a black Lamborghini with the custom plate PYROMAN, and that adoration passes to his daughter, as shown in **Blazing the Trail**. After Zoë is conceived, though, Erik puts his beloved car in storage and drives a black Maserati sedan instead, because it better accommodates a baby seat.

Due to his age and experience, Erik has more abilities than his fellow *Pyr*. In **Kiss of Fire**, for example, he causes a crowd of people to spontaneously part, in order to give Quinn clear view of Sara. This may be a variation of beguiling, but one with which Quinn was not familiar. Erik has an awareness of the other *Pyr* living in the world, as well as a sense of their locations, a skill which he refines over the course of the *Dragonfire* series.

Erik also has some ability to foresee the future which develops over the course of the series: we witnessed a glimmer of this in **Kiss of Fire** when he warned the others that the *Slayers* may have learned some new tricks and not to make assumptions about their powers. What Erik sensed, of course, was the Dragon's Blood Elixir. In **Kiss of Fury**, he admits: "I have dreamed of a dark academy, a place so foul that it has no name." In **Kiss of Fire**, he uses the Dragon's Egg to divine the location of firestorms: in **Kiss of Fury**, Sophie teaches him to use the stone as a scrying glass. After the Dragon's Egg is shattered, in **Kiss of Fate**, Erik uses the ocean as a scrying glass when he's carrying Eileen back to Chicago. In **Winter Kiss**, Eileen fills the kitchen sink and turns out the lights for him to use the surface of the water as a scrying glass.

Erik learns new tricks from the *Slayers*: after Boris shows his use of dragonsmoke as a conduit in **Kiss of Fire**, Erik practices this same feat. In **Kiss of Fury**, he uses it to defeat Sigmund. Niall described the sight of the smoke (which no human would have been able to see) like this:

It seemed to rise up, like a cobra about to strike. No, more like a thousand cobras preparing to strike. The smoke ascended into points, a many-headed hydra with teeth of venom.
— **Kiss of Fury**

Erik also learns how to take dragonfire like Quinn, and use it to fuel his own power. In **Winter Kiss**, Erik laughs at Jorge's volley of dragonsmoke.

Erik has a very long memory and recalls the *Pyr* being guardians of the Vikings' ships, the *drakkir*. He first sailed out with his father, Soren, who subsequently became leader of the *Pyr* and established the Council of Seven. His father was killed during Erik's first firestorm, when the father of his mate, an alchemist, trapped Soren and insisted that he surrender the Philosopher's Stone to be released. Erik had to kill his fatally wounded father to be merciful and the incident haunts him.

In **Whisper Kiss**, Erik realizes that he has been beguiled, something that he didn't believe was possible, in order to forget Gaspar, a contemporary of his father's, and that *Pyr's* line. He believes that the *Pyr* behind it is Gaspar's son, Salvatore, who was Erik's friend and had a talent for beguiling (like his father). Once again, Erik learns by example, knowing that a dragon shifter can be beguiled, he beguiles Chen into destroying the brand that *Slayer* been using to control the shadow dragons.

Lorenzo, the son of Salvatore, is responsible for the beguiling of Erik and Erik confronts him in **Darkfire Kiss.** Erik asks Lorenzo to join the *Pyr* but Lorenzo refuses. He also employs an illusion with mirrors to disorient Erik and challenges Erik about gathering the other *Pyr*, like Brandt. Erik sends Sloane—who is Brandt's cousin—to ask that *Pyr* to rejoin the others, even though both Erik and Sloane have promised to leave Brandt alone. He believes it's worth breaking the promise because of the dire situation, and thinks that Brandt is less likely to injure Sloane than himself. He's right: Brandt comes to fight with Erik about the command. Given the fact that the *Pyr* have been revealed in the video of Thorolf and Melissa's pictures of Rafferty and Mallory, Erik concludes that he must die and the *Pyr* have a new leader to conquer the darkfire. He also argues with Rafferty about that *Pyr* sharing information with Melissa. Erik and Brandt fight but reconcile over their shared concern for the humans that Magnus is attacking at the same time, and for Brandt's son, Brandon. Erik then helps to save London, fighting against Magnus to keep that *Slayer* from opening the Thames Barrier. Erik creates the Covenant to manage how the *Pyr* reveal themselves to humans in future.

In **Flashfire**, Erik confronts Lorenzo in his dressing room, knowing that Lorenzo's firestorm has sparked and inviting him to help the *Pyr*. Lorenzo refuses and they argue, until Erik realizes that Lorenzo is more committed to his mate than he wants the leader of the *Pyr* to know. Erik has a vision of Sigmund and Angelina (Lorenzo's dead mother) and realizes that Salvatore is going to die. Lorenzo asks for Erik's help in defending Cassie from *Slayers*, confessing at the same time that he had the third darkfire crystal in his hoard but that it's gone. Erik helps Lorenzo to ensure that his father's corpse is exposed to all of the elements, by posing as the driver of a hearse. He finds a beguiled Cassie and guesses Chen's plan to create Dragon Bone Powder from Salvatore's remains. He breaks the power of Chen's beguiling over Cassie and helps her escape for the big finish.

At the beginning of **Ember's Kiss**, Erik tells Sloane to go to Brandon's firestorm in Hawai'i but instructs Brandt to stay away. He goes to Quinn, wanting to consult with the Smith about the firestorm and learns that Sara has received a prophecy. While there, Quinn shows him a bronze mirror he's been making and Erik uses it as a scrying glass. He perceives that the mates and children will be safe, so Quinn agrees to go to the firestorm with him. Niall also goes with them, as do Eileen, Zoë, Sara, Garrett, Ewan, Rox, along with the twins Kyle and Nolan (who aren't named in that book). When Liz casts her circle, she assigns Erik to the north cardinal point.

In **Kiss of Danger**, Erik is arriving at Lorenzo's home when Drake comes to collect the darkfire crystal. In **Kiss of Destiny**, Drake is returned to Chicago by the extinguished darkfire crystal, without his men, and recognizes that he is near Erik's lair. He goes there to recover from his ordeal and share his story, and is still there when the descendants of the Dragon Legion seek him out. While he sleeps, Erik sees the footage of Jorge shaking a severed arm over a crowd, scattering blood over them.

In **Serpent's Kiss**, Erik is taunted by Chen when the *Slayer* steals JP from his prison. He begins to doubt his ability to lead the *Pyr* and forbids Rafferty to go to Thorolf, after Thorolf has attacked Rafferty. They argue and Rafferty insists on supporting Thorolf during his firestorm. Erik fears the firestorm has been faked by Chen to lure the *Pyr*. When it's clear they won't agree, Erik tries to surrender the leadership of the *Pyr* to Rafferty. All the same, Erik is one of the five *Pyr* listed by Marco and Lorenzo when they create an alliance against Chen—Thorolf and Brandon complete the list.

It's revealed that Erik has the sword known as the Avenger of the Aesir in his hoard, entrusted to him by Thorolf's father, Thorvald, after Thorolf refused its burden (and obligation.) Delaney, Erik, Brandon and Sloane fly the sword to Bangkok for Thorolf, since there's no way they'll get it through airport security or be able to ship it to him in time. Erik attends Thorolf's scale repair in Angkor where the *Pyr* confirm him as their leader again.

In **Firestorm Forever**, Erik has a vision from Sigmund about the blood moon ripening eggs, but doesn't understand it. He's attacked in his lair by Boris Vassily, the *Slayer* he believes to be dead, then by a second identical *Slayer*. He's injured but Donovan and Delaney come to his assistance. The footage of his battle is presented by Maeve O'Neill as a sign of the *Pyr's* indifference to human life. Erik later helps in the healing of Rafferty, chanting the Cantor's song with Sloane and breathing dragonsmoke. When the *Pyr* discover that Marco has the darkfire crystal, Erik fears that the Sleeper has changed sides and forbids the *Pyr* to defend his firestorm.

Erik goes to Lorenzo before that *Pyr* has an interview with Maeve O'Neill, and learns that Lorenzo intends to beguile the journalist. He smells Jorge's scent on Maeve's card before Jac flags them down with another of Boris' clones in pursuit. Erik and Marco battle the clone, and Erik sees the proof that Marco hasn't turned Slayer (his blood runs red). Jac uses the darkfire crystal to incinerate the clone. Marco and Jac use the heat of their firestorm to heal Erik's wounds. Erik has a vision of both Sigmund and Tynan, the former Apothecary, while standing in Lee's spiral garden at Sloane's home. He makes his stand against the clones at Quinn's home near Traverse City, with Marco, Quinn, Donovan and Lorenzo, on the final eclipse of the Dragon's Tail. Two *Slayers* attack them there and are destroyed. The *Pyr* gather at Erik's lair at the end of **Firestorm Forever**, for a celebratory flight and their last televised appearance.

ERINYES, THE—three sisters of Greek mythology and maiden goddesses of vengeance, also known as the Furies. They are Alecto (endless), Mageara (jealous rage) and Tisiphone (vengeful destruction). They hear complaints from mortals against other mortals and punish the culprits by harassing them. In **Kiss of Darkness**, Damien kills Tisiphone in the underworld, although Hades later revives her. In **Kiss of Destiny,** Hera limits Tisiphone's ability to avenge herself upon the *Pyr*, decreeing that she must wait for the darkfire to burn first. Tisiphone takes the form of Viv Jason while she waits in our world, but she remains a powerful immortal.

EVERETT—A *Slayer*, noted for being particularly large, who is turquoise and silver in his dragon form. We never see Everett in human form, but presumably, he is just as large. He holds the Wyvern captive in **Kiss of Fire**, and Donovan notes that he's particularly mean and not very bright. Everett is killed in **Kiss of Fire**, though his *Slayer* friend Tyson tries to avenge his death in **Kiss of Fury**.

EWAN TYRRELL—the second son of Quinn and Sara, born February 21, 2011.

FRED—Lorenzo's burly backstage doorman in **Flashfire**. Fred lets Cassie return backstage when she brings him a bottle of Scotch and does crowd control when the python escapes, again.

GARRETT TYRRELL—oldest son of Quinn and Sara, and heir to the role of Smith of the *Pyr*. Garrett is the first born of the new generation of *Pyr*, conceived during the Dragon's Tail Wars. Garrett was conceived during Quinn and Sara's firestorm, in **Kiss of Fire**, and was born April 16, 2008. Garrett shows promise early, responding to Zoë's urging that he retrieve a dish of mercury in **Winter Kiss**. He is then tutored by Quinn in old-speak, first seen in **Whisper Kiss** as Quinn lands in New York and tells Garrett about the legacy of the firestorm. As a young boy in the *Dragonfire* series, Garrett frequently mimics his father, both breathing fire and raising his hands in a echo of the traditional fighting pose. He also appears in the *Dragon Diaries* trilogy, where it is revealed that he's garnet and gold in his dragon form.

GARY—the owner of the organic food store who Rox convinces to give Thorolf a job as a delivery person in **Whisper Kiss**. Thorolf instead chooses to apprentice with Niall and learn more about being *Pyr*. Subsequently, Neo's apprentice, Jimmy, takes the job.

GASPAR—a *Pyr*, born around 650 A.D., a mercenary and a bon vivant. He was a member of Soren's High Council of Seven. Gaspar was dark-haired and dashing in his human form, very popular with women, charming and completely disinterested in commitment of any kind. He worked for whatever warlord paid the best and seduced whatever woman was in his vicinity. He never spent two nights with the same woman. His affinity was with air and he was renowned for his ability to beguile—which might have been a contributing factor to his amorous success.

Gaspar had a firestorm with a titled Venetian gentlewoman, Giovanna di Fiore, but he abandoned her after satisfying the firestorm, even to the point of leaving Venice completely. Giovanna pined for Gaspar but he refused any contact with her or his son, Salvatore. Giovanna's father adopted his grandson as his own son, and raised him with every advantage in his own house, giving Salvatore his surname di Fiore. When Salvatore came of age an into his shifting powers, Soren argued with Gaspar about the boy's training. When Gaspar still refused to acknowledge his son and teach him of his own nature, Soren dispatched his own son, Erik, to Venice to tutor Salvatore.

In **Whisper Kiss**, when Ginger is trying to compile a list of all dead *Pyr* (to identify potential shadow dragons), Erik can't recall Gaspar. He and Eileen realize that he's been beguiled, and Erik assumed it was done by Salvatore, who knows him well and is particularly skilled with beguiling. Actually, the beguiling was done by Lorenzo, Salvatore's son, to ensure that the *Pyr* can't find and recruit him.

GAULTIER—husband of Maria. This older couple adopted Quinn Tyrrell when his family was killed and raised him as their own son. He only left their home after they died.

GEOFF DAVENPORT—an interior designer in California and fan of Rafferty's antiquities shop in London. Melissa's brother, Matt, recognizes Rafferty's name from the call display when she telephones him and asks if it's the same man.

GINGER SINCLAIR—A chef turned organic dairy farmer, married to Delaney Shea, mother of Liam and Sean. Ginger is petite and curvy. She has long curly coppery gold hair, blue eyes and Delaney thinks she always looks like she's on the verge of laughter. She introduces herself as "eternal bridesmaid, go-to party organizer and best chef in four counties." Ginger grew up at Sinclair Farms, then left to train as a chef in the city. Although she had an excellent job with a restaurant, she didn't like city life much: when her grandmother confessed that the farm was becoming too much work for her, Ginger returned to Ohio. She put her mark on the farm by going organic, adding automations and innovations in the milking barn, and adding heritage varieties of cows to the herd. She built a lucrative business in bull semen and sells the milk of the Guernseys at a premium to her friend and local cheesemaker Tanya. Ginger and Delaney's story is told in **Winter Kiss**.

In **Whisper Kiss**, Ginger is working with Erik to helping Niall track down the remaining shadow dragons by compiling a spreadsheet of all dead *Pyr* that could have been raised from the dead because they weren't exposed to the four elements. She and Delaney think that Erik is ignoring her questions about Gaspar's children.

In **Darkfire Kiss**, Ginger and Delaney meet the *Pyr* in Michigan for Rafferty's scale repair and take Liam along. In **Flashfire**, Ginger and Delaney come to Venice for the repair of Lorenzo's scale. In **Serpent's Kiss**, Ginger stays at Sloane's lair with the boys while Delaney goes to Thorolf's firestorm.

In **Firestorm Forever**, after Boris' clones appear in Chicago, Donovan, Alex, Niall, Rox and their boys go to Delaney and Ginger's farm in Ohio to ensure that they're all defended.

GIOVANNA DI FIORE—a Venetian noblewoman, the mate of Gaspar and the mother of Salvatore di Fiore. When Gaspar left her and their infant son, her father adopted Salvatore and gave him the family surname.

GRAN—Ginger Sinclair's grandmother, who is given no other name in **Winter Kiss**. A practical and somewhat fierce woman, she raised Ginger after the death of her son and daughter-in-law in a car accident. Her husband had died shortly after their son's marriage, but Gran continued to run the farm, renting the tillage to her neighbor, Silas Hargreaves, in exchange for fodder for her dairy cows. She passed away after Ginger returned to the farm from the city and chef school, leaving it all to Ginger.

GREG—One of Niall's tour leaders, Greg is said by Niall and Barry to be sensible and responsible. He's leading a Silk Road tour which has been caught up in a violent snowstorm in Mongolia in **Darkfire Kiss**, and has led the group to refuge in a caravansary—although there's no contact to be had with the group, Niall uses his dreamwalker ability to check on them.

HADRIAN—one of the *Pyr* of the Dragon Legion who appear at Erik's lair at the end of **Kiss of Destiny** and who volunteers to help

Drake save Veronica from Jorge in **Firestorm Forever**. He also helps to guard Timmy. He has auburn hair and green eyes. Hadrian is emerald and silver in his dragon form, although that is not noted in *Dragonfire*. He has his firestorm in **Dragon's Mate** in the *DragonFate* series.

HAZEL WENTWORTH, DR.—a marine biologist who Liz knows by reputation. They meet at a party during the symposium at the research center when Chen is stalking Liz, and Liz agrees to send some of her unpublished papers to the senior researcher.

HERA—the ancient goddess of hearth and home, Hera intervenes in **Kiss of Destiny** to limit Tisiphone's powers in taking vengeance upon the *Pyr*. The Garden of the Hesperides is her sanctuary and she shows mercy to the pilgrim who has climbed there to pray for her intervention. Hera also turned a nymph who was Aura's mother into a tree with silver leaves outside the Garden of the Hesperides, at that nymph's request, because she had been raped by Zeus and was with child. The child nymph (Aura) was given the gift of foresight by Hera so that she could avoid her mother's fate. Hera does save the pilgrim and ensure that he heals, giving him the task of working in the Garden of the Hesperides when he insists upon serving her in gratitude. She also gives Aura the gift of mortality so that she can be Thad's mate and bear his son.

IGNATIO—Ignatio or Iggy is one of the Dragon's Tooth Warriors. Iggy is described as tall, young, and lanky, and he often teases his fellows. Alexander notes that Iggy's bantering manner means that he's often underestimated in battle, and that he is an excellent warrior. Iggy is first named in **Kiss of Danger**.

ISAAC—Samantha Wilcox's mentor and former supervisor at the CDC in **Firestorm Forever**. He's blunt and driven, as well as a brilliant researcher. He challenges her to come back to work and help in the effort to find an antidote in time for Veronica Maitland.

ISABELLE—The adopted daughter of Rafferty Powell and Melissa Smith. She is human, and the reincarnation of Sophie, the Wyvern.

In **Darkfire Kiss**, the battle with the *Slayers* causes destruction in

London and Sophie encounters the soul of a little girl whose parents have been killed. The little girl—Isabelle—wants to follow her parents to the afterlife, while Sophie wants to become incarnate to find Nikolas and help the *Pyr*. The girls decide to switch places, and Sophie slips into Isabelle's body. She then seeks out Rafferty, knowing she'll forget the transaction. She tells him that she's Sophie and indicates the black and white ring he wears. (While Zoë often touches the ring, Isabelle never touches it.) She asks him and Melissa to adopt her, advising him to call her Isabelle in future. Rafferty isn't convinced it can happen so easily as that, but the darkfire seems to be on his side, because he and Melissa do get permission to adopt Isabelle. Sara also recognizes Isabelle as the little girl from a dream she had about the Wyvern.

In **Flashfire**, Isabelle comes to Venice for the repair of Lorenzo's scale with Melissa and Rafferty. In **Serpent's Kiss**, Melissa and Rafferty leave Isabelle with Eileen at Erik's lair in Chicago while they help with Thorolf's firestorm. Isabelle's image appears in the pool where Rafferty and Melissa's reflections should be when the *Pyr* gather in Angkor for the repair of Thorolf's scale. In **Firestorm Forever,** Isabelle stays with Erik and Eileen again, as Rafferty and Melissa battle the negative publicity being generated by Maeve O'Neill. She sees Rafferty struck by the darkfire during the broadcast. Erik and Eileen take Isabelle and Zoë to Sloane's house in California before the final battle to ensure their safety.

Isabelle is also a character in the *Dragon Diaries* trilogy—Zoë is initially jealous of her because she's older and because Nick Shea is fascinated with her. The two girls later are good friends, just as they were when they were younger.

JACELYN (JAC) WILCOX—The younger sister of Samantha Wilcox and the mate of Marco, Jac first appears in **Firestorm Forever**. She has long, dark hair and blue eyes. Devastated by her nephew's death, Jac is determined to avenge Nathaniel. She feels responsible because she was taking care of Nathaniel when Jorge appeared and her nephew was infected. She moves to Seattle, the epicenter of the plague brought by Jorge, intending to hunt dragons. She begins a notebook, compiling information about the *Pyr*, and meets Marco, who has moved into an apartment in her building, when he delivers a parcel to her. (There is a continuity error in the original edition of **Firestorm Forever**. It says that Marco moved into the apartment below Jac's, but later, Marco hears what Jac is watching on television through his floor, indicating that his apartment is above hers.) Jac recognizes Marco because they work out at the same gym. The parcel contains the copy of Sigmund's book, *Habits and Habitats of Dragons: A Compleat Guide for Slayers*.

Although Marco acts as if he's passing along a package that was delivered to the lobby, maybe as an excuse to meet Jac, he's actually giving the book to Jac so she has more information to hunt dragons. Marco has researched Jac and realized her connection to the first victim of the plague. As custodian of the darkfire, he favors unpredictable choices and wonders whether Jac's thirst for vengeance might allow her to surprise Jorge. He keeps watch over her, knowing that if she does confront Jorge, she'll lose, no matter how much she works out.

Jac compiles a list in her notebook of everything she can discover about dragon shifters, from Maeve's website (*Dragons Bite*) to Melissa's documentaries, YouTube videos and the book Marco gave her. She's seeking weaknesses and not finding many, so she goes to Marco, hoping he knows more. Marco's apartment is empty, except for the darkfire crystal on the window sill—and a prophecy written on the wall with a Sharpie marker. He tells her that the darkfire crystal can kill dragons, letting her conclude that they both want to hunt dragons, and invites her to go to Easter Island with him (where the *Pyr* are battling the clones.) Jac agrees on impulse. En route to the airport, she asks Marco about the writing on the wall of his apartment, thinking it's a poem, and he recites it to her so she can add it to her book.

On Easter Island, it's Jac who grabs the darkfire crystal from Marco and uses it to injure Rafferty. Marco shifts shape and intervenes before Rafferty's human identity is revealed, carrying him away from the crowds, then using the darkfire to spontaneously manifest at Sloane's home so Rafferty can be treated by the Apothecary. Marco is so upset about Rafferty's injury—and that he's partly responsible, since he trusted Jac—that he breaks it off with Jac. She's disappointed that he's like all the other guys who dump her after sex and calls Sam for help with the cost of getting home. She and Sam reconcile a little and Jac agrees to stop in California on her way home.

Jac goes to a restaurant for dinner on Easter Island, witnesses Maeve and Jorge's first glimpse of each other, then is chatted up by Jorge, who recognizes her as the woman who injured Rafferty. Thinking that they're fellow dragon hunters, Jac reveals to Jorge that she has Sigmund's book, that Marco lives in the apartment over hers and that there's a prophecy written on the wall of Marco's apartment. Jorge lies that he lives in Portland and suggests they connect in a couple of weeks, and Jac gives him her address.

Marco, meanwhile, is trying to figure out how Jac was able to fire the darkfire crystal, since she's neither *Pyr* nor a Firedaughter. He returns to witness Jac walking with Jorge. Jorge senses Marco and leaves, and Marco, without revealing his presence to Jac, weaves a dragonsmoke barrier around the small hotel. He then sits vigil to protect her, knowing that he's at least partly to blame for her being in danger. The entire situation leaves him distrusting darkfire and unwilling to use it.

In California, Jac and Sam reconcile, finally begin talking out the issues between them. Jac takes after their mother, the romantic and the caregiver, the one who surrenders her own plans and goals to support those she loves. Jac returns to Seattle to find that her apartment has been robbed and Sigmund's book is gone. She assumes Marco retrieved it and allies with Jorge to fight dragons. He has booked her travel to Australia so she'll be at Uluru on the night of the eclipse. Marco follows Jac and she lets him into her rental cottage: they make love then their firestorm sparks with the eclipse. Marco shifts under the light of the eclipse, revealing himself to Jac as a dragon shifter. She recognizes the firestorm for what it is, thanks to Sigmund's book, and runs. Jorge gives her a ride, then shifts shape and Jac recognizes him as the dragon who spread the plague that killed Nathaniel. When Marco intervenes to save her, Jac uses the flares from the glovebox as weapons against

Jorge, tossing one into his mouth as he attacks. She does the same with a second flare, taking out one of the clones, but misses her throw on the third. When Marco appeals to Jorge to give him the Elixir, hoping to trick the *Slayer* into taking him to his lair, Jac is carried along.

Jac finds herself in what she realizes is Jorge's lair, with an unconscious Marco and the *Slayer* whose gut was blown out by her flare. He's rotating between forms and is nearly dead. The lair is an ornate library. She discovers Sigmund's book and realizes that Jorge stole it, along with a vial containing remnants of dried blood and a dark grey thorned scale. She doesn't immediately realize that this is Marco's scale, ripped free by Jorge. She watches Jorge consume the fallen clone and witnesses the effects of the Elixir as he heals. When she hears the subway, he tells her that his lair is the lost library of Ivan the Terrible, somewhere beneath the Kremlin, and reveals that he has the Dracontias, which he discovered there. Jorge smashes the scale, which awakens Marco and as they fight, Jac seizes Sigmund's book and the Dracontias.

Jac kicks Jorge when he turns on her and shoves a burning candle into his eye, giving Marco a moment to catch his breath. She also encourages Marco to put the Dracontias in his mouth, which has an immediate effect on him. Marco uses a dragonsmoke conduit to take energy from Jorge, then spontaneously manifests elsewhere with Jac.

Jac finds herself in a hotel room, with Marco in his human form and the firestorm simmering between them. He takes the Dracontias from his mouth and puts it in a glass of mouthwash but neither of them notice that it turns the mouthwash to water. They're in Virginia, near Sam's home. Despite temptation, Jac declines to satisfy the firestorm, because she knows it will result in a conception, and she's tired of being useful to others. She tells Marco that she wants to be loved, and will conceive only in love, and tells him about being the caregiver for her mom at the end, and about being taken for granted by her ambitious sister and father. Marco takes that as a challenge to win her heart—because Jac, with her bravery, loyalty and unpredictability, has restored his faith in the darkfire and the firestorm. He shares his own history with her, confiding in her, and she challenges him to survive the *Pyr's* final battle before they decide about the firestorm. She doesn't want to raise a child alone, and Marco respects that. They agree to take the Dracontias to Sam, in the hope that it will aid in her search for an antidote. Sam tells Jac that it's a foolish idea, although she keeps the stone.

In the meantime, Brandon, Chandra and Liz have followed Jac's scent to the hotel room she shared with Marco at Yulara and find her dragon hunter compilation of information about the *Pyr*. The fact that she's Marco's mate feeds their doubt about Marco and his loyalty to the *Pyr*. In order to give Jac the ability to defend herself, Marco takes the darkfire crystal from Sloane's home, impulsively bringing Rafferty to his firestorm as well. Jac and Marco use the firestorm to help heal Rafferty, and Jac has the idea that they should use it to attract *Slayers*, in order to kill them and improve the *Pyr's* chances of success in the final battle. One of the clones comes to them and proposes an alliance with Marco, suggesting that they recreate the Elixir with Jorge as the source, and rule jointly. Marco pretends to agree, planning to defend Erik and betray Boris' clone. Jac is enthusiastic about destroying Jorge.

Jac and Marco use their firestorm to help Erik when he's injured by the clone of Boris and when Marco loses a scale, Jac knows what it means and catches it. They consummate the firestorm and after the final battle, they buy the house in California from Sam, becoming Sloane's neighbors. They ultimately have three sons, although none are mentioned in *Dragonfire*: Maximilian, Powell and Rafferty.

JARED MADISON—nephew of Alex Madison and Donovan Shea, who witnessed dragons fighting as a young boy. He was defended by Sloane during Alex and Donovan's firestorm, when *Slayers* were seeking Alex's vulnerabilities.

We meet Jared again in *The Dragon Diaries*, when he plays in a band and Zoë becomes enthralled with him. He grew up with a fascination of dragons (and conviction that they are good), and was mentored by Donovan when he earned his own father's disapproval. Jared learned to fix motorcycles from Donovan and was given a bike of his own by that *Pyr*. He calls Zoë 'dragon girl' and annoys her with his greater understanding of Wyverns—and his tendency to be elusive.

JEAN—A *Pyr*, the oldest son of Thierry and Margaux, and oldest brother of Quinn Tyrrell. Jean should have been the next Smith, but he was killed by Ambrose before his wounded father's eyes. Since he was exposed to all four elements immediately after his death, he was not raised as a shadow dragon.

JEAN-PIERRE (AKA JP)—A *Slayer*, son of Mallory, and a renegade. JP is yellow topaz and silver in dragon form. In human form, he appears to be in his thirties, has dark blonde hair and speaks with a French accent. The killing of his younger brother, the *Slayer* Lucien, by the *Pyr* in **Kiss of Fire** made JP turn *Slayer* to seek revenge. The killing of his father by Jorge turned him against *Slayers*.

JP first appears in **Flashfire**, where he's been enchanted by Chen and has become the *Slayer*'s minion. Chen controls him with Dragon Bone Powder, in limited quantities, which JP uses as a stimulant. JP tries to charm his way into friendship with Cassie and Stacey. When Lorenzo finds JP with Cassie, Lorenzo beguiles the *Slayer* and warns him off. JP beguiles and ultimately seduces Stacy, Cassie's friend and travel companion, but Chen becomes impatient with JP's progress and brands him, making him a slave. JP helps Chen in the abduction of Cassie and is beaten by Lorenzo in the final battle. Erik takes the wounded JP into his custody where he remains throughout **Ember's Kiss**.

At the beginning of **Serpent's Kiss**, JP is still imprisoned in an apartment beneath Erik's loft in Chicago. Erik believes JP is dying of Chen's magic, but it's possibly the lack of Elixir that is destroying him. Chen spontaneously manifests in the makeshift prison to abduct JP and Erik catches only a glimpse of the *Slayer*, in his guise as a young man. Chen kills JP, using that *Slayer's* blood, which has the Elixir in it, to tattoo Thorolf in an attempt try to force Thorolf to turn *Slayer*.

JORGE—The most ruthless and mercenary of *Slayers*, yellow topaz and gold in dragon form, Jorge is blond in human form with pale blue eyes. Melissa describes him as looking like a "homicidal Viking" and remembers him as Magnus' muscle from Magnus' arms dealing days in the Middle East. Jorge first appears in the finale of **Kiss of Fury** with Magnus, when Magnus tries to destroy Alex's Green Machine.

Jorge is one of the *Slayers* sent by Magnus to steal the Dragon's Teeth from the Fonthill-Fergusson Foundation in **Kiss of Fate**, and kills Teresa. He stalks Eileen, working with Mallory and Balthasar, and doesn't back down from a confrontation with Magnus—he taunts Magnus, saying that if they fight to the death and Magnus wins, then Magnus will make him a shadow dragon and thus an invincible foe. Magnus recognizes the merit of this argument and challenges Jorge to learn to partially shift, letting only his nail turn to a talon. Later in the book, when Magnus is impaled on a spike by Erik and unable to free himself, Jorge negotiates with Magnus for his first sip of the Dragon's Blood Elixir. They retreat to the sanctuary together, then in the final battle with the *Pyr* at the end of that book, Jorge abandons Magnus to pursue the fleeing shadow dragons.

In **Winter Kiss**, Jorge is one of the three *Slayers* defending Magnus in his home in Ohio: the others are Balthasar and Mallory. Delaney calls Jorge one of Magnus' favorites and Magnus notes that Jorge is more golden in his dragon form due to regular sips of the Elixir. At this point, Magnus is looking for a second-in-command, while Jorge is hoping to assume command of the *Slayers* in Magnus' stead. Jorge abducts Ginger at Magnus' command, and his leg is severed from his body. Magnus withholds Elixir when Jorge demands more than a sip, in an attempt to remind the *Slayer* who is in command.

In **Darkfire Kiss**, we learn that Jorge retreated to Moscow for reconstructive surgery on his severed leg after events in **Winter Kiss**. We also learn that he had been stealing Elixir from Magnus to build a secret stash, and that Chen has stolen the last of it from Jorge. Chen sealed Jorge in his own lair with potent dragonsmoke and desperate for more Elixir, Jorge consumes the hibernating Mallory for the residue of Elixir in his body. Once freed, Jorge and Magnus match wits, each intending to use the same strategy on the other. Jorge also follows Donovan to Bardsey Island and locates the Sleeper—he taunts Magnus to come to him, and when Magnus is defeated by Donovan, Jorge consumes him, so fixed on his feast that he lets the *Pyr* seal him into the cavern with his prey.

In **Flashfire**, Erik realizes that Jorge is no longer entombed on Bardsey Island. In **Ember's Kiss**, Jorge reappears, convinced he can outwit Chen and secure more Elixir. He manifests in Chen's lair in Hale`iwa and finds a spell cast on the floor. He doesn't understand the large spiral of sand but is aware of its power. He takes one of the three dragon scales in the middle, believing he'll be able to bargain with Chen for its return. Jorge challenges Chen in the beach bar, compelling him to shift shape, which reveals the *Slayer's* nature to Brandon. Jorge then attacks Liz, hoping to eliminate Brandon's mate and weaken him further. Liz, however, as a Firedaughter, fights back, until Marco appears in dragon form and fights Jorge. When Brandon goes to Chen's lair and discovers the spell laid against him, he tries to reclaim his dragon scales, but Jorge manifests in Chen's lair. Jorge breaks two scales to cause Brandon pain but before he can break the third, Brandon shifts to fight. Jorge crumbles one scale to dust then steals Brandon's power with dragonsmoke. Brandon pretends to be more injured than he is and rotates between forms, knowing that Jorge will manifest elsewhere once he thinks the battle is over. When Jorge shimmers, just before he disappears, Brandon seizes him and is taken along. They manifest at Ka`ena Point and fight again—when Brandon realizes that Jorge's wings are destroyed, he seizes the *Slayer* and carries him far out to sea before dropping him. Jorge reappears at Liz's final test and seizes Garrett, but Liz fires the darkfire crystal at him and he releases the boy. He tries to negotiate with Brandon for Chen's corpse, offering a sip of the Elixir in exchange, but is claimed by Pele instead and taken back into the volcano as her captive.

In the Dragon Legion novella, **Kiss of Danger**, Jorge appears in the ancient world with the plan to enslave the ancestors of the *Pyr*. He tries to buy Lysander, the son of Alexander, as a slave, but is thwarted by Pelias taking the boy to train at Sparta before the sale can be completed. He has already enslaved Theo, the son of Drake, by the time Alexander fights in defense of both Pelias and Lysander. He's fed Elixir to Theo and is using the young *Pyr* as a source. Jorge seems to have chosen to return to the future when he's defeated, but reappears at the end of the story in the sanctuary of Apollo at Delphi in a last attempt to seize Theo. The darkfire sparks, hitting Jorge like lightning, and he disappears.

In **Kiss of Destiny**, Jorge tries to aid Tisiphone in her fight with Thad, but Hera intervenes. He smells the illness in the pilgrim who has come to Hera's sanctuary in hope of intervention and takes the pilgrim's arm back to the present day. He knows the illness to be highly infectious and deadly, and that it will have no known cure in the modern world. He begins a plague by shaking the arm and scattering drops of infectious blood over the a crowd, then manifests in Chen's lair.

In **Serpent's Kiss**, Jorge tries to make an alliance with Lorenzo, offering to save Thorolf if Lorenzo beguiles Chen. Although Lorenzo's beguiling isn't entirely successful, when Chen is at the point of death, Jorge begins to devour him, claiming the Elixir that is within his body.

In **Firestorm Forever**, Jorge leaves Chen's lair with his feast during an earthquake, hoping to be somewhere safe. He manifests in the lost library of Ivan the Terrible and makes it his lair. Jorge seizes four of the clones of Boris Vassily, intending to consume the Elixir within them, but one (Boris IV) escapes. Jorge then takes Veronica captive after Veronica and Drake satisfy the firestorm, planning to claim the son that she doesn't realize she's carrying and turn him *Slayer*. He stages an attack against Erik, sending the clones, while he trashes Sloane's lab and steals the vial of infectious blood so Sloane can't find an antidote. Drake and the Dragon Legion attempt to save Veronica and in the battle, but Jorge threatens to spill the infected sample over the people gathered to watch. Drake attacks at Veronica's insistance, Reed is killed and Jorge triumphs, taking Veronica to Chen's old lair along with the three clones. He lets her watch him consume the one wounded *Slayer* clone. He beguiles the second, compelling him to challenge the third to a blood duel, and chats with Veronica as they watch the fight and he snacks.

When Jorge sees the flicker of darkfire, he leaves Veronica in the custody of the last clone and goes to a bar in Sydney in his human guise. He sees the footage of the Jac attacking Rafferty on Easter Island and Marco's rescue, then goes to Easter Island himself to befriend Jac. He learns not only where she lives, but where Marco lives and that she has Sigmund's book. Jorge retreats when he senses Marco's presence, then awaits Marco in his apartment. He burns a spiral into the floor, attacks Marco with dragonsmoke, then vanishes with Sigmund's book. Jorge then deliberately infects Veronica with the virus and releases her, breaking her fingers so she can't write and strangling her so that her throat is too bruised for her to speak. He hopes to infect more people when they try to help her, but Drake intervenes and Veronica is isolated.

Still allied with Jac, Jorge arranges for her to hunt dragons at Uluru but after Jac flees Marco, Jorge's true nature is revealed to her. He taunts her to kill him, but gets more than anticipated when Marco helps her and she throws a lit flare down his throat. Jorge loses the lower half of his jaw, but seizes both Marco and Jac, taking them to his new lair. There, Jac sees the power of the Elixir as he consumes a fallen clone and his jaw grows back. Sigmund's book is there and Jac steals it, along with the Dracontias, when she and Marco escape, destroying Jorge's lair in the process. Boris IV steals the dead clone that Jorge needs to restore the Elixir in his body and the pair battle over it in Okhotny Ryad station.

When Jorge rejuvenates himself with dragonsmoke, he seeks refuge in Maeve's Manhattan brownstone. The pair make an alliance after Jorge breaks Drake's scale to prove his animosity toward the *Pyr*. He doesn't realize that Maeve doesn't acknowledge the distinction between *Pyr* and *Slayer* but wants all dragon shifters exterminated. Maeve shows him her collection of trophies from species she's exterminated. She offers him immortality for helping her eliminate the *Pyr*. Jorge claims one of the *falsa* about to hatch a clone of Boris at Machu Picchu in the final battle, and looses two clones into the fight. Sloane fights him, then injects him with the antidote to the Elixir: Jorge is missing a scale over his hip and realizes in his dying moments that Maeve claimed it from him. He also drops the stylus to open doors between realms that Maeve has given to him. The *Pyr* expose his corpse to the four elements, so Jorge is eliminated in the final battle.

JULIANE—the anchor person who is on-air when Melissa covers the story of the *Slayer* attack on London. Because she welcomes Melissa back to the network, we know that they have worked together before.

KADE—one of the *Pyr* who follow Theo and arrive at Erik's lair at the end of **Kiss of Destiny**. He is first mentioned by name in **Firestorm Forever**, where he is one of the volunteers who help Drake to save Veronica from Jorge. At the end of **Firestorm Forever**, Kade is given the magic stylus by Maeve O'Neill—when it is used to draw a door, the pen can open a portal to the realm of the Fae. Kade uses it to open a portal to Fae at the bar, Bones, in **Dragon's Kiss** in the *DragonFate* series.

KATINA—the mate and lost love of Alexander, the mother of his son Lysander, and a Waterdaughter. Alexander and Katina's story is told in the Dragon Legion Novella, **Kiss of Danger**. Katina, the mate of Alexander, was offered as a maiden to Apollo at the Korykian Cave of the Nymphs, but was refused. She was given a prophecy instead, and shortly afterward met Alexander at Delphi. She has long dark hair and is a potter, but not a skilled one. She married again after Alexander didn't come home, but at the beginning of **Kiss of Danger**, she still wears the gold ring (set with a carnelian) that Alexander gave her on their wedding day. She also wears the gold band from Cetos. After Pelias dies, she reveals her secret to Alexander to ensure that his mentor's remains can be exposed to all four elements: Katina makes it rain.

KAY MERRICK (NÉE WEATHERBY)—mate of Brandt and mother of Brandon, Kay is separated from her *Pyr* when we first meet her in **Ember's Kiss**. She's reverted to her maiden name, after divorcing Brandt while pregnant with Brandon. She runs a catering business in Australia. She's worried about her only son as there are earthquakes in Hawai`i and he's there to compete. Kay is slim with short blond hair that is going gray. She thought she was right at the time to be horrified by Brandt's ability to become a dragon, but she misses him and wishes she had apologized. Brandon's firestorm coincides with Kay's twenty-fifth Christmas without Brandt and she's feeling a little sentimental when Brandon calls to reconcile and tell her that she's going to be a grandmother. After talking to Brandon, she goes to the beach where she used to meet Brandt and finds him there. They reconcile and go to Hawai`i together to see Brandon compete, and witness his big win.

KEIR SHEA—a *Pyr*, born 1490 in Dublin, a bon vivant, wastrel, adventurer, and ultimately a buccaneer. Keir had a firestorm with Mhairi Connaught in 1551, which resulted in Donovan Shea. Subsequently, in 1563, he returned to Mhairi and she conceived Delaney—Donovan had already run away from home by this point. The brothers met when they were both young *Pyr* and felt an intuitive connection. They believed they must have been related and called each other cousins, but learned the truth centuries later in **Kiss of Fury**.

Keir is silver and peridot in his dragon form, although when he attacks Donovan in **Kiss of Fury**, Donovan has never before seen his father in dragon form. Donovan saw his father only once before that, when he sought him out and found him drunk in a pirate's lair in Tortuga in 1642. His father wasn't *Slayer* then, but he was selfish. Donovan, who had hoped to find a parent he could admire, was disappointed in the reality he found. Keir refused to shift shape anymore, because he'd decided his dragon was evil, but in human form, he wasn't much better. After Donovan left Tortuga, Rafferty sought out Keir there, only to see him killed in a brawl in a tavern before they could talk. Rafferty went to the funeral, to be sure that Keir was dead, and verified with the earth a month later that Keir's corpse was still there. The examination of Keir's former resting place reveals to Alex that three trace minerals remain in the soil when a dead *Pyr* or *Slayer* has been raised with the Elixir.

When Donovan and his father fight in **Kiss of Fury**, he's surprised that his father is impervious to injury and doesn't bleed at all, even when his arm is cut off. Keir has been made into a shadow dragon by Magnus and is the first shadow dragon the *Pyr* encounter. Keir is dismembered by Quinn and Donovan, then incinerated with dragonfire. His condition in that last fight and the fact that Rafferty saw him die in Tortuga helps the *Pyr* to figure out that Magnus has raised the dead. Although Donovan disliked his father intensely, he did inherit some of his father's reckless charm, and until his firestorm, had a similar attitude toward women.

KIRA—One of Brandon's surfer buddies in **Ember's Kiss**, Kira is petite and has dark hair that hangs to her hips and green eyes. She drives a yellow VW bug and was one of the first friends Brandon made in Hawai`i. She's starting a business, designing gear for surfers, and Brandon wears one of her wetsuits as promotion. Her nickname, and the name of her business, is Banzai Baby, a reference to the Banzai Pipeline. Kira's mom was also a surfer and realized she was pregnant with Kira while barreling the pipeline. Kira also has a sense of when the surf will be right on that beach and predicts it perfectly in **Ember's Kiss**.

KRISTOFER—a *Pyr* and one of the company of descendants that arrive at Erik's lair at the end of **Kiss of Destiny**. He follows Theo, the descendant of Drake. He is blond with blue eyes and tall, and is peridot and gold in his dragon form. Kristofer is first mentioned by name in **Firestorm Forever**, when he is one of six volunteers who offer to help Drake save Veronica from Jorge. The others are Arach, Reed, Rhys, Hadrian, Kade, and Theo himself. Kristofer is also one of the three *Pyr* Timmy can call. He has his firestorm in **Dragon's Kiss** in the *DragonFate* series.

KYLE TALBOT—son of Niall and Rox. Kyle and his twin brother, Nolan, were born April 28, 2011.

LADON—A nine-headed dragon, guardian of the golden apples in the Garden of Hesperides in **Kiss of Destiny**. Ladon is dark green in color and only allows nymphs to enter the garden. Aura steals an apple while Thad battles against Ladon. The battle is fierce until Ladon realizes that Thad is *Pyr*—he's heard about the dragon shifters, although he isn't a shifter himself. He asks to witness the firestorm, then challenges Thad about the attack on Cadmus.

LAURIE—a woman who comes to Imagination Ink in **Whisper Kiss** for a memorial tattoo from Rox to commemorate the life of her deceased sister, Anna. During this process, Niall observes Rox at her empathic best. Laurie talks about her sister while Rox does the tattoo, and confides that Anna was the rebel who was always going to get a tattoo. The design is of a Celtic cross with two peonies below it, to symbolize the sisters, and light radiating from behind it. Rox completes it in one long session, as Niall watches.

LEE—Chen's younger brother and the favored son of their father, who first appears in **Serpent's Kiss**. Lee has been imprisoned by Chen, so that he can't challenge Chen's claim of being the last of their line. He is very weak by the time the *Pyr* discover him. Lee has dark hair and dark eyes in his human form. He's gold with pale feathers, red talons, a red belly and red wings in his dragon form.

In **Serpent's Kiss**, Lee is released from his captivity in Chen's lair when Marco breaks the third darkfire crystal. Lee strikes the killing blow against Chen, driving part of the darkfire crystal into his gut and his eye. He is flung from Chen's collapsing lair and manifests on the streets of Bangkok where he finds Thorolf's lost scale. Marco takes him to meet the other *Pyr*. Lee brings the scale to Thorolf's repair at Angkor.

In **Firestorm Forever**, Sam gives Lee a ride to Sloane's shop, where he is welcomed by Thorolf. When Chandra goes into labor, Lee plants a spiral garden with Zoë's help, including plants with spirals in their blooms. They plant calendula in the middle, and sunflowers at the outer edge. Zoë compares the calendula seeds to dragon claws and the sunflower seeds to dragon eyes, and calls it a dragon garden. Lee takes over the management of Sloane's store when he searches for an antidote, and alternates cooking duties with Eileen to feed the house full of *Pyr*. (One morning, he bakes fresh croissants.)

When Drake is injured, Lee recalls the magic of his father, who was a storm-gatherer of great power. He recognizes that Chen's spiral spells were based on their father's magic, and uses the dragon garden as a focal point to draw healing power to Drake. When he chants his father's spell, pearls fall from his lips. When Drake awakens and touches the pearls, they change to raindrops, nurturing the garden, before it begins to rain.

Lee builds a spiral behind Drake's house to draw evil in preparation for the final battle during the eclipse at the end of the Dragon's Tail Wars. Theo, Niall, Delaney, Kristofer and Kade are also there to support Drake and defend his family. Lee, Niall and Delaney inoculate one of Boris' clones, and Lee breathes dragonfire to sear the wound closed. When the *Slayer* dies, the three of them incinerate him and expose his remains to the four elements. Lee attends the repair of Marco and Sloane's scales at the end of the book.

LIAM SHEA—the oldest son of Delaney and Ginger, born November 23, 2009. In the *Dragon Diaries*, he's described as having red hair and green eyes, being fair-skinned and slight. In dragon form, he's malachite and silver with red-gold claws.

LIZ BARRETT—A marine biologist, and mate of Brandon Merrick. Liz is slim and tall with long dark hair and blue eyes. She comes from a line of witches and is a Firedaughter. The women in her family know that they will face a test of their mastery of their ability to command each of the elements and that it will come within three days of a mark appearing on their skin. Liz and Brandon's story is told in **Ember's Kiss**. Like Brandon, Liz has denied her innate talent. Her mother was an Airdaughter and during her mother's test, when her mother's lack of skill in controlling fire became evident, Liz tried to help by casting fire at her mother. Instead, it killed her, and Liz lost her powers for a period after that. She's been determined to live without magic and to never have children, since the power is hereditary (although not the element of primary control). She feels her powers returning when she arrives in Hawai`i and can see auras again.

Liz and Brandon's firestorm sparks on her first night in Hawai`i during the eclipse, outside a restaurant. He later follows the spark of the firestorm to her room and they satisfy the firestorm, then he shifts shape to defend her during an earthquake. When Liz goes to find Brandon later, she gives a ride to a hitchhiker who is an elderly Chinese man. It's Chen and he tells Liz that Brandon is responsible for the earthquake and the son of the fire goddess, Pele, and that there will be more destruction. Liz has her doubts about this story, especially as she can't see Chen's aura. She wonders if he's a ghost. She sees Brandon shift shape to help his friend when they're surfing and knows he isn't evil. She also tries to help him convince his friends that they didn't see a dragon. When Sloane arrives to help Brandon, he beguiles Brandon's friends, revealing that he's *Pyr*, too. Sloane is rebuffed by the younger *Pyr*, but Liz confides in him because she thinks Brandon has been targeted by a binding spell. Sloane inadvertently reveals that consummating the firestorm means that she's conceived and Liz becomes angry with Brandon for not telling her the whole truth. Sloane also tells her that only she and the firestorm can heal Brandon, and that she will have to embrace her powers to do it. She also has a visit from the fire goddess, Pele, telling her much the same thing.

The realization that she's carrying a child makes Liz claim her powers again when she's attacked by Jorge, because she wants her son to live. Marco comes to her assistance and sees her abilities during the battle. He gives her the darkfire crystal, knowing she has the power to use it as a weapon. She uses it against Chen, as well as a binding spell that appears as a lasso of fire, but Chen summons lightning. The bolt of lightning hits Liz on the pentacle pendant that was her mother's and it's destroyed, its mark burned onto her skin. The pentacle has only three points, because Liz's mom didn't succeed at her test. The pendant took the brunt of the blow, and Brandon believes that Liz's mom was protecting her. Liz sears the exposed skin where Brandon has lost his scales, using her powers to help him heal. She suggests to the *Pyr* that they should taunt Chen instead of trying to flee from him, and set a trap to break his spell over Brandon while the *Slayer* is injured and weak.

Liz is also the one who guesses that Brandon was able to give three scales to Chen because he's lost two people he loved, in addition to losing himself. (He loses another out of his love for her.) She and the *Pyr* convince him to call his parents, Kay and Brandt, and re-establish that bond. When she hears about the spiral that was Chen's spell, she knows how to cast her own counter-spell, casting a circle, drawing a spiral that turns in the opposite direction on the beach, and positioning the *Pyr* at the cardinal points to defend them. She assigns Erik to the north, Sloane to the west, Quinn to the south and Niall to the east. The children are inside the circle and Brandon stays in human form as bait. Liz's powerful spell hauls Chen away from an attack on Thorolf, which infuriates the *Slayer*, but Liz's test begins in the middle of the fight. She triumphs, thanks to Brandon's help, and the pentacle mark burned on her skin gets its last two points.

In **Serpent's Kiss**, Marco visits Liz and Brandon. They're awakened to his presence when the darkfire crystal flares and find him in the rocking chair in the bedroom with their two sleeping sons, where the darkfire crystal is on the dresser. Realizing that he wants the crystal, Liz offers it to him and he accepts it, after inviting Brandon to join the team of five *Pyr* allied against Chen. Liz admits to herself that the crystal makes her uncomfortable because she doesn't like the unpredictable prickle of its energy. When Brandon helps the *Pyr* deliver the sword to Thorolf, Liz takes the boys to stay with Kay and Brandt. All of them attend the repair of Thorolf's scale.

In **Firestorm Forever**, Liz feels the quickening of the eggs with the clones of Boris, although she initially doesn't know what it is. She helps with the hunt for more at Uluru and identifies two under the light of the eclipse. She also becomes a being of flame herself when touched by that eclipse's light. In the ensuing fight, Liz sees how Jac uses the flares against the *Slayers* and insists that Marco isn't changing sides, even when she, Brandon and Chandra find

Jac's dragon-hunting journal. They also learn Jac's name from her luggage tag. She and Brandon hunt for dragon eggs in the Pacific between eclipses, then join the *Pyr*—Thorolf, Chandra, Sloane, Brandt, Arach, Melissa and Rafferty—at Machu Picchu for the last battle. She finds and identifies the *falsas* in the hidden chamber, guessing that the clones are inside them. Liz, Brandon and their sons attend the ritual at Erik's loft at the end of the book to repair Sloane and Marco's scales. In the public display afterward, Brandon's repaired scale is touched by the darkfire, indicating that his firestorm will burn forever.

LORENZO DI FIORE—A *Pyr* who is three shades of gold with cabochon gems in dragon form, master illusionist and magician, partner of Cassie Redmond. Lorenzo has dark curly hair and hazel eyes with gold flecks in his human form. Erik thinks he always looks as if he's on the verge of laughter and that he has an irreverence, like his mother. Lorenzo lives outside Las Vegas in comparative seclusion and is known as a perfectionist in his performances. He has no desire to embrace his *Pyr* nature as he thinks it's barbaric.

Lorenzo is the son of Salvatore and takes care of his elderly father. He is the grandson of Gaspar and his affinities are with fire and water. Lorenzo is the most adept of the *Pyr* with beguiling, and also the least enchanted with joining the *Pyr* to fight the Slayers. As a result, the *Slayers* believe him to be their best chance of a recruit. Although Lorenzo doesn't appear in the series until **Darkfire Kiss**, we have a hint of his existence in **Whisper Kiss** when we learn that Erik has been beguiled into forgetting Gaspar's line.

In **Darkfire Kiss**, Erik goes to Lorenzo's home outside Las Vegas to ask him to join the *Pyr*. He also takes issue with Lorenzo for beguiling him. Lorenzo not only declines to rejoin the *Pyr*, but challenges Erik about his leadership choices and messes with Erik's mind, too, meeting him in a hall of mirrors. Lorenzo suggests that the *Slayers* shouldn't be destroyed because the *Pyr* need an enemy—without one, he says they will destroy each other, a statement that troubles Erik. Lorenzo taunts Erik about the ramifications of the released darkfire, obviously knowing more about the unpredictable force than Erik does.

Cassie and Lorenzo's story is told in **Flashfire**. At the end of the book, Cassie and Lorenzo leave Las Vegas to live in the palazzo overlooking the Grand Canal that Lorenzo owns in Venice. The palazzo is the same building where his mother lived and worked, and Lorenzo restores it to its former splendor. He lives under the pseudonym Signor L. Rossi there, and the *Pyr* gather in the palazzo's ballroom for his scale repair.

In the **Dragon Legion novellas**, there's a flashback scene, showing Drake and the Dragon's Tooth Warriors collecting the darkfire crystal from Lorenzo's house while Lorenzo is awaiting Erik. This happens in the timeline of **Darkfire Kiss** and is facilitated by Salvatore. The crystal is returned to Erik when its power is spent.

In **Serpent's Kiss**, Lorenzo is planning a new show in Las Vegas and a return to the States, and Cassie is pregnant with their second son. He is approached by Marco to join an alliance of five *Pyr* with an affinity to air, most previously targeted by Chen, in order to save Thorolf. At the same time, Jorge proposes an alliance with Lorenzo, wanting him to beguile Chen, and Lorenzo agrees, planning to betray Jorge. Lorenzo and Thorolf defeat Chen in his lair, leaving his corpse to Jorge then are separated when Thorolf claims the sword that is his birthright and goes into Myth with Chandra. Lorenzo and Cassie's images appear in the pool where Sloane's reflection should be when the *Pyr* gather for the repair of Thorolf's scale.

In **Firestorm Forever**, Lorenzo and Cassie are going to return to the States (his new show is called *Rising from the Grave*) and Lorenzo plans to give Maeve O'Neill an exclusive interview. His expectation is that she'll want to interview him once it's revealed that he's the *Pyr* Cassie photographed changing shape, and that he'll beguile her during that interview, convincing her that the *Pyr* are good. Erik tries to change his mind without success. Lorenzo meets Maeve at his new theater, not realizing that she's the Fae

Queen. Instead of beguiling her, he is snared by Maeve's spell—trapped with a kiss—and ends up telling her a great deal about the *Pyr*. For the final battle, Lorenzo joins the team at Quinn's home in Michigan, defending Erik along with Quinn, Donovan and Marco. Lorenzo is entrusted with the syringes of antidote for the Elixir. He and Cassie and their sons participate in the scale repair at Erik's loft, and the last public display of the *Pyr* filmed by Melissa.

LOTHAIR—a *Pyr* born in 720 in northern France and one of the members of Soren's High Council. His affinity was with earth and he was a mercenary by trade. Lothair had his firestorm with Eglantine, but the names of their children are not recorded. His entire line was exterminated by *Slayers* in the wars of the Middle Ages, and one of the great *Pyr* families was lost.

LOUISA GUTHRIE—Erik Sorensson's mate in his first firestorm and the mother of Sigmund Guthrie. She was subsequently reincarnated as Eileen Grosvenor, with whom Erik had a second firestorm.

LUCIEN—A *Slayer*, who was topaz yellow in his dragon form and had particularly sharp black talons. The talons were tempered steel implants and the inspiration for the augmented talons that Quinn created for Donovan at the end of **Kiss of Fire**. Lucien cut the Wyvern at the beginning of **Kiss of Fire** with his talons when she was being tortured for information about the firestorm. Lucien was the son of Mallory and Michelle, and the older brother of Jean-Pierre (JP). He was born in Paris in 1605. His death, at the claws of Quinn and Donovan (recounted in **Kiss of Fire**) convinced his brother JP, who was still *Pyr*, to turn *Slayer* and seek vengeance.

LUKE HARGREAVES—son of Silas Hargreaves, whose farm is next to Ginger Sinclair's farm in **Winter Kiss**. Silas and Luke till some of the acreage of Sinclair Farms and provide fodder to Ginger in exchange. We are told of Luke in **Winter Kiss**, although he never makes an actual appearance in the book. He has aspirations to join both farms by marrying Ginger, and has argued with her about changing his methods on the tilled acreage to make the farm organic. He also challenged Ginger over the presence of a coyote on the farm and her caution in dealing with the predator, teasing her for having become a city girl. Ginger subsequently killed the coyote with a single shot and left the carcass for Luke to find.

LYNNE WILLIAMS—Eileen Grosvenor's sister who we meet in **Kiss of Fate**. Lynne is a former model, who gave up modeling when she married Roger. After years of fertility counseling and rough pregnancies, they have two daughters. They had a house in Notting Hill. Lynne is tall and slender, with wavy auburn hair and blue eyes, and her eyes tip upward at the outer corners. Eileen notes that her sister has dark thick lashes rather than the reddish ones that she has herself. Lynne is the one to suggest that Eileen picks men who are losers because she doesn't really want a partner at all. She says that Eileen was the only one who thought her first husband, Joe, was a keeper and suggests that Eileen only married him because she thought she should marry someone. Because Eileen has been involved with Lynne's pregnancies, she knows she can do it alone if necessary and convinces Erik that they should satisfy the firestorm, even though he fears he will soon be killed. Eileen hides the Dragon's Teeth and ensures that Lynne will find them, instructing Lynne to take them to Rafferty. Rafferty buys them, the price being enough money to send both of Lynne's daughters to university and grad school. Eileen has wrapped the teeth in Lynne's quilting fabric, and she requests the return of the fabric, which amuses Rafferty.

LYSANDER—son of Alexander and Katina. When Alexander returns home in **Kiss of Danger**, Lysander has gone with Pelias to Sparta for his training. This causes an argument between Katina and her second husband, Cetos, who has sold Lysander to a merchant as a slave and will have to return the payment. The merchant is actually Jorge, as Alexander discovers when they pursue Lysander and find Pelias battling Jorge over the boy. Jorge has been collecting the sons of the Dragon's Tooth Warriors and already has Theo, Drake's son, in his custody. Lysander shows signs of his *Pyr* heritage, being able to hear old-speak, and tries to save Alexander when Jorge is winning their battle. Alexander takes him to Delphi instead of Sparta for training.

"Pelias saw that I was *Pyr* and took me to Delphi," Alexander said. "We *Pyr* are said to be the spark cast by Apollo's killing of Pytho, so we serve at his shrine."

Katina watched their son consider this. "Is that why you're taking me to Delphi?"

Alexander smiled and put his hand on his son's head. "Yes. You will serve in the sanctuary, just as I did, and you will be taught how to manage your abilities as they develop." He flicked the quickest glance at Katina before he continued. "One day, you may be summoned to serve mankind for eight years. If that occurs, you will go."

"Why?"

"Because you will swear to it when you pledge yourself to Apollo and Gaia."
—from **Kiss of Danger**

Lysander and Theo both get the mark of the Dragon Legion on their arms from the Pythia. Both boys accompany Alexander and Katina—as well as six other unnamed *Pyr*—when they go to Damien and Petra at the end of **Kiss of Danger**.

MAEVE O'NEILL—a reporter who is actually the immortal Fae Queen Mab. She has long, dark, wavy hair and is exceptionally beautiful. Maeve first appears in **Firestorm Forever** where she is a reporter determined to expose the *Pyr* as evil. She runs a website called *Dragons Bite*. She and Jorge spot each other on Easter Island, then Jorge comes to her for sanctuary when he's wounded. They are intimate and become allies against the *Pyr*, although Maeve intends to exterminate Jorge, too. Her intention is to eliminate all species that she believes to be unnatural, leaving only the immortal Fae and the mortal humans. She shows him her trophy room—with a mermaid mirror, an elf ear and unicorn horn, among other prizes—and gives him a stylus to move between realms. She also steals one of his scales, which makes Jorge vulnerable in the final battle, and adds the scale to her trophy collection after his death. The stylus is lost in a valley near Machu Picchu when Jorge drops it. At the end of the book, Maeve gives Kade a similar stylus to open doors between the mortal realm and Fae. Maeve appears in the *DragonFate* series.

MAGDA—the aunt of Sara Keegan and former owner of the used bookstore in Ann Arbor, Michigan called *The Scrying Glass*. Once Sara's abilities as Seer are awakened in **Kiss of Fire,** she becomes aware that the bookstore is haunted by her aunt and that the quirks of the store—like the fitfully operating air conditioning unit—are her aunt's attempts to communicate with her.

MAGNUS MONTMORENCY—A *Slayer*, jade green and gold in dragon form, a collector of ancient secrets and both foe and former friend of Rafferty. He first appeared in **Kiss of Fury**, and met his match in **Darkfire Kiss**.

By the beginning of *Dragonfire*, Magnus had re-created the legendary Dragon's Blood Elixir. He began to administer it at his hidden Academy to raise the dead, enslave them by ensuring they were addicted to the Elixir, and thereby create an army of shadow dragons to serve his will. When Delaney was nearly killed in **Kiss of Fire**, he was brought to Magnus' Academy to be used for an experiment, to determine whether nearly-dead *Pyr* could be enslaved by the Elixir as readily as *Slayers*. At the end of **Kiss of Fury**, Magnus reveals himself to the *Pyr* for the first time, offering them the chance to drink the Elixir and join his forces while there's still time. When they decline, he opens his hidden Academy and reveals his shadow dragons to the *Pyr*. They see dead and beloved *Pyr* who have been turned to shadow dragons including Rafferty's grandfather, Sloane's father, three of Quinn's older brothers and Niall's twin brother, Phelan.

Magnus has history with many of the *Pyr*, particularly with Rafferty. In **Kiss of Fury**, Alex witnesses a vision of Donovan's battle against Magnus, in which Rafferty intervened to help Donovan triumph and escape. When Magnus confronts the *Pyr*, he makes reference to losing his hoard to Rafferty—this was the result of a blood duel prompted by a challenge coin, one in which Rafferty believed he had won and that Magnus was dead. Magnus, however, was not dead. He hid until he managed to heal, then rebuilt his power base in secret.

Magnus unwittingly provides information to the *Pyr*: in **Kiss of**

Fury, for example, Alex witnesses the battle between Donovan and Magnus that had occurred centuries before (courtesy of Sophie the Wyvern) and notes how Magnus draws strength from a burning flame. He appropriated its energy to use himself. She shared her observations with Donovan, which helped improve his mastery over fire.

In **Kiss of Fate**, Magnus is in London, in search of the Dragon's Teeth, which were part of the hoard he lost after battling Donovan centuries before. (The underground cavern collapsed after their fight, burying the treasure. By the time of **Kiss of Fate**, the hoard has been rediscovered during the excavation for a new subway station near Greenwich.) Magnus employs the *Slayers* Jorge, Mallory and Balthasar, and tries to claim the Dragon's Teeth from Erik and Eileen. He also persuades Sigmund to join his team, attempts to claim the children of the *Pyr* as *Slayer* recruits, and tries to convince Erik to drink the Dragon's Blood Elixir. Magnus' plan is foiled when his Academy is attacked and he retreats in the hope of defending it.

In **Winter Kiss**, Magnus is injured by Delaney when they first fight in the sanctuary of the Dragon's Blood Elixir. When he shifts between forms (a sign of distress), Delaney notices that Magnus can take the form of a green salamander. Magnus exchanges challenge coins with Rafferty again in this book—which means they will fight to the death—and they battle, with Rafferty trapping Magnus in the earth. Since the Elixir has also been destroyed and Magnus was badly wounded, Rafferty believes his old foe to be dead. He's wrong.

At the beginning of **Whisper Kiss**, Magnus is in rough shape. He manages to escape the clutch of the earth during the earthquake started by Chen, but is then captured by Chen and taken to his lair. Once there, Magnus is sealed into a jar, as Chen wants to watch him die. Chen ensures that Magnus knows he's taken over the shadow dragons, which Magnus resents bitterly. It's Rafferty who discovers the imprisoned Magnus, the first time he manages to spontaneously manifest elsewhere. He didn't give direction and realizes that Magnus summoned him. Rafferty's arrival in Chen's lair attracts Chen's attention, and Chen frees the weakened Magnus with the intent of killing the *Slayer*. He miscalculates, though, and the pair of *Slayers* fight, ultimately fleeing in salamander form.

In **Darkfire Kiss**, Magnus is living in Washington D.C. and Melissa (a reporter) is determined to expose him for his crimes as an arms dealer. Rafferty sees her enter Magnus' home and fears for her welfare—even if she is a thief, she's also human and one of the treasures of the earth. Magnus is home and witnesses the firestorm spark between Rafferty and Melissa. He decides that he will kill Rafferty's mate first, then destroy Rafferty. Rafferty, meanwhile, realizes that he and his mate can destroy Magnus together, with the truth. He reveals that the Sleeper, a hibernating Pyr entrusted to his care by his grandfather, is actually Magnus' nephew. Magnus killed his brother after Maximilian had his firestorm, then hunted both mate and child. Rafferty had taken them to refuge with his grandfather in Wales and Pwyll tricked him into thinking the child was dead. When Magnus abducts Melissa, Rafferty manages to spontaneously manifest elsewhere with a destination for the first time. Magnus threatens to open the Thames Barrier and flood London to convince Rafferty to confess the location of the Sleeper but Jorge finds the Sleeper first—when the pair reach that sanctuary, Magnus is wearying and Rafferty kills him. Delaney reminds Rafferty to ensure that what remains of Magnus is exposed to all four elements.

MALLORY—A *Slayer*, garnet red and gold with pearls in dragon form. In human form, he had chestnut hair and brown eyes and was shorter than his fellows. He was born in Aquitaine ca. 1150 and still has a French accent. Mallory had his firestorm with Michelle before turning *Slayer*, and they had two sons: Lucien and Jean-Pierre. Lucien turned *Slayer* like his father, but until Lucien's death, JP remained *Pyr* and hid from his father. Mallory thought of himself as a facilitator and ultimately became bodyguard to Magnus.

Mallory tried to beguile Eileen in **Kiss of Fate** in order to get the Dragon's Teeth from her for Magnus. (She calls him 'Frenchie' and realizes quickly that he must be a dragon shifter.) In **Winter Kiss**, Mallory is one of the three *Slayers* defending Magnus in his home in Ohio: the others are Jorge and Balthasar. He was given the Dragon's Blood Elixir by Magnus when badly injured by the *Pyr* dragonfire in **Winter Kiss**, but remains disfigured. He is sent by Magnus to taint the water supply at Ginger's farm with mercury and appears in the kitchen in salamander form. He went to Moscow with Jorge after events in Ohio, and went into hibernation in Jorge's lair on the Caspian Sea. In **Darkfire Kiss**, Mallory is murdered by Jorge and consumed for the Elixir that remains as a residue in his body.

MANDY—Viv Jason's supervisor at the coffee shop where she works until feeling the spark of the darkfire in **Darkfire Kiss**.

MARCUS MAXIMUS AKA MARCO (THE SLEEPER)—The nephew of the *Slayer* Magnus Montmorency, son of Maximilian and Cornelia, and ward of Rafferty's grandfather, Pwyll. When Magnus murdered his brother Maximilian out of jealousy for that *Pyr*'s firestorm, Cornelia and her infant son were taken into protective care by Rafferty's grandfather. The boy was enchanted to sleep until the darkfire was released, in order to hide him from Magnus, and has been hidden at Bardsey Island by Rafferty. Pwyll used the power of darkfire to cast his spell over Marcus, and trapped the rest of the darkfire within three quartz crystals.

At the beginning of **Darkfire Kiss**, Chen shatters one of the three darkfire crystals and looses the darkfire. The Sleeper stirs in his sleep and the darkfire burns brighter in the crystal in Rafferty's hoard, indicating his state. When Magnus abducts Melissa, he tries to barter with Rafferty, offering her life in exchange for the Sleeper. They fight instead and the fight moves to the refuge after Jorge locates the Sleeper and attacks. When Magnus is killed and Jorge trapped, Donovan carries the Sleeper to safety, only to have the Sleeper follow the darkfire to Rafferty's lair in London. He awakens at the end of that book when Rafferty uses the darkfire crystal to rouse him. He can see the dead and talk to them, because he sees Pwyll in Rafferty's home and facilitates a reunion between the two.

Marco is particularly tranquil and observant, and has the ability to both control and anticipate darkfire. He has dark hair and dark eyes. In dragon form, he is black with a blue-green shimmer, evocative of his bond with darkfire. His affinities are for fire and air. The *Pyr* find him enigmatic. The darkfire Marco commands gives him the ability to spontaneously manifest in other locations; he shows a tendency to suddenly appear when needed that hints at foresight, though it's not clear whether Marco or the darkfire has the ability to anticipate the future.

In **Flashfire**, Marco manifests in Lorenzo's car, asking that *Pyr* to surrender the darkfire crystal in his possession. Lorenzo admits that it's gone (Drake has claimed it) but Lorenzo goes to the house to be sure. En route, he taunts Lorenzo with the word *Diavolo*, proving that he can read Lorenzo's thoughts, a skill Lorenzo finds troubling.

It was a point of pride that he never lost control, but he *had* lost control in the theater.

And he'd threatened JP in old-speak.

Lorenzo frowned and accelerated, telling himself that it wouldn't happen again.

"Yes, it will," Marco murmured beside him.

Lorenzo glanced at his companion in wary surprise. Had he heard Lorenzo's thoughts?

"I did," Marco supplied, with a serenity that annoyed Lorenzo. "Again. It's the legacy of the darkfire, I think. I can hear the thoughts of all the *Pyr*."

—from **Flashfire**

Marco also reveals that Lorenzo's father was involved in the disappearance of the crystal. He collects the pieces of Chen's brand, acknowledging the darkfire linked to them, and disappears. Marco attends the repair of Lorenzo's scale in Venice.

In **Ember's Kiss**, Marco appears when Liz is battling Chen, shooting the *Slayer* with the darkfire crystal. He gives the darkfire crystal to Liz, whose powers as a Firedaughter are shown by her ability to use the crystal as a weapon. He advises her to embrace her powers and help Brandon. She uses the crystal to defeat Chen on their next battle.

In **Serpent's Kiss**, Marco collects a prophecy from Sara, manifesting suddenly in the home she shares with Quinn. He appears to Lorenzo in Venice when Jorge is suggesting an alliance to Lorenzo in old-speak. Marco simultaneously suggests that he and Lorenzo form the alliance of five *Pyr* mentioned in Sara's prophecy, including Erik, Thorolf and Brandon. He guards Cassie and Antonio while Lorenzo meets Jorge. Marco retrieves the darkfire crystal from Liz, appearing in the bedroom of Liz and Brandon's sons during the night. He later reveals to the *Pyr* that Chen has a brother and uses the darkfire to help Niall in his dreamwalking, giving him a glimpse into Chen's lair. He breaks the crystal, releasing the darkfire, knowing it will free Lee. He waits in a market in Bangkok, ultimately finding Lee and escorting him to the other *Pyr*. Marco attends the repair of Thorolf's scale at Angkor, appearing after the other *Pyr* are gathered in a flicker of darkfire.

In **Firestorm Forever**, Marco has his firestorm with Jacelyn. He meets her originally because of her interest in hunting dragons, having followed the darkfire's urge to move into the same building in Seattle, and is the first to recognize her link with Nathaniel. He gives her Sigmund's book—which he stole from Erik's hoard. He also has stolen the last darkfire crystal, the one that Drake returned to Erik at the end of **Kiss of Danger**, because there's a spark of darkfire in it again. The theft convinces Erik that Marco is turning against the *Pyr*. Marco receives the prophecy while he dreams in his apartment and writes it on the wall.

Jac sees both the prophecy and the crystal when she visits him, and joins Marco when he goes to Easter Island. There's a strong attraction between them and they're intimate. But Marco is horrified when Jac seizes the darkfire crystal and injures his mentor and friend, Rafferty. He abandons her to help Rafferty, which only makes it possible for Jorge to forge an alliance with Jac. The *Pyr* assume that Marco fired the crystal and abducted Rafferty, which reinforces the idea that he is betraying them. In fact, he takes Rafferty to Sloane, using the ability to spontaneously manifest elsewhere given to him by the darkfire, in order to see Rafferty healed and also to disguise his identity. (Rafferty is in dragon form but so badly injured that Marco knows he will rotate between forms, in front of a large crowd of people and television crews.)

Marco feels betrayed by the darkfire and refuses to help Sloane with the Cantor's song, which Sloane hopes will draw the darkfire out of Rafferty's body. He returns to Easter Island, argues with Jac, then finds her with Jorge. Even though he doesn't trust her, she's still a treasure of the earth, so he remains to defend her without her knowledge, breathing dragonsmoke around the hotel where she sleeps. When he returns to Seattle, he finds Jorge in his apartment. Jorge is stealing Sigmund's book and has burned a spell spiral in the floor like Chen's. Marco is trapped by the spell and has his energy drained by Jorge's dragonsmoke, while Jorge escapes with the book.

I like that Jac rattles Marco, who has always been very composed and serene. She infuriates him and challenges his assumptions, even undermining his intuitive faith in darkfire. I think she's good for him. Interestingly, while Marco lies ill in his apartment, Jac senses his protective presence. She even thinks she sees him one night when she wins a dart game at a local bar in Seattle. The darkfire rouses Marco during the second eclipse in **Firestorm Forever**, healing him, regaining his trust and giving him the power to go to Jac. She's in Australia, hunting dragons, as arranged by Jorge. The pair reconcile and are intimate again before their firestorm sparks. His identity as a *Pyr* is revealed to Jac—who has read Sigmund's book and recognizes the firestorm for what it is—and she flees, even as he feels compelled to shift to his dragon form.

Jac stumbles into Jorge's clutches, and she realizes that he's *Slayer* just before the dragonfight begins. Marco defends Jac and they fight together, until Jorge snares a wounded Marco in his dragonsmoke, draining his energy. Jorge also rips one of Marco's dragon scales free. Marco asks for the Elixir, hoping that Jorge will take him to his lair and he'll have the chance to trick the *Slayer*. Brandon hears his entreaty, which enforces the conviction of the *Pyr* that Marco intends to change sides, just before Jorge, Marco and Jac disappear. (Liz argues with Brandon about this, as she remains convinced of Marco's integrity.) Once in Jorge's lair, Marco feigns unconsciousness while Jac pumps the *Slayer* for information. Jorge is suspicious, though, and breaks Marco's lost scale. The pair fight and Marco uses dragonsmoke to drain Jorge's strength, building his own power so that they can escape the lair. With Jac's help—she shoves a burning candle in Jorge's eye and encourages Marco to put the Dracontias in his mouth—they escape the lair, leaving it burning with Jorge wounded on the floor.

When they manifest at the Holiday Inn in Virginia, near Sam's house, Marco knows that the darkfire—which helped him move through space—intends for them to take the Dracontias to Sam. He'd thought that Rafferty would need it to heal, but trusts the darkfire. Jac insists that she won't consummate the firestorm without being sure that her son will have a father, and Marco takes that as a challenge to win her heart.

"Good. It means the darkfire is working for and against us."

"What's that supposed to mean?"

"That darkfire has governed my life and darkfire has its sparks in my firestorm, too. Think about it: you're the least likely candidate to be the destined mate of a *Pyr*. What are the odds of my having a firestorm with the one mortal woman on the planet sworn to wipe my kind from the face of the earth?"

"Pretty long, I'd think."

"More than long. It's completely improbable. It defies expectation and challenges assumptions, both yours and mine." He seemed to find this reassuring.

"Like darkfire does," Jac said and Marco nodded.

"Darkfire pushes and pulls, inverts situations and challenges us to see things in new ways. Like the way you fought Jorge and the *Slayers*. Like the way we both excite and get at each other. Darkfire is lighting our firestorm and making both of us reconsider what we believe to be true."

"But that doesn't change everything. I'm still not going to

have your son."

Marco smiled the smile of a man accepting a challenge. He turned a glittering glance on Jac, one that reminded her of what he was and also what they'd done before, one that dissolved her resistance and put her body on his side. The flames of the firestorm seemed to sizzle with greater heat.

"Which only means that I'm going to have to change your mind," he murmured and Jac knew it wasn't going to be as hard for him to succeed as she might have hoped.

—from **Firestorm Forever**

With Marco's encouragement, Jac tells him about Nathaniel and about her own history. He tells her that he thought Pwyll was his grandfather—obviously this was clarified when he awakened in **Darkfire Kiss** and met Rafferty. (There is a continuity error in the original edition of **Firestorm Forever**: Marco tells Jac that he's been enchanted for "fourteen or fifteen hundred years". This is impossible, as he was born in 1055, so it's been corrected to "over a thousand years" in the new edition.) When Jac takes the Dracontias to Sam, Marco retrieves the darkfire crystal from Sloane's home. He can't separate it from Rafferty, who needs its healing power, so he takes both of them. (Rafferty is in his salamander form.) Melissa witnesses this, which adds to the *Pyr* doubts of Marco's intentions. Marco and Jac then restore Rafferty with the heat of their firestorm. Rafferty then tactfully leaves, having the energy to spontaneously manifest elsewhere. Marco and Jac resolve to wait until the end of the Dragon's Tail War before satisfying the firestorm, then are attacked by one of the Boris clones.

This clone of Boris offers Marco a deal, suggesting that they become partners, use Jorge to make a new batch of the Elixir, triumph over the *Pyr* and rule the *Slayers* together. Marco agrees, although he plans to betray the clone. He believes that the alliance will give him the inside information to ensure Erik's survival. Marco turns on the clone when Erik is cornered and Erik sees Marco's blood run red, which convinces him of Marco's loyalties. Jac helps Eileen and Zoë escape, and also destroys the clone with the darkfire crystal. Marco offers the heat of the firestorm to heal

Erik's wounds and the leader of the *Pyr* accepts. Marco loses a scale at this moment and Jac confesses her love to him after she catches it, because she knows what it means. They retreat to satisfy their firestorm in private.

For the final battle, Marco joins Donovan, Erik, Lorenzo and Quinn at Quinn's home to defend Erik in the inevitable attack by clones. He uses the darkfire crystal as a weapon until it goes dark. When the antidote to the Elixir is spilled, Marco goes to Sloane at Machu Picchu to get more. He takes two syringes, empties one into a *Slayer* brought to him by Rafferty, then returns to Michigan in time to inoculate the last clone. Erik sends him to check on the other two battles, and he witnesses the spark of Sloane's firestorm. He spontaneously manifests with Sloane, taking Sloane closer to his mate, and they end up at Quinn's place in Michigan. Sloane follows the spark from there. (Sam is in Ann Arbor.) Marco and Jac buy Sam's house in California, becoming Sam and Sloane's neighbors. Marco's missing scale is repaired at the ceremony at Erik's lair in Chicago and he participates in the *Pyr's* last televised appearance, the darkfire indicating that his firestorm will burn forever.

MARIA—wife of Gaultier. This older couple adopted Quinn Tyrrell when his family was killed and raised him as their own son. He only left their home after they died.

MARK—an unlucky name for secondary characters in *Dragonfire*. These are the 'red-shirts' of the series. Mark Sullivan was the partner of Alex Madison who was tortured by *Slayers* and killed before her eyes in **Kiss of Fury**. Mark Maitland was the husband of Veronica who was missing in action, and who Drake found dead near Cadmus' lair.

MARY—a waitress at the diner near Ginger Sinclair's farm who flirts with Thorolf in **Winter Kiss**.

MATTHEW SMITH—Melissa's older brother and an architect who first appears in **Darkfire Kiss**. He lives in California with his wife, Joanna, and children (who aren't named or numbered, but Melissa has "a niece and nephews"), and has furnished his house with Mission Style furniture. Matt says that Mel is as cool as a cucumber. He suggested to Melissa years before that they needed a code for when she called him from a dangerous location but couldn't speak openly: "The only thing missing is a piece of Mom's apple pie," is the phrase she uses to indicate that she's fine. (The other one isn't specified.) Melissa is reminded of an agate chess set she bought Matt in Mexico when she sees Balthasar in dragon form. Matt and Joanna gave Melissa earrings of freshwater pearls the Christmas before her firestorm with Rafferty, which she's wearing when she auditions to get her old job back. Rafferty and Melissa exchange their vows in Matt's garden in California.

MATT (2)—one of Brandon's surfer buddies in **Ember's Kiss**. Matt is cocky and competitive, especially when it comes to women, but loyal to his friends. Liz sees his aura as green and pulsing, and believes he's like her ex, Rob. Matt seizes Brandon's Dragon Bone Powder and throws it into the wind, prompting a violent reaction in Brandon. When Matt's leash is caught on the reef, Brandon shifts shape to save his friend, then he and Liz have to concoct a story to explain the dragon to his friends.

MAUREEN—a marine biologist and mentor of Liz Barrett, who invites Liz to attend a symposium in Hawai`i in **Ember's Kiss**. She's in her fifties and drives an old turquoise diesel Mercedes. Liz notices that her former prof has relaxed a lot since moving to the islands. Maureen hopes to entice Liz to make the same move and is inclined to be both outspoken and bossy. Maureen thinks that Liz's failed relationship with Rob, a coworker, has left her broken-hearted. She warned Liz against Rob, because he reminded the older woman of her first husband.

MELISSA SMITH—A reporter and cancer survivor, the partner of Rafferty Powell and adoptive mother of Isabelle. Melissa has green eyes that tip up at the outer corners and her skin is golden. She has short dark curly hair and is slender and tall. Melissa and Rafferty's story is told in **Darkfire Kiss**.

We meet Melissa when she enters Magnus' home in DC, hoping to steal a journal that lists his arms dealing activities. Melissa has been guided to the book by a source from her days as a foreign correspondent, a woman named Daphne who was killed by Magnus: she sees exposing Magnus and his crimes as justice for Daphne. Because of her cancer, Melissa no longer has her network job—instead, she has a blog she calls MelsRealNews where she posts the results of her research. Her plan is to post the book's contents there, but instead, Magnus catches her at home, Rafferty follows the spark of the firestorm to intervene, and she witnesses a dragon fight between Balthasar and Rafferty. She puts those pictures on her blog instead, launching a controversy within the *Pyr* about Rafferty revealing the presence of his kind to the world. When Melissa argues in favor of the *Pyr* going public, Erik is furious, but Rafferty takes her side. As a result of the firestorm between Melissa and Rafferty, the *Pyr* appear in a series of special broadcasts and Erik also creates the Covenant.

Melissa and Rafferty's firestorm is unusual because the treatment of Melissa's uterine cancer has left her unable to conceive a child. The sparks of their firestorm extinguish when the darkfire is trapped in the crystal and the crystal is claimed by Marco. Ultimately, they adopt Isabelle, a girl orphaned by the *Slayer* attack on London and one they believe to be carrying the soul of Sophie. Melissa also does a series of documentaries about the *Pyr* to improve the perception of them amongst humans, and these become a public reference in subsequent books.

in **Flashfire**, Melissa's broadcast about the *Pyr* prompt the offers to Cassie to photograph a *Pyr* in the act of shifting from man to dragon. Melissa and Cassie meet at the repair of Lorenzo's scale, and Melissa incorporates some of Cassie's photographs of Lorenzo into her specials on the *Pyr*. Melissa's documentaries are a reference for Liz in **Ember's Kiss**.

In **Serpent's Kiss**, Melissa is at Erik's lair with Isabelle when Rafferty arrives, injured after being attacked by Thorolf. She suggests another special on the *Pyr* to counter the negative publicity but Erik refuses. Melissa plans the route for the *Pyr* to deliver the sword to Thorolf, and attends Thorolf's scale repair at

Angkor with Rafferty.

In **Firestorm Forever**, Doug calls Melissa to alert her to an interview by Maeve O'Neill with a couple on Easter Island who have seen Jorge and found the nest of clone eggs there. Melissa goes to Easter Island and witnesses Jac's attack on Rafferty, his injury and Marco's disappearance with him. She then goes to Sloane's home with Thorolf and Chandra, remaining with Rafferty in the hope that he'll heal. She sees Marco take the darkfire crystal and Rafferty. She does two last broadcasts about the *Pyr*, one of Drake's scale repair (filmed behind Sloane's home) and one of the *Pyr's* last public flight in Chicago at the end of the Dragon's Tail Wars.

MEREDITH MALONEY—the former (deceased) nanny of Alex and Peter Madison, whose name Alex used for her forged identity and credit cards. The use of that name at the bank where he had installed an anti-fraud system made Peter realize that his sister might be in danger. Meredith's favorite quote was *"We have nothing to fear but fear itself"* which Alex has taken as her own creed.

MHAIRI CONNAUGHT—the mate of Keir Shea, and mother of both Donovan Shea and Delaney Connaught (later Shea). Mhairi was seduced by the charm of Keir twice, although he abandoned her to raise the sons she conceived by him. She struggled with depression all her life. Mhairi was very religious and believed the onslaught of her sons' dragon shifting abilities at puberty was a sign that they had been possessed by the devil. As a result, Donovan had run away from home by the time Keir returned to Mhairi to conceive Delaney. Mhairi was reconciled with Delaney on her deathbed and gave him the silver cross she'd always worn, making him promise to use his abilities for good. In the original edition of **Winter Kiss**, Mhairi's name is mistakenly listed as Elizabeth.

MICHAEL TYRRELL—the fourth son of Sara Keegan and Quinn Tyrrell, the Smith of the *Pyr*, born in November 2014. Sara delivers Michael—who is named for Quinn's brother, Michel—at the beginning of **Firestorm Forever**.

MICHEL—an older brother of Quinn Tyrrell. Michel was killed in the attack against the Smith orchestrated by the *Slayer* Ambrose. Michel was subsequently raised from the dead and made into a shadow dragon by Magnus. He escapes the battle with the *Pyr* in **Kiss of Fury**, then fights Quinn in Chicago in **Kiss of Fate**, also surviving that battle. Quinn kills Michel in **Whisper Kiss** when he is arriving at Niall's firestorm with Sara and Garrett. That the shadow dragon attacks when Quinn is carrying his family makes the Smith particularly decisive in dispatching him.

MIKAEL VASSILY—The first *Slayer* and father of Boris Vassily. Mikail was red and gold in dragon form, and called a treasure come to life. He had a persuasive manner and a commanding presence, was a gifted orator but was arrogant. He was the first of the dragon shifters to organize against humans and turn *Slayer* so took leadership of the *Slayers* himself. Mikael turned *Slayer* after his oldest brother, Kasper, was slaughtered by knights on the first crusade in search of exotic treasure, specifically the healing stone reputed to be embedded in the forehead of dragons. Mikael arrived too late to save his brother and the incident turned him against humans forever. He and his brother Adrik pledged a crusade against humans: when Adrik was hunted and killed, Mikael swore to spend his life taking vengeance upon mankind. His firestorm sparked shortly thereafter and it is rumored that he kidnapped his destined mate, holding her captive until the delivery of his son, Boris. He then killed her for defying him and raised his son alone. In **Kiss of Fate**, the story of Mikael's death at the claw of Soren in an alchemist's lab in 1782 is revealed, which is the root of the animosity between Erik (Soren's son) and Boris (Mikael's son).

MONA—a lover of Magnus Montmorency, whom he kills in a scene in the prologue to **Winter Kiss**. Magnus met her in Azerbaijan and found her attractive. By the time or her death, he has become tired of her demands. This scene was cut from the original edition of the book and appeared only as a free read on Deborah's website. It was returned to the 2018 edition and updated, as Mona had been renamed Daphne for **Darkfire Kiss** and been found by Magnus in Baghdad instead of Azerbaijan. There, she was a source used by Melissa Smith. Daphne's disappearance is what leads Melissa to Magnus Montmorency.

MYRDDIN—oldest son of Pwyll, born ca. 400. As a *Pyr* and the heir of the Cantor, Myrddin was the inspiration for Welsh tales of Merlin, the wizard and shapeshifter. He died in 620 and was considered by his father to have been a bright light that burned out fast. His younger brother was Owen, who was Rafferty's father.

NATHANIEL SULLIVAN—Samantha and Derek's son, and the first victim of the plague brought to Seattle by Jorge. His death haunts Jacelyn, who was with him when he became exposed, and Sam, who believes she failed her son by not finding an antidote in time to save his life. Jac has fond memories of him, and tells Marco that Nathaniel wanted to be an astronaut, that he was "a sweet, smart, lovable kid." She also thinks he was lonely and blames Sam for that. On their last day together, he used his savings to buy a necklace for Sam of the Space Needle. Sam tells Jac that Nathaniel believed he was lucky because he had two moms, her and Jac.

NEO—one of the three partners at Imagination Ink, a tattoo shop in Manhattan. He's introduced in **Whisper Kiss**. Neo loves loud music and partying and Rox implies that he's gay. Niall describes him as "a slim guy in his thirties with dyed black hair and lavish eyeliner to rival that of Rox. His earlobes held large earplugs that could have been made of ebony." Neo teases Rox for her chastity and calls her Sister Rox. As a tattoo artist, Neo is particularly gifted with portraiture: he did Rox's *Sisters of the Heart* tattoo. His apprentice, Jimmy, takes the delivery job at Garry's organic food store that Rox intended for Thorolf. Rox believes this will diminish Neo's influence as Jimmy won't be able to stay out partying when he has to get up early to make deliveries. Another artist who works at the shop is Tom, but we know little of him beyond his name.

Neo also likes to explore the underground of the city and once found a railroad turntable but couldn't find it again—Rox remembers this story when she and Niall find one in their quest to find the hidden lair of the shadow dragons. In **Firestorm Forever**, Rox mentions that Neo likes tunnels and that he once took her to

Seaview Hospital.

NEPHELE—a nymph with fair hair and a friend of Aura's in **Kiss of Danger**. She tells the other nymphs about Katina, the Waterdaughter. She changes to a cloud when Thad follows Aura and tells Aura that she likes the *Pyr*.

NIALL TALBOT—A *Pyr*, amethyst and platinum in dragon form, the Dreamwalker of the *Pyr*, and owner of an eco-tourism business located in Chinatown in New York City. Before **Winter Kiss**, Delaney was his business partner, but Delaney sold his share before going to destroy the source of the Elixir. Niall is blond with blue eyes, a little shorter than the other *Pyr*, and very muscled. He has an affinity with air as well as fire. Niall's challenge coin (which he never uses in *Dragonfire*) is a peacock rupee, struck in Birmingham in England, dated Burma 1852. It has a peacock on one side and a garland on the other. Niall is the partner of Roxanne Kincaid and father of twin boys, Kyle and Nolan, who were born 2011. Rox and Niall's story is told in **Whisper Kiss**.

Niall has an affinity with the element of air, and "whispers to the wind" which means that he asks the wind for tidings. In **Kiss of Fire**, Niall also sings to the wind, turning the storm that Boris summoned into a tornado. In **Kiss of Fury**, Niall brings the wind with him when he, Erik and Sloane intervene to save Jared from Sigmund's attempted kidnapping. Ultimately, he has a cyclone carry Sigmund far away. Niall battled his own twin brother, Phelan, who had become a shadow dragon, for the first time in **Kiss of Fury**.

In **Winter Kiss**, Niall summons a storm, letting the tornado remove Jorge, Mallory and Balthasar from the vicinity of the sanctuary of the Dragon's Blood Elixir. In Whisper Kiss, Niall takes on the task with Thorolf of hunting down and eliminating the remaining shadow dragons, which includes his twin, Phelan.

In **Whisper Kiss**, Niall smells trouble on the wind before the earthquake started by Chen. At the end of **Whisper Kiss**, Rox gives Niall a tattoo on his back of a phoenix in flight, which forms the other half of a circle with the dragon on her back when they stand beside each other. He also has a black and red yin and yang symbol tattooed by Rox on his shoulder where he lost a scale over his love for her.

"You just want me naked," Niall complained, and Rox smiled.

"You got a problem with that?"

Niall grinned. "Actually, no." He peeled off his shirt and turned, glancing over his shoulder at the reflection of his tattoo in the mirror.

The yin and yang symbol was at the lower edge of his right shoulder blade, covering the place where he had lost a scale. It looked to be held in the talons of the phoenix. The phoenix looked as if it would take flight over Niall's left shoulder. The tail feathers swept over his back, spilling around his waist and over his ribs on the front. There were clouds behind the phoenix, stylized silhouettes in shades of blue and green.

The phoenix represented the elements of air and fire.

"I still think it's the best piece you've ever done," he said with an admiration that warmed Rox like the firestorm.

The tattoo had healed beautifully, but then she'd known Niall would follow her instructions. She gave it a thorough check, then took off her own shirt. She nestled at his left side, holding up a hand mirror to see their tattoos together. She knew she'd never tire of seeing the two halves make a complete whole.

"Perfect," Niall murmured, pressing a kiss into her hair.

Rox's dragon was now colored in hues of amethyst and blue, accented in white to mimic platinum. The dragon curved like a letter C, his tail rising high on her left shoulder and his head curving up from below. Those orange stylized flames flowed behind him, but they looked more brilliant now that he was colored.

The dragon represented earth and water.

Rox liked that they each had the two elements of their own affinity represented on their backs, along with a symbol of the other's role in their partnership. She was earth and water to Niall's air and fire, but she was his Phoenix and he was her Dragon. The yin and yang symbol on his back represented the balance of their union, while the pearl on hers indicated—to Rox's thinking— the richness of the life they were making together.

Maybe even the precious gem of their son.

—from **Whisper Kiss**

In **Darkfire Kiss**, Niall feels the influence of the darkfire, because all his trips are experiencing challenges. He and Barry are working furiously to take care of their clients when Niall also feels Rafferty's firestorm. He calls to Thorolf in old-speak and takes him home, guarding over him while he sleeps. Niall, Rox and Thorolf later go to Michigan for Rafferty's scale repair.

In **Flashfire**, Niall doesn't come to Lorenzo's firestorm, but he and Rox attend Lorenzo's scale repair in Venice with their sons, who are four months old. In **Ember's Kiss**, Niall and Sloane agree that Brandon might need the support of the *Pyr* for his firestorm. He consults with Rox, who is concerned that Brandon's tattoos from a shaman indicate that he needs protection, so they go to Hawai`i. Liz places Niall at the eastern cardinal point in her protective circle, because she guesses he has an affinity with air.

In **Serpent's Kiss**, Niall has a recurring nightmare of Astrid's death, although he doesn't know which *Pyr's* memory he's sharing.

Niall didn't realize then that Rox would fill a notebook with his recurring dreams of the other *Pyr's* last moments with Astrid. He would have that same nightmare every single night for the next twenty-two months, except that it became more violent and the *Pyr's* reaction more vehement each and every time. It was as if the *Pyr's* fury was being steadily fed to become greater and more consuming.

And yet, over those same months, he didn't manage to find a single *Pyr* who had been loved by an Astrid.

Much less understand why the dream was so persistent.

—from **Serpent's Kiss**

When Thorolf's firestorm ignites, Niall realizes it was Thorolf's dream. He and Rox go to Bangkok to try to help. He and Sloane trap Thorolf with dragonsmoke after he attacks Rafferty, then Niall peeks into Thorolf's mind. He finds only fury. He's relieved when Thorolf shifts back to his human form and recognizes the *Pyr* again, but troubled by the state of Thorolf's skin, which is red and covered with spiral tattoos. Niall, Rox and Sloane also witness the healing power of the firestorm when Chandra appears and kisses Thorolf. Niall tries to dreamwalk to find out more but Marco tells him that Thorolf is in Myth, where Niall can't follow him. Instead, Marco gives Niall a vision of Chen's lair, where Thorolf was compromised with the Elixir harvested from JP. This helps the *Pyr* solve the riddle of how to help Thorolf. Niall also attends the repair of Thorolf's scale at Angkor with Rox.

In **Firestorm Forever**, Niall dreamwalks to find Drake's mate, Veronica, after she's abducted by Jorge. He finds her because she's dreaming of her son, Timmy. She reviews what she's seen and heard, which helps the *Pyr* identify where she's being held and by whom. Rox finds a video online of a dragonfight and learns the location from a former boyfriend and urban explorer, Toad. When Drake is wounded in the rescue attempt by the Dragon Legion, he is brought to Niall and Rox's apartment, and Sloane comes there to tend his injuries. Niall and Rox take their boys to Delaney's farm in Ohio and Niall tries to dreamwalk to the injured Rafferty, without success. Rox has her second set of twins there. Niall tells Ronnie in a dream about the *Pyr* plan to rescue her but remains at the farm under Donovan's protection at Erik's command. He's the one who realizes that Marco asks Jorge for the Elixir before they disappear. Sloane then asks Niall to walk in Sam's dreams, hoping that a memory of her son will provoke her to help him to find a cure for Ronnie. As Sloane anticipates, the sight of his tattoo prompts Sam to connect the dots and has her packing for California, to help Ronnie, who was her patient and responsibility until the *Pyr* rescued her. Niall, Delaney, Theo and Lee join Drake at his home in Virginia for the final eclipse, then attend the scale repair ceremony at Erik's lair in Chicago. Niall flies in the final public display and his repaired scale is touched by the darkfire, indicating that his firestorm will burn forever.

NICHOLAS SHEA—oldest son of Donovan and Alex, born May 10, 2008. Nick is named for Nikolas of Thebes, one of the Dragon's

Tooth Warriors, and the first of them to break the spell, who died in the destruction of the Academy. In the Dragon Diaries, it's revealed that he has dark auburn hair and green eyes in human form, and is yellow, shading to gold on his back, with amber eyes, in his dragon form.

NIGEL—the long-distance date that Eileen Grosvenor came to London to meet, only to discover that he was already married. She's annoyed about her run of bad luck romantically and skeptical of men when she meets Erik.

NIGEL TALBOT—a *Pyr* and the father of the twins, Niall and Phelan. He is blond and has blue eyes. Niall recalls his father as being unyielding, conservative, and stern, and he wants to be different. Nigel and his mate were attacked by *Slayers* on their wedding night and he shifted shape to defend his bride. She was so frightened by this incident that she refused to see Nigel, thus feeding the *Pyr* conviction that humans can't see the transformation without repercussions. The pair were estranged for thirteen years—he staying in London and she remaining at their country house—until their twin sons were twelve years old and becoming *Pyr*. The mother then went to Nigel for his help, and the couple were superficially reconciled, living in the same house afterward to raise the boys.

In **Whisper Kiss**, Rox is sent a dream by Zoë, the new Wyvern. Rox dreams of Nigel and Rafferty at a ball, watching Nigel's mother dance with another man. At this point, Niall and Phelan are close to thirty years old. Rafferty, unsurprisingly, urges Nigel to go to his wife and heal the rift between them, but Nigel refuses. Unbeknownst to Rafferty, Nigel has just learned of his son Phelan's decision to turn *Slayer* and has disinherited Phelan, banning him from the family forever. Nigel leaves the ball in anger, and his wife watches him go. Rox realizes that the pair are the only ones in the room who don't realize that they are in love with each other. Phelan then escorts his mother away from the ball and abducts her, sending a threat to his father in old-speak that he'll kill her if he isn't reinstated to the family. It's later revealed that Niall came to the ball to tell his mother about Phelan's decision at his father's insistence, but arrived after Phelan had abducted her. Nigel, enraged by his son's attempt to blackmail him, didn't negotiate. He killed Phelan instead and Niall became estranged from his parents, both because the sight of him reminded them of Phelan and because he couldn't accept his father's actions.

Nigel's mate isn't named in **Whisper Kiss**, and it is unclear what happened in their marriage after Niall's estrangement from them. Niall does remember that his mother grew roses at the country house, and he recalls his father's London town house—as well as the fact that he sold it after his father's death, which had been more than a hundred years before. There's an implication here that Nigel and his mate did reconcile, or at the very least, that Nigel was sufficiently in love with his mate that his life was bound to hers and that he died just after she did.

NIKOLAS OF THEBES—A Dragon's Tooth Warrior who was first to be broken free of the enchantment in **Kiss of Fury** and who fell in love with Sophie. His color in dragon form is described as anthracite and iron, and he has dark hair and dark eyes. He is intense.

> *Pyr* and *Slayers* stared at the new arrival in shock.
> He was the color of anthracite, a thousand hues of silver, gray and black, his scales gleaming in the starlight. He seemed primitive compared to the other Pyr, more reptilian.
> "He looks like a dinosaur," Jared whispered.
> "*Pyrannosaurus rex*, maybe," Alex replied.
> "I wonder whether smart women taste better," Jorge mused. Alex ignored him.
> —Nikolas appears in **Kiss of Fury**

Nikolas was enchanted by the viper Cadmus, and trapped in the Dragon's Tooth. He was freed from the spell in **Kiss of Fury** when the *Pyr* planted the Dragon's Tooth in the soil. Just as in the story of Cadmus that Sara had dreamed, the tooth sprouted like a seed, and Nikolas was the result. He was *Pyr* and had been enchanted for millennia. The *Pyr* were shocked not only by the difference between his appearance and theirs, but that Nikolas had no scent.

When he first appeared, they were uncertain whether he was *Pyr* or *Slayer*, or which side in the battle he would take. The distinction, of course, was meaningless to Nikolas, who was the very *Pyr* whose appearance Sophie had anticipated, the one with both good and evil in his heart.

In Nikolas' era, the Wyvern was close to divine and seldom seen by any *Pyr*. Nikolas fell in love with Sophie at first glance, but relations between two *Pyr* (even when one is the Wyvern) is taboo to the *Pyr* (each *Pyr* is to mate with a human). In **Kiss of Fury**, Nikolas appoints himself as Sophie's defender, thinking this the best use for his devotion.

In **Kiss of Fate**, their relationship develops further: they admit their love for each other after Sophie is attacked by Boris and they are physically intimate. Nikolas doesn't care that this is a violation of the rules, as he thinks love will overcome such obstacles. Sophie, however, discovers that making love has cost her powers. She understands her sense that Nikolas is the one who can destroy the Academy. She knows he won't go there alone, but that he will follow her to save her from certain death. Sophie flies to the Academy and Nikolas pursues her. Together, they create a maelstrom that destroys the structure and themselves are fused into a ring that looks like it's made of black and white glass. Drake insists that Rafferty should claim this ring as it changes size to fit him, in either form. Subsequently, the ring is of interest to the toddler Zoë and ultimately plays a role in the *Dragon Diaries*.

Donovan and Alex name their oldest son after Nikolas, in his memory. In **Winter Kiss**, Nikolas appears to Sara in a dream, offering a scale of the same color as Delaney's scales and urging her to help that *Pyr*. As a result, Sara persuades Quinn to go to Delaney's firestorm.

NOLAN TALBOT—son of Niall and Rox. Nolan and his twin brother, Kyle, were born April 28, 2011.

OSCAR—the voice-activated computer "heart and soul" of Peter Madison's smart house.

OLIVIA—a human and former lover of Donovan, a woman with an affection for pearls.

It was with a pearl-encrusted doublet that he first gained her attention, without any intent of doing so; a pearl pendant that saw him invited first to her home; this very pearl necklace that gained him entry to her bedchamber. His blood quickens with the prospect of what she will surrender if he fetches this pearl [beyond price] for her.
—from **Kiss of Fury**

After Donovan was betrayed by Olivia and barely escaped with his life, he avenged himself upon her. He compelled her to watch him shift shape, doing it slowly so that she couldn't misunderstand, and she was driven mad by the sight. Rafferty believed that Donovan kept the Dragon's Tooth pearl as a reminder of love and its perils. He also thought that Donovan used that pearl for the repair of his missing scale because he believed Donovan had loved Olivia. Donovan, in fact, kept the pearl because of its value and as a reminder of misplaced trust. He lost his scale due to his love of his brother, Delaney. Rafferty feared she had claimed the Dragon's Tooth from Donovan. Delaney hated Olivia: Donovan's mention of her sparks Delaney's memory of his own true nature after he had been fed the Elixir.

ORION—one of the Dragon's Tooth Warriors. Orion prefers to take action, and is inclined to be impulsive and outspoken. He is first named in **Kiss of Danger**. At the beginning of **Kiss of Darkness**, he follows the spark of his firestorm in what the Dragon's Tooth Warriors think is Rome in the early 1970's. The memory sparked by the darkfire in **Kiss of Darkness** reveals that Orion was in the tavern with Damien when he first met Petra and their firestorm sparked.

ORION (2)—the son of Damien and Petra, born at the end of **Kiss of Darkness**. He's born blond, because of his time in the underworld, and named in memory of the *Pyr* who was there when Damien and Petra's firestorm sparked.

OWEN—second son of Pwyll, the Cantor of the *Pyr*. Owen experienced his firestorm ca. 800 with Rhiannon and the couple had only the one son, Rafferty Powell.

PAUL VAN VLIET—one of Ginger Sinclair's neighbors in **Winter Kiss**. He raises dairy goats on his farm, adjacent to Sinclair Farm, and sold land to Magnus at a "sweet" price. Unbeknownst to anyone in the vicinity, the particular parcel affords a good view of the entry to the sanctuary of the Dragon's Blood Elixir. Magnus subsequently built his lair on that parcel of land.

PEG MCKAY—a tourist who photographed the hatching of five clones of Boris on Easter Island in **Firestorm Forever**. Peg contacts Maeve O'Neill and is interviewed by her. She's concerned that seeing dragons has affected her husband Arthur's angina. Melissa contacts her for a follow-up interview, and Rafferty is attacked by Jac during the filming.

PELE—a Hawai`ian fire goddess who visits Liz in **Ember's Kiss**, manifesting in Maureen's car as Liz drives through a tunnel. She reminds Liz that she's a Firedaughter and tells her that she needs to use her powers to save Brandon.

"You are wrong," Pele said sternly. "You are stronger than you know. Your gift is potent and it is needed to break the spell that awakens the Earth."

Liz swallowed. She didn't dare to look directly at Pele, but she knew the goddess was speaking of the dark magic she had already sensed. "I gave my gift away, my lady."

"You are no different from him," Pele said. "You cannot change what you are or cast it away. You gave of your power, but it is still with you. It has slumbered like embers of the fire, awaiting the moment of need."

Liz glanced at the goddess in her surprise.

Pele smiled, the raw power in her expression making Liz look back to the road. She could see a pinprick of light ahead and fixed her gaze on that. Pele's words were low and hot, insistent and inescapable. "You have only to feed the fire to bring it to a blaze again. Make no mistake: this burden is yours, Firedaughter. You have been chosen. You can triumph or you can fail."

"But my test..."

"Comes to you in this place, where only you can make the difference." Pele flicked her robes again, sending an array of sparks into the darkness. "There is a certain elegance to it that reveals the hand of the greatest goddess of all. You must embrace the fire that is yours to command."

"Fire kills," Liz insisted, her nostrils as filled with the scent of the ashes that had been her mother as if she still stood on that hill. "Fire burns and destroys."

Especially when she tried to command it.

"Fire purifies," Pele insisted. "Fire is your weapon of choice. Fire sears and fire heals. You know this, Firedaughter. It is your legacy."

—from **Ember's Kiss**

When Liz faces her final test and summons the fire, Pele appears and seizes the *Slayer*, Jorge, taking him back into the volcano as her captive.

PELIAS—Alexander's mentor when he trained as a warrior in Sparta. He took Alexander to serve at the sanctuary at Delphi once he knew that Alexander was *Pyr*. He told Alexander, however, that he wasn't *Pyr* himself. Pelias collects Lysander for his training in **Kiss of Danger**. By the time he and Lysander are attacked by Jorge en route, Pelias has told Lysander about the *Pyr* and about his father. Pelias defends the boy and Alexander arrives in time to help. Pelias sacrifices himself to save Alexander, giving him power with his own dragonsmoke. He confesses to Katina on his deathbed that he is *Pyr* but has lost the ability to shift shape, because he hid his powers for so long. He also tells her that she has healing powers, and instructs Lysander to find all the pieces of Alexander's lost and broken scale, and to keep them safe. When Alexander learns that his mentor was *Pyr*, he says they must expose Pelias' remains to all four elements and learns that Katina is a Waterdaughter.

PETER MADISON—brother of Alex Madison, who is Donovan Shea's mate, husband of Diane and father of Kirsten and Jared.

Peter installed security systems for banks and was considered a straight arrow by his sister. His remote second home was used by Alex and Donovan as a refuge during their firestorm and the rebuilding of the Green Machine.

PETER — one of the Dragon's Tooth Warriors with an inclination to be negative. He is first named in **Kiss of Danger**. In **Kiss of Destiny**, Thad mentions Peter's surprise when his firestorm sparked in their travels, but neither he nor Drake know whether Peter consummated the firestorm.

PETRA — The lost love of Damien, and an Earthdaughter. Petra and Damien's story is told in the Dragon Legion Novella, **Kiss of Darkness**. She is trapped in the timelessness of Hades, eternally pregnant with Damien's child. She has long dark hair and can sing beautifully. She can also turn mortals to stone.

Petra and Damien experienced their firestorm when she was singing in a tavern, and he told her what it was. He also shifted shape, showing his nature to her, and Petra willingly surrendering, thinking that a son would bind this glorious dragon man to her forever. She knew her own powers meant that she could never find happiness with a mortal man, and hoped that she and Damien could be happy because they were both different. But Damien learned that Petra had turned their neighboring villagers to stone and abandoned her, fearing her powers and the prophecy he'd been given at Delphi.

When he finds her in Hades, he doesn't initially realize that she's still pregnant: she drowned when the ship sank that was taking her to a sanctuary. She explains that she'd turned the villagers to stone to defend him, because they were going to ambush and kill him. After they escape the underworld, she gives birth to Damien's son, who they name Orion.

PHELAN TALBOT — the twin brother of Niall Talbot, killed by their father not just because he turned *Slayer* but because he attacked their mother. Phelan always relied upon charm to get what he wanted, and is deceitful and lazy. Phelan is turned to a shadow dragon by Magnus and first reappears to Niall in **Kiss of Fury**. In **Winter Kiss**, Niall and Phelan battle again—Ginger sees the similarity between the two dragons, but she thinks the silver in Phelan's scales looks tarnished and the amethyst appears clouded. In **Whisper Kiss**, Phelan tries to convince Rox that he's Niall. He plans to abduct her out of jealousy that Niall has a firestorm and he won't. He's also fueled by Chen's Dragon Bone Powder which disguises the reality of his being a shadow dragon.

Niall's scales were different from earlier in the afternoon, too. Instead of shining with inner light, looking like faceted gems, they were clouded and dim. The platinum edges didn't gleam and sparkle—they looked more like tarnished silver. He looked more like a dead fish than a piece of jewelry.

And there was a smell about him, a rotten, dead smell, one that made Rox gag. She spit out the scarf and it fell toward the pavement. As she stared at it, shocked that he had flown so high so fast, she saw his sunglasses tumbling toward the pavement, as well.

She looked into his face and her heart stopped cold. His blue eyes had become black, soulless pits. She couldn't even see the difference between the pupil and the iris—they were all black. He saw her surprise and laughed, revealing an impressive array of sharp and yellowed teeth. There was a mark of a tiger on the side of his throat, one that hadn't been there earlier.

He wasn't Niall, after all.

—From **Whisper Kiss**

Niall finds it difficult to kill his twin until he's certain that Phelan can't be healed, as Delaney was. It's Rox who realizes that there's no spark of the divine left in Phelan and proves as much to Niall, giving him the conviction to kill his evil brother.

PWYLL—a *Pyr* and grandfather of Rafferty Powell, born ca. 150 AD. Pwyll was the Cantor, a poet and a spellcaster. His mate was in a convent when their firestorm sparked and he seduced her there, resulting in Myrddin, born ca. 400. Their second son was Owen, Rafferty's father. Because both of Pwyll's sons had died by the time Rafferty reached puberty, Pwyll collected the boy from his mother and took him to his lair, to train him in the art of being *Pyr*. Rafferty ultimately left Pwyll to seek his fortune and ended up in the service of Magnus in Venice, who recognized him as the heir to the Cantor and wanted to learn Pwyll's songs.

When Rafferty saved Cornelia, the pregnant mate of Magnus' brother Maximilian after Magnus killed Maximilian, he took her to Pwyll. Pwyll sheltered her and hid her until the birth of her son, Marcus. Magnus felt the birth of her son and pursued Cornelia to Wales, but Pwyll told him that both mother and child had died in the birth. He showed the corpses to Magnus. In reality, the dead baby was a human child that Pwyll had substituted for Marcus in order to protect the *Pyr* infant. Pwyll and Rafferty argued about the older *Pyr's* deception and parted badly. They never spoke again, even though Rafferty heard Pwyll's song when he was dying roughly a hundred years after the incident. The knowledge of the Cantor was believed to be lost, because Rafferty had refused to apprentice with his grandfather after the murder of the human infant.

By this time, Marcus had been enchanted and subsequently became known as the Sleeper. Pwyll's crystal containing the darkfire appeared in Rafferty's hoard after Pwyll's death and Rafferty defended the Sleeper out of duty.

Pwyll was roused as a shadow dragon by Magnus and battled against Rafferty in **Kiss of Fury**. He was killed by Rafferty in **Whisper Kiss**.

At the end of **Darkfire Kiss**, Marcus is awakened and has the power to speak with the dead, courtesy of the darkfire. He reconciles Rafferty and Pwyll.

In **Flashfire**, Lorenzo reveals that Pwyll taught him the flashfire song, in exchange for Lorenzo defending one of the darkfire crystals in his hoard. The crystal has disappeared and Lorenzo fears the ramifications of that. This would seem impossible— Pwyll died in 1152 and Lorenzo was born in 1585—but Pwyll may have taught Gaspar, Lorenzo's grandfather, or might have appeared in a vision to Salvatore or Lorenzo.

In **Firestorm Forever**, Sloane has a vision of Pwyll's ghost, who teaches him the chant to snare the darkfire in the crystal once again. Sloane sings with Erik, under Pwyll's guidance, and Rafferty is healed:

He could discern a shady figure there, an older man he didn't know.

"This," the apparition whispered in old-speak. He began to chant a song that Sloane found both familiar and unpredictable. It was Pwyll's ghost!

Sloane echoed the chant, learning the tune and the sound of the words. He didn't understand the words themselves and guessed they were Welsh. He didn't know why Pwyll had appeared to him and not to Erik, but he didn't care.

He sang and Erik followed his lead.

The darkfire recognized the chant. From the first note, the blue-green light leapt and snapped, apparently in response to the summons. Erik closed his claw over Sloane's, making his own link to the crystal, and sang with vigor. Sloane and Erik continued together, compelled to keep the slow rhythm of the Cantor's chant. The darkfire glittered like a river of ice crystals, and it flowed toward the crystal, albeit at the speed of a glacier. Finally, Sloane saw its icy swirl inside the crystal itself.

The Cantor's chant was deep and low, as relentless as the movement of the earth's crust. Sloane and Erik sang together, holding the notes longer than Sloane could have believed possible, summoning the darkfire as best they were able. Sloane heard Drake add his voice to theirs and the walls of the house rumbled with their song. Quinn and Lee lent their voices to the chorus, too. The floor vibrated beneath them, as if the earth itself resonated, and the darkfire moved steadily into the stone.

The chant was filled with ancient power. The darkfire's hue brightened where Sloane's dragonsmoke touched Rafferty, creating a glow at those points. The chant seemed to be congealing the darkfire into a brilliant glowing orb of blue-green. Sloane could see the same effect in Erik's dragonsmoke. The darkfire had dimmed beneath Rafferty's scales at the most distant points from the dragonsmoke, as if extinguished there.

Encouraged, Sloane sang with greater vigor, well aware that the eclipse had passed its zenith. The shadow seemed to slide off the moon more quickly, or maybe he was just too aware of how much darkfire still lingered beneath Rafferty's scales.

Suddenly the shadowy outline of Pwyll disappeared.

The lights went out.

Before Sloane's eyes, the river of darkfire glowed as if it were phosphorescent. It danced and glimmered, and the dragonsmoke conduit sparkled along its length with the distinctive hue of darkfire. Sloane sang and the darkfire snapped, racing down the dragonsmoke to embed itself in the crystal.

The eclipse was over.

—from **Firestorm Forever**

PYTHIA AT DELPHI—The oracle of Apollo, the Pythia is a maiden who lives in the shrine and keeps herself pure in order to share her visions as prophecies. Katina, the mate of Alexander, was offered as a maiden to Apollo at the Korykian Cave of the Nymphs by her parents, because of her gift as a Waterdaughter, but was refused. Her parents then took her to Delphi for a prophecy because they were uncertain of her future.

> *Your future lies in fire and earth;*
> *the world's in the son you birth*,"

She met Alexander at Delphi where he was serving in the sanctuary, experienced the firestorm and later bore him a son, Lysander.

In the *Dragonfire* world, the *Pyr* served at Delphi, because they were believed to be the spark cast by Apollo's killing of Pytho. Alexander tells Lysander that there are three sayings carved on the walls of the sanctuary: 'Know Thyself', 'Nothing in Excess', and 'Make a pledge and mischief is nigh.'

At the end of **Kiss of Danger**, Katina and Alexander return to Delphi and receive another prophecy from the Pythia:

"Evil must face its just defeat,
By Pyr *trained to soldiers elite.*
Apollo makes this task your price,
A life of service will suffice.
You, naiad-spawn, lost and found,
Have gifts beyond any count.
Here you will learn skills still unknown;
Here you will bear sons more of your own;
Here you and Pyr *will live as one;*

They understand that they will both serve at the shrine.

In **Kiss of Darkness**, Damien and Petra parted ways, even though she was pregnant, after he received a prophecy at the shrine:

A lost child mourned for many years
A mother who will shed no tears
A dragon warrior turned to stone
A woman abandoned, all alone.
Firestorm's promise will fade to naught
Until stone and fire pay death's cost.
After a Pyr *sacrifice is made*
Destiny's promise can be claimed.

Petra revealed to Damien that she was an Earthdaughter and had turned their neighbors to stone. He feared that he would be the sacrifice and left her. When the darkfire reminds him of this in a vision, Damien realizes that the dragon warriors turned to stone were the Dragon's Tooth Warriors on the mission to stop Cadmus.

QUINN TYRRELL—A *Pyr* and the Smith of the *Pyr*, Quinn is sapphire and steel in dragon form, and has dark hair and blue eyes in human form. He partnered with Sara Keegan after their firestorm, and they live in Traverse City, Michigan. Quinn is an artisan blacksmith—his business is called *Here Be Dragons*—while Sara runs a used bookstore, which she moved from Ann Arbor to Traverse City. Quinn was married centuries earlier to Elizabeth, despite their not having a firestorm, but she was murdered by the *Slayer* Ambrose. Sara and Quinn's story is told in

Kiss of Fire.

Quinn is the youngest son of the previous Smith, Thierry and his mate Margaux. Quinn had four older brothers, but his entire family was exterminated in Béziers in 1209 when Quinn was four by Ambrose in the crusade against the Cathars. Quinn was adopted and raised by a childless peasant couple, Maria and Gauthier. After their death, he wandered in search of his own identity, and was saved from the gallows by Ambrose. Quinn's affinities are to fire and earth.

As the Smith, Quinn has some specific powers, including the ability to strike a talisman, the power to command metal, and the ability to conjure fire out of nothing. He refers to his power over metal as "singing its song", and uses that ability to reshape metal (like Ambrose's challenge coin) or convince locks to open. In **Kiss of Fire**, he starts a fire in Erik's beloved Lamborghini to ensure he gets the attention of the leader of the *Pyr*. (It works.)

Quinn also has the ability to repair the armor of the *Pyr*. Love makes the *Pyr* vulnerable as they each lose a scale after falling in love, and that scale doesn't grow back. Quinn can repair the damage, but only with the assistance of the mate and the four elements. He replaces one of his own scales at the end of **Kiss of Fire**:

> The lost scale was directly over his heart, and a large section of flesh was left unprotected. Sara caught her breath and met the knowingness in Quinn's gaze, not daring to believe the implication of what she saw.
> He had lost the scale because he had lost his heart.
> He was vulnerable because he loved her.
> Sara was both frightened and happy about this revelation. She wanted Quinn to be strong and invincible. She wanted his love, but she didn't want to ever be the reason he lost a battle. She stepped closer and reached up to the tender spot. Quinn bent down so that she could reach. She ran her fingers over it gently, feeling how he shivered at her touch. The skin was sensitive, having been shielded for so very long.

What had she done by falling in love with him?

Sara was afraid; then she understood what he had made. He was trying to restore his armor, so that he could better defend them both. She tested the fit of the wrought-iron scale, not surprised to find that it was perfectly sized and shaped to fit the space.

It was made of iron, which came from the earth.

It had been shaped in the fire.

There were two elements to go.

"But how will we attach it?" she asked. "I can't breathe dragonfire. I don't want to make you vulnerable, Quinn."

"My father believed that his love for my mother made him stronger," Quinn said. "Or maybe it was her love for him that was the charm."

"But how can that be? If you're vulnerable like this..." Sara choked on her words and looked down at the scale, feeling powerless and not knowing what to do. The pregnancy hormones took over, making her eyes fill with tears.

"I'm stronger, because of you."

She looked up and the first tear fell. To her surprise, Quinn touched her cheek with infinite tenderness. That first tear fell on his talon. He transferred the glistening bead to the scale she held.

It sizzled and Sara saw the edge of the iron waver and glow, exactly the way that Quinn glowed before he transformed from man to dragon.

Was it instinct or intuition or plain old logic that told her what to do next? Sara would never really be sure, but she reached up and put that makeshift scale in place. She heard the sizzle of her tear against Quinn's skin and saw him draw up, as if he felt a pang.

The scale looked black and wrong, even though it was attached.

But they had only allowed for three elements.

Air was left.

Sara reached up and kissed the scale, letting her love for Quinn flow through her touch. Then she whispered the words, fanning the scale with her breath. "I love you, Quinn Tyrrell," she said, then said it again. She touched her lips to the scale once more.

The scale shimmered as she lifted her head, as if it were lit by an inner fire or as if it had just come from the forge. Its light became brighter and brighter, until Sara had to close her eyes.

When she looked again, that one scale might have been made of polished sterling. It shone brilliantly, like a badge of honor upon Quinn's chest.

Four elements, present and accounted for.

Four elements, healing a *Pyr* as readily as they could destroy him. By working together, she and Quinn had done it!

Quinn threw back his head and bellowed, a sound of jubilation and pride that made Sara's heart sing and the floor of the shop vibrate.

She laughed as he shifted back to human form before her eyes. Then he caught her in his arms and swung her around, as happy as she had ever seen him. She pushed away his shirt and examined his chest. He had a freckle there that he hadn't had before, but when Sara looked closely at it, it had a silvery gleam.

—from **Kiss of Fire**

In **Kiss of Fury**, Quinn and Sara go to Donovan's firestorm, and Quinn fights with Donovan in his first battle with Keir. Both Quinn and Sara take on the responsibility of sharing information with Alex and convincing her of the merit of the firestorm, the *Pyr*, and Donovan. Quinn also begins to suspect the variables necessary to repair a missing scale—he repaired the armor of Niall, Sloane and Donovan, but only Donovan's repair held. Rafferty suggests that the date of the repair, which was the eclipse heralding Donovan's firestorm, means that the repair can only be done during the firestorm. Quinn has a dream in which the Wyvern opens a portal to his dead father, who then shares knowledge of the Smith with Quinn which Quinn compares to old-speak in his thoughts. Thierry teaches Quinn that the repair must occur during the firestorm and requires the assistance of the mate to adhere for good. Delaney removes Donovan's repaired scale, proving this to be truth. Quinn also sings to the metal of the head gaskets in Alex's prototype Green Machine, changing their shape to make the engine more viable. He ultimately repairs Donovan's armor with the loose scale and Alex's contribution, a jet pin of a swan from her grandmother.

In **Kiss of Fate**, Quinn feels the breaking of the Dragon's Egg just as Sara does. We see the first of the conflict that will haunt him throughout *Dragonfire*: he wants to go to Erik's firestorm, but he also wants to protect Sara (and later, his sons) by staying away. Quinn is the one who feels this most keenly of the *Pyr*. When Delaney attacks Sara, provoked by Magnus' command, Quinn's worst fear seems to be realized. He defends her but becomes very wary of going to firestorms. Quinn repairs Erik's missing scale with his father's runestone, which Eileen has retrieved for him.

In **Winter Kiss**, Quinn has felt Delaney's firestorm but because of that *Pyr's* previous attack, hasn't even told Sara that there is a firestorm. He's determined to keep his family safe, but Sara's dream and her belief that he needs to repair Delaney's armor convinces him to go. Quinn insists that Donovan has to go as well, and suggests that the two of them defend each other's backs and each other's families. Quinn helps in the destruction of the sanctuary and later repairs Delaney's missing scale with one of the amber earrings Ginger inherited from her mother. He fashions the other into a ring, which Ginger wears as a sign of her commitment to Delaney.

In **Whisper Kiss**, Quinn and Sara go to Niall's firestorm, Quinn's doubts once again overcome by Sara's dreams. When they arrive in New York, they're attacked by the shadow dragon made of Quinn's brother Michel, and Quinn destroys him, driven to decisiveness by the proximity of Sara and Garrett. Quinn also recognizes the power of the old spell woven into Chen's tiger brand. He repairs Niall's missing scale, the repair reinforced by the tattoo Rox has given Niall on the exposed patch of skin.

In **Darkfire Kiss**, Quinn is aware of the crackle of darkfire that accompanies the spark of Rafferty's firestorm. Once again, he declines to go to the firestorm to protect his family, because Sara is pregnant again. He repairs Rafferty's scale—with the loose scale and Melissa's tears—at his studio in Michigan on New Year's Eve and all the *Pyr* attend with their mates and children.

In **Flashfire**, Quinn goes to Venice to repair of Lorenzo's scale with Sara and the boys.

In **Ember's Kiss**, Sara sees the prophecy for Brandon's firestorm on the mirror in burning letters and writes it down before it disappears. Concerned by the portent, Quinn creates a smooth circle of wrought iron for Erik to use as a scrying glass, wanting his guarantee that the mates and children will be safe if he and Sara attend the firestorm. Erik says they'll be safe, so they go. Quinn and Sara stand in the south in the protective circle Liz draws for her spell and later, Quinn repair Brandon's scale.

In **Serpent's Kiss**, Sara receives the prophecy for Thorolf's firestorm by automatic writing—she types it into her computer when she's working on the inventory for her bookstore. Both she and Quinn are startled when Marco appears, takes the prophecy and disappears with it. Sara and Quinn attend the repair of Thorolf's scale in Angkor virtually, their images (along with those of their three sons) appearing where Thorolf's reflection should be.

"We gather to heal one of our own," Quinn said and the other *Pyr* raised their wings high. He breathed dragonfire into a small jeweler's forge. The flames shone in the depths of the pool, but also rose as if the fire sat on the surface. Rox caught her breath as its golden light touched the scales of the gathered *Pyr*, making them look like the jeweled treasures she knew them to be. They were virtually motionless and she ran a hand over Niall to reassure herself that she wasn't dreaming.

He caught her hand gently in his claw, gave her fingers a squeeze, and lifted her hand to his chest. She felt his own repaired scale, along with the gift she'd given him to see it done. She also felt the beat of his heart beneath her palm.

Quinn breathed more dragonfire on his forge, the flame heating to silver in its brilliance. He reached up with one claw and to Rox's surprise, his talon passed through the water, as if the surface was a portal to another world. Thorolf surrendered the loose scale to him, and Rox caught her breath as Quinn took it to his side of the barrier. He heated it, that spiral glowing with dark malice.

Would it make T sick again?

Chandra leaned forward to address Quinn. "You need a gift from me," she said softly. "Let me give it to you."

She offered an arrow head with the rune carved in it to Quinn, holding it out in her bare hands to the flame Quinn had conjured. Rox had heard all about Chandra's past and her runes. Still she wasn't sure what to expect, but Quinn coaxed the fire to burn hotter. White flames erupted from the surface of the water to lick the stone in Chandra's hands. The arrow head heated to white. Chandra caught her breath in pain and Rox saw three tears fall to the water.

They were gold, though, instead of clear.

Quinn laughed with delight as he caught them, and his claws came through the surface of the water.

Thorolf caught his breath in awe. "Tears of amber," he whispered.

Chandra flashed him a smile. "Probably the last ones," she said. "I'm fresh out of magic."

"You won't regret surrendering it for me," Thorolf said with a vehemence that made Rox shiver. She'd always known that if he came to care for anything, his love would be potent stuff.

Quinn worked the teardrops of amber into the surface of the scale with his usual dexterity and Rox could see how proud he was of his work. Thorolf took flight, then hovered low over the surface of the water, the brightness of his reflection making Rox narrow her eyes.

"Fire!" Quinn declared and pressed the arrow head into the gap in Thorolf's armor. Rox knew that fire was one of Thorolf's affinities. Thorolf tipped his head back, grimacing at the pain, then blew a plume of dragonfire over the pool.

—from **Serpent's Kiss**

In **Firestorm Forever**, Quinn is with Sara as she delivers their fourth son, Michael: they agree to have one more son, since Quinn was fifth in his own family. He hasn't told her about the firestorm that has sparked, not wanting to distress her until the baby arrived. They drive to Sloane's lair in California, stopping to do some art shows on the way, which Quinn has been planning. Quinn breathes dragonsmoke to help with Rafferty's healing, then joins the Cantor's song with Sloane to drive out the darkfire. He goes with Erik to pick up Thorolf and the captive clone at Lassen Volcanic National Park. When the *Pyr* gather and Sloane buys Sam's house to have more space, Quinn and Sara stay there with their boys. Quinn is part of Melissa's special documenting Drake's scale repair. In the final battle, he fights clones at his lair in Traverse City with Erik, Lorenzo, Donovan and Marco, then attends the scale repair in Chicago. His own repaired scale is one of the ones touched by darkfire at the *Pyrs'* final appearance, indicating that his firestorm will burn forever.

RAFFERTY POWELL—A *Pyr* who is opal and gold in dragon form, Rafferty is the romantic of the *Pyr*, partner of Melissa Smith and adoptive father of Isabelle. Rafferty is tall and broad in his human form, with long chestnut hair and dark eyes. He has a house in Hampstead Heath and a business in London as an antiquities dealer. Rafferty tends to aid firestorms while he awaits his own. He also allies frequently with Erik to ensure the survival, longevity and the good of the *Pyr*. He is one of the survivors of Soren's original Council of Seven. Because of his age, the younger *Pyr* often have looked to Rafferty as a mentor, most particularly Donovan and Thorolf. Rafferty's strongest affinity is to the earth, and he frequently requests the cooperation of Gaia in song. Rafferty is the one *Pyr* who learns to change to a salamander and spontaneously manifest elsewhere. It's possible that he's able to do this because of his lineage—he's from the same family as Myrddin, who was said to be a shape-shifter who could take many forms.

In **Kiss of Fire**, it's Rafferty who figures out that Sara can be rescued from the cabin where the *Slayers* have imprisoned her from below. He sings to the earth to create a tunnel in the earth, thereby letting Quinn bypass the dragonsmoke. Rafferty also corrects some of the misinformation taught to Quinn by Ambrose, notably about the hiding of his clothing when he shifts shape. Rafferty proposes an exchange of information between the *Pyr*, offering to teach Sara how to defend herself against beguiling in exchange for Quinn teaching the others how to use the energy of dragonfire instead of being burned by it. He tells Sara that he's twelve hundred years old.

In **Kiss of Fury**, Rafferty has been assigned by Erik to help

Donovan to abduct Alex: he drives the hearse that they use as a getaway car. It's revealed that Rafferty and Donovan met when Donovan took Olivia's challenge to steal a large pearl from Magnus' hoard, and Rafferty fought in Donovan's defense. Rafferty also dreams of the prophecy linked to Donovan's firestorm: in his dream, it's given to him by his grandfather, Pwyll. He hears the disturbance of Delaney in the earth, and later sings to the Dragon's Tooth when it's planted. Donovan admits that his dragon tattoo is the result of a bet he lost with Rafferty in Atlantic City about twenty years before. He beguiles Alex's sister-in-law Diane when she starts to panic. Rafferty battles against his grandfather, who has been changed to a shadow dragon by Magnus, but doesn't defeat him. When Nikolas escapes the spell of the Dragon's Tooth, Rafferty sings that same song as when the pearl was planted, welcoming him to the *Pyr* side.

In **Kiss of Fate**, Rafferty awaits Erik's firestorm with the leader of the *Pyr*, both of them staying in his London home. They argue, because Rafferty desperately wants a firestorm and Erik resents having a second one. Rafferty learns about the rediscovery of the Dragon's Teeth, when he's invited to view them and recognizes what they are, although he and Erik are uncertain how to claim them. Rafferty feels the destruction of the Dragon's Egg so forcefully that he fears he's having a heart attack and asks Gaia for tidings. After Eileen claims and hides the Dragon's Teeth, she sends her sister to Rafferty with them, and Rafferty buys them. He then plants the seeds in his garden with the help of Niall and Thorolf and sings to them, entreating them to join the *Pyr* when they shake free of their enchantment. When they awaken, he flies to the hidden Academy with them and sings to aid in its destruction, where he witnesses the sacrifice made by Sophie and Nikolas. Afterward, Rafferty wears the black and white ring created by their deaths. When the Academy falls, Rafferty also destroys the shadow dragon made of his grandfather, Pwyll.

In **Winter Kiss**, Rafferty is one of the first of the *Pyr* to arrive at Delaney's firestorm and takes an active role in explaining the *Pyr* to Ginger, as well as encouraging Delaney to think of the future. He also leaves the prophecy about this firestorm written on a napkin for Ginger to find. Zoë pulls the ring into her mouth and gives Rafferty a vision, which leads him to an understanding of Saros cycles and the making of the Elixir. Rafferty's enemy is Magnus Montmorency, who has used his ability to spontaneously manifest elsewhere to escape each of their battles to date. Rafferty tries to do the same and manifests in the sanctuary of the Elixir, where he and Magnus exchange challenge coins and fight. (He also wishes to be in salamander form, though, and is not.) He pretends to be more injured than he is, in order to help Delaney and Ginger, and ultimately imprisons an injured Magnus in the earth, thinking he's ended their duel to the death.

In **Whisper Kiss**, Rafferty comes to Niall's firestorm, and again argues the merit of the *Pyr*, the firestorm and Niall to that *Pyr's* destined mate. He sings in competition with Chen to free Niall when the earth is devouring him, and recognizes that there's another dragon shifter with an affinity to the earth urging Gaia to action. Rox dreams of a conversation between Nigel and Rafferty, in which Rafferty was urging that *Pyr* to make amends with his wife. Rafferty sings the song of steel in the hidden lair of the shadow dragons which causes the collapse of the tunnel. He learns that Magnus was injured in Ohio but hasn't died, and tries to manifest in Magnus' presence — once again, he succeeds, in time to see Chen release Magnus from his prison. He is unable to follow the pair when they disappear.

Rafferty's firestorm with Melissa is recounted in **Darkfire Kiss.** Rafferty tracks Magnus to his lair in Washington DC, intending to finish their duel to the death. He's trying to manifest inside the house when he sees a woman break into Magnus' lair. Concerned for her, he follows and intervenes when she's challenged by Magnus. In this battle, Magnus uses dragonsmoke as a weapon, which is new to Rafferty. Rafferty fights Magnus, ensuring the woman can escape, then follows her. She has stolen a book from Magnus and the *Slayer* Balthasar pursues her at Magnus' command. Rafferty fights Balthasar and is shocked to realize that the woman is photographing them. After defeating Balthasar, Rafferty follows her to get the pictures, and she surrenders the chip from the camera. He destroys it and they're intimate. He takes

Magnus' book while she's sleeping and leaves her, not believing that the sparks he sees are his firestorm.

The next day, Erik contacts Rafferty, enraged that images of Rafferty and Balthasar have appeared on the blog of one Melissa Smith. Rafferty realizes that he's been tricked—she surrendered the wrong chip to him—and returns to Melissa's home, with Thorolf assigned to accompany him. Their firestorm sparks, which outrages Rafferty. He sees Melissa as an opportunist who has targeted the *Pyr* for her own advantage. His firestorm is also tinged by darkfire, an unpredictable force. Magnus also appears at the townhouse, trapping Rafferty and Thorolf in Melissa's house with dragonsmoke, then beguiles Melissa into accompanying him. They leave in a helicopter flown by Balthasar. Rafferty sings to the earth, causes a crack to open in the ground and escapes the house. At the end of the street, a water main has broken, sending a plume of water into the air. He uses that as cover to shift and follow the helicopter.

Rafferty attacks the helicopter in his dragon form and saves Melissa, landing in Arlington cemetery. They introduce each other and Rafferty recognizes her from the television news. He respects her plan to prove she hasn't lost her reporting skills by exposing Magnus. They realize they both have good reasons to pursue Magnus before Magnus attacks Rafferty. In the moment of defeating Magnus, Rafferty reveals the existence of the Sleeper, the son of Magnus' brother Maximilian who has been under his protection since Pwyll died. Jorge intervenes, spontaneously manifesting to steal Magnus away just before he dies. Rafferty retreats to his London lair with Melissa. Erik is already furious over the YouTube video of Thorolf, but there will be another one shortly of Rafferty and Magnus.

In Rafferty's lair, Melissa and Rafferty surrender to the firestorm, but it's not satisfied. Rafferty is astonished, but Erik arrives to chasten him, with Eileen and Zoë. Rafferty and Erik argue, Rafferty defending Melissa's plan to reveal Magnus and restore her career. Once she understands the meaning of the firestorm, Melissa tells Rafferty about her cancer, and the fact that she can't conceive a child. Erik attributes this to darkfire and Rafferty tells Melissa about darkfire. Melissa suggests that the *Pyr* go public to improve their PR and Erik is shocked by the very idea. Rafferty thinks it's a good plan and tells Melissa about his own past, about Pwyll, Myrddin and the Sleeper. Melissa tells him about the breakdown of her marriage.

Rafferty helps Melissa to photograph Magnus' book so that his crimes can be revealed. She stores the images remotely and queues up her blog posts. As she anticipates, her former producer contacts her and she gives him access to the back-up file. Magnus manifests in Rafferty's lair after the blog posts start to go live and abducts Melissa, compelling Rafferty to learn to spontaneously manifest elsewhere himself. He uses the Cantor's song, his affinity with the earth and the ring from Sophie and Nikolas to guide his course. He reaches Melissa, who is trapped in a small room, and breaks them free. He also loses a scale, because he loves Melissa, and entrusts it to her, although she doesn't know what it means. Rafferty realizes that they're beneath Highgate cemetery as an earthquake begins. He suggests that Melissa call Doug and be the reporter on the scene, which she does.

Rafferty manifests in a trapped subway and helps the people there escape, then pursues Magnus through space. Magnus manifests at the Thames Barrier and overcomes the people working there to open the floodgates. He offers to stop if Rafferty reveals the location of the Sleeper and teaches him the Cantor's spell. Rafferty refuses. They fight, then Jorge summons Magnus in old-speak from the Sleeper's refuge. Both Magnus and Rafferty manifest in that cave, where Donovan is already battling Jorge. Rafferty smashes Magnus while the Slayer is still in salamander form, killing him. Rafferty retrieves his challenge coin. Magnus rotates between forms, dying in his dragon form, and Jorge is distracted by the feast of Elixir offered by his corpse. Donovan carries the Sleeper to safety while Rafferty sings to the earth, encouraging it to seal Jorge inside the cave that was the Sleeper's refuge.

Rafferty then returns to London and Melissa. He manifests in a ruined church and meets a little girl named Isabelle whose parents have been killed. He realizes that Sophie's soul has returned:

"This way!" the little girl insisted, catching at Rafferty's hand. She tugged him toward a house that had collapsed even more completely than the church, climbed a pile of rubble, and peered through a broken window. "They're in there. See?"

Rafferty bent down beside her and looked. He saw two pairs of feet in a bed that had a ceiling dropped on it. He frowned, smelling that both people were dead. Then, realizing that the child was watching him, he nodded with purpose. "We had better get some help."

"No," the little girl said. "Isabelle's parents are dead." She fixed a clear gaze upon him. "Isabelle wanted to die, too. She wanted to go with them. She didn't want to stay."

Rafferty thought that perhaps her strange way of expressing herself had to do with the trauma, and he made to reassure her.

"It is how it must be," she said with conviction. "Isabelle is gone, too. I wanted to stay." She held Rafferty's gaze steadily. "So I traded with Isabelle."

"I don't understand what you mean. Aren't you Isabelle?"

"I am now. I look like Isabelle outside."

"Not inside?" Rafferty asked.

She shook her head. She smiled up at him, and her confidence caught at his heart. "I remember you, Rafferty. You used to call me Sophie, but you should call me Isabelle now."

Rafferty gasped. He stared. Was she truly telling him that the soul of Sophie had taken the body of this Isabelle? That they had traded to each get their desire? It was incredible, but the little girl watched him with knowing eyes.

"Isabelle's parents are dead," she said, as if she were the one explaining something simple to a child. "I want to live with you now, Rafferty."

"It's not that simple," Rafferty said, his words falling quickly. "There are authorities and procedures and..."

He fell silent when she reached out and almost touched the white and black ring on his finger. Did she know what it was? Could she know what it was?

She looked up, and he was sure she did know. She smiled a mysterious smile, one that reminded him very clearly of Sophie.

"I want to live with you," she insisted, then dropped her voice to a conspiratorial whisper. "But you will have to call me Isabelle now."

—from **Darkfire Kiss**

Rafferty and Melissa return to his home to find the *Pyr* gathered after successfully closing the Thames Barrier. The Sleeper has also appeared there but remains unconscious. Melissa encourages Rafferty to sing the Cantor's song with the darkfire crystal and he does, which awakens Marco, the Sleeper. He reveals that Pwyll told him of the three darkfire crystals and that it would be his task to hunt the crystals one day, and that Pwyll's tutelage continued in his sleep. He claims the darkfire crystal from Rafferty, and Erik has a vision of his grandfather's ghost. Melissa and Rafferty adopt Isabelle and get married in the garden of her brother's home in California, then Melissa begins a series of documentaries on the *Pyr*, endorsed by Erik.

Melissa stood back and turned to look at the horizon. Her heart leapt at the sight of Rafferty in his dragon form, flying toward her. His wings beat lazily, his opal scales glinting in the light of the setting sun. He was magnificent, powerful, and beautiful, like a jeweled treasure come to life.

And he was her mate.

"God, the camera loves this guy," Doug breathed, and Melissa fought a smile. The camera wasn't alone in that.

Rafferty turned with easy grace, then spiraled down to land elegantly beside Melissa. He flapped his wings; he coiled his tail; he looked into the camera with those glinting eyes; and he exhaled a small stream of dragonfire.

The Covenant, Erik's new decree and part of the compromise with Melissa, insisted that Rafferty could reveal himself only in dragon form, and he could not speak to humans while in that form.

Melissa turned to the camera again. "The *Pyr,* ancient dragons, reveal themselves with a message for our kind. As guardians of the earth, they count humans among the earth's treasures that they are committed to protecting. But we have put the earth in peril, just as we once imperiled the *Pyr*. We need to change our ways, to help defend the gift of this earth instead of destroying it. Come with me as we visit the elements, each in its turn. Come with me to learn how we can join forces with the *Pyr* and make our world a better place."

Melissa turned to Rafferty. He reared back, arching his neck and displaying the scaled beauty of his chest. His tail slid across the earth, stirring the dust. He reached out a glittering talon to Melissa, and she put her hand on his claw. She smiled at the camera with complete confidence, then stepped into his embrace.

He caught her close, roared, then soared into the darkening sky with her in his grasp. Melissa laughed as the wind danced around them, flicking her skirt and running through her hair. She felt alive and powerful as she never had before. She was optimistic in a way she'd never imagined she'd be again.

It was because of Rafferty and the gift he brought to her, the gift of his faith in the future.

—from **Darkfire Kiss**

In **Flashfire**, Rafferty and Melissa are in the Middle East, because she's on assignment. They attend the repair of Lorenzo's scale in Venice.

In **Serpent's Kiss**, Rafferty is perceived to be *Slayer* by Thorolf, who attacks and injures him. Rafferty's faith in Thorolf and the firestorm means that he stands beside the *Pyr* and tries to figure out what Chen has done to him. He uses his ability to spontaneously manifest elsewhere to take Chandra and Thorolf to her sanctuary in Myth. He and Erik disagree about the correct choice—Rafferty wants to help Thorolf but Erik thinks that would be stepping into Chen's trap—and Erik resigns the leadership of the *Pyr* to Rafferty. Thorolf attacks Rafferty again, breaking two of his ribs, but Rafferty's faith is rewarded when Chandra arrives and the heat of the firestorm begins to heal Thorolf. He later helps Thorolf to follow Chandra and they let the firestorm's heat restore Rafferty before Thorolf battles Chen. When he's injured, Rafferty leaves him in Chandra's care, returning to Melissa, Rox and Niall to restore himself. He helps with the plan to get the sword to Thorolf, then makes the final delivery with Lorenzo. Rafferty and Melissa attend the repair of Thorolf's scale at Angkor, where Rafferty insists that Erik take the leadership of the *Pyr* again.

In **Firestorm Forever**, Rafferty takes Isabelle to Chicago when Melissa decides to go to Easter Island and do a broadcast about the clones that hatched there. Jac seizes the darkfire crystal from Marco and shoots it at Rafferty in his dragon form, seriously injuring him. Marco shifts shape and takes Rafferty to Sloane before his human form can be revealed, but the darkfire injury isn't easily treated. The Pyr discover that a combination of breathing dragonsmoke to give Rafferty strength and chanting to put the darkfire back into the crystal is most effective. Pwyll's ghost appears to Sloane to save Rafferty with his song, which the *Pyr* repeat. When Marco steals the darkfire crystal from Sloane's home to defend Jac, Rafferty comes along in his salamander form, and the heat of the firestorm heals Rafferty completely. He returns to Sloane's home, manifesting in Lee's garden right after Drake is healed by the *Pyr*. Rafferty helps in the final battle at Machu Picchu, then attends the scale repair and final appearance of the *Pyr* in Chicago. When Marco breaks the darkfire crystal, the darkfire strikes Rafferty's ring first—the one of Sophie and Nikolas—then his repaired scale, indicating that his firestorm will burn forever.

RAYNOR—the son of Thorolf and Chandra, born in February 2015 at Sloane's home in California. Chandra takes him to the final battle of **Firestorm Forever**, carrying him in a baby sling.

REED—one of the *Pyr* who arrive at Erik's lair at the end of **Kiss of Destiny** and who volunteer to help Drake save Veronica from Jorge in **Firestorm Forever**. Reed is smoky quartz and silver in his dragon form. He dies in the first attempt to save Veronica and is exposed to the four elements by Arach and Kristofer.

RHYS—one of the *Pyr* who arrive at Erik's lair at the end of **Kiss of Destiny** and who volunteer to help Drake save Veronica from Jorge in **Firestorm Forever**. He is garnet and silver in dragon form and has dark hair and dark eyes. Rhys has his firestorm in **Dragon's Heart** in the *DragonFate* series.

RICK—One of Brandon's surfer buddies in **Ember's Kiss**. Rick has dreadlocks.

ROB—Liz's former boyfriend mentioned in **Ember's Kiss** who dumped her. Maureen thinks that Rob broke Liz's heart and that the fact that they work in the same lab isn't helping Liz move on, but Liz has decided that Rob is cocky and self-absorbed. Maureen also warned Liz against Rob, because he reminded the older woman of her first husband.

ROXANNE KINCAID—A tattoo artist, partner of Niall and mother to twin boys, Kyle and Nolan, as a result of the firestorm. Rox and Niall subsequently had a second set of twin boys, Ahern and Ruark. Rox is tiny but fierce, with dark hair and blue eyes, and protective of those she loves. She is vegetarian and straight edge. She disguises her pretty features by dressing as a punk and wearing a lot of black makeup. She has a lifelong love affair with dragons and has covered the walls of her apartment with paintings of dragons. She has a husky voice, which Niall finds really attractive.

Rox ran away from home as a teenager to escape her step-father's abuse, hoping to find her older sister, Suzie, who had run away earlier for the same reason. Instead, she ended up on the streets, and was taken in by Chynna, owner of the tattoo shop Inspiration Ink. She worked in the shop in exchange for room and board. Once Chynna saw Rox's talent, she made Rox her apprentice. Subsequently, Rox and another of Chynna's projects, Neo, became partners in Imagination Ink. Inspired by Chynna, Rox likes to pay it forward by doing favors for others.

Rox is the one mate who has always loved dragons and been inspired by them. She's painted murals of dragons on the walls of her apartment, which astonish the *Pyr* when they first see them. Here's Niall's reaction in **Whisper Kiss**:

He was shocked by the artwork. The walls were filled with framed posters of dragons, and one wall was actually painted in a fresco of a dragon in flight.

No, they weren't posters—they were original paintings. He'd never seen so many images of dragons, let alone so many that were so beautiful. Each dragon was unique, each image rendered with a loving hand and an eye for detail.

The living room, otherwise, had only a pair of vintage couches. They were slightly different, but covered in the same natural cotton. Their backs were low enough that they didn't obstruct the view of the art. The floor was hardwood, polished to a sheen and devoid of any rugs. White rice-paper blinds covered the windows, which must have been large, judging by the expanse of closed blinds. The only color was from the art, which seemed to glow on the walls.

No doubt about it, the dragons held court.

Niall couldn't stop looking at the paintings. He moved around the room, examining each in turn, well aware of Rox's nervous silence as she watched him.

There was one dragon perched on a mountain aerie; another flew low over a lake as clear as a mirror, his scaled belly reflected perfectly in the water. There were two fighting each other, their tails locked together and their teeth bared. There was a dragon sleeping beside his hoard, one eye open a slit as an intrepid woman ventured closer. The fresco was of a moonstone and silver dragon, raging on the attack. Each dragon was so realistic that Niall wouldn't have been surprised to hear the rumble of old-speak in his thoughts.

He gradually realized they had been created by the same hand. There were commonalities in the way the scales were articulated, the way the eyes had been drawn, the assumption of the musculature beneath the scaled skin. He saw an R in the bottom corner of one, an *R* executed with flourishes, and he knew why Rox was self-conscious. He remembered Thorolf's tattoo.

He turned to look at her.

She was watching him, her arms folded across her chest, her eyes filled with doubt as she nibbled one thumbnail. He'd never seen her uncertain, and his heart clenched with the reason why she felt vulnerable.

"Did you create all of these?" He heard the wonder in his own voice and didn't try to hide his awe.

Rox nodded once; then she swallowed.

"They're wonderful." Niall couldn't help but look again. The level of detail was fascinating, and he could have studied each work for hours on end. "Do you sell your work?"

"No." There was no question in her tone. "These dragons are

for me."
—from **Whisper Kiss**

Rox first sees Thorolf shift in a bar, when he gets in a fight. She covers for him and takes him home, although her initial thought that he's her fantasy man come to life is quickly shattered by Thorolf's truth. All the same, Rox is convinced that everyone deserves a second chance, or as many second chances as they need to get it right. She fails to make much difference in Thorolf's attitude, but remains optimistic. At the beginning of **Whisper Kiss**, she's found Thorolf a delivery job with an organic grocery, but Thorolf chooses to apprentice with Niall instead. Rox believes this story to be a lie, suspecting that Thorolf is moving in with another woman, and goes to Niall Talbot to confirm Thorolf's story. Even though Niall and Rox think that they have little in common when they first meet, Niall proves to be the dragon Rox has been waiting for. Ironically, Thorolf is the one to see the truth of their shared assumptions first: he accuses Niall of sounding like Rox when the two *Pyr* argue in Ginger's barn in **Winter Kiss**.

Rox is referred to as the Phoenix in the prophecy governing her firestorm with Niall, and in the dream that she has thanks to Niall's Dreamwalker skills, she sees herself rising from the ashes of her past, which no longer can hurt her. Subsequently, Niall has a phoenix tattooed on his back, to indicate Rox, which she has the dragon on her back colored to match Niall's hues. She also is reunited with her lost sister, thanks to Niall, who locates Suzie with his newfound skills. Rox and Niall's story is told in **Whisper Kiss**.

In **Darkfire Kiss**, Rox and Niall attend the repair of Rafferty's scale at Quinn's studio in Michigan. In **Flashfire**, Niall and Rox attend the repair of Lorenzo's scale in Venice with their twin sons, Kyle and Nolan, who are just four months old.

In **Ember's Kiss**, Rox recognizes and explains that the artist who did Brandon's tattoos is a shaman, and she identifies the spiral one as a protective talisman. When she and Niall decide to go to Brandon's firestorm, she suggests that they leave Kyle and Nolan with her sister, Suzie, but Niall wants his whole family together. Rox also recognizes that there's something unusual about the mark on Liz's arm and asks Liz about it.

In **Serpent's Kiss**, Rox keeps a log of Niall's nightmare about Astrid, trying to help him solve the mystery of who she is, and why he's having the recurring dream. She recognizes that Thorolf's scales have been tattooed, which is why they look dark. (The Elixir used for those tattoos is why his scales are clouded.) She realizes that the tattoos are turning him *Slayer* against his will. She attends Thorolf's scale repair at Angkor with Niall, as well as their sons Kyle and Nolan, and plans to paint the scene when she returns home.

At the beginning of **Firestorm Forever**, Rox is pregnant. She discovers the video online of the clones of Boris and recognized the location where Ronnie is being held captive. With the help of her friend Toad, she identifies it as Seaview Hospital on Staten Island, which is abandoned. She remembers how to get in by the underground tunnels, thanks to a visit she made there once with Neo, and shares that information with Drake. She takes refuge at Delaney's lair with Niall, Donovan, Alex and their sons, and delivers her second set of twins (Ahern and Ruark) in Ohio. She and Niall attend the scale repair at Erik's lair in Chicago and she watches the *Pyrs'* final display for Melissa's documentary.

RUARK TALBOT—son of Rox and Niall, twin brother of Ahern, younger brother to Kyle and Nolan. Ahern and Ruark were born in March 2015.

SAHIR—the original name of Cinnabar.

SALVATORE DI FIORE—A *Pyr* and Lorenzo's father. Salvatore was the son of Gaspar and Giovanna di Fiore, but never acknowledged by his *Pyr* father. He was adopted by his grandfather (his mother's father) and raised as a nobleman in Venice. When he came into his *Pyr* powers, Soren sent his son, Erik, to Venice to tutor Salvatore and the two became good friends.

Salvatore had a firestorm with Angelina, a Venetian courtesan, and the result of that firestorm was Lorenzo. Like his father, Salvatore was challenged by the notion of commitment. Unlike his father, he returned repeatedly to his mate. One of the couple's great joys was sharing dragonflights together, but one of their flights was ultimately witnessed by one of Angelina's disapproving neighbors. Angelina was attacked by a mob while Salvatore was absent and her house was burned. She was killed in defense of her only son, and Salvatore arrived too late to save her. He blamed himself for her death.

Once Lorenzo grew up and established himself, Salvatore had less interest in the world. By the time we meet him in **Flashfire**, he's been hibernating for years, brooding over the loss of Angelina. Lorenzo has ensured his father's protection as the older *Pyr* has become increasingly frail. Because of the influence of darkfire, Salvatore gained the ability to visit what he called 'the realm of the Wyvern', where he saw dreams and memories of his own as well as those of others. In this realm, he reconnected with Angelina and finally died, leaving this realm to join her forever in that one.

In **Kiss of Danger**, it is revealed that Salvatore stole the darkfire crystal from Lorenzo's hoard and gave it to Drake, because he had a dream that this was his responsibility. He believes this dream to have come from the Wyvern.

SAMANTHA WILCOX—a biological researcher, mother of Nathaniel Sullivan, sister of Jac Wilcox and mate of Sloane Forbes, Sam retreats to California after the death of her son and the dissolution of her marriage to Derek. She abandons her career, convinced that she failed her son by not finding an antidote to the virus in time to save his life. She buys the house next to Sloane's, just because it's available, and takes up tarot card reading. She is blond with blue eyes. Sam begins an affair with her neighbor, Sloane, but breaks it off when she sees his dragon tattoo. She blames dragons for her son's death and won't associate with anyone who admires them. Sam and Sloane are repeatedly intimate and repeatedly interrupted by his duties to the *Pyr*, but he challenges Sam to reconsider her choices and to grieve for her son.

Because of his influence, she reunites with her sister, Jac, and they begin to rebuild their relationship.

Sam returns to work at the CDC when Veronica is released by Jorge and diagnosed with the virus. She's determined to make the most of this second chance, and is infuriated when the *Pyr* steal Ronnie away. When she dreams of Sloane's tattoo, she connects the proverbial dots and returns to California. She argues with Sloane when she realizes that he's a dragon shifter himself, but then works with him in pursuit of an antidote. Drake explains to her about the firestorm and she appreciates Sloane's noble impulses and they make peace. Sam makes the breakthrough to find the antidote, then is awed that Sloane cedes all credit for their work to her. She returns to the CDC to have the antidote tested, manufactured and distributed, but misses Sloane. Ronnie has given Sam the scale that Sloane lost and she keeps it as a momento.

Jac gives Sam the Dracontias, arguing that it will provide a cure, but Sam is skeptical and the sisters argue again. When Sam watches Melissa's special about the repair of Drake's armor, she's thinking about Sloane and is awed when he comes to her. They're intimate and she gives him the Dracontias, as well as the idea that it might be an antidote for the Elixir. She's in the research labs at the university hospital in Ann Arbor when the *Pyr* conclude their final battle, and Sloane follows the spark of the firestorm to her. She decides to move back to California with him, knowing that their oldest son will be the Apothecary of the *Pyr*.

SARA KEEGAN—A former accountant turned used bookstore owner, Sara is practical. She has long fair hair and is delicately built, with green eyes. She was a finance person who traveled constantly, and even had to cancel out of a long-planned trip with her parents to see Machu Picchu to work. When her parents were killed in an accident on that trip, she re-evaluated her priorities, deciding to move to Ann Arbor and run the New Age bookstore left to her by her eccentric aunt. In **Kiss of Fire**, she has her firestorm with Quinn Tyrrell, the Smith, and is revealed as the Seer of the *Pyr*. She is the mother of Garrett, Ewan, Thierry, and Michael.

The only thing Sara has left of her parents is their wedding rings. She inherited both the bookstore and a house from her aunt Magda, and lives in the apartment on the upper floor of the house. The shop is located in Nichols' Arcade, which is where she is first attacked by a dragon—it's Ambrose who assaults her, and Quinn who defends her, without realizing the identity of her dragon attacker. Ambrose leaves a coin on the threshold of her shop which Quinn finds. The shop also seems to have a ghost, which Sara suspects is her Aunt Magda. Books fall off shelves of their own accord and the air conditioning unit seems to have a mind of its own. She even finds her aunt's tarot cards under a chair. All of this is an attempt by the aunt to persuade Sara to consider that she has psychic gifts.

When Quinn is exhibiting his wares at the outdoor art exhibition, Sara visits his booth and buys a doorknocker made of wrought iron, unaware that Quinn has created it as a talisman for his firestorm. It is a mermaid that Sara finds particularly beautiful. This mermaid heats to red hot when Sara is endangered, acting as a beacon to Quinn.

Quinn breathed fire into the forge, sending its flames higher and hotter than coal and coke could have made them. The heat would have driven him away in human form, even with his protective gear, but his dragon form welcomed the fire.

With his talons, he removed the mermaid door knocker from the fire where she waited. She was red-hot, gleaming and glowing, on the verge of turning into liquid. He finished the end of her tail with sure strokes. He had known when the iron took this feminine shape beneath his hand that his turn had come; he had known that he could finish the work only in dragon form.

His firestorm was coming.

The others, good and bad, would follow the beacon of its heat.

This time, he would triumph.

This time, he would protect what was his to defend.

He exhaled mightily, sending sparks dancing throughout his workshop, infusing the hot iron with his desire. The mermaid glittered as if she were made of fire, caught in a magical wind of Quinn's making. She looked to be filled with sparks, but in truth, she was filled with the power of his will.

He was the Smith.

His talisman was struck.

Let them try to stop his firestorm.

—from **Kiss of Fire**

In **Kiss of Fury**, Sara is pregnant with Garrett when she and Quinn go to Donovan's firestorm. She takes the lead in explaining about the *Pyr* and the firestorm to Alex, who is wary of dragons. The two become friends. She has two dreams, one of men sprouting from seeds and one of pearls being planted, both visions from the Wyvern. She doesn't immediately realize that the dreams are about the Dragon's Tooth Warriors, but in the second dream, she hears the name *Cadmus* and researches it. As a result, the *Pyr* bury the large pearl Donovan once claimed from Magnus' hoard and Nikolas sprouts from it, the first of the Dragon's Tooth Warriors.

In **Kiss of Fate**, Sara feels the breaking of the Dragon's Egg, although (like Quinn) she isn't sure what has happened, only that it's frightening. They decide to go to Erik's lair. When Sara tries to help Sloane to heal Delaney there, her pregnancy awakens the command Magnus has buried in Delaney's mind and Delaney tries to seize her unborn child. Quinn defends her and Delaney attacks Alex, also against his own will, then chooses to become an outcast so he doesn't injure the mates of his fellows or their sons. At the end of the book, Sara lends Sigmund's book to Eileen as a resource for the reference she's compiling about the history of the *Pyr*.

In **Winter Kiss**, Quinn refuses to go to Delaney's firestorm because of Delaney's aggression toward Sara during her pregnancy. But Sara dreams of Nikolas and Sophie seeking each other. In her dream, Nikolas gives her a scale that is copper and emerald, like Delaney's dragon scales, and interprets this as a sign that Quinn must go to Delaney to repair his scales. She's also aware that the dream is slightly different from the ones sent to her by Sophie, and speculates that the *Pyr* have a new Wyvern.

In **Whisper Kiss**, Sara dreams of the prophecy linked to Niall and Rox's firestorm, which claims that Niall can become the Dreamwalker. She doesn't know that the partial eclipse has triggered Niall's firestorm and puts it aside, assuming it refers to the next total eclipse. She has a dream the next night and receives a second prophecy referring to Chen's ancient charm. Quinn has a dream the same night about his brother, Michel, who has been turned into a shadow dragon, and they choose to go to Niall's firestorm. Sara witnesses Quinn's destruction of Michel and is one of the mates threatened by Chen in the big finish.

In **Darkfire Kiss**, Sara notices that the mermaid doorknocker made by Quinn—and hanging on the door of her bookstore in Traverse City—is glowing when she leaves the shop. It looks as if it's made of blue glass instead of wrought iron. She knows this is a warning of some kind and returns to the shop, taking out Sigmund's book, *The Habits and Habitats of Dragons: a Complete Guide for* Slayers, and looks up 'blue flames'. That leads her to the entry for darkfire, which she doesn't find encouraging. She used her aunt Magda's tarot cards for guidance, and turns up the card Death, which she knows is an indication of profound change. Quinn then tells her that there's a firestorm tinged by darkfire, that it's Rafferty's, and that they won't be going. This is because she's pregnant and he doesn't want to put her at risk. Sara subsequently dreams of a little girl and wonders if she's carrying the Wyvern—at the end of the book, when the *Pyr* gather for Rafferty's scale repair, she recognizes Isabelle as the girl from her dream.

In **Flashfire**, Sara and Quinn attend the repair of Lorenzo's scale in Venice. Sara spends time in Lorenzo's library, and both she and Quinn babysit the twins for Niall and Rox.

In **Ember's Kiss**, Sara sees the prophecy for Brandon's firestorm on the mirror in burning letters. She writes it down before it disappears and when she and Quinn go to Hawaii, she shows it to Liz. She and Quinn stand in the south in the protective circle Liz draws for her spell. They both attend the repair of Brandon's scale.

In **Serpent's Kiss**, Sara receives the prophecy for Thorolf's firestorm by automatic writing—she types it into her computer when she's working on the inventory for her bookstore. Both she and Quinn are startled when Marco appears, takes the prophecy and disappears with it. Sara and Quinn attend the repair of Thorolf's scale in Angkor virtually, their images (along with those of their three sons) appearing where Thorolf's reflection should be.

In **Firestorm Forever**, Sara delivers her fourth son, Michael, and she and Quinn agree to have one more, since Quinn was fifth in his own family. They decide to drive to Sloane's lair in California, stopping to do some art shows on the way. When the *Pyr* gather and Sloane buys Sam's house to have more space, Quinn and Sara live there. Sara is with Chandra when she delivers her son, and sees Chandra's vision of Snow.

SEAN SHEA—the second son of Ginger and Delaney, born May 14, 2012.

SEAN SINCLAIR—Ginger's father. He died in a car accident with his wife Elena when Ginger was about a year old. The couple had no other children, and Ginger was raised by his mother. The amber and silver earrings that Ginger wears in **Winter Kiss** and offers for the repair to Delaney's scale were given by Sean to Elena.

SIGMUND GUTHRIE (BORN SIGMUND SORENSSON)—Erik's son by his first firestorm, a *Pyr* scholar with a passion for unearthing and compiling lost dragon lore, and one who turned *Slayer*. Sigmund was born in 1770. Sigmund is malachite green and silver in his dragon form, and slender. He has blue eyes, which remind Erik of Louisa, Sigmund's mother, when father and son meet in **Kiss of Fire**. Sigmund is missing a scale, which he says is due to his love of his mother. He blames Erik for Louisa's death.

Sigmund is the author of *The Compleat Guide to Slaying Dragons*, a compilation of dragon lore that he published for *Slayers* to better eliminate *Pyr* like Erik. It is a rare volume, and Sigmund reveals in **Winging It** that he printed and published the book himself, by hand. He insists to Zoë that there was only ever a single copy.

In **Kiss of Fury**, it becomes clear that Sigmund is under the talon of Boris Vassily. He waits for Alex Madison to return to her apartment and attacks her there, but fails to kill her because of

Donovan's intervention. Sigmund removes the engine from the hidden prototype of the Green Machine, at Boris' command. Sigmund subsequently tries to kidnap Alex's nephew, Jared Madison, from his home. In defense of his son, Peter Madison stabs Sigmund with a letter opener in the space where he was missing a scale, then Sloane, Niall and Erik came to the boy's rescue.

Sigmund's failures make Boris wonder if he's really a spy for Erik: he threatens Sigmund and makes the offhand comment that inspires Sigmund to undertake a new project.

Boris scowled at the car overhead. "If only I could clone myself a dozen times, we would be rid of the *Pyr* and their pesky humans."

There was a pause, one that caught Boris' attention. He turned to find Sigmund looking thoughtful, even as he rubbed the red mark on his throat.

"Maybe I can do something about that," Sigmund said. "Would that count as competence?"

Boris snorted, even though the possibility made his pulse leap. Dozens of himself! Encouragement didn't motivate well as fear.

"It's all so much idle speculation," he said, using his bored tone. "Let me know if you can manage it." He pointed at the car overhead. "Now, get to work before I really get annoyed."
– from **Kiss of Fury**

In **Kiss of Fate**, Sigmund realizes that his father is having a second firestorm and wants to thwart it. He makes a deal with Magnus to destroy Erik's new mate in exchange for a sip of the Elixir, then corners Eileen in a research library. Sigmund is fatally wounded in the subsequent dragon fight, but thanks to Eileen's efforts, he and Erik take a step toward reconciliation. Sigmund asks Eileen to persuade Erik to do the death ritual so he can't be made into a shadow dragon and Erik does. Later, Eileen finds Soren's runestone in the pocket of the coat she put over Sigmund when he was dying. Erik asks Sigmund how to destroy the Elixir when Sigmund is dying and he doesn't manage to answer before he passes, but he later appears in Erik's dreams to provide more information about the Elixir—and to hint that Eileen carries the new Wyvern.

In **Winter Kiss**, Magnus reveals that the experiment on Delaney with the forcible injection of the Elixir was Sigmund's research project. In **Darkfire Kiss**, Sigmund appears in a vision to Erik, telling him that the Sleeper awakens and referring to the three darkfire crystals of the Cantor. Typically, he hints at more than he confesses, and his visit frustrates Erik.

In **Flashfire**, Sigmund brings the ghost of Angelina to Erik in a vision, translating her confession (which is in Venetian) for Erik. She tells him of Salvatore's promise to ensure Lorenzo's happiness, and Erik realizes that Lorenzo is in love with Cassie. Erik also sees Angelina with Salvatore and guesses that Salvatore has either died or will soon, his promise kept, and that he'll be reunited with his beloved.

In **Firestorm Forever**, Sigmund appears in a recurring dream of Erik's, warning that the blood moon will ripen the eggs. Erik doesn't know what this means. The "eggs" are the clones of Boris Vassily created by Sigmund, which will hatch during the eclipses that mark the end of the Dragon's Tail Wars. Since Boris and Erik have exchanged challenge coins, all thirteen clones will try to kill Erik. Sigmund tries to warn his father. Sigmund also appears with the ghost of Tynan in a vision to Erik, when Erik is standing in Lee's garden at Sloane's home. It's implied that Sigmund has brought Tynan to Erik. Tynan tells Erik that the Apothecary (Sloane) is the one who can choose to heal the earth.

Sigmund makes cameo appearances in the *Dragon Diaries*, using his powers help his half-sister Zoë develop her own and save the *Pyr*. In this, Sigmund earns his redemption.

SLOANE FORBES—A *Pyr*, Sloane is tourmaline and gold in dragon form, owner of a greenhouse and nursery specializing in herbs, and the Apothecary of the *Pyr*. His scales are said to be magnificent, shading from green to purple to gold and back again over his length from nose to tail. In human form, Sloane has dark hair and dark eyes, and is tall and slim. He's said to be wiry, and that his fighting prowess is underestimated. His affinities are to fire and water, and he is serene for a dragon. His firestorm with Samantha is told in **Firestorm Forever**.

In **Kiss of Fire**, Donovan tells Quinn that Sloane is their healer, and that he has herbal ointments to heal injuries. Quinn notices that Sloane also chants as he's tending Donovan's wounds, much as he sings to metal. It's Sloane who realizes that the *Slayers* have some new power to heal—it proves to be the Elixir. Sophie teaches him another healing chant when she tends Erik after his injury.

In **Kiss of Fury**, Sloane comments that Donovan heals fastest of the *Pyr*, when he's treating his injuries with an unguent. Quinn has tried to repair Sloane's armor without success. Sloane has also identified a manuscript in his collection that he thinks holds the key to the *Slayers'* new power, but can't decipher the code—until the Wyvern sends him a vision of the translation. It's only a glimmer but it's enough to start Sloane on the right track and he translates the text. It's about the spark of the Great Wyvern and what happens when *Pyr* die and an old procedure for making a dead *Pyr* rise and turn *Slayer*. This can only be done if the corpse hasn't been exposed to the four elements within half a solar day, but the *Pyr* know that this death ritual isn't consistently practiced anymore.

Sloane, Niall and Erik defend the house of Alex's brother, Peter, when the *Slayers* attack, and Sloane is the dragon that her nephew Jared sees outside. When the shadow dragons reveal themselves, one of them is Tynan, Sloane's father, and he has a hard time slaughtering him (just as Magnus intended). Jared steps into danger, wanting to help "his dragon, and later, Sophie compels him to forget what he's seen. Donovan joins the battle against the shadow dragon that was Sloane's father and, once the shadow dragon is dismembered, Sloane helps to incinerate the remains with dragonfire. Sloane chooses to see the positive in Delaney's choices, and offers to try to heal him.

In **Kiss of Fate**, the *Pyr* gather for the eclipse and Sophie encourages Sloane, saying that he's made progress, but Delaney has doubts. Sloane and Delaney are planting seeds in his greenhouse when they feel the Dragon's Egg break and they go to Chicago to learn more. Sloane tells the *Pyr* about the Dragon's Blood Elixir because he's finished translating the manuscript, and hypnotizes Delaney to try to learn more about the Academy.

In **Winter Kiss**, after Delaney consummates his firestorm with Ginger but the sparks still fly, a chance comment from Ginger makes Sloane recall a book in his collection. He goes home to retrieve it, then returns to Ohio—it is clear that Rafferty already knows about the volume. Sloane tells the *Pyr* that even though he's broken the code of the book, he doesn't understand the verses in it. With Alex's help, he figures out how to destroy the Dragon's Blood Elixir with nitric acid.

In **Whisper Kiss**, Sloane comes to New York at Niall's summons, to try to answer the question of whether Phelan can be redeemed. Rafferty reveals that Sloane always prefers tea to coffee. Rafferty, Sloane and Thorolf manage to save Niall when Chen targets him and tries to have the earth swallow him. Sloane is part of the group that go into the underground tunnels to seek Chen and the lair of the shadow dragons but Chen distracts him and guides him away from the others. By the time he finds his way back, Thorolf has been injured. When Rox is injured by Phelan, Sloane tries to heal her, but she remains cold and unconscious.

The wound missed the tattoo, slicing from Rox's right shoulder down to her waist. Her skin was puffed and bluish white, the cut silvery as if touched by frost. She was cold, but the wound was frigid, as though generating a chill of its own.

"Worse than I thought." Sloane swore under his breath as the two of them stared and Niall's heart sank. Sloane eased his finger along the cut, exploring its depth. He shook his head and frowned. "Nothing in it. Nothing I can pull out, anyway."

Niall leaned toward Rox and felt the firestorm glimmer between them. Its heat was feeble, which terrified him. The firestorm wasn't satisfied—was it fading because Rox was going to die?

Niall put his hand on Rox's shoulder and the glow became a bit brighter. Niall felt the others come into the room, but he was focused on Rox. The firestorm had no sparks, no flame—just a radiance.

Like that of glowing coal.

Dying coals.

Sloane caught his breath. "Touch the wound," he commanded with quiet force. "There's no time to look it up. Just try."

Niall laid one hand alongside Rox's cut. The firestorm's sparks sputtered weakly and disappeared, as if the flame had been doused.

Frightened, he put his other hand beside the first one, bracketing the cut between his index fingers. Three sparks danced between his hands and Rox's skin for a moment before there were no more. The glow remained, though, and he dared to hope it was brighter.

"Not much, but we'll work with it." Sloane put his hands on top of Niall's and began to chant. Niall heard the Apothecary's song and let it fill his thoughts. He let it drive his intent; he begged it to fulfill his wish.

And when he understood its rhythm, he added his voice to Sloane's. They sang together with force and yearning.

The firestorm responded, kindling a greater heat beneath Niall's hands. There were still no visible flames, but Niall felt as if someone had stirred those coals.

As if they might not die after all.

They needed fuel. Niall slid his hands up and down Rox's skin, trying to coax the toxin from her body, and he sang louder. He let the memory of her kisses fill his thoughts, recalled the vigor of the burning firestorm, and tried to summon her to the bonfire they could make together.

The firestorm sparked, its radiance growing.

Niall knew the moment that Delaney came to stand behind him. He felt the weight of Delaney's hand on his shoulder and when he glanced up, he saw that Delaney had put his other hand on Sloane's shoulder. Delaney added his voice to the chant.

The firestorm's flame erupted beneath Niall's hands.

He sang even louder and with more force, determined to bring Rox back from wherever she had gone. He knew there was a shadow in her past, and knew she had triumphed over it before.

Phelan's touch must have reopened that old wound, revealing its hidden depths. Niall coaxed the flame with all his heart and soul. He sang Sloane's song of healing and marveled at the power of the crackling firestorm.

Rafferty added his baritone to their chorus, Erik's voice giving their song another voice of strength. Quinn lent his voice to the effort, as well. Niall dared to hope that they could heal his mate, that the firestorm could be rekindled to burn bright enough. Ginger, Eileen, and Sara added the weight of their hands and the force of their wills.

The flames danced beneath his hands, simmering and sizzling, taking on the sensual turn that he associated with the firestorm. The way the influence of his friends helped Rox brought tears to Niall's eyes.

He kept singing, his voice becoming even more urgent.

Sloane changed his song as the wound began to weep a dark fluid. He called to the toxin, summoning it forth, removing it as it revealed its dark shadow. It looked vile, like oil, but had a shimmer like mercury. Delaney's low voice reminded Niall of how Delaney had been able to follow the firestorm's song through the darkness. They worked together until the wound ceased to weep dark fluid.

Then the flames abruptly died.

A white line glowed coldly on Rox's back. She was utterly still, cold, and motionless.

Had she died? Niall felt for her pulse in fear. It was there, slow and feeble, but fluttering at her throat.

"It found an answering shadow within her," Sloane said with disgust. "It found a resonance in her mind."

"What the hell does that mean?" Niall demanded.

"That Rox has an old wound. The shadow found it and fed it."

"But the firestorm should be able to heal it," Niall protested. "It was working so well."

Sloane put a hand on his shoulder. "It began the process. It removed the taint so that it couldn't spread farther, but it had already taken root."

"But how do we finish what we started? How do we save her?"

"I don't know."

—from **Whisper Kiss**

Niall then learns to dreamwalk, to locate Rox's painful memory and eradicate it so that she can be healed. Once he's done, Sloane's unguents work on Rox's wound. Sloane also sees Rox's back piece in this scene and later asks her to give him a tattoo, a caduceus with two dragons instead of two snakes, on his left bicep. The tattoo is a reminder of his father's warning, that the Apothecary's responsibility is to heal, regardless of the cost to himself. Here's Sam's first impression of the tattoo:

"A caduceus," she whispered and he was intrigued that she recognized the symbol. "But with dragons." She shuddered and pulled away, evading his gaze. "Why?"

"Because I thought it was cool," he said lightly, which wasn't entirely a lie. He watched her, noting how she tried to hide her revulsion.

"A symbol of the dead? Of the god who was the patron of *thieves*?" She shook her head. "Why would you think that was cool? And with dragons!" She drew back to look at him. "What kind of life do you live?"

Sloane was intrigued. Most people assumed the caduceus was the symbol of health care, although that was really the Rod of Asclepius, which featured only one snake. The caduceus did have a darker meaning, one he found appropriate for his inherited role among the *Pyr*.

It was also evocative of his father's warning, murmured so long ago.

—from **Firestorm Forever**

The tattoo evokes a quote from William Godwin's *Lives of the Necromancers*: 'It is said the wand would wake the sleeping and send the awake to sleep. If applied to the dying, their death was gentle; if applied to the dead, they returned to life.' This foreshadows the choices Sloane will make in **Firestorm Forever** to eliminate the *Slayer* clones.

In **Darkfire Kiss**, Sloane watches over Eileen and Zoë when Erik meets Lorenzo. When Sloane feels the spark of the darkfire, he recalls his father's desire to see the mythic flame, but he doesn't share his father's fascination for it—he distrusts it instead. He also goes to Brandt on Erik's command to warn his cousin about

Lorenzo, but argues with Erik about this plan first, since it will break the blood oath he swore to Brandt. He escorts Brandt to Erik when that *Pyr* decides his real argument is with the leader of the *Pyr* and manages to intervene so that the two make peace. He also shares his father's conviction that there is good in darkfire when the *Pyr* doubt as much. When Rafferty's scale is repaired at Quinn's studio, Sloane brings Sara a book on mystical herbalism.

In **Flashfire**, Sloane defends Eileen and Zoë when Erik meets with Lorenzo, then takes them to Donovan for protection. He arrives in Venice with Marco to attend Lorenzo's scale repair ceremony.

In **Ember's Kiss**, Sloane approaches Brandon at the beach bar after his friends have seen him in dragon form and Brandon recognizes that Sloane is *Pyr*. Sloane beguiles Brandon's friends to keep them from hunting down the dragon. Sloane then tells Brandon that he should beguile anyone who has seen his dragon and Brandon takes offense, both because he doesn't know how to beguile anyone and because he doesn't want to deceive his friends. Liz has recognized that Brandon needs help to heal and asks the Apothecary to help. She tells Sloane about the Dragon Bone Powder as well as confirming that their firestorm is satisfied. Sloane makes a reference to the son they've conceived, thinking Brandon has explained everything to her already, and Liz doesn't take well to the news that she's going to have a child. He challenges Brandon when that *Pyr* is trapped in Chen's lair, telling him that he has to accept his nature to have the help of the *Pyr*. Brandon does and Sloane goes to defend Liz.

In **Serpent's Kiss**, Sloane leaves his research to treat Rafferty after Thorolf injures him. (He's seeking an antidote to the virus spread by Jorge.) Sloane, Rafferty, Melissa, Erik and Eileen figure out that Chen has held Thorolf captive and is turning him *Slayer*. Thanks to Chandra sharing visions, Sloane learns the source of the virus. He helps with the transport of the sword to Thorolf and attends the repair of Thorolf's missing scale at Angkor.

I knew from the beginning of *Dragonfire* that Sloane's firestorm would be triggered by the last eclipse in the Dragon's Tail cycle and that the Apothecary would heal the world. I didn't initially guess that he'd have to heal his mate to even give their firestorm a chance of success. In **Firestorm Forever**, Sloane continues to seek the antidote for the virus brought by Jorge and heals his mate in advance of their firestorm. He begins an affair with his new neighbor, Sam Wilcox, who he finds mysterious and intriguing. She walks away when she sees his dragon tattoo. Sloane is called to Chicago to treat Erik's wounds after the leader of the *Pyr* is attacked by one of Boris' clones. When he returns home, he smells that Sam has come to his house and also discovers that Jorge had destroyed his research and stolen his samples. He checks on Sam and things heat up between them again, but Sloane is summoned to New York to tend Drake's injuries after the failed attempt to rescue Veronica.

When Sloane returns to California, he seeks out Sam at the market where she does tarot readings and asks for a reading. He realizes that she's not very good at readings, which supports his sense that she's hiding and hurt by some incident. He does a reading for her, surprising Sam with his insight, and they're intimate again. At her place, he finds evidence of Nathaniel and realizes her connection and her profession, as well as the reason she distrusts dragons. They talk about healing and he tells her about his father, as well as why he's called the Apothecary. They're about to be intimate again, but Sloane receives a message with a link to the video about Rafferty being injured by Jac on Easter Island. He hurries home to find Rafferty injured on the floor of his house, with Marco beside him. Marco refuses to sing the darkfire song with Sloane to try to help Rafferty and leaves Sloane alone with the injured *Pyr*. The last thing Sloane needs is another challenge, but he has one anyway and he does his best to save Rafferty with the Apothecary's song—fearing all the while that it won't be enough.

Erik, Thorolf, and Quinn arrive at Sloane's home with their mates and children to help with Rafferty's recovery. Rafferty is stable but still unconscious. Sam ends up giving Lee a ride to Sloane's place and inviting Sloane home with her—he needs a break from work and the *Pyr* filling his house, but senses that something has changed in her. Her sister Jac has visited and she's begun to deal with her grief over the loss of her son, Nathaniel. To Sloane's pleasure, she confides in him, but then tells him that she's going back to Atlanta to help in the effort to find a cure for Veronica Maitland. Sloane believes that he's helped her to heal enough that she can return to her life and that maybe that was was the point of their relationship. He knows it isn't fair to hope for more, since he could have a firestorm at any time. He buys Sam's house from her for the sake of space and some of the *Pyr* move over there.

Just when Sloane is about to lose hope completely, he has a breakthrough in his quest for an antidote to the virus spread by Jorge—he realizes that Drake didn't catch the virus from Veronica and wonders if Drake, as the only living being from the same era as the virus, has antibodies for it. This gives him more tests to run and new hope for an antidote. Chandra delivers her son at Sloane's house, and the *Pyr* steal Veronica away from Sam's care to try Sloane's cure on her.

At the next eclipse, the darkfire crackles beneath Rafferty's scales and Sloane has a vision of his father. The *Pyr* breathe dragonsmoke in an effort to give Rafferty strength, but instead, the energy is claimed by the darkfire and injures him even more. Marco's firestorm ignites and Pwyll's ghost appears to Sloane. Pwyll teaches Sloane the darkfire song to draw the darkfire out of Rafferty. The *Pyr* snare it in dragonsmoke, then compel it back into the crystal, and Rafferty sleeps more easily.

Thorolf captures one of the clones and brings it to Sloane's lab, so Sloane can test the antidote on him. He's having some success in treating Ronnie, but frustrated by interruptions and the loss of Sam. Marco appears in Sloane's home and seizes both the darkfire crystal and Rafferty, who is clinging to it. Sloane finds himself defending Marco to his fellow *Pyr* who fear that Marco is turning *Slayer*. Sloane insists that he needs Sam's help to succeed in creating an antidote and argues with Erik about revealing details about the *Pyr* to her. Sloane insists, and the leader of the *Pyr* leaves California. Sloane also fears that Jorge has learned Chen's spell and is using Drake's scales to injure that *Pyr*. Sloane asks Niall to dreamwalk to Sam and show her his tattoo. When he does,

Sam doesn't remember anything about her dream, except Sloane's tattoo. She connects the dots and returns to California, furious that he's somehow involved in the theft of her patient, Ronnie.

The *Pyr* heal Drake in Lee's spiral garden, and Sloane learns some of the chant Lee was taught by his father. Rafferty reappears, healed by Marco's firestorm. When Sam appears, Sloane and Sam join forces against the virus, which Sloane has identified as the same virus discussed by Thucydides. Sam guesses that Sloane is a dragon shifter and they argue.

"Of course I am," he snapped. "I heal my own kind."

"That's just wrong," Sam muttered.

"Is it? What you don't seem to understand is that we are divided, into *Pyr* who defend the treasure that is the human race, and *Slayers* who would exterminate both *Pyr* and humans from the face of the earth."

"Which are you?" She shivered at the coldness that filled his gaze.

"You have to ask?" Sloane's disgust was clear. "I am the Apothecary of the *Pyr*," he said with some pride. "I heal my kind. I protect humans and heal them when I can. When I can't, I ask for help." His gaze bored into hers and Sam found it very easy to believe in that moment that Sloane could become a fire-breathing dragon. "Why do you think I invited you here?"

"You didn't invite me. I had that dream..." Sam's voice faded to nothing as she gaped at him. "That's how you communicated with Veronica, too, isn't it? You infected her dreams!"

"Her dreams weren't *infected*. Dreams can be a good way to communicate with people, without leaving any discernible signs."

"This is all about hidden power, isn't it? It's all about subversion and conspiracy..."

Sloane's eyes flashed and he jabbed a finger toward Veronica. "Does that look like subversion to you? You said yourself that she was healing! How can you look at Ronnie and doubt my intentions?"

There was that. He had helped her. Sam bit her lip, sat down, and forced herself to take a soothing sip of tea. That gold dragon wouldn't have helped, which implied that maybe there *were* two

kinds of dragon shifters.
—from **Firestorm Forever**

Drake tells Sam about the firestorm and she realizes that Sloane is trying to protect her by not pursuing a relationship with her. They reconcile and continue to work together. When Sam suggests that the *Pyr* might all be immune to the virus, Sloane tests it on himself because time is of the essence. Determined to save Sloane, Sam tries the Dracontias brought to her by Jac as a last resort—and it eradicates the virus from the blood samples. Sam prepares to take the cure back to the CDC for replication and distribution, amazed that Sloane will let her take all the credit. Sloane comes to her defense when she releases the clone in the lab and loses his scale over his love for her. Ronnie finds it and saves it for him, knowing what it means. She later gives it to Sam.

Drake's scale repair ceremony is held behind Sloane's home in California and is recorded by Melissa. He goes from there to Sam, missing her, and she gives him the Dracontias. They agree that it might counteract the Elixir, making it possible to kill *Slayers* who have had the Elixir. Back in his lab, Sloane creates an antidote to the Elixir with the stone. He joins the *Pyr* at Machu Picchu for the final battle, then his firestorm with Sam sparks. Marco takes him to Traverse City, then Sloane flies to Ann Arbor himself, following the spark of the firestorm to his mate. *Dragonfire* ends in Ann Arbor, just as it began there with Quinn and Sara's firestorm.

SNOW—the pet falcon and familiar of Chandra, which resides mostly in Myth. Snow brings Chandra warnings, both when there will be an attack and when the portals between the realms are going to be sealed. When Chandra becomes mortal at the end of **Serpent's Kiss**, she surrenders her access to Myth and Snow flies to Apollo, leaving the mortal realm in his custody. In **Firestorm Forever**, Snow brings Chandra a vision during her labor to deliver Raynor, helping Chandra and Thorolf solve the riddle of the eggs containing Boris' clones. In **Firestorm Forever**, Chandra sees Snow as an owl, not a falcon, but she also sees the bird as a condor, suggesting that Snow has shapeshifting abilities like Chandra's.

SOLVEIG—Thorolf's mother, who appears in his vision of his own birth in **Serpent's Kiss**. She died delivering his younger brother when he was five years old, and the baby died, too. Thorolf blamed his father for her death and they argued before parting badly.

SOPHIE—The Wyvern at the beginning of the *Dragonfire* series, Sophie is more ethereal in appearance than the other *Pyr*, silver and white with long trailing feathers. Her appearance is compared to that of a swan, and Quinn thinks she looks like she's made of spun glass or sheer silk. In human form, Sophie has silvery-blonde hair and is slender, with turquoise eyes. She likes to spontaneously appear, which not all of the *Pyr* appreciate, as well as suddenly disappear, which they like even less. She has the ability to cast dreams and to change into a salamander. Sophie is unusual for a Wyvern as she is more involved in the daily affairs of the *Pyr*. Previous Wyverns were remote and mysterious, but Sophie believes the stakes are such that she has to lend a talon to the fight against the *Slayers*.

At the end of **Kiss of Fire**, Sophie reveals that she can pass through *Slayer* dragonsmoke without injury. Sara suggests that Sophie could have saved herself, but Sophie insists that Quinn and Sara had need of a quest together to solidify the relationship after their firestorm. This incident shows both the Wyvern's ability to see the future, and Sophie's inclination to put others before herself.

In **Kiss of Fury**, Sophie used the television to show Alex an incident from Donovan's past, with Olivia, Magnus and the Dragon's Tooth. She also lets Alex watch her shift shape, doing it very slowly. Also in this book, Sophie meets Nikolas and is immediately aware of him in a new and exciting way.

In **Kiss of Fate**, Sophie and Nikolas consummate their relationship, even though it's a violation of the taboo against intimacy between Wyvern and *Pyr*. Nikolas believes they have a future, but Sophie realizes that the act has cost her powers. She can't shift to a salamander or harness a dream anymore. She remembers her conviction that Nikolas is the one who can destroy the Academy and chooses to sacrifice herself for the good of the

Pyr. She flies to the Academy and Nikolas pursues her. Together, they destroy it, their bodies fusing together into a ring that looks like it's made of black and white glass.

Erik and Eileen conceive during that firestorm and by the end of the book, Eileen knows they will have a daughter. Erik hopes that Zoë will be the new Wyvern. Sophie makes cameo appearances in Zoë's dreams in the *Dragon Diaries*, the spin-off paranormal young adult series which chronicles Zoë's coming of age as the new Wyvern, and is reincarnated as Isabelle, who is adopted by Rafferty and Melissa in **Darkfire Kiss**.

SOREN—father of Erik Sorensson; leader of the *Pyr*; founder of the High Council of Seven; one of the Drakkir. Soren had an ongoing dispute with Mikail Vassily, the *Pyr* who recommended that dragon shifters turn against humans. Mikail was a compelling speaker and many of the discontent followed him, making him leader of the *Slayers*. Soren established the High Council of Seven in 1220 in an attempt to rally the remaining *Pyr*.

Many years later, after the numbers of *Pyr* and *Slayers* were vastly diminished, Soren and Mikail were trapped by the father of Louisa Guthrie, an alchemist in search of the Philosopher's Stone. Guthrie tried to compel either or both dragons to surrender the prize by forcing them to fight each other. Soren was triumphant over Mikail, but Guthrie broke his promise and didn't release Soren. Instead, he tried to remove the mythic gem he believed to be embedded in Soren's forehead. When Erik arrived to intervene, his father was so badly injured that he begged Erik to kill him, which he did.

Soren had a runestone which was his talisman, and it was inscribed with the Helm of Awe. In **Kiss of Fate**, when Eileen puts the runestone on Erik's forehead while he's sleeping, Erik dreams of the day his father gave him the runestone on Erik's first voyage with the Drakkir.

Erik felt a hand on his shoulder, knew his father had come to stand beside him. They had sailed together on that first journey,

Soren watching over his only son. The memory made Erik smile, made him appreciate the connection that had been between them. It eroded the bitterness of what he had been compelled to do, flooding out the anger that had made it impossible to simply remember his father.

"*We are* Pyr," Soren said, his old-speak deep with authority. "*This world is both our treasure and our burden.*"

Erik turned to see his father smile that secretive smile, the one that stole over his lips as if he had remembered a mysterious pleasure. His eyes glinted with confidence and pride; then he pushed something hard into Erik's hand.

Erik knew what it was, felt his fingers tighten on the runestone. He knew it was his father's talisman and was surprised to be given it.

"*Dream upon it,*" Soren advised. "*It will guide you true, give you the strength you need, provide direction when you are lost.*"

Soren nodded once, narrowing his eyes to survey the endless stretch of the sea, and his joy in adventure was obvious. "*Who knows what we shall find? Who knows what we will learn?*" He turned that sparkling gaze upon Erik. "*But it is all ours to claim, to savor, to defend. Our gift and our responsibility.*"

He squeezed Erik's shoulder once and his smile broadened. "*Remember to dream.*"

Then Soren turned to scan the horizon once more with pleasure and anticipation. With optimism. He ducked his head and turned to hail one of his fellows, leaving Erik alone with the view and the echo of his father's old-speak.

And the runestone. Erik opened his hand to find his father's prize cradled in his palm. It was marked with the Helm of Awe, the most powerful sigil of protection known to the Vikings.
—Kiss of Fate

STACY—Cassie's friend and roommate for the trip to Las Vegas in **Flashfire**. They've been friends since kindergarten. The trip to Vegas was booked by Stacy for her wedding, but her fiancé Scott dumped her (as Cassie had predicted) so the two friends use the reservation for a girls' vacation. She's five-eleven, curvy, blonde and likes sparkle. She admonishes Cassie to stop working, and is first beguiled then seduced by JP. She is ultimately told about the

Pyr, with Erik's approval, and stays with Cassie and Lorenzo in Venice when she visits Italy.

STEVE (1)—a friend of Ginger's in Ohio, who marries her friend Tanya. Introducing them is one of Ginger's matchmaking victories.

STEVE (2)—a technician who works for Erik at his pyrotechnic display company and is described by Erik as the most talented and thorough member of the team. In **Whisper Kiss**, Erik gives Steve the responsibility of managing a display for the Fourth of July while he (and Eileen and Zoë) travel to New York for Niall's firestorm.

SUZIE KINCAID—Rox's older sister, who ran away when she was abused by their step-father. The two sisters each wear a silver promise ring to indicate their vow to watch out for each other forever. Suzie has dark hair like Rox but her eyes are green, and she's just as outspoken as Rox. Rox believes her sister is the pretty one, but Niall disagrees. At the end of **Whisper Kiss**, Niall locates Suzie in Beverly Hills and brings her back to Rox so that the sisters are reunited. He reveals that Suzie had changed her name, which was why Rox couldn't find her, but Suzie's new name isn't mentioned. Suzie has apparently married well both she and her partner are elegantly and expensively dressed. (He isn't named either.) The four of them then go back to the family home to reconcile with Rox and Suzie's mom, who threw out the stepfather after both of her girls ran away and has been looking for them both. Niall found Suzie by using his Dreamwalker skills, honed during his firestorm with Rox.

TANYA—an artisan cheesemaker and friend of Ginger's, Tanya and Ginger met at chef school and Tanya followed Ginger to rural Ohio. Tanya buys the milk from Ginger's Guernseys and also from the Van Vliet's goats for her cheeses. Ginger introduced Tanya to Steve, once again showing her abilities as a matchmaker. Ginger and Delaney meet at the stag-and-doe for Tanya and Steve at the beginning of **Winter Kiss**, and subsequently attend Tanya and Steve's wedding together as a couple.

TERESA MACCRAE—Eileen's roommate in college, Teresa is working at the Fonthill-Fergusson Foundation at the beginning of **Kiss of Fate**. Teresa is petite, with long dark hair that she wears coiled up. She favors stiletto heels and looks sleek and expensive. Eileen is annoyed with Teresa for saying she doesn't have time to meet while Eileen is in London, then Teresa abruptly suggests they meet at the foundation at night, which makes Eileen feel as if she wants something. Teresa wants Eileen to assess a trunk of what appear to be massive teeth, found during the excavation for a new subway line. These are the Dragon's Teeth, although neither woman knows that right away. Teresa just knows that an antiquities dealer, Rafferty Powell, is very interested in acquiring them, and she wants to make sure they aren't sold too cheaply. The foundation is attacked by Magnus' men and Teresa is shot, before Eileen manages to escape with the Dragon's Teeth and Erik's help. At the end of **Kiss of Fate**, Eileen contributes to a fund for new perennial gardens and landscaping at their alma mater and makes the contribution in Teresa's memory.

THADDEUS (THAD)—A *Pyr* and one of the Dragon's Tooth Warriors, Thad is both practical and inclined to invoke divine assistance. His story is told in the Dragon Legion Novella, **Kiss of Destiny**. Thad didn't have a close relationship with his father and was raised by his mother—his father simply appeared to deliver him to Delphi for training when he was eight years of age. He never saw either of them again. He has dark hair and dark eyes, is black with golden lights in his dragon form, and his affinities are to fire and earth. His destined mate is Aura, who is an immortal nymph at the beginning of their story.

Thad is a romantic who wishes to make a permanent connection with his mate. When he meets Aura, though, she's skeptical. As daughter of a nymph and of a man who deceived her mother, Aura is determined to wait for true love or do without. She's impressed by stories told of Damien's dedication to Petra, and decides to test Thad—she takes him to the Garden of the Hesperides, planning for him to eat one of the golden apples which will compel him to tell her the truth. Instead, he battles Ladon, the dragon custodian of the tree bearing the golden apples, to earn the right to an apple. Aura is convinced that Thad is telling the truth after he eats the apple, but she also sees that there is no child in her future so thinks he's wrong about the firestorm. The pair subsequently battle Tisiphone and the *Slayer* Jorge outside the garden—Jorge seizes the arm of a sick pilgrim who has come to beg the assistance of the goddess Hera at her garden. Jorge takes the diseased limb back to the future, thereby launching the plague that the *Pyr* battle in **Firestorm Forever**, while Hera gives Aura a gift for her service and loyalty. Aura chooses to become mortal to be with Thad and bear his son. The transition also makes her an Airdaughter and the fourth elemental witch to partner with one of the *Pyr*. Thad remains in the past—along with Alexander and Damien—to start a new lineage of dragon warriors. Their descendants come to Erik's lair to pledge to follow Drake at the end of **Kiss of Destiny**.

THEO (1)—the oldest Theo in the *Dragonfire* series is the son of Drake. When Drake and the Dragon's Tooth Warriors were enchanted, they were trapped for centuries. By the time the spell was broken in **Kiss of Fate** and they were released, everyone they knew and loved had passed away, including Drake's wife Cassandra and his son Theo. He mourned their loss deeply, and regretted that they never knew his fate. The conviction that they must have believed that he'd abandoned them was the reason he accepted Timmy's request for help in finding his missing father.

Theo appears in **Kiss of Danger**, after Alexander has left the Dragon Legion to pursue his mate, Katina, and is seeking his own son, Lysander. Theo has been enslaved by the *Slayer* Jorge and fed the Elixir, in order to generate more Elixir for the *Slayer*. This is part of Jorge's plan to enslave all the ancestors of the *Pyr*. Jorge feeds upon Theo as Alexander watches in horror, using his dragonsmoke to drain lifeforce from the boy. By the end of the story, Jorge has been sent back to the future and Theo is to serve in the sanctuary of Apollo along with Alexander's son, Lysander. The presence of Elixir in Theo's body is never explored further, although the implication is that Theo did not suffer from withdrawal or need Elixir in the future.

THEO (2)—the second Theo in the *Dragonfire* series first appears in **Kiss of Destiny**. After Drake and the Dragon's Tooth Warriors travelled through time, and each *Pyr* was left at the sparking point of his own firestorm, Drake was the only one returned to the present time. He subsequently learned that the time-traveling *Pyr* had changed history: not only have the *Pyr* multiplied in the past and present and established the Dragon Legion, but his own line has continued. By tradition, the oldest son in each generation of the *Pyr* descended from Drake's son Theo is also named Theo. Drake meets this Theo, the current leader of the Dragon Legion, in Erik's loft at the end of **Kiss of Destiny**. Theo is carnelian and gold in his dragon form, and has dark hair and dark eyes. He also appears in the *DragonFate* series and will have his own firestorm in that series.

THIERRY DE BÉZIERS—A *Pyr*, the Smith of his time and the father of Quinn Tyrrell. Thierry's mate was Margaux and he made a lifetime commitment to her, one that startled and inspired Erik Sorensson. Thierry was assassinated by Ambrose, who had vowed to eliminate the line of the Smith, after the love of his life, Margaux, chose Thierry over him. Thierry and Margaux had five sons, and the oldest four were killed on the same day as their parents. Only Quinn, then four years old, survived. His challenge coin was a Roman gold coin and Quinn remembers Thierry amusing his children by making the coin disappear and by playing with sparks.

Because Quinn was so young when Thierry died, he didn't learn the secrets of the Smith from his father. The Wyvern, Sophie, sends Quinn a dream of his father in **Kiss of Fury**, in which Thierry tells Quinn how to repair the scales of his fellow *Pyr*.

THIERRY TYRRELL—the third son of Sara Keegan and Quinn Tyrrell, the Smith of the *Pyr*. Sara is pregnant with Thierry in **Ember's Kiss** and he is born June 11, 2012.

THORKEL—Thorolf's grandfather and a member of the High Council established by Soren. Erik remembers Thorkel as being passionate and unpredictable, but loyal. Thorkel was the one who suggested to Soren that the empty spot on the High Council of

Seven be filled by Erik. Thorkel had the Avenger of the Aesir sword forged.

THOROLF—The bad boy of the *Pyr*, and a former project of Rox's, Thorolf is a *Pyr* who enjoys all the pleasures life has to offer. He was born in Norway in 1160, son of Thorvald, son of Thorkel. Thorolf is tall with long blond hair and blue eyes and is a powerful fighter, although he can't swim. In dragon form, Thorolf is moonstone and silver, as well as very large and muscled. His affinities are to fire and air, and he loves a good fight, as well as other pleasures of the flesh—in fact, Rox accuses him of caring only about "sex, sex, and beer".

Thorolf first appears in **Kiss of Fate** when he is discovered by Niall, identified as *Pyr* because of his reaction to the breaking of the Dragon's Egg. He's working as a bike courier at this time, and calling himself T. He's been living with Rox for three years, since she saw him shift and took him under her proverbial wing. Niall challenges Thorolf and leads him to Erik, compelling Thorolf to fly from New York to the UK. Thorolf botches the landing on the roof of Lynne's house in Notting Hill. Erik recognizes him immediately, though, and remembers Thorolf's forebears:

Erik stood in the middle of the roof and eyed the new arrival, who was still breathing quickly in his fear. Niall, at the opposite end of the roof, rolled his eyes with dismay.

The new arrival locked his arms around the chimney and hung on. Eileen was amused by his terror. She also understood that Erik had placed the new arrival close to her only because he trusted him.

He might be trying to provoke the silver *Pyr* into embracing his powers, but he was certain that he wouldn't hurt Eileen. That was quite a vote of confidence.

"You couldn't just meet on the ground somewhere?" he asked. Eileen could see that he was shaking. He pushed a hand through his wet hair and spared her a glance, cursing under his breath as he eyed the distance to the ground.

"You are lucky that I was so fond of your grandfather," Erik said, subtly reminding the younger of his manners.

"Say, 'Thank you very much, Erik,' " Eileen whispered.

"Right. Thanks, dude. Don't mind if I don't shake hands. I'll just hold on to this chimney here."

"Do you have a name?" Erik asked.

"My friends call me T."

"T?" Erik couldn't disguise his distaste. "Your name is *T*?"

"As in teetotaler," Niall said, and chuckled.

The tall, tattooed man beside Eileen blushed scarlet. She could see the redness of his face even in the darkness. He even shuffled his feet a bit. "Well, no, not really, but my real name is weird."

Erik's expression was cold. His features could have been carved of stone.

"I'm thinking that your real name is the way to go in present company," Eileen murmured.

The new arrival flashed her a smile, showing a measure of charm now that he wasn't terrified. "No kidding." He cleared his throat. "How about Thorpe? That's pretty close and I can live with it..."

"What name did your father bestow upon you?" Erik demanded.

The man beside Eileen swallowed. "Well, I—"

"What name?"

The new arrival looked down then across the garden. He couldn't evade Erik's stare for long, though. "Thorolf," he finally admitted. He winced and nudged Eileen, evidently thinking she was an ally. "Weird, don't you think?"

"It's old, though," Eileen said. "Old names are strong."

"Thanks a lot."

"It's ancient," Erik interjected. "As is the word *weird,* and of similar origin. You were named Thor's Wolf, servant of the god who is foretold to slaughter Jormungand, the World Serpent, at Ragnarok. A weighty legacy, perhaps too weighty for one who chooses to be named T."

—from **Kiss of Fate**

Thorolf has several tattoos: a Celtic knot around his neck, a Helm of Awe on his left bicep, a blue dragon spiral on his right arm, and a large blue and black dragon on his left hand, with a tail coiling around his wrist. Roxanne Kincaid did this last tattoo when

Thorolf was asleep (actually, he was passed out drunk) in an attempt to remind him of the majesty of his own nature. One of the first things that Rox and Niall realize they have in common is their desire to improve Thorolf, but Rox sees quickly that Niall's methods are more effective than hers.

In **Winter Kiss**, Thorolf accompanies Niall and Sloane to defend Delaney during his firestorm, and is the first of the other *Pyr* to talk to Ginger. (He chats with her while Delaney, Niall and Sloane fight Balthasar and Mallory in dragon form.) He demonstrates his considerable appetite, eating his way through the kinds of pie served in a diner near Ginger's farm, as well as ensuring there are no leftovers from any meal. He argues with Niall, who is disgusted by Thorolf's refusal to master his abilities and accuses him of wanting to just fight, drink, and screw.

In **Whisper Kiss**, Niall has agreed to mentor Thorolf, and the pair are working together to eliminate the shadow dragons. Because Thorolf is unreliable and the shadow dragons are attacking without warning, Niall suggests that Thorolf move into the apartment over the eco-tourism business. Rox thinks Thorolf is lying to her when he moves out of her place—even though their relationship is platonic, she's protective of him and has found him a job. She meets Niall when she tries to find out the truth and their firestorm sparks. Niall doesn't forget to tutor Thorolf: when they head into the tunnels beneath the city, he encourages Thorolf to use his senses and determine what lies before them. Chen tries to brand Thorolf in the tunnels beneath the city where the shadow dragons have been imprisoned, but only manages to injure him.

In **Darkfire Kiss**, Thorolf is the first of the *Pyr* to be recorded as he shifts shape. The incident happens when he's fleeing dragonsmoke after the *Slayer* attack on Melissa's home. He also attracts three bolts of lightning, a sign from the darkfire that he's found his affinity with air, and a signal that Chen notices. He dreams again of Chen as a seductive woman and is determined to defeat the *Slayer* and eliminate his influence.

In **Flashfire**, Thorolf meets Viv Jason in Bangkok, and chases the thief who steals her wallet. The thief is Chandra, disguised as a boy, who wants to know Viv's current identity. Thorolf corners the thief and begins to shift shape. When his eyes change to dragon eyes, the kid throws Viv's wallet at him and jumps off a roof into a canal. Thorolf figures the kid is hungry so takes a US fifty dollar bill out of his own wallet, makes it into a paper airplane, and throws it to the kid. He then returns to Viv and surrenders to temptation.

In **Ember's Kiss**, Chen becomes annoyed with Viv for taking so long to claim Thorolf and attacks Thorolf in his sleep, in the apartment he shares with Viv in Bangkok. Viv changes to a viper to fend off Chen, then convinces Thorolf he's had a nightmare.

In **Serpent's Kiss**, Viv keeps her word and delivers Thorolf to Chen, who keeps the *Pyr* captive for almost two years, infecting him with Elixir. Chen then releases Thorolf, expecting the *Pyr* to rally around him. He's not counting on Chandra, who is hunting Viv Jason, or the firestorm which sparks between Thorolf and Chandra. Chandra finds Thorolf first, when he returns to his old apartment in search of Viv. He doesn't realize that almost two years have passed and thinks the new tenant is trying to deceive him. Chandra arrives and intervenes in time, but the firestorm sparks and distracts them both. When he kisses Chandra, Thorolf sees her shift shape, becoming many women, and is awed by her.

They're pursued and Thorolf shifts instinctively when he fears Chandra is threatened, but does so in a crowded market, revealing himself to the humans there. Rafferty comes to Thorolf's firestorm and tries to intervene, but Thorolf perceives the *Pyr* as enemies, thanks to the Elixir in his system and attacks Rafferty. He even tosses his challenge coin at Rafferty, not recognizing the *Pyr* and thinking he's a *Slayer*. Chandra's presence drives back the influence of the Elixir and he realizes his mistake with horror, as Rafferty returns his coin. He realizes he has spiral tattoos all over his body, which he doesn't remember getting, and Rafferty points out that they aren't normal tattoos if they fade in the presence of the firestorm. Chandra then reveals that she's sworn a vow of chastity and won't surrender to the firestorm. Thinking they have things to work out, Rafferty spontaneously manifests elsewhere, taking Thorolf and Chandra to her sanctuary.

Thorolf is surprised to discover that her refuge is Myth. In Myth, Chandra shows Thorolf the past, using the memories of ghosts. Thorolf dreams of his own birth, remembers his father, and sees Chandra come to choose him as a hero. Thorolf's father recognizes Chandra as one of the Vanir and Thorolf realizes his mate is a goddess. He also blames her for setting him on a path that ended with the death of a woman he loved and him parting badly from his father. They argue and he abandons her, furious, remembering his last argument with his father about his refusal to accept the Avenger of the Aesir. Meanwhile, Niall realizes that his recurring dream of the dying Astrid is Thorolf's memory. When Chandra catches up with Thorolf, she bares herself to him, tempting him, and surrenders more of her truth. He realizes that she doesn't believe in love because she hasn't experienced it—everything is an exchange to her—and that makes him want to teach her.

Thorolf is left behind when Chandra leaves him to pursue something, but he follows and finds her on the verge of executing Viv. He intervenes, Viv escapes and Chandra kicks his ass. Meanwhile, Erik has had a vision and the *Pyr* are bringing the sword that is Thorolf's legacy to him. Thorolf awakens in Bangkok, very impressed with his mate. In her absence, the Elixir grows stronger and when Rafferty approaches, Thorolf once again mistakes his old friend for a *Slayer*. This time, he breaks Rafferty's ribs. Niall, Sloane and Rafferty trap Thorolf in dragonsmoke, but the confusion only fades for Thorolf when Chandra arrives and kisses him, the firestorm doing its magic again. Thorolf challenges her to prove her nature to his fellow Pyr, and Chandra shows them two visions: one of Damien and Tisiphone in the Underworld (in **Kiss of Darkness**) and a second of Jorge stealing the pilgrim's arm (from **Kiss of Destiny**).

Chen appears and snatches Chandra, as the firestorm is destroying his plan to claim Thorolf and the mate is usually the weak link. Rafferty offers to spontaneously manifest and take Thorolf to her. Thorolf finds the pair fighting on a mountainside and asks Chandra to hold Rafferty in his salamander form. He fights Chen as Rafferty basks in the heat of the firestorm: Chandra drives the Elixir from Thorolf's scales with her touch and the firestorm's heat. Chen then breathes smoke and targets the gap in Thorolf's scales, stealing his strength. Rafferty takes the pair to Myth, leaving Chandra to heal Thorolf. They begin to satisfy the firestorm but Thorolf sees Ulrike, the woman who betrayed his beloved Astrid, among Chandra's guises when she shifts shape before his eyes. When they argue, he flees and finds Viv Jason. Viv deceives Thorolf into releasing her from the mirror spell cast by Chandra and attacks him, then delivers him to Chen again.

Chandra invades Thorolf's dreams while they're in Chen's lair and apologizes, then encourages him to fulfill his destiny. He realizes that she's declined to return to Asgard and is committed to the firestorm, so he's convinced.

She met his gaze and he noted that her eyes were brown this time, brown with a circle of gold around the iris. "In every culture, there is a concept of evil, of some wicked force against humans. In the west, it's often presented as a dragon. As a result, in every culture, there is an archetypal hero." She smiled. "A dragon slayer, to defend humans and defeat evil so that peace and justice can reign."

"And that's where I come into it?"

"If you're going to pick a dragon slayer, I think it makes sense to pick one who can fight fire with fire," she said, her eyes glowing. Her fingertips slid down his chest, creating a burning line of desire. Thorolf guessed her destination when her fingers passed his waist. "I think you should pick the strongest and most resilient of all the candidates, the one who comes from a lineage of noble and principled warriors, the one who carries all the traits of a hero in his heart, mind and body."

"But I had just been born when you chose me."

Chandra shook her head. "No, I chose you long before that."

"How could you know?"

"There was a time when I could see past, present and some of the future. There was a time when I saw the man you would become, even when you were just a gleam in your father's eye. In

the spark of his firestorm, I saw his son, and I knew that you were the one."
—from **Serpent's Kiss**

They defeat Chen with Lorenzo's help, then leave the *Slayer* to be consumed by Jorge. Rafferty appears with the Avenger of the Aesir and Thorolf leaps into Myth with Chandra to defeat Jormungand, the Midgard Serpent. He's doused in the venom of that serpent in its death throes, and the toxin finds the gap in his scales. Chandra rekindles the heat of the firestorm to save him, and admits that she's surrendered her immortality for him. Being loved for himself, not for what he could do for another person, is the one thing Thorolf has desired and his mate gives it to him. They satisfy the firestorm, then Thorolf has a vision of his father in which they reconcile, a gift from Chandra to him. Thorolf's missing scale is repaired by Quinn at Angkor, with three amber tears shed by Chandra.

In **Firestorm Forever**, Thorolf and Chandra are teaching self defense classes in Bangkok and Chandra is pregnant when Rafferty is injured by the darkfire crystal. They go to Sloane's place in California to help treat Rafferty. Chandra has developed a taste for kim chee during her pregnancy and is having dreams. Her current one is of Australia and twin boys—this proves to be a reference to the clones hatching at Uluru, and Chen's brother Lee. Thorolf goes to Easter Island and to Australia, leaving Chandra in California, but doesn't find anything new. Their son Raynor is born in California, then they both go to Uluru for the eclipse. Thorolf and Brandon capture a clone and Thorolf takes him to Sloane.

When they're seeking the location of the last batch of clones, Chandra dreams of Snow flying through the jungle to a hidden city, which leads them to Machu Picchu. Thorolf remembers that the first incident of the Dragon's Tail Wars was Ambrose's murder of Sara's parents at Machu Picchu. Thorolf attends Drake's scale repair, then joins the final battle at Machu Picchu. He also attends the final public ceremony in Chicago and has his repaired scale touched by darkfire, indicating that his firestorm will burn forever.

THORVALD—Thorolf's father and Thorkel's son, Thorvald argued with Thorolf when his son refused to accept the Avenger of the Aesir. He entrusted the sword to Erik on his deathbed. Thorvald makes an appearance in Thorolf's vision in **Serpent's Kiss**, when Chandra shows Thorolf his own birth.

His father was dressed in furs and leather, his shoulders covered with snow, his beard long and fair, his eyes as bright a blue as a summer sky. A deer was flung over his shoulder, his hunting knife jammed into his belt. He looked vital and male, a man providing for his family in the midst of winter. He also looked younger than Thorolf remembered him, but then, the day father and son parted was the memory that haunted him. That was decades away from this moment, and he wished with sudden force that they hadn't disagreed.

That he hadn't been judged and found wanting.

Thorolf felt his mother's pulse skip at his father's appearance and recognized that the firestorm had continued to light the days and nights of these two.

"A boy, Thorvald," she whispered and Thorolf's father grinned. He shut the door behind himself and slid the deer to another table.

The midwife stood and bowed deeply, even as Thorvald came to his wife's side. He bent and kissed her cheek, pushing the damp hair back from her face. His smile was filled with such tenderness and affection that Thorolf's heart clenched. He'd seldom seen this side of his father's nature. "I knew it would be a son, Solveig," he said with a confidence Thorolf recalled. "And I knew he would be strong. My fear was all for you."

He bent and kissed her, and Thorolf watched as she closed her eyes in relief. A tear slid from the corner of one eye and Thorvald captured it with one roughened finger, lifting it to his own mouth as he watched her. "Nectar of the gods," he said, as he always had when he'd removed Solveig's tears.

As Thorolf remembered, it made her smile.

It was remarkable to witness this moment, this emotion in a man who had usually hidden all of his emotions from view.

—from **Serpent's Kiss**

Thorolf also blames his father for the death of Astrid, the woman he loved. Dragons razed the village where she lived and her neighbors killed her for bringing their destruction. Thorolf learned that his father directed the dragons to that village because he believed Astrid was distracting Thorolf from his duties. He gave Thorolf the Avenger of the Aesir then, but Thorolf threw it away. Thorvald also reveals Chandra's identity as one of the Vanir to Thorolf, when he dreams of his own birth and sees her arrive to choose him as a hero. At the end of **Serpent's Kiss**, Thorolf has another vision of his father and they reconcile.

TIMMY—the son of Veronica Maitland and her deceased husband, Mark. Timmy was introduced in **Harmonia's Kiss** when he asked for Drake's help in locating his missing father. Drake responded to the boy because Timmy reminded him of his own lost son, Theo. Timmy is eleven when Veronica and Drake have their firestorm in **Firestorm Forever**, and is an avid fan of the *Pyr*. He figures out Drake's true nature, agrees to keep it secret and loves his first dragonflight.

TOAD—an urban explorer and former boyfriend of Rox. She contacts him in Firestorm Forever when a video is posted online of a dragonfight, hoping he can identify the location. He does—it's Seaview Hospital on Staten Island, and proves to be the location where Jorge is holding Ronnie.

TRUDY—a coworker and contemporary of Maureen's at the Institute in Hawai`i where Liz attends a symposium in **Ember's Kiss**. Trudy has dark hair and a disapproving manner, especially with regards to surfers.

TYNAN FORBES—Sloane's father and the Apothecary before Sloane. Tynan was intrigued by darkfire, which he'd only read about, and wished to see it before he died, but did not. He preferred herbal cures and lived in a small town in Ireland. Tynan and Sloane argued when Sloane wanted to go to medical school in London, as Tynan didn't believe the *Pyr* could learn healing for their kind at an institution for humans. Tynan was turned into a shadow dragon by Magnus and battled against Sloane and

Donovan in **Kiss of Fury**. His shadow dragon was destroyed in that book. He warned Sloane that the responsibility of the Apothecary had to be fulfilled, regardless of the cost. Sloane got his caduceus tattoo in **Whisper Kiss** to ensure he never forgot his father's warning. In **Firestorm Forever**, Sloane remembers his father's sense of humor and fondness for practical jokes. Sloane has visions of his father's ghost, like this one:

He looked into one corner and thought he could discern his father, sitting before the fireplace here as he had in that house in Ireland. Tynan lifted his head and smiled slightly at Sloane.

"It is the role of the Apothecary to heal, no matter the price to himself," Tynan said in old-speak, and Sloane remembered the day his father had first given him this warning. *"It is the role of the Apothecary to give, to choose where to give, to sometimes decide who will live and who will die. It is the task of the Apothecary to guide the dying to their release and summon the injured back to life. The task is not easy, but it must be done. You will be the Apothecary in dire times and you will be tested. Do not forget your abilities, my son."*

Tynan nodded once. The darkfire illuminated his figure with a blue-green aura, then leapt to Sloane's tattoo. It slid over the lines of the caduceus, making the tattoo burn all over again, then winked out.

—from **Firestorm Forever**

Tynan's ghost also appears in a vision to Erik, telling him that the Apothecary can choose to heal the earth. Sloane feels his father's presence when he makes the hike to the final battle at Machu Picchu. The mist reminds him of Ireland and he draws strength from his father's conviction that good triumphs.

TYRONE—or Ty, one of the Dragon's Tooth Warriors. He is first named in **Kiss of Danger**. Ty is said to have practically raised himself, since he was orphaned young, and tends to be grim rather than optimistic.

TYSON—A *Slayer* and friend of Everett, born ca. 1100. Tyson was amber and silver in his dragon form, and stocky and dark in his human form. Alex in **Kiss of Fury** noticed the droplets, leaves and even bugs caught in the amber of his scales, which made them glimmer in the light. His nature was violent, although he was very loyal. He was not particularly bright: when his scent was first discerned in **Kiss of Fury**, the *Pyr* believed he was a young dragon, but upon seeing him, Donovan knew Tyson was old. The discrepancy was caused by Tyson's lack of learning and failure to develop intellectually (or perhaps emotionally). In **Kiss of Fury**, Tyson was part of the attack on Gilchrist labs and held Mark down to kill him as Alex was forced to watch. He tried to avenge his friend, the *Slayer* Everett, by attacking Donovan during his firestorm—the pair exchanged challenge coins and Tyson was subsequently killed by Donovan.

ULRIKE—one of Chandra's mortal guises, supposedly a friend of Astrid but the one who betrayed her and Thorolf, and brought the dragon attack to the village. Thorolf blames her for Astrid's death when he finds out.

URSULA—one of Lorenzo's stage assistants in **Flashfire**. She and Anna bind Lorenzo for his escape trick, and see him shift shape when it goes wrong. He chooses not to beguile them. Ursula shows Cassie the way out after the firestorm is consummated in Lorenzo's dressing room and escorts Erik backstage. She also gets Cassie backstage again when Cassie brings her a gift of French perfume and finds her a complimentary seat to the performance. Ursula and Anna unveil Lorenzo's car after his final stunt, while Lorenzo watches from Venice.

VERONICA MAITLAND (RONNIE)—the wife of a missing serviceman who asks Drake to find her husband in **Harmonia's Kiss**; mother of Timmy. Ronnie has dark hair and blue eyes. In **Harmonia's Kiss**, Ronnie has taken her son to the Middle East to try to discover the fate of her missing husband, Mark, who is in covert operations. Timmy solicits the help of Drake. Drake follows Mark's scent to find the lair of the viper, Cadmus, and finds Mark's remains. Cadmus was the viper who had enchanted Drake and the Dragon's Tooth Warriors centuries before, and still is alive, infecting the world of men with his toxic song. Drake and his men kill Cadmus during this encounter, silencing him forever. Drake brings a family photograph back to Ronnie as evidence of her husband's fate, but also found renewed purpose in defending the treasure of humanity as a result of their exchange.

Ronnie and Drake have their own firestorm in **Firestorm Forever**. Their firestorm is sparked by the first eclipse and Drake comes immediately to Ronnie. They satisfy the firestorm before one of the clones attacks and Drake shifts shape to defend Ronnie. She's runs when Drake tells her to, but is captured by the clone and taken to Jorge. Her home is burned to the ground as a result of the dragonfight. Drake is left injured but alive. Her son, Timmy, is at his friend's for the night and is safe. Drake promises him that he'll find Ronnie.

Ronnie is held captive by Jorge at an abandoned hospital, where she learns that Jorge intends to steal her son and turn him *Slayer*. At first, she's skeptical that she can even be pregnant, but time proves Jorge right. Niall dreamwalks to her, asking her to review what she's seen so the Pyr can locate her and rescue her. They solve the riddle, but the rescue fails, because Jorge fakes out Drake. Ronnie is then taken to Chen's old lair, where Jorge compels her to watch the clones fight each other at his bidding. Back in her new prison cell, Ronnie has nothing to do as her pregnancy continues. Jorge finally infects her with the virus when she's four months pregnant, ensures that she can't communicate by bruising her throat and breaking her fingers, then releases her outside a hospital. Drake arrives and speaks for her, guessing that she's been infected and ensuring that she's placed in quarantine. She's relieved that he's been watching over Timmy and that he's planning for them to make a home together.

Sam comes to the hospital to try to save Ronnie and they connect. When Ronnie reveals that she's a research librarian, Sam gets her a computer with a WIFI connection so she can search for more information and also stay in contact with Timothy. Two months later, when Ronnie develops a fever, they all think the virus is entering its final phase and that she will die. Niall dreamwalks to Ronnie again, warning her that the *Pyr* are going to rescue her the next morning when she's supposed to be moved to the CDC, and she's glad that she'll be with Drake again.

At Sloane's home, Ronnie is given the current antidote, which brings down her temperature but doesn't cure her. Drake tells her of his history as she convalesces and Sloane continues his research, since Drake alone is proven to be immune to the virus. Ronnie tells him about her parents' objection to her marriage to Mark and her grandmother's support, explaining why she continues to wear her grandmother's pearls. Sam is convinced to come to California to help pursue a cure for Ronnie—when Sloane shifts shape to defend Sam from the clone, Ronnie finds his lost scale and knows the Apothecary is in love. She gives it to Sam. Sloane creates an antidote which cures Ronnie and her son. By the time of Drake's scale repair, she has had their son, and wears a domino mask for the recording of the repair by Melissa and her crew. She offers her grandmother's pearls to repair Drake's scale. Ronnie and Drake's son is not named in *Dragonfire*, though he attends the final ceremony in Chicago with them and Timmy.

VIV JASON—a slender redhead with attitude, Viv first appears in **Darkfire Kiss** when she feels the influence of the darkfire. She walks out of her job in a coffee shop, having waited for this moment, and travels to Chen's lair in Tibet to ally with him. She enters his lair in the form of a green serpent, evading all his traps, then shifts to her human form. Chen isn't sure what she is, but he recognizes her power over the element of fire. Since they both want to destroy the *Pyr*, he agrees to ally with her.

In **Flashfire**, Viv meets Thorolf after her wallet is stolen by a pickpocket and Thorolf pursues the thief. He doesn't yet know that the thief is Chandra, and that she's trying to find out what name Viv is using. Viv and Thorolf begin a sexual relationship at her instigation.

In **Ember's Kiss**, Chen becomes impatient with Viv's progress and attacks Thorolf in Bangkok, in the apartment he shares with Viv. She changes to her snake form to fight off Chen, and insists to Thorolf that he's had a bad dream. Viv's alliance with Chen is broken, when the *Slayer* realizes her true intent.

Viv Jason is actually Tisiphone, one of the Erinyes, who was killed by Damien in the Dragon Legion Novella, **Kiss of Darkness**. Hades revived her and gave her the right to avenge herself upon the *Pyr*, but Hera cursed her to wait in **Kiss of Destiny** when she attacked Thad:

> *Across the centuries and the years,*
> *You will wait and shed your tears,*
> *Until the darkfire is freed again,*
> *Your vengeance can cause the* Pyr *no pain.*
> *I close the portal, for once and all,*
> *To see those I love out of your thrall.*
> *When darkfire will burn once again,*
> *Vengeance can be yours only then.*
> *When daughters of all elements are mates*
> *Then will the dragons face their fates.*

Tisiphone is flung through space and time by Hera to modern Manhattan. Viv Jason is the mortal woman who offers to help her when she manifests beside Brooklyn Bridge. Tisiphone kills Viv and assumes her identity to await the spark of darkfire and her opportunity to seek vengeance upon the *Pyr*.

By the beginning of **Serpent's Kiss**, Viv has seduced Thorolf completely, who has no idea she's anything other than a human woman. Chandra, however, is aware of her powers and mistakenly believes Viv to be one of the Liliot. (It's Chandra's quest to destroy Viv and save the *Pyr*.) Viv attacks Thorolf in her viper form and delivers him to Chen, keeping her side of the deal. Two years later, after Thorolf has been poisoned and released by Chen, Chen confronts her in a house that she's thinking of buying, demanding that she trap Thorolf again. When she declines, he casts her into Myth, where Chandra calls her by name (Tisiphone) and compels her to take her viper form, revealing her own powers. Thorolf intervenes in their fight, attacking Chandra so Viv can escape. Viv doesn't escape completely: she is trapped in a mirror spell of Chandra's, unable to flee but also protected from

Chandra's plan to kill her. The mirror is broken by Thorolf and Chandra collects the shards, then tells the *Pyr* what she's done and why. She challenges Thorolf to fix his mistake. Viv manages to reassemble the mirror pieces with her own sorcery. She knows she can be freed by someone else looking into the mirror so when Thorolf seeks her out, she cries to manipulate him. He looks, believing in her again, then realizes his mistake when her tears turn to blood. Viv is released but in her true form as one of the Erinyes. Chandra kills her, ensuring that she can't rise again, but not before Viv bites Thorolf.

XAVIER—A *Slayer*, garnet red in dragon form. He was injured in **Kiss of Fire**, taunted Sloane that *Pyr* could be forcibly converted to *Slayers*—which the *Pyr* did not believe at the time—and was killed in that same book.

ZACH—Melissa's ex-husband who left her when she was diagnosed with cancer. His surname is never mentioned, but Melissa's inability to have children was the reason he left the marriage. Melissa also remembers that he called her an "ice queen".

ZETA—a slave girl in Cetos' household in **Kiss of Danger**.

ZOË SORENSSON—A *Pyr* and the daughter of Erik Sorensson, leader of the *Pyr*, by his second mate, Eileen. She has dark hair and green eyes like her father. As the daughter of a *Pyr*, Zoë is believed to be the next Wyvern but (like all *Pyr*) won't come into her powers until puberty.

Throughout the *Dragonfire* series, the *Pyr* (especially Erik) are watchful for signs that Zoë is the new Wyvern. In **Winter Kiss**, Eileen comments on the connection between Zoë and her father, Erik, when Erik asks the toddler to help him scry. Zoë also dispatches a number of dreams in **Winter Kiss**: she gives Rafferty a vision of an eclipse with the number 6585.322 superimposed upon it, leading him to information about the Saros cycles that govern the creation of Dragon's Blood Elixir. Sara dreams of Nikolas seeking Sophie without success, and also of him giving her a copper and emerald scale. They interpret this to mean that Delaney has lost a scale and that they must go to that *Pyr*'s firestorm so Quinn can repair Delaney's armor. The same night, Donovan dreams of his first meeting with Delaney, when they recognized that they were of the same kind and no longer alone: he comes to the same conclusion as Quinn. Zoë also fusses in **Winter Kiss** after Mallory is discovered in his salamander form on the lip of the sink, until she seizes Garrett's hand and passes him a vision. The toddler takes Thorolf to the mercury that was left on Delaney's pillow and the women realize that Zoë is telling them that the well has been poisoned by Mallory.

In **Whisper Kiss**, Zoë touches Erik's forehead, where his father's runestone is embedded, and destroys the beguiling, helping him see that he was beguiled by Lorenzo. On the drive from Chicago to New York, Zoë dispatches dreams to the *Pyr* (unbeknownst to her parents, also in the car): though trapped in a toddler's body with its limitations, she is aware of her role as the Wyvern, the history of the *Pyr* and her responsibility to her kind. She sends Rox a vision from the past, so Rox witnesses Phelan's deception of his and Niall's mother, which proves to Rox that Phelan can't be redeemed; she sends Sara a prophecy about Niall's firestorm, which convinces Quinn to go to Niall's firestorm (with Sara and Garrett); she encourages both Donovan's and Delaney's foreboding so that they also come to the firestorm; and she sends Niall a dream of Rox's troubled childhood so he understands her better. In the same book, with the help of the assembled *Pyr*, Zoë guides Niall's hand into the wound Phelan gave Rox, leading him to discover his Dreamwalker skills and heal his mate. She also uses old-speak for the first time in this book, reminding Erik in the battle with Chen that he has learned that the *Pyr* can beguile other dragon shifters.

In **Darkfire Kiss**, Zoë has begun to talk and Eileen tells Sloane that Erik has complained that she's not acknowledging his old-speak anymore. She doesn't respond to Sloane's either. Eileen notes that her eyes have changed color too, from blue to the same green as Erik's. Sloane wonders if these changes are the influence of the darkfire. In **Flashfire**, Sloane takes Eileen and Zoë to

Donovan for protection while Erik helps with Lorenzo's firestorm, and later they attend Lorenzo's scale repair in Venice. In **Ember's Kiss**, Zoë picks up Brandon's fallen scale, when he loses it while Liz is casting a spell, and leaves the protective circle to do so. She puts it in the pocket of her pink overalls, then takes Garrett's hand, producing the scale later for the repair of Brandon's armor.

In the Dragon Legion novella, **Kiss of Destiny**, Zoë gives Drake a drawing at the very end, when he awakens in Erik's lair. It's of the fountain where he and Thad were taken by the darkfire crystal before Thad was taken to their firestorm. Shortly after this exchange, the descendants of the Dragon Legion appear at Erik's lair to pledge themselves to him.

To [Drake's] surprise, Zoë appeared suddenly beside him. She could move with her father's silence and stealth, and her gaze was fixed upon him with the same intensity. "I made this for you," she said, then put a large piece of paper on the table before him. Drake was too surprised to speak. Children did not give him gifts. In fact, no one had given him a gift in a long time. She stared at him for a moment, then followed her mother to the fridge.

It was a drawing.

The drawing was clearly the work of a child, but still Drake recognized the location. There was a black oval in the middle with blue spraying out of a block in the center of the oval. Drake knew it was a fountain. There were green curly lines around it, evoking the shrubbery of a park, and the sky was colored in black with yellow dots for stars. Two stick figures sat on the lip of the fountain, and Drake guessed that they were men. One held a blue-green rectangle in his hand and there were rays of blue and green emanating from it.

It was Thad and Drake, just before Thad had felt the spark of his firestorm.

Drake looked at the little girl with shock. Zoë was drinking a glass of milk, more interested in how many chocolate chips were in her cookie than the attitude of her father's friend. Eileen must have noticed his expression because she came to his side.

"It's the park at the university, I think," she said. "We pass it every day." She frowned. "We've never been there at night."

"Who are the men, Zoë?" her father asked quietly.

She shrugged and bit into her cookie. "They wanted to be there." Her gaze barely flicked at Drake, then she finished her snack and went to her room, picking up her pack at her mother's reminder.

"It's Thad and me," Drake said. "This is where the stone brought us the second to last time."

"So close," Erik mused. "But not so close that you could sense my presence, or that I would be much aware of yours."

"Were you?"

Erik slanted a glance at him. "I felt a glimmer a few weeks ago, but it disappeared. I thought I had imagined it, because it was so fleeting. How could you be here and gone again so quickly as that?" He pressed his fingertips to one temple and closed his eyes.

"The darkfire is changing everything," he whispered, then grimaced.

—from **Kiss of Destiny**

In **Serpent's Kiss**, Erik sees Zoë's reflection in the water with Eileen when he attends Thorolf's scale repair at Angkor. In **Firestorm Forever**, Zoë dreams of Sigmund's words to Erik just before one of the clones attacks Erik in his lair. She later goes to California with her parents and helps Lee plant his "dragon garden". Zoë is in the car when Eileen is driving away from Lorenzo's place and Jac drops onto the roof, and is the one who unlocks the car door for her.

Zoë's coming of age as the new Wyvern is told in the *Dragon Diaries* trilogy.

FAMILY TREES

FAMILY TREES

In the following family trees, the names of destined mates are noted if known. Any partnership between a *Pyr* and his destined mate that has been documented in any of the *Dragonfire* Novels is marked with a dragon an includes the title of their book. The *Pyr* who formed the High Council of Seven each have a **7** beside their names, and those known to have turned *Slayer* are annotated with an **S**. There were likely many other *Slayers* whose choice is not recorded here.

You can also download the family trees from the Dragonfire website and print them out yourself.

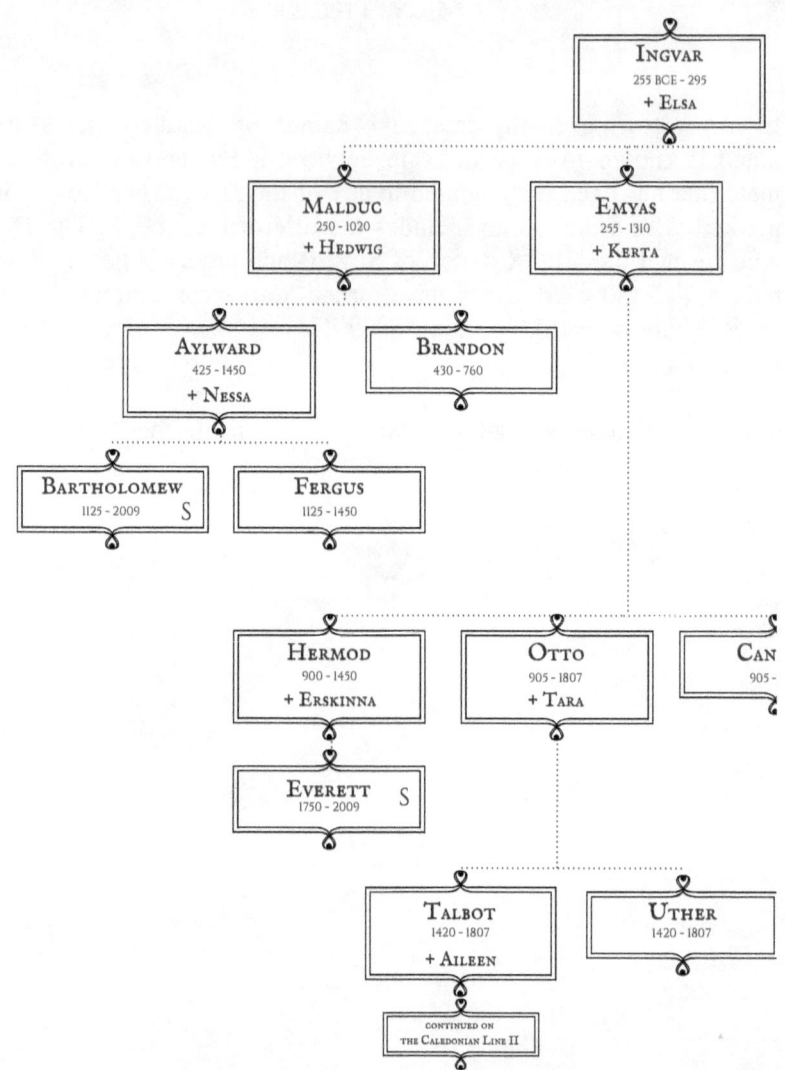

INGVAR
255 BCE - 295
+ ELSA

MALDUC
250 - 1020
+ HEDWIG

EMYAS
255 - 1310
+ KERTA

AYLWARD
425 - 1450
+ NESSA

BRANDON
430 - 760

BARTHOLOMEW
1125 - 2009   S

FERGUS
1125 - 1450

HERMOD
900 - 1450
+ ERSKINNA

OTTO
905 - 1807
+ TARA

CAN
905 -

EVERETT   S
1750 - 2009

TALBOT
1420 - 1807
+ AILEEN

UTHER
1420 - 1807

CONTINUED ON
THE CALEDONIAN LINE II

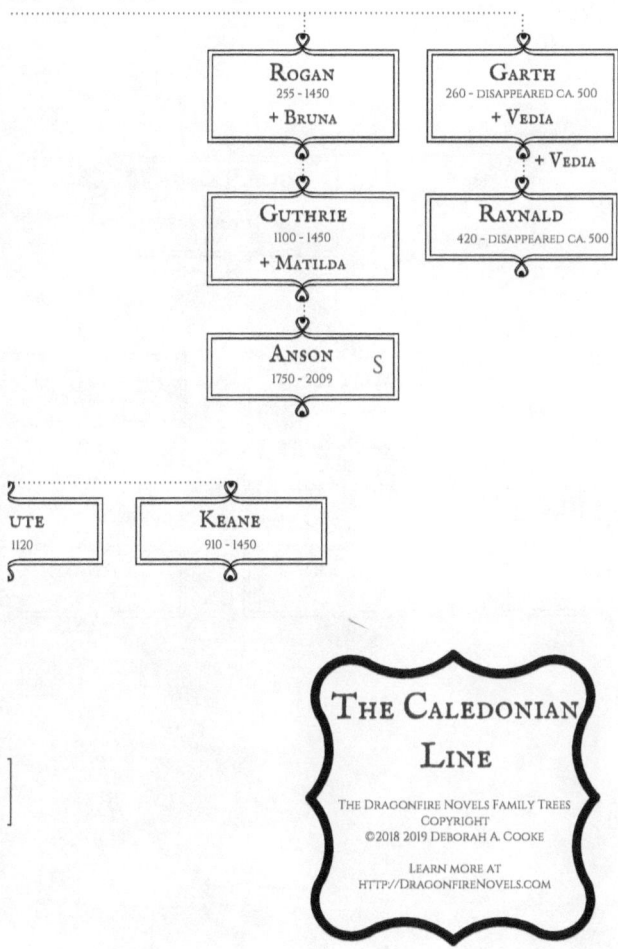

ROGAN
255 - 1450
+ BRUNA

GARTH
260 - DISAPPEARED CA. 500
+ VEDIA

+ VEDIA

GUTHRIE
1100 - 1450
+ MATILDA

RAYNALD
420 - DISAPPEARED CA. 500

ANSON S
1750 - 2009

UTE
1120

KEANE
910 - 1450

THE CALEDONIAN LINE

THE DRAGONFIRE NOVELS FAMILY TREES
COPYRIGHT
©2018 2019 DEBORAH A. COOKE

LEARN MORE AT
HTTP//DRAGONFIRENOVELS.COM

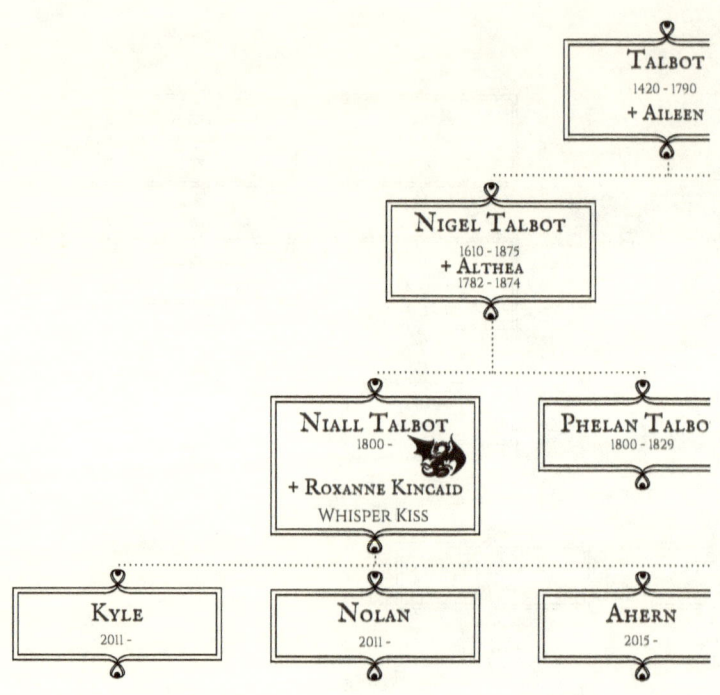

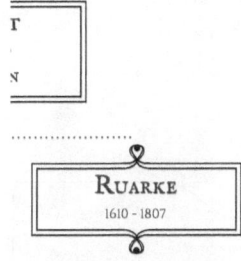

RUARKE
1610 - 1807

OT
S

RUARK
2015 -

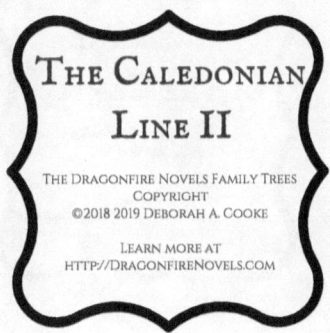

THE CALEDONIAN
LINE II

THE DRAGONFIRE NOVELS FAMILY TREES
COPYRIGHT
©2018 2019 DEBORAH A. COOKE

LEARN MORE AT
HTTP//DRAGONFIRENOVELS.COM

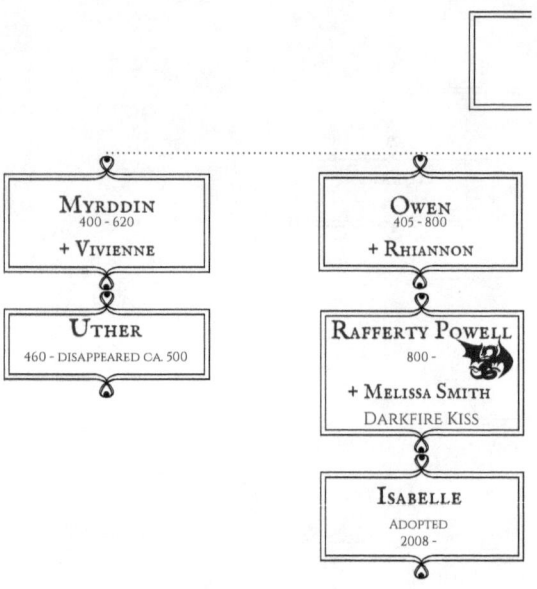

MYRDDIN
400 - 620

+ VIVIENNE

UTHER
460 - DISAPPEARED CA. 500

OWEN
405 - 800

+ RHIANNON

RAFFERTY POWELL
800 -

+ MELISSA SMITH
DARKFIRE KISS

ISABELLE
ADOPTED
2008 -

THE LINE
OF THE CANTOR

THE DRAGONFIRE NOVELS FAMILY TREES
COPYRIGHT
©2018 2019 DEBORAH A. COOKE

LEARN MORE AT
HTTP://DRAGONFIRENOVELS.COM

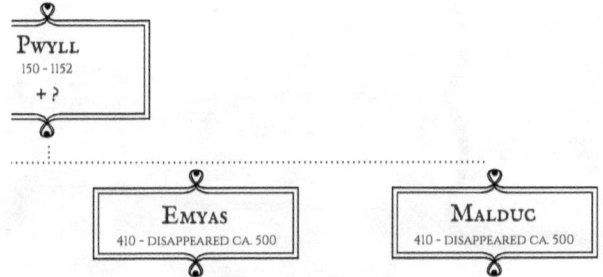

PWYLL
150 - 1152
+ ?

EMYAS
410 - DISAPPEARED CA. 500

MALDUC
410 - DISAPPEARED CA. 500

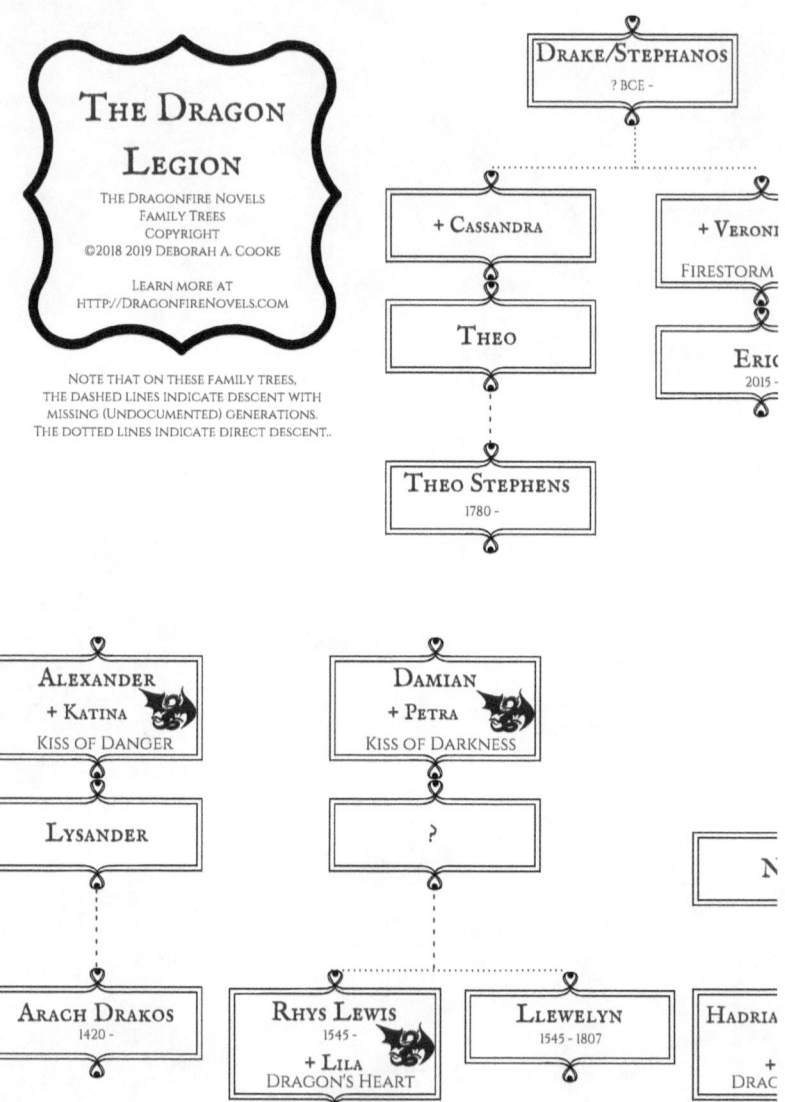

THE DRAGON

LEGION

THE DRAGONFIRE NOVELS
FAMILY TREES
COPYRIGHT
©2018 2019 DEBORAH A. COOKE

LEARN MORE AT
HTTP://DRAGONFIRENOVELS.COM

NOTE THAT ON THESE FAMILY TREES,
THE DASHED LINES INDICATE DESCENT WITH
MISSING (UNDOCUMENTED) GENERATIONS.
THE DOTTED LINES INDICATE DIRECT DESCENT..

DRAKE/STEPHANOS
? BCE -

+ CASSANDRA

+ VERONI

FIRESTORM

THEO

ERIC
2015 -

THEO STEPHENS
1780 -

ALEXANDER
+ KATINA
KISS OF DANGER

DAMIAN
+ PETRA
KISS OF DARKNESS

LYSANDER

?

N

ARACH DRAKOS
1420 -

RHYS LEWIS
1545 -
+ LILA
DRAGON'S HEART

LLEWELYN
1545 - 1807

HADRIA

+
DRAC

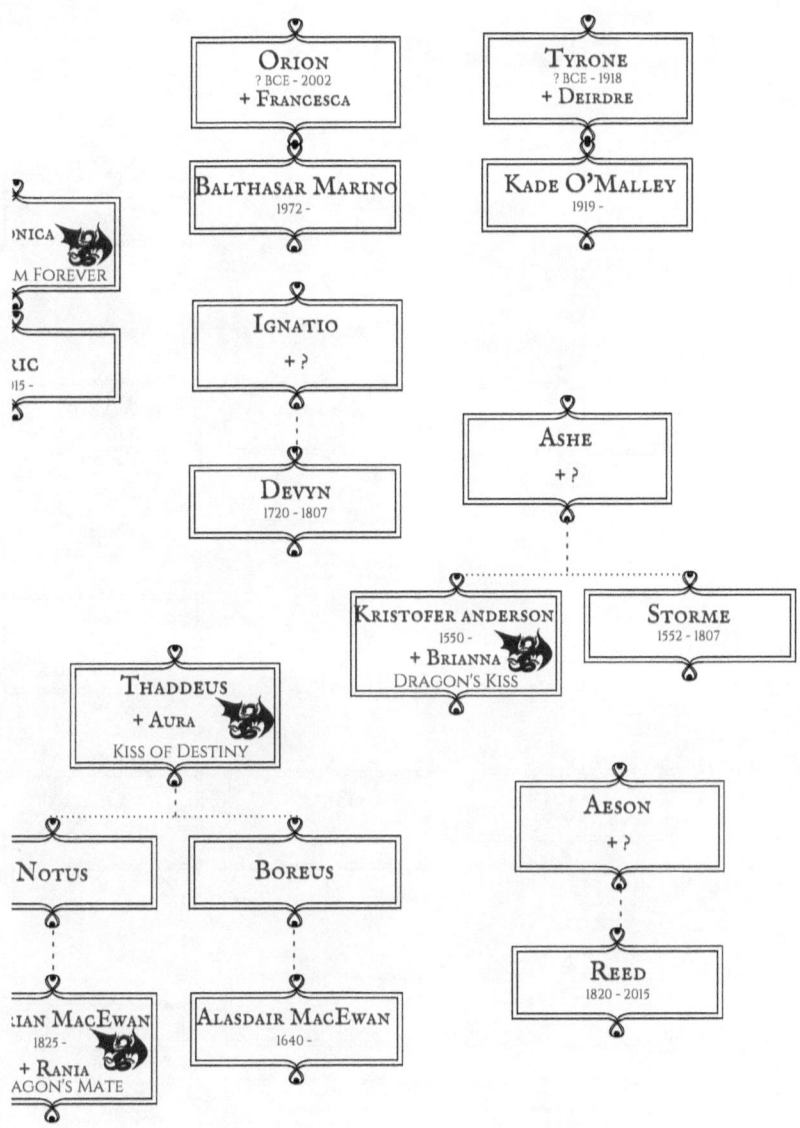

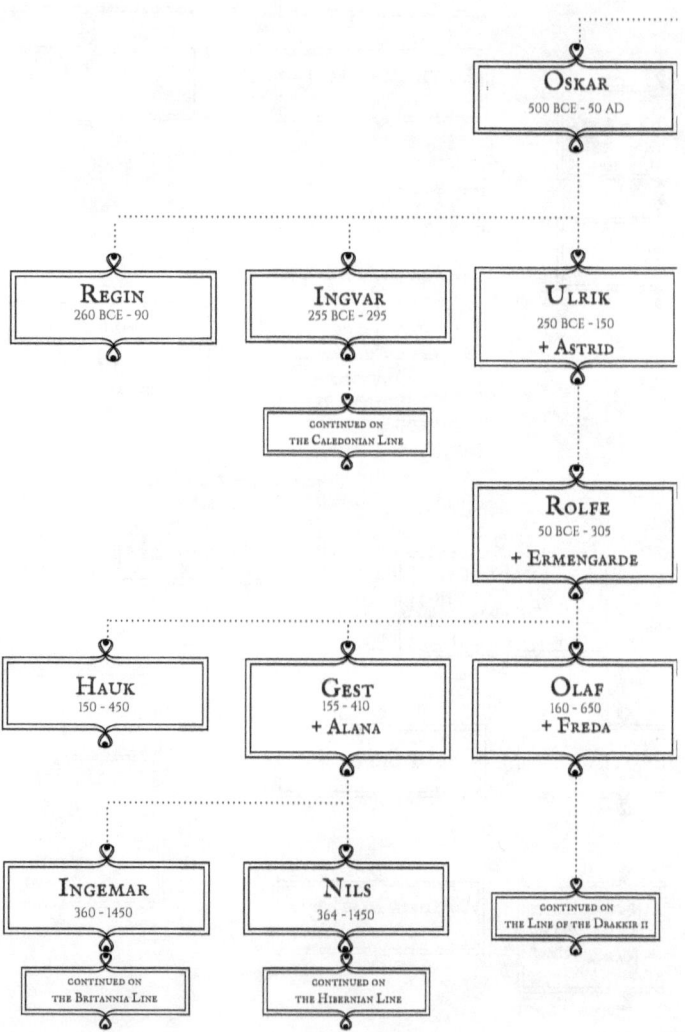

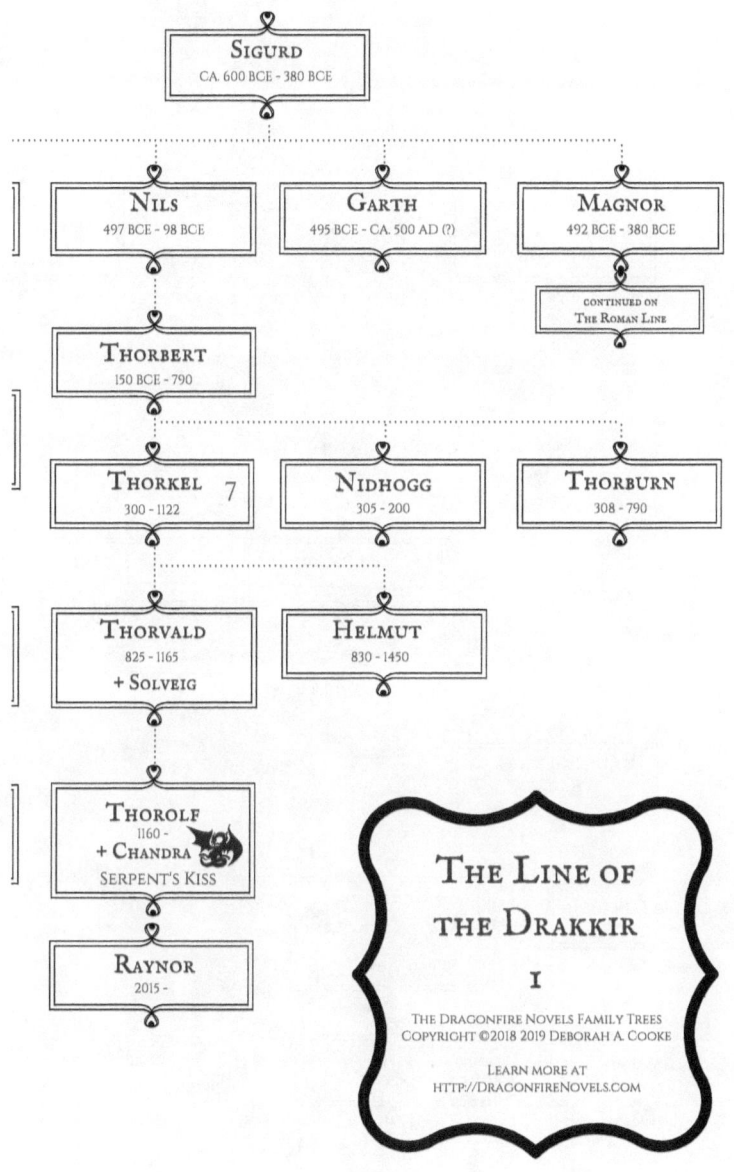

SIGURD
CA. 600 BCE - 380 BCE

NILS
497 BCE - 98 BCE

GARTH
495 BCE - CA. 500 AD (?)

MAGNOR
492 BCE - 380 BCE

CONTINUED ON
THE ROMAN LINE

THORBERT
150 BCE - 790

THORKEL 7
300 - 1122

NIDHOGG
305 - 200

THORBURN
308 - 790

THORVALD
825 - 1165
+ SOLVEIG

HELMUT
830 - 1450

THOROLF
1160 -
+ CHANDRA
SERPENT'S KISS

RAYNOR
2015 -

THE LINE OF
THE DRAKKIR

I

THE DRAGONFIRE NOVELS FAMILY TREES
COPYRIGHT ©2018 2019 DEBORAH A. COOKE

LEARN MORE AT
HTTP://DRAGONFIRENOVELS.COM

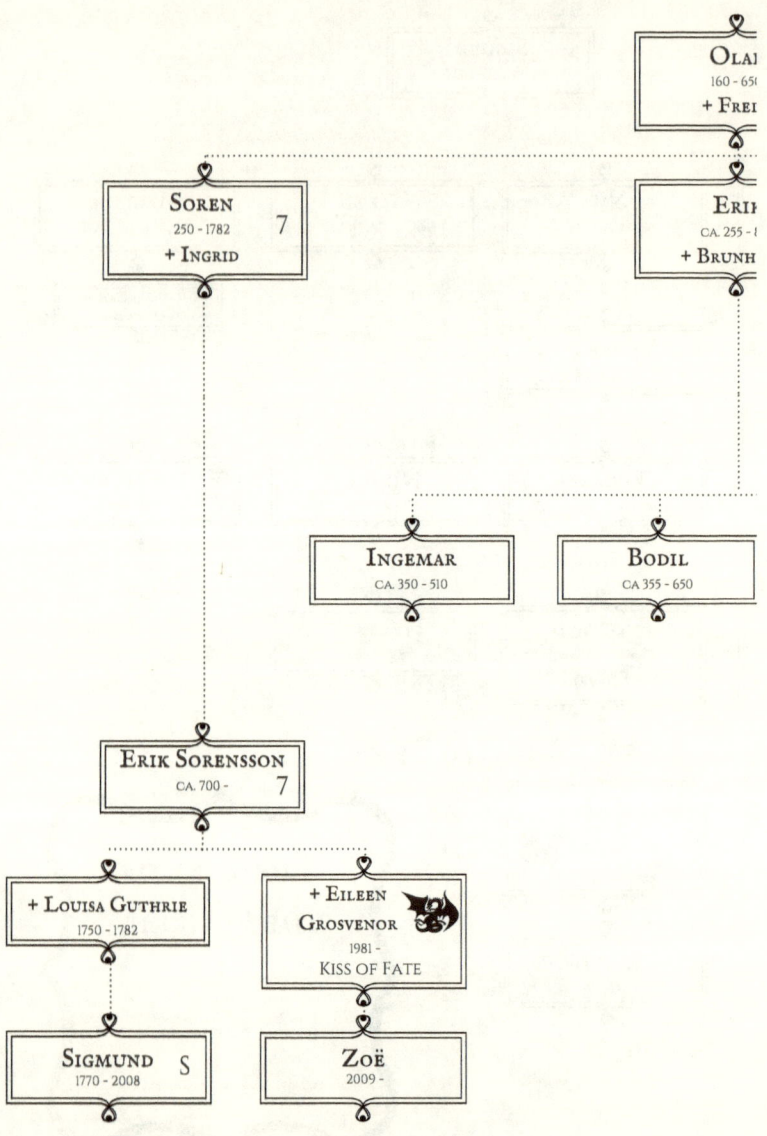

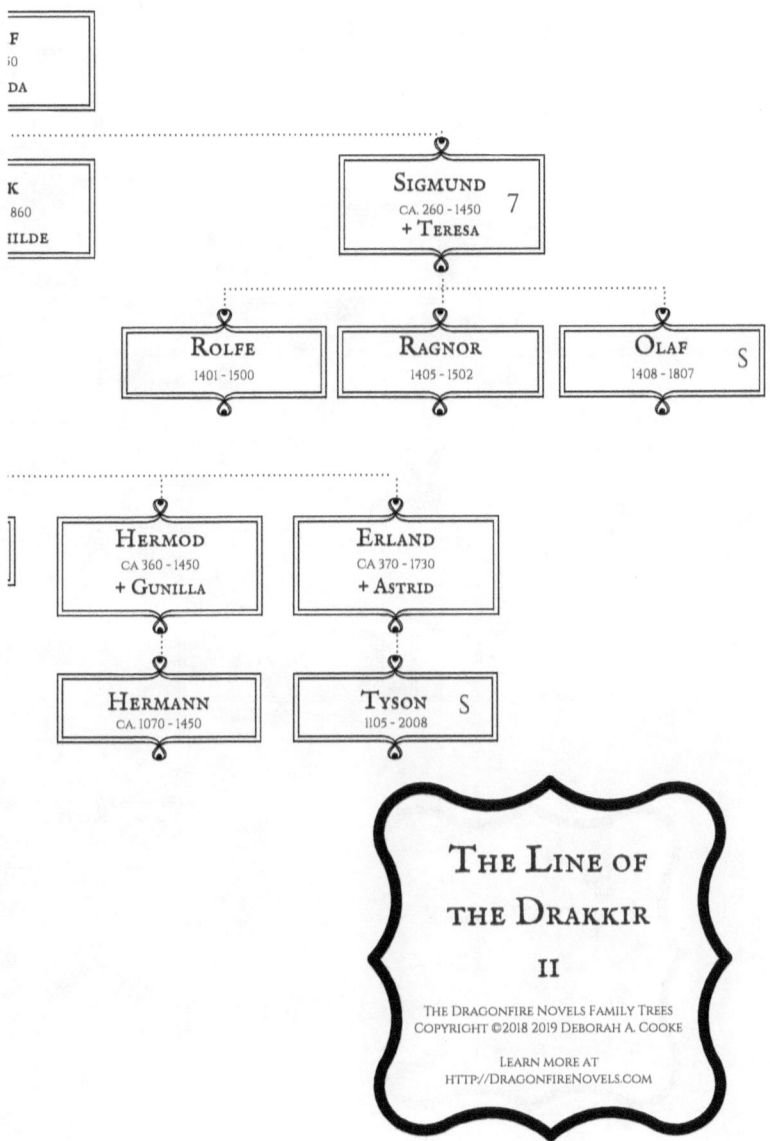

F
50
DA

K
860
IILDE

SIGMUND
CA. 260 - 1450   7
+ TERESA

ROLFE
1401 - 1500

RAGNOR
1405 - 1502

OLAF
1408 - 1807   S

HERMOD
CA 360 - 1450
+ GUNILLA

ERLAND
CA 370 - 1730
+ ASTRID

HERMANN
CA. 1070 - 1450

TYSON   S
1105 - 2008

THE LINE OF
THE DRAKKIR

II

THE DRAGONFIRE NOVELS FAMILY TREES
COPYRIGHT ©2018 2019 DEBORAH A. COOKE

LEARN MORE AT
HTTP://DRAGONFIRENOVELS.COM

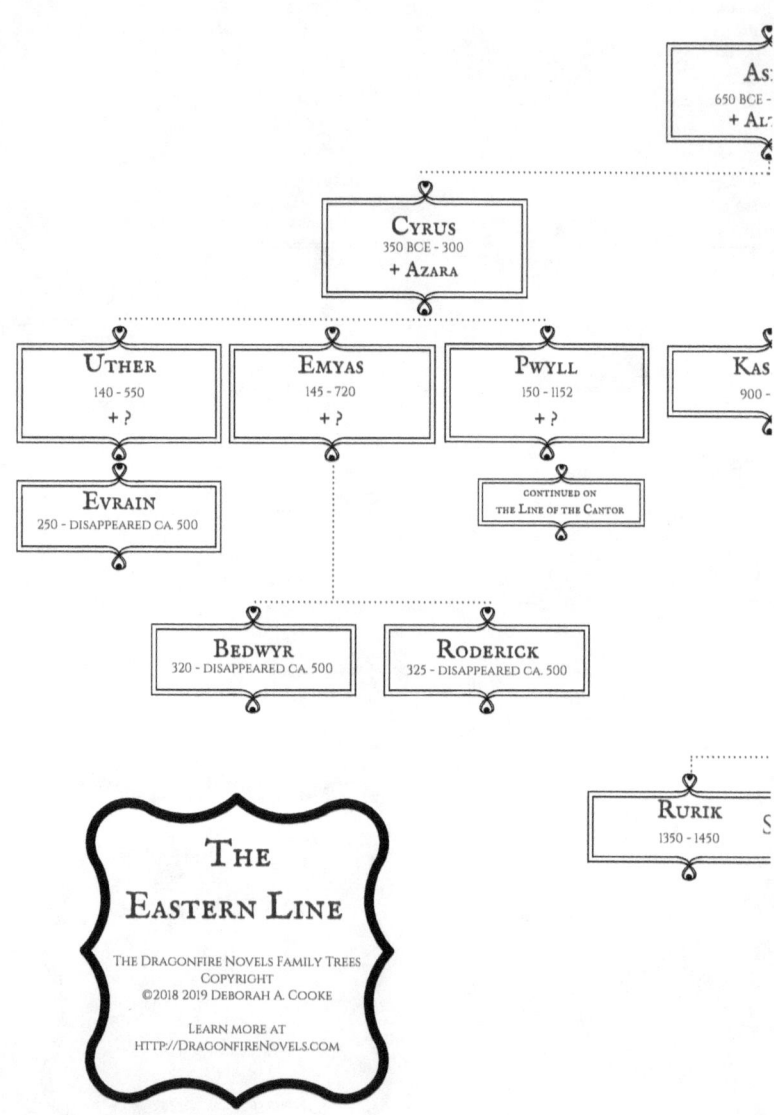

AS:
650 BCE -
+ AL

CYRUS
350 BCE - 300
+ AZARA

UTHER
140 - 550
+ ?

EMYAS
145 - 720
+ ?

PWYLL
150 - 1152
+ ?

KAS
900 -

EVRAIN
250 - DISAPPEARED CA. 500

CONTINUED ON
THE LINE OF THE CANTOR

BEDWYR
320 - DISAPPEARED CA. 500

RODERICK
325 - DISAPPEARED CA. 500

RURIK
1350 - 1450

S

THE
EASTERN LINE

THE DRAGONFIRE NOVELS FAMILY TREES
COPYRIGHT
©2018 2019 DEBORAH A. COOKE

LEARN MORE AT
HTTP://DRAGONFIRENOVELS.COM

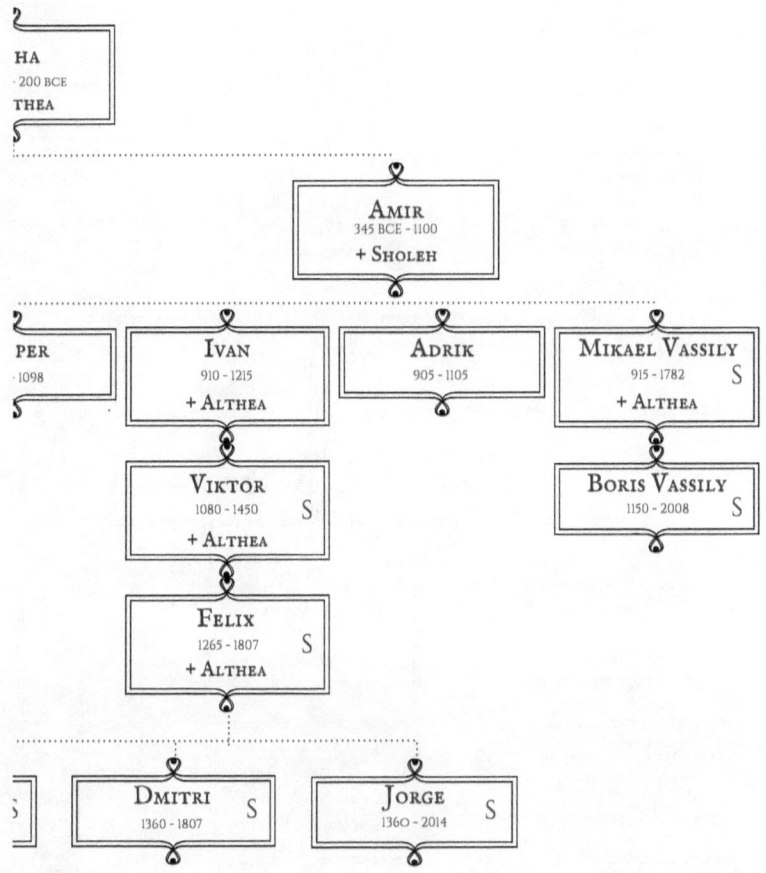

HA
· 200 BCE
THEA

AMIR
345 BCE - 1100
+ SHOLEH

PER
· 1098

IVAN
910 - 1215
+ ALTHEA

ADRIK
905 - 1105

MIKAEL VASSILY
915 - 1782   S
+ ALTHEA

VIKTOR
1080 - 1450   S
+ ALTHEA

BORIS VASSILY
1150 - 2008   S

FELIX
1265 - 1807   S
+ ALTHEA

DMITRI
1360 - 1807   S

JORGE
1360 - 2014   S

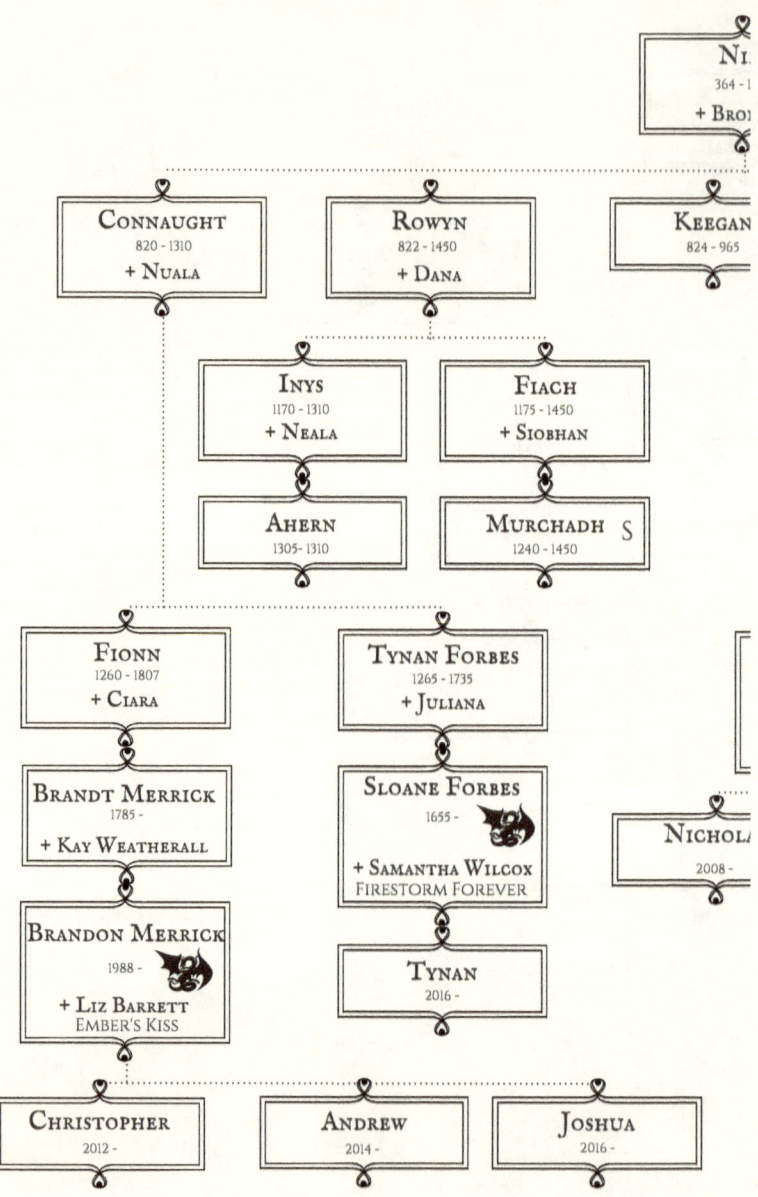

NI.
364 - 1
+ BRO

CONNAUGHT
820 - 1310
+ NUALA

ROWYN
822 - 1450
+ DANA

KEEGAN
824 - 965

INYS
1170 - 1310
+ NEALA

FIACH
1175 - 1450
+ SIOBHAN

AHERN
1305 - 1310

MURCHADH S
1240 - 1450

FIONN
1260 - 1807
+ CIARA

TYNAN FORBES
1265 - 1735
+ JULIANA

BRANDT MERRICK
1785 -
+ KAY WEATHERALL

SLOANE FORBES
1655 -

+ SAMANTHA WILCOX
FIRESTORM FOREVER

NICHOLA
2008 -

BRANDON MERRICK
1988 -
+ LIZ BARRETT
EMBER'S KISS

TYNAN
2016 -

CHRISTOPHER
2012 -

ANDREW
2014 -

JOSHUA
2016 -

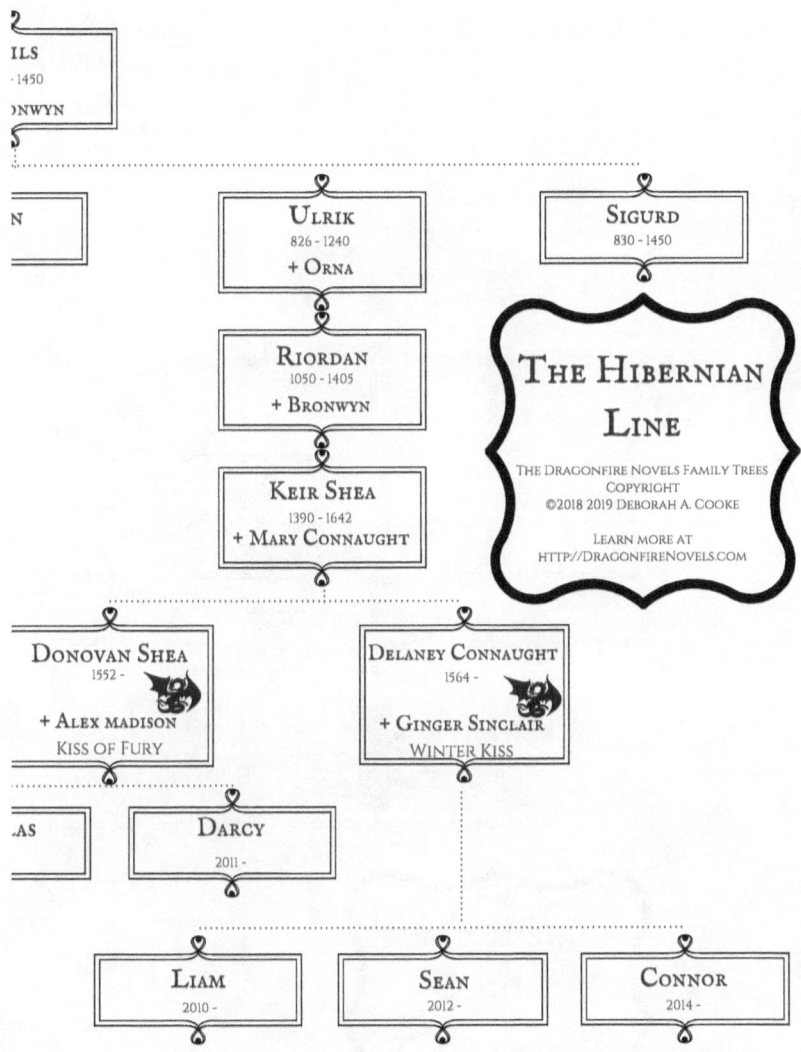

ILS
- 1450
ONWYN

ULRIK
826 - 1240
+ ORNA

SIGURD
830 - 1450

RIORDAN
1050 - 1405
+ BRONWYN

THE HIBERNIAN
LINE

THE DRAGONFIRE NOVELS FAMILY TREES
COPYRIGHT
©2018 2019 DEBORAH A. COOKE

LEARN MORE AT
HTTP//DRAGONFIRENOVELS.COM

KEIR SHEA
1390 - 1642
+ MARY CONNAUGHT

DONOVAN SHEA
1552 -
+ ALEX MADISON
KISS OF FURY

DELANEY CONNAUGHT
1564 -
+ GINGER SINCLAIR
WINTER KISS

AS

DARCY
2011 -

LIAM
2010 -

SEAN
2012 -

CONNOR
2014 -

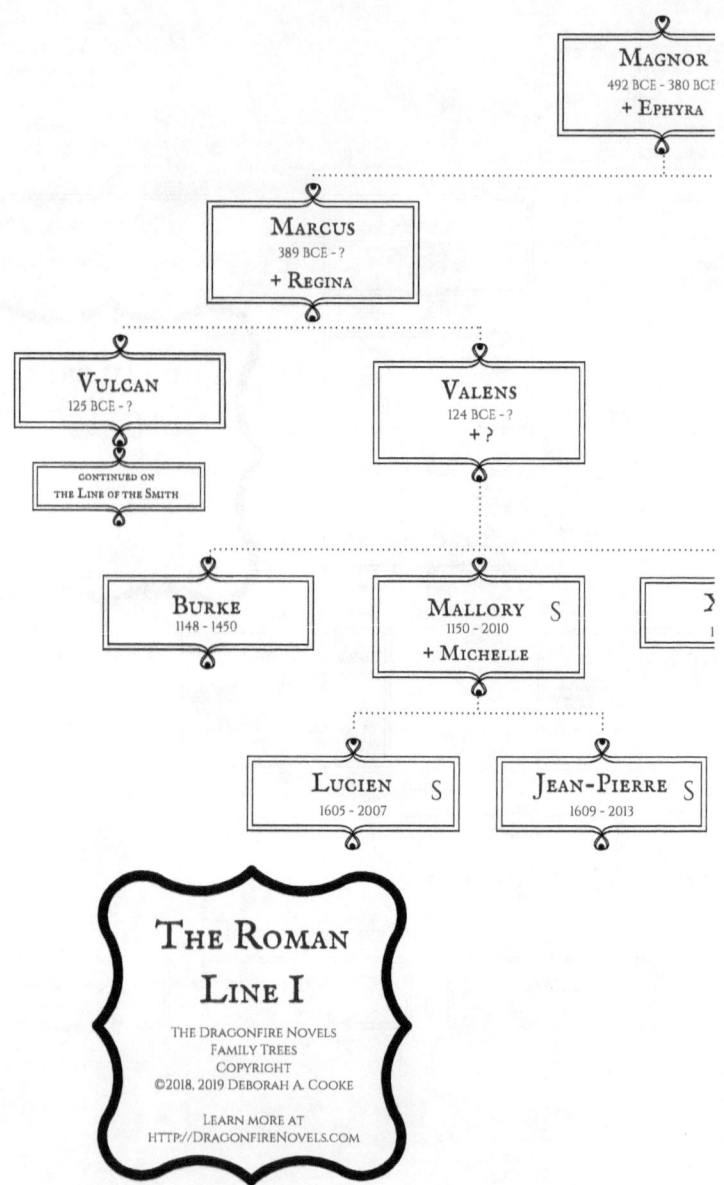

MAGNOR
492 BCE - 380 BCE
+ **EPHYRA**

MARCUS
389 BCE - ?
+ **REGINA**

VULCAN
125 BCE - ?

CONTINUED ON
THE LINE OF THE SMITH

VALENS
124 BCE - ?
+ ?

BURKE
1148 - 1450

MALLORY S
1150 - 2010
+ **MICHELLE**

LUCIEN S
1605 - 2007

JEAN-PIERRE S
1609 - 2013

THE ROMAN LINE I

THE DRAGONFIRE NOVELS
FAMILY TREES
COPYRIGHT
©2018, 2019 DEBORAH A. COOKE

LEARN MORE AT
HTTP//DRAGONFIRENOVELS.COM

CONTINUED ON
THE ROMAN LINE II

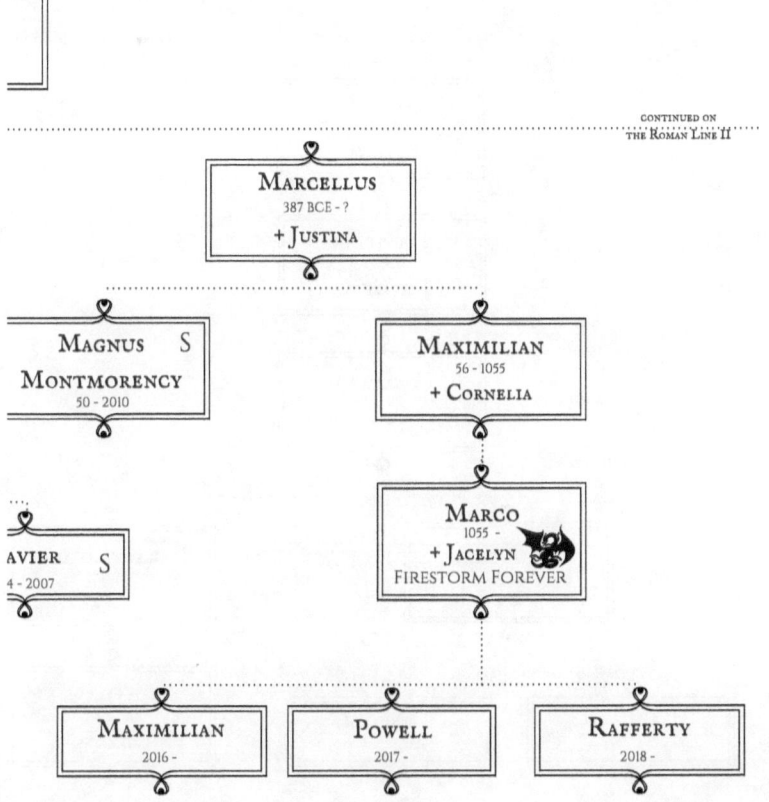

CONTINUED ON
THE ROMAN LINE I

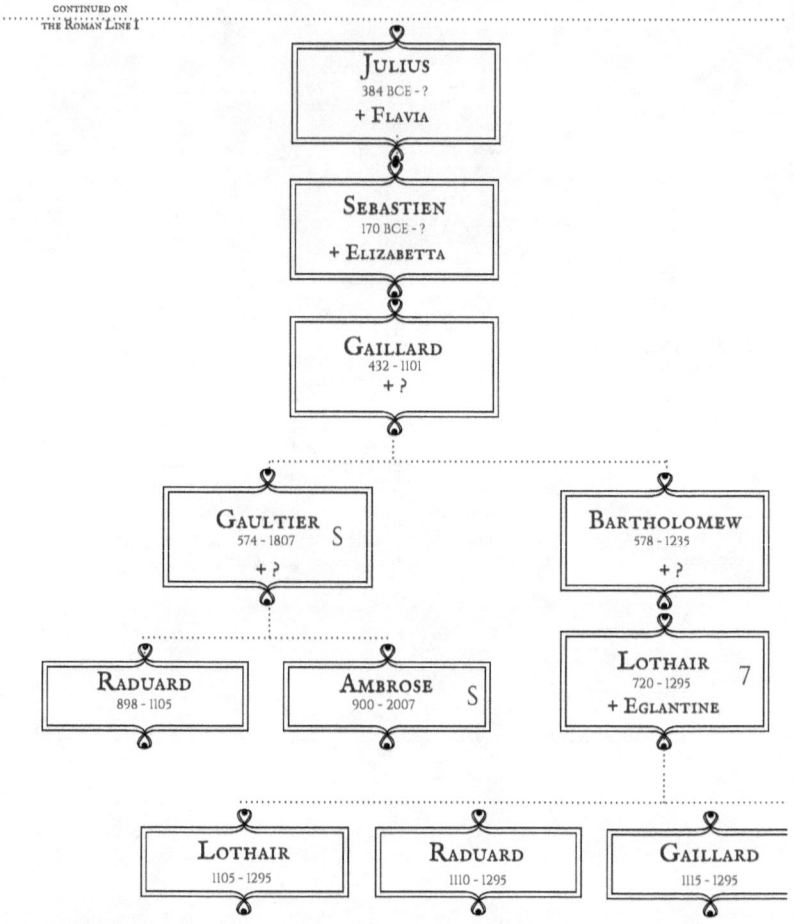

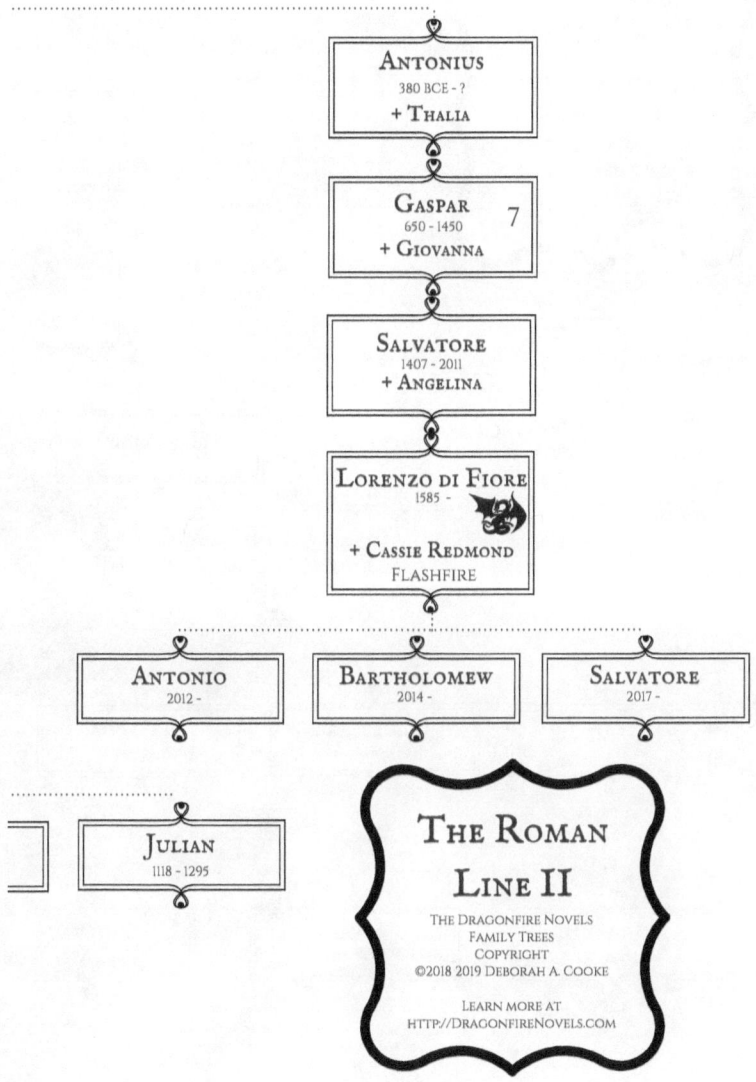

ANTONIUS
380 BCE - ?
+ **THALIA**

GASPAR 7
650 - 1450
+ **GIOVANNA**

SALVATORE
1407 - 2011
+ **ANGELINA**

LORENZO DI FIORE
1585 -

+ **CASSIE REDMOND**
FLASHFIRE

ANTONIO
2012 -

BARTHOLOMEW
2014 -

SALVATORE
2017 -

JULIAN
1118 - 1295

THE ROMAN LINE II

THE DRAGONFIRE NOVELS
FAMILY TREES
COPYRIGHT
©2018 2019 DEBORAH A. COOKE

LEARN MORE AT
HTTP://DRAGONFIRENOVELS.COM

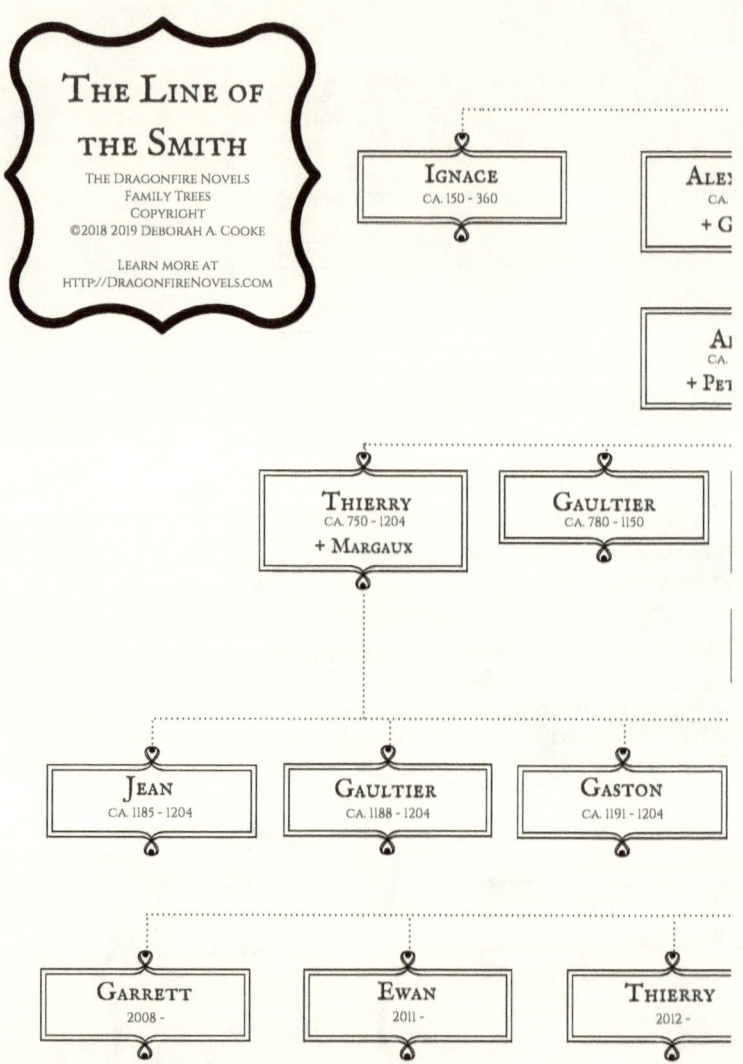

THE LINE OF THE SMITH

The Dragonfire Novels
Family Trees
Copyright
©2018 2019 Deborah A. Cooke

Learn more at
Http://DragonfireNovels.com

IGNACE
CA. 150 - 360

ALE
CA.
+ G

A
CA.
+ PET

THIERRY
CA. 750 - 1204
+ MARGAUX

GAULTIER
CA. 780 - 1150

JEAN
CA. 1185 - 1204

GAULTIER
CA. 1188 - 1204

GASTON
CA. 1191 - 1204

GARRETT
2008 -

EWAN
2011 -

THIERRY
2012 -

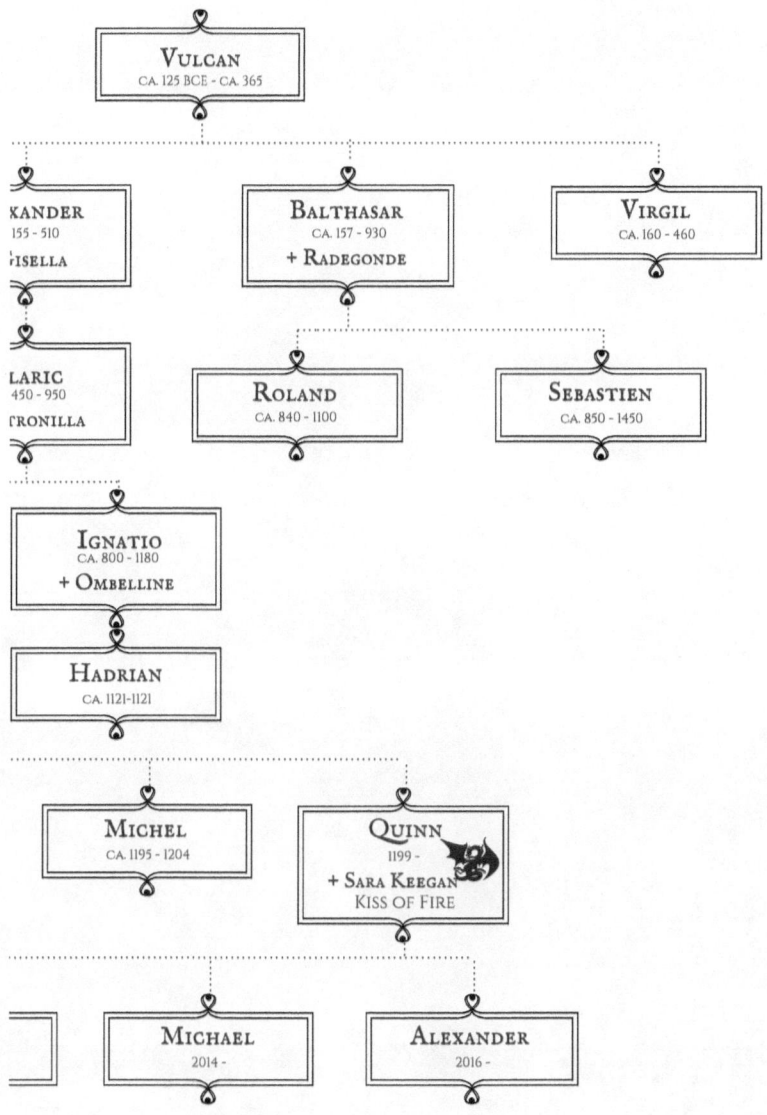

VULCAN
CA. 125 BCE - CA. 365

XANDER
155 - 510
ISELLA

BALTHASAR
CA. 157 - 930
+ **RADEGONDE**

VIRGIL
CA. 160 - 460

LARIC
450 - 950
RONILLA

ROLAND
CA. 840 - 1100

SEBASTIEN
CA. 850 - 1450

IGNATIO
CA. 800 - 1180
+ **OMBELLINE**

HADRIAN
CA. 1121-1121

MICHEL
CA. 1195 - 1204

QUINN
1199 -
+ **SARA KEEGAN**
KISS OF FIRE

MICHAEL
2014 -

ALEXANDER
2016 -

INTERVIEWS
WITH THE PYR

In 2009, I presented six interviews with the *Pyr* on my website. Each of the first six dragon shifter heroes in the *Dragonfire* series was interviewed on some facet of the *Pyr* nature. Their replies reflect their understanding of their own world at this point in time i.e. before the darkfire had sparked and its influences were entirely understood. All six interviews are presented again here for your reference.

QUINN TYRRELL ON HEREDITARY ROLES

DC: Hello, Quinn. I understand you're the Smith of the *Pyr*—what does that mean?

QT: The Smith repairs the armor—that is, the scales—of the *Pyr*. It's a hereditary role, so only the son of a Smith can become a Smith. It's also a learned role, because the son of the Smith has to learn about the forge and develop his skill, like any armorer, in order to do the best work possible.

DC: Is there only one Smith at a time?

QT: It tends to work out that way. Generally, the oldest son of the Smith will become the next Smith. I had four older brothers, though, all of whom trained with my father. They all were killed, however, when I was just a boy. I ultimately became the next Smith without the benefit of my father's training, by honing my innate skills and training with human blacksmiths.

Like so many artisanal crafts, there's the physical challenge of learning the skills -of working with the iron and the forge and the hammer—but also a mystical elements and arcane knowledge to give the work power. I had no one to teach me that knowledge and thought it was lost forever with my father's death.

DC: Then how did you learn it?

QT: I was lucky, in that the Wyvern saw fit to send me some dreams which put me in touch with my father and his skill. I couldn't have learned those things without an apprenticeship with a *Pyr* Smith, and although the connection is tenuous, I've managed to learn a great deal more this way, because of Sophie's gift to me.

It makes me a better Smith.

And being with Sara makes me a better *Pyr*.

DC: Do you ever have to choose between your immediate family and the greater *Pyr* family?

QT: All the time. It's the hardest part of my role, I think. I don't want to ever put Sara in danger, but usually my fellow *Pyr* need their scales repaired in the midst of their firestorms. That means *Slayers* and that means trouble. I can't leave Sara home, not now that we know the dragonsmoke barrier can be crossed, because she'd be undefended. I have to take her with me, right into danger, and you can imagine how happy I am about that.

DC: Probably not very happy at all.

QT: When she's pregnant, it's worse. My protective urges are at full power as soon as I sense she's conceived, and that's usually the time I also feel a firestorm brewing.

DC: Is Sara afraid to go?

QT: She understands my commitment to the *Pyr*, and that my skills are imperative to them. What's interesting is that as our relationship has evolved, we've changed sides on the argument—I used to insist that I had to go, but as our family grows, it's now Sara who says we have to go.

We work as a team, and it's a good team, good for both of us.

DC: What about the other traditional roles of the *Pyr*? Are they hereditary, like that of the Smith?

QT: Well, there aren't that many roles any more, given the loss of our formal hierarchies and social structures in the Middle Ages. Only vestiges remain of what was once our society.

Sloane, for example, is the Apothecary of the *Pyr*. My understanding is that he earned that ancient role because of his talent for healing and his knowledge of the lore. You'd have to ask him whether there can be only one Apothecary or not. It's possible that the Apothecary was once a hereditary role that mutated into an apprenticeship due to some Apothecary's lack of a son. I'm not sure, but Sloane would know.

Erik is, of course, the leader of the *Pyr*. While this role isn't hereditary in strict terms, it was his father who first created and held that role. Erik would have to have been a pretty lousy leader to have not stepped into that role.

But then, our numbers are so diminished. We don't have as many candidates and opportunities as once we did. All the more reason to make more *Pyr*.

DC: Speaking of which, I was talking to Niall about affinities. Can you tell me about yours?

QT: I have an affinity with fire and with earth. But because of my time at the forge and maybe because of my role as Smith, I have stronger control over the element of fire than my fellows. I can take an assault of dragonfire and withstand major injury. It's a case of mind over matter, and I'm trying to teach the other *Pyr* to have more control over their own link with fire.

DC: And earth?

QT: My connection with earth manifests in an innate

understanding of metals. I sing the song of steel, of silver, of wrought iron, and when I sing, I can turn the metal to my will. It takes time, but it's very satisfying.

DC: Which is why you're also an artisan blacksmith?

QT: You can't live on a firestorm! And I like the idea of sending my work, filled with my force of will, into the homes of humans. Many of my pieces are protective talismans, and in these times, we can all use a little extra protection.

DC: Well, said. Thank you, Quinn, for your time and patience today. If you don't mind, I'd like to admire the work in your studio a bit before I leave.

DONOVAN SHEA ON *PYR* VS. *SLAYER*

DC: Hi, Donovan. Thanks for meeting with me. Can you tell me, first off, who are the *Slayers*?

DS: *Slayers* are *Pyr* gone bad. It's that simple.

There's an old saying that *Pyr* are born, but *Slayers* are made. What we mean by that is that *Slayers* choose the darkness—they choose to turn their back on the Great Wyvern's plan for us in this world.

In basic terms, the true *Pyr* follow our mandate to defend the earth, including humans as one of the treasures of the earth. The Slayers believe that humans are destroying the earth and so must be eliminated.

DC: It's not a crazy argument...

DS: But it's wrong! And we know that it's wrong because the Great Wyvern withdraws the spark of her approval from those who turn *Slayer*.

DC: How so?

DS: Their blood turns black, which Sloane says is indicative of their turning away from the Great Wyvern's divine spark. They also become infertile.

DC: I thought you were all infertile until your firestorms, that only your destined mate can conceive your son or sons?

DS: Technically, that's true. The difference is that *Slayers* never get a firestorm, but they can still sense when one of the *Pyr* has one. I think that jealousy drives a lot of their need to interfere in firestorms, even beyond their greater goal of ensuring there are no more *Pyr* created.

DC: Then how do they get more Slayers?

DS: Traditionally, they recruited *Pyr* to choose the darkness over the light.

There has been another way, though, by using the Dragon's Blood Elixir. I think Delaney should tell you about that, because he knows a lot more about it. He was, after all, forced to consume the Dragon's Blood Elixir himself.

DC: Other than wanting to eradicate humans and stop firestorms, what characterizes Slayers?

DS: They're selfish and greedy. They tend to choose their individual ambitions over the good of everyone. That's why all this talk about saving the planet by eliminating humans is probably just talk—most *Slayers* I've met want to eradicate everyone except themselves. They want to be king of the world, at any price, which isn't that positive of a goal.

The good thing is that they are all deceitful and would sell each other for a nickel. That gives us a chance to beat them.

DC: It seems as if things have heated up between the *Pyr* and *Slayers* recently. Why is that?

DS: Well, there are a bunch of prophecies, which isn't really my thing. The point is that the world is at a kind of balance point. It's about the nodes of the moon, and you'd have to check this with my mate, Alex, to make sure I have the details right. We're in a phase called the Dragon's Tail, which is the descending node of the moon. In astrological terms, it's a period when the karmic balance must be restored. It's a chance to make a change and set the world on a new course.

The cycle of the moon's nodes is 19 years long—this Dragon's Tail began in 2006 and culminates in September 2015. We don't have that long to get it right!

DC: More star stuff. Don't eclipses have something to do with firestorms?

DS: Yes. There's a traditional idea within the *Pyr* that firestorms which are particularly important to us begin on a full lunar eclipse. There have been a lot of firestorms since 2006 that have begun that way, and you've been writing about them.

DC: Why would these be particularly important firestorms? Just because they're happening within the Dragon's Tail?

DS: I think maybe it's because of Rafferty's conviction. He says that a firestorm is a chance to make a strong partnership, for the the *Pyr* and his mate to be stronger together than either can be apart. He talks about two halves coming together to make a greater whole. So, it makes sense to me that our doing this in this time makes us stronger, and better equipped to defeat the *Slayers* forever.

It's certainly what happened to me. I know I would be much less strong without Alex.

DC: Because you became the foretold Warrior as a result of your firestorm?

DS: It wasn't just the firestorm. Alex and I felt the firestorm and

could have just had sex, made a baby, moved on. The fact that we made a permanent union, that we each share our skills in solving problems, makes us a force to be reckoned with. It gave me the power to become the Warrior, and our partnership gives me the strength to use that ability when I need to.
It's good stuff!
DC: What does it mean to be the foretold Warrior?
DS: It means that I can summon the elements as weapons and command them.
It means that I can kick butt.
DC: Don't the *Slayers* have weapons of their own? I thought they were developing the ability to cut dragonsmoke.
DS: That is not good, and it's because of the Elixir.
Let me just backtrack and explain dragonsmoke. Dragonsmoke is a boundary mark. We can breathe dragonsmoke and weave it as a barrier around a place we want to secure—like the location of a hoard, or the sanctuary of one's mate. You have to work at breathing good dragonsmoke, at exhaling it slowly and evenly, at weaving it tightly. A good dragonsmoke barrier has a resonance that only *Pyr* and *Slayers* can hear—think of the ping of a crystal glass. It's like that, but higher, too high a tone for humans to hear. Traditionally, a *Pyr* or *Slayer* could only cross a dragonsmoke barrier with the express permission of the dragon who breathed it.
What's happened recently , though, is that *Slayers* who have drunk the Dragon's Blood Elixir can cut dragonsmoke without there being any indication that the barrier has been compromised. They do this by hovering between forms—also very challenging—and letting only their right index finger change to a talon. They use that talon as a knife. I don't think it's easy to learn, even after drinking the Elixir, but the fact that they can do it at all is troubling.
Some dragons who can really control their dragonsmoke can use it as a weapon—they breathe it and surround their opponent, then use the dragonsmoke as a conduit to steal the life force of their adversary. That's pretty challenging stuff, given that the meditative state used for breathing dragonsmoke isn't usually the mood you're in when you're fighting.
It figures that a *Slayer* would have come up with that one.
DC: Sounds like the rules are changing.
DS: All the time. I like to think it's a sign of desperation on the part

HERE BE DRAGONS: THE DRAGONFIRE COMPANION

551

of the *Slayers*, but that Elixir was really potent stuff.

DC: You mentioned that humans can't hear the resonant ring of a good dragonsmoke mark. Why is that?

DS: The *Pyr* have sharper senses than humans do. We can see farther and in greater detail. We can feel each other's firestorms, no matter where they happen, like a distant bonfire. Our sense of smell is very keen—we can smell Slayers and guess their distance, for example. That's another thing—the Elixir has given some *Slayers* the ability to disguise their scent, which means they can surprise us. Not good.

And we can hear sounds you can't—higher ranges, lower ranges, more distant and muted sounds. Our communication between each other is an old, very low, kind of talking which is called old-speak. Some *Pyr* and *Slayers*—especially those with an affinity for air—can cast their old-speak far and wide, while others can slide it into the thoughts of other *Pyr* and *Slayers*. Never been my forte, but I can do basic old-speak.

Of course, Alex isn't a fan. She likes to know what's going on, so I don't use it as much as I used to!

DC: I like that you make that concession to her! Thank you, Donovan, for telling us more about the *Pyr*. Fingers crossed that you kick all the butt you need to by 2015!

ERIK SORENSSON ON THE *PYR*

DC: Good morning, Erik. I know that you're pressed for time today, so let's dive right in. Who are the *Pyr*?

ES: Good morning, Deborah. The *Pyr* are dragon shape shifters. We are an ancient race, and our own stories suggest that we date back to the creation of the planet. Of course, there is no documentation to prove this claim, but my partner Eileen notes that every human civilization has stories of dragons. She believes—because she is convinced that human stories are a reflection of human observations and beliefs—that this supports the notion of our being at least an old of a species as humans.

DC: So, you're just another species that coexists with human society?

ES: I should think not! The *Pyr* were created, according to our stories, to defend the treasure that is the earth itself. We are the guardians of the four elements—earth, fire, water, and air—and charged with ensuring the future of the planet.

DC: In human stories, dragons guard treasures of precious gems and gold. Are you saying that the *Pyr* value more basic things?

ES: We defend the earth and its elements, but we are not without our hoards. Even a *Pyr* does not live by air, earth, fire and water alone, and many of us do have a taste for luxury.

DC: And how are the *Pyr* different from humans?

ES: As noted, we have the ability to transform ourselves into dragons. This is generally a decision on the part of the *Pyr*, but the change can be involuntary under duress, or the effects of an eclipse. It is a fighting pose, so some *Pyr* shift automatically to their dragon form when sensing a threat.

DC: Are *Pyr* born with their powers?

ES: We are born as *Pyr*, but do not come into our capabilities until puberty. The ability passes through the male line, which is to say that every *Pyr* is the son of another *Pyr*—and that *Pyr*'s destined human mate.

DC: Does that mean there are no female *Pyr*?

ES: At any point in time, there can be one female *Pyr*. She is the daughter of a *Pyr* (and that *Pyr*'s destined mate) and is known as the Wyvern. The Wyvern has additional talents and plays a unique role within *Pyr* society. She is usually a seer and capable of perceiving the implication of events far beyond that of any other *Pyr* or human. She can dispatch dreams, targeting individual *Pyr* and humans, and sending them the information they need. She can change into additional forms, characteristically adding a third form of a salamander to her repertoire. She can move through space and time by will, appearing instantly in a given place. This is somewhat startling, and also gives her the power to move through dragonsmoke—essentially she manifests on the other side of the smoke barrier.

This means that the Wyvern is very sensitive. Traditionally, the Wyvern has remained remote and kept herself apart from even *Pyr* society. Her influence has been felt, but in many times and places, she has not been seen. Sophie, the most recent Wyvern, chose to become more actively engaged in our battle with the *Slayers*. I fear she paid a tremendous price for her decision. I would never have suggested that she pursue the path that she did, which is probably why she didn't ask my advice.

DC: You're referring to the developments in **Kiss of Fate**. Does this mean that there won't be another Wyvern?

ES: No. The role of the Wyvern is much like that of the Smith, in that it is a task that a soul undertakes for one lifetime. I believe that Sophie will be reborn—perhaps in human form, perhaps in *Pyr* form—because the divine spark that gave her life will continue to burn. She will not be the Wyvern in that next life, that I guarantee.

DC: You sound very certain of that.

ES: I am *Pyr*. I have a daughter, conceived during my firestorm. There is no further explanation necessary.

DC: Well, I'm a bit confused. Does that mean that your daughter is Sophie reborn? Are they both the same person inside?

ES: Actually, that is an interesting question. Because of the loss of our lore and the fact that the Wyvern traditionally kept herself apart from our society, we weren't certain. I knew that Zoë had to be the new Wyvern simply because of her gender. Rafferty was skeptical that she could be the Wyvern because her nature is so different from that of Sophie. Even as a very young child, we can all see that Zoë is very direct, which is quite different from the evasiveness that characterized Sophie. On the other hand, it has also become clear that Zoë already possesses some of the powers traditionally associated with the Wyvern.

So, it seems that the position of Wyvern is one that a soul chooses to accept for a lifetime. Sophie, then, has completed her tour of duty—to use a human parallel—but unfortunately, I don't know what has happened to her soul. Perhaps she has chosen not to reincarnate. Perhaps it isn't time. I don't know, but I do wish her every happiness. Our world is not the same without her presence.

DC: But you said Zoë was conceived during your firestorm. What is the firestorm?

ES: I understand that you intend to speak to Rafferty, as well. As the firestorm is a matter close to his own heart, I will let him explain it to you.

DC: Do the *Pyr* have any other powers?

ES: One talent that many *Pyr* manage to develop is that of beguiling. Beguiling is a kind of hypnosis, the ability to persuade a human that things are other than that human believes. To beguile, the *Pyr* conjures a flame in his eyes. The human stares at the flame, because humans are fascinated by fire, and it is possible for the *Pyr* to introduce new thoughts to that human while the human is transfixed.

Beguiling can be useful in disguising our presence within human society, but there have been those who abuse its power, and use beguiling to deceive. I have mixed feelings about beguiling and advise its use sparingly.

DC: But don't the *Pyr* have affinities to certain elements? Can you tell me more about that?

ES: I have already said too much. You must understand that we do not exist openly in human society, but rely upon our ability to blend in. It is not in my nature, nor is it my inclination, to explain all of *Pyr* history to you, simply because you have asked. I have an obligation to defend those I lead, after all.

Perhaps Niall will explain the nature of affinities to you. His affinity with air is very strong.

DC: It sounds as if there are particular challenges to your role as leader of the *Pyr*.

ES: Humans have a metaphor about herding cats. I assure you that gathering dragons and building consensus between them is several orders of magnitude more difficult! I believe in respecting the convictions and decisions of other *Pyr*, but there are times...

My father invented the notion of a ruling council of *Pyr*. It is an idea that I have brought into use again, although in a more fluid form. It is my observation that *Pyr* do not respond well to having the will of others imposed upon them, and I have learned a great deal in recent centuries about persuasion. Although I have a core group of *Pyr* upon whom I can rely, it is an ongoing challenge to gather those who have chosen to exile themselves.

DC: Maybe you should just beguile them!

ES: A *Pyr* cannot beguile another *Pyr*.

Unfortunately.

I know where the others are, though, and will use all of my powers to gather them in time. As you might well imagine, individual *Pyr* can be stubborn.

DC: I can easily imagine that! You have a lot on your proverbial plate right now. Can you explain the crisis facing the *Pyr* at this time?

ES: It is the final crisis, the final challenge from the *Slayers* over the future of the planet. The magnitude of that challenge means that I cannot discuss it further today. Perhaps Donovan could better explain it to you, as he has been actively engaged in the battle.

DC: Thank you, Erik, for your time, and also your authorization for me to interview the other *Pyr*.

DELANEY SHEA ON THE DRAGON'S BLOOD ELIXIR

DC: Hi Delaney. Thanks for joining me today. The other *Pyr* keep saying I should talk to you about the Dragon's Blood Elixir. What can you tell me about it?

DS: Well, it's nasty stuff. The Dragon's Blood Elixir was created by the Magnus, who has since become the leader of the *Slayers*. It confers immortality upon those *Pyr* and *Slayers* who consume it. They also heal more quickly and are able to learn some skills that have traditionally belonged only to the Wyvern. Some of them learn to cut dragonsmoke, for example, and others to spontaneously manifest in other places. Some learn to hover on the cusp of transformation, half man and half dragon. It's really strong stuff.

The catch is that one sip isn't enough. The Elixir is like a drug, one with effects that wear off, so those who have drunk it will always need more. And they have to go to Magnus for it, because he controls the source. No surprise that he's never been in much of a hurry to tell anyone that part.

DC: So, there are *Pyr* and *Slayers* who have drunk the Elixir, and have become hooked on it?

DS: No. The power of the Elixir has only been seductive to *Slayers*, maybe because they can't see beyond their own ambitions. The true *Pyr* haven't wanted it, either because it's evil, because immortality is unnatural, or because we guess that there's a trick. Magnus never did play a straight game.

DC: I'll guess that those *Slayers* who have drunk it are harder to kill.

DS: You'd be guessing right!

But it's not just *Slayers*, you know. Magnus came up with this scheme to build himself an army that was completely obedient to him. He learned through all his research that when *Pyr* and *Slayers* die, there's a chance of what humans might call limbo—we have to be exposed to all four elements within half a solar day (12 hours) to be dead. But the spark of the Great Wyvern leaves the body of the dead *Pyr* immediately. We have a tradition of personally ensuring that any fallen *Pyr* is given the full exposure, but the root of the tradition wasn't clear until recently. (So much *Pyr* lore was lost in the Middle Ages, after we were nearly hunted to extinction.)

What Magnus learned was that he could forcibly administer the Elixir to the remains of these *Pyr* and *Slayers* who were dead but not exposed to all four elements within the required time period. They were re-animated, like zombies, and completely susceptible to his will. They have no moral code, no real life force or spark of the divine anymore, and can't feel pain. They fight until they can't anymore, no matter what happens to them, like automatons. We call them shadow dragons, since they're shadows of their former selves.

DC: That sounds pretty creepy.

DS: The worst is when you confront a shadow dragon that's been made of someone you knew when he was alive. It's really hard to kill that shadow dragon, because of the resemblance—and the shadow dragon might have been made of a decent *Pyr*. Magnus uses that against us deliberately, setting the shadow dragons we know upon us.

DC: How is it that you know so much about the Elixir?

DS: Well, I was an experiment, the only *Pyr* to be forced to consume the Elixir. I was nearly killed in the defense of Quinn's mate (**Kiss of Fire**) and the *Slayers* took my body. Magnus had me taken to his secret academy and force-fed the Elixir. Not only had I not been exposed to all four elements, but the spark of life wasn't completely extinguished in me. There was enough left for me to fight the Elixir and to be aware of the pain it created in my body.

DC: But were you turned into a shadow dragon?

DS: Not quite, again because I wasn't dead. I was drawn to Donovan's firestorm, maybe because he's my brother, and that seemed to kindle the spark of life within me. I was able to fight Magnus' command that I should destroy Donovan's mate (**Kiss of Fury**), but I still didn't trust myself. I exiled myself from the *Pyr* after a nasty incident during Erik's firestorm (**Kiss of Fate**), and decided to eliminate the Elixir myself forever. I was heading into that suicide mission when my own firestorm sparked—and Ginger changed everything.

DC: That's pretty bold to take on a mission like that.

DS: My life wasn't worth living as it was. My body raged for more Elixir, especially during eclipses, and drinking more of that crap was the last thing I wanted to do. I thought that if I could ensure that no other *Pyr* had to endure what I did, that my death would be worthwhile.

DC: But Ginger changed everything.

DS: You bet she did. You know, I never used to believe in the healing power of love. Guess I had that wrong.

DC: Let's talk about something more cheerful! I'm intrigued by these Dragon's Teeth Warriors who appeared in Erik's story (**Kiss of Fate**). Do you know anything about them?

DS: The Dragon's Tooth Warriors are a military group who were enchanted eons ago, around the time of the ancient Greeks. They were turned into teeth, like the teeth of a dragon. And the story was that these teeth could be sown, like seeds, and they would turn back into an army of men ready to fight. No surprise that Magnus thought they would be a great addition to his army of shadow dragons, so he really wanted the teeth. In the course of Erik's story, they were freed from their enchantment, although they're really different from us modern *Pyr*.

DC: How are they different?

DS: They don't talk much. They have a tougher moral code. They're great fighters and have trained a lot together. They seem to anticipate each other's moves without any communication that even we can hear. They're a force to be reckoned with, that's for sure.

DC: Do you know where they are?

DS: Last I heard, they were getting used to our world. I have feeling we'll hear from them again, once they come to terms with what's happened to them.

I hope so. We could use them on our side.

DC: You mentioned the challenge of facing a shadow dragon you've known before—did you have to do that?

DS: No, it didn't happen to me. My brother, Donovan, had to fight our father, Keir, but given their history, I don't think it was as hard for him as it might have been otherwise. Quinn faced his older brothers and Rafferty, his grandfather. The toughest fight, though, is between Niall and his twin brother Phelan—Phelan's a shadow dragon, but he had already turned *Slayer* before he died. He looks just like Niall but isn't nearly as good of a friend to have. Phelan is one vicious shadow dragon.

DC: You and Niall are good friends?

DS: The best! We've been buddies for a long time, and were

partners in an eco-tourism business, too. I sold my half of the business out to him, so I could take on the Elixir without leaving any unfinished ends. He really argued with me about my choice, which is what makes him such a good friend—he's not afraid to tell me that he thinks I'm wrong.

DC: But you didn't listen to him?

DS: (laughs) Niall argued that life was always worth living, but he wasn't as persuasive as Ginger. That's probably a good thing!

DC: Thanks Delaney, for sharing your experience with us. It must have been a nightmare. Good for Ginger that she helped you to heal!

NIALL TALBOT ON AFFINITIES

DC: Hi Niall. Thanks for making the time to talk to me. Can you tell me a bit about the affinities that the *Pyr* have for the elements?

NT: Hi Deborah. As guardians of the elements, we have a connection with all four elements. It seems that most of us have a stronger connection with two elements. For most of us, one of those elements is fire—we do breathe fire, after all! It's pretty key to the whole dragon shape shifting thing. But in addition to that, most of us appear to have a connection with a second element.

DC: That sounds a bit vague.

NT: It's not always obvious. I've been lucky, because my own affinity for the element of air has always been strong. I couldn't not know about it. It's been a part of my life for as long as I can remember. I could whistle up a wind by the time I was twelve. Other *Pyr* aren't so lucky. They have to work at figuring out their affinity.

DC: What's the point of having an affinity?

NT: It's easier to be able to command that element. Of course, I had to work at my ability to conjure storms and to bend them in the right direction. It doesn't all come naturally! But practice and patience make a big difference.

DC: How are affinities with other elements manifested?

NT: Rafferty has an affinity for the earth. He can sing to the earth—it's more like a chant, really—and collect news from Gaia, in much the same way as I ask questions of the wind. He can also move the earth, coaxing it to open or close. Magnus, the leader of the *Slayers*, has the same affinity, but uses it for dark purposes.

Even though some of us have the same affinities, they come to light in different ways. Erik, for example, also has an affinity for air, but he has prophetic visions. Erik can see into the future because of his gift. I can't do that, but he can't summon a tornado.

Donovan and Delaney both have affinities with water—again it manifests slightly differently for each of them. Delaney has compassion for others while Donovan has an intuitive understanding of others. Donovan can anticipate reactions, which is part of what makes him a great fighter, and the Warrior of the *Pyr*. Sloane has an affinity for water, too, and his expresses itself in his ability to heal. He's the Apothecary of the *Pyr*.

DC: You're talking about the roles of the individual *Pyr*. Do these result from affinities?

NT: Not necessarily. But a *Pyr* who undertakes a role, either a hereditary one or an assumed one, usually relies upon his affinities to better fulfill that role.

DC: Do affinities run in families? Donovan and Delaney are brothers, and they both have an affinity with water.

NT: You know, I'm not sure. My twin brother, Phelan, never exhibited an affinity, so I'm not sure what his was. Fire was obvious, but otherwise, I don't know. Of course, Phelan was never much interested in anything that required effort on his part.

DC: Phelan turned *Slayer* before his death, didn't he?

NT: I don't want to talk about that.

DC: Sorry! Is there anything else you can tell me about traditional roles in the *Pyr*?

NT: I really need to get back to work. I've got a ton of bookings to take care of, and since Delaney left the partnership, I'm on the run all the time.

Maybe you'd better talk to Quinn about that.

DC: Do you miss Delaney in the eco-tourism company you used to run together?

NT: You bet. But it is what it is, and he's happy with Ginger. That's the best thing I can hope for any friend of mine—happiness and a great relationship. Gotta go!

DC: Thanks for talking to me, Niall. Don't work too hard!

Rafferty Powell on the firestorm

DC: Good morning, Rafferty. Thanks for meeting with me. Can you explain the firestorm to me?

RP: I would like nothing better. The firestorm is the mark of a *Pyr* meeting his destined mate. That mate is always a human woman, and the consummation of their relationship will result in the conception of the *Pyr*'s son.

That all sounds very biological, but I assure you, the firestorm is a magical moment in the life of a *Pyr*. It occurs only once in the life of each *Pyr*, and should be savored as the rare opportunity that it is.

DC: Only once?

RP: I'm not suggesting that the *Pyr* are celibate otherwise! But it is only during the firestorm that the *Pyr* can conceive a son and heir.

DC: And that happens the first time he and his mate are intimate?

RP: Yes. And that's part of the issue. There are some *Pyr* who perceive the firestorm simply as a biological urge to make more *Pyr* and one that must be satisfied. There are those who consummate the firestorm, then move on. But in my many centuries of observing firestorms, I have noticed that the Great Wyvern chooses those mates who offer something to us. A firestorm can result in an enduring relationship, one that makes the individual *Pyr* stronger and gives balance to his life. It can also empower him.

DC: You make it sound as if it doesn't always work out that way.

RP: It is always risky to care for another individual, regardless of your species. Love makes us vulnerable. For the *Pyr*, love actually makes us physically vulnerable—we lose a scale in our dragon form when we care for another. There's literally a hole in our armor, and a blow struck there can kill us.

DC: Wow. Is there any way to repair that damage?

RP: I like that the mate is the only one who can offer the solution. In surrendering a physical token that is of emotional importance to her, the *Pyr*'s scale can be repaired with that token. It is also necessary for the four elements to be accounted for in the repair ceremony.

DC: How so?

RP: There are four elements, as you know—fire, water, earth and air. Both parties in the firestorm typically bring two elements, or affinities with two elements, to the partnership. By forming a permanent union, one represented by the repairing of the *Pyr*'s scale, a balance is formed in the relationship that is an echo of the four elements in the world at large. We are the guardians of the elements, you know, so I think that balance makes us stronger.

I think you should talk to Niall about the *Pyr* and their affinities with specific elements.

DC: I'll do that. How does a *Pyr* know when he's having his firestorm?

RP: It's impossible to miss! Sparks literally fly between the *Pyr* and his destined mate, and the heat of the firestorm burns in his blood. It burns hotter as time passes, increasing the demand to fulfill it. I don't think anyone has ever resisted a firestorm's call for long.

The other issue, of course, is that all of the *Pyr* can feel a firestorm burning. We are drawn to it, like moths to the flame. Not everyone comes with good intentions though — *Slayers* often try to interfere in a firestorm. The most effective way of doing that is to kill the human mate.

DC: So, the *Pyr* ends up trying to seduce his mate while he's also defending her?

RP: Often, yes. I understand it can be a very intense courtship.

DC: Have you had your firestorm?

RP: No. But I am content to wait until the Great Wyvern decrees my time to have come. I believe that a firestorm is worth waiting for.

DC: But you said you'd been observing firestorms for centuries. Are the *Pyr* immortal?

RP: No. We are not immortal. First of all, we do not come into our powers until puberty. After that — which can be a trying period for all concerned — we age very slowly until we have our firestorm. I am 1200 years old.

DC: And very patient!

RP: Well, good things are worth the wait. And the firestorm comes with a price, as well. Once a *Pyr* has had his firestorm, his aging processes accelerate. There are those who perceive this as a negative, and try to evade their firestorms because of it. I think, though, that it is part of the Great Wyvern's plan to encourage us to make a lasting bond with our mates, and I think that when we do so, there is no point to life without that mate. I could tell you numerous stories of *Pyr* who died shortly after—if not concurrently—with their human mates, simply out of a lack of will to continue. It is my conviction that they are together then, somewhere, although of course I have no evidence of that.

DC: You sound like a romantic.

RP: I was raised at my grandfather's knee, listening to stories of adventure and romance. Romance and a conviction in the power of true love is what sustains me and gives meaning to my life.

DC: So, do *Pyr* have only one child and heir, the one conceived in the firestorm?

RP: Not necessarily. That woman has the ability to bear that *Pyr*'s children. She is the only woman with whom he can be fertile, and all of the children they conceive will be *Pyr*. That's a good argument for a lasting relationship, in my opinion. I like the idea of large families!

DC: What about the roles that some of the *Pyr* have? Are those hereditary, or are they earned?

RP: I think you should talk to Quinn about that. He is the Smith of the *Pyr*, and can explain to you how he came to assume that role.

DC: Thank you, Rafferty, for sharing your vision with us. I wish you luck with your own firestorm, whenever you feel its power.

Harmonia's Kiss

Enchanted for thousands of years, the shapeshifters known as the Dragon's Tooth Warriors have awakened to find the world a vastly different place. Their leader, concerned for their morale, dares to take them on a mission to confront the fullness of everything they've lost.

Little does Drake realize that this dangerous mission will give him a renewed purpose. And if they succeed, these *Pyr* will have to question everything they thought they knew about the past—and confront a quest for the future.

I

Summer Solstice
June 2010

It was time.

Erik Sorensson, leader of the *Pyr*, waited at the standing stones of Callanish, as agreed. It was close to midnight, the sky filled with dark clouds and the wind chilly off the Atlantic.

He waited alone. He leaned against the tallest stone, the one that might have been a finger pointing to the heavens, and listened.

Erik had no doubt that the Dragon's Tooth Warriors would keep to their commander's agreement. They were ancient, these warriors, remnants of a time long before his own. Erik was old, but the Dragon's Tooth Warriors were far, far older.

So much older that they were almost incomprehensible to him. He wondered what they wanted of him.

He expected it was permission.

But for what? He needed every talon in this fight against the *Slayers* and was impatient to have the Dragon's Tooth Warriors committed to his ranks. He knew they had endured a great trauma and wanted to give them time.

The problem was that Erik didn't have a lot of time.

He hoped they requested something he could grant.

Erik sensed the Dragon's Tooth Warriors before he saw them. They had no scent, these ancient warriors. His awareness of their arrival was more a prickling at the edge of his thoughts, more a manifestation of his gift of foresight than the raw ability to smell his fellows.

Erik scanned the eastern sky and saw their silhouettes appearing through the clouds. The moonlight touched their dark figures, painting them with silver as if they came from a dream.

In a way, they did, having been awakened after centuries of spellbound sleep.

As always, the Dragon's Tooth Warriors were rigorously disciplined. It was as if a single mind drove their actions. Erik knew it was their military training, but still, he was impressed.

He wanted them pledged to the cause of the *Pyr*.

They approached in perfect formation, a single dark dragon at the fore of the company, then a pair immediately behind him. Two pair followed those two, leading several rows of their ranks. They numbered less than twenty, of all the hundred who had once been, but were still a fearsome force. Erik knew they were powerful fighting machines, partly because of their discipline, partly because of their devotion to the whole of the company.

That in itself spoke of a different era, when the individual was of less import than the survival of the collective.

Even the beat of their wings was synchronized. They were virtually indistinguishable from each other. That didn't change with proximity. Whenever he stood amongst them, Erik was struck that they were all dark, as dark as obsidian, and only different in subtle ways. Even in human form, they were markedly similar in appearance.

Their commander had taken the name of Drake, although Erik had no doubt it was not the name he had once been called. Erik knew that whatever Drake promised him was a vow from the entire company. His word was his bond, and whatsoever he commanded would be done. That said, Erik found Drake particularly hard to read, and he watched the commander's approach with some trepidation.

Not for the first time, he wondered what Drake wanted of him. This time, though, Erik wondered whether he could deliver it.

Drake did not imagine that this would be an easy victory. He knew only that he had no choice but to lead his men in a confrontation of their past.

And to do so, it was imperative that he ask the permission of the leader of the *Pyr*. The risks were not small, especially given the mood of his men, and further, Erik Sorensson was the closest thing to an oracle in these times.

Drake wanted not just permission but an augury of success. His own powers of foresight were minimal, but he felt dread at what might await his men if they returned home. At the same time, he sensed they had to go.

He needed advice.

He landed before Erik with precision. As soon as his feet

touched the ground, he folded his wings neatly behind his back and inclined his head in deference. He held the pose while the rest of the company landed silently behind him, keeping their formation.

Only when they had all landed and all bowed their heads did Drake speak. "We thank you for your time, Leader of the *Pyr*." Drake's voice had always been deep, his words formal. He was a *Pyr* of few words, always had been, but on this night, he had need of eloquence. "We appreciate the gift of your counsel."

Erik nodded slightly, his eyes glittering. Drake sensed Erik's power and was reassured that this leader was not so different from those he had served in the past. "And I thank you for this courtesy of consultation."

"Will you sit with me and tell me of your concern?" Erik gestured to the circle of stones, and Drake surveyed the unfamiliar site. He immediately liked the resonance of the stones and felt relief. This place murmured of timelessness.

Like Delphi.

Perhaps Erik already knew of his request.

Erik shifted shape first, taking his human form in a shimmer of blue. Drake summoned his own change and saw that same blue light dance over his hide. His men took their cue from that, a blue glimmer slipping over the entire company of Dragon's Tooth Warriors. It was evidence that they were all of the same kind, regardless of the differences between them.

Drake saw it as a portent of agreement.

In the blink of an eye, nineteen men stood behind Drake, each one olive skinned, dark haired, and dark eyed. Erik chose a stone and leaned his hips against it, then Drake faced his leader. He did not lean, but remained at attention.

Erik met Drake's steady gaze. "You are a corps of fighting men, drawn unwillingly from your own age into our own," he said with care. "I sense that this is not a coincidence. I sense that we have need of your skill in these days, and I would know what you need in order to pledge your men to our battle."

"You have the power of an oracle," Drake said and bowed. He appreciated that Erik was giving him a way to begin.

"And I believe that the Great Wyvern sends us the tools we need to triumph over adversity. The *Pyr* face a challenge in these times, and I have dreamed that you hold the key." Erik's eyes were no less bright in human form. "What would you ask of me?"

Drake chose his words with care. He did not want to appear unappreciative or indifferent, but he knew what he knew. "I am not certain that we can currently be of use to the *Pyr* in their quest," he said quietly. "I am concerned by the change in my men."

Erik waited in silence, but Drake knew he had the *Pyr*'s attention.

"At your suggestion, we have traveled," he continued. "We have learned of the customs of this time. I had hoped that this would aid my men in accepting their fate, but it has not been so."

"What do you mean?"

Drake felt his lips tighten. "I know that you have need of every talon in this battle, but I fear that pledging my men to your quest will only lead to their slaughter. Already we are much diminished from our original count. Casualties are too high when we engage without our hearts. A warrior must want to win, must believe in the merit of his cause to fight his best."

"And your men do not?"

Drake shrugged. "How can they? All has been stolen from them. They are consumed with dreams of returning home."

"What do you propose?"

"To take them home." Drake straightened. "To confront them with the truth, however harsh it might be. They are practical men, and I believe that seeing this reality is imperative."

"Why have you not done this already?" Erik asked.

"It might break them," Drake acknowledged. "Or it might renew their purpose. The risks are not small, but I fear we must confront the past to have any future."

Erik pursed his lips, unable or unwilling to hide his disappointment. He glanced over the waiting company, and Drake appreciated that the leader of the *Pyr* gave consideration to his concerns. He fixed Drake with a compelling glance. "Tell me of your history, for I know little of it."

Drake nodded, relieved that Erik wanted more information before he decided. That was the mark of a good leader. "In our time, we were an elite corps, gathered from throughout the known world, a force created to fight a particular kind of vermin."

"Vermin? What kind of vermin?"

"Our own kind, turned to darkness, to greed, and slaughter."

Drake found understanding in Erik's gaze. "These vermin used their abilities to enslave men, and they did so by casting a potent spell. I suppose it to be a precursor to what you call beguiling. They survived upon the power of having others beholden to them, not upon food or regular sustenance, although many offerings were made to them by their devout followers. And truly, they had no care for any riches other than this influence. In time, they lost the ability to shift shape and remained in dragon form, for in that form, they could best enchant men. We called them vipers, for they were more toxic than any other creature."

"How so?"

"In lands where they held sway, there was always pestilence and famine and war, for these vipers were said to be in the service of Ares."

"God of war," Erik mused.

"And one much inclined to violence and strife. Men, however, had no ability to destroy the vipers who caused their misery."

"Why not?"

"Any warrior, no matter how valiant, was charmed before coming close enough to strike. Each enchanted man became trapped in the form of a tooth, each added another tooth to the viper's maw. Such vipers secreted themselves deep in the earth, matched the rhythms of their bodies to that of the elements, and lived long. Their spell emanated from such depths that it became part of the rhythm of the land and the flow of the wind. It whispered in men's dreams, turning their thoughts, and ultimately it pulsed in their veins. These spells were insidious and potent."

"But you hunted them?"

Drake bowed. "We were the best weapon against them."

"Why?"

"There was once a warrior of our own kind known as Cadmus, one who led an army of men to retrieve his sister from Zeus. He was the first to find a viper. His men were dispatched to gather water at the Castalian Spring. The viper resided there and suffered none to take of the water he called his own. He killed the men of Cadmus, rather than enchanting them. Infuriated to lose so much of his company, Cadmus killed the viper himself in retaliation." Drake met Erik's gaze. "Because he was *Pyr*, he had more resistance to the spell. We have a power to close our minds to the enchantment, although always there is danger that we will lose our focus and be lost."

Erik nodded in understanding.

"Athena was enamored of Cadmus' mission and so she gave him magical counsel. She bade him cut the viper's teeth loose and gather them. Later, when he had need of more troops, she bade him sow those teeth in the soil. An army of fighting men sprang from the furrows, primed for battle. He threw a stone into their midst to distract them from himself, and they fell upon each other in violence. He managed to intervene, but only five survived to make a truce. They became the founding men of Thebes, later known as Spartans or 'sown men.'"

"A useful army," Erik commented.

Drake drummed his fingers on the stone. "There were others, of course, teeth gained in similar manner by Jason, who slayed a viper with the aid of Medea's spell. That company, though, destroyed themselves without remorse. Not a one survived."

"So those who awaken from the spell are volatile."

"And why not? They have lived in the hearing of a malicious song for a long time, trapped so that they cannot escape its poison yet fired by its call to do damage. I understand their rage well, for I have felt it. To be freed from the spell gives one a tremendous desire for vengeance and violence."

Erik nodded again. "Yours was turned against Magnus and his hidden Academy," he said, evidently recalling the night the spell had been broken.

"It is a fleeting strength," Drake noted. "For it is soon replaced by despondency."

"How so?"

"Because life and love have become as dust while one slept."

Erik flicked a glance over the company of men, his gaze assessing and sympathetic.

Drake cleared his throat to continue. "Cadmus, though, was no mere soldier. He began to hunt vipers, for material reward. He also kept the teeth for himself. And in order to do so more effectively, he gathered a force of *Pyr* like himself."

"Because you could approach the vipers."

Drake nodded. "It worked most well, and many vipers were destroyed in the world due to our efforts."

"But?"

Drake's brow lifted an increment. "But ultimately, one viper snared us within his spell."

"How?"

"Cadmus turned. He became what he had destroyed. He was plagued by bad luck throughout his life and came to believe it was a punishment for the death of the first viper, for slaughtering one of his own kind. He believed the vengeance of Ares to be upon him. I believe that he remained too long in dragon form, that he studied the power to enchant, perhaps initially out of curiosity, but that ultimately the power seduced him."

"I will assume that you hunted him," Erik said quietly.

"You would guess correctly." Drake eyed the leader of the *Pyr*, wondering how much more he had guessed. "But you might also guess that he, of all foes, knew how best to enchant even *Pyr*. He took his spell beyond the range of human hearing. He slid it into old-speak, and so it was that he snared us all."

"But someone cut you free?"

"Not precisely." Drake shook his head. "Cadmus aged and grew more feeble. He had had his firestorm and could not slow the aging process as much as might have been possible otherwise. Over time, all that remained was his ability to enchant. He lost his teeth. He lost his talons. His scales softened and grew pale, and he dragged himself deeper into the earth. He remained a viper but a toothless one, more of a worm."

"He was weaker?"

"So weak that he could not physically defend his hoard of teeth when another hunted him." Drake frowned, knowing that this next piece of the tale would be of import to Erik. "He did, however, manage to cast some spell over that company of *Pyr*, even in his dotage."

"Who were they?"

"Magnus Montmorency and his minions. First of those you call *Slayers*. They managed to leave the lair of Cadmus, but the residue of his spell clung to their thoughts."

Erik caught his breath.

"His song was potent." Drake watched the leader of the *Pyr* steadily. "That is why I would lead my men home. I believe that they need to know for certain that Cadmus has died. I believe that looking upon his remains, such as they are, is the only thing that will give them hope for the future."

"It is not a foregone conclusion," Erik said softly.

Drake inclined his head in acknowledgment of that truth. "But the alternative is that I lead my men into battle, without their hearts engaged. The alternative is that I lead them to certain death."

"I do not like it." Erik's eyes narrowed. "Their spirits might be broken by seeing that their homes are lost forever."

"Indeed, they might. Unfortunately, I see no real alternative."

Erik considered the leader of the Dragon's Tooth Warriors. "You will go, regardless of what I say," he guessed.

Drake shook his head. "I make my argument and await your decision. You are leader of the *Pyr*, and the closest being to the oracles upon whom we once relied."

"You invite me to learn from your counsel," Erik suggested.

"I invite you to cast a prophecy," Drake corrected. "To guide both of us in this choice."

The pair eyed each other for a moment. "It is not like that," Erik said abruptly. "I cannot command my visions of the future, nor can I direct them…"

"Can you not?" Drake asked quietly. It was unthinkable to him that such a power should rely upon luck. Indeed, he did not believe in luck. He believed in fate, and destiny, and the insatiable desire of the divine to meddle in earthly matters. The Great Wyvern might play with any of them. She might challenge them or break them, but she always had a purpose.

Even if it was her own entertainment.

Erik heaved a sigh. He cast a glance over the company of warriors, who stood silent and attentive. He pulled a coin from his pocket, one that gleamed silver in the moonlight. "An Olaf Tryggvason penny," he said at Drake's enquiring glance. "I have carried it for longer than I can recall. I shall try to scry with it."

It was, Drake realized, Erik's challenge coin. He knew the coin would be imbued with the power of the leader of the *Pyr* and his prophetic abilities. This would offer a glimpse of the future, of the will of the divine.

Whatever that might be.

He bowed his head in deference to his leader's choice.

Erik placed the coin on his left palm and held it out, letting the moonlight illuminate it. He narrowed his eyes and focused upon the coin, the slowing of his breath telling Drake that he was trying to summon a vision. He murmured softly, the way his nostrils abruptly flared telling Drake that he saw something in the radiant silver of the coin.

Drake stepped closer, eager to know but not wanting to disturb Erik from his trance.

Erik closed his hand abruptly over the coin and shoved it into his pocket, his gaze locking upon Drake. "You must go. You are right in that there is no choice. May the Great Wyvern smile upon your quest."

"Will you tell me what you have seen?"

Erik shook his head tersely. "It is not my place to do so. But if there is anything else you need of me, you have only to ask."

"I ask only for your goodwill."

"You have it. You have always had it."

Drake nodded, then backed away, unable to deny the shadow that had touched his heart. What had Erik seen? He cast only the slightest glance toward his men, and they shimmered on the cusp of change in unison.

As he shifted shape himself and took the lead, Drake stifled his dread. One way or the other, all would be resolved shortly. He could only hope that he was not leading his men into torment.

He'd done that once before.

Far behind him, Erik Sorensson gripped the coin in his pocket. Drake was right in that his men had to confront the past to find their future. The course was not without risk, however.

For the viper who had charmed them still drew breath.

They could be enchanted again. They could be destroyed. They could turn *Slayer*, against their own will. Or they could return to Erik to add their force to his fight, their resolve bolstered.

Erik knew which answer he liked best.

Just as he knew the choice was not his to make.

II

Dust, all dust.

Drake sat in a café in a modern Middle Eastern city and faced the truth. Everything he had known, everything he had loved, was lost to time. He had known it would not be easy for him and his men to revisit the lands they had known so well, so many centuries before. But the experience of coming home was far worse than expected.

Home. That was a cruel joke. The cities they remembered were ruins, if they survived at all. The homes they had built were lost to the hills. The verdant valleys they had known were barren. The people they had loved, the children and wives, brothers and parents and neighbors, were lost without a trace. The past was dust and ash, desolation that hung a weight on Drake's heart.

He had seen each of his men survey what had once been familiar without recognition. He had watched hope die, over and over again. Theirs was an irrational hope, they all knew it, but they each sought some crumb of what they had lost. They had marched off to war thousands of years before and never returned. While they had been trapped in enchantment, lives had ended, borders had shifted, the world had changed.

They were perennially homeless now. All the money in the world, all the traveling possible, couldn't take them back to where they longed to be.

Ever.

First Lidio had confronted his truth. Then Aeson, then Cletus, Milo, and Alexander. Disappointment had roiled through the ranks like a plague, but instead of bolstering the men, it had devastated them.

Drake had been wrong.

He had felt the full weight of that disappointment himself on this day. Once he had known this region as well as the back of his hand. Once he had known every face, every building, every elderly man anxious to chat. Once this area had been his refuge and his home.

But there was no longer any trace of his village or his modest house. The olive trees were dead and gone, the vineyards had been torn up, the laughter of children was silenced. The harbor was paved, and there were concrete buildings at every corner. The human enemies they had marched off to fight were not just gone, but forgotten.

The truth of it utterly destroyed Drake's own morale. He could not lead his men onward in good conscience. There was no future. Life had no meaning for them. The only experience before them was death.

Drake ordered another round of drinks. To what other purpose would he use the coins in his pocket? There was no point in battle, no point in love, no point in life.

Not anymore.

It seemed like yesterday that he had seen Cassandra meet an invading army at the town's gate, her feet bare and her hair unfurled. That hadn't been a hundred feet from this very spot. She'd been armed only with her defiance and her wits, with her sense of injustice. He had lost his heart with one glance.

He had felt the simmer of the firestorm's burn that day and had known she was his destined mate even before he knew the color of her eyes. He would have loved her even without the firestorm's heat. It wasn't impressive for a man with an army at his back to be confident. It had awed him as a warrior to see Cassandra, though, so sure of her own power that she had been unafraid.

She had been a marvel.

And the memory of her passion and her love, the recollection of her kiss and the sweet hope of reunion, had driven him on and on.

But she was gone.

Dust.

Drake would never see her again. Her smile, her laugh, her bravado, all gone forever. His son, too, lived only in his own memory.

Had they believed that he had deserted them? There had been no one to send word of the enchanted company, no human who had known their fate. The prospect sickened Drake, made him drain his glass.

He felt the tingle of a distant firestorm but could not summon the interest in defending it. Let the new *Pyr* have their firestorms. Let the new *Pyr* fight for justice and truth and survival of the earth herself.

He wanted only to die.

This place would suit well enough.

Drake and his men sat in silence and drank red wine in a café in the sun. Drake didn't care what happened to them next and his men shared his view. He was a leader without direction, a leader of men who were rudderless, and he didn't care about that either. The wine's tart taste was just another reminder of the past.

He was barely aware of the young boy who came into the café, scanned the men, and headed directly for him.

"Do you know my father?" the boy demanded, his words startling Drake. He would have been six or seven years old, this earnest boy, with his dark hair and dark eyes.

He looked just like Theo.

Drake's throat tightened.

"Do you?" he demanded again, just as Theo would have done. Cassandra's persistence had found expression in their son.

Drake would have liked to have ignored the child, to have gone back to his drinking, but he couldn't do it. He was too full of the awareness of what he'd lost and this child was too similar to his own son.

He put down his glass. "Who is your father?"

The boy recited the name and rank of a serviceman, his pride in his father more than clear.

Drake shook his head. "I do not know him."

The boy studied him for a long moment, looking so intently into his face that the commander wondered what he saw. Then he pulled out the chair beside Drake, inviting himself to the table. He pointed to the glass. "What is that?"

"It is wine. You should not drink of it." It was easy to speak to the boy as he had once spoken to his own son, albeit in a different language and a place that was centuries away.

The boy picked up the glass and sniffed it, then wrinkled his nose. "I don't want any." He pushed it away from both of them. Then he turned that sharp gaze on his older companion again. "Do you know who killed my father then?"

Drake was startled. "Are you certain that he was killed?"

"He's missing." The boy's lips set. "It's been two months, and it only took us two days to come here. He would come home if he could, wouldn't he?" He looked to Drake for confirmation.

Drake felt a lump in his throat, for he knew that all fighting men would return home if they had the power to do so. He would have traded everything in this moment to return home. "I am certain he would. A man of honor does not abandon his family."

"I *know* he would come home."

The child's conviction tore at Drake's heart. Had Theo believed the same of him? Had Cassandra?

The child looked around the café, studying the Dragon's Tooth Warriors. "I have to find him. I thought you would know where."

"Why?"

"Because you are like him. You are soldiers, and soldiers know where to find other soldiers, even if they're secret soldiers." The boy looked up suddenly. "And they kill other soldiers, too."

"I did not kill your father."

The boy nodded, apparently confident of this fact, and eyed the others. Before he could begin an interrogation, a woman raced into the café, her eyes wide with fear.

She was lovely, with dark hair and blue eyes, slender but not boyish. The sight of her made something spark within Drake, made him sit even straighter.

"Timmy!" Her expression changed to relief at the sight of the boy. She was dressed in western clothing and her accent was American. "You're not supposed to go out without me. You know that." She came to the boy's side and took his hand, chiding him gently. "I'm so sorry that he interrupted you," she said, offering a shy smile to the commander.

Drake saw more than she likely wanted him to see. He saw that this alluring woman had lost weight recently, for the gold ring on her left hand was very loose. There were shadows beneath her eyes, which were reddened from tears. He guessed that she was struggling to be strong in the face of adversity, but she hugged the boy a little more tightly than was deserved.

Her fear touched him, touched him where he would have preferred to remain untouched.

Before Drake realized what he was doing, he had gotten to his feet and inclined his head. "I assure you that he was no trouble."

"Well, I apologize." Her gaze swept over him, and he wondered what she saw. "We have to go to the embassy, Timmy, in case there's news."

When she would have turned away, Drake wasn't quite ready to see her leave. "He says his father is missing."

She froze, her heart in her eyes when she looked back at him. She swallowed, then nodded, her lips tight.

"For long?"

"Almost two months!" She made a gesture of futility with one hand, and the words spilled from her lips. "It was crazy to come here, everyone said so, and I guess it's not going to make any difference to anything, after all." She sighed. "I thought that if I was here, I could find out the truth, but that was stupid."

Drake heard her anguish, and it made his heart clench.

It cracked his armor.

He could help this woman.

All the same, he was cautious—many asked for truth when they actually wanted a palatable lie. The world was a harder place than it should be. That, at least, had not changed.

"Do you want to know the truth, no matter what it is?"

She looked at him then, really looked at him. He saw the intelligence in her eyes and the strength she had not yet realized was hers. She knew what he was asking, and she straightened before she nodded curtly. "I need to know for sure. I *have* to know."

The commander saw the way she held her son protectively close and understood that she would do anything to defend the memory of her lost husband. He recognized that gesture and that feminine strength. The sight made a lump rise in his throat.

The stranger didn't look at all like Cassandra. She didn't speak like Cassandra or carry herself the same way. She wasn't quiet and mysterious, as Cassandra had been—she was forthright, honest, perhaps too trusting. But her conviction that she could change a situation that appeared to be beyond retrieval reminded him of his lost wife, of the woman who had stolen his heart away, all those centuries before.

This woman's determination reminded him of Cassandra's conviction that she could accomplish deeds that no one else had managed. That extraordinary faith in her ability to make a difference, against all odds, lived on in this stubborn foreigner, who had brought her son a third of the way around the world in a desperate bid for the truth.

Who was he to doubt his powers when she was convinced she could shape the world to her will? She might be wrong, but he admired her fortitude.

Her determination made Drake realize that the despondency that had claimed him, this uncharacteristic indifference, was the work of a viper.

And why not? They were said to breed in darkness, said to bring war and pestilence and famine upon the lands they occupied. Why not here, where all had gone awry? How could he have forgotten to listen?

Drake listened then. He strained his ears, using the full capacity of his keen *Pyr* senses.

And the chant was there. Soft, persistent, but there. He heard the soft murmur of the viper, so well heeded in this place. His eyes widened slightly as he recognized that his despondency—and that of his men—had been wrought by the spell. They had almost been enthralled again, so consumed with their losses that they had nearly lost everything that remained.

Erik was right. There was purpose in their awakening in this time. They could continue their mission. The Dragon's Tooth Warriors could do what they did best, hunt and destroy vipers.

And he would guess his last coin that this woman's quest was linked to his own. It could be no accident that she had found him, no coincidence that she had touched him with so few words.

It was fate.

Drake looked into the eyes of this woman and instead of seeing the past, he saw the future. He would do something for her.

He would make a difference to this boy.

He would get her truth, no matter what it cost him.

And in so doing, he guessed that he would find his own path forward.

"My name is Drake," he said, although that was only his new name. His old name was as dust, just as his old life had been. Drake suited him well enough.

"Mr. Drake?" she asked.

"General Drake," the boy corrected.

Drake felt himself smile a little, and the curve felt unfamiliar on his lips. "Just Drake." She was softer than his Cassandra, this woman, and he was wary of frightening her.

"I'm Veronica," she said, slipping her hand into his. Her fingers were small, her skin soft, her perfume tantalizing. Something else awakened in Drake, a desire he'd thought never to feel again. "Veronica Maitland." She shrugged and started to blush, then pulled her hand away quickly. "Everyone just calls me Ronnie."

He would call her Veronica in his thoughts, at least. The name was perfect for her, for it meant "little truth," or "honesty."

Just what she had brought to him.

"I will find your husband, Mrs. Maitland," Drake said.

Her throat worked for a moment before she spoke. "They say, they say, that his mission was…"

"I will find him," Drake interrupted firmly. "Take your son home and leave this to me. I will ensure that you know the truth, whatever it is."

"I don't have much money…"

"I will require no compensation."

She eyed him, then nodded, her grip tight on her son's shoulders. "How will I find you, Drake?"

He felt his sense of purpose grow as he beckoned to his men. There was no time to drink and mourn the past. They would do what they did so well.

"Have no fear," he said. "I will find you when I know."

III

It was not a trail a mortal man could have followed.

Drake and his men followed the last known trail of Ronnie's husband, the murmur of the viper growing louder with every step. Drake had seen the difference in his men immediately, as soon as he had brought the viper's song to their attention. They had enlivened and become invigorated, no longer mourning the past.

Drake also knew his instinct about Veronica's husband was right, that the two stories were tied together, that the man he sought had been but a casualty in the web of influence spun by the viper.

Drake was relentless in his pursuit. He felt the vibration of the viper's monologue beneath his feet. Now that he was aware of it, Drake saw the poison at work everywhere he looked. He heard whisperings of jealousy and hatred on every side. He saw hunger and poverty. He heard the resonance of despondence and a sense of futility. His features set, and he worked ever closer to the source, indifferent to his own exhaustion.

He would not disappoint Veronica.

He would keep his promise to her.

He would bring her the news, whatever it was, the news that none had dared to bring to Cassandra.

Even with his resolve, it took him days to sort the old echoes from the new ones. The murmuring was so pervasive and had been expressed for so long that the very stones seemed to vibrate with its hatred. It resonated from a deep, deep source.

And with every step, the spell became more seductive. It was harder to free his thoughts from the viper's web of influence as the song became louder. He counseled his men and reminded them of the ways they could close their thoughts to such wickedness.

It was the strongest spell they'd ever faced, and he gave them permission to back away if any of them needed to do so.

They were resolute and followed him closely.

So far.

Drake followed one dead end and then another, gradually narrowing down the possibilities. As days passed, Drake began to espy signs that his men were falling under the spell of the viper's increasingly loud enchantment.

On the third day, two collapsed in spasms and did not move again. The others were spooked for a moment, then their discipline bolstered them.

Drake did not doubt that he would lose more. They all knew the stakes and the importance of their quest. He could feel them closing their minds to the pervasive chant.

This viper was old.

He would not be easily defeated.

Drake pressed on. The world around him grew more destitute, and he knew they were drawing ever closer to the viper's lair. There was barbed wire atop the walls and mines below the streets, wounded children, and heavily armed men. There was fear in the eyes of many and signs of starvation on hands and faces.

And as the viper's spell became more distinct, it became more familiar.

Cadmus, Drake realized with shock, had not died.

They would be confronting a foe who had defeated them before.

Drake had always believed that men were inherently good. He chose to believe that silencing the viper would turn the tide in this land, just as it had in so many others. He was not unafraid. While he had slept for centuries, enchanted, the viper had refined his words and built his strength. Challenging Cadmus would bring out the strongest arsenal that worm had at his disposal.

Cadmus would want to win.

Drake was similarly determined to win. It was impossible to guess who would triumph.

Three more men balked at continuing, one collapsing and the others determined to assist him.

Cadmus must have become aware of their presence, must have changed his tune specifically to poison the thoughts of Drake and his men. The song wound into old-speak, the words resonating in Drake's own thoughts when he didn't specifically force them out.

Cadmus must be seeking to enchant the Dragon's Tooth Warriors before they could manage an assault on him.

That must mean there was a chance they could win.

Although Drake took encouragement from that, he would not force his men onward. Each man's choice must be his own. He dared to hope that Cadmus had grown even softer and slower. He dared to hope that if he could deny the seductive spell of Cadmus' words, he could triumph.

And change the world for the better.

When the litany that had only been rhythmic and alluring became more audible, Drake halted at an apothecary. At his command, the Dragon's Tooth Warriors stuffed cotton wool into their ears. That would dull the sound. With any luck, the cotton would make the words incomprehensible.

And save his men.

Drake had led them awry once and would not do as much again.

He gave the command, but did not use cotton himself. His second, Alexander, looked ready to question the choice. Drake lifted a finger to silence him before he spoke. "I will not imperil you all again."

Alexander bowed slightly. "Sir, with respect, the exposure we have endured makes us more susceptible, all of us—"

"He is *mine*," Drake interrupted, speaking through clenched teeth. He heard the rare heat in his words and felt himself shimmer on the cusp of change as he held Alexander's gaze. "I ask only that you guard my back, for as long as you are able. If you choose to halt, there is no shame in it."

Alexander inclined his head and took a step back in deference.

Drake knew his second didn't agree with his choice, but didn't care. He pivoted and led them onward.

The words became more clear as the sun set. The shadows grew longer and the stone more chilly. Drake's pursuit was relentless. He sensed that he had found the true trail and he was not going to rest until he followed it to its terminus.

Where the viper would be.

Delay could give the monster the chance to change his location, or to better defend himself. Drake quickened his pace. They strode through a market, the stalls closed for the night and the crowds gone. He felt three more of his men fall behind and respected their choice.

Drake ducked through a café, marched down an alley, ignored a man who would have kept him from entering an old office building. Drake heard the words growing louder with every step, although he refused to listen to their meaning.

Instead he thought of Cassandra.

And Veronica. He thought of strength in the face of adversity, he thought about good triumphing over wickedness, and that armed him against the viper's chant.

Drake halted when he saw traces of blood on a concrete step. Drake sniffed it, knew it was human, and suspected he knew whose blood it was. The mark was dry and dark, days old.

Too old.

Drake sighed deeply. He should have guessed that a man of merit, one bent on eliminating evil, would have found his way to the viper and those under the viper's influence. He did not imagine that Maitland's quest had ended well.

But he had promised Veronica the truth. The chant grew in intensity, wafting over the threshold ahead of him, beckoning him onward.

To doom or to triumph?

Alexander's nostrils flared as he bent to smell the blood. Alexander was the best tracker among them, his senses even more keen than most *Pyr*. "Same bloodline as the boy," he murmured and Drake nodded. He gestured at the door and Alexander's lips tightened.

Two more warriors hesitated on the threshold, refusing to follow Drake as they shook with fear. The memory of the enchantment, of the powerlessness to escape the viper's venomous song, was too great. Drake ceded the loss without comment. He would not lead a man unwillingly into this danger.

Beyond the door was a basement, one lit with only a single bulb. Drake paused to assess it. There were steel doors on either side of the basement, making it essentially a corridor that bent at the end. The walls were cinderblock and it was colder than a tomb.

The viper's words wound into Drake's thoughts, insidious and horribly compelling. He concentrated on the memory of his wife and his son. He fixed his thoughts on Veronica and her son. He thought of hope, as opposed to despair, and he chose to believe that good could triumph.

He thought about Timmy living in a better world.

Drake indicated the doors and strode onward. The Dragon's Tooth Warriors stopped to investigate each door, silently following routine, as Drake pressed on. A man came into the basement behind them, waving an assault rifle. The warrior at the back of the group struck him hard and he went down without having fired a shot.

But more men erupted suddenly into the basement, some coming from the street, others from the doors in the corridor. Drake gave a minute nod. The cadence of evil was strong here. He knew he was close to the source and that these men, who listened continually to the viper's words, could not be redeemed.

There was a flash of blue, then the Dragon's Tooth Warriors shifted shape and the carnage began. They made steady progress through the ranks of the men, their impassivity in marked contrast to the men's panic. The last Dragon's Tooth Warrior secured the door to the street with fire and fear.

There would be no escape for these lost men.

Drake continued, peering around the corner, Alexander at his side. More doors lined the continuation of the corridor, but it terminated in a steel fire door. That door had no handle and a man stood on either side of it, weapon at the ready.

One fired at Drake, his shock and dismay at facing dragons clear.

Drake and Alexander charged the pair, raging dragonfire. The men fired again and again, but their shots went wild in their fear. Drake and Alexander ripped them to shreds, casting their bodies aside. Three of the Dragon's Tooth Warriors came around the corner to support their commander. Drake saw their resolve, saw their satisfaction in finding purpose again.

Drake listened, but he heard nothing except the enchanting litany of hatred. He nodded and Alexander ripped the door from its hinges.

Four men were secreted there, braced for a fight, and they fired instantly upon Drake and his men. Drake breathed a stream of brilliant dragonfire, setting their clothes and their bodies alight. He could smell the wickedness on them and had no patience with their obstruction.

Was Veronica's husband alive?

When the dust settled, Drake saw that there was a labyrinth hidden beneath the building. Cadmus must have sensed their proximity for his words grew in volume.

Drake indicated the various corridors, dispatching men to

ensure their vacancy. He could smell blood, the blood of those they had slain, and he could feel the chill of the earth. He peered into the shadows, his keen gaze put to full use. He caught a whiff of terror, human terror, and turned his steps in that direction.

He had torn open the door to what proved to be a cell before he smelled something else.

Drake smelled death.

The man on the floor was still, and Drake knew with a glance that it was a mercy. He had been battered and abused, his body burned and tormented. He was nude, but Drake feared he knew the fallen man's identity.

Drake shifted shape and stepped into the room, wary. This had been a handsome man, trim and muscular. His skin was cold, his body stiffening, and Drake regretted that he had not arrived sooner.

How much of him would have been left, even days before? He felt respect for this fallen soldier, for Cadmus' song was strong here. It would take a man of uncommon bravery to venture so near to a viper's den. It had taken one of cunning and boldness to infiltrate this place, alone.

It would take a man determined to eliminate evil, regardless of the price.

Drake wished he had known this man.

There was something in the dead man's hand. Drake knelt beside him and carefully removed it, smoothing it against his own palm. It told him the man's identity more clearly than anything else could have done. Why had those in thrall to Cadmus' song left him this token? It couldn't have been out of kindness, not with that hateful spell making every heart pump in rhythm.

Maybe they had wanted to break his spirit, as well. Drake considered the man's expression, which was determined even in death, and doubted their success.

He tucked the photograph into his pocket with care.

"*Take him to the embassy,*" he instructed Alexander in old-speak.

"*I will not leave you.*"

Drake leveled a look at his second. "*This viper is mine.*"

Alexander stared at Drake for a moment, then inclined his head.

"*I condemned you all once,*" Drake said more kindly. "*Now I *defend you, as is my responsibility. He is our work left undone, and I would finish what was begun."*

Alexander stepped back, more willingly this time, and a shudder rolled through his body in the same instant. The viper was affecting him, even with his ears blocked.

"Go in haste," Drake instructed. *"If I do not return by sunrise, the command is yours."*

Alexander caught his breath, then moved quickly to do as instructed. No sooner had they moved Maitland's body than Drake shifted shape again. The viper's song grew louder and more seductive. Drake roared, then swung his tail. The cinderblock wall cracked along the mortar lines on the first blow, crumbling on the fourth strike.

The words poured from the darkness beyond. The space was small. Although he would have preferred to have continued in dragon form, for his keener senses, the constraints of space did not allow it. He shifted, with reluctance.

Drake stepped through the gap in human form, smelled the dank darkness, and jammed cotton into his ears before he moved forward with purpose. Cadmus' song grew more vehement, winding into Drake's thoughts as if there was no impediment.

Could he hold fast to do what had to be done?

He would triumph or he would die in the attempt.

Either way, Veronica would have her truth.

IV

The spell of enchantment slid into Drake's head, filling his mind with thoughts that were not his own. Every step made the words more persuasive. Every level he descended seemed to add to the resonance of the spell.

Was he not tired? Was he not worn down by his efforts? His shoulder was sore, his feet hurt and his knuckles were bleeding. Could he not simply sleep? He could sit down, right in this cave, and rest for a while.

It would be harmless.

Inevitable.

Sensible.

Drake shouldered on, knowing a spell when he heard one.

The tunnels became darker and colder, secreted deep in the earth. He found marks of the viper's passing and felt the vibration of its hateful song beneath his feet. He thought of all the suffering it had created and marched on.

Why did he want to save humans, when they could do so much ill to each other? He could imagine what had been done to Cassandra, and to Theo, all at the hands of the people of their village. They had always been afraid of him and his powers. Had that fear been turned against his family? Had they been destroyed because of their association with him?

Because of his absence?

He should never have left them. He should never have hunted vipers. He should never have meddled in events that were not his to influence.

He could stop now.

Drake felt Cadmus' words find a resonance within him, turning his love for his family into something far less fine, but he fought the spell with all his heart and soul.

And what of now? What need had he of a purpose to his life? He could join Cadmus. He could use his powers for vengeance. He could kill more men than had already died on this day. He could extract a blood toll in honor of Veronica's loss.

Then he could claim this entire territory as his own. He could bend it to his will and empower himself.

All he had to do was raise his voice in the viper's spell. All he had to do was surrender to the truth that life was harsh and unyielding, that one gained only what one took.

These were not his impulses and they never had been. Drake gritted his teeth and ignored the summons. He climbed ever deeper into the earth, steeling himself with the memory of women facing adversity.

Cassandra at the gate.

Veronica with her hand on her son's shoulder.

Both of them with fire in their eyes. Both of them knowing the odds were long and not caring.

Surely he could do the same.

Drake didn't know how far he had traveled or how deep he had delved when he saw a light ahead of him. It was yellow and feeble, and just the sight revolted him.

He shifted shape, silent and wary, then carried on into the viper's den. Drake froze at the sight of Cadmus.

The ancient *Pyr* had lost his scales. He was pale and soft and bloated, only his eyes gleaming with the coals of that old fire. He looked like the worm he was, pale yellow like a maggot. There was a smell about him, one that revolted Drake more than the sight of him.

Cadmus smiled and his teeth were gone, his gums blackened. "Finally, my apprentice has arrived," he said, his voice melodic, even when he ceased his spell.

"I am no apprentice of yours."

"No? Not when we have so much in common?" Cadmus gestured to one side and Drake saw a skeleton in the shadows. The skin was long gone, the dust heavy upon the frame. "Dust," Cadmus whispered. "After the firestorm, we all age more quickly. When one's mate is dust, what point is there?"

"Harmonia," Drake murmured, tearing his gaze from the site of what she had become. He would remember her in her glory, on her wedding day. He recalled her with gems in her hair and embroidery on her hems, the necklace given by her father gleaming at her throat. He would remember the gods and goddesses themselves reclining on golden couches, celebrating the match. "She was radiant."

"She was a curse upon me!" Cadmus retorted.

"She loved you! She was your destined mate."

"She was poison." Cadmus moved restlessly, and Drake saw the movement was painful for him. "She was her father's daughter first. Whose viper did I kill? That of Ares himself. And whose daughter did I wed?"

"That of Ares himself," Drake admitted.

"And she wore those gems he had wrought for her and brought naught but misery into my life." Cadmus was bitter in his hatred and his eyes burned. "Every child of mine met with misfortune. Every possession we gathered was destroyed. She was no gift but a curse. She was Ares' vengeance for my killing of his viper."

Cadmus eased closer, leaving a line of slime on the floor of the cavern. "And what of you? Is your precious Cassandra not lost to you, stolen by the gods while you slept? Do you imagine that she was faithful? Whose idea was it that you rode to war? Maybe she had a lover..."

"No!" Drake shouted. He recognized that this too was the viper's spell, being presented for his benefit. He leapt at the old viper and slashed at his hide. Cadmus, devoid of armor or the ability to defend himself, cried out in pain.

He still had the weapon of his words, though.

"Women!" Cadmus whispered. "The natural mates of men and our enemies every time. They enchant us with their wiles and turn us from our true purpose."

"No," Drake insisted, striking another blow upon the bloated old worm. "They remind us of what is important. They show us truth. They and their love turn us from the allure of Ares." He leaned closer, fighting his reaction to the stench of Cadmus. "Harmonia was the child of Aphrodite, too. That you did not heed her song of love meant that you were the curse in that match."

"No!" Cadmus cried. "It was not my fault!"

Drake struck his old commander again, slicing at that old hide as the blood flowed. He was massive and filled with hatred, unwilling to surrender his grasp upon life, but Drake was determined.

"No!" Cadmus murmured, dropping his voice to a murmur of old-speak. *"Join me. Be my successor. Take what is rightfully yours...*"

Drake had no taste for this spell. He ripped the throat of his foe, then kicked his broken carcass aside. Cadmus' body cycled between forms, switching from ancient man to old dragon, with increasing speed. Drake watched in horror, even as he caught his breath.

Then Cadmus finally was still.

"It is not the right of any man or *Pyr* to take what is not his own," he declared, then spat upon the commander he had once respected beyond all others. He felt sick.

But at the same time, he felt lighter. He was more optimistic. He knew that there was a place for himself and his men in this world.

He understood that the light of the firestorm could keep a *Pyr* from turning to the darkness, that Harmonia could have brought Cadmus the balance he had needed.

If only Cadmus had accepted the truth of her kiss.

Drake was prepared to take the lesson.

Veronica, with her clear blue eyes, had given that gift to her husband. Perhaps it was her love that had armored him against the viper's vile spell. With her spirit, she had pulled Drake back from the darkness, had saved him from succumbing to that old spell. Drake would never forget her gift.

Drake took no souvenirs of this place, no tokens of battle, no proof of what he had done. He had the only memento he needed.

The one that was for Veronica.

V

Ronnie Maitland was packing her bags.

She didn't know what had been in her head when she'd decided to bring Timmy to the Middle East. She didn't know how she could have imagined that she could learn the truth about Mark's death when there was no official record, when the government and the military wouldn't tell her anything. She knew Mark had been involved in covert operations and she knew the risk. He had warned her that it might end this way.

It had been so much easier to be strong when Mark had e-mailed her regularly.

But it had been seven and a half weeks, and she had known that it was more than a mission taking longer than it should have done. She knew the truth in her heart, and she had been angry that no one would tell her what had happened.

Timmy deserved the truth.

She deserved the truth.

But she'd been foolish to come here, to leave all that was familiar on a quest that she saw now was doomed to failure. She'd been stupid to trust Drake, too, without having any idea who he was or what his affiliation might be.

She'd waited a week for Drake to bring her the story she'd already guessed, but there was no sign of him. Why had she trusted him? No one at the embassy knew him—or if they did, they weren't admitting it. She shouldn't have been so gullible.

She shouldn't cry, even though everything was going wrong.

There was something about Drake, though, something about his impassivity or maybe his confidence. Drake had a sense of authority, a resolve about him that made Ronnie believe him. He was like a rock. He was the kind of man who had seen a lot, who understood more than anyone should, yet had not lost his soul.

He could probably kill a man with his bare hands, yet she'd trust him with her son.

Maybe that was proof that she was losing it.

Drake had been right about one thing—Ronnie should go home. This was no place for her or for Timmy. She packed quickly and recklessly, knowing that she had to return to routine.

She'd have to wait for news. She'd go home and she'd try to

meet more women on the base, even though she'd always stunk at making quick connections with other women. She'd try to carry on for Timmy's sake. She had to be strong. Mark would expect that of her.

Plus she had to figure out what she was going to do. She'd have to get a job, find a home, settle them into a new life someplace. It felt wrong to be planning a future without Mark. It felt as if she was betraying his memory, or the power of their love, just by thinking about it. She remembered his insistence before departing on this tour of duty, his demand that she would live life without him. She knew that she had made the promise he had asked of her without ever believing that she would have to keep it.

Could there be a future without Mark? Ronnie doubted it.

But she'd promised. It might have been the last promise she'd ever have a chance to make to Mark, and she was going to keep it.

Somehow.

There was a decisive knock on the door of the hotel room, and Timmy ran to open it before she could stop him. She heard him greet someone and knew she'd missed another opportunity to teach him to be cautious.

Mark would have known how to get his attention.

Ronnie felt suddenly overwhelmed. How was she going to raise their son alone?

Why did she have to?

"You are foolish," Drake said, his low voice carrying through the living room of the hotel suite. Ronnie's heart stopped cold, and she stared at the man she'd not really expected to see again.

He looked exactly the same, and she was relieved that she hadn't imagined him. His hair was salt and pepper, cut short, and his eyes dark. It was impossible to guess his age. He was tanned and fit and moved with the economy of an experienced warrior. He was dressed as earlier in khaki but carried no weapons. She had assumed he was in the service, as well, maybe that of another country, but realized this time that his outfit was devoid of insignia.

Maybe he, like Mark, worked in covert operations.

Ronnie dared to hope. She'd understood what he meant earlier, that Mark might have been captured and imprisoned, tortured even, that he might not still be the man she remembered, but Ronnie believed in the power of love.

She'd take Mark any way she could have him. It had to be better than him being gone forever.

Drake crouched down in the doorway to address Timmy, his gaze so steely that the boy took a step back.

"It is your duty to defend your mother," Drake said, his voice stern but not harsh. "A child opens the door to anyone who knocks, but you must be the man of the household. You must think. You must be sure. You must defend your mother and your home. You must not allow peril to cross the threshold unchallenged."

He had a strange way of expressing himself, a formal use of language as if English wasn't his first language. Ronnie wondered where Drake was from.

Then she swallowed, fearing his meaning. If Timmy had to be the man of the house, did he mean that Mark wasn't coming home the way he had been when he'd left?

Or at all?

Ronnie had said that she wanted the truth.

But the idea of what he might have come to tell her dropped the bottom out of her world.

She crossed the room, pasting a smile on her lips and managing by some miracle to speak lightly. "Hello, Drake. I didn't think I'd see you again so soon."

He inclined his head slightly as he straightened to consider her. She had the feeling that he was assessing her, deciding how much information she could take. She held his gaze, letting him see her determination to know it all, and saw his minute nod.

His gaze flicked to Timmy, then back to her, as if they were in league together. Did Drake have children himself? He seemed to have an intuitive understanding of how to deal with Timmy.

Did he have a wife, one who worried about him?

Ronnie bet he did.

"A matter of jurisdiction was resolved today," he said quietly.

She didn't understand him immediately, but caught her breath at the intensity of his gaze.

He'd found Mark.

Ronnie guessed that the resolution hadn't been so easy, but her heart began to pound with the certainty of what he had come to tell her.

"What's jurisdiction?" Timmy demanded, looking between the two of them in confusion.

Ronnie put her hand on his head and ruffled his hair. She fought the sense that it would just be the two of them from now on. She still didn't know for sure. There was still hope.

Even if Drake's unflinching gaze made her stomach twist in knots.

"Go watch TV for a minute," she said, her words coming thick.

"But..."

"Do as your mother instructs you," Drake said, his quiet words as inflexible as iron.

Timmy went.

Ronnie wondered how Drake had circumvented military protocol, how he had ensured that this matter of jurisdiction—as he had called it—was resolved. She wondered who he was and who he worked for, but guessed that he would never tell her.

Drake watched Timmy throw himself on the couch, and Ronnie saw something flicker in his eyes. She decided that she was right about him having a family, too. She'd bet that he'd do anything to defend them.

No wonder she liked him.

No wonder she responded to him so intuitively.

Then he turned to her, as composed and impassive as ever.

"I am sorry," Drake said softly as he handed her an envelope. There was something in it, something thin, and Ronnie had a terrible sense that she knew what it was. "The embassy will undoubtedly contact you to make the arrangements."

Ronnie fingered the envelope, but didn't open it. Drake watched her nervous fingers, then he ducked his head in farewell and turned to leave.

"Thank you, Drake," she said, feeling that it was inadequate and knowing that her voice sounded high. She clutched the envelope as if it was the only anchor in her world.

Drake glanced over his shoulder, looking so world-weary that she wondered how often he had made a similar visit. His gaze seemed haunted, and she regretted that she had unwittingly sent him on a path that had brought him pain.

"A deed done correctly requires no thanks," he said.

Ronnie swallowed. "That's not true. Thank you."

He almost smiled, one corner of his mouth moving just slightly, and Ronnie once again felt that connection with him.

On impulse, she reached up and kissed Drake's cheek. He was shaved smooth, so smooth that his cheek felt leathery beneath her lips, and she sensed the raw power in him.

She froze and stared, astonished by what she had done. She wasn't usually so impetuous, but there was something about this man, something that made her believe he'd walked in danger just to keep his promise to her. She held his gaze, wondering how he'd respond to her impulsive gesture. Her heart was pounding and her mouth was dry.

She watched his throat work soundlessly for a moment. He lifted one hand to the place where her lips had been and seemed overwhelmed.

By a chaste kiss.

Then Drake blinked. "I wish the tidings had been better."

There was kindness in his tone, a kindness that left tears forming behind her eyes. She still was keenly aware of Drake, though, of the strength of his hands, of the utter stillness of him, of his gaze upon her.

Not missing a thing.

"Time is said to heal," he whispered, but there was no conviction in his tone.

Ronnie looked up at that. What had he lost? Maybe he understood more of what she was feeling than she'd thought. "Will I see you again?"

Drake held her gaze for a minute that stretched through infinity. Just when she thought he might say something, he abruptly pivoted and left.

There was her answer. And really, what would be the point? Ronnie knew Drake wouldn't tell her what he'd found — which really told her everything she needed to know.

She shut the door and leaned her back against it, her heart leaping as she considered the envelope. She took a deep breath and opened it.

Just as she had feared, there was a photograph inside.

It was the shot of the three of them taken the previous Christmas, the one Mark had taken right before he'd told her that he was taking another tour of duty. She and Timmy were laughing and Mark was pointing at the camera, his mouth open as the timer finally went off. The lights of the tree glittered white behind them and the torn foil wrapping paper was scattered around their knees. She was holding her son and her husband close, both of them within reach.

It was the photo that Mark had said he'd carry right against his heart.

It was the photo he had said they would have to pry out of his cold, dead hands.

That was how she knew.

Ronnie caught her breath and pressed the photograph between her hands. She tried to be strong, but failed. She raised her hands to her mouth and cried.

Even though her worst nightmare had come true, Ronnie was fiercely glad that she knew Mark's fate. It was kinder to be sure that he would never return than to be waiting for the sound of his tread on the front step forever.

It still wasn't easy, and she wept as if her heart was breaking.

Because it had.

VI

Ronnie didn't see Drake stride into the courtyard of her hotel. She didn't see him spit at the pavement, as if he would rid himself of the distasteful flavor of a task that had needed to be done. She didn't know that he could hear her weeping, much less that the sound tore at his heart. She didn't see him summon his men with a flick of his wrist or hear him inform them of their destination in old-speak.

She certainly didn't see the entire company leap into the night sky, shift shape to powerful dragons and fly westward in pairs.

She had no idea that the Dragon's Tooth Warriors flew to the lair of Erik Sorensson, leader of the *Pyr*, to pledge their service to his command.

Their mission here had been successfully completed, yet they would undertake more quests for the good of the world. They would defend firestorms, they would fight vipers, and they would be another weapon in the arsenal of the *Pyr*.

Ronnie would never have imagined that their exchange had been anything other than one-sided, but she had given Drake the greatest gift of all. She had restored his faith. She had dismissed his despondency and his despair. She had reminded him not just of what he had lost, but its merit. She had given him hope, and a purpose.

She had given him a kiss to treasure, a touch to remind him of his priorities from that day forward. He knew that he would feel the softness of her lips against his skin forever. He knew that she had meant nothing by it, that it had been a gesture of appreciation, but it meant the world to him.

It reminded him of Harmonia's birthright, the perfect balance to Ares' strength. It was evidence of how a *Pyr* could temper his abilities and use them for good. It was a reminder to keep the light of the firestorm at the fore of his thoughts.

Drake hoped that in return, one day when Veronica Maitland's grief had diminished, one day when she least expected it, she would meet a man who didn't exactly remind her of her lost husband but who kindled the same feelings within her as that man once had.

Drake hoped that maybe, just maybe, Ronnie would one day

see her future instead of her past.

It would take time, but Drake intended to hope for her healing. He'd hope for her son to grow up strong and proud.

And one day, one day after her tears had dried, Drake would make a point of finding her again. Veronica Maitland might be glad to see him. She might not.

The choice would be hers.

In the interim he'd know, with every blow from his talons and every volley of dragonfire he exhaled, that he was continuing the fight that he and his kind would pay any price to win.

Don't miss

THE DRAGONFATE NOVELS

A new series featuring the *Pyr*.

MAEVE'S BOOK OF BEASTS

The DragonFate Novels #1

Careful what you wish for…

A mysterious book given to Sylvia by a handsome stranger plunges her into a hidden world, awakening her ability to see a paranormal realm and the Others who live in it. It also makes her a target for the Dark Fae who want the book back—and who will kill her to reclaim it. The stranger, Sebastian, becomes Sylvia's reluctant defender—but his ability to influence her dreams is almost as dangerous as the fact that he's a vampire. On the run with Sebastian, Sylvia learns about the plan of Maeve, Queen of the Dark Fae, to eliminate all other paranormal creatures. Possession of the book means that Sylvia is caught in the middle of a war between the Dark Fae and the Others, with a predator as her only ally. If she can decipher the book, will that help the Others to fight for their survival? Should she trust Sebastian? Or does the vampire who ignores all the rules have a secret plan of his own?

Available Now!

DRAGON'S KISS
The DragonFate Novels #2

Her kiss could be his doom…

When dragon-shifter Kristofer feels his firestorm ignite, he eagerly follows its spark to his destined mate. To his surprise, the heat leads him to a Valkyrie intent on claiming his soul. Even so, Kristofer has never met a woman as alluring as the fierce warrior before him. Trusting in the firestorm, he must convince her to fight with him instead of against him.

Trading the life of a dragon shifter for that of her sister Valkyrie is an easy choice for Bree…until she meets Kristofer. Experience taught her that dragons are evil, but in him she sees a bold and noble warrior. Finding his confidence as irresistible as his touch, Bree fears she is being tricked into abandoning her sister. But how can she take Kristofer's life when his very presence makes her burn with desire?

When they're compelled to join forces, Kristofer seizes the chance to convince Bree that they're stronger together. Yet as a sinister plan unfolds, an ancient dragon is roused from his slumber. With danger closing in, can Kristofer convince Bree to surrender her immortality for their forbidden love? Or will Bree's distrust of dragons prove justified?

Available Now!

ABOUT THE AUTHOR

eborah Cooke sold her first book in 1992, a medieval romance published under her pseudonym Claire Delacroix. Since then, she has published over fifty novels under the names Claire Delacroix, Claire Cross and Deborah Cooke. *The Beauty*, part of her successful Bride Quest series of historical romances, was her first title to land on the New York Times List of Bestselling Books. Her books routinely appear on other bestseller lists and have won numerous awards. In 2009, she was the writer-in-residence at the Toronto Public Library, the first time the library has hosted a residency focused on the romance genre. In 2012, she was honored to receive the Romance Writers of America's Mentor of the Year Award.

Currently, she writes paranormal romances and contemporary romances under the name Deborah Cooke. She also continues to write medieval romances as Claire Delacroix. Deborah lives in Canada with her husband and family, as well as far too many unfinished knitting projects.

www.deborahcooke.com
www.dragonfirenovels.com
www.dragonsofincendium.com
www.delacroix.net

www.ingramcontent.com/pod-product-compliance
Lightning Source LLC
Chambersburg PA
CBHW031019030726
47497CB00004B/920